A Passion
for Him

A Passion
for Him

SYLVIA DAY

KENSINGTON PUBLISHING CORP.
www.kensingtonbooks.com

KENSINGTON BOOKS are published by

Kensington Publishing Corp.
119 West 40th Street
New York, NY 10018

All Kensington titles, imprints, and distributed lines are available at special quantity discounts for bulk purchases for sales promotions, premiums, fund-raising, educational, or institutional use.

Special book excerpts or customized printings can also be created to fit specific needs. For details, write or phone the office of the Kensington special sales manager: Kensington Publishing Corp., 119 West 40th Street, New York, NY 10018, attn: Special Sales Department; phone 1-800-221-2647.

KENSINGTON and the k logo are Reg. U.S. Pat. & TM Off.

ISBN-13: 978-0-7582-9044-1
ISBN-10: 0-7582-9044-6

First Kensington Trade Paperback Printing: November 2007

10 9 8 7 6 5 4 3 2

Printed in the United States of America

To my dear friends, Shelley Bradley and Annette McCleave. Thank you both for the friendship, support, and brainstorming you shared with me while I wrote this book. They were invaluable and deeply appreciated.

Acknowledgments

To Kate Duffy, for her forbearance and guidance. When I needed help, she was there for me. I couldn't have finished this book without her.

To Nadine Dupont, for her assistance with the French words used in this book. Any errors are mine alone.

To the fabulous gals on my wicked chat loop, for their aid and friendship.

To Patrice Michelle, Janet Miller, and Mardi Ballou, for their commiseration.

I'm grateful to you all. Thank you so much!

Chapter 1

The man in the white mask was following her.

Amelia Benbridge was uncertain of how long he had been moving surreptitiously behind her, but he most definitely was.

She strolled carefully around the perimeter of the Langston ballroom, her senses attuned to his movements, her head turning with feigned interest in her surroundings so that she might study him further.

Every covert glance took her breath away.

In such a crush of people, another woman most likely would not have noted the avid interest. It was far too easy to be overwhelmed by the sights, sounds, and smells of a masquerade. The dazzling array of vibrant fabrics and frothy lace . . . the multitude of voices attempting to be heard over an industrious orchestra . . . the mingling scents of various perfumes and burnt wax from the massive chandeliers . . .

But Amelia was not like other women. She had lived the first sixteen years of her life under guard, her every movement watched with precision. It was a unique sensation to be examined so closely. She could not mistake the feeling for anything else.

However, she could say with some certainty that she had

never been so closely scrutinized by a man quite so . . . compelling.

For he *was* compelling, despite the distance between them and the concealment of the upper half of his face. His form alone arrested her attention. He stood tall and well proportioned, his garments beautifully tailored to cling to muscular thighs and broad shoulders.

She reached a corner and turned, setting their respective positions at an angle. Amelia paused there, taking the opportunity to raise her mask to surround her eyes, the gaily colored ribbons that adorned the stick falling down her gloved arm. Pretending to watch the dancers, she was in truth watching him and cataloguing his person. It was only fair, in her opinion. If he could enjoy an unhindered view, so could she.

He was drenched in black, the only relief being his snowy white stockings, cravat, and shirt. And the mask. So plain. Unadorned by paint or feathers. Secured to his head with black satin ribbon. While the other gentlemen in attendance were dressed in an endless range of colors to attract attention, this man's stark severity seemed designed to blend into the shadows. To make him unremarkable, which he could never be. Beneath the light of hundreds of candles, his dark hair gleamed with vitality and begged a woman to run her fingers through it.

And then there was his mouth . . .

Amelia inhaled sharply at the sight of it. His mouth was sin incarnate. Sculpted by a master hand, the lips neither full nor thin, but firm. Shamelessly sensual. Framed by a strong chin, chiseled jaw, and swarthy skin. A foreigner, perhaps. She could only imagine how the face would look as a whole. Devastating to a woman's equanimity, she suspected.

But it was more than his physical attributes that intrigued her. It was the way he moved, like a predator, his gait purposeful and yet seductive, his attention sharply focused. He did not mince his steps or affect the veneer of boredom so esteemed by Society. This man knew what he wanted and lacked the patience to pretend otherwise.

At present it appeared that what he wanted was to follow her. He watched Amelia with a gaze so intensely hot, she felt it move across her body, felt it run through the unpowdered strands of her hair and dance across her bared nape. Felt it glide across her bared shoulders and down the length of her spine. *Coveting.*

She could not begin to guess how she had attracted his attention. While she knew she was pretty enough, she was not any more attractive than most of the other women here. Her gown, while lovely with its elaborate silver lace underskirts and delicate flowers made of pink and green ribbon, was not the most riveting on display. And she was usually disregarded by those seeking a romantic connection, because her long-standing friendship with the popular Earl of Ware was widely assumed to be leading to the altar. Albeit very slowly.

So what did this man want with her? Why didn't he approach her?

Amelia canted her body to face him and lowered her mask, staring at him directly so he would not have to wonder if she was looking at him. She left him no doubt, hoping his long legs would resume their deliberate stride and bring him to her. She wanted to experience all the details of him—the sound of his voice, the scent of his cologne, the impact of proximity to his powerful frame.

Then she wished to know what he wanted. Amelia had lived the entirety of her motherless childhood being secreted from place to place, her governesses changed often so that no emotional attachment could form, she was cut off from her sibling and anyone who might care for her. Because of this, she distrusted the unknown. This man's interest was an anomaly, and it needed to be explained.

Her silent challenge caused a sudden, visible tension to grip his body. He stared back, his eyes glittering from the shadows of the mask. Long moments passed, time she barely registered because she was so focused on his response to her. Guests walked past him, momentarily obstructing her view and then revealing him again. His fists clenched along with his jaw. She saw his chest expand with a deep breath—

—just as she was bumped roughly from behind.

"Excuse me, Miss Benbridge."

Startled, her gaze turned to identify the offending individual and found a wigged man wearing puce satin. She muttered a quick dismissal of his concern, managed a brief smile, and swiftly returned her attention to the masked man.

Who was gone.

She blinked rapidly. *Gone.* Lifting to her tiptoes, Amelia frantically searched the sea of people. He was tall and blessed with an impressive breadth of shoulder. His lack of a wig provided an additional means of identification, but she could not find him.

Where did he go?

"Amelia."

The low, cultured drawl at her shoulder was dearly familiar, and she shot a quick, distracted glance at the handsome man who drew abreast of her. "Yes, my lord?"

"What are you looking for?" The Earl of Ware mimicked her pose, craning his neck in much the same fashion. Any other man would have looked ridiculous, but not Ware. It was impossible for him to appear anything less than perfect from the top of his wigged head down to his diamond-studded heels six feet below. "Would it be too much to hope that you were looking for me?"

Smiling sheepishly, Amelia abandoned her visual hunt and linked her arm with his. "I was seeking a phantom."

"A phantom?" Through the eyeholes of his painted mask, his blue eyes laughed at her. Ware had two expressions—one of dangerous boredom and one of warm amusement. She was the only person in his life capable of inspiring the latter.

"Was this a frightening specter? Or something more interesting?"

"I am not certain. He was following me."

"All men follow you, love," he said with a faint curve to his lips. "At the very least with their gazes, if not with their legs."

Amelia squeezed his arm in gentle admonishment. "You tease me."

"Not at all." He arched one arrogant brow. "You often appear lost in a world of your own making. It is supremely appealing to men to see a woman content with herself. We long to slip inside her and join her."

The intimate timbre of Ware's voice was not lost on Amelia. She glanced up at him from beneath her lashes. "Naughty man."

He laughed, and the guests around them stared. So did she. Merriment transformed the earl from the epitome of an ennui afflicted aristocrat to a vibrantly attractive man.

Ware began to stroll, expertly carrying her along with him. She had known him for six years now, having met him when he was ten and eight. She'd watched him grow into the man he was today, watched him take his first steps into liaisons and the way relations with women had changed him, although none of his inamoratas held his attention long. They saw only his exterior and the marquessate he would rule upon his father's passing. Perhaps he could have lived with that depth of interest, if he had not met her first. But they *had* met, and become the closest of friends. Now lesser connections displeased him. He kept mistresses to relieve his physical needs, but he kept her close to see to his emotional ones.

They would marry, she knew. It was unspoken between them, yet understood. Ware simply waited for the day when she would finally be ready to step beyond the boundaries of friendship and into his bed. She loved him for that patience, even though she was not *in* love with him. Amelia wished she could be; she wished it every day. But she loved another, and while death had stolen him from her, her heart stayed true.

"Where are your thoughts now?" Ware asked, his head tilting in acknowledgment of another guest's greeting.

"With you."

"Ah, lovely," he purred, his eyes lit with pleasure. "Tell me everything."

"I am thinking that I shall enjoy being married to you."

"Is that a proposal?"

"I'm not certain."

"Hmmm . . . well, we are getting closer. I take some comfort in that."

She studied him carefully. "Are you growing impatient?"

"I can wait."

The answer was vague, and Amelia frowned.

"No fretting," Ware admonished gently, leading her out a pair of open French doors to a crowded terrace. "I am content for now, so long as you are."

The cool evening breeze blew across her skin, and she inhaled deeply. "You are not being entirely truthful."

Amelia came to a halt at the wide marble railing and faced him. Several couples stood nearby, engaging in various conversations, but all were casting curious glances in their direction. Despite the shadows created by the cloud-covered moon, Ware's cream-colored jacket and breeches gleamed like ivory and enticed admiring perusals.

"This is not the place to discuss something as auspicious as our future," he said, reaching up to untie his mask. He removed it, revealing a profile so noble it should have graced a coin.

"You know that will not dissuade me."

"And you know that is why I like you so well." His slow smile teased her. "My life is regimented and compartmentalized. Everything is orderly and firmly in its place. I know my role and I fulfill the expectations of Society exactly."

"Except for courting me."

"Except for courting you," he agreed. His gloved hand found hers and held it. He adjusted his stance to hide the scandalous contact from the curious. "You are my fair princess, rescued from her turret tower by an infamous pirate. The daughter of a viscount hanged for treason and sister to a true femme fatale, a woman widely considered to have murdered two husbands before marrying one too dangerous to kill. You are my folly, my aberration, my peccadillo."

He brushed his thumb across her palm, making her shiver. "But I serve the opposite purpose in your life. I am your anchor. You cling to me because I am safe and comfortable." His gaze lifted to look over her head at the others who shared the terrace with them. He bent closer and murmured, "But on occasion, I remember the young girl who so boldly demanded a first kiss from me, and I wish I had responded differently."

"You do?"

Ware nodded.

"Have I changed so much since then?"

With his mask dangling from one hand and her hand captured in the other, he turned abruptly and led her down the nearby flight of stairs to the garden. A gravel pathway bordered low yew hedges, which in turn bordered a lush center lawn and impressive fountain.

"The passing of time changes all of us," he said. "But I think it was the passing of your dear Colin that changed you the most."

The sound of Colin's name affected Amelia deeply, provoking feelings of overwhelming sadness and regret. He had been her dearest friend, who later became the love of her heart. He was the nephew of her coachman and a Gypsy, but in her sheltered world they were equals. They had been playmates as children, then found their interest in each other changing. Deepening. Becoming less innocent.

Colin had matured into a young man whose exotic beauty and quiet strength of character had stirred her in ways she had not been prepared for. Thoughts of him had ruled her days, and dreams of stolen kisses had tormented her nights. He had been wiser than she, understanding that it was impossible for a peer's daughter and a stableboy to ever be together. He had pushed her away, pretended to feel nothing for her, and broken her adolescent heart.

But in the end he had died for her.

Her silent exhale was shaky. Sometimes, just before she drifted into sleep, she permitted herself to think of him. She opened her heart and let the memories out—stolen kisses in the woods, passionate longing and budding desire. She had never felt that depth of emotion again and knew she never would. Some childish infatuations faded away. Her love for Colin had been built with firmer stuff, and it stayed with her. No longer a raging fire, but a softer warmth. Adoration enhanced by gratefulness for his sacrifice. Trapped between her father's men and agents of the Crown, she could have been killed had Colin not spirited her away. A reckless, love-fueled rescue that had delivered her to safety at the cost of his precious life.

"You are thinking of him again," Ware murmured.

"Am I so transparent?"

"As clear as glass." He squeezed her hand, and she smiled fondly.

"Perhaps you think my reticence stems from my lingering affection for Colin, but it is my affection for you that restrains me."

"Oh?"

Amelia could see that she had surprised him. They turned back toward the manse, following the subtle urging of the path. Brilliant light and the glorious strains of stringed instruments spilled out in abundance from the many open doorways, enticing strolling guests to linger close to the festivities. Others wended their way through the rear garden as they did, but all resisted straying too far.

"Yes, my lord. I worry that perhaps I will steal you from your great love."

Ware laughed softly. "How fanciful you are." He grinned and looked so handsome, she gazed a moment longer to admire him. "I admit to curious musings when you wear that faraway look, but that is the extent of my interest in affairs of the heart."

"You have no notion of what you are missing."

"Forgive me for being callous, but if what I am missing is the melancholy that clings to you, I want none of it. It is attractive on you and lends you an air of mystery that I find irresistible. Sadly, I fear I would not fare so well. I suspect I would appear wretched, and we cannot have that."

"The Earl of Ware wretched?"

He gave a mock shudder. "Quite impossible, of course."

"Quite."

"So you see, you are perfect for me, Amelia. I enjoy your company. I enjoy your honesty and our ability to converse freely about nearly everything. There is no uncertainty or fear of reprisal for a careless act. You cannot hurt me, and I cannot hurt you, because we do not attribute actions to emotions that are not there. If I am thoughtless, it is not because I seek to injure you, and you know this. Our association is one I will appreciate and value until I take my last breath."

Ware paused when they reached the bottom step that would lead them back up to the terrace. Their brief spell of privacy was nearly at an end. Her desire to spend unhindered time with him was an added impetus to marriage. It was only the sexual congress that would end their evenings that she resisted.

The memory of feverishly exchanged kisses with Colin haunted her, and she could not bring herself to risk disappointment with Ware. She dreaded the possibility of awkwardness intruding on their closeness. The earl was comely and charming and perfect. How would he look when he was flushed and disheveled? What sounds would he make? How would he move? What would he expect of her?

It was apprehension that goaded these ponderings, not anticipation.

"And what of the sex?" she asked.

His head swiveled toward her, and he froze with his foot poised above the step. The depth of his blue eyes sparkled with merriment. Ware backed down from the stair and faced her directly. "What of it?"

"Do you not worry that it will be . . . ?" She struggled to find the correct word.

"No." There was a wealth of assurance in the negation.

"No?"

"When I think about sex with you there is no worry involved. Eagerness, yes. Anxiety, no." He closed the small gap between them and bent over her. His voice came as an intimate whisper. "Do not hesitate for that reason. We are young. We can wed and wait, or we can wait and then wed. Even with my ring on your finger, I will not ask you to do anything you do not wish to. Not yet." His mouth twitched. "In a few years, however, I may not be so accommodating. I must reproduce eventually, and I do find you supremely alluring."

Amelia tilted her head, considering. Then she nodded.

"Good," Ware said with obvious satisfaction. "Progress, however incremental, is always good."

"Perhaps it is time to post the banns."

"By God, that is more than an incremental move forward!" he cried with exaggerated verve. "We are actually getting somewhere."

She laughed and he winked mischievously.

"We will be happy together," he promised.

"I know."

Ware took a moment to once again secure his mask, and her gaze wandered as she waited. Following the line of the marble railing, she found a profusion of ivy climbing the brick exterior. That visual trail led to another terrace farther down, this one unlit in an obvious gambit to deter guests from lingering away from the ballroom. It appeared, however, that the lack of welcome was too subtle for two attendees, or perhaps they simply did not care to heed it. Regardless, the reason *why* they were there was not what caught Amelia's attention. She was more interested in *who* was there.

Despite the deep shadows that blanketed the second patio, she recognized her phantom follower by the pure white of his mask and the way his garments and hair blended into the night around him.

"My lord," she murmured, reaching out blindly to clutch Ware's arm. "Do you see those gentlemen over there?"

She felt his attention turn as she directed.

"Yes."

"The dark-clad gentleman is the one who held such interest in me earlier."

The earl looked at her in all seriousness. "You made light of the matter, but now I am concerned. Was this man an annoyance to you?"

"No." Her gaze narrowed as the two men parted and set off in opposite directions—the phantom away from her, the other man toward her.

"Yet something about him disturbs you." Ware rearranged her grasping hand to rest upon his forearm. "And his assignation over there is curious."

"Yes, I agree."

"Despite the years that have passed since you were freed from your father's care, I feel caution would be wise. When one has an infamous criminal for a relation, every unknown is suspect. We cannot have odd characters following you about." Ware led her quickly up the steps. "Perhaps you should stay close to me for the remainder of the evening."

"I have no cause to fear him," she argued without heat. "I think it is more my reaction to him that surprises me, as opposed to his interest in me."

"You had a reaction to him?" Ware paused just inside the door and drew her to the side, out of the way of those who entered and exited. "What sort of reaction?"

Amelia lifted her mask to her face. How could she explain that she had admired the man's powerful frame and presence without lending more weight to the sentiment than it deserved? "I was intrigued. I wished he would approach me and reveal himself."

"Should I be concerned that another man so quickly captured your imagination?" The earl's drawling voice was laced with amusement.

"No." She smiled. The comfort of their friendship was priceless to her. "Just as I do not worry when you take interest in other females."

"*Lord Ware.*"

They both turned to face the gentleman who approached, a person whose distinctively short and portly frame made him recognizable despite his mask—Sir Harold Bingham, a Bow Street magistrate.

"Sir Harold," Ware greeted in return.

"Good evening, Miss Benbridge," the magistrate said, smiling in his kindly way. He was known for his tough rulings, but was widely considered to be fair and wise.

Amelia quite liked him, and the warmth of her returning pleasantries reflected this.

Ware leaned toward her, lowering his voice for her ears only. "Will you excuse me a moment? I should like to discuss your admirer with him. Perhaps we can learn an identity."

"Of course, my lord."

The two gentlemen moved a short distance away, and Amelia's gaze drifted over the ballroom, seeking out familiar faces. She spotted a small grouping of acquaintances nearby and set off in that direction.

After several steps she stopped, frowning.

She wanted to know who was behind the white mask. The curiosity was eating at her, niggling at the back of her mind and making her restless. There was such intensity in the way he had looked at her, and the moment when their eyes had met lingered in her thoughts.

Turning abruptly on her heel, she again walked outside and down the steps into the rear garden. There were many other guests about, all seeking relief from the crush. Rather than going straight along the path she had taken with Ware or to the right where the second terrace waited in the dark, she turned to the left. A few feet off to the side, a marble reproduction of Venus graced a semicircular space filled with a half-moon bench. It was bordered by the same low, perfectly shaped yew hedges that surrounded the lawn and fountain, and it was presently unoccupied.

Amelia paused near the statue and whistled a distinctive warble that would bring her brother-in-law's men out of hiding. She was guarded still, and suspected she would always be. It was an inevitable consequence of being the sister-in-law of a known pirate and smuggler such as Christopher St. John.

At times she resented the inherent lack of privacy that came with having one's every movement watched. She could not help but wish that her life was simple enough to make such precautions unnecessary. But at other times, such as tonight, she found relief in the unseen protection. She was never left exposed, which enabled her to view her phantom in a different light. Having St. John's men nearby also afforded her the opportunity to elicit help in relieving her curiosity.

Her foot tapped impatiently atop the gravel as she waited. That was why she did not hear the man's approach. She did,

however, feel him. The hairs on her nape tingled with awareness, and she turned swiftly with a soft gasp of surprise.

He stood just barely within the entrance of the circle, a
tall, dark form that vibrated with a potent energy that seemed
barely restrained. Beneath the pale light of the moon, the
man's inky locks gleamed like a raven's wing, and his eyes
glittered with the very intensity that had goaded her to seek
him out. He wore a full cape, the gray satin lining providing
a striking backdrop to his black garments, enabling her to
fully appreciate the size and power of his frame.

"I was looking for you," she said softly, her chin lifting.

"I know."

Chapter 2

Her phantom's voice was deep, low, and distinctly accented. Foreign, which complemented his swarthy complexion.

"Do not fear me," he said. "I wish only to apologize for my lack of manners."

"I am not frightened," she replied, her gaze darting past his shoulder to where other guests were clearly visible.

He stepped aside and bowed, gesturing her out with a grand sweep of his arm.

"That is all you have to say to me?" she asked, as she realized that he intended for them to part.

His beautiful mouth pursed slightly. "Should there be more?"

"I . . ." Amelia frowned and glanced away a moment, trying to gather her thoughts into coherent words. It was difficult to think clearly when he stood in such close proximity. What had been compelling at a distance was nearly overwhelming now. He was so somber. . . . She had not expected that.

"I do not mean to detain you," he murmured, his tone soothing.

"Lack of manners," she repeated.

"Yes. I was staring."

"I noticed," she said dryly.

"Forgive me."

"No need. I am not upset."

She waited for him to take some action. When he stepped out of the small circle and again gestured toward the main part of the rear garden, she shook her head in denial. Her mouth curved at his apparent haste to be rid of her.

"My name is Miss Amelia Benbridge."

The man stilled visibly, his only movement the lift and fall of his chest. After a moment's hesitation, he showed a leg in a courtly bow and said, "A pleasure, Miss Benbridge. I am Count Reynaldo Montoya."

"Montoya," she breathed, testing the name on her tongue. "Spanish, yet your accent is French."

His head lifted, and he studied her closely, his gaze caressing the length of her body from the top of her elaborate coiffure down to her kid slippers. "Your surname is English, yet your features are enhanced by a foreign touch," he pointed out in rebuttal.

"My mother was Spanish."

"And you are enchanting."

Amelia inhaled sharply, startled by how the simple compliment affected her. She heard such platitudes daily, and they held as much meaning as a comment on the weather. But Montoya's delivery altered the words, imbuing them with feeling and an underlying urgency.

"It appears I must apologize again," the count said, with a self-deprecating smile. "Allow me to escort you back before I make a further fool of myself."

She reached out to him, then caught herself and clutched the stick of her mask with both hands instead. "Your cloak . . . Are you departing?"

He nodded, and the tension in the air between them heightened. There was no reason for him to linger, and yet she sensed that they both wanted him to.

Something was holding him back.

"Why?" she asked softly. "You have not yet asked me to dance or flirted with me or made a casual remark about where you intend to be in the future so that we might find one another again."

Montoya reentered the small circle. "You are too bold, Miss Benbridge," he admonished gruffly.

"And you are a coward."

He drew up sharply just a few inches from her.

A cool evening breeze blew across the top of her shoulder, carrying with it one of the long, artful curls that hung down her back. The count's gaze focused on the glossy lock, then drifted over the swell of her breasts.

"You look at me as a man looks at his mistress."

"Do I?" His voice had lowered, grown softer, the accent more pronounced. It was a lover's tone, or a seducer's. She felt it move over her skin like a tactile caress, and she relished the experience. It was rather like exiting a warm house on a frosty day. The sudden impact of sensation was startling and stole one's breath.

"How would you know that look, Miss Benbridge?"

"I know a great many things. However, since you have decided not to acquaint yourself with me, you will never know what they are."

His arms crossed his chest. It was a challenging pose, yet it made her smile, because it signaled his intent to stay. At least for a short while longer. "And what of Lord Ware?" he asked.

"What of him?"

"You are, for all intents and purposes, betrothed."

"So I am." She noted how his jaw tensed. "Do you have a grievance with Lord Ware?"

The count did not reply.

She began tapping her foot again. "We are having visceral reactions to one another, Count Montoya. As attractive as you are, I would venture to say that you are accustomed to snaring women's interest. For my part, I can say with absolute certainty that a similar situation has never happened to me before. Stunning men do not follow me about—"

"You remind me of someone I used to know," he interrupted. "A woman I cared for deeply."

"Oh." Try as she might, Amelia could not hide her disappointment. He had thought she was someone else. His interest was not in *her*, but in a woman who looked like her.

Turning away, she sank onto the small bench, absently arranging her skirts for comfort. Her hands occupied themselves with twirling her mask between gloved fingertips.

"It is my turn to apologize to you." Her head tilted back so that their gazes met. "I have put you in an awkward position, and goaded you to stay when you wanted to go."

The contemplative cant to his head made her wish she could see the features beneath the pearlescent mask. Despite the lack of a complete visual picture, she found him remarkably attractive—the purring rumble of his voice . . . the luscious shape of his lips . . . the unshakable confidence of his bearing . . .

But then he was not truly unshakable. She was affecting him in ways a stranger should not be able to. And he was affecting her equally.

"That was not what you wished to hear," he noted, stepping closer.

Her gaze strayed to his boots, watching as his cape fluttered around them. Dressed as he was, he was imposing, but she was unafraid.

Amelia waved one hand in a careless affectation of dismissal, unsure of what to say. He was correct; she was too bold. But she was not brazen enough to admit outright that she found the thought of his interest gratifying. "I hope you find the woman you are looking for," she said instead.

"I am afraid that isn't possible."

"Oh?"

"She was lost to me many years ago."

Recognizing the yearning in his words, she sympathized. "I am sorry for your loss. I, too, have lost someone dear to me and know how it feels."

Montoya took a seat beside her. The bench was small, and due to its curvature it forced them to sit near enough that her skirts touched his cape. It was improper for them to be seated so close to each other, yet she did not protest. Instead she breathed deeply and discovered he smelled like sandalwood and citrus. Crisp, earthy, and virile. Like the man himself.

"You are too young to suffer as I do," he murmured.

"You underestimate death. It has no scruples and disregards the age of those left behind."

The ribbons that graced the stick of her mask fluttered gently in the soft breeze and came to rest atop his gloved hand. The sight of the lavender, pink, and pale blue satin against his stark black riveted her attention.

How would they look to passersby? Her voluminous silver lace and gay multicolored flowers next to his complete lack of any color at all.

"You should not be out here alone," he said, rubbing her ribbons between his thumb and index finger. He could not feel them through his gloves, which made the action sensual, as if the lure of fondling something that belonged to her was irresistible.

"I am accustomed to solitude."

"Do you enjoy it?"

"It is familiar."

"That is not an answer."

Amelia looked at him, noting the many details one can see only in extreme proximity to another. Montoya had long, thick lashes surrounding almond-shaped eyes. They were beautiful. Exotic. Knowing. Accented by shadows that came from within as well as from without.

"What was she like?" she asked. "The woman you thought I was."

The barest hint of a smile betrayed the possibility of dimples. "I asked you a question first," he said.

She heaved a dramatic sigh just to see more of that teasing curve of his lips. He never set his smile completely free. She wondered why, and she wondered how she might see it. "Very well, Count Montoya. In answer to your query, yes, I enjoy being alone."

"Many people find being alone intolerable."

"They have no imagination. I, on the other hand, have too much imagination."

"Oh?" He canted his body toward her. The pose caused his doeskin breeches to stretch tautly across the powerful muscles of his thighs. With the gray satin spread out beneath him in contrast, she could see every nuance and plane, every hard length of sinew. "What do you imagine?"

Swallowing hard, Amelia found she could not look away from the view. It was a lascivious glance she was giving him, her interest completely carnal.

"Umm . . ." She tore her gaze upward, dazed by the direction of her own thoughts. "Stories. Faery tales and such."

With the half mask hiding his features she couldn't be certain, but she thought he might have arched a brow at her. "Do you write them down?"

"Occasionally."

"What do you do with them?"

"You have asked far too many questions without answering my one."

Montoya's dark eyes glittered with warm amusement. "Are we keeping score?"

"You were," she pointed out. "I am simply following the rules you set."

There! A dimple. She saw it.

"She was audacious," he murmured, "like you."

Amelia blushed and looked away, smitten with that tiny groove in his cheek. "Did you like that about her?"

"I loved that about her."

The intimate pitch to his voice made her shiver.

He stood and held his hand out to her. "You are cold, Miss Benbridge. You should go inside."

She looked up at him. "Will you go inside with me?"

The count shook his head.

Extending her arm, she set her fingers within his palm and allowed him to assist her to her feet. His hand was large and warm, his grasp strong and sure. She was reluctant to release him and was pleased when he seemed to feel similarly. They stood there for a long moment, touching, the only sound their gentle inhalations and subsequent exhales . . . until the gentle, haunting strains of the minuet drifted out on the night zephyr.

Montoya's grip tightened and his breathing faltered. She knew his thoughts traveled along the same path as hers. Lifting her mask to her face, Amelia lowered into a deep curtsy.

"One dance," she urged softly when he did not move. "Dance with me as if I were the woman you miss."

"No." There was a heartbeat's hesitation, and then he bowed over her hand. "I would rather dance with you."

Touched, her throat tightened, cutting off any reply she might have made. She could only rise and begin the steps, approaching him and then retreating. Spinning slowly and then circling him. The crunching of the gravel beneath her feet overpowered the music, but Amelia heard it in her mind and hummed the notes. He joined her, his deep voice creating a rich accompaniment, the combination of sound enchanting her.

The clouds drifted, allowing a brilliant shaft of moonlight to illuminate their small space. It turned the hedges silver and his mask into a brilliant pearl. The black satin ribbon that restrained his queue blended with the inky locks, the gloss and color so similar they were nearly one and the same. Her skirts brushed against his flowing cape, his cologne mingled with her perfume; together they were lost in a single moment. Amelia was arrested there, ensnared, and wished—briefly—never to be freed.

Then the unmistakable warble of a birdcall rent the cocoon.

A warning from St. John's men.

Amelia stumbled, and Montoya caught her close. Her arm lowered to her side, taking her mask with it. His breath, warm and scented of brandy, drifted across her lips. The difference in their statures put her breasts at level with his upper abdomen. He would have to bend to kiss her, and she found herself wishing he would, wanting to experience the feel of those beautifully sculpted lips pressed against her own.

"Lord Ware is looking for you," he whispered, without taking his eyes from her.

She nodded, but made no effort to free herself. Her gaze stayed locked to his. Watching. Waiting.

Just when she was certain he wouldn't, he accepted her silent invitation and brushed his mouth across hers. Their lips clung together and he groaned. The mask fell from her nerveless fingers to clatter atop the gravel.

"Good-bye, Amelia."

He steadied her, then fled in a billowing flare of black, leaping over a low hedge and blending into the shadows. He headed not toward the rear of the manse but to the front, and was gone in an instant. Dazed by his sudden departure, Amelia turned her head slowly toward the garden. She found Ware approaching with rapid strides, followed by several other gentlemen.

"What are you doing over here?" he asked gruffly, scanning her surroundings with an agitated glance. "I was going mad looking for you."

"I am sorry." She was unable to say more than that. Her

thoughts were with Montoya, a man who had clearly recognized the whistle of warning.

He had been real for a moment, but no longer. Like the phantom she'd fancied him as, he was elusive.

And entirely suspect.

"Would you care to explain what happened last night?"

Amelia sighed inwardly, but on the exterior she offered a sunny smile. "Explain what?"

Christopher St. John—pirate, murderer, smuggler extraordinaire—returned her smile, but his sapphire eyes were sharp and assessing. "You know very well what I am referring to." He shook his head. "At times you are so like your sister, it is somewhat alarming."

What was alarming was how divinely handsome St. John was, considering how devilishly his brain worked. Despite the years she'd lived within his household, Amelia was still taken aback by his comeliness every time she saw him.

"Oh, what a lovely thing to say!" she cried, meaning every word. "Thank you."

"Minx. Fess up now."

Any other man would have difficulty prying information out of her that she didn't wish to share. But when the raspy-voiced pirate became cajoling, he was impossible to resist. With his golden hair and skin, thin yet carnal lips, and jeweled irises, he reminded her of an angel, for certainly only a celestial being could be formed so perfectly from head to toe.

The only outward sign of his mortality were the lines that rimmed his mouth and eyes, signs of a life that was fraught with stresses. They'd softened a great deal since his marriage to her sister, but they would never fully dissipate.

"I noted a man's uncommon interest. He noted that I'd noted, and approached me to explain."

Christopher leaned back in his black leather chair and

pursed his lips. Behind him was a large window that over-looked the rear garden, or what would have been a rear garden if they'd had one. Instead, they had a flat, brutally trimmed lawn that made stealthy approach of the manse impossible. When one had a great deal of enemies, as St. John did, one could never lower their guard, especially for frivolous aesthetic reasons. "What explanation did he offer?"

"I reminded him of a lost love."

He made a sound suspiciously like a snort. "A clever, sentimental ruse that almost embarrassed Ware and caused a terrible scandal. I cannot believe you fell prey to it."

Flushing with renewed guilt, she nevertheless protested. "He was sincere!" She did not believe anyone could pretend melancholy so well. That was not to say that she wasn't aware of something amiss, but she did believe his emotional response to her.

"My men followed him last evening."

Amelia nodded, expecting as much. "And?"

"And they lost him."

"How is that possible?"

St. John smiled at her astonishment. "It's possible if one is aware that he is being followed and is trained in how to evade shadows." His smile faded. "The man is no lovelorn innocent, Amelia."

She rose, frowning, which forced St. John to rise as well. Her floral skirts settled around her legs, and she turned to face the rest of the room, lost in thought. Appearances could be deceiving. This room and the criminal who owned it were prime examples. Decorated in shades of red, cream, and gold, the study could belong to a peer of the realm, as could the manse it was a part of. There was nothing here to betray its primary purpose—that of being the headquarters of a large and highly illegal smuggling ring.

"What would he want with me?" she asked, remembering the previous night's events in crystal clarity. She could still smell the exotic scent of his skin and hear the slight accent to his words that made her insides quiver. Her lips tingled from the press of his, as did her breasts with the memory of the hardness of his abdomen.

"Anything from a simple warning to me, to something more sinister."

"Such as?" She faced him and found him watching her with knowing eyes.

"Such as seducing you and ruining you for Ware. Or seducing you and luring you away to use as leverage against me."

The word "seducing" used in conjunction with the mysterious, masked Montoya did odd things to her. It should, perhaps, frighten her, but it didn't.

"You know as well as I how fortuitous it is that you met Ware while in your father's captivity and that he is willing to disregard your scandalous past and familial connections." His fingers drummed almost silently upon the desktop. "Your son will be a marquess and your children will have every advantage. Anything that jeopardizes your future is cause for concern."

Amelia nodded and looked away again, hoping to hide how the reduction of her relationship with Ware to the material benefits made her feel. She was well aware that she stood to gain the most from their union. As Ware's friend, she wanted only the best for him. Marriage to her was anything but. "What do you want me to do?"

"Do not venture off by yourself. If the man approaches you again, do not allow him within a few feet of you." The severity of his features softened. He wore cerulean blue today, a color that complemented both his tawny coloring and the beautifully embroidered waistcoat that hugged his lean waist. "I do not mean to chastise you. I want only to keep you safe."

"I know." But the entirety of her life had been spent in gilded cages. She found herself torn between loving the security of it and resenting the restrictions. She tried to behave, tried to follow the rules set for her, but at times it was difficult to conform. She suspected that was due to her father's blood in her veins. It was the one thing she most wished to change about herself. "May I be dismissed? Ware will be along shortly to take me for a ride in the park, and I must change."

"Of course. Enjoy yourself."

Christopher watched Amelia leave the room and then resumed his seat, only to stand a moment later when his wife entered in a profusion of pale pink skirts. As always, the sight of her made his heart race with a mixture of attraction and pure joy.

"You look a vision this afternoon," he said, rounding the desk to embrace her. As she had since the moment they had first met, Maria melted against him, a lush warm weight that he adored.

"You say that every day," she murmured, but her smile was filled with pleasure.

"Because it's true every day." He cupped her spine and molded her curves to his hardness. They fit together like two matching puzzle pieces, despite their disparity in height.

Maria shared the same glossy raven tresses as her younger sibling, but that was the extent of their physical similarities. Amelia took after her father, the late Viscount Welton, with his emerald green eyes and tall, slender build. Maria, who gratefully claimed a different pater, took after their Spanish-blooded mother with her sloe eyes, short stature, and full figure.

St. John and his wife made a striking couple; their contrasting appearances complemented each other in ways oft commented on. But they drew the most attention for their reputations. The former Lady Winter was still known as the "Wintry Widow," a woman who was widely rumored to have murdered her first two husbands. Christopher was her third and last husband, the husband of her heart, and he was frequently celebrated for remaining alive.

You have survived another night in your wife's bed, they jested.

Christopher would smile and say nothing. It wasn't true, but he would not refute the misconception. Few would understand how he died in her arms every night and was reborn.

"I overheard the end of your conversation with Amelia," she said. "I think you are looking at the situation from the wrong perspective."

"Oh?" This was where their true similarities lay. As different as they were on the exterior, on the interior they were alarmingly alike, both criminally minded and quite wily. "What am I missing?"

"You are seeing only what interest the masked man had in Amelia. What of her interest in him? That is where my worry stems."

He frowned down at her, absently admiring the artfully arranged curls that tumbled about her ears and shoulders, and her full bosom which swelled enticingly above her low, ribbon-edged bodice. "She has always been curious. That is how she met Ware to begin with."

"Yes, but she allowed this man to kiss her. A stranger. Why? She has been pining for her Gypsy sweetheart all these years and keeps Ware at bay. What was the fascination with this man that goaded such a response in her?"

"Hmm . . ." Lowering his head, he took her mouth in a long, luxurious kiss. "Would you mourn for me with such devotion, were I to pass on?" he queried, his lips moving against hers.

"No." Maria smiled with the hint of mystery that kept him endlessly enthralled with her.

"No?"

"Nothing or no one could ever take you from me, my darling." Her small hands brushed over his chest. "I will die alongside you. It is the only way I will allow you to go."

Christopher's heart swelled with love so fierce, it sometimes overwhelmed him. "So our young Amelia was drawn to this man in ways she has not been to anyone else. What do you suggest we do about that?"

"Watch her more closely, and find that man. I want to know him and his intentions."

"Done." He smiled. "Have you any plans for the rest of this afternoon?"

"Yes. I'm quite busy."

He hoped he hid his disappointment. While he had a great many items on his list of things to accomplish, he would not have minded an hour or two of his wife's company. There was something delicious about making love in the middle of the day with the drapes thrown wide and the sun shining in. Especially when she took the top and writhed above him in the daylight.

Sighing dramatically, Christopher released her. "Enjoy yourself, love."

"That depends on you." Her dark eyes shined wickedly. "You see, my schedule says 'lovemaking' from two to four. I will need your help to accomplish that task."

Christopher was instantly aroused. "I am at your service, madam."

She stepped back and glanced down at the front of his breeches. "Yes, I see that you are. Shall we retire?"

"I should like that," he purred, his blood hot.

A knock intruded from the open doorway. They both looked over.

"Hello, Tim," Maria said, smiling at the giant whose great head was ducked to fit beneath the threshold.

He bowed in greeting, then rumbled, "Did you still wish to speak with me?"

"Yes." Tim was one of Christopher's most trusted lieutenants. He was also infinitely patient and had a way with women. His fondness for the fairer gender was obvious. They sensed it and were far more open with him than they were with other men. They listened to and trusted him, which would facilitate keeping Amelia in line.

Christopher looked down into Maria's uplifted face. "Don't undress," he whispered for her ears only. "I want to unwrap you myself."

"As if I'm a gift," she teased.

"You are. My most prized possession." Kissing the tip of her nose, he stepped back from her. "I must discuss Tim's new assignment to watch Amelia."

Her answering smile was a sight to behold. "You are so clever to anticipate my concerns. You never require my input in matters."

"But I do," he refuted, "and I value it." His voice lowered with promise. "Shortly, I shall show you how much."

Maria's fingertips brushed along his palm as she moved away and their hands separated. "See you at dinner, Tim," she said, sashaying past him as he entered the room.

"Yes, ma'am."

Tim looked at Christopher with a wry smile. "I know that look. This will be quick, eh?"

"Yes. Very. I want you to shadow Miss Benbridge."

"I 'eard about last night. No worries. She's in good 'ands with me."

"I would not ask you if I weren't confident in that." Christopher patted him on the shoulder as he headed out the door. "See you at dinner."

"Lucky bastard," Tim said after him.

Christopher grinned and sprinted up the stairs.

Chapter 3

France, a month earlier

"So," Simon Quinn said, setting his fork down. "The time has come."

"It has." And not a moment too soon in Colin Mitchell's estimation. He'd waited years for this day. Now that it had arrived, he found that sitting decorously at the table for dinner was nigh impossible. In mere hours he would set sail for England and the love of his life. He wished he were already there. With her.

All around them, revelry was the order of the day. Although raised in a boisterous Gypsy camp, Colin preferred quiet evenings. It was Quinn who sought out these loud venues. He claimed they made eavesdropping impossible and solidified their carefully affected mien of ennui and nonchalance, but Colin suspected the predilection was goaded by another reason entirely. Quinn was not a happy man, and it was easier to feign contentment when surrounded by gaiety.

Still, this establishment was one Colin tolerated better than most. It was clean, well lit, and the food was delicious. Three massive chandeliers hung from the wooden-beamed ceiling above them, and the air was redolent of various appetizing dishes and the perfumes of the many buxom serving wenches. Raucous laughter and a multitude of conversations fought to be heard over the frenetically playing orchestra in the far corner, which left them in relative privacy among the din, just two finely attired gentlemen enjoying an evening meal out.

"I had thought you might have grown beyond your feelings for the fair Amelia," Quinn said with a faint hint of his Irish brogue still evident. He lifted a glass of wine to his lips and studied Colin carefully above the rim. "You've changed a great deal from the young man who came to me searching for her so many years ago."

"True." Colin knew Quinn did not want him to go. He was too valuable a player in Quinn's games. He could become anyone, anywhere. Men trusted him and women found him irresistible. Perceptive creatures, they sensed that his heart was locked away, and it made them try harder to win him. "But that is one part of me that has not changed."

"Perhaps *she* has changed. She was a girl when you left her."

"She changed while I knew her." He shrugged. "It only deepened my feelings." How could he explain all of the many facets he had seen in her over the years?

"What allure does she possess that enslaves you so? The contessa adores you, and yet she is merely a diversion to you."

A vision of the lovely Francesca came to mind, and Colin smiled. "As I am a diversion to her. She enjoys the game, never knowing who will appear at her doorstep or which disguise I will be hidden beneath. I suit her reckless inclinations, but those extend only to the bedroom. She is too proud a woman to accept a man of my breeding in a capacity other than the one I fill presently."

Once, on assignment for Quinn, Colin had been chased into the first open door he'd come to during a ball. The room had been occupied by Francesca, who was adjusting her appearance and enjoying a small respite from the crush.

He had bowed, smiled, and proceeded to divest himself of wig and clothing, turning his specially tailored garments inside out. The contessa had found the act of changing from a white-haired, black-clad gentleman to a dark-haired, ivory-clad rogue quite diverting. She'd eagerly assumed the ruse of his companion, exiting to the hallway with her hand firmly attached to his forearm, which effectively stumped the two scowling gentlemen who stumbled upon them in their search.

She'd taken him to her bed that night and kept him there the last two years, unconcerned when his employment forced him to leave her for weeks or months at a time. Theirs was an affair of convenience and mutual understanding.

I sometimes envy the woman who has such a tenacious hold on your heart, she once said to him.

Colin had swiftly turned the direction of her thoughts elsewhere. He could not bear to think of Amelia while in the company of another woman. It felt like a betrayal, and he knew from experience that Amelia would be deeply wounded.

"Amelia holds the same allure for me as her sibling holds for you," Colin said, meeting Quinn's widening eyes. "Perhaps if you can explain to me why you still pine for Maria, it will help to answer your question regarding my feelings for Amelia."

A self-deprecating smile curved the Irishman's mouth. "Point taken. Will you return to her as Colin Mitchell or as one of your other aliases?"

Heaving out his breath, Colin glanced around the dining parlor at the many guests and overtly friendly serving staff. To Amelia, he was a part of her past . . . a deceased part of her past. A childhood friend who had grown into a young man who loved her with every breath in his body. She had loved him similarly, with the same wild, saturating, unrestrained adolescent passion. He had tried to stay away, tried to push her away, tried to convince himself that they would both grow beyond such impossible aspirations. As he was a Gypsy and a stableboy in her father's employ, there was no possibility of a future between them.

In the end, he had been unable to keep his distance. Her father, the late Viscount Welton, had been the worst sort of monster. Welton had used Amelia as leverage against her sister, selling the stunningly beautiful Maria to marriage-minded peers, whom he then killed for the widow's settlements. When Welton's machinations put Amelia in danger, Colin had attempted a daring rescue during which he'd been shot and left for dead.

How did one rise from the grave? And once he managed that task, would she accept him back into her life in the role he wished to fill—that of lover and husband?

"If she will have me, she will be the Countess Montoya," he said, referring to the title he had invented expressly for her. Over the years he'd built and strengthened the roots of that assumed nobility, purchasing properties and establishing wealth under that guise. He would not have her married to the common Colin Mitchell. She deserved better. "But perhaps it is her attachment to Colin that will win her heart."

"I will miss you," Quinn said, his blue-eyed gaze pensive. "In fact, I am not certain how I will manage without you."

Quinn had been enlisted by agents of the Crown of England to manage tasks more cautious agents wouldn't. He was not "officially" recognized, nor was Colin, which freed them both from the restrictions under which others labored. In return for their unacknowledged efforts, they kept most of the spoils, which made them exceptionally wealthy.

"You will find a way," Colin said, smiling. "You always do. You still have Cartland. In some respects, he is far more accomplished than I. He can track better than a canine. If something is lost, he is the best man to find it."

"I have my concerns about him." Quinn rested his elbows on the carved wooden arms of his chair and steepled his fingers together.

"Oh? You never said as much to me before."

"You were still in my employ then. Now I can speak to you as a friend who shares a joint past."

The logic to that was odd, but Colin played along. "What worries you?"

"Too many seem to die around Cartland."

"I thought that was by design."

"Occasionally," Quinn admitted. "He lacks the remorse that most would feel upon taking a life."

"You mean to say that *I* feel," Colin said wryly.

Quinn grinned and attracted the attention of a woman the next table over. His smile changed from one of amusement to one of sensual promise. Colin looked away to hide his chuckle. It amazed him that a man so widely lauded for his comeliness could hide such a covert livelihood.

"You never did enjoy that part of your employment," Quinn continued.

Colin lifted his glass in a mock salute and then swallowed the blood red contents in one uncouth swallow. "I always feared that every life I ended would cling to me in some way, taint me, and that eventually they would make me unsuitable for Amelia."

"How romantic," Quinn jeered softly. "One of the qualities I most loved in Maria was her ability to survive in the gutter. I could not live my life with a lily-white female. The weight of the façade would quickly fatigue me."

"You assume that the man you sit across from now is the real Colin and the one who longs for Amelia is the façade. Perhaps the opposite is true."

Quinn's gaze narrowed beneath boldly winged brows. "Then maintain the ruse a little longer."

Tensing, Colin set his empty glass down and listened alertly. "What do you want?"

He would do anything for Quinn, but the sudden portent of danger set him on edge. His bags were packed and loaded aboard the ship. In a few hours he would set sail and begin his true life, the one he had interrupted six years ago to become a man of means. A man of title, prestige, wealth. A man worthy of Amelia Benbridge.

"I have been told that Cartland is meeting often with confidants of Agent-General Talleyrand-Périgord."

Colin whistled. "Cartland is one of the most impious men I have ever met."

"Which is why his association with the equally impious agent-general is concerning. I want to search his lodgings tonight," Quinn said, "while you are still here to see to my safety. I simply need you to delay him if he attempts to retire early."

"Since he is aware that I depart at dawn, he will find it odd if I approach him."

"Be covert. Most likely he will cause you no grief. He is not known for being reclusive."

Nodding, Colin ran the posed scenario through his mind and could find nothing that would interfere with his removal from France. A few hours of his time and he would alleviate his feelings of guilt for abandoning Quinn. Cartland spent more time awake in the night hours than he did during the day. Chances were more than good that Colin would sit in a carriage watching the door of one establishment or another and go directly from there to the wharf.

"Of course I will help you," he agreed.

"Excellent." Quinn gestured to an attendant for more wine. "I am indebted to you."

"Nonsense," Colin dismissed. "I can never repay you for what you have done for me."

"I expect to be invited to the wedding."

"Never doubt it."

Quinn raised his refilled glass in a toast. "To the fair Miss Benbridge."

Filled with anticipation for the future, Colin drank eagerly to that.

* * *

"What are you about?" Colin muttered to himself just a few hours later as he clung to the shadows of an alleyway and followed Cartland at a discreet distance.

The man had left his mistress's home an hour past and had been strolling rather aimlessly ever since. Because he continued to move in the general direction of his lodgings, Colin followed. He could not have Cartland returning while Quinn might still be there.

The night was pleasant, the sky clear but for a few clouds. A full moon hung low, providing ample illumination when not blocked by a building. Still, Colin would much rather be in his cabin at the moment, sleeping away the hours until he could stand at the bow and breathe deeply of the crisp sea air.

Cartland turned a corner, and Colin fell behind, counting silently until the appropriate lapse had passed and he could round the building as well and continue his leisurely pursuit.

He made his move and paused, startled to find a private courtyard ahead. Cartland stood there, engrossed in discussion with someone who appeared to have been waiting. Two brick posts held lanterns marking the entrance to the outdoor retreat. A small fountain and a neatly trimmed, tiny lawn were the only other items in the space.

Colin hung back, drawing his cloak around him to better disguise his frame in the darkness. He was not an easy man to hide, not at a few inches over six feet in height and sixteen stone, but he had learned the art of concealment and practiced it well.

Oddly enough, while he could attribute his size to his laborer parents, Cartland was also quite large, and his breeding was more refined. He worked for a living only because his father had bankrupted them, and he made certain that everyone knew he was above certain tasks. Killing was not one of them. That was a duty he enjoyed far too much for

Colin's taste, which was why they associated with each other only when forced to by necessity.

Creeping along the damp stone wall, Colin moved closer to the two men, hoping to hear something that would help to explain this assignation.

"... *you may tell the agent-general* ..."

"... *forget your place! You are not* ..."

"...*I will see to it, Leroux, provided I am compensated* ..."

The debate seemed to grow more heated with Cartland gesturing roughly with one hand, while the gentleman with whom he spoke began to pace. The sound of heels tapping restlessly along cobblestones helped to disguise Colin's stealthy approach. Cartland's evening garments were covered by a short cape secured with a jeweled brooch that gleamed in the lantern light. The other man was hatless, coatless, and much shorter. He was also highly agitated.

"You have not followed through with your end of our arrangement!" Leroux snapped. "How dare you approach me for more money when you have yet to accomplish the task you were previously paid for!"

"I was underpaid," Cartland scoffed, his features hidden beneath the rim of his tricorn.

"I will inform the agent-general of your ridiculous demands, and advise him to seek someone more trustworthy to work on his behalf."

"Oh?" There was a smugness to Cartland's tone that alarmed Colin, but before he could act, it was too late. The light of the moon caught the edge of a blade and then it was gone, embedded deeply within Leroux's gut.

There was a pained gasp and then a thick gurgle.

"You can pass along something else for me as well," Cartland bit out, as he withdrew the dagger and thrust it home again. "I am not a lackey to be set aside when I have outlived my usefulness."

Suddenly a dark form leaped from the shadows and tackled Cartland, knocking his hat aside. The blade slipped free and clattered to the cobblestone. Leroux sank to his knees, his hands clutching at the welling blood.

Rolling and writhing upon the ground, the would-be rescuer fought brutally, delivering blows that echoed off the buildings around them. Material ripped and venomous words were exchanged as Cartland gained the upper hand. Pinning his assailant to the ground, he reached for the knife lying just a few feet away.

"Cartland!" Colin abandoned his attempt at stealth and rushed toward the fray, tossing his cloak over his shoulder to bare the hilt of his small sword.

Startled, Cartland pulled back, revealing a face etched with bloodlust and cold, dark eyes. The man beneath him took the opening and swung his fist hard and fast, clipping Cartland in the temple and sending him reeling to the side.

Colin ran through the posts that marked the entrance and pulled his blade free. "You have much to answer for!"

"It won't be to you," Cartland cried, kicking out with his feet.

Sidestepping the assault, Colin lunged, piercing Cartland's shoulder. The man roared like a wounded animal and flailed in fury.

Circling, Colin turned his head to look at the unfortunate Leroux. His open, sightless eyes betrayed his demise.

It was too late. The man who had the ear of Talleyrand-Périgord was dead.

The dreaded feeling of portent once again hit Colin hard.

Distracted, he failed to anticipate the blow that came to the back of his knee, tumbling him to the ground. By instinct, he rolled to the side, avoiding another assault from Cartland, but coming up against the corpse and the pool of blood quickly spreading around it.

Cartland scrambled for his discarded knife, but the other

man was there first, sending it skidding across the cobblestones with a well-placed kick. Colin was struggling to his
feet when alarmed shouts sounded from the nearby street.
All three of them turned their heads.

Discovery was near at hand.

"A trap!" Cartland hissed, leaping to his feet. He stumbled toward the low stone wall and threw himself over it.

Colin was already in motion, running.

"Halt!" came a cry from the alleyway.

"Faster!" urged Leroux's would-be rescuer, fleeing alongside him.

Together they took a different alley than the one Colin had
arrived through . . . the one that was presently filling with
authorities who pursued with lanterns raised high.

"Halt!"

When they reached the street, Colin ran to the left in the
direction of his waiting coach; the other man fled to the
right. After the explosion of activity in the small courtyard,
the relative stillness of the night seemed unnatural, the rhythmic pounding of his footfalls sounding overly loud.

Colin weaved in and out among various buildings and
streets, taking alleys whenever possible to lessen his chances
of being apprehended.

Finally, he returned to Cartland's mistress's house and
caught the eye of his coachman, who straightened and prepared to release the brake.

"Quinn's," Colin ordered as he vaulted into the carriage.
The equipage lurched into motion, and he hunched over,
tearing off his blood-soaked cloak and tossing it to the
floorboards. "Damn it!"

How the hell could such a simple task spin so far beyond
his control?

Keep Cartland from returning home too early. A bloody
simple task, that. One that should not have involved witnessing a murder and the drawing of his blade.

The moment his carriage drew to a halt before Quinn's door, Colin was leaping out. He pounded with his fist upon the portal, cursing at the lengthy delay before it opened.

A disheveled butler stood with taper in hand. "Sir?"

"Quinn. *Now.*"

The urgency in his tone was clear and undeniable. Stepping back, the servant allowed him entry and showed him into the lower parlor. He was left alone. Then a few moments later Quinn entered wearing a multicolored silk robe and bearing flushed skin. "I sent for you hours ago. When you did not reply, I assumed you had boarded your ship and gone to sleep."

"If you've a woman upstairs," Colin gritted out, "I think I might kill you."

Quinn took in his appearance from head to toe. "What happened?"

Colin paced back and forth before the banked fire in the grate and relayed the night's events.

"Bloody hell." Quinn ran a hand through his inky locks. "He will be desperate, running from both us and them."

"There is no 'us,'" Colin snapped. He pointed at the longcase clock in the corner. "My ship sets sail within a few hours. I've come only to wish you good riddance! Had I been caught tonight, I might have been delayed for weeks or months while this mess was sorted out."

More pounding came to the door. They both paused, hardly daring to breathe.

The butler rushed in. "A dozen armed men," he said. "They searched the carriage and took something from inside it."

"My cloak," Colin said grimly, "soaked with Leroux's blood."

"That they would come for you here would suggest that Cartland has offered you up as the sacrificial lamb." Quinn growled as commands were shouted from outside. "Answer that," he said to the waiting servant. "Delay them as long as possible."

"Yes, sir." The butler departed, closing the parlor door behind him.

"I am sorry, my friend," Quinn muttered, moving to the clock and shoving it aside, revealing a swinging panel behind it. "This will lead you to the stables. You may find trouble at the wharf, but if you can board your ship, do so. I will manage things for you here and clear your name."

"How?" Colin rushed over to the hidden portal. "Cartland was working with the French in some capacity. There must be some level of trust in him."

"I will find a way, never doubt it." Quinn set a hand on his shoulder as voices were heard in the foyer. "Godspeed."

With that, Colin rushed through the door, and it was immediately shut behind him. Scraping sounds accompanied the moving of the clock back to its original position. He heard no more than that, because he was moving blindly through the dark tunnel, his hands held out to either side to feel his way.

His heart racing, his breathing labored, he fought against a rising panic. Not because capture was at hand, but because he had never been so close to reclaiming Amelia. He felt as if she were within his grasp and that if he were unable to board his ship, he would be losing her all over again. He'd barely survived the first time. He doubted his ability to survive another.

The tunnel became dank, the smell unpleasant. Colin reached what appeared to be a dead end and cursed viciously. Then the sounds of skittish horses caught his ear, and he glanced up, noting the faint outline of a trapdoor above him. He kicked around with his foot until he found the short stool; then he pulled it closer and stood upon it.

Quiet as a mouse, he lifted the door just enough to look through the strands of straw that covered it. The stable was still, though the perceptive beasts it housed shifted restlessly in response to his agitation. Throwing the hatch wide, he climbed out and sealed the door again. Colin grabbed the nearest bridle and horse, then opened the stable doors.

He walked his mount outside, eyes wide and ears open as he searched for those who might be hunting him.

"You, there! Halt!" cried a voice coming from the left.

Grabbing two fistfuls of silky mane, Colin pulled himself up and onto the horse's bare back.

"Go!" he urged with a kick of his heels, and they burst out to the mew.

The early morning wind whipped the queue from his hair. He was hunched low over his mount's neck, as they raced through the streets, breathing heavily in unison. Colin's gut knotted with anxiety. If he made it to the ship without incident, it would be a miracle. He was so close to leaving this life behind, damn it. So close.

Colin galloped as near to the wharf as he dared, then dismounted. He freed his horse, then traversed the remaining distance on foot, moving in and out among the various crates and barrels. Sweat coated his skin despite the chill of the ocean breeze and his lack of outerwear.

So close.

Later, he would not remember the climb up the gangplank or the journey from the deck to his cabin. He would, however, never forget what he found inside.

The door swung open, and he entered, gasping at the sight that greeted him.

"Ah, there you are," purred the unctuous voice of a stranger.

Pausing on the threshold, Colin stared at the tall, thin man who held a knife to his valet's throat. One of Cartland's lackeys or perhaps one working for the French.

Regardless, he was caught.

His valet stared at him with wide horrified eyes above a cravat tied around his mouth as a gag. Bound to a chair, the servant was visibly trembling, and the acrid smell of urine betrayed just how frightened he was.

"What do you want?" Colin asked, holding both hands up to display his willingness to cooperate.

"You are to come with me."

His heart sank. *Amelia.* In his mind, she was retreating. Fading.

He nodded. "Of course."

"Excellent."

Before he could blink, the man moved, shoving his valet's head back and slitting his throat.

"*No!*" Colin lunged forward, but it was too late. "Dear God, why?" he cried, his eyes stung by frustrated, hopeless tears.

"Why not?" the man retorted, shrugging. His eyes were small and pale blue, like ice. Swarthy skin and late-night bristle on his jaw made him look dirty, although his simple garments appeared to be clean. "After you."

Colin stumbled back out the cabin door, inwardly certain that he would die this night. The deep sadness he felt was not due so much to the loss of his life, such as it was. It was mourning for the life he had dreamt of sharing with Amelia.

His hands were shaking as he gripped the railings that supported the stairs leading back up to the deck. A sickening thud and low groan behind him made him jump and turn too quickly. He tripped and landed on his arse on the second-to-bottom step.

There at his feet lay his captor, facedown with a rapidly swelling lump protruding from the back of his head.

Colin's gaze lifted from the prone body and found the man who had fought with Cartland in the courtyard earlier. He was short of stature and stocky, his body heavily muscled and clothed in nondescript attire of various shades of gray. The man's features were blunt, his dark eyes wizened and jaded.

"You saved my life," the man said. "I owed you."

"Who are you?" Colin asked.

"Jacques."

Just the one name, no more than that.

"Thank you, Jacques. How did you find me?"

"I followed this man." He kicked at the fallen body with the tip of his boot. "It is not safe for you to remain in France, monsieur."

"I know."

The man bowed. "If you have something of value, I would suggest you offer it to the captain as enticement to set sail immediately. I will manage the bodies."

Colin heaved out a weary breath, fighting the flickering hope inside him. The chances of him actually making it to English soil were negligible.

"Go," Jacques urged.

"I will help you." He pushed heavily to his feet. "Then you should disembark before you are associated with me."

"Too late for that," the Frenchman said, his gaze direct. "I will remain with you until you are settled and this matter of my master's death is resolved."

"Why?" Colin asked simply, too weary to argue.

"Arrange our departure now," Jacques said. "We will have plenty of time to talk on the journey."

Unbelievably, within the hour they were out to sea. But the Colin Mitchell who stood at the mist-covered bow was not the same one who had shared a farewell dinner with Quinn.

This Colin had a price on his head, and the cost to pay it could be his life.

Chapter 4

*T*he fence was directly ahead. After making certain that the guard was still far enough away to miss seeing her, Amelia hurried toward it. She did not see the man hidden on the other side of a large tree. When a steely arm caught her and a large hand covered her mouth, she was terrified, her scream smothered by a warm palm.

"Hush," Colin whispered, his hard body pinning hers to the trunk.

Her heart racing in her chest, Amelia beat at him with her fists, furious that he had given her such a fright.

"Stop it," he ordered, pulling her away from the tree to shake her, his dark eyes boring into hers. "I'm sorry I scared you, but you left me no choice. You won't see me, won't talk to me—"

She ceased struggling when he pulled her into a tight embrace, the powerful length of his frame completely unfamiliar to her.

"I'm removing my hand. Hold your tongue or you'll bring the guards over here."

He released her, backing away from her quickly as if she were malodorous or something else similarly unpleasant. As for her, she immediately missed the scent of horses and the hard-working male that clung to Colin.

Dappled sunlight kissed his black hair and handsome

features. She hated that her stomach knotted at the sight and her heart hurt anew until it throbbed in her chest. Dressed in an oatmeal-colored sweater and brown breeches, he was all male. Dangerously so.

"I want to tell you I'm sorry." His voice was hoarse and gravelly.

She glared.

He exhaled harshly and ran both hands through his hair. "She doesn't mean anything."

Amelia realized then that he was not apologizing for scaring the wits from her. "How lovely," she said, unable to hide her bitterness. "I am so relieved to hear that what broke my heart meant nothing to you."

He winced and held out his work-roughened hands. "Amelia. You don't understand. You're too young, too sheltered."

"Yes, well, you found someone older and less sheltered to understand you." She walked past him. "I found someone older who understands me. We are all happy, so—"

"What?"

His low, ominous tone startled her, and she cried out when he caught her roughly. "Who?" His face was so tight, she was frightened again. "That boy by the stream? Benny?"

"Why do you care?" she threw at him. "You have her."

"Is that why you're dressed this way?" His heated gaze swept up and down her body. "Is that why you wear your hair up now? For him?"

Considering the occasion worthy of it, she had worn one of her prettiest dresses, a deep blue confection sprinkled with tiny embroidered red flowers. "Yes! He doesn't see me as a child."

"Because he is one! Have you kissed him? Has he touched you?"

"He is only a year younger than you." Her chin lifted. "And he is an earl. A gentleman. He would not be caught behind a store making love to a girl."

"It wasn't making love," Colin said furiously, holding
her by the upper arms.

"It appeared that way to me."

"Because you don't know any better." His fingers kneaded
into her skin restlessly, as if he couldn't bear to touch her,
but couldn't bear not to either.

"And I suppose you do?"

His jaw clenched in answer to her scorn.

Oh, that hurt! To know there was someone out there
whom he loved. Her Colin.

"Why are we talking about this?" She attempted to
wrench free, but to no avail. He held fast. She needed distance from him. She could not breathe when he touched her,
could barely think. Only pain and deep sorrow penetrated
her overwhelmed senses. *"I forgot about you, Colin. I
stayed out of your way. Why must you bother me again?"*

He thrust one hand into the hair at her nape, pulling her
closer. His chest labored against hers, doing odd things to
her breasts, making them swell and ache. She ceased struggling, worried about how her body would react if she continued.

"I saw your face," he said gruffly. *"I hurt you. I never
meant to hurt you."*

Tears filled her eyes and she blinked rapidly, determined
to keep them from falling.

"Amelia." He pressed his cheek to hers, his voice carrying an aching note. *"Don't cry. I can't bear it."*

"Release me, then. And keep your distance." She swallowed hard. *"Better yet, perhaps you could find a more
prestigious position elsewhere. You are a hard worker—"*

His other arm banded her waist. *"You would send me
away?"*

"Yes," she whispered, her hands fisted in his sweater. *"Yes,
I would."* Anything to avoid seeing him with another girl.

He nuzzled hard against her. *"An earl . . . It must be
Lord Ware. Damn him."*

"He is nice to me. He talks to me, smiles when he sees me. Today, he is going to give me my first kiss. And I'm—"

"No!" Colin pulled back, his irises swallowed by dilated pupils leaving deep black pools of torment. "He may have all the things that I never will, including you. But by God, he won't take that from me."

"What—?"

He took her mouth, stunning her so that she couldn't move. Amelia could not understand what was happening, why he was acting this way, why he would approach her now, on this day, and kiss her as if he were starved for the taste of her.

His head twisted, his lips fitting more fully over hers, his thumbs pressing gently into the hinges of her jaw and urging her mouth to open. She shivered violently, awash in heated longing, afraid she was dreaming or had otherwise lost her mind. Her mouth opened, and a whimper escaped as his tongue, soft like wet velvet, slipped inside.

Frightened, she stopped breathing. Then he murmured to her, her darling Colin, his fingertips brushing across her cheekbones in a soothing caress.

"Let me," he whispered. "Trust me."

Amelia lifted to her toes, surging into him, her hands sliding into his silken locks. Unschooled, she could only follow his lead, allowing him to eat at her mouth gently, her tongue tentatively touching his.

He moaned, a sound filled with hunger and need, his hands cupping the back of her head and angling her better. The connection became deeper, her response more fervent. Tingles swept across her skin in a wave of goose bumps. In the pit of her stomach a sense of urgency grew, of recklessness and flaring hope.

One of his hands slipped, caressing the length of her back before cupping her buttock and urging her up and into his body. As she felt the hard ridge of his arousal, a deep ache blossomed low inside her.

"Amelia... sweet." His lips drifted across her damp face, kissing away her tears. "We shouldn't be doing this."

But he kept kissing her and kissing her and rolling his hips into her.

"I love you," she gasped. "I've loved you so long—"

He cut her off with his lips over hers, his passion escalating, his hands roaming all over her back and arms. When she couldn't breathe, she tore her lips away.

"Tell me you love me," she begged, her chest heaving. "You must. Oh, God, Colin..." She rubbed her tear-streaked face into his. "You've been so cruel, so mean."

"I can't have you. You shouldn't want me. We can't—"

Colin thrust away from her with a vicious curse. "You are too young for me to touch you like this. No. Don't say anything else, Amelia. I am a servant. I will always be a servant, and you will always be a viscount's daughter."

Her arms wrapped around her middle, her entire body quaking as if she were cold instead of blistering hot. Her skin felt too tight, her lips swollen and throbbing. "But you do love me, don't you?" she asked, her small voice shaky despite her efforts to be strong.

"Don't ask me that."

"Can you not grant me at least that much? If I cannot have you anyway, if you will never be mine, can't you at least tell me that your heart belongs to me?"

He groaned. "I thought it was best if you hated me." His head tilted up to the sky with his eyes squeezed shut. "I had hoped that if you did, I would stop dreaming."

"Dreaming of what?" She tossed aside caution and approached him, her fingers slipping beneath his sweater to touch the hard ridges of his abdomen.

He caught her wrist and glared down at her. "Don't touch me."

"Are they like my dreams?" she queried softly. "Where you kiss me as you did a moment ago and tell me you love me more than anything in the world?"

"No," he growled. "They are not sweet and romantic and girlish. They are a man's dreams, Amelia."

"Such as what you were doing to that girl?" Her lower lip quivered, and she bit down on it to hide the betraying movement. Her mind flooded with the painful memories, adding to the turmoil wrought by the unfamiliar cravings of her body and the pleading demands of her heart. "Do you dream about her, too?"

Colin caught her wrist again. "Never."

He kissed her, lighter in pressure and urgency than before, but no less passionately. Soft as a butterfly's wings, his lips brushed back and forth across hers, his tongue dipping inside, then retreating. It was a reverent kiss, and her lonely heart soaked it up like the desert floor soaked rain.

Cupping her face in his hands, he breathed, "This is making love, Amelia."

"Tell me you don't kiss her like this." She cried softly, her nails digging into his back through his sweater.

"I don't kiss anyone. I never have." His forehead pressed against hers. "Only you. It's only ever been you."

Amelia jerked awake with a violent start, her heart racing with the remnants of adolescent passion and yearning. Tossing back the covers, she sat up, allowing the chilly night air to seep through her thin night rail to her perspiration-damp skin. She lifted shaking fingertips to her lips, pressing hard against the swollen curves in an effort to stem their tingling.

The dream had been so vivid. She imagined that she could still taste Colin, a heady exotic flavor that she craved to this day. It had been years since she'd been plagued with such recollections. She'd thought they were fading, that perhaps she might be healing. Finally.

Why now? Was it because she had agreed to proceed with the wedding? Was Colin's memory rearing up and demanding that the love of her life not be set aside?

Amelia closed her eyes and saw a white mask above shamelessly sensual lips.

Montoya.

His kiss had made her tingle as well. From head to toe and everywhere in between.

She had to find him. She *would* find him.

"What does he say?"

Colin refolded the missive carefully and tucked it into a drawer of his desk. He looked at Jacques. "He believes Cartland is leading a group of men here in England."

"He will not want to bring you back alive." Jacques walked over to the window and brushed the sheer panel aside to look down at the front drive.

The town house they occupied was a rental in fine shape. It was a short distance from the city, near enough to be convenient, but far enough away to ensure that no one would find them noteworthy. The distance also allowed them to ascertain if they were being followed or not, which Colin had been just a few nights past. The night he had danced with and kissed Amelia.

"It is good that you stay indoors during the day," Jacques said, turning back to face him again. "You are being hunted on all sides."

Shaking his head, Colin closed his eyes and leaned into the back of his chair. "It was foolish of me to seek her out that way. Now I have attracted St. John's attention, and he will not rest until he knows why I displayed such interest in her."

"She is a beautiful woman," Jacques said, his voice laced with a Frenchman's innate appreciation of such delights.

"Yes, she is."

Beyond beautiful. Dear God, how was it possible for a woman to be so perfect? Stunning green eyes framed by sooty lashes. An imminently kissable mouth. Creamy skin, and the fully ripened curves of a woman grown. All carried with an air of latent sensuality that he had always found alluring.

He could admit now that his attendance at the ball had been goaded by his hope that he would see her and find his attraction unfounded. Perhaps absence had made his heart too fond. Perhaps he had embellished her memory in his mind.

"But that is not why you love her," Jacques murmured.

"No," Colin agreed, "it's not."

"I have rarely seen a woman with such yearning in her soul. Although I watched her as you did, she did not take note of my interest, only of yours."

That was his fault, he knew. Repeated glimpses of her profile had only whetted his appetite to see her directly. *Look at me*, he'd urged silently. *Look at me!*

And she had, unable to resist when followed with such ravenous attention.

The eye contact had cut him to the quick, piercing across the distance between them and stabbing deep into his heart. He'd felt it, the yearning Jacques spoke of. That longing elicited a primal response in him to deliver it, whatever *it* was that she wanted. Whatever she needed.

"You could take her from the other man," Jacques said.

He knew that, too. Had felt the wavering in her as they had danced and then again when they had kissed.

"I wish I'd never followed Cartland that night!" Colin growled, the frustration inside him a writhing, powerful thing. "Everything would be different."

She would be in his bed now, writhing and arching beneath him as he rode her hard and deep, awakening the wanton he sensed was waiting just beneath the surface. In his mind, he could hear her voice hoarse from crying out his name, her satin skin covered in a fine sheen of sweat.

He would push her beyond reason, take her body places she never knew it could go . . .

"The twists in our lives happen for a reason," Jacques

said, returning to the desk and sitting across from him. "I could have lived the whole of my life without leaving France, yet I was destined to follow you here."

Colin pushed the lewd images from his thoughts and opened his eyes. "You are a good man, Jacques, to carry your debt beyond the grave."

"Monsieur Leroux saved the life of my sister and with her, the life of my niece," he said quietly. "I cannot proceed knowing his murderer has not paid for the crime."

"And how do we make him pay?"

The Frenchman smiled, bringing warmth to his hard features. "I would like to kill him, but that would put you at a marked disadvantage. With me as your only witness, you would find it extremely difficult to prove your innocence."

Colin said nothing to that. Jacques had already helped far beyond what he had any right to ask.

"So he must confess." Jacques shrugged. "I will take what pleasure I can from doing whatever is necessary to garner that confession."

Nodding, Colin looked toward the window. Night had fallen hours ago. Shortly, he could leave and make discreet inquiries in his efforts to find Cartland before the man found him. But first, he would need some rest. "I will retire for a few hours, then set out and see what I can discover. Someone will have a loose tongue, to be sure. I just have to find him."

"Perhaps you should contact the man you worked for here," Jacques said carefully. "The one who directs Quinn."

Colin had never met Lord Eddington, never exchanged a word or correspondence. All communications passed through Quinn, and as far as Colin knew, Eddington was unaware of the identities of the men working under Quinn. There would be no way to prove that he was a confidant. "No. That is not possible," he said grimly. "We do not know one another."

The Frenchman blinked, apparently so taken aback by

the news that he lapsed into his native language. *"Vraiment?"*

"Truly."

"Well, then . . . that rules out that course of action."

"Yes. Unfortunately, it does." He pushed to his feet. "We will talk more when I awake."

Jacques inclined his head in agreement and waited until Colin had left the room. Then he moved to the desk, where he opened a drawer and pulled out the white half mask.

Colin would not be attending any balls or masquerades, so his continuing possession of the mask betrayed its sentimental value. Jacques had watched his new friend with Miss Benbridge and knew the woman meant a great deal.

So he would watch her when he could and keep her safe, if possible. If God was kind, Jacques would finish his task, Cartland would have his comeuppance, and Colin would have the woman he loved.

As a child, Amelia had learned how to socialize with giants.

Of course, at that time, they had been imaginary. The man standing before her was quite real, but she knew he was the same sort of giant as the one in her mind—gentle and kind beneath a gruff, formidable exterior.

"This is extortion!" Tim cried, looming over her.

Amelia set a hand at her neck to rub the ache caused by craning so far back. "No," she denied. "Not really. Extortion gives you only one choice. I am offering you options."

"I don't like yer options." He crossed his great arms over his barrel chest.

"I do not blame you. I don't care for them very much either."

She moved toward the nearby padded window seat. The upper family parlor was packed with people, all employees of St. John. Some played cards, others talked and laughed boisterously, and still others napped where they sat, exhausted from running errands all day long.

"It would have been much easier for everyone if the man had simply stated his intentions directly." Amelia shook out her skirts of yellow shot silk taffeta and settled as comfortably as possible in her evening attire. "But he did not, and so we must guess. I am not very good at guessing, Tim. I haven't the patience for it."

Looking up at him from beneath her lashes, she smiled prettily.

Tim snorted and scowled. "Don't you 'ave something else to worry your 'ead o'er? Wedding gowns and such?"

"No. Not really."

She should be consumed with the planning of her forthcoming nuptials. From waking to sleeping she should have no time for anything else. It was the most anticipated match of the Season and, if she maneuvered well, it could be a wonderful launch for her new position as a future marchioness.

Instead she was consumed by thoughts of her masked admirer. She was tenacious when intrigued and told herself that if she could only discern the man's motives, she would be free to concentrate on more pressing matters.

It was prewedding nervousness. The need for one last peccadillo. A farewell to childhood whimsy.

She shook her head. There were a hundred names she gave to why she was so distracted by the masked Montoya. But the reason's true identity eluded her.

"Well, *yer* not doing any searching," Tim grumbled. "Not on my watch."

"Fine," she said agreeably. "Just inform me when you find him."

"No." Tim's jaw took on that obstinate cant that was more bark than bite. He wore green wool trousers this evening and a black waistcoat trimmed with green thread.

It was the most colorful ensemble she had ever seen him wear. His coarse gray hair was restrained in a braided queue, and his Vandyke was neatly trimmed.

Amelia adored him for the effort, knowing the care he displayed was due entirely to affection for her. He wanted to make her proud while he was following her about at the Rothschild ball this evening. He would not be attending, of course, merely watching from the outside perimeter, yet he'd taken pains with his appearance.

She was proud of him, regardless.

"Very well, then." She heaved a dramatic sigh. "I shall search for him myself and drag you along with me, since you are to be my nursemaid."

Tim growled and several heads turned in their direction. "All right," he snapped. "I'll tell you when, but not where or 'ow. But you should be forgetting about that man. 'E won't be troubling you again, I promise you that."

"Lovely." She patted the space next to her and held her tongue regarding any further discussion on the matter. She would see Montoya again, alone. Whether that was within St. John's captivity, or outside his reach. She had to. Something within her wouldn't allow the matter to rest. "Come and tell me about Sarah. Will you be making an honest woman out of her soon?"

The floor vibrated with Tim's heavy footsteps, and when he sat, the seat creaked in protest. Amelia smiled. "Was your mother a sturdy woman?"

His returning grin was infectious. "No. She was tiny, but then, so was I."

She laughed and he flushed, so she changed the subject. "About Sarah . . . ?"

Sarah was Maria's longtime abigail, a soul of discretion and loyalty. Tim had been soft on the maid for years, yet neither appeared to be hastening toward the altar.

"She won't 'ave me," he answered glumly.

Amelia blinked. "Whyever not?"

"She says my work is too dangerous. She won't be widowed with children. Too 'ard."

"Oh." She frowned. "I do not understand that, to be honest. Love is too precious to waste. Waiting for the right time, the right place . . . Sometimes that never comes and you will have missed out on what little happiness was yours to claim."

Tim stared at her.

"Do not discount me because I am young," she admonished.

"Ye've yet to 'ave life knock you down."

"I have had it hold me back, restrain me, keep me from the things I have wanted."

" 'Tis different to see something through glass than it is to 'old it in your 'and and 'ave it taken from you." His eyes were kind. "Cease pining for yer stableboy. The earl is a good man to turn a blind eye to this." Tim waved his arm in a sweeping gesture that encompassed the whole room.

Amelia sighed. "I know. I do love him. But it is not the same."

"If the Gypsy 'ad lived, you would 'ave grown out of yer liking for 'im."

"I do not believe so," she refuted, seeing Colin clearly in her mind, laughing, his dark eyes bright with joy and affection. Then later, flushed and intent with passion. They'd done no more than kiss, but the ardor was there. The need. The sensation that the feeling would escalate into a blinding brilliance that might well be unbearable.

That sense of . . . anticipation . . . stayed with her. Unfulfilled. Untapped.

Until Montoya kissed her.

Then it had simmered inside her. Just for an instant, but long enough to reawaken what had long been dormant. *That* was what she could not explain. Not to anyone, not to herself. She had considered what, if anything, was similar about her two attractions. It was rather alarming to decide that she was attracted to the forbidden. To what she could not have. Should not have.

In the voluminous folds of her skirts, Amelia's hand clutched the secret bundle in her pocket that she carried with the mad hope that she might see Montoya again.

"The Earl of Ware has come to call," the butler intoned from the doorway.

Tim stood and held out his hand to her. "A good man," he said again.

Nodding, she released the note in her pocket and set her fingers within his palm.

The man in the white mask was following her.

The mask was the same, but the man wearing it was not. This man was shorter, stockier. His garments, though of the same austerity as Montoya's, were of lesser quality.

Who was he? And why did he hold such interest in her?

Amelia was crestfallen, but prayed she hid it well. Although she had known it was a possibility that Montoya had approached her for a reason beyond attraction to her, she had chosen to believe that it was personal, in the best possible way. His mourning for his lost sweetheart had been so like her own. She had felt a connection to him that she had previously felt only with Ware and Colin.

Had it all been a lie?

She suddenly felt alone and very naïve. The ballroom was a crush, the earl whose arm she held was charming and devoted, and someone was speaking to her, but she felt as if she were an island in a vast sea.

"Are you unwell?" Ware whispered.

Shaking her head, she tried to look away from the man in the white mask and was unable to. She damned herself for looking for Montoya. If she had not, she could have kept the fantasy of his interest alive within her. Now that it was gone, she felt its loss keenly.

"Should we stroll?" Ware suggested. He bent over her in

a highly intimate pose made acceptable by his smile and a wink at the gentleman speaking to them. "Lord Reginald's discourse is coaxing me to sleep, as well."

Amelia fought a smile, but felt it tugging at the corner of her lips. She turned her gaze from the masked man who watched her so closely and met Ware's concerned blue eyes. "I should like that, my lord."

He made their excuses and began to lead her away. As often happened when he sheltered her, her heart swelled with gratitude. She prayed that the feeling would grow into love and thought perhaps after they consummated their marriage it might turn into that. He would have a care for her in that regard, too, she knew.

She glanced at him, and he caught her gaze and held it. "Everything I do for you, sweet Amelia, is for the occasional moments when you look at me as you are doing now."

Blushing, she looked away and watched the man in the mask moving, circling the room at the same pace she was, keeping himself directly opposite her.

"Would you excuse me for a moment?" she asked Ware, smiling.

"Only a moment."

A female guest walked past them, her appreciative gaze roving the length of Ware's tall frame.

"You provocative devil, you," Amelia teased.

He winked, stepped back, and kissed her gloved hand. "Only for you."

She rolled her eyes at the blatant lie, then made her egress, heading toward the hallway that led to the retiring rooms. She took her time, making certain it would be easy to follow her, then slipped down the hall. There were plenty of guests mingling about. Music swelled from the open ballroom doors. Candlelight flickered in sconces along the wall. She felt safe.

Taking a deep breath, she pivoted on her heel and faced him.

He stood several feet back. Amelia arched a brow and gestured him closer. He smiled and approached, but stopped a discreet distance away.

"Y-your mask . . ." she began.

"*His* mask," he corrected with a definite French accent.

"Why? Does he want me, or St. John?"

"I do not know who St. John is."

Amelia hesitated a moment, inwardly debating the wisdom of her actions; then she reached into her pocket. She withdrew what she hid there and held it out to him.

The Frenchman's head tilted to the side as he considered her. He took what she offered and sketched a gallant bow. "Mademoiselle."

"Give him that," she said. Then, lifting her chin, she walked past him and returned to Ware's side.

Chapter 5

"For God's sake! Why did you go?"

Colin paced back and forth before the fire in his study and growled low in his throat.

"Because," Jacques said easily.

"Because? *Because!*" Colin glanced down at the object in his hand, a miniature of Amelia as only a lover should see her. *En dishabille,* one shoulder provocatively bare almost to the nipple, her hair loose and flowing, her lips red and slightly parted. As if she'd been fucked long and well.

Who was this made for? Not for him certainly. It would have been commissioned many months ago.

"She looked beautiful, monsieur."

Pausing before the fire, Colin leaned heavily against it, wishing he could have seen her. "What color was she wearing?"

"Yellow."

"She approached you?"

"In a fashion." Jacques sat on the settee and tossed one arm over the back, at ease. Which was completely opposite of Colin's own turmoil. "I admire her."

Colin released his breath in a rush. "Damn it. I wanted to keep my distance."

"Why? To keep her safe? She is heavily guarded." The

Frenchman's fingertips drummed silently against the wooden lip which framed the back of the settee. "Why is that?"

"Her sister and her sister's husband are both notorious criminals. They fear she will be used against them, just as I do." Leaving the grate, Colin sank heavily into his seat behind his desk.

"I thought her father was a man of some consequence."

"A viscount, yes." At Jacques's raised brows, he continued. "His avarice was exceeded only by his cruelty. He could see nothing beyond his own wants and desires. He married a lovely widow to gain access to her daughter, Amelia's sister. He sent Maria to the finest schools, then sold her into marriage to men he eventually killed to obtain their widow's settlements."

"*Mon Dieu!*" Jacques's fingers stilled. "Why did she not flee?"

"Lord Welton had Amelia and was using her to gain Maria's cooperation."

The Frenchman's face hardened. "I hope he has met his reward. There are very few things in this life that I find more detestable than crimes against one's family."

"His lordship was tried and hanged. In the course of her efforts to free her sister, Maria met Christopher St. John, a known pirate and smuggler. Together, they were able to manage a rescue and implicate Welton in the murders of Maria's two husbands."

Colin ran a hand through his hair. "The tale is far more complicated than that, but suffice it to say that St. John and his wife are two people with a multitude of enemies."

"Considering Miss Benbridge's past and present circumstances, it is even more curious that she would approach me as she did."

"Amelia was never one to do what was expected." His gaze returned to the miniature in his hand. It was an irresistible enticement that he must find a way to ignore.

"What did she give you?"

"An invitation." A private request to meet with her at the Fairchilds' musicale. Another chance to see her and speak with her.

"Will you go?"

"I think it would be best if I leave Town," he said, considering alternative locations. He could travel to Bristol, where Cartland's brood originated, and see what might be of interest there. A man like Cartland would not have a sterling past. There could be something Colin could use to lure the man into the open. "We cannot risk remaining in one location too long."

"And I was just beginning not to thoroughly detest London," Jacques said wryly.

Colin knew that although the Frenchman tried valiantly to hide it, he found England distasteful and obviously longed to go home.

"You do not have to come with me." Colin smiled to soften his words. "Frankly, I do not know why you are here."

Jacques shrugged his sturdy shoulders. "Some men are born to lead. I was born to serve." He stood. "I will begin packing our belongings."

"Thank you." Colin closed his fist around the precious image of Amelia, then put it away in his drawer next to the mask. "I will join you."

Rising to his feet, he told himself distance from Amelia was the best thing he could do for her.

But the image of her portrait refused to leave his mind, gnawing at his soul in a way he wondered if he would survive.

Amelia had always been known for her wanderings. Her unusual childhood led her to detest solitude as much as she craved it. She was never one to sit still for long, and she often made excuses to be alone, even at the most intimate of dinner parties. Ware understood her restless wanderlust, which was why he was always quick to suggest a stroll and a breath of fresh air.

So when she begged a few moments' absence to use the retiring room, Ware paid her no mind, nor did Lady Montrose, who acted as her chaperone. They both smiled and nodded, freeing her to attend her assignation.

If Montoya came.

She moved through the downstairs as silently as possible, slipping once into a conveniently located alcove when the sound of approaching voices made discovery a very real hazard. With a racing heart, she waited for the guests to pass.

Would he appear? Would he have found a way? His attendance at the masquerade led her to believe that he was a man of some consequence. A casual introduction to Lady Fairchild would have sufficed to be extended an invitation to tonight's event. However, she had inquired about him and was answered with a blank stare.

He had not been invited.

That did not mean he would not be here.

If his interest in her was related to St. John, she imagined he would have the knowledge required to gain entry to the house and find the private sitting room. She could not decide if that meant it would be best for him not to come. With the household she lived in and the man she was promised to marry, she could not afford any more trouble. But her heart recklessly ignored the situation as a whole and concentrated solely on what it wanted. She wasn't certain what she would do if he responded to her invitation; she knew only that she wished he would.

Anticipation and heady expectation filled her at the thought. She had dressed with purpose this evening, choosing a gown made of dark, thick sapphire damask accented with delicate silver lace at the bodice, elbows, and underskirts. With sapphires in her hair, at her throat, and adorning her fingers, she looked older and worldlier.

If only she felt that way inside. Instead she felt as she had as a young girl—breathless with the desire to see Colin and eager to feel the emotions that only he roused in her. She had thought she would never feel similarly again. It was both thrilling and frightening to feel that way about a masked stranger.

Finally, she reached the small sitting room she had specified in the note. Sarah had learned of the room from her cousin who worked in the Fairchild household. The abigail passed the information on to Amelia, wanting her to have a quiet place to retreat if necessary.

Pausing a moment with her hand on the knob, Amelia took a deep breath and attempted to calm her riotous nerves. It was hopeless, so she abandoned the effort. Opening the door, she slipped inside. The drapes were open, allowing a sliver of silver moonlight to slant in through the sash.

She waited just inside the door, giving her eyes the time necessary to adjust to the reduced lighting. She held her breath expectantly, her ears straining to listen above the rushing of blood, hoping that he would be there and call out to her.

But there was nothing more than the ticking of the clock on the mantel.

Amelia moved to the window and turned, taking in the contents of the room. Two settees, one chaise, two chairs, tables of various sizes scattered about . . . There was more, but no Montoya.

She sighed, and her hands moved restlessly over her voluminous skirts. Perhaps she had arrived too early, or he was having some difficulty gaining entry. She looked out the window, half frightened by the thought that he might be standing outside. But there was no Montoya there either.

A few minutes. She could spare that much.

As she began to pace, the clock ticked relentlessly. Her heart rate slowed and her breathing settled into a natural rhythm. Disappointment weighed on her shoulders and the corners of her mouth. After ten minutes passed, Amelia knew it was impossible to linger, though she thought she might wait all night if not for those who would seek her out in worry.

She walked toward the door. "Well . . . Now there is nothing to distract from the wedding plans," she muttered.

"Who was the miniature created for?"

Amelia paused with her hand on the knob, shivering as that dark, deep voice wrapped around her like a warm embrace. Gooseflesh covered her bared skin, and her lips parted on a silent gasp. Wide-eyed, she pivoted slowly to face the room. It was then that she saw the faint glow of the white half mask and cravat in the far corner. Montoya wore black again, enabling him to hide in the shadows of the unlit room.

"Lord Ware," she answered, slightly dazed by her phantom's sudden appearance and the realization that he had been there the whole time. Watching her. Why the mask? What was he hiding?

"Why was it created?" he asked gruffly. "It is not a gift commonly given from a virginal bride to her fiancé."

She took a step toward him.

"Stay there and answer the question."

Amelia frowned at his curtness. "I wanted him to see me in a different way."

"He will see you in all ways, in the flesh." There was bitterness in his tone, and the sound of it softened her apprehension, which enabled her to say what she might not have said otherwise.

"I wanted him to see that I was willing to share that side of myself with him," she admitted.

The sharp alertness that tensed his frame was palpable. "Why would he doubt it?"

"Must we talk about him?" Her foot tapped impatiently. "We have so little time since you spent all of it hiding in that corner."

"We are not talking about him," Montoya said silkily. "We are discussing why an intimate gift meant for your fiancé found its way into my possession. Did you intend for me to see you in a different way as well?"

Amelia caught herself fidgeting nervously and hid her hands behind her back. "I think you see me differently," she murmured, "regardless."

His smile flashed white in the darkness. "So if I, a stranger, can see you as a sexual creature, why would your future husband have difficulty doing the same?"

She held her breath, considering his perceptive probing. "What is it that you want me to say? It is inappropriate for me to discuss private matters."

"Sending me a provocative image of you is appropriate?"

"If it troubles you so, return it." She held out her hand.

"Never," he growled. "I will never give it back."

"Why not?" She raised one brow in challenge. "Do you seek to use it against me?"

"As if I would ever allow anyone else to see it."

Possessiveness. Clear as day. He was possessive over *her*. Amelia was both startled and pleased.

"Why does Lord Ware not see you as you wish to be seen?" he asked, finally approaching.

His tall form stepped out of the shadows and into the moonlight, setting her heart racing. There was something so predatory, yet elegant in the way he moved, his tails swaying gently with his determined stride. Power leashed and clad in a civilized veneer. It made his allure even more seductive, made her want to see him unrestrained and free. His features were austere, his beautifully etched lips enticing her to kiss him.

That is what I want, she realized suddenly. *That is why I needed to see him again.*

She was willing to be honest with him in order to achieve that aim. "We are longtime companions."

"Is it not a love match?" he asked, stopping a few feet away.

"I should not answer that."

"And I should not be here. You should not have lured me."

"You had me followed."

He shook his head. "No. Jacques took it upon himself. I am leaving Town. I need distance from you, before this matter progresses any further."

"How can you leave? Are you not haunted by our dance in the garden?" Her hand lifted to the sapphires at her throat. "Don't you think about the kiss we shared?"

"I cannot cease thinking of it." He pounced and caught her hard against him, as if something in him had broken free of its bonds. "Waking. Sleeping."

She felt his gaze heating her mouth. She licked the lower curve and breathed in the scent of his skin. He smelled exotic, spicy, purely male animal. Something instinctive inside her stirred in response.

"Do it," she goaded, her chest moving against his with rapid pants.

Montoya whispered a low curse. "You do not love him."

"I wish I did." Tentatively, her hands slipped beneath his coat and settled at his waist. His skin was hot, so feverish, she could feel the heat through his garments.

"Is your heart already taken?"

Her exhale was shaky. "In a fashion."

"Why me?"

"Why the mask?" she retorted, hating the feeling of being stripped bare by his questions.

He stared down into her upturned face. "My visage is not one you would wish to see."

She was deeply disquieted by the finality in his tone. The feeling of incertitude disturbed her to the point that she released him and attempted to step back. He held fast.

"Let us settle this now," he said, reaching up to brush callused fingertips along her cheekbones. "What do you want from me?"

"Did you approach me because of St. John?"

Montoya shook his head. "My motives were simple. I saw a beautiful woman. I lost all sense of manners and stared, which made her ill at ease. I attempted to apologize. That is all." His hands cupped her spine and stroked downward, arching her into him.

He was so hard, so solid, Amelia wanted to cling to him and touch him without impediments. Only one man had ever held her this closely. Only a short time ago, she would have said her ability to enjoy such an embrace with every fiber of her being had passed with Colin. Now, she knew that wasn't true.

How extraordinary to have found Montoya.

Or more aptly, how extraordinary that he had found her.

"That night . . . You recognized that others were coming," she pointed out.

"I did." The line of his lips hardened. "I am a man encumbered by a tainted past. It is why you should not send for me."

"You did not have to come." A tainted past, one that allowed him to recognize covert signals that most aristocrats would fail to notice. *Who was he?*

The corner of his mouth twitched with amusement, and she touched it with her fingertip. She could not see any deformity through the eyeholes of the mask or around his mouth. What she could see were dark eyes of a slightly exotic slant and a mouth made for sin. The curvature, shape, and firmness were perfection. She could imagine hours of kissing him and never growing bored. Whatever else may be wrong with him, she thought she might be able to bear it.

She touched the edge of the mask. "Let me see you."

"No!" He pushed her hand away roughly, then caught it

again and kissed the back. The press of his lips left tingles, even through her glove. "Trust me. It would be difficult to bear the truth of it."

"Is that why you will not court me?"

Montoya stilled. "Would you wish me to?"

"Do you feel this way about many women?" Her gaze dropped to his throat where she watched him swallow hard. "I have felt this way about only one other man, and he is lost to me, as your love is to you."

Suddenly his embrace tightened, and he pressed his lips to her forehead. "You have mentioned a lost loved one before," he rasped.

"Sometimes it feels as if a piece of me is missing. It is unbearable. I do not understand why I feel so vividly about him after all these years, as if he might return, as if some part of me expects him to." Her hands fisted in his coat. "But when I am with you, I think only of you."

"Do I remind you of him?"

She shook her head. "He was vital and unrestrained; you are more subdued, but in a . . . primitive way." Her smile was sheepish. "That sounds silly."

"The primitiveness comes in response to you," he said, nuzzling his jaw against her temple. He was so close, the smell of him inundated her senses and made her giddy. Joy, hot and sweet, filled her. The sensation of being alive after years of numbness. She felt guilty for that, burdened by a sense of betraying Ware, but she could not fight the attraction to Montoya. It was too strong, too heady and intoxicating.

"I would be willing to explore it . . ." she offered shyly.

"Are you propositioning me, Miss Benbridge?" he asked with a low laugh that she adored from the moment she heard it. It was the kind of laugh one worked to hear again. Already her mind was sifting through anecdotes she could share that might make him merry.

"I want to see you again."

"No." He cupped her nape and held her cheek to his chest, wrapping his big body around her. It was safe in his embrace. Warm. Delightful. Could two people spend hours hugging? A derisive snort escaped her. Hours of kissing and hugging. She was deranged.

"Was that a snort?" he teased.

She flushed. "Do not attempt to change the subject."

"We should part," he said, sighing with what sounded like regret. "You have already been absent from the festivities too long."

"Why did you not say something when I first arrived?"

Montoya tried to retreat, but she held him to her. There was power in her proximity, she thought. The two halves warring within him—the part that wanted to hold her and the part that wanted to push her away—seemed stalemated when she was near.

Amelia smiled a woman's smile. "You could not allow me to walk away, could you?"

"Is that vanity I hear?"

"Is that evasion?"

The flash of a rakish dimple made her stomach flutter. "If my circumstances were different, nothing could keep me from making you mine."

"Oh?" She looked up at him from beneath her lashes. "Would you come bearing honorable intentions, or would you seduce me as you are doing now?"

"Sweet . . ." He laughed again. "The only seduction at work here is yours."

"Truly?" Her breasts were full and heavy, pressing uncomfortably against her corset. Her mouth was dry, her palms damp. She *felt* seduced. Could it be that his body was responding to her as well? "What am I doing to you?"

"Why?" His smile was charming. "So you can do more of it?"

"I might. Would you like that?"

"When did you become so flirtatious?"

"Perhaps I have always been so," she rejoined, batting her lashes coyly.

Montoya turned pensive. "Can Ware manage you?" He caught her wrists and pulled her hands away from his waist.

"I beg your pardon?" Amelia frowned as he evaded her and moved toward the door.

"You are mischievous baggage." His gaze narrowed as his hand wrapped around the knob.

"I am not baggage." She set her hands atop her pannier.

"You will forever land into trouble if not watched carefully."

She arched a haughty brow. "I have been watched my entire life."

"And yet here you are, luring strangers with tantalizing miniatures and holding a highly inappropriate assignation."

"You did not have to come!" She stomped one slippered foot, irritated by his condescending tone.

"True. And I shan't come again."

His tone was too familiar. He had asked her if he reminded her of Colin. Up until this moment, he had not. They were built differently, their voices were inflected with dissimilar accents, and their strides boasted different kinds of confidence. Colin had a bit of a stomp, as if to forcibly establish his presence. Montoya had sultriness to his gait, a more understated way of defining his dominance.

But in their mulish determination to set her aside, they were the same. As a young girl, she'd no choice but to tolerate it. That was not the case now.

"As you wish," she said, moving toward him with a deliberate swaying of her hips. "If it is so easy for you to walk away and leave me behind, it would be best if you go."

"I did not say it would be easy," he bit out.

Amelia set her hand atop his where it gripped the knob. "Good-bye, Count Montoya."

He turned his head, and she lunged, pressing her lips to his. He froze, and she took the advantage, tilting her head to deepen the contact. His breathing grew labored, his skin hot. Still, he did not move. She was unsure of how to proceed, and without his participation the kiss became awkward. Then she thought perhaps she was overthinking the thing.

Closing her eyes, Amelia allowed instinct to take over. Her hands settled lightly upon his tense shoulders, and he shuddered. She licked his lower lip, and he groaned. Her stomach churned madly with delight and fear. What if they were caught? How would she explain?

Then she did not care because it was too delicious taking him as she wanted. He did nothing to help her, but he did nothing to stop her either. Stretching her arms up, she reached behind him and tugged off her glove; then she curled her fingers around his nape. The moment their bare skin touched she was lost to him. His mouth opened on a gasp, and she pushed her tongue inside, licking the taste of him as she would a favorite treat. She tugged on his queue, and he growled.

His tongue stroked along hers, a practiced, smooth glide that made her moan into his mouth. The tiny sound broke him. He moved so quickly, she barely registered it. The next she knew, she was pinned to the door by over six feet of aroused male, and he was kissing her back, ardently and possessively.

"Damn you," he cursed in a harsh whisper. "I can't have you."

"You will not even try!"

"I have done nothing but try. *Nothing.* That does not change the fact that my circumstances make me unsuitable and dangerous for you."

Montoya cupped her nape and slanted his mouth hungrily over hers. It was a dark kiss, rife with sensual intent. Delicious. She sagged into the door and took it, all of it. Every thrust of his tongue, every nibble of his teeth, every caress of his beautiful lips. She took it and begged for more with pleading whimpers that drove his fervency to greater heights.

There was a mask between them and endless secrets. There was the wall that existed between strangers who shared nothing of each other beyond a single moment in time, yet the connection she felt with him was there, threading through all of that.

Was it mere lust? How could it be when she could not see all of him? But this thrumming in her veins, the ache in her breasts, the dampness between her thighs . . . Lust was there, part of the greater whole.

"Amelia," he breathed roughly, his warm breath gusting across her damp skin. His parted lips drifted across her face, from jaw to cheekbone. Then higher. "I want to strip you bare, lay you on my bed, and kiss you all over."

She shivered, both at the serrated way he said her name and the images his words invoked in her mind. "Reynaldo."

"I must leave Town or that will happen, and I cannot lay claim to you if we progress that far. Not now."

"When?" Tormented by yearning and a body that was wracked with unappeased desire, she would promise anything in this moment to see him again.

"You have Ware, a friend of long acquaintance who can give you things that I cannot."

"Perhaps you and I can be friends."

"You do not know me well enough to say that."

"I want to know you." Her voice was a throaty purr. Never in her life had she sounded like that, and it affected him. She could tell by the way he wrapped himself around her in an even tighter embrace. "I would like you to know me."

He pulled back, and she realized she found the mask attractive. Arousing. How odd, but true, nevertheless. She did not find it alarming, but rather comforting. She felt too open, and the sight of the mask shielded her as well as him.

"The only thing you need to know about me," he said in a rasp, "is that there are those who want me dead."

"Such a statement might frighten other women away," she retorted, tugging his mouth back down to hers, "but I live with people who have similar problems. Some would say I live a similar circumstance simply by association."

"You won't change my mind," he grumbled, licking at her parted lips, his body acting in opposition to his words.

"*I* was attempting to leave the room; *you* detained me."

"You kissed me!" he accused.

Amelia shrugged. "Your mouth was in the way. I could not avoid it."

"You *are* trouble." Bending his head, he kissed her one last time. Softer. Lingering. Her toes curled in her slippers. "*Now*, we must part, before we are discovered."

She nodded, knowing it was true, understanding that she had been absent far too long. "When will I see you again?"

"I cannot say. After your wedding, perhaps. Maybe never."

"Why?" She'd asked that question endlessly tonight and still couldn't collect the answer. Did he not understand how precious it was to feel this alive around another being? She had not realized that she was dormant until she'd met him.

"Because Ware can give you things that I cannot."

She was about to retort, when the doorknob jiggled. Her breath caught and held. She froze. Montoya did not.

He moved quickly, pulling back from her and fading again into the shadowy corner. She stumbled away from the door when it pushed open behind her. Turning, Amelia faced the intruding party.

"My lord," she breathed, curtsying.

Ware entered with a frown. "What are you doing in

here? I have been searching the house for you." He studied her carefully; then his jaw tautened. "You have something to tell me, don't you?"

She nodded and held a shaking hand out to him. He took it and drew her out of the room, pausing a moment to sweep the contents with his gaze. Finding nothing amiss, he led her away from Montoya and into a future that was far less orderly than it had been mere days ago.

Chapter 6

"So that is the whole of it," Amelia said, her fingers fidgeting with her teaspoon.

The Earl of Ware reached over and stilled his fiancée's restless movement by covering her hand with his own. "No need to be nervous," he murmured, his mind sifting through everything she had related.

"You are not angry?" Her green eyes were wide with a mixture of surprise and apprehension.

"I am not pleased, but I am not angry." He smiled ruefully and settled back more firmly in his chair.

They were seated on the terrace of the St. John house, enjoying tea before their customary ride through the park. It was with some trepidation that he had passed the hours waiting to speak with her. He knew what a woman looked like after a heated assignation, so while Amelia's revelation was in keeping with his own suspicions, he was sorry to have them confirmed.

"I do not know what to do," she said, sounding forlorn. "I fear I am out of my depth."

"And I fear I am not going to be much help," he admitted. "We are friends, love, but I am a man first and foremost. It does not sit well with me to hear that you feel things for this stranger that you do not feel for me."

As her hand twisted and gripped his tightly, a becoming

blush spread across her cheeks. "I do not like myself very much at this moment. You are dear to me, Ware. You always have been, and I have not acted as you deserve. I pray you can find it in your heart to forgive me."

He stared pensively over the rear "garden." The word barely applied to the outdoor space that surrounded the St. John manse. Only low-lying flowerbeds alleviated the stark severity of the spacious lawn.

"I forgive you," he said. "And I admire your honesty. I doubt I would have the fortitude to reveal so much were I in your stead. However, I cannot have a fiancée who is engaging in such behavior, especially in public venues."

She nodded, looking like a chastened schoolgirl. While the scolding was required, he took no pleasure in it.

"You will have to decide, once and for all, whether you wish to wed me or not, Amelia. If you choose to proceed with our arrangement, you must act in good faith and deport yourself properly." Ware pushed to his feet and rolled his shoulders back to alleviate the tension there. "Damnation, I do not like feeling as if you are being coerced to marry me!"

Amelia stood as well, her floral muslin skirts falling to a graceful drape. "You are angry." She held up a delicate hand to stem his reply. "No. I understand. You have the right to be. Had you acted similarly, I would have been equally furious with you."

Blowing out her breath, she walked to the marble terrace railing and leaned her weight upon her hands. He joined her, the lawn to his back, she to his side.

She was lovely this afternoon, as she was every afternoon. Her dark hair was arranged in artless, powdered curls that swayed around her shoulders. Her skin was pale as cream, her eyes as green as jade, her lips red like dark wine. He had once jested that she was the only woman he thought of in poetic prose, and she'd laughed with him, delighted at what she called his "fancifulness." He was only fanciful with her.

"If we wed," she murmured, "do you intend to be faithful to me?"

"That depends on you." He considered her carefully. "If you lie there and pray for a swift finale, I probably will not be. I enjoy sex, Amelia. I crave it. I would not give up the pleasure of sexual congress for anything, even a wife."

"Oh." She looked away with a sigh.

A stray breeze blew by, rolling a tight curl along the tender, bared skin where her neck met her shoulder. She shivered, not with cold, but from the sensation. Ware noted that reaction, as he noted everything about her. Cataloguing the finer details for future use. Amelia was a tactile, sensual creature. Something he appreciated and had been gentle not to exploit, biding his time for the day when she would be his and he could teach her how to embrace that side of herself. With him alone.

Now, he had much to consider.

"I believe we could enjoy each other," he offered, teasing her fingers on the ledge with his own. "I think sex between us could be much more than a chore, but only if you open yourself to me completely in that way. No shyness, no reserve. If our marital bed is welcoming, I will not go elsewhere. I am not a man given to the pursuit of conquests. I simply want to fuck and have a splendid time doing it. If I can do that with one woman, more the better in my estimation. Less work."

The coarse word shocked her, he could tell, but it was the right word for how he liked his bedsport, and it was best she know that now. There would be no brief groping and grunting in the darkness. There would be illumination, flushed and sweaty skin, and many hours.

"Is that what passion in the bedroom is?" she asked, with what appeared to be genuine curiosity. "Animal urges given free rein? Is there nothing more involved in the process?"

It took him a moment to comprehend the question. "Are

you referring to the glances your sister shares with St. John? Or how the Westfields look at one another?"

"Yes. They are . . . indecent, yet romantic."

"You are not the only one to see such affection and covet it." The inquisitiveness in her gaze made him smile.

"Do you?"

Ware shrugged and crossed his arms over his chest, leaning his hip into the railing. "On occasion. But I do not pine for it or suffer from its lack. I think, however, that you do."

As honest as ever, she nodded.

"I begin to see that my straightforward approach to wooing you was not the best," he mused aloud. "I assumed that the miserable end to your first love affair would make you inclined to appreciate a more . . . *grounded* relationship. But you want the opposite, do you not?"

She pushed away and began to pace, which was her wont when agitated. At times like this, she reminded him of a caged cat prowling in its boredom. "I do not know what I want, that is the problem." The look she gave him pinned him in his place.

"I am content. There is nothing more that I need."

"Are you truly content?" she challenged. "Or do you simply accept that friendship is all that one can hope for in your position?"

"You know the answer to that."

"Who would you wed, if not for me?"

"I've no notion, nor do I care to think about it until absolutely necessary. Are you suggesting I consider alternatives to you?"

Coming to a halt, Amelia released a sound that reminded him endearingly of a kitten's growl. "I want to be mad for *you!* Why is the choice not mine to make?"

"Perhaps you suffer from bad taste?" He laughed when she stuck her tongue out at him. Then he lowered his voice and stared at her with heavy-lidded eyes. "If it's the mask that arouses you, I can wear one to bed. Such games can be fun."

When her eyes went big as saucers, he winked.

Her hands went to her hips as she bristled; then her head tilted to the side. "Perhaps it is the mystery that intrigues me so? Is that what you are suggesting, my lord?"

"It is a possibility." Ware's smile faded. "I intend to make inquiries about your admirer. Let us see if we can unmask him."

"Why?"

"Because he is not for you, Amelia. A foreign count? You have always longed for a family. You would not move away from your sister now that you are reunited, so what future do you have with this man? And let us not discount the fact that he may seek to wound me through you."

She began pacing again, and he watched, admiring the inherent grace in her movements and the way her skirts swirled enchantingly around her long legs. "Everyone appears to believe that Montoya has no interest in me as an individual, only in the people connected to me. I admit I find it rather insulting to learn that those who claim to love me find it impossible to imagine a man desiring me for myself."

"I can more than imagine it, Amelia. I feel it. Do not take my courtesy as a lack of desire for you. You would be wrong."

Heaving out her breath, she said, "St. John is also attempting to find him."

He expected as much. "If the man is hiding in the rookeries, St. John might succeed. But you said the count was finely dressed and cultured. He sounds as if he is a denizen of my social circles, rather than the pirate's. My search may prove more fruitful."

Amelia paused again. "What will you do if you find him?" There was more than a small measure of suspicion in her voice.

"Are you asking me if I will hurt him?" The question was not frivolous, as he was a swordsman of some renown. "I might."

Her beautiful features crumbled. "I should not have said anything to you."

Straightening, Ware moved toward her. "I am pleased you spoke the truth. Our relationship would have been irreparably damaged if you had presented a lie to hide your guilt." As he reached her, he breathed deeply, inhaling the innocent scent of honeysuckle. He had long suspected that her body resembled the flower she favored, fragrant and sweet as honey upon the lips.

He cupped her face in both hands and tilted her gaze upward to lock with his. Something new swirled in the emerald depths and he found himself falling into them. "But that does not change the fact that the man knew you were mine and took liberties regardless. A grave insult to me, love. I can forgive you, but I cannot forgive him."

"Ware . . ." Her lips parted, the seam glistening in the soft afternoon light.

Leaning over her, he bent to take her mouth. Her breath caught as she recognized his intent.

"Good afternoon, my lord."

They sprung apart as Amelia's sister and her husband joined them on the terrace, followed shortly by a maid bearing a new tea service.

"It is a lovely day," the pirate said in his distinctive raspy voice. "We thought we would join you in the sunshine."

Ware understood the warning. With a slight bow of his head, he stepped back farther. The former Lady Winter smiled at his perceptiveness. It was a bedroom smile, the one a woman shared with her lover after a bout of great sex. For Mrs. St. John, it was her only smile, and it was a lauded part of her appeal.

"We would enjoy the company," Ware said, leading Amelia back to their table.

He spent the rest of the afternoon trading inanities with the St. Johns and, later, with those he and Amelia passed during their drive through the park. But part of his mind was actively occupied with the logistics of his hunts—the one for Amelia's favor and the other for the masked man who sought to steal it from him.

"Are you certain the man's name is Simon Quinn?"

"Aye," the tavern keep said, setting another pint on the bar.

"Thank you." Colin accepted the ale and moved to a table in the corner. The report of a man searching for him was disturbing, even more so because the one making the inquiries was using Quinn's name. It could be Cartland, or one of the men with him, though the owner of the tavern was fairly certain the man did not have a French accent.

There was nothing Colin could do aside from settling in to wait, using techniques of concealment in which he was well versed. A man of his size could never hide completely, but he could make himself less noticeable by sprawling low to disguise his height and breadth of shoulder. He also left his hair unrestrained, which roughened his overall appearance.

The establishment itself made it easy to lose oneself among the crowd. The lighting was kept low to hide a multitude of faults and dirt. The dark-stained walnut furnishings—round tables and spindle-backed chairs—only added to the dimness of the interior. The air was filled with the smells of old and new ale and crackling grease from the kitchen. Patrons wandered in and out. Several were regulars whom Colin had spoken to previously.

Long ago, in his past life, he had frequented such places with his uncle, Pietro. Those lazy afternoons off had been spent listening to the imparted wisdom of a good and decent man. Colin missed him, thought of him often, and wondered how he was faring. Pietro had instilled strength of character in him and a belief in honor that had stood him in good stead these many years.

Colin's hand fisted on the table.

One day, they would be reunited, and he would show his uncle how he had heeded those early teachings. He would free Pietro from his life of servitude and establish him in comfort. Life was too short, and he wanted his beloved uncle to enjoy as much of it as possible.

"Evenin'," greeted a voice to his side, drawing Colin from his introspection.

Beside him stood an elderly gentleman who spent most of his life in the taverns on this street, offering companionship to those who would buy him a drink or something to eat. Occasionally, the man overheard something worth selling, and Colin was willing to pay for it, as he was well aware.

"Have a seat," Colin replied, gesturing to the chair opposite his own.

Hours passed. He used the time to question those who found him familiar from his previous sojourns there. Many hoped to earn a coin or two by passing along information of note. Sadly, there was nothing of interest about Cartland, but Colin bought a pint for anyone who talked with him and used their company to deepen his disguise.

Then, quite miraculously, the man he most hoped to see appeared in a swirl of heavy black cape. Simon Quinn paused at the bar and exchanged words with the keep, then turned with wide eyes to find Colin waving from the corner.

"By God," Quinn said as he approached, unclasping the jeweled frog that secured his cloak to his neck. "I have been searching all over London for you, half-starved, and you have been here in my lodgings the entire time?"

"Well"—Colin grinned—"the last few hours, at least."

Quinn muttered a curse under his breath and sank wearily into the seat across from him. A pint was brought over, then a plate of food. Once he was fully settled, he said, "I come bearing both good and bad news."

"Why am I not surprised?" Colin said dryly.

"I have been betrayed in France."

Colin winced. "Did Cartland forfeit the names of every-one?"

"It would appear so. I believe that is how he was able to prove his loyalty."

"The man has loyalty to no one but himself."

"Very true." Quinn stabbed a piece of meat, brought it to his mouth, and chewed angrily.

"So that is the bad news, then. What is the good?"

"I have been able to secure a promise of a pardon for all of us, including you."

"How is that possible if they hunt you as well?"

Quinn's smile was grim. "Leroux was valuable to the agent-general, enough so that the capture of his killer is of greater concern than the routing of English spies. I was allowed to leave on the promise that I would return with the murderer—whoever that may be. To guarantee my return, they hold the others Cartland betrayed."

Colin straightened. "By God . . . we must work swiftly, then."

"Yes." Quinn finished off his pint. "And there are conditions to complicate matters. First, I must persuade Lord Eddington to release a French spy whom he has in captivity. Then, we must convince a member of Cartland's group—a man named Depardue—to vouch that Cartland has confessed to the crime."

The first seemed unlikely, and the second seemed highly difficult, but Colin would take what opportunities were given to him and gladly.

I want to know you, Amelia had said. If only he had the chance to make that happen.

"You seem unduly pleased by this," Quinn said around a bite. "It is not much."

"I saw Amelia," Colin confessed. Held her, touched her, tasted her.

Quinn stilled with a forkful of food lifted halfway to his mouth. "And?"

"It is complicated, but hopeful."

Setting his utensils down, Quinn gestured for more ale. "How did she take your emergence from the grave?"

Colin smiled ruefully and explained.

"A mask?" Quinn asked when he finished. "Out of all the guises you are capable of donning, you chose a *mask?*"

"Originally, it suited the masquerade. Later, she saw it on Jacques and it drew her to him. It seemed appropriate to wear it a third time under those circumstances."

"She is more like her sister than I thought." Quinn's lips curved into the slight smile he always wore when referring to Maria. "However, I fail to see how the situation is hopeful. Amelia has no idea who you are."

"That is a bit of a problem," Colin agreed.

"A bit? My friend, you are the master of understatement. Trust me, she will not take the news well. She will take it as lack of affection. When she discovers that you were not chaste and pining for her the entire time, she will have her proof that you do not love her."

Colin heaved out a sigh and sank back into his chair. "This was *your* plan! *You* said that I should become a man of means in order to make her happy."

"Also to make you happy. You would always doubt your worth if you came to her as an underling." Quinn smiled at the serving girl who brought over the fresh pint, then sat back and studied Colin for a long moment. "I hear she is betrothed to the Earl of Ware."

"Not yet."

"She could be a marchioness, despite her father's scandal and her sibling's reputation. Quite an accomplishment."

Glancing around the room, Colin's gaze paused a moment on every patron, taking stock of each one. "Yes, but she does not love him. She still loves me. Or rather, the boy I used to be."

A lovely blonde entered the room from the staircase that led to the bedchambers above. Dressed in deep purple and wearing a black ribbon and cameo at her throat, she reminded Colin of a doll. Her delicate features and slender build roused protective instincts, her heavy-lidded eyes and full, red lips inspired carnal musings.

His brows lifted as she turned her head and locked eyes with him. Her smile made him frown in confusion, and he watched her approach with much curiosity, pushing to his feet when she came to a halt behind Quinn.

She set her hands on the Irishman's broad shoulders. "You should have told me you were back, *mon amour,*" she said, her voice inflected with an unmistakable French accent.

The look Quinn shot Colin was intriguing, bearing more than a trace of irritation. He did not stand, merely caught the blonde's hand and tugged her around, directing her to a chair he pulled closer with his foot. Considering Quinn's love of females, his apparent disinterest in such a beautiful woman was beyond surprising. In close proximity, she was a delight. Pale blue eyes were framed by long, thick chocolate lashes and accented by finely arched brows.

"Is this him?" she asked, studying Colin with an appreciative eye.

Quinn growled.

She smiled wide, revealing straight white teeth. She offered her hand and said, "I am Lysette Rousseau. You are Monsieur Mitchell, *oui?*"

Colin glanced at Quinn, who cursed under his breath and resumed his meal. "Perhaps," he replied with caution.

"Excellent. Should it become necessary to kill you, it will be much easier now that I have catalogued your appearance."

Blinking, he asked, "What the devil did you just say?"

"Provoking wench," Quinn muttered. "He is innocent."

"They all say that," she replied sweetly.

"It is true in this case," Quinn argued.

"They all say that, too."

"Pardon me." Colin glanced between them. "What are you talking about?"

Quinn gestured toward Lysette with an off-hand jerking of his fork. "She is an additional part of my guarantee. She is to return to France with either Cartland, you or me."

"Or a confession," she purred. "A confession from any of you would suffice. See? I am not so difficult to please."

"Christ." Resuming his seat, Colin examined the French-woman. It was then that he noted a hardness to her eyes and mouth that he had missed before. "How do you find these femmes fatales, Quinn?"

"They find me," Quinn grumbled, biting into a potato with gusto born of frustration.

"You see only the negatives," Lysette said, gesturing for service. "There are three of us at this table, all searching for the same thing. I am here to assist you."

Quinn glared. "If you think holding a sword over my head is endearing, you are sadly mistaken."

Colin was not so quick to dismiss her. "How can you help?"

"In many ways." The blonde took a brief moment to order wine from the attending serving girl. "Think of the places I can go where you cannot. All the people who might speak to me but not to you. All the wiles I employ as a woman that you cannot employ as a man. Why, the possibilities are endless!" She lifted a delicate hand to the cameo at her throat, and he found it nearly impossible to imagine her killing anyone.

"How does your participation relate to Depardue?" Colin asked.

Something dark passed over her features. "If he resolves this, it will save me the trouble."

"The agent-general is determined to leave nothing to chance," Quinn explained. "Depardue watches Cartland.

Lysette watches me. They perform the same service. She is an added . . . warranty."

Colin winced. "I cannot imagine Depardue appreciates the intimation that he might not be successful." He looked at Lysette, wondering what the lure of such a position would be. "Why are you doing this?"

"My reasons are my own. A word of advice"—she stared at him intently—"you can trust nothing about me except this: I want Leroux's killer brought to justice."

Exhaling harshly, Colin drummed his fingertips atop the table. "I do not like this. While Cartland hunts me, we have a serpent in our midst."

Quinn nodded his agreement.

Lysette pouted as she accepted the goblet she had ordered previously. "I would rather be Eve than the snake."

"Eve was alluring," Quinn retorted.

Colin choked, never having heard the Irishman say an unkind word to a female before.

"What have you accomplished up to this point?" she asked, dismissing Quinn's rudeness and directing her attention to Colin.

"My days are spent evading Cartland and anyone who sounds French, and my nights are spent searching for him."

"That is the most ridiculous plan I have ever heard," she scoffed.

"What do you suggest I do, then?" he challenged. "I know nothing."

"So you must learn." Lysette took a dainty sip of the blood red wine and licked her lips. She sat with a ramrod straight spine and uplifted chin, the hallmarks of good breeding and proper schooling. "You cannot do that while hiding, which is exactly what Cartland will expect you to be doing. Why do you not contact the man you both work for? Surely, he has the resources to help you bring this to a swift end."

"That is not his purpose," Quinn argued. "We are responsible for the managing of our assignments. If we are caught, the cost is ours to pay. I expect your arrangement is similar."

For a moment, it seemed frustration marred the French-woman's lovely features, and then it was gone, replaced by a honeyed, careless smile.

Colin could not help but wonder at her, and contemplate how much of a risk she presented. She was so slender and feminine, yet he knew from tales of Amelia's sister that appearances could be very deceiving. "Do you have other suggestions, mademoiselle? Perhaps you think I should search in the bright light of day?"

"Will you wear a mask?" Quinn asked, finally pushing his plate aside.

"Why would he?" She raked Colin with an assessing glance from the top of his head, down the length of his outstretched legs, to his booted feet. "It would be a shame to conceal such comeliness." Her mouth curved seductively. "I should like to view all of it."

Quinn snorted. "Now, you see, love. That is why you are not Eve. You lack the sense required to see the man is taken."

"You may wear a blindfold," she offered Colin with a wink, "and call me by whatever name you prefer."

Colin laughed for the first time in days.

"Watch out for her," Quinn warned.

"I will leave that task to you. I leave for Bristol in the morning. Cartland's past may be affecting his present. I hope that something can be discovered that might give me some advantage."

"Good thinking." Quinn's lips pursed with thought. "Lysette and I will stay behind and make inquiries here."

"I am not comfortable allowing him to go off alone," she said, with an underlying note of steel to her voice.

"You will grow accustomed." Quinn lounged in his chair with his usual insolent grace—his body canted to the side, his arm slung across the spindle back, his legs spread wide.

"As handsome as you are," she sniffed, "I sometimes find it difficult to like you."

Quinn grinned. "So we are in accord. Mitchell will search elsewhere. You and I will work together in Town."

"Perhaps I wish to go with him instead." Lysette's smile did not reach her lovely eyes.

"Oh, would you?!" Quinn's exaggerated pleasure made Colin laugh again. "How delightful. At least for me, if not for Mitchell. Sorry, chap." He shrugged one shoulder and set his hand on the table.

Before either of them could anticipate the action, Lysette was on her feet and Quinn's discarded knife was piercing the table with precision . . . directly between his casually splayed fingers.

He froze and stared at how close he had come to losing a finger or two. "Damnation."

She leaned over him. "Do not mock or underestimate me, *mon amour*. It is not wise to prick my temper."

Colin stood. "Thank you for the kind offer of your companion's company," he said hastily, "but I must respectfully decline."

Lysette looked at him with a narrowed glance.

"You trust me not at all," he said, "but I promise you this: I have every reason to clear my name and no reason to flee."

For a moment, she did not move. Then her mouth lifted slightly at the corner. "Your woman is here."

He said nothing, but an acknowledgment wasn't necessary.

She waved him off with a graceful toss of her wrist. "You will not stray far. Good luck to you."

After a quick bow, Colin reached into his pocket and tossed coins on the table. "I will pray for you," he said to Quinn, squeezing his friend's shoulder as he passed.

Quinn's reply was a blistering curse.

Chapter 7

It was a small but fine house in a respectable neighborhood. The Earl of Ware had owned it for three years now, and during that time, it had rarely been unoccupied.

Tonight the lower windows were dark, but candlelight flickered from one upper sash. He pushed his key into the front door lock and allowed himself entry. The home was maintained by two servants, a husband and wife pair who were trustworthy and discreet. They were abed now, and since he did not require their services, Ware did not disturb them.

He set his hat on the hook, followed by his cloak. Beneath that he wore the evening garments he had donned for another night in an endless string of nights spent at balls and routs. Except this evening had been slightly different. Amelia was different. *He* was different. The awareness between them had changed. She saw him in a new light, as he saw her in altered fashion as well.

Climbing the steps to the upper floor, he paused a moment outside the one door where light peeked out from the gap at the bottom. Ware exhaled, taking a moment to relish the thrumming of blood in his veins and the quickening of his arousal. Then he turned the knob and entered, finding his dark-haired, sloe-eyed mistress reading quietly in bed.

Her gaze lifted to meet his. He watched her breathing

quicken and her lips part. The book was shut with a decisive snap, and he kicked the portal closed behind him.

"My lord," Jane breathed, tossing back the covers, revealing a shapely figure. "I was hoping you would come tonight."

Ware's mouth curved. She was hot for it, which meant the first fuck could be hard and swift. Later, they would take their time, but now such dalliance would not be necessary. A circumstance that suited his mood.

From the moment he had first seen the stunning widow, he'd wanted her. When her last arrangement with Lord Riley ended, Ware approached her with haste before anyone else could lure her away. She was flattered and, later, enthusiastic. They suited each other well, and the sex was pleasurable for both.

He shrugged out of his coat; she untied the belt of her robe. Within moments he was deep inside her—her hips on the edge of the mattress, his feet on the floor as he drove powerfully into her writhing body. His frustration and unease were forgotten in the maelstrom of carnal sensation, much to his relief.

But the surcease did not last long.

An hour later he rested on his back with his hand tucked behind his head, his sweat-drenched skin cooling in the evening air.

"That was delicious," Jane murmured, her voice throaty from passionate cries. "You are always so primitive when aggravated."

"Aggravated?" He laughed and tucked her closer to his side.

"Yes. I can tell when something is troubling you." Her hand stroked down the center of his chest.

Ware stared up at the ornate ceiling moldings and thought again of how well the room suited her, with its rose and cream colors and gilded furnishings. He had encouraged her to spare no expense and to think only of her own comfort, having found over the course of several mistresses that a woman's taste in décor spoke a great deal about her. "Must we talk of things unpleasant?"

"We could work your frustrations into exhaustion," she teased, lifting her head to reveal laughing dark eyes. "You know I will not complain."

He brushed back the damp strands of hair that clung to her temple. "I prefer that solution."

"But it would be only a temporary measure. As a woman, I might be able to assist you with your problem, which I suspect is feminine in nature."

"You *are* helping me," he purred.

Her raised brows spoke of her skepticism, but she did not press him.

Exhaling harshly, he shared his thoughts aloud, trusting Jane as a friend and confidante. She was a sweet woman, one of the sweetest he knew. She was not the kind of soul who sought to hurt others or advance herself at another's detriment.

"Do you realize that a man of my station is rarely seen as a man?" he asked. "I am lands, money, and prestige, but rarely more than that."

She listened quietly but alert.

"I spent my youth in Lincolnshire, raised to think of myself only as Ware and never as an individual. I had no interests outside of my duties, no goals beyond that of my title. I was trained so well that it never occurred to me to want something of my own, something that had nothing to do with the marquessate and everything to do with me."

"That sounds like a very lonely way to live."

He shrugged and shoved another pillow under his head. "I had no notion of any other way."

When he held his silence, she prompted, "Until?"

"Until one day I traversed the perimeter of our property and chanced upon an urchin preparing to fish in my stream."

Jane smiled and slid from his arms and the bed, donning her discarded robe before moving to the console and pouring a libation. "Who was this urchin?"

"A servant from the neighboring property. He was waiting for the young lady whose father he worked for. They had struck up a friendship of sorts, which intrigued me."

"As did the young lady." She warmed the brandy expertly by rolling the glass over the flame of a taper.

"Yes," he agreed. "She was young, wild, and free. Miss Benbridge showed me how different the world looked through the eyes of one who suffered under no one's expectations. She also completely disregarded my title and treated me just as she treated the urchin, with playful affection."

Jane sat on the edge of the bed and drank lightly, then passed the goblet over to him. "I think I would like her."

"Yes." He smiled. "I believe she would like you, as well."

They would never meet, of course, but that was not the point.

"I admire you for marrying her," she said, "despite the sins of her father."

"How could I not marry her? She is the person who taught me that I had value in and of myself. My aristocratic arrogance is now tempered with personal arrogance."

Laughing, Jane curled over his legs. "How fortunate for the rest of us."

Ware ran a hand through his unbound hair. "I will never forget the afternoon when she said, quite innocently, that I was devilishly handsome, which was why she sometimes halted her speech midsentence. No one had ever said such a thing to me. I doubt anyone had ever felt it. When they stuttered it was because of intimidation, not admiration."

"I tell you that you are comely, my lord," she said, the sparkle in her eyes giving proof to her words. "There are few men as handsome as you are."

"That may be true. I do not compare myself to other

men, so I would not know." He drank in large swallows. "But I suspect my attractiveness has more weight when I believe in it myself."

"Confidence is a potent lure," she agreed.

"Because she had no expectations of me, I was able to be myself with her. It was the first time in my life that I spoke without considering the confines of my station. I practiced wooing with her and said things aloud that I had never allowed myself to even consider." He looked down the foot of the bed and into the fire in the grate. "I suppose I grew into my own by knowing her."

Running her fingertips down his bare thigh, she asked, "Do you feel as if you owe a debt to her?"

"Partly, but our relationship has never been one-sided. We practiced deportment together and conversation. I had experience with such things; she was so sheltered."

"You gave her polish."

"Yes. We both gained."

"And now she belongs to you," Jane pronounced, "because you helped to create her."

"I—" Ware frowned. Was that where this disgruntlement came from? Did he simply feel proprietary? "I am not sure that is it. She was in love once—or so she says—and she still pines for him. I do not resent that. I accept it."

"Perhaps 'appreciate' would be a more apt word?" Her lips lifted in a kind smile. "After all, she cannot burden you with elevated feelings if they are engaged elsewhere."

He tossed back the rest of his brandy, filling his belly with fire, then thrust the goblet at her in a silent demand for more. "If that were true, why am I so annoyed by her fascination with another man?"

As she accepted the glass, her brows rose. "Annoyed? Or jealous?"

Ware laughed. "A little of both?" He waved one hand carelessly. "Perhaps my masculine sensibilities are piqued because she never felt such interest in me? I cannot say for certain. I only know that I doubt myself again. I am wondering if my decision to give her the space and time to heal was an error in judgment."

Jane paused halfway to the console. "Who is this other man?"

He explained.

"I see." She refilled his glass and warmed the liquor, then returned to him. "You know I cared deeply for my late husband."

Nodding, Ware patted the spot next to him. She crawled up beside him, baring her lithe legs to his view. "But I was tempted to marry another, whom I did not love."

"You jest," he scoffed. "Women want nothing so much as they want devotion and pronouncements of undying affection."

"But we are also pragmatic. If you offer Miss Benbridge all the practical things she covets that this other man cannot provide, she will be more tempted to select you."

"I pointed out that his foreign title would require her to leave her sister behind."

"Verbally, you did, yes. Now make it even more difficult by proving it in fact. Take her to see your properties, purchase a home near her sibling . . . things of that nature. Then, consider her love of romance and mystery. Put that into play, as well. You can seduce her easily. You have the skill and she is susceptible. Flowers, gifts, stolen kisses. Your competition is working in the shadows. You have no such limitations."

"Hmm . . ."

"It could be fun for you both. A chance to learn more about each other than you now know."

He reached over and linked his fingers with hers. "You are so clever."

Jane's mouth curved in her winsome smile. "I am a woman."

"Yes, I am ever aware of that fact." Reaching to the side,

98   *Sylvia Day*

Ware set his goblet atop the bedside table and pulled her beneath him. He kissed her, then moved lower, nudging the edge of the robe aside to take a nipple in his mouth.

"Oh, that's nice," she sighed.

Lifting his head, he grinned. "Thank you for your help."

"My motives are not entirely altruistic, you know. Perhaps you will become aggravated during your attempts to woo Miss Benbridge. I do so love it when you are less than controlled."

"Minx." He gave a mock growl and she shivered.

Which prompted Ware to spend the rest of the hours until morning playing the primitive lover to both their delights.

Amelia peeked around the corner of the house, her lower lip worried between her teeth. She searched for Colin in the stable yard, then heaved a sigh of relief when she found the area empty. Male voices drifted on the wind, laughter and singing spilling out from the stables. From this she knew Colin was hard at work with his uncle, which meant that she could safely leave the manse and head into the woods.

She was becoming quite good at subterfuge, she thought as she moved deftly through the trees, hiding from the occasional guard in her journey toward the fence. A fortnight had passed since that fateful afternoon when she had caught Colin behind the shop with that girl. Amelia had avoided him since, refusing to speak with him when he asked the cook to fetch her.

Perhaps it was foolish to hope that she would never see him again, given how closely their lives were entwined. If so, she was a fool. There was not an hour of the day that passed without her thinking of him, but she managed the pain of her grief as long as he stayed away from her. She saw no reason for them to meet, to talk, to acknowledge each other. She traveled by carriage only when moving to a new home, and even then, she could deal exclusively with Pietro, the coachman.

Espying the waited-for opening, Amelia hopped deftly over the fence and ran to the stream, where she found Ware coatless and wigless, with his shirtsleeves pushed up. The young earl had caught some color to his skin these last weeks, setting aside his life of book work in favor of hard outdoor play. With his dark brown locks tied in a queue and his cornflower-colored eyes smiling, he was quite handsome, his aquiline features boasting centuries of pure blue blood.

He did not set her heart to racing or make her ache in unfamiliar places as Colin did, but Ware was charming and polite and attractive. She supposed that was a sufficient enough combination of qualities to make him the recipient of her first kiss. Miss Pool told her to wait until the right young man came along, but Colin already had, and had turned to another instead.

"Good afternoon, Miss Benbridge," the earl greeted with a perfect bow.

"My lord," she replied, lifting the sides of her rose-hued gown before curtsying.

"I have a treat for you today."

"Oh?" Her eyes widened in anticipation. She loved gifts and surprises because she rarely received them. Her father simply could not be bothered to consider such things as birthdays or other gift-giving occasions.

Ware's smile was indulgent. "Yes, princess." He offered his arm to her. "Come with me."

Amelia set her fingers lightly atop his forearm, enjoying the opportunity to practice her social graces with someone. The earl was kind and patient, pointing out any errors and correcting her. It gave her a higher polish and a deeper confidence. She no longer felt like a girl pretending to be a lady. Instead she felt like a lady who chose to enjoy her youth.

Together they left their meeting place by the stream and wended their way along the shore until they reached a larger clearing. There Amelia was delighted to find a blanket stretched out on the ground, the corner of which was held down by a basket filled with delicious smelling tarts and various cuts of meat and cheeses.

"How did you manage this?" she breathed, filled with pleasure by his thoughtfulness.

"Dear Amelia," he drawled, his eyes twinkling. "You know who I am now, and who I will be. I can manage anything."

She knew the rudiments of the peerage, and saw the power wielded by her father, a viscount. How many more times the magnitude was the power wielded by Ware, whose future held a marquessate?

Her eyes widened at the thought.

"Come now," he urged. "Have a seat, enjoy a peach tart, and tell me about your day."

"My life is dreadfully boring," she said, dropping to the ground with a sigh.

"Then tell me a tale. Surely you daydream about something."

She dreamt about kisses given passionately by a dark-eyed Gypsy lover, but she would never say such a thing aloud. She rose to her knees and dug into the basket to hide her blush. "I lack imagination," she muttered.

"Very well, then." Ware situated himself on his back with his hands clasped at his neck and stared up at the sky. He looked as at ease as she had ever seen him. Despite the rather formal attire he wore—including pristine white stockings and polished heels—he was still a far more relaxed person than the one she met weeks ago. Amelia found that she rather liked the new earl and felt a touch of pleasure that she had wrought what she considered to be a positive change in him.

"It appears I must regale you with a story," he said.

"Lovely." She settled back to a seated position and took a bite of her treat.

"Once upon a time . . ."

Amelia watched Ware's lips move as he spoke, and imagined kissing them. A now-familiar sense of sadness shivered through her, an effect of leaving her beloved romantic notions behind and embracing unfamiliar new ones, but the sensation lessened as she thought of Colin and what he had done. He certainly did not feel any sadness about leaving her behind.

"Would you kiss me?" she blurted out, her fingertips brushing tart crumbs from the corners of her lips.

The earl paused midsentence and turned his head to look at her. His eyes were wide with surprise, but he appeared more intrigued than dismayed. *"Beg your pardon. Did I hear you correctly?"*

"Have you kissed a girl before?" she asked, curious. He was two years older than she was, only one year younger than Colin. It was quite possible that he had experience.

Colin had an edgy, dark restlessness about him that was seductive even to her naïve senses. Ware, on the other hand, was far more leisurely, his attractiveness stemming from innate command and the comfort of knowing the world was his for the taking. Still, despite her high regard for Colin, she could see how Ware's lazy charm appealed.

His eyebrows rose. *"A gentleman does not speak of such things."*

"How wonderful! Somehow, I knew you would be discreet." She smiled.

"Repeat the request again," he murmured, watching her carefully.

"Would you kiss me?"

"Is this a hypothetical question, or a call to action?"

Suddenly shy and unsure, Amelia looked away.

"Amelia," he said softly, bringing her gaze back to his. There was deep kindness there on his handsome patrician

*features, and she was grateful for it. He rolled to his side
and then pushed up to a seated position.*

"Not hypothetical," she whispered.

"Why do you wish to be kissed?"

She shrugged. "Because."

"I see." His lips pursed a moment. "Would Benny suffice? Or a footman?"

"No!"

*His mouth curved in a slow smile that made something
flutter in her belly. It was not an outright flip, as was caused
by Colin's dimples, but it was certainly a herald of her new
awareness of her friend.*

*"I will not kiss you today," he said. "I want you to think
upon it further. If you feel the same when next we meet, I
will kiss you then."*

*Amelia wrinkled her nose. "If you have no taste for me,
simply say so."*

*"Ah, my hotheaded princess," he soothed, his hand
catching hers, his thumb stroking the back. "You jump to
conclusions just as you jump into trouble—with both feet. I
will catch you, fair Amelia. I look forward to catching you."*

*"Oh," she breathed, blinking at the suggestive undertone
to his words.*

"Oh," he agreed.

Amelia was awakened by the knock that came to her
bedchamber door. She lay curled in a ball, her eyes closed,
her sleep-foggy mind praying that she could drift back into
sleep and rejoin her vivid dreams. Dreams that reminded
her of the rare connection she had with Ware and how precious that bond was to her.

But the knocking came again, more insistent. Harsh reality intruded, and she mourned the loss of her nocturnal
reminiscences.

"Amelia?"

Maria. The one person in the household that she could not ignore.

Calling out in a sleep-husky voice, Amelia struggled to a seated position and watched as the portal swung open and her sister stepped into view.

"Hello, poppet," Maria said, gliding toward her with an elegance she had long envied. "Sorry to wake you. It is late morning, however, so I did wait. Sadly, the length of my patience is probably not as long as you would like."

"I do so love that gown on you," Amelia replied, admiring the cream-colored muslin and its appeal next to Maria's olive skin.

"Thank you." Maria took a seat on the slipper chair near the window. "Did you have a good evening?"

Visions of Ware, dashing in evening attire, filled Amelia's mind. Last night had been one in an endless string of nights spent at balls and routs. Except last evening had been marginally different. She was different. *Ware* was different. The awareness between them had changed, and she knew instinctively that it would never be the same.

He was pressing forward, maneuvering expertly, forcing her to see their situation in cold, hard facts. After an entire childhood filled with falsehoods and evasions, she was normally grateful for his candor. In this instance, however, it served only to increase her feelings of guilt and confusion.

"It was a lovely evening," she replied.

"Hmm . . ." The sound was clearly skeptical. "You have been melancholy of late."

"And you are here to talk about it."

"Lord Ware almost kissed you on the terrace yesterday afternoon, and yet last night you did not appear any more eager to see him than usual. How could I not ask you about it?"

Closing her eyes, Amelia's head dropped back onto the pillow.

"If you would share your burdens with me," Maria coaxed, "perhaps I could help. I should like to."

Opening her eyes, Amelia looked up at the satin lining of her canopy and remembered an earlier time. Her room was decorated in various shades of blue, from pale to dark, just as her childhood bedchamber had been. She'd made the choice consciously, an external declaration of her decision to pick up where her relationship with her sister had been cruelly severed. Her father had stolen years from them, but in this room she felt as if she reclaimed them.

"There is nothing to help me with, Maria. There is nothing to mend or alter."

"What of your masked admirer?"

"I will not be seeing him again."

There was a pregnant pause, then, "The last you spoke of him was not with such finality in your tone. You saw him a second time, did you not? He sought you out."

Amelia turned her head to meet her sister's gaze. "*I* lured him to me, and he was angry at me for doing so. He intends to leave Town now, to keep his distance and to prevent me from reaching out to him again."

"He shows a care for your reputation by this action, but you are upset by it." Confusion filled Maria's dark eyes. "Why?"

Tossing up her hands, Amelia said, "Because I do not want him to go! I want to know him, and it pains me greatly that I will not be given that chance. I am distressing Ware and you, yet I cannot seem to set aside my fascination nor can I ignore how weary I am of being left behind. I had enough of such treatment with my father."

"Amelia . . ." Maria held out a hand to her. "What is it about this man that has captured you so? Is he comely? No . . . don't become angry. I simply wish to understand."

Amelia sighed. Lack of sleep and inability to eat were taking their toll. She could not fight the feeling that Montoya was slipping away, that every moment when she did nothing took him farther from her. It frustrated her and made her snappish.

"He wore the mask again," she said finally. "I've no notion of what he looks like beneath it, but I do not care. I am moved by the way he talks to me, the way he touches me, the way he kisses me. There is reverence in his handling of me, Maria. Longing. Desire. I do not believe such depth of affection can be feigned. Not the way he expresses it."

Frowning, Maria looked away, lost in thought. Dark ringlets swung around her bared shoulders and betrayed how unsettled she felt. "How can he feel such things for you after only a few moments' acquaintance?"

"He says I remind him of a lover lost to him, but in truth I sense he wants me for myself in addition to that." Amelia's fingertips plucked at the edge of her bed linens. "He originally approached me because of her, but when he came again it was for me."

"How can you be certain?"

"I am certain of nothing, and now I suppose I never will be." She looked toward the open door to her boudoir, afraid her features would reveal too much.

"Because he is departing." Maria's voice softened. "Did he say why or where he intends to travel?"

"He says he is in danger of some sort. Deadly danger."

"From St. John? Or someone else?"

Amelia's hands fisted into the counterpane. "He has nothing to do with your husband. He said as much and I believe him."

"Shh," Maria soothed, standing again. "I know you are distraught, but do not vent your frustration on me. I want to help you."

"How?" Amelia challenged. "Will you help me find him?"

"Yes."

Frozen with disbelief, Amelia stared at her sibling. "Truly?"

"Of course." Maria's shoulders went back, a sure sign of her determination. "St. John's men look for him, but we have an advantage. You are the only person to manage close proximity to this man."

Amelia was speechless for a moment. She had not expected anyone to champion her desire to pursue Montoya, and she could not have selected a better person to help her than Maria, who was afraid of nothing and well versed in finding things that did not wish to be found. "Ware searches for him, too."

"Poor Count Montoya," Maria said, sitting on the edge of the bed beside her and collecting her hands. "I pity him. He espies a pretty woman and because of it, becomes hunted from all sides. St. John will seek him in a criminal's fashion. Ware will seek him in a peer's fashion. So you and I must seek Montoya in a woman's fashion."

"And how would that be?" Amelia asked, frowning.

"By shopping, of course." Maria smiled, and the entire room brightened. "We will visit all the purveyors of masks that we can find and see if any recall the count. If he always covers his face, he must procure a great many of the things. If not, perhaps it was a recent purchase and he left an indelible impression. It is not much, but it's a start. We will have to take care, of course. If he is in danger, finding him will bring that danger to us. You must trust me and listen to me implicitly. Agreed?"

"Yes." Amelia's lower lip quivered, and she bit it to hide the betraying movement. Her hands tightened on her sister's. "Thank you, Maria. Thank you so much."

Maria caught her close and kissed her forehead. "I will always be here to help you, poppet. Always."

The quiet declaration gave Amelia strength, and she clung to it as she slipped from the bed and began to prepare for the day ahead.

Chapter 8

There was a leisurely pace to the pedestrians, carts, and carriages that traveled down the street. The day was sunny and comfortably warm, the air cleansed from a brief spate of early morning rain. Colin, however, was far from relaxed. Something about the day did not sit well with him.

"You should not worry so much," Jacques said. "She will be fine. No one has connected you to your past or to Miss Benbridge."

Colin smiled ruefully. "Am I so transparent?"

"*Oui*. In your unguarded moments."

Staring out the carriage window, Colin noted the many people going about their daily business. For his part, his business this afternoon was leaving Town. His carriage was presently wending its way toward the road that would lead them to Bristol. Their trunks were loaded and their account with the rental property was settled.

He remained *un*settled.

The feeling that he was leaving his heart behind was worse than before. His mortality was something he began to feel more keenly each day. Life was finite, and the thought that the entirety of his would be spent without Amelia in it was too painful to bear.

"I have never shared a carriage with her," he said, his gloved fingers wrapping around the window ledge. "I have never sat at a table with her and shared a meal. Everything I have done these last years was in pursuit of a higher station, one that would afford me the privilege to enjoy all the facets of her life."

Jacques's dark eyes watched him from beneath the rim of his hat. He sat on the opposite squab, his compact body as relaxed as Colin had ever seen it, but still thrumming with energy.

"Soon after my parents died," Colin murmured, staring out at the view of the street, "my uncle accepted the position of coachman to Lord Welton. The wages were dismal and we were forced to leave the Romany camp, but my uncle felt it was more stable than the Gypsy life. He had been a dedicated bachelor prior to my arrival, but he took the burden of my care very seriously."

"So that is where your honor comes from," the Frenchman said.

Colin smiled slightly. "I was wretched at the change. At ten years of age, I felt the loss of my friends keenly, especially following so soon after the loss of my father and mother. I was certain my life was over and I would be miserable forever. And then, I saw her."

In his mind's eye, he remembered the day as if it were yesterday. "She was only seven years old, but I was awed. With her dark curls, porcelain skin, and green eyes, she looked like a beautiful doll. Then she held out a dirty hand to me, smiled a smile that was missing teeth, and asked me to play."

"*Enchanté,*" Jacques murmured.

"Yes, she was. Amelia was a dozen playmates in one—adventurous, challenging, and resourceful. I rushed through my chores just so I could be with her." Sighing, Colin leaned his head back against the squab and closed his eyes. "I remember the day I first rode as rear footman on the carriage. I felt so mature and proud of my accomplishment. She was happy for me, too, her eyes bright and filled with joy. Then,

I realized that while she sat inside, I stood outside, and I would never be allowed to sit with her."

"You have changed a great deal since then, *mon ami*. There is no such divide between you now."

"Oh, there is a divide," Colin argued. "It just is not a monetary one any longer."

"When did you know that you loved her?"

"I loved her from the first." His hand fisted where it rested atop his thigh. "The feeling just grew and changed, as we both did."

He would never forget the afternoon when they had played in the stream, as they often did. He in his breeches, she stripped to her chemise. She had just reached fifteen years, he ten and eight. He had stumbled across the pebbled shore, attempting to catch a fleeing frog, when he'd fallen. Her delighted laughter turned his head, and the sight of her had changed his life forever. Bathed in sunlight, drenched in water, her beautiful features transformed by merriment, she had seemed a water nymph to him. Alluring. Innocently seductive.

His breath had caught in his throat; his body had hardened. Heated cravings burned in his blood and dried his mouth. His cock—which had become an aching, demanding torment as he'd matured—throbbed with painful pressure. He was no innocent, but the physical urgings he'd appeased before were merely annoying when compared to the need wrought by the sight of Amelia's seminude body.

Somehow . . . sometime, when he hadn't been looking, Amelia had grown into a young woman. And he wanted her. Wanted her as he'd never wanted anything before. His heart clenched with his sudden longing; his arms ached to hold her. Deep inside him, he felt an emptiness and knew she would fill it. Make him whole. Complete him. She'd been everything to him as a child. He knew she would be everything to him as a man.

"Colin?" Her smile had faded as tension filled the air between them.

Later that evening, Pietro noted his somberness and questioned him. When he'd spilled out his discovery, his uncle reacted with novel ferocity.

"Stay away from her," Pietro growled, his dark eyes burning in their intensity. "I should have ended your friendship long ago."

"No!" Colin had been horrified at the thought. He couldn't imagine his life without her.

Pietro slammed his fist on the table and loomed over him. "She is far above you. Beyond your reach. You will cost us our livelihood!"

"I love her!" As soon as the words left his mouth, he knew they were true.

Grim-faced, his uncle had dragged him out of their quarters in the stables and taken him into the village. There, he'd thrust Colin into the arms of a pretty whore who delighted in exhausting him and wringing him dry. A mature woman, she was unlike the marginally experienced girls he'd dallied with before. She made certain he was spent. He left her bed with muscles turned to jelly and a need for a long nap.

When he'd staggered into the nearby tavern hours later, his uncle had met him with a jovial smile and fatherly pride. "Now you have another woman to love," he'd pronounced, slapping him affectionately on the back.

To which Colin had corrected, "I'm grateful to her, yes. But I love only Amelia."

Pietro's face had fallen. The next day, when Colin saw Amelia and felt the same lustful longing as he'd experienced at the stream, he'd known instinctively that the sexual act would be different with her. Just as she'd made the days brighter and his heart lighter, he knew she would make sex deeper and richer, too. The hunger he felt for that connection was inescapable. It gnawed at him and gave him no rest.

Over the next few months, Pietro told him daily to leave

her be. If he loved her, his uncle said, he would want the best for her, and a Gypsy stableboy could never be that.

And so he eventually found the fortitude to push her away out of love for her. It had killed him then.

It was killing him anew now.

The carriage dipped, swayed, and rumbled over the streets beneath it, every movement a signal that he was moving farther and farther away from the only thing he'd ever wanted in this world.

"You will return to her," Jacques said quietly. "It is not the end."

"Until we finish this matter with Cartland, I cannot even consider having her. There is a reason Quinn continued to use Cartland even though he was troublesome—he is an excellent tracker. As long as he is searching for me, I have no future."

"I believe in destiny, *mon ami*. And yours is not to die at that man's hands. I can promise you that."

Colin nodded, but in truth, he was not so optimistic.

The white-gloved fingers that were curled around the carriage windowsill belonged to Montoya. Amelia knew it with bone-deep surety.

As the nondescript equipage passed her, she chanced a stray glance through the open window and spotted Jacques. Frozen in surprise, a shiver of discovery moved through her and filled her with hope. Then she noted the many trunks strapped to the back of the coach.

Montoya was leaving Town, just as he'd said he would.

Fortuitously for her but unfortunate for him, his driver had chosen to travel along the very street she and Maria traversed in their search for him.

"Maria," she said urgently, afraid to tear her gaze away for fear she would lose sight of him.

"Hmm?" her sister hummed distractedly. "I see masks in the display here."

Before Amelia could protest, Maria slipped into the nearest store, the merry chiming of bells heralding her departure.

A multitude of pedestrians milled around them, though many steered clear due to Tim, who towered over everyone and guarded his charges with an eagle eye.

"Tim." Amelia lifted her hand and pointed at the carriage, which continued to move farther away. "Montoya is in that black travel coach. We must move swiftly or we shall lose him."

The sensation of something precious sifting through her fingers caused a sort of anxiety she had never felt before. She grabbed her skirts and followed at a near run.

A hackney discharged its passengers a few yards up the street. Amelia hurried toward it with one hand lifted in a frantic wave.

Realizing her intent, Tim cursed under his breath, grabbed her elbow, and dragged her along. "Halt!" he roared as the driver raised his whip.

The man turned his head and froze at the sight of Tim. Swallowing hard, he nodded. When they reached the coach, Tim yanked the door open and thrust her up into it. He looked at the two lackeys who followed them. "Go back with the others and find Mrs. St. John. Tell her what happened."

Sam, a red-haired man who had been in St. John's employ for years, gave a jerky nod. "Aye. Be careful."

Tim lunged into the coach, forcing Amelia back into the interior. "I don't like this," he said gruffly.

"Hurry!" she urged. "You can chastise me on the way."

He glowered and cursed again, then yelled instructions to the driver.

The hackney lurched into motion, pulling away from the milling pedestrians and into the traffic of the street.

The doorbells were still chiming when Maria came to an abrupt halt just inside the door of the shop.

A tall, elegantly attired gentleman blocked her way to the deeper interior. At his side, a lovely blonde was wearing the very latest in French fashion. Maria's gaze moved from one to the other, noting what a handsome couple they made.

"Simon!" Maria gaped in startled recognition.

"*Mhuirnín.*" As he captured her hand and lifted it to his lips, the tender affection in the beloved voice was palpable. "You look ravishing, as always."

Simon Quinn stood before her looking more sinfully delicious than any man had a right to. Dressed in buff-colored breeches and a dark green coat, his powerful frame drew the eye of every woman within viewing distance. He bore the form of a laborer, while clad in superbly tailored garments fit for the king himself.

"I was not aware that you had returned to London," she chastised gently. "And I admit I am more than slightly piqued that you did not seek me out immediately."

The Frenchwoman smiled a smile that never reached her cold, blue eyes. "Quinn . . ." She shook her head, setting the festive ribbons that adorned it to swaying. "It appears your poor treatment of women is an unfortunate recurring trait in you."

"Hush," he snapped.

Maria frowned, unaccustomed to Simon being curt to lovely females.

The bells chimed again, and she attempted to step out of the way when her arm was caught by a grasping hand. Taken aback, she pivoted in a swirl of deep rose-colored skirts and found Sam looking far too anxious beside her.

"Miss Amelia saw 'is coach," the lackey blurted out, "and ran after 'im. Tim's with 'er, but—"

"Amelia?" It was then that Maria realized her sister was not beside her. She rushed back out the door and onto the crowded street.

"There," Sam said, pointing at a hackney moving down the street.

"She saw Montoya?" Maria asked, her gut knotting with apprehension. Lifting her skirts, she pushed her way through the milling pedestrians. Simon and the blonde came fast on her heels, and more of St. John's men barreled through directly after them. They were causing somewhat of a melee, but she did not care. Reaching Amelia was her only concern.

When it became apparent that there was no hope of catching up to them on foot, she stopped. "I need my carriage."

"I sent for it," Sam assured from his position at her side.

"Seek out St. John and explain." Her mind rushed ahead, planning out the possibilities of the next few hours. "I will take the rest of the men with me. Once we find Amelia, someone will be sent back with our direction."

Sam nodded his agreement and departed to collect his mount.

"What the devil is going on?" Simon asked, a frown marring the space between his brilliant blue eyes. The blonde, for her part, looked only vaguely interested.

Maria sighed. "My sister has become enamored of a masked stranger she met at a ball several nights ago, and she is chasing him."

The sudden tension that gripped Simon's frame increased her anxiety. If he sensed some danger from the situation, she knew it must be more than worry for a sibling that drove her.

"I have been fretting over it ever since," she continued, "but she cannot be swayed. I attempted to reason with her, but she is determined to find him. As is St. John. I offered to assist Amelia in her search as a way to control at least a part of the whole affair, but apparently she spotted him on the street a few moments ago and is now giving chase."

"Good God!" Simon cried, eyes wide.

"Oh, this is delightful!" Miss Rousseau said, her eyes finally showing some signs of life.

"I will come with you," Simon said briskly, gesturing to

his footman who waited nearby. The boy rushed off to fetch Simon's carriage.

"You do not have to become involved," Maria said, heaving out her breath. "You are presently engaged. Enjoy your day."

"You are upset, *mhuirnín*. And perhaps I can help. We were on our way out of Town for holiday, as it was. Miss Rousseau does not mind the alteration of our destination."

"No, no indeed," the Frenchwoman said, smiling. "In fact, I should like to come along. Foolish young lovers are always so diverting."

Simon growled, the sound so edgy that Maria reconsidered her continuing protests and held her silence instead. Simon had been her lieutenant for many years, and his assistance would be tremendously valuable. Whatever the situation was between him and Miss Rousseau, it was for them alone to work out. She had enough trouble of her own to manage.

It was a few moments longer before the gleam of highly polished black lacquer heralded the approach of the St. John town coach. Maria hoped that the distance to be traveled was not one that would need the sturdier travel carriage.

Simon's equipage drew up behind hers, and with laudable haste they were all in hot pursuit.

Colin vaulted down from his travel coach with relief, his long legs cramped from the many hours spent traveling from London to the small posting inn just past Reading. He stood in the courtyard a moment and surveyed his moonlit surroundings. Jacques alighted behind him, and together they entered the inn to secure their lodging for the night.

The dim interior was quiet. Only a few patrons remained in the main room; the rest had retired. The necessary arrangements were quickly dealt with, and shortly, Colin found himself in a small, sparsely furnished room that was clean and comfortable.

As soon as he was alone, melancholy descended in a cold, weighty mantle. He was a day's ride away from Amelia, with the morrow bringing even more distance between them. Frustrated by the progression of events, he prayed sleep would offer him a brief respite, but after years of dreaming of Amelia, he did not hold out much hope.

He was reaching to close the curtains when the door opened behind him. Gripping the hilt of the dagger hidden in his coat, he canted his torso to make himself a smaller target.

"Montoya."

Amelia's sweetly feminine voice caused him to freeze in midturn. He had hoped to be followed, but not by her. Now the danger that stalked him shadowed her as well.

"I had to see you," she murmured. "Your carriage passed me in the street, and I could not allow you to go."

Only years of training and living by his wits leashed his surprise, preventing him from ruining everything by facing her. Instead he closed the drapes, dimming the gentle light of the moon before turning toward her. If he was fortunate, the banked fire in the grate would keep his face mostly in shadow, lessening the possibility of recognition.

Mentally prepared only for her reaction to him, Colin was completely vulnerable to his own reaction to her. The sight of her by the door—and near a bed—hit him like a blow, freeing a possessive, primitive growl from his tightened throat. She shivered at the sound, her lips parting with quickened breaths.

His hands clenched into fists at his sides. Did she know what she did to him?

She stood proud and undaunted before the door, a beribboned hat tied at a jaunty angle, her slender body encased in a gown of shimmering satin and delicate white lace. The innocent cut of the dress made the years fall away, made him hard as a rock and hot to claim her. He loved her deeply and completely with lingering traces of his boyish adoration, but he also lusted for her with every drop of the wild Gypsy blood in his veins.

"Tell me you did not travel alone," he bit out, hating to think of such beauty unattended. She was a treasure to be secured and valued. The thought of her on the journey without a guard, unwittingly in jeopardy, tied him in knots.

"I am protected." Her eyes glittered in the muted light, and she queried in a whisper, "Are you angry with me?"

"No," he said hoarsely, his heart thudding with rhythmic violence in his chest.

"The mask . . ." She inhaled audibly. "Most men look especially dashing in evening attire. You—"

"Amelia—"

"—move me always. Whatever you wear, wherever we are."

His eyes closed as her praise rippled through him. He took an involuntary step toward her, then jerked to a halt. The room was suddenly too small and airless; the need to divest them both of every stitch of cloth was nearly overwhelming. His craving for her grew more ferocious, clawing and biting in its desire to be appeased.

"Are you happy to see me?" she asked in a small voice.

Colin shook his head, his eyes opening because he couldn't bear not to see her. "It kills me."

Tenderness swept over her finely wrought features and called to something deep inside him.

"It is the yearning I sense in you that lures me." She stepped closer, and he lifted a hand to halt her progress before she came too near. "As long as you want me, I will want you in return."

"I would have ceased wanting you long ago," he rasped, "if such a thing were possible."

Her head tilted to the side as she considered him. "You lie."

Unable to resist, he smiled at that. She was audacious still.

"You enjoy wanting me," she said, with purely female satisfaction.

"I would enjoy having you more," he purred.

When her gaze shot to the bed, his cock swelled to full arousal. Her tongue darted out to lick her lower lip, and a rough, edgy sound rumbled from his chest.

"Come with me," she entreated, her gaze returning to his. "Meet my family. My sister and her husband can assist you. Whatever plagues you, they can help to resolve."

Colin's gut tightened. He should say no . . . He should avoid bringing any danger into her life . . .

But the possibility of having her *now* . . . No more waiting, no more hiding . . .

It was night, a bed was near, and they were alone. His deepest fantasy made reality.

He stepped toward her. "There is something I must tell you. Something you will find difficult to understand. Do you have time to hear me out?"

She lifted her gloved hand and extended it to him. "As much as you need."

"What of those who came with you?"

"He is drinking below." She smiled. "I lied, you see. I pointed out a different patron and said I suspected he was you. So Tim is occupied with watching him, while I inquired discreetly and found you. You have a unique form— so tall and broad. The maids noticed you when you came in."

"What of your reputation, then? A young woman of obviously fine breeding making inquiries about a bachelor."

"Once I learned where you were, I described my relief at finding my brother who is wearing dark green."

Colin glanced down at his blue garments. *Dear God, was it true? Could he have her?*

She beamed with obvious pride in her cleverness.

"You have gone to a great deal of trouble to find me, Miss Benbridge."

"Amelia," she corrected. "And yes I have."

He smiled. "Turn around, then, and face the door."

Amelia frowned. "Why?"

"Because I need to approach you, and I am not certain how much of my face can be seen in this light." When she hesitated, he said, "*You* pursue *me*. You want me. I will be yours, in every sense, but in return you must listen to me without question. Does that frighten you?"

She swallowed hard, her irises overtaken by dilated pupils. Then she shook her head.

"It excites you," he murmured. Hot, potent lust intoxicated him, easing the relentless drive that set him on edge. He had always led the way with her. It was highly arousing to lead the way in their bedsport, as well. "Turn."

Complying, she faced away from him, and Colin approached with a rapid stride, freed from the fear of untimely recognition. He pressed up against her, breathing in the scent of honeysuckle, placing his palms flat to the panels on either side of her head.

The vein in her throat fluttered with her increasing heartbeat, arresting his attention.

The sound of the bolt sliding home stiffened his frame and drew his gaze away.

How simple the action was, that of locking the door, but it aroused him as nothing ever had. She *wanted* him to take her, to strip her bare, to fuck her sweet little body until he was spent and conquered.

Though he knew it, he still wanted her to say the words aloud.

"There is no chance that you will depart this room as virginal as you entered it," he murmured, his tongue stroking over her racing pulse.

In answer, she reached for the chair by the door and pushed back hard against him, creating a gap that allowed her to wedge the spindle back beneath the knob.

"Do you anticipate interruptions?" he asked, with laughter in his voice and heart. "Or do you simply wish to keep the world at bay?"

The thought of Amelia forsaking the world at large to be with him made his chest tight. She had promised to do so as a young girl. Would she recommit to that promise as a woman?

"You assume I wish to lock others out." Her mouth curved in a woman's smile. "Perhaps I wish to lock you in."

Colin threw back his head and laughed at that, his arms banding her torso and squeezing her tightly. "Ah, love. How glad I am that you remain so spirited."

"The threat of lovemaking is not sufficient to repress me," she retorted.

No, but his identity might be. The thought was sobering. He inhaled sharply. "Amelia, I must share my face and past with you before we can proceed."

The tension that gripped her was palpable. "Will it change how I feel about you?"

"Most definitely, yes."

"Do not reveal anything."

He blinked. "I beg your pardon?"

"Right now, in this moment, I feel as if I could not breathe without you near." Her voice was low and earnest. "I've no desire to be disillusioned. Not after these last years when nothing was vital to me. It seems almost as if I walked through life wearing a veil. Only when I am with you do I see the world in all its many colors."

Pressing his cheek to hers, he whispered, "You should place greater worth upon your virginity. I cannot take you—"

She turned her head and pressed her lips to his. The sudden rush of sensation was dizzying. Then unbearably arousing. He felt her moving, but was unable to break the contact to discover why. His tongue stroked across her lips, licking the innocently sweet flavor that was innate to her. The taste was addicting, destroying him. He was helpless to resist it. When her bare fingertips wrapped around his wrist and lifted his hand to her breast, he knew there was no fighting her. He could not simply blurt out who he was. The revelation required more tact than that.

"I can see you with my heart," she said breathlessly, her lips moving against his. "I want to have you while I feel for you as I do at this moment—wild and hot and free. Does that make me reckless and naïve? Do you find me foolish and fast?"

With every word that left her mouth he grew harder and less controlled. *Wild. Hot. Free.* The combination was a potent allure for a Gypsy male. Amelia had lived outside the boundaries of Society for so long, she found it easier than most to ignore its constrictions. He suspected that contributed to their affinity. At heart, they were both desperate to run laughing through the fields without any restraints.

Colin reached around her and unfastened the jeweled brooch that secured her lace fichu. "Can I cover your eyes?" he asked in a dark voice. "Would that dampen your ardor?"

She tried to turn her head to meet his gaze, and he stopped her with a kiss. "I would not have the revelation occur during the act. I want nothing to mar our first time together. I have waited too long for it and desired it too deeply to see it ruined."

Nodding, she held still as he twisted the expensive lace loosely, then tied it around her head in a makeshift blindfold.

"How does that feel?"

"Strange."

"Do not move." Colin backed up and shed his coat. He unwound his cravat, then began to work on the carved ivory buttons of his waistcoat.

"Are you undressing?" she asked.

"Yes."

He watched a shiver move through her and smiled. How erotically beautiful she looked with her kiss-swollen lips and covered eyes. His to savor and enjoy. Pietro had attempted to dissuade him away from Amelia by insisting that

Englishwomen lacked the fire a Gypsy man needed. Colin hadn't believed it then; he certainly did not believe it now.

Her lovely breasts lifted and fell with her rapid breathing; her hands clenched rhythmically at her sides. She was ripe and ready, an oasis in the desert of his barren life.

Shrugging out of his waistcoat, Colin tossed it over the back of a chair and returned to her. "I want you to speak your thoughts to me. Tell me what feels good, what doesn't. I will know if you lie. Your body will betray you."

"Then why should I speak?"

"For your benefit." He caressed her shoulders, then reached for the tiny row of cloth buttons that followed the line of her spine. "Speaking aloud will force you to think in minute detail about what I am doing to you. It will anchor you to the pleasure and this moment."

"Anchor me to you."

"Yes, that, too." He kissed her throat. "It will empower you, be the telling of your desires. You may hesitate to touch me or wonder what is allowed or what is not allowed. But if you sense how the sounds of your pleasure in turn please me, you will know that this is a joining of two lovers playing equal parts."

"It sounds so intimate," she breathed.

"For us, my love, it will be."

Chapter 9

Ware entered Christopher St. John's study shortly after ten in the evening. The infamous pirate was pacing between the back of his desk and the window beyond that with a sort of restlessness the earl had never seen in him before. Sans coat and bearing a skewed cravat, St. John looked rumpled and anxious, which set the hairs on Ware's nape to rising. After seeing the travel coach hitched in the front circular drive, it was apparent that a journey of some distance was planned.

"My lord," St. John greeted absently.

"St. John." He cut straight to the heart of the matter. "What has happened?"

Rounding the desk, the pirate moved to the nearby console and held up a decanter in silent query. Ware shook his head in the negative and sank onto one of the matching settees that sat perpendicular to the grate. He was here to collect Amelia for the evening's social rounds. It was unlike her to leave him waiting. Her punctuality was one of the many traits he enjoyed in her.

"There is no way for me to relate the day's events without awkwardness," St. John began, pouring a hefty ration.

"Never mind that. I prefer bluntness to anything else."

Nodding, St. John took the seat opposite and said, "Mrs. St. John and Miss Benbridge went into Town today. I was told they meant to spend the day shopping. I have since learned that they were hunting the masked man who has so captured Amelia's interest."

Ware's brows rose. "I see."

"By some stray chance, Count Montoya—if that truly is his name—was seen departing London. Miss Benbridge hailed a hackney and set off in pursuit. My wife followed shortly after."

"Bloody hell."

"Would you care for that drink now, my lord?"

The earl seriously considered it, then shook his head. "I have made some inquiries of my own regarding this matter. I had hoped Lady Langston would shed some light on the man's identity; however, no invitation was ever issued to a Count Montoya."

St. John's lips pursed grimly. "I am at a loss for how to view this situation. If the man meant to hurt her in some fashion or seduce her, why leave London?"

There was jealousy and possessiveness laced with all the other emotions Ware was presently experiencing, but there was also resignation. Some part of him had known that Amelia held off on marriage to him because of a need for . . . *more*. He had no idea what she felt was missing, but in truth their relationship could not progress any further and still end happily without first resolving that lack.

"I am surprised to find you still at home," the earl said. "Amelia is not my wife, yet I feel a pressing need to go after her."

The glare the pirate shot at him was cutting. "I am near maddened with the need to follow, but I have no notion of their direction. I am awaiting word."

"Forgive me, I meant no offense. I was merely making an observation." He considered his options, then said, "I should like to go with you, if you have no objection."

St. John seemed ready to argue; then his scowl cleared

and he nodded. "If you wish to come along, do. But your formal attire will be a burden."

Ware stood, as did the pirate. "I will change and pack lightly. If you depart before I return, please leave a note so that I may follow."

"Of course, my lord." St. John offered a commiserating smile. "I must apologize to you, as well. Your courting of Amelia has done much for her. Mrs. St. John and I are both exceedingly grateful, as is Amelia."

"St. John." Ware laughed ruefully. "At this moment, the matter of my pride is secondary to Amelia's safety."

They clasped hands in a gesture of mutual respect. Then the earl hastened to depart before he was left behind. As his carriage rolled away from the St. John residence, Ware began a mental list of what to bring with him.

His small sword and pistol were among the items he catalogued. If Amelia's honor was to be impugned, he considered it his right and duty to correct the slight.

As Colin spread open the back of Amelia's gown, his thoughts were already rushing ahead, considering how this one night would change their lives forever. "Do you have an abigail with you?"

The blindfold might make some women more timid and hesitant. Not so with Amelia. Her voice came sure and strong. "No. I saw your carriage and gave chase."

Warring with the primitive need to mark her as his, his heart still wanted to protect her even at great cost to himself. "There will be no way to hide that you have been ravished. In the heat of passion, our better sense deserts us. What you want now, you may regret in the morning."

"I know my own mind," she said stubbornly.

"You will give up Ware." He gently withdrew one of her arms from a sleeve, then repeated the movement on the other side. "And you will belong to me."

"I think it more likely that you will belong to me."

Smiling, he bent at the knees and pulled her gown down with him. Amelia stepped out of the garment without urging, balancing her weight by leaning against the door. He deliberately delayed the joy of seeing her stripped from her outer garments. He took his time laying the dress over the back of a wing chair in an effort to spare it the most wrinkling.

"You are so calm," she murmured. "So controlled. You must have many affairs."

"This is not an affair." He turned his head, raking her lithe body with a heated glance. Still too many garments, but he knew that he was seeing her as no other man ever had.

She set her hand on her hip, and a finely arched brow lifted above the fichu. "Perhaps I want an affair."

"Well, you are not having one with me," he growled, reaching her in two strides and lifting her feet from the floor. "You will not be having one ever, because no other man will come after me in your bed."

Amelia laughed and wrapped her arms around his neck. "My . . . how delightful you are when you become possessive."

He pressed his lips to her ear. "Wait until my cock is inside you. See how delightful my possession is then."

"Tease," she said breathlessly, with a slight note of anxiety. "At this rate, the sun will be rising before I am naked."

"You do not have to be naked to be fucked," he whispered, deliberately challenging her to revive her spirits. "I could toss up your underskirts, undo my breeches, and pin you to the door."

"If your intent is to frighten me, you should know that I am difficult to scare." The anxiousness was gone from her voice, banished by her impressive inner fortitude. "I have lived in the most rustic of places. I have seen all sorts of animals doing all sorts of things to each other."

He buried his grin in her tender throat.

"Do not find amusement at my expense," she said. "Your threat is groundless. You would not take my virginity in so callous a manner. You worship me too much."

"So I do, Your Highness." Setting her back on her feet, Colin dropped to his knees and kissed her feet.

As she laughed, he moved upward, sliding beneath the masses of skirts, pressing open-mouthed kisses up the length of her stocking-clad legs. Her laughter turned into a gasp, then a soft whimper.

The intimate smell of her drove him insane, and with a tentative finger, Colin tested her, gritting his teeth at finding her slick and hot. Startled by his bold caress, Amelia stumbled and fell into the door with a soft thud.

"Not while I am standing!" she protested.

Pressing a final kiss to the back of her knee, Colin crawled free and stood before her. He gently turned her, then set to work on her tapes and stays, taking the brief respite to regain his control. He focused on his breathing and hers instead of the animal need that clawed inside him.

Finally, she was left with only her chemise, a garment made of material so fine he could almost see clear through it. It was enough to drive him to madness, the far-too-vague hints of her body beneath.

"I want you to remove the rest," he said, stepping back.

"Why?"

"Because it will please me."

"It is not as easy as you intimate. I have never been naked before a man."

"Do it, Amelia," he ordered, near desperate to see all of her.

With no further hesitation, she reached down and removed her shoes. The hem of her chemise lifted as she reached for the ribbons that secured her stockings. His mouth watered at the sight, every movement she made erasing similar memories from his past. No other woman could compete with the innocent, unaffected fashion in which Amelia undressed. Her movements were not practiced or planned with an eye for seduction, but they aroused him unbearably, nevertheless.

Aching with lust for her, he freed the placket of his breeches and took his cock in hand. He was thick and hard, slick at the tip with wanting her. Stroking leisurely down the length, he groaned in need.

Amelia froze at the sound, unsure of what she had done to distress him. "What is it? What's wrong?"

"Nothing is wrong," Montoya assured in a gruff voice that belied his words. "Everything is perfect."

She listened carefully, regulating her breathing in order to take in every nuance of sound. "What are you doing? I hear you moving."

"I am fondling my cock."

Images filled her mind, incomplete due to her inexperience, but arousing regardless. The flesh between her legs throbbed in response, making her squeeze her thighs together in a vain effort to ease the ache. "Why?"

"Because it pains me, love. I am hard and ready for you. Harder and thicker than I have ever been."

"Can I touch it?"

He made a choked noise, and the sounds of his movements became more pronounced. "Bare yourself first."

Amelia finished undressing with haste, forcibly shoving aside thoughts of her imperfections. Unlike Maria, she was not lushly curved and built for a man's pleasure. She was taller, thinner, and smaller-breasted. She was too active, enjoying riding and fencing more than card games and teas.

"Dear God," he gasped when she dropped her chemise to the floor.

Her hands moved to cover herself, but he moved swiftly, catching her wrists. "Never hide from me."

"I am nervous," she retorted.

"My love . . ." He wrapped her against him, and she felt his erection between them. Smooth as silk, but hard as a rock and hot to the touch. Despite the shock of it, her body delighted in the feel and grew slicker.

"You are so beautiful, Amelia. Every inch of you. I dreamed of seeing you like this, naked and willing. How sorry those fantasies were compared to the reality."

She pressed her forehead to his chest and said, "You are being kind."

Montoya brought her hand to his cock and wrapped her fingers around it. "This is not how a man feels when he finds his lover inadequate."

Amelia moved, squeezing and caressing, exploring. His breath hissed out between his teeth. "You will make me spend," he gritted out.

"If it would please you to do so, go ahead," she replied, wanting to give him pleasure. Wanting to satisfy him in a way that would brand him as hers.

"Minx."

She stilled as a big, warm hand cupped her breast. Immediately, her nipple, already tight and hard from the chill of the open air, pebbled further.

"See how you fit so perfectly within my palm," he murmured, his hips beginning to thrust into her movements. "You were built for me, Amelia." She whimpered as his thumb and forefinger surrounded her nipple and tugged on it, sending pangs of intense pleasure straight to her womb. Everything tightened and coiled, making her move restlessly.

"And how quickly you respond to me." He leaned back, and a moment later she cried out as hot, wet suction surrounded the tender peak of her breast. Her hands gripped his cock convulsively, and he growled against her skin, the vibration driving her wild.

His powerful arms banded her waist, supporting her as

he pushed her backward and worshipped her breast, his tongue curling around her nipple as his cheeks hollowed with drawing pulls.

Just as he had said, every thought left her mind, leaving her a creature of lust and desire. The lack of reason bound her tighter to him. There was only one other man she had ever considered sharing herself with in this way. That Montoya was scarred and haunted had no bearing on the emotions he aroused in her.

"Tell me you love this," he said, as he moved to her other breast. "Let it out, Amelia. Do not be silent."

His teeth nipped the hard peak and she cried out. He began licking her, his tongue stroking with maddening leisure. It was not enough, not nearly. She began to writhe, whimpering, arching her back in an attempt to push deeper into his mouth.

"What do you need?" he asked in a dark whisper. "What do you want? Tell me, and I will give it to you."

Desperate, she begged, "Suck it . . . please . . . I need—"

She gasped as he obliged, his lips closing around her. In her hands his cock throbbed, and a hot trickle of moisture tickled the backs of her fingers. She touched it, found its source at the tiny hole at the head. The pad of her thumb smoothed it around, and he shuddered and suckled her harder.

With her sight stolen from her, every other sense was heightened. As his skin heated, her nostrils filled with his unique scent, increasing her desire. Her sense of touch was painfully acute; even the slight rustle of the air prickled across her flesh.

"Please," she cried, wanting more.

With one last lingering suck, Montoya straightened and pulled her up with him. Then he lifted her into his arms and moved toward the waiting bed.

* * *

Simon was in a foul mood by the time Maria's coach pulled off the main road and into the courtyard of an inn just shy of Reading. Two of St. John's outriders traveled on ahead, freed of the burden of the slow-moving carriages. If they were fortunate, they would return with a more solid direction or perhaps even a sighting.

The entire day had been a study in frustration. The hackney carrying Amelia had discharged her and her guard shortly after collecting them, unwilling to travel beyond the city. They had then secured another carriage and continued on. That progression of events was to be expected. What most concerned Simon were the reports of an inordinate number of French-speaking riders moving in the same direction ahead of them.

It could be nothing, or it could be Cartland.

Simon had longed to disclose the whole of the matter to Maria over dinner, but he felt a similar level of loyalty to Colin, who had risked his life for Simon on more than a few occasions. So he said nothing, holding his tongue when they parted ways to retire for the night.

In the meantime, neither he nor Lysette had any of the items required for comfortable travel. They had no change of clothes and no servants. They did not even have the proper equipage, which led him to having an aching arse and a sore back.

At least Colin had mentioned traveling to Bristol, which gave Simon an advantage. He subtly urged Maria in that general direction, while quietly sending a lone footman back to his lodgings to inform his valet of their change of plans. The servant would manage the settling of the accounts, the packing of their things, and the rounding up of Lysette's maid and belongings.

Thinking of the Frenchwoman, his gaze moved to where she sat before the fire. By necessity, they shared a bedchamber, the size of their party enough to take up the last remaining rooms. Maria had complained mightily about the poor quality of the inn, arguing that St. John had various lackeys scattered around the area who would take them in and provide them comfortable lodging. Simon's insistence that they remain near the road was unreasonable to her, and he appreciated the validity of the argument. However, he had no desire for Maria to realize that he had lied about the planned holiday, a ruse that would be revealed if he donned the same garments.

A soft sigh drew his attention back to Lysette. She was curled up in a wing chair, stripped to her chemise with her legs tucked up close and a blanket across her lap. Pale blonde curls were loosened from a previously stylish arrangement and left to lie carelessly against pale, creamy skin. She was reading, as she often did, devouring historical volumes of text with a voracity he found intriguing. Why such interest in the past? They had merely intended to make discreet inquiries, and she had brought a book along with her anyway.

Frowning, Simon moved to the bed and stripped down to his smalls. Then he crawled between the sheets. With lowered lids, he studied her, admiring her delicate golden beauty while considering why it was that he found her so unappealing. It was, to his knowledge, the only time in his life that he had found external attractiveness incapable of distracting from the internal flaws. Considering that Lysette rivaled Maria in loveliness, it was a startling realization to come to.

The women were similar in many ways, and that only emphasized their differences. Maria had a solid core within her, a spine of steel that was created by her unwavering determination. Lysette seemed sometimes as if she was uncertain of her life's path. He could not understand why she appeared to relish her role one moment, and then despise it the next.

His instincts were clamoring, and he had come to rely on

them implicitly. Something told him that all was not right in Lysette's world. She was a hired killer, and her icy disposition supported her chosen profession. Yet her apathy for others was sometimes belied by brief flashes of confusion and remorse. He suspected she was a bit touched, and it was difficult to feel both sympathy and dislike toward the same woman.

"How did you come to work for Talleyrand?" he asked.

She jumped and glared at him. "I thought you were sleeping."

"Obviously not."

"I do not work for Talleyrand."

"Who then?"

"That is none of your business," she said smartly.

"Oh, I think it is," he drawled.

Her gaze narrowed as she looked at him. "Whom do you work for?" she countered.

"I work for no one. I am a mercenary."

"Hmm . . ."

"Are you?" he prodded, when she said no more than that.

Lysette shook her head, once again looking a bit lost. Her clothes were finely crafted and expensive, her manners and deportment faultless. She had begun life in far better circumstances than these. He knew why Maria had turned to a life of crime, but why had Lysette?

"Why don't you find a rich husband and enjoy yourself draining his coffers?" he asked.

Her nose wrinkled. "How boring."

"Well, that would depend on the husband, would it not?"

"Regardless, that does not sound appealing to me."

"Perhaps life as a mistress would suit you better?"

"I do not like men very much," she pronounced, startling him. "Why are you asking me such questions?"

Simon shrugged. "Why not? There is nothing else for me to do."

"Go to sleep."

"Do you prefer the company of women?"

She stared at him a moment. Then her eyes widened. "No! *Mon Dieu*. I prefer the company of books, but in lieu of that, men are my second choice. Most especially in the manner to which you are referring."

He smiled at her horror.

"Why don't you think about Cartland?" she suggested, "And leave me in peace."

His humor fled. "You think he will find Mitchell?"

"I think it would be impossible for him not to with this large a number of pursuers. He was given a sizeable contingent of men. I would be surprised if he was not watching all the major roads in and out of London." Her beautiful features lost all traces of humanity. "I would not have come with you if I thought of this as merely a family affair."

"Of course not," he murmured, the tiny flare of warmth he'd felt for her fading as rapidly as it had come. Such was the way of their relations—one minute he found her marginally attractive, the next he could not abide her. "And what of this man who rides with Cartland? Depardue? Do you think about him?"

"As little as possible."

There was something more there; he could tell by the edge that had entered her voice. "He is your rival, is he not?"

Her lips whitened, then, "No. He is not. If he succeeds, it does not reflect negatively on me."

"So why not allow him to proceed and spare yourself the blight on your soul?"

"I do what I must," she said with a trace of defensiveness. "You do not like that I can set aside my emotions to accomplish the tasks set before me, but the ability keeps me alive."

Heaving out his breath, Simon slid down to lie on his back. "Surviving in the manner that you and I do does not mean we have to be heartless. What would be the point of living if we have no heart?"

He heard the book slam shut. "Do not seek to lecture me!" she snapped. "You have no notion of what my life has been like."

"So tell me," he said easily.

"Why do you care?"

"I told you, there is nothing else to do."

"Do you want to have sex?"

His head shot up in surprise. She stared back with both brows raised.

"With you?" he asked, incredulous.

"Who else is here?" she retorted.

To his chagrin, Simon realized that as much as he enjoyed a quick, meaningless tumble, he had no real desire to tumble Lysette. However, damned if he wouldn't rise to the occasion. "I suppose we could . . ."

Her eyes widened at his obvious reluctance. Then she laughed, a sweet, lilting sound that he found enchanting. Who knew such a cold creature could have such a warm laugh? "You don't want to sleep with me?" she asked, grinning.

Simon scowled. "I can manage the task," he bit out.

Lysette looked pointedly at the general area of his cock. "It does not look that way to me."

"Never cast aspersions on a man's virility. You force him to prove it by fucking you raw."

A shadow passed over her features. She swallowed hard and looked away.

His irritation fled. Sitting up, he said, "I was jesting."

"Of course."

Scrubbing a hand over his jaw, Simon cursed inwardly. He did not understand the woman at all. She was too mutable. "Perhaps we should restrain our conversations to safer subjects?"

She looked at him. "Yes, I think you are right."

He waited for her to say something; then finally he took the lead. "I intend to capture Cartland and bring him together with Mitchell. Then you can see for yourself the differences between the two. If I know Cartland at all, he hopes to eliminate Mitchell before his secret is revealed."

"If there is such a secret to tell."

"Why do you not believe us?"

"Do not take offense," she said easily. "I do not believe Cartland either."

"Who do you believe, then?" he snapped.

"No one." Her chin lifted. "Tell me you would do differently in my place."

"You met Mitchell. He is an earnest young man with a good heart."

Her gaze hardened. "I am certain there are those who would laud Monsieur Cartland as well."

"Cartland is a lying murderer!"

"So you say. But did he not once work for you? Do you not have a grievance against him for revealing your traitorous activities in France? You have motive to want him dead, which leaves anything you say against him suspect."

Cursing under his breath, Simon plopped back onto the pillow and yanked up the counterpane.

"Are you going to sleep now?" she asked.

"Yes!"

"*Bonne nuit.*"

His response was a frustrated growl.

Chapter 10

A melia shivered as her bare back touched the cool counter-pane and Montoya's warmth left her. If she kept her gaze trained downward, she could see a tiny sliver of the room and the glow of the fire in the grate. But she did not want to see, so she squeezed her lids shut.

In her mind's eye, she pictured Montoya as a rather exotic-looking man. Strong, handsome, and rather severe. The desire she felt to lighten his burdens and bring him some comfort was a goading force. She wanted to hear him laugh and press kisses to the dimples she saw far too rarely.

Suddenly, an image of Colin burst forth in all its glory, vivid and powerful. She stiffened in surprise.

"What is it?" Montoya murmured, the cessation of sound telling her that he had stopped undressing.

Inhaling sharply, Amelia brought her thoughts back to the present. Perhaps it was to be expected that she would think fondly of her first love at this moment, the one where she embarked on a similar journey with another. She lacked the experience to know.

"I am cold without you," she lied, holding her arms out to him.

"In a moment, you will be hot and damp," he purred, the bed dipping as he joined her atop it.

She felt the warmth of him along her side and then the

gentle press of his firm lips to her shoulder. His hand drifted along the length of her, following the slight curves and valleys of her figure.

"I fear I am dreaming," he said softly. "I am afraid to blink in case I open my eyes and find you gone."

Amelia's hand came to rest on the flat plane of her belly just below her navel. "I feel flutters here," she confessed.

His hand covered hers and squeezed gently. "I will be there soon. Deep inside you." His fingertips tiptoed across her skin and touched the curls between her legs.

It tickled, making her laugh. When he pressed his lips to hers, she felt his returning smile. "I love you," he breathed before taking her mouth.

Her heart stopped, delaying her reaction to the deepening intrusion of his fingers. A callused fingertip parted her and her thighs squeezed together instinctively.

Gasping, Amelia turned her head away, the reaction to those whispered words hitting her with stunning force. She had never thought to hear those words again, not from the lips of a lover. Tears welled, burning her eyes.

"Open your legs," he urged, kissing her throat. "Allow me to pleasure you."

She began to quiver, the assault to both her senses and her heart rattling her to the core. "Reynaldo . . ."

"No." He came over her then, kissing her hard. "Call me anything but that. Lover or darling—"

". . . sweetheart . . ."

"Yes . . ." His tongue thrust deep, caressing hers, making her moan into his mouth. "Open," he said ardently. "Let me see you . . . touch you . . ."

Unable to deny him when he spoke with such passion, Amelia spread her legs and then arched upward as he stroked against the tender, throbbing point that begged for his attention.

"Oh!"

Montoya's kisses became more luxurious as he continued

to fondle her with devastating skill. His callused fingertips rubbed her slick, aching sex in time to the rhythmic plunges of his tongue.

Awash in pleasure, yet struggling against the building tension that strained her body, she writhed and clutched at him. Beneath her grip his forearm muscles flexed with his movements, increasing her erotic awareness of how intimately he touched her.

Then one finger dipped lower, circling the clenching opening to her sex.

"How slick you are," he breathed reverently. "How greedily you suck at my fingertip." To prove his point, he pushed in the tiniest bit. Amelia cried out as her body spasmed around the gentle invasion.

"Dear God, you are so tight and hot," he praised gruffly. "You will kill me when I push inside you."

Amelia reached for his cock, wondering how she would accommodate him. He was so thick and hard. Her untried body was burning from the press of one finger.

Montoya groaned when she wrapped her hand around him. He was slick, too. With need and desire for her.

"You are ready to come," he said. "Feel how hard your clitoris is?" The pad of his thumb pressed lightly against the swollen protrusion and circled. In response, her body tightened around the single finger slowly easing into it.

She whimpered as he stepped up the pace, his finger thrusting in and out, deeper and deeper. His expert manipulation of her clitoris caused her skin to dampen with sweat and her breasts to ache. Desperate mewling poured from her throat, and she clung to him, trying to bring him closer.

"Tell me what you need," he whispered, his lips to her ear. "Tell me how to please you."

"My nipples . . ."

"They are beautiful. Puckered so wantonly. Eager to be sucked."

"Yes!" Amelia arched upward in blatant invitation.

"Say it, my love." His finger pushed deeper and touched her maidenhead. "Say what you want."

"I want . . ."

"Yes?" He continued to rub inside her.

"I want your mouth on my breasts."

"Umm . . . with pleasure," he purred.

She gasped when he obliged, the burning heat searing her tender flesh. Tension gripped her limbs, tightening with every tug of his lips, every thrust of his finger, every circle of his thumb.

The climax stole her breath when it hit. Her body went rigid, her heart slammed against her ribs, her blood rushed through her ears.

And deep inside her, at the extremity of her orgasm, Montoya broke through the barrier between them. Amidst the onslaught of sensation, the loss of her virginity was barely noticed, and the tear that leaked from the corner of her eye was not from pain, but pleasure so intense she could hardly bear it.

As awareness returned after the rush, she heard his hoarsely voiced endearments and praise. Her first thought was of how grateful she was to share the sexual act with a man who felt such passion for her and inspired a returning desire for him. What might have been an act of duty was instead a joy.

There were a hundred emotions warring for dominance within her, all struggling to be freed through words. But her throat was too tight to release them.

Instead, she wrapped her arms around him and held him to her breast.

Colin listened to the sound of Amelia's heart slowing and knew he had never loved her more. She was a goddess in her passion, a creature of lust and longing, her beautiful body flushed and glistening. Earthy. Wild and hot, as she had longed to be. Built for sex.

With him.

No other man could unlock her. She said she felt nothing

when he was gone. She felt alive when he was near. Warm and soft, wet and willing. Eager to be touched.

"That was"—she gave a soft, breathy sigh—"wonderful."

He rubbed his face against her breast and laughed, his heart filled with joy. He, too, felt reawakened after being dormant too long. She had pursued him, needing his desire to set free her own.

"Your whiskers burn," she complained, pushing at his head.

The image in his mind of such an obvious sexual mark on her made his cock throb in frustrated protest at its deprivation.

But the fantasy he had nurtured over the years was not of his own gratification. He wanted *hers*, needed it. Before the night was over he would bind her to him with pleasure, enslave her with desire, teach her all the many facets of sexual culmination. Her love was the ultimate prize, but her lust was vital, too.

"Can I burn you in other places?" he asked, lifting his head.

Her tongue darted out to wet her lower lip. Colin took over the task, licking across the plump curve with the very tip of his tongue. It was an enticement, an intimation, a hint.

From the way her breath caught, she comprehended his intent. "You jest."

"Never. I want to taste you, Amelia. On the outside and on the inside."

He could almost hear her brain working. Considering.

"I find it easier to conceive of my tasting you in that fashion," she said slowly, "more so than I can the reverse."

His arms shook at the thought, and he rolled to his back to avoid collapsing atop her.

"You would like that," she mused aloud, noting his reaction. "Does a woman's mouth feel so different from her quim?"

"I love that you are inquisitive. I pray you will always be."

"One day I should like to teach you something."

"Siren. You already have me bewitched. Must you reduce me further?"

Her hand brushed lightly across the ridges of his abdomen and circled his upthrust cock. He exhaled harshly as she sat up and turned to face him. Reaching out, he caught her shoulder and stayed her. Despite her inability to see, she turned her head toward him. Her free hand reached for the fichu.

"Not yet," he said.

"I am ready now."

"I am not."

She seemed prepared to protest, then changed her mind. Instead, she stroked gently up the length of his shaft. He grit his teeth and fisted the counterpane.

"I want to do to you," she murmured, "what you did to me."

"You know men are less fastidious than women when we reach orgasm."

"But the sensation is the same, is it not?"

He smiled. "I would imagine so."

Amelia sat up and tucked her legs beneath her. With two hands, she fondled him, squeezing and caressing. The sensation originated at his cock, burned up his spine, and seared his heart. There was reverence in her touch. Awe.

The edge of a nail traced the line of a vein, and he groaned, a low, pained sound.

"Tell me what you like," she breathed. "Tell me how to please you best."

"You already please me best." Colin caressed the elegant curve of her spine.

"Then tell me how to please you better."

"If you did that, I would spend in your hands."

"Or my mouth?" Her head tilted to one side in question.

"Not tonight," he choked out. His bollocks drew up, and he pulled them down with a quick tug.

She felt blindly until she comprehended what he had done. "Why did you do that?" Her cool fingers touched his balls, rolling them gently, then tugging them.

Unlike when he had performed the task himself, Amelia's ministrations had the opposite result. Colin felt as if his testicles were attempting to crawl up inside his body. He pushed her hand away. "Bloody hell, do not do that!"

"That was amazing," she said, with that awed tone that drove him to madness.

Pushed to the edge of reason, Colin rolled over her and settled between her thighs. The makeshift blindfold twisted with his movements, but he caught it quickly and pulled it into place.

"You feel so good." Amelia's small hands moved across his shoulders. "You are so big and hard . . . everywhere."

He heard anxiety in her voice and sought to alleviate it. "I will please you," he promised, supporting his weight on one forearm and reaching low to massage the tender flesh of her cunt with the heel of his other palm. She moaned and rolled her hips into the pressure. "What you felt before is nothing to how it will feel when I am inside you."

Her slender arms wrapped around his neck and pulled him near. "I want that. I want that with you."

"Yes." He licked along the shell of her ear, making her shiver. "You are a sensual woman. It's there in the way you move, the way you look at me, the way you are built."

"I am too slender," she said in a quiet voice.

"You are perfect. Some women are fashioned to suit all men. You were crafted for me alone. My blood runs hot, my passions high; therefore you were made for endurance. Your limbs graceful, but lithe. Your curves lush, but not limiting."

He pushed a finger inside her, testing her soreness. Her answering moan of welcome was all the encouragement he needed. Fisting his straining cock, he positioned the thick head at the tiny slitted entrance to her body. Cum was dribbling from the tip, the shaft too eager and determined to lubricate his way. It wasn't necessary. Amelia was so wet and hot. With the veriest roll of his hips, the fat crown slipped inside her.

"Oh, God . . . !" she breathed, her mouth opening on gasping breaths.

Colin's entire body strained with the pleasure of her grip. The scalding heat inside her swept upward from his cock and over his skin. Sweat misted, then pooled in the small of his back as his back bowed with the effort he maintained to keep his entry slow. She would need time to adjust to his size and the novel intrusion of a man's body into hers.

Amelia's hands caught his hips, and her hips began a tiny rolling motion that nearly unmanned him.

"Bloody hell!" he gasped, jolting as his seed spurted out in a desperate bid to relieve the torturous pressure in his bollocks.

"I need you deeper," she begged, and he was so grateful for her that he took her mouth in a lush, frantic kiss. Her lips closed around his tongue, sucking it with such fervor his cock swelled in jealousy.

Using his weight, Colin pinned her to the bed, sinking another inch inside her, his hands cupping her face and gentling her ardor.

"Amelia . . ." He groaned and nuzzled his sweat-slick cheek against hers. "You are making it impossible for me to initiate you as you deserve."

"I ache inside," she cried, holding him so tightly. "And you are not there yet."

"You are tiny and untried, and I am thick and hard. If I go too quickly, it will bring you pain now and soreness later."

"You are too big . . ."

"No, damn it all!" He did not want to be surly, but her hungry cunt was tugging on the head of his cock, goading his primitive instincts to take over and leave the gentlemanly ones behind.

"Then let me watch. Perhaps if I can see, I would be less anxious. This moment is too intense without my sight. Every noise, every touch is magnified."

Colin went rigid. Now was not the time, and yet he could not bear for any part of this night to distress her. He was in heaven. He wanted nothing more than for her to be also. "I am afraid of what will happen if you see me now. If you turned me away, I do not think I would survive it."

Her lower lip quivered. Then she asked, "Do you have one of your masks with you?"

"You ask me to withdraw?" He stared down at her with wide eyes. "Are you insane? I am *inside* you."

"Not all the way," she argued. "Not as I need you to be." Her voice took on the pleading, cajoling note that he had never been able to resist.

She would kill him, he realized with an odd mixture of pride and wryness. She would never be passive in the bedroom, just as she had never been passive out of it. He half feared the day when she'd be fully awakened sexually. How would he survive the full assault of her feminine wiles? He wasn't yet buried to the hilt and he felt like he was dying.

"It excites me," she whispered, releasing the stunning statement with panting breaths. "The sight of you in the mask." Her fingers came up and traced the shape of his lips. "You have such a wicked mouth. I have dreamt of it. Longed for it to move across my skin and whisper hot words of wanting."

Shuddering with desire, Colin pushed restlessly into her streaming cunt. She was melting around his cock. Her nipples were hard against his chest, her stomach was quivering against his.

"It would please me to watch you. Do not deny me." Her hands cupped his buttocks and tugged, pulling him fractionally deeper.

She became tighter the deeper he went, her virgin tissues resisting the remolding of her body to fit his.

"Please . . ." she breathed with such heartrending yearning. "Do not leave me in the darkness at this moment in my life."

Cursing, Colin wrenched himself free, his body shaking with its need. He rolled from the bed and stalked on nerveless legs to the armoire where his valise waited. Reaching inside it, he withdrew the mask, which he had kept as a tangible reminder of the stolen moments he had shared with Amelia.

He stared down at the gleaming white item in his hands with a building resentment for its purpose—that of keeping Colin Mitchell away from the woman he loved.

How he wished he would have seen where this deception would lead when he first purchased the mask! One look at Amelia—a sip of water for a man dying of thirst—was all he had expected the ruse to provide.

"Hurry," she urged in the throaty voice of a consummate seductress. The feminine allure so practiced and studied in other women was simply innate to her.

Colin lifted the half mask to his face and tied the black satin ribbons that would hold it in place, then retied the ribbon that restrained his queue. Turning his head, he looked at her and knew he would not leave this room as the same man who had entered it.

She reclined against the piled pillows, her legs and arms crossed modestly, the blindfold gone. In her verdant gaze he saw lust, longing, and appreciation of such magnitude that he could scarcely breathe.

Pivoting on his heel, he faced her directly, affording her a clear view of his raging cock and taut musculature. He watched her swallow hard and understood how intimidating the sight of him must be. She was a tall woman, but he was still much taller. He was more than twice her size, his body hardened by both his common lineage and frequent physical activity.

And he was in full rut. Thick veins pulsed with his raging blood, and he fisted the shaft to ease the pain of it.

"Does the sight of me this way arouse you," he asked, "or frighten you?"

Amelia licked her lips. "I am not frightened," she whispered. "I am nervous and perhaps apprehensive, but I do not fear you."

"You are a strong woman," he praised, striding swiftly toward her.

Without preliminaries, he kneeled on the bed and climbed over her, tugging her arm out of the way so he could claim a nipple with his mouth. He attended the stiff peak with hard, rhythmic suction, urging her silently to make some sound of her delight.

Her hands cupped the back of his head and held him to her breast. "Come inside me," she whispered. "I hate this feeling of uncertainty and ignorance."

Sitting back on his heels, Colin pulled her legs over either side of his own, spreading her thighs wide to expose her cunt to his gaze. With the angle of the pillows and her semi-reclined position, she had a clear view. Before she could register the size of her tiny pink slit compared to the girth and length of his cock, he was in her, pushing the thick head into the tender opening.

She whimpered and dug her nails into his thighs.

Holding her hips, he took her, rocking gently but relentlessly deeper and deeper. His gaze moved between the place of their joining and her beautiful face.

With his back shadowing her from the rapidly dwindling glow of the fading fire, he could not discern color, but he saw the telltale shimmer of sweat on her brow, and her eyes glistened with a sheen of tears.

"Am I hurting you?" he gasped, his fingers bruising her as she responded to his voice by rippling along the buried length of his cock. She was so damn tight and hot, it felt as if he were fucking into a tightly closed fist.

"No . . ." Her voice was thready and faraway sounding.

Colin lifted one of her hands from his skin and set it over her distended clitoris. "Stroke yourself," he instructed.

To his utter delight she obliged without embarrassment, her long, slender fingers circling the slick flesh with only slight hesitation.

Her lovely cunt responded as he had known it would, clenching and grasping at him with renewed fervor. With every suck, he pushed deeper, groaning with the ecstasy of it, gulping in desperate breaths of air filled with the scents of sex and honeysuckle.

She began to writhe and mewl in a show of such wanton craving, he would wonder later how he managed to work inside her completely without coming at the midway point. Finally, with a last desperate lunge, he hit the end of her, the sensation of being balls-deep inside her enough to make his eyes tear.

Amelia cried out as Montoya's hot, heavy length finally struck deep. A flare of torturous relief spread outward from the aching spot inside her that begged to be rubbed, and then coiled tight again.

When he held still, she struggled, circling her hips, grinding against the root of his shaft. The growl that left him was more animal than human, and her body shivered in response, spurred to greater lust by the sound.

He held her still with powerful hands, his gaze burning from within the eyeholes of the mask. His beautiful mouth was hard, his jaw taut.

"Why won't you move?" she cried.

"Because I am about to blow, and I refuse to go without you."

"I am ready!" Her voice was high with her distress, her womb clenching and tightening in a way that was nearly painful.

With effortless strength, he scooped her up and lifted to his knees, impaling her deeper on the rock-hard length of his cock. Amelia clung to his broad shoulders, her mouth suckling across the salty, whisker-roughened expanse of his throat. The room spun as he rearranged their positions, every movement sliding her over him until she bit him in retaliation for her sexual frustration.

Montoya cursed and pushed her away from him.

"Ride," he said roughly.

He sat on the edge of the bed, her legs astride his, his erection buried deep. So deep. Canting his arms back, he supported his torso and gave her full access to use him as she willed. The display he made was searingly erotic, his abdomen laced tight with muscle, his furred chest damp with sweat.

And the mask. Dear God, the mask added a dark, alluring mystery that urged her to recklessness.

"I—"

"Now!" he barked, making her jump.

Her shoulders went back and her chin lifted in answer to his challenge. She thought this must be difficult for him for reasons she had not considered before. He made love with the expertise of a man who had his choice of women, which suggested the marring of his face might have been a recent event. Perhaps she was the first woman to welcome him to her bed since the injury was inflicted. The thought added poignancy to an already remarkable event.

Amelia decided in that moment that she would love him well, with all that she had, better than any other woman ever could. She would reach for the turmoil she sensed inside him and soothe it with her passion, showing him with her body that it was his heart that lured her to him.

Setting her hands on his shoulders for balance, she pushed

onto her knees and lifted, sliding her sex upward along the length of him. When she lowered, the feel of the broad head of his cock stroking over that quivering spot inside her made her gasp and shake violently.

"That's it," he praised in a dark whisper, watching her through thick black lashes. "See how well I fit you? I was made for your pleasure."

Biting her lower lip, she repeated the movement, venturing slowly as she found the way of it. Her thumb brushed across a scar that marred his shoulder, the wound so old, it had long since turned silver. She caressed it as she undulated, feeling the circular shape surrounded by ragged edges. In the back of her mind the injury bothered her, prodded at her . . .

Then he spoke, and everything else scattered from her mind.

"Sweet Amelia. You are mine."

Amelia rose and wrapped her arms around his torso, tilting her head to fit her mouth over his, lifting and falling, moaning at the feel of her swollen nipples brushing across the light dusting of coarse hair on his chest.

Claiming him as he claimed her.

Montoya thrust one hand into her tresses, holding her close as he murmured encouragement into her mouth, his hips circling beneath her in breathtaking thrusts, stealing her wits.

Stealing her heart.

As she gained confidence, she moved faster, breathing hard from her exertions, drops of sweat trickling down between her bouncing breasts.

"I want you this way daily." His words were heavy, slurred with pleasure. "I want you to feel empty when I am not inside you. Hungry. Starved for me."

Amelia knew it would be that way. She was mindless with lust, grinding, writhing, pumping onto his thick, straining erection as if she had done this before. As if she knew what she was doing.

His teeth nipped her throat and she cried out, everything clenching inside her until he cursed from the feel of it.

He was driving her to this madness—with his big body reclined, his eyes heavy-lidded behind the mask, his lips glistening from her mouth. He looked like a pagan sex god. Exotically beautiful. Endlessly controlled. Content to lie back and be pleasured by a wanton whose sole focus was the pursuit of orgasm.

With her lips against his cheek, she whispered, "Fuck me," surprising herself with how easily the crude word rolled off her tongue.

A brutal shudder wracked Montoya's frame in response.

"Make me *come*," she coaxed breathlessly, riding him still. "I want it . . . I want *you*. Wild. Deep. I need you with me—"

Before she could blink, he had twisted, pinning her to the bed. Feet on the floor and fists in the counterpane, he drove powerfully into her, every perfect downstroke wrenching a cry of rapture from her throat.

He loomed over her, watching her through the mask, his chest heaving, his abdomen lacing, his buttocks clenching beneath her calves as she lifted to meet his every plunge. His body was a study in sexual power. Built to fuck a woman into addiction.

The coiling tension in her womb tightened, forming a hard knot that made her head thrash against the brutal pleasure. And then it broke free in a riot of sensation, burning across her skin, seizing her lungs, spasming inside her in endless rapid ripples that worshipped his straining cock.

The guttural roar that ripped from his throat brought tears to her eyes and a name to her lips. He paused in midstroke, rigid, and she mewled a protest, undulating beneath him in delirious pleasure.

He resumed, increasing the strength and speed of his thrusts until he swelled inside her, groaning through gritted teeth. Embedded in her to the deepest point, his body jerked in time to the hot, thick wash of his ejaculations inside her.

It was savage and primitive and beautiful. He curled around her, his weight supported on his forearms beneath her back, his skin sticking to hers with their mingled sweat.

"I love you," he whispered ardently, his tongue licking the trails of her tears. "I love you."

Amelia reached for the ribbons that secured the mask.

Chapter 11

It was dark in the room, the banked fire incapable of casting a shadow more than a foot away from the grate. Sight was difficult, and yet Simon's instincts urged him to heed their warning.

Moving cautiously, he turned his head and found the space in the bed beside him to be empty. He exhaled carefully, maintaining the deep, even rhythm of sleep.

Something had woken him, and since he was sleeping with a woman who would kill him if necessary, he knew ignoring the disturbance would not be wise.

He looked toward the window and saw the gleam of silver moonlight on strands of golden hair. Lysette had the drapes parted a scant inch or two and was presently staring out the window.

"What are you doing?" he whispered, sitting up.

Her head might have turned toward him, but he could not be sure.

"I heard noises outside."

"What do you see?"

The curtain closed. "Three riders. One went inside briefly, I assume to wake the innkeeper. Then they continued on."

Shivering, Simon threw off the covers and moved to the grate. "I doubt anyone would go to such trouble for directions at this time of night."

"My thoughts exactly."

"Could you hear them? Were they French?"

There was a brief flare of light as she lit a match; then the wick of a single taper took over the illumination. "I think they were English."

He frowned into the flickering fire. "Perhaps I should wake Maria."

"No need. They rode forward, not backward. Whatever they are looking for, it has yet to be found."

As heat began to radiate outward from the grate, Simon stood and faced Lysette. She looked tired, and a crease marred the side of her lovely face. She wore her cloak over her chemise and clutched it to her chest with white-knuckled fingers.

He gestured toward the bed. "Fine. Let's go back to sleep. I am still sore from that blasted carriage and could use a bit more time on my back instead of my arse."

Lysette nodded wearily and sank into the chair she had been reading in earlier. *"Bonne nuit."*

"Bloody hell." Scowling, he asked, "Did you fall asleep there?"

She blinked up at him. *"Oui."*

"On purpose?"

"Oui."

Simon ran a hand through his hair and prayed for patience. "I do not bite or snore or drool. I mean no offense when I say that I have no interest in tumbling you. The bed is perfectly safe."

"The bed may be," she said, watching him impassively, "but I have some doubts as to whether you are."

He opened his mouth to argue, then threw up his hands. "Bah! Rot in the chair, then."

Freezing, he hurried back to the bed and crawled between now-cooled linens. Curling into a ball, he prayed the warmth of the renewed fire would reach the bed soon.

"Curse you," he grumbled, glaring down the length of the bed at her. "It would be much warmer if there were two of us in here."

"You have more reason to want me dead than alive," she pointed out in a far too reasonable tone.

"At this moment, truer words were never spoken," he snapped. "The only reason I am not strangling you is because killing you would rob me of your body heat!"

Her pretty lips thinned primly.

"This is ridiculous, Lysette." He sat up, too frustrated to even attempt sleep. The impracticality of sleeping in the cramped wing chair after a long day of travel was so out of character for her. She was faultlessly practical, as was everyone who lived by their wits. "Why would I kill you now, when I have not before?"

She shrugged, but the way her gaze darted nervously belied the careless gesture.

Heaving out a long-suffering sigh, Simon once again tossed back the covers and stalked toward her. When she wielded a knife from between the edges of her cloak, he was not surprised.

"Put that away."

"Stay back."

"I am not attracted to you," he reiterated slowly. "And even if I was, I have no need to force myself on an unwilling woman."

Lysette frowned suspiciously. "I am fine in the chair."

"Liar. You look exhausted, and I cannot afford to drag you along while I attempt to clear Mitchell's name. You must carry your own weight."

She bristled at that. "I will not be a burden."

"Damned if you won't after a night spent sleepless and frozen. You will become ill and useless."

Pushing to her feet, she said, "I can take care of myself. Go back to bed and leave me in peace!"

Simon opened his mouth to argue further, then shook his head instead. He once again climbed between the sheets and turned his back toward the other side of the bed. A few moments later, the taper was extinguished. Shortly afterward he heard delicate snoring.

Faced with a deepening puzzle, Simon lay awake for some time.

Amelia studied the masked man in repose beside her and wondered how deeply he slept.

"We will wait until the sunrise to remove it," Montoya had said earlier.

"Why not now?" she countered, desperate to see beneath the now intrusive barrier. Her heart was smitten and her body no longer innocent. But what they shared could be no more than infatuation—it could not be love—if she did not see all sides of him.

"I want nothing to mar this evening," he had explained, withdrawing from her body and moving to the washstand behind the screen in the corner. He'd returned with a damp cloth and washed between her thighs, then cleansed himself before joining her in the bed. "In the morning, I will bare myself to you, strengthened by the memories of a blissful, perfect night in your arms."

In the end, she had reluctantly agreed, unwilling to be at odds with him over the matter of a few hours.

With his back to the headboard and her body curved to his side, he had asked her to share a beloved memory from her past. She had chosen a tale about Colin, relating how she had conquered her fear of heights by climbing a tree during a game of hide-and-seek.

"He passed below me several times," she said, her cheek resting over Montoya's heart. "I half hoped he would find me quickly, because it was frightening clinging to that limb, but the desire to surprise him was too great to give myself away."

His hand caressed up and down the length of her back.

"You wanted to win," he corrected, laughing that low, deep laugh she had adored from the moment she heard it.

"That, too." She smiled. "When he finally forfeited, I was so pleased with myself. Colin spent his allowance on a new ribbon to mark the conquering of that fear."

Montoya sighed. "He must have loved you a great deal."

"I think he did, although he never told me. I would have given anything to hear those words from him." Her fingers sifted through the hair on his chest.

"Actions speak louder than words."

"I tell myself that. I still have that ribbon. It is one of my greatest treasures."

"What do you imagine your life would have been like now, if you two had never been parted?"

Lifting her head, she'd met his questioning gaze. "I have imagined it in hundreds of scenarios. The most likely one, I think, would be that St. John would have taken Colin under his wing."

"Would you be married?"

"I have always hoped so. But that would depend upon him."

"He would have asked you," Montoya said with conviction.

Amelia smiled. "What leads you to be so certain?"

"He loved you deeply. I have no doubt. You were simply too young for him at the time, and he was not in a position to offer for you." He brushed the backs of his fingers along her cheekbone. "Do you love him still?"

She hesitated, wondering at the wisdom of confessing a lingering affection for one man while warming the bed of another.

"Always tell me the truth," he urged softly, "and you will never be wrong."

"Part of me will love him forever. He helped to mold me into the person I am today. He is weaved into the very fabric of my life."

Montoya had kissed her then, sweetly and with deep reverence. Breathless and enamored, she asked him to share a part of his past with her, expecting that he might speak of his lost love. He did not.

He chose to speak of his livelihood and the dangerous work he had done for the Crown of England. He shared how he'd traveled the length and breadth of the Continent, never having a true home or family, until the day he sought to resign and was instead embroiled in a life-threatening intrigue.

"That is why I attempted to maintain my distance from you," he said. "I did not want to taint your life with my mistakes."

"Is that how your face was scarred?" she asked, her fingertips lightly following the edge of the mask where it touched his skin.

He went rigid. "Beg your pardon?"

Instantly contrite for having distressed him, Amelia rushed to say, "I can understand your fear, but your disfigurement will not alter my affection for you."

"Amelia . . ." He seemed at a loss for words.

The conversation had died then, and they had simply clung to each other as Montoya fell asleep. She remained awake, her mind shifting through a multitude of thoughts. She planned what to say to Ware and Maria and mentally rehearsed how she would ask St. John for his assistance. She catalogued the various aches and pains that heralded her new awareness as a woman and speculated on how her relationship with Montoya would proceed once they were freed from all the unknowns that plagued them. She also wondered at her outrageous behavior of the last week and what it meant.

Only Maria truly understood what a monster Lord Welton was. That his blood ran through Amelia's veins made her ill at times. Externally, she was clearly his issue. Was she also like her father in ways she could not see? It was terrifying to realize that everything she had done these last few days had been selfishly motivated. She had disregarded the feelings and concerns of those who cared for her—Ware, Maria, and St. John—in favor of her desire to be with Montoya. Was she truly her father's daughter?

Amelia gazed into the licking flames and thought of the mask, ruminating about the man beneath it. The urge to peek beneath the guise was pressing. She tried to excuse the action with the reasoning that it was the mystery of his identity that had goaded her to act so rashly, not a defect in her character.

But what if Montoya was a light sleeper? What if he caught her and became angry? She dreaded the thought of exchanging furious words.

Perhaps she could test the depth of his slumber in some way . . . ?

Her hand lifted from the hard expanse of his abdomen, and her fingertips ran lightly along his thigh. The muscle twitched, but he made no other movement. Amelia tried again, caressing him with deeper pressure. This time, he moved not at all.

She became hopeful. He had loved her long and well, and extended journeys were known to make many a traveler weary.

Raising her head, her gaze roamed admiringly over the sculpted beauty of his chest. The scar on his shoulder was more visible now, the room lightened considerably by the fire Montoya had stoked into a hearty blaze to banish the pervasive chill. She studied the bullet hole with sympathy, guessing by the size and many radiating lines that it had been a nasty wound.

She kissed the evidence of injury, her lips brushing featherlight over the damaged flesh. The tempo of his breathing changed, and his nipples tightened while she watched in awe.

How fascinating the human body was. Tonight she had learned so much about her own. Amelia felt the sudden urge to know everything about his.

With the memories of his lovemaking still fresh and burning in her mind, she extended her tongue and licked across the tiny bead of darkened flesh. His skin was salty, the texture firmer than hers. She loved it, as she was beginning to love all of him.

Mimicking his earlier ministrations to her breasts, Amelia wrapped her lips around his nipple and sucked gently. He stirred, but not in the way she had anticipated.

Her thigh was draped over his, her knee bent and leg raised. As his cock swelled, she felt it, and she turned her head to see the thickening outline of his erection beneath the bedclothes. Her blood heated and began to move sluggishly. More surprising yet, her mouth watered.

She glanced at his face beneath lowered lashes. In the shadows of the eyeholes he appeared to be sleeping, with no telltale shimmer from liquid eyes to betray his cognizance.

Did she dare to explore further?

Her curiosity raging, she did not debate the question long. She slid downward, pulling the counterpane with her, eventually exposing his glorious cock to her avid gaze.

"You play with fire, love."

Montoya's voice startled her. She looked up at him and found him watching her with slumberous, burning eyes.

"How long have you been awake?" she asked.

"I've yet to fall asleep." His wicked mouth curved, revealing his dimple.

"Why did you keep your silence?"

"I wanted to see how far you would go." His hand lifted, his fingertips catching and caressing a stray curl of her hair. "Curious kitten," he murmured.

"Do you mind?"

"Never. Your touch is vital to me."

Considering that permission to proceed, she returned her attention to his erection. Amelia ran one fingertip from tip to root and smiled when it jerked at her touch.

"I find it astonishing that you fit in me," she confessed.

Remembering the rapturous feel of her cunt around his cock, Colin could not find the voice to reply. He was ferociously aroused and leashing himself by sheer will alone. When she'd begun to touch him, he had thought it by chance. Then she'd lifted her head and branded him forever with the feel of her lips upon the wound that had nearly killed him. It was the gunshot that had separated them so many years ago. The shot he'd taken while trying to save her.

Amelia slid lower still, stopping at eye level with his groin and leaving a trail of moisture along his leg. The evidence that the mere sight of his body was enough to arouse her to slickness made his bollocks tighten, forcing a perfect bead of semen to grace the tip of his cock.

His lungs seized as she eyed it hungrily. Would she be so bold?

A heartbeat later the question was answered as her tongue darted out and licked the droplet away.

Colin exhaled harshly at the whiplash of pleasure.

She studied him with narrowed eyes, a look he had come to know well over the years. It was a calculated glance, one she gave when considering how to tackle a challenge he presented. He smiled, understanding that she never sought to best him, only to equal him and be his match.

"You never answered me before," she said, circling the base of his cock with her thumb and forefinger. "Does a woman's mouth feel so different from her quim?"

"Yes."

"In what way?"

"In many ways. A cunt hugs every inch of a cock. It expands and contracts in ripples, and it is as soft as the finest silk. In contrast, a woman's mouth hugs through suction, not design. The pad of the tongue is textured and the muscle is agile. It can stroke like a finger, which stimulates the sensitive spot"—he pointed to the place on the underside of his cockhead—"here."

"Which do you prefer?" Her grip slid upward, then down again, making his teeth clench.

"Both have unique pleasures."

"That is not an answer," she murmured, caressing him again.

"It is difficult to think when you are fondling me," he managed.

She ceased and waited impatiently for him to gather his wits.

"My preference changes with my mood. There will be occasions when I will want to lose myself in you. I will want to hold you close and feel your body moving beneath mine. I will want to suck on your nipples and feast at your mouth. I will want to watch your face as you orgasm and hold you in the aftermath."

As he spoke he felt her grow wetter, hotter against the flesh of his leg. His voice deepened in response. "At other times, I will want to be serviced. I will want to lose myself to the pleasure in a way I cannot when I must see to your needs as well. The sight of your supplication will satisfy the primitive male in me, while my surrender to your care will be complete. I will be helpless and open, completely at your mercy."

The smile she gave him was impish. "I should like that."

"You might, or you might not. Many women do not. They fail to see the power in the act. They feel demeaned and used. Others simply do not like the taste of a man's seed."

"Hmm . . ."

He knew that hum and its portent. She wanted to know which type of woman she would be. Sadly, they had run out of time.

"We must dress you and return you safely to your room before you are seen. When the hour is appropriate to protect your reputation, we will meet and I will bare myself to you—my face and my secrets."

"I am not finished with you," she complained with a seductive pout that hardened him to full, raging arousal.

"It will be with exquisite pleasure that I offer myself to your sexual experimentation, love," he said hoarsely. "But such play requires time free of interruptions. We do not have the luxury tonight."

"You speak of our future liaisons with such surety," Amelia said, staring at his cock and resuming her ministrations.

Colin set his hand over hers and stilled her movements. "I cannot think otherwise and advise you not to either."

"But you have not made your intentions known."

Fueled by heady lust and burning possessiveness, he promised, "My intention is to tear down everything that stands between us. Then I want to woo you properly, with great fanfare. I want to dazzle you with extravagance, and lay the world at your feet." His thumb caressed the back of her hand. "Then, when every recessed corner of your heart is filled with love for me, I will wed you."

He loved her. He could not imagine never having her, not after this night. Yet he could make her no promises with a price on his head.

Despite this, at the pinnacle of the orgasm of his life, he had pressed against her womb and emptied his seed inside her. He no longer had any time. The clock was ticking.

Colin watched her lovely face and could not guess her thoughts. "Amelia?"

She laid her cheek upon his thigh. "Do not wait until life meets some inner criteria to seize the day," she whispered. "I have learned that sometimes tomorrow never comes."

Her melancholy cut him, and he held his arms out to her,

groaning his pleasure when she draped her nude body over his. Sexual desire simmered into the more complicated need to cling to something precious, yet unsecured.

Dawn approached, but neither was capable of releasing the other.

Chapter 12

It was a knock that woke her. At first groggy with the remnants of sleep, Maria took a moment to recognize her surroundings. Then the memories of the day before and the long, sleepless night rushed back in a deluge. She sat up abruptly, tossed back the covers, and rushed to the door.

"Christopher!" With joy, she flung herself into her husband's arms, and he crushed her to him, lifting her feet from the floor and stepping into the room.

"How did you find me so quickly?" she asked, as he kicked the portal closed behind him.

"It would have been quicker, damn you, if you had stayed in one of my inns and not this hovel! Why the devil are you here?"

"Simon insisted." She had tried to suggest they use one of the many homes Christopher owned across the entire length and breadth of the country. They were not grand. They were small cottages, inhabited by those who lived off pensions provided by St. John. The homes were safe, comfortable, and usually located in quiet corners where few questions were asked and fewer visitors came by. Nicknamed "inns" for both the accurate description of the service provided and also for the anonymity afforded by so generic a name, they were responsible for saving many lives.

"Damn him, too," Christopher said. Then he took her mouth, his head tilting to fit his lips to hers.

When she was limp and breathless, he muttered, "Vexing wench. Why must you torment me by being so troublesome?"

"This is not my doing!" she protested, tossing his hat aside.

"Damned if it isn't." He carried her to the bed and tossed her upon it, his gaze heating at the sight of her clad in only a chemise. Shrugging out of his fawn-colored coat, he said, "If you had not indulged Amelia in her fancy, we would not be taxed with chasing her, and I would not have spent the frigid night in a carriage."

"She would have gone alone, I know it." Maria crawled beneath the covers.

Christopher rebuilt the fire. Then he discarded his waistcoat, removed his boots, and climbed into bed with her, wearing his breeches and shirtsleeves.

"Tell me how you found me with such haste," she said, curling into his side.

"When Sam returned with the news of where you had gone, he mentioned Quinn. I sent men to find his lodgings, and when they discovered where he was staying, they found his valet packing. I followed him and he led me here."

Frowning, Maria lifted her head. "How is that possible? We had no notion that we would be staying at this establishment until we chanced upon it."

"Quinn must have known. His valet and the abigail of his French companion came directly to this place. You did say he insisted."

"He insisted we stay near the road." But, now that she thought of it, she remembered that it was Simon who'd begged that they take shelter at the first inn they came to just before Reading. She had protested the sorry appearance of the lodging, but he had complained of a sore arse and growling stomach.

"I do not understand." She sat up and faced her reclining spouse. "Our meeting in the shop was unplanned, I am certain of it. Even if I were wrong about that, there was no way for Simon to know Amelia would run off as she did."

"But, if he knew who Amelia was chasing and where the man might be headed . . ." Christopher's words faded, leaving her to draw her own conclusions.

"He told me they were already intent on a holiday, yet you say his valet and belongings were not yet ready. Why the ruse? Why pretend to help me, when he had his own motives for following?"

"We will have to ask him those questions in a few hours, when we rise."

"A few hours?!"

He yawned and tugged her back into his arms. "His room is guarded, and the hour is still relatively early. I sent riders ahead to follow the trail. There is nothing pressing that cannot wait the duration of a much-needed nap. I require some sleep this morn or I will be useless the rest of the day. Besides—and you must forgive me for pointing this out—you do not look rested either."

Maria settled into her husband's embrace with lingering reluctance. She was a woman who acted swiftly. Doing so had kept her alive. "I cannot sleep well without you near," she confessed.

He hugged her tighter and pressed a kiss to her forehead. "It pleases me to hear that."

"I must have become accustomed to your snoring."

His head lifted. "I do not snore!"

"How would you know? You are asleep when you do it."

"Someone would have mentioned it to me before now," he argued.

"Perhaps you exhausted them so that they slept right through it."

Growling, he rolled and pinned her beneath him. She blinked up at him with mock innocence. No one dared to tease the fearsome pirate, except for her. Goading his ire was a delicious temptation she could not resist, because the more she agitated him, the more sexually focused he became.

"If you need exhausting, madam," he bit out, reaching between them to unfasten his breeches, "I am more than capable of managing that task."

"You said you were useless and required a nap."

He shoved up the hem of her chemise and cupped her sex in his hand. Instantly, she was wet for him. Hot and creamy with desire. She moaned as he stroked her, and he smiled arrogantly, pulling away to position his cock.

"Does this feel useless to you?" he purred, pushing the hard length into her.

"Oh, Christopher," she breathed, awash in heated delight. After nearly six years of marriage, her ardor for him had not lessened one bit. "I love you so. Please don't fall asleep before I come . . ."

"You will pay for that," he said in a voice slurred with pleasure.

He made certain she did. And it was wonderful.

Colin was rinsing off his razor when a stray noise caught his attention and arrested his movements. He listened carefully, his nerves already stretched by the upcoming confrontation.

Amelia had returned to her chamber some time ago, but he doubted she slept. She was too curious, too impatient by nature. Knowing her as well as he did, he imagined she paced her room and glanced repeatedly at the clock, counting down the minutes to the time when he would reveal his identity to her.

There. It came again. The perceptible sound of scratching at the door.

Setting his blade on the washstand, he grabbed a cloth and was drying his face when his valet opened the door. Jacques entered bearing a grim expression.

"Miss Benbridge has been found, *mon ami.*"

Colin stilled. "By whom?"

"Riders this morning. They spoke with the giant who came with her and then turned about."

Heaving out his breath, Colin nodded. "Did you arrange the private dining room as I requested?"

"*Mais oui.*"

"Thank you. I will be down in a moment."

The door shut with a quiet click, and Colin hastened his toilette. He had promised Amelia an explanation, and he intended to give it to her without interruption.

Nodding to his valet, he presented his back and shrugged into the coat he had selected that morning. It was a striking garment, reminiscent of a male peacock's beautiful plumage. The cost of the intricately embroidered ensemble, which included breeches and silver-threaded waistcoat, was obvious. The Colin Mitchell who Amelia remembered so fondly would never have been able to purchase clothing so expensive. He wore it now as an outward display of his rise in the world. His dream of becoming a man capable of affording her was now a reality, and he wanted her to see that straightaway.

Suitably attired and inwardly certain, Colin left his bedchamber and took the stairs to the main room. It took only a moment to find the large man who had accompanied Amelia. The giant sat with his back to the wall and his eyes trained on his surroundings. As Colin approached him, the man's gaze sharpened with examining intensity.

"Good morning," Colin greeted, coming to a halt directly before the table.

"Morning," came the deep, rumbling reply. "I am Count Montoya."

"I gathered as much."

"There is much I need to explain to her. Will you give me the time and opportunity to do so?"

The man pursed his lips and leaned back his chair. "What do you 'ave in mind?"

"I have reserved the private dining room. I will keep the door ajar, but I beg you to remain outside."

The man pushed to his feet, towering over Colin's not inconsiderable height. "That will suit both me and my blade."

Colin nodded and stepped aside, but as the giant moved to pass him, he said, "Please give her this."

He handed over the items in his hand. After a brief pause, they were taken from him. Colin waited until Amelia's guard had ascended the stairs; then he moved to the private dining room and mentally prepared for the most difficult conversation of his life.

The moment Maria entered the main room of the inn, Simon knew he was in trouble. She bore the glow of a woman well fucked, but if that had not given away the end of his gambit, her change of clothes would have. Confirmation came when Christopher St. John entered the space a few steps behind his wife.

"What a lovely way to begin the day," Lysette said with laughter in her voice. Much as he usually detested her enjoyment of drama, today it was a relief after her odd behavior the night before.

Simon heaved a resigned sigh and pushed to his feet.

"Good morning," he greeted, bowing to the striking couple. The combination of St. John's golden coloring and Maria's Spanish blood was an attractive one.

"Quinn," St. John said.

"Simon," Maria murmured. She lowered into the chair her husband held out for her and linked her hands primly atop the table. "You know the identity of the man behind the mask. Who is he?"

Resuming his seat, Simon said, "He is Count Reynaldo Montoya. He was in my employ for several years."

"*Was?*" the pirate asked. "No longer?"

Simon related the events with Cartland.

"Dear God," Maria breathed, her dark eyes wide with horror. "When Amelia said the man was in danger, I never imagined it would be to this degree. Why did you not tell me? Why the lie?"

"It is complicated, Maria," he said, hating that he had betrayed the trust she bestowed so rarely. "I am not at liberty to divulge Montoya's secrets. He has saved my life many times over. I owe him at least my silence."

"What of my sister?" she cried. "You know how much she means to me. To know that she was at risk and not warn me . . ." Her voice broke. "I believed you and I were closer than that."

St. John reached over and clasped his wife's hand. The gesture of comfort pained Simon deeply. Out of all the women in the world, Maria was the dearest to him.

"I wanted to help you find her and then send her to safety with you," Simon said, "leaving Montoya and I to finish this business."

Maria's gaze narrowed in her fury. It radiated from her, belying the girlish image created by her delicate floral gown. "You should have told me, Simon. If I had known, I would have managed the situation far differently."

"Yes," he agreed. "You would have tasked dozens of men with the search, which would have alerted Cartland and put her at greater risk."

"You do not know that!" she argued.

"I know *him*. He worked for me. I know all his strengths. Finding lost people and items is his forte. Lackeys scouring the countryside would attract the attention of a simpleton, and Cartland is far from that!"

It was the pirate's raspy drawl that cut through the building tension. "How do you signify, Mademoiselle Rousseau?"

Lysette waved one delicate hand carelessly. "I am the judge."

"And the executioner, if need be," Simon grumbled.

St. John's brows rose. "Fascinating."

Maria pushed back from the table and stood. Simon and St. John stood as well.

"I have wasted enough time here," she snapped. "I must find Amelia before anyone else does."

"Allow me to come with you," Simon asked. "I can help."

"You have helped quite enough, thank you!"

"Lysette witnessed three riders making inquiries in the dead of night." Simon's tone was grim. "You need all the assistance you can muster. Amelia's safety lies within your purview, but Cartland and Montoya lie within mine."

"And mine," Lysette interjected. "I do not understand why we do not contact the man you work for here in England. He would seem to be an untapped, valuable resource."

"St. John likely has a larger, more reliable web of associates," Simon argued. "One more swiftly galvanized into action."

"Maria." St. John set his hand at the small of her back. "Quinn knows the appearances of both men. We do not. We would be blind without him."

She looked at Simon again. "Why does Montoya wear the mask?"

Careful to keep his face impassive, Simon used the excuse that Colin gave him. "He wore the mask for the masquerade. Later, he wore it to make it more difficult for Miss Benbridge to pursue him. He did not want to jeopardize her. He cares for her."

Maria lifted her hand to stem anything else he might say.

"We have an added complication," the pirate said. All eyes turned to him. "Lord Ware may follow."

"You jest!" Maria cried.

"Who is Lord Ware?" Lysette asked.

"Bloody hell," Simon muttered. "The last thing we require is the injury of a peer."

"He asked to accompany me," St. John said grimly. "But

the departure of Quinn's valet made waiting impossible. Still, he asked for direction, and while I was deliberately vague in hopes that he would reconsider, he may prove more tenacious than other men of his station."

Maria exhaled sharply. "Even more reason to keep moving, then."

"I sent the town carriage back to London," the pirate said. "Pietro is loading the travel coach as we speak. We should make better time."

Simon, unfortunately, did not have a change of equipage, but his bruised arse would have to make do.

With the sunrise lighting their way, they hastened toward Reading.

The moment the knock came to her bedroom door, Amelia ran to open it.

"Tim!" she cried, startled at the sight of her visitor and not very pleased. Perhaps he intended for them to leave now, which would necessitate her explaining about Montoya and her deception of the night before.

He took one look at her wild hair and disarrayed clothing and cursed with a viciousness that made her wince. "You lied to me last night!" he accused, pushing his way inside.

She blinked. How did he know?

Then she saw the items in his hand, and the answer to the question lost importance. "Let me see," she said, her heart racing at the possibilities. Tim had the mask. How? Why?

Tim stared at her for a long, taut moment, then offered her the mask and the missive with it.

> *My love,*
> *You have the mask. When next you see me, I will not be wearing it.*
> *Your servant,*
> *M*

The sudden realization that Montoya could have fled after she departed made her feel ill.

"Dear God," she gasped, clutching the mask to her chest. "Is he gone?"

He shook his head. "'E waits for you downstairs."

"I must go to him."

Amelia hurried to the untouched bed where her corset and underskirts awaited donning. Montoya hadn't the time to dress her completely. His fear for her discovery in his room had driven him to haste. She had hoped to ask a chambermaid for help, but Tim would have to manage the task.

"I think you should wait until St. John comes," he said. "'E's on 'is way now."

"No," she breathed, pausing in midmovement. Her time with Montoya was too precious. The addition of her sister and brother-in-law would only add to the confusion she felt. "I must speak with him alone."

"You've already been alone with 'im," he barked, shooting a pointed glance at the untouched bed. "St. John will 'ave my 'ead for that. I don't need to give 'im any more to be angry o'er."

"You do not understand. I have yet to see Montoya's face. You cannot expect me to face such a revelation with witnesses who are in foul temper." She held a shaking hand out to him.

He stared at it for a long moment with his jaw clenched tight and his fists clenched tighter. "A moment ago, I admired 'im for seeking me out. Now I want to rip 'im to pieces. *'E should not have touched you.*"

"I wanted him," she said with tears in her eyes. "I pushed him. I was selfish and cared only about my own desires."

Just as her father would have done, curse him. And curse his blood which tainted her. Everything around her was in disarray because she could think only of herself.

"Don't cry!" Tim complained, looking miserable.

His discomfort was her fault. Somehow, she had to make everything right. The starting point was Montoya, as he was the pivotal figure who had begun this descent into madness.

"I have to go to him before they arrive." She shrugged out of her unfastened gown, wiggled into her corset, and presented her back. "I shall need your assistance to dress."

Tim muttered something as he stalked toward her, and by the glower he wore, she thought herself fortunate to have missed it.

"I think I'll wed Sarah after all," he growled, yanking on her stays so tightly, she lost her ability to breathe. "I'm too old fer this."

Gasping and lacking the air required to speak, she swatted at him to fix it. He scowled, then appeared to notice that she was about to faint, and why. He grumbled an apology and loosened the tapes.

"I 'ope yer 'appy," he snapped. "You've driven me to the altar!"

Amelia pulled on her underskirts. After Tim tied them to her, she caught up her dress from where it pooled on the floor and thrust her arms into the sleeves.

Tim's thick fingers fumbled with the tiny buttons that secured the gown.

"I love you." She looked over her shoulder. "I do not know if I have ever told you that, but it's true. You are a good man."

The flush of his skin spoke volumes.

"'E'd best marry you, if that's what you want," he said gruffly, his gaze on his task. "Otherwise, I'll string 'im up and gut 'im like a fish."

It was some sort of peace offering, and she accepted it gratefully. "I would help you, if it came to that."

He snorted, but a quick glance over her shoulder revealed a wry curve to his lips. "'E doesn't know what trouble 'e's got 'imself into with you."

Amelia shifted impatiently. "I pray we can keep the man alive long enough to show him."

The moment Tim announced he was done, she pulled on stockings and shoes, and rushed toward the door. As she took the stairs with all the decorum she could muster, her breath shortened until she felt dizzy.

The next moments of her life would alter the future forever; she felt it in her bones. The feeling of portent was so strong, she was almost inclined to flee, but could not. She needed Montoya with a depth and strength she had thought she would never feel again. Part of her heart screamed silently at the betrayal of her first, dear love for Colin. The other half was older, wiser and understood that affection for one did not negate the affection she felt for the other.

Her hand shook as she reached for the doorknob of the private dining room. In the best of circumstances she would be nervous. She was about to face the man who had seen her and touched her in ways no one else ever had. The added tension brought on by the revealing of his face only deepened her disquiet and concern.

Taking a deep, shaky breath, Amelia knocked.

"Come in."

Before she lost her courage, she entered with as confident a stride as she could affect. She paused just inside, taking in the lay of the room with its cheerily blazing fire, large circular table draped in cloth, and walls covered in paintings of the countryside. He faced away from her before a window, his hands clasped at the small of his back, his broad shoulders covered in exquisite colorful silk, his silky black locks restrained in a queue that ended just between his shoulder blades.

The sight of his richly clad form in the simple country room was glaring. Then he turned, and her body froze in shock.

It cannot be him, she thought with something akin to panic. *It is impossible.*

Her heart ceased beating, her breath seized in her lungs, and her thoughts stuttered as if she had taken a blow to the brain.

Colin.

How was it possible . . . ?

As her knees gave way, she grappled blindly for a nearby chair but missed. She crumpled to the rug, a loud gasp filling the highly charged air as her instincts rushed to the fore and forced her to breathe.

"Amelia." He lunged toward her, but she held up a hand to stop him.

"Stay away!" she managed, through a throat clenched painfully tight.

The Colin Mitchell she knew and loved was dead.

Then, how is it, an insidious mental voice questioned, *that he is here with you?*

It can't be him . . . It can't be him . . .

She repeated that litany endlessly in her mind, unable to bear the thought of the years between them, the life he must have led, the days and nights, the smiles and laughter . . .

The betrayal was so complete, she could not credit that Colin was capable of it. Yet, as she stared at the dangerously handsome man who stood across from her, her heart whispered the agonizing truth.

I would know him anywhere, it said. *My love.*

How could she have missed the signs?

Because he was dead. Because I grieved long and deeply.

Freed from the confines of the mask, Colin's exotic Gypsy features left no doubt that it was he. He was older, the lines of his face more angular, but the traces of the boy she had loved were there. The eyes, however, were Montoya's—loving, hungry, knowing eyes.

The lover who'd shared her bed was Colin . . .

A wracking sob escaped her, and she covered her mouth with her hand.

"Amelia."

The aching tone in which her name was spoken made her cry harder. The foreign accent was gone, leaving behind the voice she heard in her dreams. It was deeper, more mature, but it was Colin's.

She looked away, unable to stand the sight of him.

"Have you nothing to say?" he asked quietly. "No questions to ask? No insults to hurl?"

A hundred words struggled to leave her mouth, and three very precious ones, but she leashed them tightly, unwilling to bare the depth of her pain. She stared at a small, square painting of a lake that adorned the wall. Her lower lip quivered, and she bit it to hide the telltale movement.

"My body has been inside yours," he said hoarsely. "My heart beats in your breast. Can you not at least look at me, if you will not speak to me?"

Her silent reply was the tears that flowed in a steady, endless stream.

He cursed and came toward her.

"No!" she cried, stilling him. "Do not come near me."

Colin's jaw clenched visibly, and she watched the muscle tic with an odd disconnection. How strange to see Montoya's maturity and polish within her childhood love. He looked the same and yet different. He was bigger, stronger, more vital. He was stunningly attractive, blessed with a novel masculine appeal few could rival. She used to dream of the day they would be wed and she could call him her own.

But that dream had died when he had.

"I still dream of that," he murmured, answering the words she had not realized she'd spoken aloud. "I still want that."

"You allowed me to believe you were dead," she whispered, unable to reconcile the Colin she remembered with the magnificently dressed man standing before her.

"I had no choice."

"You could have come to me at any time; instead you have been absent for years!"

"I returned as soon as I was able."

"As another man!" She shook her head violently, her mind filling with memories of the last weeks. "It was a cruel game you played with my affections, making me care for a man who does not exist."

"I exist!" He stood tall and proud, his shoulders back, his chin lifted. "I played no role with you. Every word that left Montoya's mouth, every touch, was from *my* heart. The same heart beats in both men. We are one and the same. Both madly in love with you."

She dismissed his claim with a wave of her hand. "You affected an accent and allowed me to believe you were disfigured."

"The accent was a façade, yes. A way to keep you from guessing the truth before I could tell you properly. The rest was a creation of *your* mind, not mine."

"Do not blame this farce on me!" Amelia struggled to her feet. "You allowed me to grieve for you. Have you any notion of what I have suffered these last years? How I have suffered these last weeks, feeling as if I was betraying Colin by falling in love with Montoya?"

Torment shadowed his features, and she hated the vicious satisfaction she felt at the sight of it. "Your heart was never fooled," he said roughly. "It always knew."

"No, you—"

"Yes!" His dark eyes burned with an inner fire. "Do you recall whose name you cried at the height of orgasm? When I was deep inside you, clasped in the very heart of your body, do you remember which lover's name came to your lips?"

Amelia swallowed hard, her mind shifting through the myriad of sensations that had assailed her untried body. She remembered the look of the bullet scar on his shoulder, the way the feel of it had plagued her in some fashion she could not pinpoint.

"You were driving me mad!" she accused.

"I wanted to tell you, Amelia. I tried."

"Later, you could have. I nearly begged you!"

"And have this discussion directly after we made love?" he scoffed. "Never! Last night was the culmination of my deepest, most cherished fantasies. Nothing could have induced me to ruin that."

"It is ruined!" she yelled, shaking. "I feel as if I have lost two loves, for the Colin I knew is dead, and Montoya was a lie."

"He is not a lie!"

Colin came toward her, and she hastily caught the back of a chair and pulled it between them. The sturdy wooden seat was no deterrent, however, and he shoved it aside.

She turned to flee, but he caught her, and the feel of his arms around her trembling body was too much.

Amelia hung in his embrace, devastated.

"I love you," he murmured, his lips to her temple. "I love you."

For so long she'd prayed to hear those words from his lips, but they were too little now and far too late.

Chapter 13

As her coach pulled into the courtyard of the inn specified by the outriders, Maria collected her hat and gloves in preparation for alighting.

"It is a rare sight to see you so anxious," Christopher murmured, his heavy-lidded gaze making him appear deceptively slumberous. She knew him too well to believe that.

"I am relieved we have found her and that she was of sound mind enough to drag Tim along with her, but there are still the matters of Montoya and Ware to address." Maria sighed. "As miserable as my youth was, I am grateful to have been too busy to indulge in reckless love such as this."

"You were waiting for me," Christopher purred, catching her hand before she gloved it and kissing the back.

She cupped his cheek and smiled. "You were worth the wait."

The coach rolled to a halt, and Christopher vaulted down. As she accepted his assistance, she said, "I am surprised that Tim is not out here to greet us."

"As am I," he agreed. He glanced up at the coachman. "Pietro, make arrangements for the horses, then unload Miss Benbridge's valise."

Pietro nodded and pulled away, taking the carriage to the stables several yards away.

"You think of everything," Maria praised, wrapping her arm around his.

"No, I think of you," he corrected, looking down at her with the melting intensity that had shattered her defenses so many years ago.

They waited for Simon and Mademoiselle Rousseau to join them. Then they all entered the quiet inn.

"I will inquire about Tim," Christopher said, striding to the counter. A moment later, he gestured for one of the lackeys at her side to join him. Together, the two men followed the innkeeper out of the room.

"What is going on?" Mademoiselle Rousseau wondered aloud.

"Let us order food," Simon said. "I am half-starved."

"You are always half-starved," she muttered.

"It requires a great deal of energy to tolerate you, mademoiselle," he retorted.

The bickering duo walked away, leaving Maria waiting with a lackey. She frowned as Christopher reappeared with Tim in tow.

Maria noted the grim look on Tim's face and moved forward to meet them. "Where is Amelia?"

"Apparently," Christopher drawled, "her phantom admirer has decided to step out from behind the mask."

"Oh." She glanced at Tim, who looked both pained and furious. "What is it?"

"They are speaking in the private dining room," Christopher explained, "with an open door for propriety's sake. From the sounds of it, it is not going well for the man."

"Why not?"

"When 'e approached me," Tim rumbled, "I thought 'e looked familiar, but I couldn't place 'is face. It came to me when I overheard them talking."

"What came to you?" she asked, looking between both men. "Who is he? Do we know him?"

"Remember the pictures I drew for you in Brighton?" Tim asked, harkening back to the days of her "courtship" with Christopher. After a failed attempt to retrieve Amelia, Tim had put both his excellent memory and talent for rendering to good use by drawing images of the servants who had spirited Amelia away.

Nodding, Maria recalled the stunningly beautiful drawings. "Yes, of course."

"The man she's speaking to is one of them."

Frowning, she tried to recall them all. There had been a drawing of Amelia and Pietro, as well as of a governess and a young groomsman . . .

"That is not possible," she said, shaking her head. "That young man was Colin, the boy who died trying to save Amelia."

"Pietro's nephew, was he not?" Christopher asked with one brow raised. "If there are any doubts about the man's identity, I am certain Pietro can help us to dispel them."

"Bloody hell," she breathed. Pivoting on her heel, she looked for Simon and found him sinking into a chair. She marched toward him.

He glanced up and saw her coming, his blue eyes first sparkling with welcome, then narrowing warily. The smile that curved his sensual lips faded as resignation passed over his features. She knew then that it was true, and her heart ached for the torment her sister must be feeling.

"Out with it," she snapped, as he stood before her.

Simon nodded and pulled out the empty seat that waited between him and Mademoiselle Rousseau. "You might want to take a seat," he said wearily. "This might take some time."

"Release me, Colin."

Amelia held back a sob by dint of will alone. The feel of

his big, powerful body pressed so passionately against her back was both a balm and a barb. Her nerves were raw; her emotions fluctuated between wild, heady joy and a feeling of abandonment too close to what she had felt in her father's negligent care.

"I cannot," he said hoarsely, his hot cheek pressed ardently to hers. "I am afraid if I let you go, you will leave me."

"I want to leave you," she whispered. "As you left me."

"It was the only choice that afforded me the opportunity to have you. Can you not see?" The tone of his voice was a rough plea. "If I had not left and made my fortune elsewhere, you would never be mine, and I could not bear it, Amelia. I would do anything to have you, even give you up for a time."

She tugged at his arms. Every breath she took was filled with the scent of him, a scent that awakened her body to memories of the passionate night behind them. It was an unbearable torment. "Release me."

"Promise to stay and hear me out."

Amelia nodded, knowing she had no choice. Knowing they had to find some closure to this so they could both move on with their lives.

Facing him with an uplifted chin, she tried to keep her face impassive despite the tears she could not stop. For his part, Colin made no effort to hide his torment. His handsome features were wracked with painful emotions.

"I might have felt differently," she said flatly, "if you had told me of your desire to build a different life for yourself, if you had made me a partner in your plans instead of cutting me out."

"Be honest, Amelia." He clasped his hands behind him as if to prevent reaching out for her. "You would never have allowed me to go, and if you had begged me to stay, I would not have had the strength to deny you."

"Why could you not stay?"

"How was I to afford you with a servant's meager pay? How was I to give you the world when I had nothing?"

"I could have borne any livelihood if only you were there to share it!"

"And what of the nights?" he challenged. "Would you feel the same while shivering because we must ration our meager stipend of coal? And what of the days? Where we must rise before the sun to work ourselves to exhaustion?"

"You could have kept me warm, as you did last night," she retorted. "A lifetime of such nights . . . I would damn the coal to hell if my bed was warmed by you. And the days. The passing of each hour would bring me closer to you. I could have tolerated anything if it led me back to you."

"You deserve better!"

Amelia stomped her foot. "It was not for you to decide that I was incapable of living such a life! It was not for you to decide that I was not strong enough!"

"I never doubted that you would make such an effort for me," he argued, his frame vibrating with an edgy intensity so reminiscent of the Colin of old. "What I doubted was *my* strength, *my* capability to live in that manner!"

"You did not even try!"

"I couldn't." Colin's voice grew more impassioned. "How could I bear looking at your cracked and reddened hands? How could I bear the tears that would come in the unguarded minutes when you longed for a moment's comfort?"

"Love requires sacrifice."

"Not when the entirety of the sacrifice is made by you. I could not live with myself knowing that my selfishness brought you to an unhappy end."

"You don't understand." Her hand lifted to cover her heart. "I would have been happy as long as I had you."

"And I would have hated myself."

"I see that now." Grieving anew, Amelia wondered how she could have been so wrong about their love for each other. "If we had never met, you would have been happy with the life you had, wouldn't you?"

"Amelia—"

"Your discontent stems from me and the expectations you imagined I had for you."

"No, that is not true."

"It is." The pain in her chest intensified until she could hardly breathe. "I'm so sorry," she whispered. "I wish we had never met. We might have been happy."

His eyes widened. "Dear God, do not say such a thing! Never. You are the only thing that has ever brought me happiness."

Suddenly, she felt so old and so tired. "Leaving your country and your family, traversing the Continent risking your life to gather information for the Crown . . . That is what you call happiness? You are deluded."

"Damn it," Colin growled, snatching her by the shoulders. "You are worth it, all of it. I would do it again a hundred times over to become worthy of you."

"I never thought you were unworthy, and you did not harbor these feelings of inferiority until you met me. That is not love, Colin. I do not know what that is, but I know what it is not."

Made anxious by Amelia's sudden composure, Colin considered ways to keep her connected to him. Last night they had been as close as two lovers could ever hope to be, and now they were as distant as strangers. "Whatever doubts my revelation may inspire, do not belittle my feelings for you. I love you. From the moment I first saw you, I loved you, and I have never stopped. Not for a moment."

"Oh?" Amelia wiped at her tears with hands so steady, he felt a prickling disquiet. "What of the times when you gained the expertise at lovemaking you displayed so beautifully last night? Were you in love with me then?"

"Yes, damn you." He pulled her closer, pressing the full length of his heated body to hers. "Even then. Sex is sex to a man, nothing more. We require the spending of our seed to be healthy. It has nothing to do with elevated feelings."

"Simply slaking your needs as you did behind the store when we were younger?" She shook her head. "Last night, with every touch . . . every caress . . . I wondered how many women you must have entertained in order to acquire such skill."

"Jealous?" he lashed, bleeding inside and frightened by her rapid retreat. She spoke with no inflection, no feeling, as if she cared not at all. "Do you wish it had been you who served my baser needs with no emotion or caring? No affection or concern?"

"I am jealous, yes, but also sad." Her beautiful eyes were empty. "You lived a full life without me, Colin. At times, you were likely content with your lot. You should not have come back. Those women did not make you wish to be someone you are not, as I do."

"I never think of them," he vowed, cupping her beloved face in his hands. "Never. All the while I thought of you and how deeply I wanted you. I wished they were you. It was an ache that never faded. I learned, yes. I became skilled, yes. For *you!* So that I could be everything to you, so that I could satisfy *you* in every way. I wanted to be all you needed, all you wanted."

"How miserable," she said. "It breaks my heart to know that I have prevented you from being happy."

Furious at his helplessness and confused by the turns the conversation was taking, Colin held her still and took her mouth, thrusting strong and sure into the hot, moist depths.

He tasted her pain and sorrow, her bitterness and anger. He drank it all, stroking across her tongue with his, before sucking fiercely.

Clutching his forearms with both hands, she moaned and trembled in his arms. Her body could not resist his, even now. It was a weakness he hated to exploit, but he would if necessary.

"My mouth is yours," he said hoarsely, brushing his wet lips back and forth across hers. "I have shared kisses with no one but you. Never."

He caught her hand and held it over his heart. "See how strongly it beats? How desperately? Because of you. Everything, *everything* I have ever done has been with you in mind."

"Stop . . ." she panted, her breasts thrusting against his arm with her labored breathing.

"And my dreams." He pressed his temple to hers. "My dreams have always been yours. I aspire to be a better man to be worthy of you."

"And when will that day come, Colin?"

He pulled back, frowning.

"All these years, and yet you still found reasons to put me aside until last night when I forced your hand." Amelia sighed, and he heard a note of finality in the forlorn sound. "I think we saw in each other only what we wanted to see, but in the end the gulf between us is too wide to cross with mere illusions."

Colin's blood froze, a not inconsiderable feat with her body pressed so tightly to his. "What are you saying?"

"I am saying that I am tired of being left behind and forgotten until some preordained time arrives. I have lived the whole of my life under such a cloud and refuse to do so any longer."

"Amelia—"

"I am saying that when we leave this room, Colin, it will be farewell between us."

The slight scratching on the open door drew Simon's attention from the maps spread out across his desk. He looked up at the butler with both brows raised. "Yes?"

"There is a young man at the door asking for Lady Winter, sir. I did tell him that neither she nor you were at home, but he refuses to leave."

Simon straightened. "Oh? Who is it?"

The servant cleared his throat. "He appears to be a Gypsy."

Surprise held his tongue for the length of a heartbeat. Then Simon said, "Show him in."

He took a moment to clear away the sensitive documents on his desk. Then he sat and waited for the dark-haired youth who entered his study a moment later.

"Where is Lady Winter?" the boy asked, the set of his shoulders and jaw betraying his mulish determination to get whatever it was he came for.

Simon leaned back in his chair. "She is traveling the Continent, last I heard."

The boy frowned. "Is Miss Benbridge with her? How can I find them? Do you have their direction?"

"Tell me your name."

"Colin Mitchell."

"Well, Mr. Mitchell, would you care for a drink?" Simon stood and moved to the row of decanters that lined the table in front of the window.

"No."

Hiding a smile, Simon poured two fingers of brandy into a glass and then turned around, leaning his hip against the console with one heel crossed over the other. Mitchell stood in the same spot, his gaze searching the room, pausing occasionally on various objects with narrowed eyes. Hunting for clues to the answers he sought. He was a finely built young man, and attractive in an exotic way that Simon imagined the ladies found most appealing.

"What will you do if you find the fair Amelia?" Simon asked. "Work in the stables? Care for her horses?"

Mitchell's eyes widened.

"Yes, I know who you are, though I was told you were dead." Simon lifted his glass and tossed back the contents. His belly warmed, making him smile. "So do you intend to work as her underling, pining for her from afar? Or per-

haps you hope to tumble her in the hay as often as possible until she either marries or grows fat with your child."

Simon straightened and set down his glass, bracing himself for the expected—yet, surprisingly impressive—tackle that knocked him to the floor. He and the boy rolled, locked in combat, knocking over a small table and shattering the porcelain figurines that had graced its top.

It took only a few moments for Simon to claim the upper hand. The time would have been shorter had he not been so concerned about hurting the lad.

"Cease," he ordered, "and listen to me." He no longer drawled; his tone was now deadly earnest.

Mitchell stilled, but his features remained stamped with fury. "Don't ever speak of Amelia in that way!"

Pushing to his feet, Simon extended his hand to assist the young man up. "I am only pointing out the obvious. You have nothing. Nothing to offer, nothing with which to support her, no title to give her prestige."

The clenching of the young man's jaw and fists betrayed his hatred for the truth. "I know all of that."

"Good. Now"—Simon righted his clothing and resumed his seat behind the desk—"what if I offered to help you acquire what you need to make you worthy—coin, a fitting home, perhaps even a title from some distant land that would suit the physical features provided by your heritage?"

Mitchell stilled, his gaze narrowing with avid interest. "How?"

"I am engaged in certain . . . activities that could be facilitated by a youth with your potential. I heard of your dashing near rescue of Miss Benbridge. With the right molding, you could be quite an asset to me." Simon smiled. "I would not make this offer to anyone else. So consider yourself fortunate."

"Why me?" Mitchell asked suspiciously, and not without a little scorn. He was slightly cynical, which Simon thought

was excellent. A purely green boy would be of no use at all.
"You don't know me, or what I'm capable of."

Simon held his gaze steadily. "I understand well the
lengths a man will go to for a woman he cares for."

"I love her."

"Yes. To the point where you would seek her out at great
cost to yourself. I need dedication such as that. In return, I
will ensure that you become a man of some means."

"That would take years." Mitchell ran a hand through
his hair. "I don't know that I can bear it."

"Give yourselves time to mature. Allow her to see what
she has missed all of these years. Then, if she will have you
anyway, you will know that she is making the decision with
a woman's heart, and not a child's."

For a long moment, the young man remained motionless,
the weight of his indecision a tangible thing.

"Try it," Simon urged. "What harm can come from the
effort?"

Finally, Mitchell heaved out his breath and sank into the
seat opposite the desk. "I'm listening."

"Excellent!" Simon leaned back in his chair. "Now here
are my thoughts . . ."

"Why did you say nothing to me?" Maria asked when
the tale was finished, staring at Simon as if he were a stranger.
She felt as if he were.

"If I had told you, *mhuirnín*," Simon said softly, "would
you have withheld the information from your sibling? Of
course not, and the secret was not mine to share."

"What of Amelia's pain and suffering?"

"Unfortunate, but not something I could alleviate."

"You could have told me he was alive!" she argued.

"Mitchell had every right to make himself worthy of
Amelia's esteem. Do not fault him for pursuing the woman
he loves in the only manner available to him. Of all men, I

understand his motivations very well." He paused a moment, then spoke in a calmer voice. "Besides, what he did with his life was no concern of yours."

"It is a concern of *mine,*" drawled a voice from behind them, "now that it affects Miss Benbridge."

Maria turned in her chair and faced the man who approached. "Lord Ware," she greeted, her heart sinking.

The earl was dressed as casually as she had ever seen him, but there was a tension to his tall frame and a tautness to his jaw that told her leisure was far from his mind. His dark hair was unadorned but for a ribbon at his nape, and he wore boots instead of heels.

"This is the fiancé?" Mademoiselle Rousseau asked.

"My lord," Christopher greeted. "I am impressed by your dedication."

"Until she tells me otherwise," the earl said grimly, "I consider Miss Benbridge's welfare one of my responsibilities."

"I have not had this much fun in ages," the Frenchwoman said, smiling wide.

Maria closed her eyes and rubbed the space between her brows. Christopher, who stood at her back, set his hand on her shoulder and gave a commiserating squeeze.

"Would someone care to fill me in?" Ware asked.

She looked at Simon. He raised both brows. "How delicately should I phrase this?"

"No delicacy required," Ware said. "I am neither ignorant nor cursed with a weak constitution."

"He does intend to marry into our family," Christopher pointed out.

"True," Simon said, though his gaze narrowed. He relayed the events leading up to the present moment, carefully leaving out names like Eddington's, which could not be shared.

"So this man in the mask is Colin Mitchell?" Ware asked,

scowling. "The boy Miss Benbridge fancied in her youth? And she does not know it is him?"

"She knows it now," Tim muttered.

"Mitchell is telling her as we speak," Christopher explained.

There was a thud behind them, and they all turned to find Pietro, who stood gaping with a dropped valise at his feet. "That isn't possible!" the coachman said heatedly. "Colin is gone."

Maria glanced at Simon, who winced.

"This grows more fascinating by the moment," Mademoiselle Rousseau said.

"You are a vile creature," Simon snapped.

Looking up at Christopher, Maria signaled her intent to stand, and he stepped back. "I should go see how things are progressing."

"No need," he murmured, his gaze trained beyond her.

All heads turned toward the hallway that led to the private dining room. Amelia appeared with reddened eyes and nose and disheveled hair, the picture of tormented heartbroken loveliness.

Mitchell came into view directly behind her, and the sight of him took Maria aback, as it did everyone who saw him. Elegantly attired and proud of bearing, he left no traces of servitude clinging to his tall frame. He was an arrestingly beautiful man, with dark, sensual eyes framed by long, thick lashes and a voluptuary's mouth framed by a firm, determined jaw. He, too, looked devastated and gravely wounded, and Maria's heart went out to both of them.

"Amelia . . ." Ware's cultured drawl was rough with concern.

Her verdant gaze met his and filled with tears.

A low growl rumbled from the earl's chest.

"Colin." Pietro's agonized tone deepened the trauma of the day's revelations.

Distracted by the many unfolding events, Maria did not foresee Ware's intent until he stalked up to Mitchell and asked, "Do you consider yourself a gentleman?"

Mitchell's jaw tightened. "I do."

Ware threw a glove down at Mitchell's feet. "Then I demand satisfaction."

"I will give it to you."

"Dear God," Maria breathed, her hand at her throat.

Christopher left her side. He drew to a halt beside the earl and said, "I would be honored to serve as your second, my lord."

"Thank you," Ware replied.

"I will serve as Mitchell's," Simon said, joining them.

"No!" Amelia cried, her horrified gaze darting between the grim masculine faces. "This is absurd."

Maria pulled her away. "You cannot intercede."

"Why?" Amelia asked. "This is not necessary."

"It is."

"I have a home in Bristol," Ware said. "I suggest we retire there. Our audience will then be made up of those we trust."

Mitchell nodded. "That was my destination, so the location is convenient for me as well."

"I caused this." Amelia looked pleadingly at Maria. "My selfishness has led to this end. How do I stop this?"

"What is done, is done," Maria said, rubbing her hand soothingly down Amelia's spine.

"I want to go with them."

"That would not be wise."

Christopher turned to her, and she saw in his face that he disagreed. She did not understand why he would wish them to go, but she could learn his motives later. As it was, she trusted him implicitly and knew that his first concern was always for her health and happiness.

"I want to go," Amelia said again, with more strength.

"Shh," Maria soothed. "We can discuss this over a hot bath and a change of clothes."

Her sibling nodded, and they moved away to order heated water and a tub. With everyone distracted with their own thoughts, no one noted the man who occupied a shadowed seat in the far corner. He attracted even less attention when he left.

Stepping outside, Jacques tugged the brim of his hat down and sauntered across the drive toward the carriage that waited a short ways down the lane.

He opened the door and looked inside. "Mitchell was just challenged to a duel."

Cartland smiled. "Come in and tell me everything."

Chapter 14

It never ceased to amaze Amelia how a man as vibrant and impossible to ignore as Christopher St. John could fade into oblivion when he chose to. As it was, she hardly noticed that he shared the same squab with Maria as they traveled to Bristol. He held his tongue as she poured out her heart, and she was grateful to him for his silence. Few would believe that the notorious criminal could tolerate hours upon hours of a weeping woman's lamentations over love, but he did and he did it well.

"You told him you would not see him again?" Maria asked gently.

"Until Ware challenged him, that had been my intent," Amelia said from behind the handkerchief she held to her nose. She had refused to talk about anything yesterday on the ride to Swindon. Only today did she feel capable of discussing Colin without crying too copiously to speak. "We will be happier apart."

"You do not look happier."

"I will be, over the duration of my life, as will Colin." She sighed. "No one can be happy pretending day after day to be someone they are not."

"Perhaps he is not pretending," Maria suggested softly.

"Regardless, the new Colin harbors the same doubts as the old. Despite all that he has accomplished, he still believed Ware was the better choice until just days ago. He continues to make decisions regarding my welfare without consulting me. I had enough of such treatment in my childhood."

"You are allowing your past to cloud your present."

"You champion his actions?" Amelia asked with wide eyes. "How can you? I can find nothing good in what he has done. He is wealthy, yes—that is obvious in the quality of everything he owns—but accepting that end as being worthy of my grief and heartache puts a price on my love, and I cannot abide that."

"I do not champion his actions," Maria murmured, "but I do believe he loves you and that he thought he was acting in your best interests. I also believe that you love him. Surely, there is something good in that?"

Amelia ran a hand over her skirts and gazed out the window. Behind them, Colin rode in his carriage with Jacques, Mr. Quinn, and Mademoiselle Rousseau. Ware led their procession in his coach. She was trapped between the two, both figuratively and literally.

"I have come to the realization that passion is not as the poets would have us believe," she said.

There was a suspicious choking sound from the opposite squab, but when she shot a narrowed glance at St. John, his face was studiously impassive.

"I am quite serious," she argued. "Prior to these last weeks, my life was orderly and comfortable. My equanimity was intact. Ware was content, as were both of you. Colin, too, had an existence that was progressing in its own fashion. Now all of our lives are in disarray. You've no notion of how it pains me to realize that my resemblance to Lord Welton is more than skin deep."

"Amelia. That is absolute nonsense." Maria's voice was stern.

"Is it? Have I not done exactly as he would do? Cared only for my own pleasure?" She shook her head. "I would rather be a woman who lives for duty than one who lives for her own indulgences. At least I would have honor then."

Concern filled Maria's dark eyes. "You are overwrought. It has been a long journey and the inn in Swindon had little to recommend it, but we are almost to Bristol, and then you must rest for a day or two."

"Before or after the duel?" Amelia asked testily.

"Poppet—"

There was a distant shout heard outside, and then the carriage turned. Leaning forward, she looked out the window and watched a long, manicured lane empty into a circular drive graced by a sizeable center fountain. The lavish manse beyond that was breathtaking with its graceful columns and massive portico flanked by abundant, cheery flowerbeds.

The line of carriages rolled to a halt before the steps, and the front door opened, allowing a veritable swarm of gray-and black-liveried servants to flow out. St. John exited first. He then assisted Maria and Amelia down to the graveled drive.

"Welcome," Ware said, as he joined them. His mouth curved in a rakish half smile as he lifted Amelia's gloved hand to his lips. He looked dashing in his garb of pale blue breeches and coat the exact color of his eyes, and the strained smile she returned had true appreciation for his charm behind it.

"Your home is lovely, my lord," Maria murmured.

"Thank you. I hope you will find it even lovelier once you are inside."

In unison, they turned to look toward Colin's coach. Amelia steeled herself inwardly for his appearance, expecting that he would look at her as he had done all of yesterday—with entreaty in his dark eyes.

Sadly, no preparation on her part could mitigate the effect he had on her as he vaulted down from his carriage and approached with an elegant stride that was entirely sensual. Damn the man. He had always moved with an animal grace that made her tingle all over. Now that she knew how well that latent sexuality translated to bedplay, the response was worse.

She looked away in an effort to hide the irresistible attraction she felt.

"My lord," Colin said, his smooth voice roughened by obvious dislike. "If someone could kindly provide direction to the nearest inn, I will be on my way. Mr. Quinn will return later to make the necessary arrangements."

"I would like you to stay here," Ware said, startling everyone.

Amelia looked at him with mouth agape.

"That is impossible," Colin protested.

"Why?" Ware challenged with both brows raised.

Colin's jaw tightened. "I have my reasons."

"What is it?" St. John asked, a note in his voice alerting Amelia. Apparently he saw something in the exchange that she did not. "Allow me to help you."

"That will not be necessary," Colin said stiffly. "Keep Miss Benbridge safe. That is all the assistance I require."

"If you are in danger," Maria said, "I would prefer to keep you close. Perhaps we should stay at the inn as well."

"Please," Ware said in his customary drawl, as composed as ever. "Everyone will be safer here than in a public venue with frequent traffic."

"St. John," Colin said. "If I could have a moment of your time."

St. John nodded and excused himself. The two men moved a short distance away and spoke in tones too low to overhear. They became more animated, the conversation more heated.

"What is going on?" Amelia asked Maria.

"I wish I knew," Maria replied.

"Allow Mrs. Barney to show you to your rooms," Ware said, gesturing to the housekeeper who waited on the lower step with a soft smile.

"I want to know what is happening," Amelia said.

"I know you do," Ware murmured, setting his hand at her lower back and leading her toward the manse. "And I promise to tell you everything as soon as I know it."

"Truly?" She looked up at him from beneath the brim of her hat.

"Of course. When have I ever lied to you?"

She understood the message. *I am not Mitchell*, it said. *I have always been true to you.* Grateful for him, Amelia offered a thankful, shaky smile. Maria joined her, and together they followed Mrs. Barney into the house.

Colin watched Lord Ware lead Amelia toward the manse and fought the urge to wrench her away. It was unbearable to see her with another man. It ate at him as acid would, burning and stinging and leaving a gaping hole behind.

"I think you should stay," St. John said, drawing Colin's attention away from Amelia's departing back.

"You do not understand," Colin argued. "We have been followed ever since we left Reading. If I keep my distance from Miss Benbridge, I will draw the danger away from her."

St. John looked grim. "Unless she has a mind to follow you again," he pointed out. "Then she will be far more vulnerable than if she were to remain here."

"Bloody hell. I did not think of that." Lifting a hand to the back of his neck, Colin rubbed at the tense muscle that pained him. "In her present mood, I do not think she will go to the trouble."

"But you cannot be certain, and neither can I. Therefore, I think it best to err on the side of caution."

"Can you not deter her in some way?" Colin asked. "Cartland cannot be allowed anywhere near her. If he suspects how much she means to me, he will exploit her."

"Have *you* been able to deter her? Do not expect miracles from me." St. John smiled. "My wife is considered the Deadliest Woman in England, and she taught her sibling everything she knows. Amelia can cross swords with the best of men, and she can throw a knife better than anyone, even me. If she decides to follow you, she will find a way."

Colin blinked, then gave a resigned exhalation. "Oddly enough, I am not as surprised by that revelation as I should be."

"I would have liked to have met their mother. She must have been extraordinary."

"I do not have the time to socialize," Colin growled. "I must be either the hunter or the prey, and the latter role does not suit me."

St. John nodded. "I understand."

"I wish Mademoiselle Rousseau would believe Jacques's witness of the events of that night, but she refuses. I cannot collect why. Why dismiss him so completely? How can she trust Cartland's word over anyone else's?"

"I do not know what it is she seeks, but I will lend you whatever support you need. There is little that requires your attention tonight. Allow my men to begin the search in town. You can pick it up tomorrow. I think one night of domesticity will soothe Amelia enough to keep her from haring after you."

The thought of spending an intimate evening in the company of Amelia and Lord Ware was a torment unparalleled.

"Will you stay?" the earl asked, joining them. "Rooms are being prepared for you and your acquaintances as we speak."

"Thank you." It was all Colin could manage. "I will tell the others." He turned on his heel and walked away.

St. John watched him go, noting the stiffness of his posture and the anger evident in his stride. "He loves her."

"I see that."

Turning his head, St. John found the earl watching Mitchell

with a narrowed glance. "I know why I think he should remain. I cannot collect why you do."

"Our differences will be more obvious in direct contrast." Ware met his gaze. "I am the best choice for her. If I doubted that for a moment, I would step aside. I want her happiness above all else. I do not think he is capable of giving it to her."

"He is a formidable opponent in the challenge ahead. Mitchell has lived by his wits and his sword for several years."

"I am not without skill of my own," the earl said easily, "regardless of the civilized manner in which I acquired it."

St. John nodded and followed Ware's urging to move into the house. Tim was overseeing the removal of both trunks and servants from the trailing coach. Mitchell was scowling at Quinn, who was assisting a grinning Mademoiselle Rousseau down from their carriage.

For his part, St. John wondered if other men went through such difficulties when attempting to marry off a younger sibling. Shaking his head, he climbed the stairs and moved directly to the suite assigned to him where he knew he would find his wife. Together, they would strategize the events of the coming few days.

The thought made him smile.

Bathed, dressed, yet inwardly shaky, Amelia slipped out of her bedchamber and hurried down the long gallery. Maria had told her to nap in preparation for afternoon tea, but Amelia could not sleep. What she felt was the urge to roam, to stretch her legs, to breathe fresh air and clear her head. As a child, she had learned that a brisk walk was capable of alleviating many ills, and she felt in strong need of that now.

"Amelia."

She paused at the sound of her name. Turning, she found Lord Ware exiting a room a few doors behind her. She curtsied. "My lord."

He shot a pointed glance at her walking boots. "May I join you?"

She briefly considered voicing a kind objection, then thought better of it. As much as she wished to be alone with her thoughts, Ware deserved an explanation and the opportunity to chastise her, if he so wished. "I would be honored."

He smiled his charming, dashing smile and came toward her. He was dressed as a country gentleman, and the more leisurely appearance suited him well. It reminded her of their meeting in Lincolnshire, and the smile she returned to him was genuine.

"How lovely you are," he murmured, "when your smiles reach your eyes."

"It is because you look so handsome," she returned.

Ware lifted Amelia's hand to his lips and his gaze beyond her shoulder, where he saw Mitchell at the end of the hall, watching them both with daggers in his eyes. Tucking Amelia's hand around his arm, he led her away toward the stairs, which would take them to the lower floor and the rear garden.

He felt his rival's stare burning a hole in his back for the entire way.

Colin watched Lord Ware's proprietary handling of Amelia with something so akin to blood rage, it frightened him.

He could not bear it.

"You must find something to occupy yourself with, *mon ami*," Jacques said, startling Colin with his sudden, silent appearance. "You will act regrettably if you think endlessly of her."

"I have always thought endlessly of her," he bit out. "I know of no other way to live."

"She requires time. I admire your fortitude in giving it to her."

Colin's fists clenched. "It is not fortitude. I simply do not wish to kill a man in front of her."

"*Alors* . . . you must leave. Distract yourself with a task."

Inhaling sharply, Colin nodded. He had been set upon that end when he chanced upon Amelia with Ware. He forced himself to look away from where the couple had stood mere moments ago. "That was my intent. I was seeking you out."

"What do you want me to do?" the Frenchman asked, looking grim as always.

"I cannot go into town. There is some concern that Miss Benbridge will follow, and while I find that highly unlikely, the request is valid, so I must stay for now."

"I understand."

"St. John is sending a man to rally those who work for him in Bristol. Go and direct the search. Tell them what to look for, what to expect. If you find anything of import, send for me."

Jacques nodded and set off immediately. The Frenchman took the main staircase; Colin took the servants'. It emptied by the kitchen, and he ignored the startled glances sent his way as he exited out the delivery door and headed toward the stables.

Every step he took grew heavier, his heart weighed upon by the upcoming confrontation that would cut him nigh as deeply as the one with Amelia had.

He entered silently and inhaled deeply, finding the smells of hay and horses both familiar and soothing. The many beasts inside snorted and shifted restlessly as his scent filled the air and disturbed their equanimity. Glancing about, he looked for the groomsmen's quarters. His stride faltered when he found the doorway. A man leaned against the jamb, watching him with wounded, angry eyes.

The years had been kind to Pietro. Aside from a slight pouch at the belly, the rest of his body was still fit and strong. Strands of silver accented his temples and beard, but his skin was smooth and free of wrinkles.

"Uncle," Colin greeted, his throat tight with sorrow and affection.

"My only nephew is dead," Pietro said coldly.

Colin flinched at the repudiation. "I have missed you."

"You lie! You let me think you were dead!"

"I was offered the chance at a different life." Colin held out his hands in a silent plea for understanding. "I had one chance to accept and no time to second-guess."

"And what of me?" Pietro demanded, straightening. "What of my grief? Was that nothing to you?"

"You think I was not grieving?" Colin bit out, stung by the condemnation of yet another person he loved. "I might as well have been dead."

"Then why did you do it?" Pietro came forward. "I have tried to see what would make you do such a thing, but I don't understand."

"I had nothing to offer anyone before. No way to create a life of comfort for those I loved."

"Comfort from what? The only discomfort in my life has been my mourning for you!"

"What of freedom from work?" Colin challenged. "What of a life of travel and discovery? I can offer you those things now, when I could not before."

Pain wracked Pietro's handsome features. "I am a simple man, Colin. A roof over my head . . . food . . . family. Those are all I need to be happy."

"I wish my needs were as simple." Colin moved to the nearest stall and set his crossed arms along the top of it. "I need Amelia to be happy, and this was the only way I could conceive of to have her."

"Colin . . ." He heard his uncle sigh. "You love her still."

"I have no notion how *not* to love her. It is ingrained in me, as much a part of me as my hair and skin color."

Pietro joined him at the stall door. "I should have raised you in the camp. Then you wouldn't want things that are beyond your reach."

Colin smiled and looked aside at him. "Amelia and I would have met at some point, at some time."

"That is your Romany blood talking."

"Yes, it is."

There was a long silence, as each attempted to find the right thing to say. "How long have you been in England?" Pietro asked finally.

"A few weeks."

"A few weeks and you didn't come to me?" Pietro shook his head. "I don't feel that I know you at all. The boy I raised had more care for the feelings of others."

Aching from the pain he had inflicted, Colin reached out and set his hand atop Pietro's shoulder. "If my love is in err, it is not due to lack of it for you but to a surfeit for her. I would have done anything, gone anywhere, to become worthy of Amelia."

"You seem to have accomplished what you set out to do," Pietro said quietly. "Your clothes and carriage are fine indeed."

"It seems a waste now. She is as angry as you are. I do not know if she will forgive me, and if she does not, all is lost."

"Not all. You'll always have me."

Tears came to Colin's eyes, and he brushed them away with jerking movements. His uncle looked at him a moment, then heaved out his breath and embraced him.

"There is still some of the Colin of old in you," he said gruffly.

"I am sorry for the pain I caused," Colin whispered, his throat too tight to speak any louder. "I saw only the end, not the interim. I wanted everything, and now I have nothing."

Pietro shook his head and stepped back. "Don't give up yet. You've worked too hard."

"Can *you* forgive me?" If he could manage to win back the love of one, perhaps there was a possibility that he could win back the other.

"Maybe." A grin split the depths of his uncle's beard. "I have six horses to groom."

Colin's mouth curved wryly. "I am at your service."

"Come on." Pietro put his arm around Colin's shoulders and urged him toward the groomsmen's quarters. "You'll need to change your clothes."

"I can buy more if these are ruined."

"Hmm . . ." His uncle looked at him consideringly. "How wealthy are you?"

"Obscenely."

Pietro whistled. "Tell me how you did it."

"Of course." Colin smiled. "We have time."

It was late afternoon. The sun was dipping to the west and supper was being prepared. Ware's guests would eat earlier tonight than they would in Town, then spend the evening in the parlor, attempting to ignore the tension simmering between all parties. It would no doubt be unpleasant, but Ware understood the emotional undercurrents that were affecting everyone but him. He cared for Amelia and thought her the most suitable bride for his needs. That was his only tie to all of the rest.

"Mitchell stayed," he said to Amelia, as they strolled through the rear garden.

"Oh."

She stared straight ahead. With a sigh, he drew to a halt, which forced her to do the same.

"Talk to me, Amelia. That has always been the core strength of our friendship."

With a shaky smile, she canted her body to face his. "I am so sorry to have done this to you," she said remorsefully. "If I could go back and alter the events of this last week, I would. I would go back years and have married you long ago."

"Would you?" He tugged her closer, and set his hands lightly on her hips. Behind her, a profusion of climbing roses hugged an archway that led to a pond. Dandelion seeds drifted in the breeze, creating an enchanting backdrop for an enchanting woman.

"Yes. All these years I mourned him and he was thriving." Something deliciously like a growl escaped her. "He finds it far too easy to leave me behind. I am sick of being left behind. First my father, now Colin."

Amelia wrenched away and began to pace, her long legs moving with a lithe, determined elegance.

"I have never left you," he said, pointing out what he knew to be his greatest strength. "I enjoy your company far too much. There are precious few people in this world about whom I feel similarly."

"I know. Bless you. I love you for that." She managed a brief smile. "That is what has decided my mind. You will be steadfast and supportive. You do not seek to be someone you are not. You inspire me to be decorous and deport myself in a manner befitting a lady. We rub along well together."

Ware frowned, considering. "Amelia. I should like to discuss your thoughts on decorum and deportment in greater detail. Forgive me, but I find it rather odd to mention those traits as being most attractive. I would think our friendship and ease of association would lure you most."

She halted, her pale green skirts settling gently around her feet. "I have come to realize something these past days, Ware. I have reckless tendencies, just as Welton did. I require a certain environment in order to restrain those selfish impulses."

"And I provide this environment."

Amelia beamed at him. "Yes. Yes, you do."

"Hmm . . ." He rubbed his jaw. "And Mitchell inspires your reckless nature?"

"'Goads' would be a more apt word choice, but yes, he does."

"I see." Ware smiled wryly. "His role sounds more fun than mine."

"Ware!" She looked affronted, which made him laugh.

"Sorry, love. I must be honest. In one breath, you point out that I do not seek to be someone I am not—in opposition, I presume, to Mr. Mitchell. Then in the next breath, you say that I inhibit a part of your nature that you are not proud of. Is that not seeking to be someone you are not . . . in a fashion?"

Her lower lip quivered in that way it had when she was upset. She set her hands on her hips and demanded, "Do you *want* me to be with him?" she cried. "Is that what you are saying?"

"No." All traces of amusement left him, and he bared the emotions he kept hidden below the surface. "I do not think he is the man for you. I do not think he deserves you. I do not believe he can provide a life that would content you. But that does not mean I want to live with only half of you."

Amelia blinked. "You are angry."

"Not at you," he said gruffly, reaching for her again. He gripped her by the elbows and pulled her close. "But I may eventually become so and I do not want that. I resent that I can have only the one side of you. If you choose me, Amelia, I can make you happy. The question left is whether you can make me happy, and I wonder if that is possible if I am forever waiting for the return of that precocious girl who asked me to kiss her."

"Ware . . ."

She cupped his cheek with her hand, and he nuzzled into it, inhaling the sweet scent of honeysuckle that clung to her.

"I do not deserve you," she whispered.

"Is that not what Mitchell said to you?" he asked, altering his hold to embrace her fully. Resting his cheek against her temple, he said, "I will leave you now. I have arrangements to make, and you require time to think."

"I do not want you to fight him."

"It is too late to change that end, Amelia. But I demand first blood, nothing more."

He felt relief relax the tautness of her spine. "Thank you," she said.

Ware brushed away the lone tear that stained her cheek, and stepped back.

"I am available to you at all times. Do not hesitate to seek me out if you have a need."

Amelia nodded, and watched Ware turn about and head toward the manse. When he disappeared from her view, she glanced around her, feeling lost and alone. No one knew how she felt, how deeply wounded she was by Colin's reappearance after all these years.

She stilled, her heartbeat stumbling for a moment over a sudden realization.

There was one person who loved Colin as she had. One person who would be equally devastated by his betrayal.

Knowing Pietro would need comfort as she did, Amelia lifted her skirts and hurried toward the stables.

Chapter 15

Francois Depardue assumed a vaguely bored expression as he entered the inn in Bristol. He took the stairs to the guest rooms above and knocked on the appropriate door. A shout of permission for entry was heard from the interior, and he answered it by stepping inside.

"Well?" Cartland asked impatiently, glancing up from the maps he had spread across the small, round table.

It was with great effort that Francois bit back an angry retort. With every day that passed, he disliked the brash, arrogant Englishman more and more. He'd argued with and then begged his superiors to have Cartland held in custody until he could ascertain who was truly guilty of Leroux's murder, but to no avail.

If he is lying, they said, *he will be close at hand for you to eliminate.*

They had insisted that Cartland join the search, and the Englishman had immediately assumed that he was in charge. He was an excellent tracker and even better killer, but those skills were tempered by his mistaken belief in his own superiority.

"It appears that Mitchell will be staying with Lord Ware. The manse is heavily guarded for some distance around. I would guess that is due to the presence of Christopher St. John."

Cartland smiled. "The earl is likely concerned that Mitchell will flee like the coward he is before the challenge can be met."

"So you say," Francois said.

The Englishman's features darkened. "I think the presence of Mademoiselle Rousseau has spoiled your temper."

Lysette. Francois smiled at the thought of her. Once, she had been harmless, but he and his men had ensured that she would never be harmless, or innocent, again. Aside from his sincere desire to see justice brought to Leroux's killer, his one pleasure in this miserable assignment was the thought of crossing paths with Lysette again.

His blood heated in anticipation. She would fight him, she always did, and she improved with every encounter. The harder she resisted him, the more he enjoyed it. Now that the *Illuminés*, on whose behalf she worked, had tasked her with ensuring either Cartland or Mitchell paid for Leroux's death, he imagined his inevitable domination of her body would be that much sweeter.

Perhaps the *Illuminés* thought he would welcome their assistance, but he did not like being second-guessed, which was how he viewed their interference.

"Do you have any suggestions for how we should proceed?" Francois asked.

"We could possibly lure the bulk of the guards away, using me as bait. Then we can attack the manse at night and kill him."

"But that will not tell me who is guilty, will it?"

Pushing to his feet, Cartland snapped, "I am obviously innocent, or they would not have sent me to find Mitchell!"

"Why, then, is Mademoiselle Rousseau here?" Francois smiled. "You think she is merely present to observe and support my efforts? Surely you are not so stupid. It was well planned to send you with me and Quinn with her. Nothing has been left to chance. You think your spy"—he gestured

to the stocky man in the corner with a jerk of his chin—
"gives you an advantage, but you are wrong."

"What do you suggest we do?" Cartland's face flushed.

Francois debated a moment, then shrugged. "Mitchell is
dueling over a woman. Perhaps she is the key to his confession."

The Englishman paled. "You think to take St. John's sister-
in-law? Are you insane?"

"Surely he cannot be as fearsome as is rumored," Francois scoffed.

"You've no notion," Cartland muttered. Then his features took on a mien of wily determination. "Then again . . .
perhaps you are right." He smiled smugly. "I will think of a
way. Give me time."

Francois shrugged, but inwardly he was making his own
plans. "Fine. I will go eat downstairs. Either of you care to
join me?"

"No. We both have work to do."

"As you wish."

Cartland watched Depardue leave with a narrowed
glance.

"He is becoming more trouble than he is worth," he muttered. "Since killing him myself is out of the question, we
must find another way to hasten the man to his reward."

"Send him to capture the girl, then," Jacques replied easily. "Since it was his idea, he should not object."

Grinning, Cartland considered the beauty of the plan. If
Mitchell or St. John took care of Depardue for him, it would
only strengthen his own protestations of innocence.

"Can you arrange for him to gain entry?"

"*Mais oui.*"

"Excellent. See to it."

Amelia found Pietro leading a bridled horse from the
nearby corral to the stable yard. For a long moment, she

was struck dumb by the resemblance he bore to Colin. With her memories of her childhood love arrested in the past, she had not noticed before. Now that she had seen him as a man, the similarities were unavoidable and agonizing. Tears welled, and though she tried to blink them back, they were plentiful and blurred her vision. She wiped them angrily away.

"Miss Benbridge." Pietro looked at her with commiseration in his dark eyes. "It hurts. I know."

She nodded. "How are you faring?"

"I'm angry," he admitted, "but grateful to have him back. If you still love the boy he was, perhaps you feel the same?"

"I am glad he is alive," she managed. "Is there anything you need?"

A smile lifted the corner of his mouth. "It is sweet of you to think of me during this time. I can see why he adores you as he does."

Her face heated at the gentle praise.

"He has loved you a long time, Miss Benbridge." Pietro's deep, slightly accented voice soothed her, though his words did not. "From the beginning, I tried to discourage him, but he wouldn't listen. I think it says a great deal that you both care so deeply for each other after all these years apart."

"That does not change the fact that he feels inferior to me"—she released a shaky breath—"or that I do not like the person I become trying to convince him of his worth."

He watched her for a long moment, then nodded. "Will you help me?"

"Of course." Amelia stepped closer. "What do you need?"

"Can you lead this horse into the stable for me? I have a few more to round up before the sun sets."

She accepted the proffered reins. The smile he gave her was strange, but presently everything in her life felt odd.

"Thank you," he murmured, then walked away.

Amelia turned and moved through the open stable door.

The moment she stepped inside, she realized Pietro's intent. She paused, her breath caught in a mixture of surprise and volatile lust.

Colin worked with his back to her, but his identity was never in question. His torso was bare, his legs clad in worn coarse breeches, his calves hugged lovingly by polished Hessians. Powerful muscles bunched and flexed beneath sweat-sheened skin as he stroked a brush rapidly over a horse's flanks.

The sudden assailment of memories from their youth almost brought her to her knees. The sight of scratches left by her nails in the golden flesh added a carnal claim to his beautiful body that she longed to enforce.

As she watched, he stilled. Her exhale was a pant, and his head swiveled to face her in a lightning quick movement.

"Amelia."

He straightened and pivoted, baring the chest she had worshipped with both mouth and hands.

Dear God, he was divine. So handsome and virile, he made her heart ache.

"Are you alone?" he asked.

"Utterly."

Colin flinched and stepped toward her.

"Please do not come closer," she said.

His jaw tightened and he halted. "Stay. Talk to me."

"What is there to say? I heard your reasons. I understand why you acted as you did."

"Is there hope for us? Any at all?"

She shook her head.

Agony transformed his features. "Look at me," he said in a broken voice. "Look at where we are. This is where I would be if I had not left—tending St. John's horses while you lived your life in a manse I am not allowed to enter. How could we have been together? Tell me that."

Amelia covered her mouth to stifle a sob.

"What if I gave it all away?" His words were laced with

a desperation that broke her heart into even smaller pieces. "What if I resumed my place as a servant in your household? Would you have me then?"

"Damn you," she cried, her shoulders straightening in self-defense. "Why must you change yourself to suit me? Why can you not simply be who you are?"

"This *is* who I am!" He spread his arms wide. "This is the man I have become, but he is still not what you want."

"Who cares what I want?" She stalked toward him. "What about what you want?"

"I want *you!*"

"Then why are you so quick to leave my side?" she snapped. "If you want me, fight for me. Do it for you, not for me."

Amelia thrust the reins at him.

He caught her hand and held it. "I love you."

"Not enough," she whispered, yanking free. Then she turned and ran from the stable in a flurry of skirts and lace.

Colin stared after her for long moments, attempting to reason what more he could do, what more he could say to win her love back. He had done everything, lost everything . . .

A dark shape filled the doorway, and he pushed his roiling emotions aside. "St. John."

The pirate stared at him with knowing eyes. "There was a lone rider spotted on a hill nearby. He is being followed back to town."

Colin nodded. "Thank you."

"Supper will be served shortly."

"I do not think I can bear it." The thought of the façade he would have to wear while Ware publicly laid claim to Amelia was too much.

"I will make your excuses, then."

"I owe you a great deal."

St. John hesitated a moment, then stepped farther inside. "Did you ever have the misfortune to meet Lord Welton?"

"Once. Briefly."

"What do you recall about him? Any impressions that lingered?"

Frowning, Colin thought back to the long-ago day. "I remember thinking he had no warmth in his eyes."

"Nothing like Miss Benbridge."

"Bloody hell. Nothing like her at all."

"Yet she seems to think they are similar creatures," St. John murmured. "Or at least that she is capable of becoming more similar. Any action she takes that is prompted by her desires rather than her reason is a suspected weakness."

Colin digested the information carefully. With him, Amelia was a creature of passion. She always had been. But they had been separated at the same time she'd learned of her father's treacherous nature. Certainly the revelation of Welton's true evil would have changed her, altered her in some way. In his heart he was attempting to woo the girl of old, but she was not that same girl any longer. He had to take that into consideration.

"Ware is the reasonable choice," Colin said, but he no longer thought the earl was the best choice. Amelia's vitality came from the passionate fire within her. It needed to be celebrated, as it would be with Colin. Not extinguished by the decorum Society would demand from Ware's wife.

"Yes," St. John agreed. "He is."

The pirate made his egress as silently as he'd arrived, leaving Colin with a great deal to consider.

Amelia sat stiffly during dinner, highly conscious of the fact that Colin took his meal in his room. The discussion she'd had with him in the stables prodded at her and gave her no rest. She was poor company, speaking little and casting a dark cloud over everyone's already somber mood. Despite her best efforts, she could not forget the sight of Colin working in the stable, a station he might still occupy if he had stayed in her employ. It was a shocking revelation to her, and she did not know what to think of it.

She retired early and hoped exhaustion would claim her, but fate was not so merciful. Unable to sleep, Amelia spent long hours tossing about in her bed. She finally abandoned the effort and left the confines of her disheveled linens. Donning her robe over her night rail, she slipped downstairs to the library.

The hour was late, all parties abed, leaving her the massive manse to herself. There were many times she roamed the St. John house at night, finding comfort in the silence and feeling of aloneness so reminiscent of her youth. Her imagination wandered, creating stories and tales in her mind, her memories picking up various passages from favorite books until she found herself at the library.

The door was slightly ajar, the flickering light of a blazing fire betraying the presence of someone inside. A shiver of awareness coursed over her skin in a wave of gooseflesh, urging her to forsake thoughts of reading and return to the safety of her bed. She debated a moment, internally examining why she would proceed when she valued stability so highly.

Ever since Colin had returned to her life, she had been acting with reckless disregard for anything but her own wants and needs. The correlation to her pater could not be ignored, and her jaw clenched with determination. It was most likely Ware in the library, and his presence would ground her and mitigate the riot of emotions she did not know how to deal with.

She pushed open the door.

Entering on silent feet, she noted the shirtsleeve-clad arm hanging over the side of a wing chair and the large hand holding a crystal goblet at a careless angle. From the darkened color of the skin, she knew she had incorrectly guessed the occupant's identity, but she did not retreat. Something about the way the glass was held alarmed her. The amber liquid inside was tilted perilously close to the rim, threatening to spill onto the English rug.

The room was warm and comfortable, the walls lined floor-to-ceiling with bookcases displaying a mixture of worn volumes and priceless artifacts. Overstuffed furniture was scattered around the space, as were many side tables. It was a library that was actually used, rather than serving as merely an ostentatious display of wealth. Despite the inevitable upcoming confrontation with the man in the chair, she was soothed by the smells of parchment and leather, and took comfort in the silence inherent in a place of learning and discovery.

Amelia rounded the wingback and found Colin sprawled within its cradle, his long legs stretched out to rest his booted feet atop a footstool, his torso sans a coat and waistcoat, his throat bared by a missing cravat. He looked at her with heavy-lidded, emotionless eyes and lifted the goblet to sculpted lips. There was a scratch near his brow and a trail of dried blood below it.

"What's wrong?" she asked softly. "How were you hurt?"

"Stay away," he said in low, rough tone. "I am in a dark place, Amelia, and I have consumed more liquor than is wise. I cannot say what I will do if you come too close."

Draped on the carved wooden arm of a nearby chair were his waistcoat, coat, and weapons—a small sword and dagger.

"Where did you go?"

"I have yet to leave." He turned his head to look into the fire.

She heard the sadness and despair beneath the words, and her heart hurt for him. For her. "I am glad you did not go out."

"Are you?" Colin's head turned. In the light of the flickering fire, his beautiful face was hard, his dark eyes cold. "I am not."

"What could you have done in this condition?"

"There is no reason for me to evade Cartland. I should turn myself over to him and spare everyone the jeopardy my presence creates."

"Your life is the reason!" she protested. "If you concede, you will die."

A wry smile tugged at the corner of his lips. "Without any hope of having you, perhaps such a fate would be merciful."

"Colin! How can you say such a thing?" She covered her mouth and fought the tears that welled.

He cursed softly. "Go away. I am not fit company, as I warned you."

"I am afraid to leave you." She feared that he would do as he threatened and surrender.

"No, you are not. You already left me, remember?"

Amelia almost said more, but his dangerous mood stilled her tongue. She had seen St. John in similar moods at times and had always wondered at Maria's fortitude in seeking him out when he was so afflicted.

He needs me, Maria would say in explanation.

It was obvious that Colin needed comfort, too. And Amelia had distanced herself from him, which left him only the bottle to turn to for solace.

She approached him with shoulders squared, lifting the hem of her robe to her lips where she wet it. Reaching him, Amelia raised his chin with one hand and used the other to smooth away the blood. He was still, his eyes watchful, the tension that gripped him reaching out and surrounding her as well, making every nerve ending tingle and every breath a pant.

With an edgy snarl, Colin turned his head and pressed his lips to the sensitive skin of her wrist. She froze, unable to move as his tongue stroked over her now madly fluttering vein.

His glass hit the rug with a soft thud and a splash, and then he was on her, wrapping his big body around her and pulling her to the floor.

"I want you." His hot open mouth moved ravenously over the tender flesh of her throat. "So badly, it's eating me alive."

"Colin . . ." The feel of him, over six feet of potently aroused male, ignited her simmering passion to a raging fire. "We shouldn't . . ."

"Nothing can stop it," he said, his hand pushing open the halves of her robe and cupping her breast. "You belong to me."

Her gaze turned to the door she had left open when she entered. "The door—"

His lips surrounded her nipple through her night rail. Amelia gasped and clutched his hair.

"Remember that night," he whispered against her breast. "Remember how I felt inside you. Remember how deep . . . how I filled you . . ."

She quivered in longing, her blood hot, her breasts heavy and aching. His callused fingertips rolled and tugged at her nipple, sending waves of pleasure along the length of her body.

"Colin—"

He came over her and took her mouth, inundating her senses with the taste of brandy and the exotic spice that was uniquely his. She moaned in delight, sucking at his thrusting tongue in a desperate effort to drink in more of him.

Distantly, she felt his hands on her thighs. The chill of the evening air over feverish skin betrayed the lifting of her gown. As everything tightened and coiled in anticipation of his touch, Amelia whimpered into his mouth. His knee intruded between hers, urging her legs apart. Shameless, she complied, spreading her thighs to give him access to the throbbing flesh at the apex.

Colin lifted his head and watched her as he cupped her sex in his hand. "You melt for me," he breathed, his chest lifting and falling rapidly. He pushed two fingers inside her, and she arched in helpless pleasure. "You were made for me."

The feel of him there, where she ached, was too much. Wrapping her arms around his shoulders, she breathed, "Come in me. Fill me."

His gaze darkened, the irises swallowed by dilated pupils. "There is so much I can do to your body, Amelia. So many ways to impart pleasure. Shall I show you what you will miss when we part?"

"You left me first."

"I came back." His seductive tone was in sharp contrast to the pain she saw on his features. "Will *you* come back? If I love you well enough . . . if I addict your body to mine . . . will you come back to me?"

Her lower lip quivered and he licked across it, his breath hot and scented of liquor. His fingers advanced and retreated, plunging shallowly into her clenching sex, building her ardor with tender skill. It was searingly intimate, but in a different way than before. The emotions they bared were not hope and pleasure but despair and pain.

"It would be worth everything," he said in a serrated whisper, "if there was any chance that you might love me again."

"I never stopped." She cried softly, tears trailing down her temples to wet her hair. "Lack of love for you is not the problem."

Colin pressed his cheek to hers. "My greatest regret is that I could not be enough for you, despite my best efforts."

Amelia turned her head and pressed her lips to his, unwilling to argue again about their differences when he was already hurting. He took her kiss with tangible desperation, his heart beating so violently, she could hear it over her own racing pulse. All the while his shoulders flexed beneath her touch, the muscles working to propel his fingers into her drenched, aching sex. She cried out softly, a thready sound of female surrender and lust.

The sound changed him; she felt it. The wounded boy from her past gave way to the determined man of her present. Desperation altered to dominance; despair altered to desire. When his head lifted and he met her gaze again, he had the devil in his eyes.

"If only you could see what I see," he murmured, gentling his fingers, pulling free of her to slide across her clitoris with a slick, expert touch.

She gasped, her hips lifting involuntarily in an effort to increase the pressure of his teasing rubbing.

"Always hungry," he whispered, "always passionate. You burn for me, Amelia, as if you had Gypsy blood in your veins."

Colin nipped at her chin, then slid lower, licking along her throat until he reached the obtrusive ruffled neckline of her night rail. He moved, taking a kneeling position, hovering over her in a way that made her feel ravished. She was splayed beneath him, her clothes in disarray, his fingers touching her as only a husband should. The wantonness of her pose only increased her ardor, made her hotter and more desperate.

He pushed up her gown, higher and higher, until her stiffened nipples were kissed by the air and then by his mouth. His tongue was an instrument of pleasure and agony. The gentle licking over the tight peak made her clutch at his hair and pull him closer. As he suckled her, his cheeks hollowed, goading the sensations bombarding her until there was no way to register them all.

Colin. Her beautiful, exotic Colin was making love to her as she had never dreamed he would, and she could not resist him. His need and longing tapped into her own, freeing her of her inhibitions, making her a willing supplicant to his demands.

"Such beautiful breasts," he praised, kissing across the valley between them to pay a like service to her neglected, jealous nipple. Colin cupped the swollen flesh with his hand, plumping it with gentle kneading, rolling the beaded point between thumb and forefinger. "You are so sweet and soft. I could lose myself in you for days . . . weeks . . ."

The thought of being the recipient of the full force of his

desires was as arousing as his touch, and Amelia rode his hand, the need to orgasm becoming a driving urge. "Please . . ."

His teeth bit into her nipple, eliciting a gasp of surprise. Then he traveled lower to circle her navel with the point of his tongue. "Not yet."

"Now," she begged, her need so intense, she could hear how wet she was. "Please . . . now."

Colin reared up to a kneeling position, leaving her bereft of his warmth and touch. He smiled as she protested, revealing the rakish dimples she had always loved. His shirtsleeves were tugged from the confinement of his breeches and pulled over his head, baring a sculpted chest and abdomen that made her mouth water. His skin was dark and stretched tightly over a highly defined musculature. She loved his body, always had. She adored the way hard labor made him powerful and strong.

"The way you look at me will keep us up all night," he said with darkly sensual promise.

He reached for the placket of his breeches and freed the straining length of his erection. Whatever arguments of reason she might have uttered died a fiery end, her entire focus narrowing to encompass only the man before her. He was a sensual fantasy come to life with his glistening torso bared to the waist and his thick, hungry cock curving upward in proud enticement.

Licking her lips, she sat up and reached for him.

"Amelia . . ." His tone was a warning, but he made no move to deter her as she angled him down to meet her waiting mouth.

"Just a taste," she whispered, licking her lips. "One taste . . ."

Her tongue swept across the tiny hole at the tip.

Colin's breath hissed out between his teeth.

The skin was softer than anything she had ever touched before, and the taste of him, salty and primitively male, was an aphrodisiac. With a moan, Amelia circled the wide, flared head with her lips and gave a tentative suck.

"Dear God," he groaned, shuddering. His hands came up to cup the back of her head.

Emboldened by his response and a wild desire to have him at her mercy, Amelia tilted her head and licked the pulsing length from top to bottom. The point of her tongue followed the path of a pulsing vein to the thick crest. She licked around and around, tasting the thick essence of his seed.

Colin was certain he would die of the pleasure Amelia bestowed with such enthusiasm. She seemed lost in the act, less focused on him and more on her own enjoyment. Her beautiful face was flushed, her green eyes glassy with arousal, her lips red and swollen and stretched tightly around his girth.

"Yes," he whispered, as she moaned and sucked harder. "Your mouth is heaven . . . take me deeper . . . yes . . ."

His body ached with the force under which he leashed it. He was trembling, burning, gasping for air. The sight of his cock sliding in and out of the ring of her lips was killing him. An hour ago, he had thought he would never touch her again, never hold her or feel her hot and wet around his cock as she climaxed beneath him. The pain of that loss was nearly too much to survive. To lose all hope and be left with nothing, only to see this—his breeches barely parted, his cock engorged and throbbing with need, and Amelia . . . the love of his life . . . servicing his lust with such passionate fervor. It made the ecstasy of her luscious mouth agonizingly intense.

"My love . . . I won't last . . ." His voice was so guttural, he barely understood himself, but she knew. She collected his meaning. He felt it in the way she touched him, saw it in the way she looked at him.

"Do it," she breathed, her words warm against his wet

skin. Her hand fisted around him and pumped, drawing up his bollocks and making his thighs quake with the intensity of his rising climax. She cupped him there, her fingers sliding through the rough hair and fondling his sack.

He cursed, the tension in his spine painfully acute. "I will flood you—damn it . . ."

Her eager mouth flowed over the aching head of his cock in a burning caress of drenching heat and hungry suction. His lungs seized, his vision darkened, his fingers tightened on her scalp.

He was moving on instinct alone; his hips bucked and thrust, running his cock over her flickering tongue and against the back of her throat. Her clenched hand prevented him from moving too deep, kept him from taking too much. Amelia moaned in sensual supplication, the vibration tingling up the length of his erection and freeing his coiling orgasm.

Colin growled as he erupted, his cock jerking with every wrenching pulse of semen, his fingers tangling in her hair. Over the mad beating of his heart and harsh, panting breaths, he heard her seductive mewls and desperate swallows as he came such as he'd never come before, pumping hard and fast into the milking depths of her mouth until he was completely and utterly spent.

She released him with a last, lingering suck, her lips shiny with his seed and curved in a purely woman's smile. Colin stared down at her in a daze, his thoughts lost in an alcohol-soaked, orgasm-induced fog. His heart, however, was as alive as it had ever been.

Had he truly thought sex would temper his love for her and make it more manageable? He loved her more now than ever, with a reckless, saturating abandon.

Lose her? *Never.*

Pushing her back, he slid down. He parted her thighs with his palms and buried his face in the slick, humid paradise of her glistening sex. Colin licked her, parting the pouty lips to stroke across her clitoris.

"Colin!" she cried out, her voice filled with startled, embarrassed pleasure.

He smiled against her, then kissed her deeply, turning his head to push his tongue inside the tiny, clenching slit that was made to hold his cock. The taste of her intoxicated him, addicted him.

"No . . . *Please.*"

There was something in her voice, a note of panic that urged him to lift his head. He stared at her, saw the wild light in her eyes and asked, "What is it?"

"Please. Stop."

He frowned, noting the high flush on her cheeks and the trembling of her thighs beneath his hands. She was hopelessly aroused, yet she stayed him.

"Why?"

"I cannot think . . ."

Reason. Conscious thought. She wanted it. Servicing him gave her power. Being serviced by him took it all away.

"You think too much," he said hoarsely. "Give in. Free the woman who took me to her bed without care for anything or anyone."

She struggled beneath him. "You want t-too much . . ."

"Yes," he growled. "All of you. Every piece . . ."

He was in her then, giving her pleasure with avid lips and tongue, eating at her, drinking her in, inhaling the primal scent of her deep into his lungs. The innate hunger he felt for her stirred in response, rousing and climbing, swelling his cock as if she had not just drained him.

Amelia twisted beneath Colin, clawing at his shoulders, begging for mercy in a voice roughened by pure female lust. She was on the edge of a steep cliff that terrified her, and he was pushing her, giving her no quarter, allowing her no space to retreat.

His tongue was an instrument of torturous pleasure, lashing and flickering, driving her higher and harder. His lips circled her clitoris, sucking and pulling. And the noises he made. The wet smacking, the rumbling purrs, the groans of need that made her slicker and hotter.

Thick skeins of dark hair tickled her inner thighs, moving as he did, narrowing her focus until all she knew was the tightening of her womb and the helpless rolling of her hips.

He demanded her response, forced it from her, turned her into a mindless creature of desire and need and desperate wanting.

"No . . . no . . . no . . ." she gasped, fighting him even as her fingers tangled in his locks and pulled him closer.

So that he could not leave her again.

Colin cupped her buttocks and lifted her, altering the angle, urging her thighs to widen so that he could take everything. He thrust his tongue hard and fast into the spasming opening, and she climaxed violently, her arms falling heavily to the floor, her nails clawing at the rug.

"Colin!"

She was devastated, destroyed. But he was not done with her. Before she could catch her breath, he was over her, inside her, pushing deep into the heart of her with the thick, hot length of his cock.

"Yes." He groaned, sliding his arms beneath her shoulders, holding her in place as he lunged with sensual grace and seated himself to the hilt. "Jesus . . . you feel so good."

He ground his hips against her, rubbing deep inside her, making her feel every throbbing inch of him.

Gasping, writhing, Amelia accepted his possession with ravenous greed, her swollen tissues parting for his relentless drives with a quivering welcome. He gripped her throat with one hand, her hip with the other, pinning her down. Dominating her. Possessing her. Branding her as his.

"Mine," he growled, sliding in and out of her, the movements of his hips leisurely, though nothing else about him was.

There was a look on his flushed and sweat-dampened face. Part agony, part pleasure. So austere and focused. So intent. His eyes blazing with heat. His handsome features stretched tautly with strain. It was searingly erotic. Intimate.

Colin was making love to her. He was alive and in her arms, in her body. Whispering words of love and desire, making dreams come true that she had thought were forever dead to her.

Again the tension built and coiled, causing her to tighten around his straining cock and ripple along its length, making him curse and growl. She felt the chafing rubbing of his waistband between her thighs, heard the sound of his boots digging into the weave of the rug, realized he was still partly dressed just as she was.

The image in her mind of how they must look—she with parted robe and lifted night rail, he with boots and breeches lowered just enough to free his beautiful cock, both locked on the floor in carnal congress—took her to orgasm.

"There," he purred, watching her with a feral smile of possession, thrusting strong and sure, extending her pleasure until she thought it might kill her. The surge of sensation was unbearable, tingling across her skin until it was too tight and sensitive.

When she was limp and whimpering, he sought his own pleasure, his dark head thrown back, his neck corded tightly, his cock so thick and hard.

Amelia watched him as he had watched her, her legs wrapped around his working hips, her hands at his waist. Pulling him into her.

His pace picked up, his grip tightened. She felt the climax coming, felt it grip him in a fist, felt it tighten his lungs. It burst from him in shocking spurts of molten liquid inside her, again and again, the breaking dam heralded by his ragged, extended groan and jerking, wrenching shudders.

"Dear God," he gasped, quaking, rubbing his pelvic bone against her swollen, oversensitive clitoris and making her come again. Suffusing her body with delight that seeped into her bones and heart and soul. Making them one.

"My love," he breathed, rubbing his big body against hers, drenching her in the scent of his skin. "I won't release you. You're mine—"

She stemmed further words with a desperate kiss.

Chapter 16

Amelia woke to a hand held over her mouth. Scared beyond measure, she struggled against her assailant, her nails clawing at his wrist.

"Stop it!"

She stilled at the command, her eyes opening wide, her heart racing madly as her sleep-fuzzy brain came to an awareness of Colin looming over her in the darkness.

"Listen to me," he hissed, his gaze darting to the windows. "There are men outside. A dozen at least. I don't know who they are, but they are not your father's men."

She yanked her head to the side to free her mouth. "What?"

"The horses woke me as the men walked by the stable." Colin stepped back and yanked off her counterpane. "I snuck out the back and came round to fetch you."

Embarrassed to be seen in only her night rail, Amelia yanked the covers back over her.

He yanked them off again. "Come on!" he said urgently.

"What are you talking about?" she asked in a furious whisper.

"Do you trust me?" Colin's dark eyes glittered in the darkness.

"Of course."

"Then do as I say, and ask questions later."

She had no notion of what was happening, but she knew

he wasn't jesting. Sucking in a deep breath, she nodded and slipped from the bed. The room was lit only by the moon-light that entered through the window glass. The heavy length of her hair hung down her back in a thick, swinging braid, and Colin caught it, rubbing it between his fingers.

"Put something on," he said. "Quickly."

Amelia hurried behind the screen in the corner and dis-robed, then slipped the chemise and gown she had worn earlier over her head.

"Hurry!"

"I cannot close the back. I need my abigail."

Colin's hand thrust behind the screen and caught her elbow, tugging her from behind it so that he could drag her to the door.

"My feet are bare!"

"No time," he muttered. Opening her bedroom door, he peered out to the hallway.

It was so dark, Amelia could barely see anything. But she heard male voices. "What is going—"

Moving with lightning speed, Colin spun and covered her mouth again, his head shaking violently.

Startled, it took her a moment to understand. Then she nodded her agreement to say nothing.

He stepped out to the hallway with silent steps, her hand in his. Somehow, despite her shoeless state, the floorboard beneath her squeaked, when it hadn't under Colin's boots. He froze, as did she. Below them, the voices she had heard were also silent. It felt as if the house were holding its breath. Waiting.

Colin placed his finger to his lips. Then he picked her up and hefted her over his shoulder. What followed was a blur. Suspended upside down, she was disoriented and unable to discern how he managed to carry her from her second-floor bedroom to the lower floor. Then a shout was heard up-stairs as she was discovered missing, and pounding feet thundered above them. Colin cursed and ran, jostling her so that her teeth ached and her braid whipped his legs so hard, she feared hurting him. Her arms wrapped around his lean hips, and his pace picked up. They burst out the front door and down the steps.

More shouting. More running. Swords clashed and Miss Pool's screams pierced the night.

"There she is!" someone shouted.

The ground rushed by beneath her.

"Over here!"

Benny's voice was music to her ears. Colin altered direction. Lifting her head, she caught a glimpse of pursuers, and then more men intercepted them, some she recognized, others she didn't. The new additions to the fray bought them precious time, and soon she could not see anyone on their heels.

A moment later she was set on her feet. Wild-eyed, she glanced around to catch her bearings, and found Benny on horseback and Colin mounting the back of another beast.

"Amelia!" He held out one hand to her, the other expertly holding the reins. She set her hand in his, and he dragged her up and over, belly down across his lap. His powerful thighs bunched beneath her as he spurred the horse, and then they were off, galloping through the night.

She hung on for dear life, her stomach heaving with the jolting impacts. But it did not last long. Just as they reached the open road, a shot rang out, echoing through the darkness. Colin jerked and cried out. She screamed as her entire world shifted.

Sliding, falling . . .

Amelia awoke to a hand held over her mouth and a whisper in her ear.

"Shh . . . Someone is in the house."

Colin's voice anchored her in the semidarkness. For the space of several heartbeats, the horror and fear from the vivid dream lingered. Then the feel of Colin's body pressed to her back and his strong arms around her provided much needed comfort.

Awareness seeped in slowly. She noted the elaborate moldings on the ceiling and felt velvet beneath her calf.

They were on the settee in the library. From the look of the fire in the grate—now reduced to mere embers—she had been asleep for at least a couple of hours.

Turning in Colin's embrace, she faced him and pressed her mouth to his ear. "Who is it?" she whispered.

Colin shook his head, his dark eyes glittering.

Amelia held still, absorbing the tension that gripped his frame. Then she heard it. The sound of a booted foot falling on the parquet floor.

Boots. At this hour.

Her heartbeat leaped from the steady rhythm of slumber to a racing tempo. Unlike her dream, this time it was Colin who was endangered.

He pressed his lips to hers in a quick, hard kiss. Then he slid silently off the edge of the couch. On his knees, he fastened his breeches. He drew his discarded shirtsleeves over his head, then reached for his small sword.

She, too, slid to the floor and belted her robe.

"Secure the door when I leave," he whispered, pulling his blade free of its scabbard with torturous slowness to avoid making any sound.

Denying him with a shake of her head, Amelia crawled over to where a faint glimmer betrayed the jeweled hilt of his dagger lying atop his waistcoat and coat. The moment her hand wrapped around it, he was behind her.

"No."

"Trust me." She turned her head to press her cheek to his.

His jaw clenched. "My sanity hinges on your safety."

"You think I feel differently about you?" She touched his cheek with a shaking hand, tracing the faint line that marked the spot where a dashing dimple appeared when he was happy. "Rest easy. My sister is the Wintry Widow."

There was a long pause, his throat working as he considered what she was saying.

"Let me help," she breathed. "How will we ever move forward together if you always leave me behind?"

She knew how the thought of her in danger tormented him, because she felt likewise about him.

Finally, Colin managed a jerky nod. With a swift kiss to his parted lips, she pulled the dagger free of its sheath.

I love you. The words were spoken soundlessly, his lips against hers.

Amelia lifted his hand and kissed the back.

Colin wrenched away from her and moved to the door. At some point while she was sleeping, he had closed it. Now, he turned the knob and cracked it just wide enough to see. The well-oiled hinges made no sound.

In the blink of an eye, he was gone. She counted to ten, then slipped out after him.

Bolstered by the feel of the dagger hilt, Amelia crawled along the runner toward the stairs, her senses acute. The sound of the wind blowing and the nocturnal call of a preying owl grounded her to the moment. She breathed shallowly, her emotions suppressed by the instinct to survive and the need to protect Colin. There was a sudden silence, as if the house held its breath, and then she heard the barest hint of sound—a stealthy footfall straight ahead.

She paused. Pushing to her knees, she huddled in the darkness.

A clear shot, just one.

To her right, a movement caught her eye. Holding the blade and aiming the hilt, Amelia prepared to throw. Her arm was steady, her nerves taut but manageable. She had never killed before, but if it became necessary, she would act first and face the consequences later.

Her arm went back, her focus narrowed on a slim shaft of moonlight lying directly across the bottom step.

Although there was no discernable sound of progress, Amelia sensed the intruder moving closer to that tiny beam of light.

Closer . . . closer . . .

Suddenly, Colin lunged. She knew it was him by the white of his shirt, as he arced through the moonlight. He crashed into a body so well concealed by shadows that Amelia had been unable to see the outline of it at her present angle. A loud crash heralded the colliding of the two figures into a breakable object.

She leaped to her feet. Crossing the hallway, she reached the opposite wall, improving the chances of a successful strike.

It was too dark to identify one form or the other. With both figures tangled in a writhing mass of limbs, she could do nothing but pray.

Mercifully, a door opened on the upper floor. She bit back a sob of relief. The light cast by an approaching lantern bearer was sufficient illumination to catch an uplifted blade too short to be Colin's small sword. Amelia pulled back her arm and threw, putting weight behind the volley with an oft-practiced lunge.

It spun hilt-over-blade in a lightning quick roll. A pained grunt rent the air. The knife that had been aimed at Colin clattered noisily, yet harmlessly, to the parquet.

St. John rushed down the staircase with a pistol held in one hand and a lantern held aloft in the other. Maria was directly behind him with a foil at the ready.

Light spilled across the foyer, revealing Amelia's target. Clutching his chest, the intruder sank to his knees. The hilt of the dagger protruded from between his clutching hands. He swayed morbidly for a long moment, then fell forward.

"Bloody hell," Colin breathed, rushing to her side. "Beautifully done."

"That was excellent, Amelia," St. John said with much pride, his gaze on the body lying slumped at his feet.

"What in hell is transpiring out here?" Ware demanded, descending the staircase. Mr. Quinn and Mademoiselle Rousseau joined the gathering in short order.

"Depardue," the Frenchwoman said. She lowered to a crouch and set her hand on his shoulder, pushing him gently to his back. *Comment te sens-tu?*"

The Frenchman groaned softly and opened his eyes. "Lysette . . ."

She reached for the dagger and withdrew it. Then stabbed him again, this time through the heart.

The sound of the blade scraping across a rib bone and a sharp abbreviated cry from Depardue made Amelia shudder violently. "Good God!" she cried, feeling ill.

The Frenchwoman's arm lifted and fell again. Mr. Quinn lunged and yanked her back, the dagger pulling free with her retreat and hitting the floor. "Enough! You killed him."

Mademoiselle Rousseau fought her confinement, hurling expletives in French with such venom, Amelia took an involuntary step backward. Then the woman spat on the corpse.

The display left everyone in stunned silence for a long moment. Then St. John cleared his throat. "Well . . . that one is no longer a threat. However, there must be more of them. I doubt the man would come alone."

"I will search the downstairs." Colin looked at Amelia. "Go to your room. Lock the door."

She nodded. The sight of the dead man and the rapidly spreading pool of blood at her feet made her stomach churn. Now that help was at hand, the full effect of her actions began to seep into her consciousness.

"I found something."

All eyes turned toward the direction of the foyer, where Tim appeared, carrying Jacques by the scruff of his neck.

"'E was sneaking about outside," the giant rumbled.

No one could fail to note the Frenchman's fully dressed state.

"I was not 'sneaking' about!" Jacques protested.

"I think 'e let that one"—Tim jerked his chin toward Depardue—"in."

"Do we have a traitor in our midst?" St. John asked ominously.

A cold chill swept across Amelia's skin.

"*Ça alors!*" Mademoiselle Rousseau threw up her hands, one of which was covered in blood. "Should we be wasting time on him when there could be others outside?"

Tim looked at St. John. "We caught three more, not including these two."

Colin's face hardened. "We will question all of them, then. Someone will tell us something of import."

Mademoiselle Rousseau snorted. "*Absurde.*"

"What do you suggest we do?" Simon asked with exaggerated politeness. "Torture him slowly over many days? Would that better slake your blood lust?"

She waved her hand carelessly. "Why exert yourself? Kill him."

"*Salope!*" Jacques yelled. "You would eat your own young."

St. John's brows rose.

"She works with me," the Frenchman cried, struggling in Tim's grip. "I, at least, can bear witness to Mitchell's innocence in the matter of Leroux's murder. She has nothing of value."

"I beg your pardon?" Colin said, his frame stiffening. "Did you say you both work together?"

Amelia wrapped her arms around her waist, shivering.

"*Ta gueule!*" Mademoiselle Rousseau hissed.

Jacques's smile was maliciously triumphant.

"I think we should separate them," Colin suggested.

St. John nodded.

"I will take Lysette," Simon said with a hard edge to his voice.

When the Frenchwoman shivered with apparent apprehension, Amelia looked away and fought a flare of sympathy for the woman.

"Come along, poppet," Maria murmured, linking arms with her. "Let us gather tea and spirits for the men. We have a long night ahead of us."

Colin stared at the man he'd thought was a friend and attempted to comprehend the fullness of the plot being explained to him. "You have been working with Mademoiselle Rousseau from the beginning? Before you met at the inn a few days ago?"

Jacques nodded. He was bound to a damask and gilded chair in Ware's study, his calves tied to the legs, his hands restrained behind the back. "We did not meet at the inn. I have known her for some time now."

"But you both acted as if you had just become acquainted," Simon argued. When Mademoiselle Rousseau had proven to be more stubborn in holding her silence, he had left her bound and guarded in a guest room and joined the rest of the party in questioning her coconspirator.

"Because we had to make you believe that this matter was about Cartland and his murder of Leroux," Jacques explained.

"Is that not what this has all been about?" St. John asked, frowning.

"No. The *Illuminés* sought to end your inquiries and activities in France, which have become increasingly troublesome. I was sent to discover the identity of your superior."

Colin froze. "The *Illuminés?*" He had heard whispers of a secret society of "enlightened" members who sought power through hidden channels, but the rumors were unsubstantiated. Until now. "What do they have to do with Leroux?"

"None of this had anything to do with Leroux," the Frenchman snapped. "In fact, Cartland's murder of Leroux has been a complication."

"How so?" Simon asked from his position on the settee. Dressed in his evening robe and holding a cheroot in one hand, he looked the part of a man at leisure, which was definitely not the case.

"The *Illuminés* learned that Mitchell was returning to England," Jacques said. "I secured a cabin aboard the same ship with the intent to befriend him on the journey. It was hoped that our association would eventually lead to a disclosure of the identity of the man you work for here in England. I followed Mitchell the night we were to set sail, and I took advantage of the opportunity presented to me. I used the situation to build a friendship with Mitchell."

"Fascinating," St. John murmured.

"And what of Lysette?" Simon asked.

"Mitchell was my target," the Frenchman said. "You were hers. The *Illuminés* do not like to leave anything to chance."

"Bloody hell." Colin growled his frustration. "And what of tonight? What role did Depardue play?"

"He was responsible for discovering the truth regarding Leroux's death, which is a personal matter to the agent-general."

"So I am still wanted in France," Colin said, "and someone must pay for Leroux's death. My predicament has not changed, merely your and Mademoiselle Rousseau's role in it."

Jacques smiled grimly. "Yes."

"And now Depardue is dead."

"Do not regret that outcome, *mon ami*. As Mademoiselle Rousseau can attest, he was a far from honorable man. I would never allow you to suffer for his crimes. I assured you of that from the beginning."

"But you allowed Depardue into my house," Ware pointed out. "Why?"

"Cartland sent him to find Miss Benbridge," Jacques explained. "I agreed to assist him, but my intent was not to let him succeed. I had hoped to be the one to 'discover' him and kill him, thereby deepening your trust in me."

"I do not understand." St. John stepped closer. "Why does Cartland trust you?"

"Because of Depardue. When Mitchell and I were still in London, I searched for Cartland. I found Depardue and told him I was working with Lysette to apprehend Leroux's killer. Lysette's involvement made Depardue wary. This created an opening with Cartland, who needed alternate French support because Depardue did not believe him."

"Where is Cartland now?" Colin asked.

"At the inn, waiting for word."

Colin looked at Quinn, who stood.

"I will change swiftly," Quinn said.

St. John rose. "I shall come along, as well."

"I will stay here with the women," Ware offered. Then he smiled. "Though I doubt they need my protection."

Colin left the room and moved toward the library with a rapid, eager stride. Quinn fell into step beside him.

"It appears that your vindication is at hand," the Irishman said.

"Yes. Finally." Anticipation thrummed through Colin's veins and made his heart race. The divide separating him from Amelia still existed, but the scent of their lovemaking clung to his skin and gave him hope. She loved him. The rest would come in time.

He and Quinn parted ways by the staircase, and Colin returned to the library to collect his coats. His fist curled around the empty sheath that normally held his dagger, and his mind returned to the moment when Amelia had come to his aid, defending him to the death. Earlier today he had thought it impossible to love her more than he did. Now he realized he was falling in love with her all over again. With the woman Amelia had grown into.

For the first time, Colin was absolutely certain there was no other man in the world better for Amelia. And even if that were not the case, damn them all regardless. She belonged to him. With perseverance he might convince her to believe that, too.

Resolute and determined, he shrugged into his garments and left the room. Ware was standing at the foot of the staircase, staring down at the location where Depardue's body had lain not long ago. The scene was tidied now, but Colin suspected the memory would haunt the earl for years to come.

At the sound of footfalls, Ware turned his head, and his gaze narrowed upon seeing Colin.

"If you capture Cartland," Ware said, "you will have no further business here." His jaw tightened. "Except for one."

"Shall we meet at dawn?" Colin suggested. The duel was one more impediment to his future with Amelia. He wanted it dispatched immediately. "We will both have been awake through the night. No advantage for either of us."

"Perhaps you will fight at length or return wounded," the earl said grimly. "However, if neither of those conditions applies, dawn will suit me well."

Colin bowed and hastened toward the stables, spurred by the thought that the sun could rise upon an entirely new life for him. He found St. John waiting with a dozen men. Quinn appeared shortly after.

Within a half hour, a troop of over a dozen riders was on its way into town.

Chapter 17

Cartland heard the sounds of many booted feet approaching his room and reached for the gun resting on the table before him. Sending Depardue along with four others had been a gamble he would have preferred to avoid, but sometimes such risks reaped the greatest rewards.

Holding a pistol lightly in one hand, he waited for the knock and then called out for entry. The door opened, and one of his men entered in a rush.

"I cannot be certain," the man said; "perhaps I am overcautious, but a group of three heavily armed gentlemen entered the tavern below."

Cartland tucked his weapon into his waistband and reached for his coat. "Better to be cautious than foolhardy." He caught up his small sword and moved swiftly toward the door. "Are the others below?"

"Yes, and two in the stables."

"Excellent, come with me."

Moving with long, rapid strides, Cartland made his egress by way of the servants' staircase. Straight ahead was the rear exit, but he turned left instead and went through the kitchen to the delivery door. It always paid to be careful.

The door was ajar, allowing the cool night breeze into the hot kitchen. Cartland saw nothing but darkness beyond the small pool of spilling light, but he rushed outside to the alley in a near run to give himself a better chance of escape if a trap was set.

Once he was shrouded by the enveloping moonlit night, he felt safer.

Until he heard the pained grunt of the lackey who ran just behind him.

Startled, Cartland stumbled over a loose bit of gravel. He spun, pulling his gun free as he did so, his gaze wild and seeking.

"So good to see you again," Mitchell called out.

The light of the moon illuminated the narrow alley and the prone body on the ground with the knife hilt protruding from its back. The lackey groaned and writhed and was absolutely useless to Cartland.

"You!" he sputtered, unable to see the man who hunted him.

"Me," Mitchell agreed from the shadows.

The echo created by the surrounding buildings made it difficult to determine where Mitchell was.

Meanwhile, Cartland was out in the open.

Brandishing his firearm, Cartland said, "The French won't believe that I am at fault. They trust me."

"Allow me to worry about that."

There was a thud to the left, and Cartland fired in that general direction. When a large, round rock rolled down the shallow incline to rest against his booted foot, he knew he'd been tricked. Had he not been so panicked, he would have known better. His heart sank into his gut, frozen by terror.

Mitchell's laughter filled the night. Then the Gypsy appeared in a flurry of a swirling cape like some phantom apparition. In each hand was a weapon. One was a pistol, which left Cartland with no options beyond death or surrender. His useless, smoking gun fell from his nerveless fingers and clattered to the alley floor.

"I can help you," he offered urgently. "I can speak on your behalf and clear your name."

Mitchell's teeth flashed white in the darkness. "Yes, you will—by returning to France and paying for your crimes."

Amelia jolted awake just before dawn. Her heart was racing as if she'd run a great distance, but she could not discern why.

She lay abed for a long moment, blinking up at the canopy above her. Her bleary gaze lingered upon the gold tassels that framed the edges, and she attempted to regulate her panting by concentrating on every breath.

Then she heard an unmistakable noise that filled her with dread—the sound of swords clashing outside.

For a moment, she feared the men had not succeeded with their early morning capture of Cartland, but the lack of shouting and mayhem dispelled that thought.

The duel!

She called out for her abigail as she leaped up from the bed. "Anne!"

Hurrying to the window, she threw the drapes wide, cursing under her breath to see the pale gray-and-pink sky.

Amelia rushed to her armoire and pulled out a shawl. "Anne!"

The door opened, and she turned in an agitated flurry. "Why did you not wake me before—Maria!"

"Amelia."

The note of sympathy in Maria's voice caused gooseflesh to flare across Amelia's arms. "No!" she breathed, rushing past her sister to the gallery.

"Poppet! Wait!"

But she did not. She ran with all the strength she had, nearly crashing into an industrious chambermaid before skittering around the corner and stumbling down the stairs. As she approached the lower floor, the unmistakable ring of clashing foils iced her blood. Amelia was nearly to the French doors that led to the rear terrace and the lawn beyond that when she was caught in a crushing embrace and restrained. She attempted a scream, but was gagged by a massive hand over her mouth.

"Sorry," Tim muttered. "I can't let you distract 'em while they're fighting. That's 'ow men are killed."

She shuddered violently at the thought of either man being injured. Struggling like a madwoman, Amelia fought for freedom, but even grown men could not best Tim. As the sounds of fighting continued, tears welled and coursed freely. Every clang of steel clashing against steel struck her like a blow, causing her to jerk repeatedly in Tim's arms. He cursed and pressed his cheek to hers, murmuring things meant to soothe, but nothing could alleviate her distress.

Then . . . silence.

Amelia froze, afraid to breathe in case the sound would overpower the heralds of whatever was transpiring outside.

Tim carried her to a nearby window and pushed up the sash a bare inch. A damp, chilly breeze blew through the tiny gap, making her shiver.

"You are the better man."

Colin's voice drifted to her ears, and her lips quivered against Tim's palm.

"You are the reasonable choice," he continued in a grim tone. "You have been steadfast and true to her. Unlike my estate, your wealth and title are long-standing. You can give her things that I cannot."

Amelia hung limply in Tim's arms, sobbing silently.

"Most importantly, her affection for me is not something she welcomes, while she gratefully embraces her future with you."

Her head turned to the side, her tear-stained cheek pressing against Tim's thundering heart.

Colin was leaving her, as he had so many times before.

Tim's hand fell away from her mouth.

"Release me," she whispered, her spirit broken. "I will not go outside."

He set her down and she turned away.

"Poppet." Maria waited at the bottom of the stairs with her arms wide open. Amelia walked gratefully into them, her knees weakening, forcing them both to sit on the bottom step.

"I had hope," Amelia whispered, her chest crushed by grief such as she had not felt since she first believed Colin had died. "I hate myself for having hope. Why can I not learn from the past? Those I love do not stay in my life. They all leave. Every one of them. Except for you . . . only you stay . . ."

"Hush. You are overwrought."

Strong arms curved beneath her as Tim lifted her up. She curled against his chest as he carried her back to her bedchamber with Maria in tow.

Colin straightened from his low bow, his eyes meeting Ware's as the earl mimicked his movements. He felt the hot trickle of blood weeping from the shallow wound caused by Ware's blade, but he did not care. Ware had satisfaction, but that was all he would have. It would have to be enough for the earl, for Colin intended to take the spoils.

"But regardless of everything that recommends you, my lord," Colin continued, "I concede only this duel. Not Miss Benbridge. Her deeper affection is for me, as always. And I believe my feelings for her are quite obvious to one and all."

"Which is why you abandoned her for several years?" the earl scoffed.

"I cannot alter the past. However, I can assure you that from the present moment onward, nothing on Earth can take her from me."

Ware's blue eyes narrowed, and thick tension filled the air between them. Then the corner of the earl's mouth lifted. "Perhaps you are not the man I thought you were."

"Perhaps not."

They bowed again, then quit the lawn, both men heading in the separate directions their lives would now take them.

The next half hour of Amelia's life—or was it an hour?—passed in a daze. Maria forced tea upon her, as well as a hefty dose of laudanum.

"It will calm you," her sister murmured.

"Go away," she muttered, slapping at the many hands that sought to soothe her brow.

"I will read quietly," Maria said, "and send your abigail away."

"No. You go, too."

Eventually they gave up and went away, leaving Amelia to curl into herself and fall back into a dreamless, drug-induced sleep.

Sadly, the respite did not last long. Far too soon another hand brushed the curls back from her face.

"I suppose I have only myself to blame for your lack of faith."

Colin's voice brushed across her skin like a tangible caress. She rolled into him, grasping with her hands. He caught them with his own and squeezed.

"You were supposed to sleep straight through this morning," he murmured, pulling the blankets back from her. "I wanted to spare you any possibility of distress."

She was lifted and cradled to a warm, hard chest. The scent of his skin, so alluringly masculine and uniquely Colin, urged her to bury her tear-streaked face in his cravat.

She was distantly aware of being carried. It felt as if they descended a staircase, and then fresh air was drifting over her skin, making her shiver.

"There's a blanket in my carriage," he murmured. "A minute more and then you will be comfortable again."

A moment later she was jostled into a carriage, and it set off with a lurch, the wheels crunching across gravel. She was held securely in Colin's lap and covered warmly. Tears leaked out between her closed eyelids, and she prayed that she would never wake from such a wonderful dream.

His firm lips pressed tightly against her forehead. "Sleep." Drugged by the laudanum, she did.

It was the sudden cessation of motion that woke Amelia. Blinking, she fought off the remnants of sleep.

"The horses are fatigued and I am near starved." Colin's deep voice pulled her from half awareness to full cognizance in an instant.

The duel . . .

Bolting upright, the top of her head made sharp contact with his chin, causing them both to cry out.

"Ow, damn it," he muttered, rearranging her atop his lap as if she weighed nothing at all.

Wild-eyed, Amelia took in the luxurious appointments of Colin's travel coach and then leaned out the window. They were in the courtyard of what appeared to be an inn.

She glanced at him and found him rubbing his chin. "Where are we?"

"On our way."

"To where?"

"To be wed."

Amelia blinked. "What?"

His smile revealed his dimples and reminded her of the boy she had fallen so deeply in love with. "You said that we had no hope of moving forward together if I was forever leaving you behind. Since I had no further reason to enjoy Lord Ware's hospitality, it was time for us to go."

She stared at him for a long moment, trying to collect what it was that he was saying. "I do not understand. Did you not duel this morning?"

"Yes, we did."

"Did he not win? Did you not say he was the better man? Dear God, am I losing my mind?"

"Yes, yes, and no." Colin tightened the arm banded around her waist and pulled her closer. "I allowed him first blood," he explained. "He had a right to it. When I took you, you were still his."

Amelia opened her mouth to protest, and he covered her lips with his fingertips. "Allow me to finish."

She stared at him for a long moment, absorbing the sudden gravity reflected on his countenance. Then she nodded and slipped free of his embrace, moving to the opposite squab so that she could think properly.

It was then she noted that she was dressed in her night rail. For his part, Colin was beautifully attired in a velvet ensemble of dark green. She still encountered difficulty correlating the Colin before her with the Colin of old, but she had no difficulty loving him, regardless. The sight of him filled her with pleasure, just as it always had.

"There is no point in denying that Ware can offer you things that I cannot," Colin said, his dark eyes watching her with a mixture of love and determination. "That is what you overheard this morning. However, I have come to realize that I don't care."

"You don't?" Amelia's hand went to her fluttering stomach.

"No, I don't." He crossed his arms, revealing the powerful muscles she found endlessly arousing. "I love you. I want you. I intend to have you. Every other consideration be damned."

"Colin—"

"I've stolen you, Amelia. Run away with you, just as I have always wanted to do." He smiled again. "Within a fortnight, you and I will be husband and wife."

"Do I have no say in the matter?"

"You can say 'yes' if you like. Otherwise, you have no say."

Amelia laughed even as tears fell.

Colin leaned forward and set his elbows on his knees. "Tell me those are happy tears."

"Colin . . ." She gave a shaky sigh. "How can I say yes? Discarding Ware so callously for my own pleasure is exactly the sort of behavior my father excelled at. I could not live with myself if I acted so selfishly. Perhaps I would even grow to resent you for tempting me into such reckless deportment."

"Amelia." He straightened. "If I tell you that Ware would want nothing more than your happiness, it might alleviate your concern and goad your agreement, but that is not what I want."

She frowned.

"Yes, we are acting impetuously," he continued. "Yes, we are seizing the day and our love without a care for the world. That is who we are. That is our affinity. You and I are not ones to restrain our joys."

"People cannot live in that manner."

"Yes, they can. As long as doing so brings no pain to others." His voice grew more impassioned, arresting her. "Ware does not love you, not as I do. And you do not love him. I also suspect that you do not love yourself, not as you should. You accused me of molding myself into someone I am not, yet you are guilty of the same offense. You seek to mold yourself into a woman of decorum and duty, but that is not who you are! Do not be ashamed of the facets of you that I love so much."

"Welton was an awful man," she cried. "I cannot be like him."

"You never could be." Colin caught up her hands. "You are filled with love for life and family. Your father was filled with love only for himself. Two very different things."

"Ware . . ."

"Ware knows what I am doing. He could stop us if he wishes, but he won't. Regardless, I am altering myself to have you. I am taking this day and you, and forsaking all of the rest. It is frightening, yes. We will both have to leave the cages we created for ourselves and venture into the unknown. But we will have each other."

Cages. She had been caged for so long, one part of her hating the restrictions, the other part grateful that they restrained her from being too much like Welton. "You know me so well," she whispered.

"Yes, I know you better than anyone. You told me to believe that I was worthy of you. Now it is your turn to believe that you are worthy of me. Trust that you are free from whatever defect of character your father suffered. Trust that I am smart enough to love a wonderful woman."

He pressed his lips to her knuckles. "Make the leap with me, Amelia. I am holding on to our love with both hands, despite all the reasons why I shouldn't. Do the same. Embrace your wild nature and run with me. Be free with me. We shall all be happier for it."

She gazed at him for a long moment, her vision blurring with tears. Then she threw herself into his arms.

"Yes," she whispered with her cheek pressed to his. "Let's be free."

Christopher, Simon, and Ware were engrossed in a discussion when Maria burst into the room with her skirts held in one hand and a missive in the other.

All three men rose immediately. Christopher and Simon both stepped toward her with frowns marring their handsome features. Ware merely raised his brows.

"I found this atop Amelia's pillow! Mitchell has absconded with her."

Simon blinked. "Beg your pardon?"

"Truly?" Christopher smiled.

"He says he intends to marry her." She glanced down at the note to read it again. "They are already headed north."

"We must hurry or we will miss the nuptials," Ware said.

"You knew?" Maria stared at him with wide eyes.

"I hoped," he corrected. "I am pleased to see the man has come to his senses."

Maria opened her mouth, then shut it again.

"Well, let's not dally," Christopher said, catching her elbow and spinning her back around toward the door. "We have packing to see to. Tim can guard Mademoiselle Rousseau and Jacques while we are absent."

"North," Simon muttered. "May I ride in your carriage, my lord?"

"Certainly."

Still finding it difficult to believe, Maria glanced over her shoulder at Ware.

"This is a happy occasion, Mrs. St. John," he drawled, following directly behind them. "You should be smiling as I am."

"Yes, my lord."

She looked at Christopher, who nodded. With that, she shrugged and laughed aloud. Then she lifted her skirts and raced her husband up the stairs.

Epilogue

"We set sail in a few hours," Quinn said, fingering a coined tassel on a multicolored pillow. "My trunks and valet are aboard, and Lysette is safely restrained in my cabin."

They sat in the family parlor of Colin's new town house in London. It was a large room, beautifully decorated in shades of soft blue and gold. Around the room, Amelia had added colorful touches of his heritage—pillows encased in glorious scarves, small carved figurines, and bowls of Romany trinkets given to them by Pietro as wedding gifts. The style was unfashionable and would be considered horrifyingly gauche by many, but they both loved the space and spent a great deal of time curled up together there.

Embrace who you are, she had said, with a new confidence that aroused him unbearably. She, too, was embracing the reckless side of herself that she had fought to contain for so long. Fears of becoming too much like her father were banished, just as Colin's fear of being unworthy of her no longer had power to dictate his actions.

Colin leaned back in his chair and asked Quinn, "Did the French agree to release your men in a trade for the return of Mademoiselle Rousseau and Cartland?"

"And Jacques. They want him, too. But I am only taking Lysette with me for now. They can have the other two back after I am certain they will honor their end of the agreement."

"I do not envy you that trip," Colin said, wincing. "I cannot imagine Mademoiselle Rousseau makes a very good prisoner."

"She is miserable, but I am enjoying the whole thing immensely."

Colin laughed. "Because you're a cad. When will you return?"

"I am not certain." Shrugging, Quinn said, "Perhaps after I ensure that the others are released. Or perhaps not even then. Maybe I will travel some."

"You are good to your men, Quinn. It is a trait I have always admired in you."

"They are not my men any longer. I have resigned." He nodded at Colin's raised brows. "Yes, it's true. My work for Eddington was diverting for a time, but now I must find new ways to amuse myself."

"Such as?"

"Some sort of trouble will come up." Quinn grinned. "Seeing you in your evening finery reminds me that a life of social indulgence is not for me. It would bore me to tears."

"Not with the right woman."

Quinn threw his dark head back and laughed, a rich, full sound that brought a smile to Colin's lips.

"Even when I was maudlin with love for Maria," Quinn said, pushing to his feet, "I thankfully never spouted such nonsense."

Colin rose with him, flushing sheepishly. "One day, I hope to remind you of your protestations and watch you eat your words."

"Ha! That day will be a long time coming, my friend. Likely, neither of us will live long enough to see it."

As Quinn turned to leave the room, Colin felt more than a small measure of sadness at their parting. Quinn was a wanderer by nature; therefore, they would see each other far less often. After all they had endured and experienced together, he thought of Quinn as a brother and would miss him accordingly.

"Farewell, my friend." Quinn clapped him on the back when they reached the foyer. "I wish you much joy and many children in your marriage."

"I wish you happy, as well."

Quinn touched his brow in a smart salute, and then he was gone. Off to find his next adventure.

Colin stared at the closed front door for a long moment.

"Darling."

Amelia's throaty purr sent a wave of heat across his skin.

He turned to face her with a smile and found her paused at the top of the stairs, dressed in only her robe. Her hair was beautifully, intricately arranged with twinkling diamonds weaved among the powdered strands.

"You have yet to dress?" he asked.

"I was nearly finished."

"It does not appear that way to me."

"I had to stop when Anne brought me the finishing touches to my ensemble . . . and the final piece of yours."

"Oh?" His smile widened. He knew well that look of seductive mischief in her eyes.

Her left arm lifted gracefully, the emerald of her wedding ring glinting in the candlelight from the foyer chandelier, her delicate fingers wrapped with lustrous black satin and dangling a familiar white mask.

Every muscle in his body hardened.

"If you like," she murmured, "we can go to the masquerade as planned. I know it took you some time to dress."

He strode toward the stairs. "It would take me considerably less time to undress," he purred.

"I should like you to wear this."

"I set it out for a reason."

"Wicked man."

Colin took the steps two at a time and caught her up, relishing the feel of her soft, unfettered body pressed to his. *"I'm* wicked? It is you, Countess Montoya, who lures me away from a staid social outing in favor of a night of licentious revelry."

"I cannot resist." She lifted the mask to his face and secured the ribbons. "I have a passion for you."

"Indulge it," he growled, his lips to her throat. "I beg of you."

Her laughter was filled with joy and love. It filled his heart then, and over the course of many hours afterward. Along with other, equally wondrous sounds.

Don't miss *Ask for It*, the first book in Sylvia Day's Georgian series.

London, April 1770

"A re you worried I'll ravish the woman, Eldridge? I admit
   to a preference for widows in my bed. They are much
more agreeable and decidedly less complicated than virgins
or other men's wives."

Sharp gray eyes lifted from the mass of papers on the enormous mahogany desk. *"Ravish*, Westfield?" The deep voice
was rife with exasperation. "Be serious, man. This assignment is very important to me."

Marcus Ashford, seventh Earl of Westfield, lost the wicked
smile that hid the soberness of his thoughts and released a
deep breath. "And you must be aware that it is equally important to me."

Nicholas, Lord Eldridge, sat back in his chair, placed his
elbows on the armrests, and steepled his long, thin fingers.
He was a tall and sinewy man with a weathered face that had
seen too many hours on the deck of a ship. Everything about

him was practical, nothing superfluous, from his manner of speaking to his physical build. He presented an intimidating presence with a bustling London thoroughfare as a backdrop. The result was deliberate and highly effective.

"As a matter of fact, until this moment, I was not aware. I wanted to exploit your cryptography skills. I never considered you would volunteer to manage the case."

Marcus met the piercing gray stare with grim determination. Eldridge was head of the elite band of agents whose sole purpose was to investigate and hunt down known pirates and smugglers. Working under the auspices of His Majesty's Royal Navy, Eldridge wielded an inordinate amount of power. If Eldridge refused him the assignment, Marcus would have little say.

But he would not be refused. Not in this.

He tightened his jaw. "I will not allow you to assign someone else. If Lady Hawthorne is in danger, I will be the one to ensure her safety."

Eldridge raked him with an all-too-perceptive gaze. "Why such passionate interest? After what transpired between you, I'm surprised you would wish to be in close contact with her. Your motive eludes me."

"I have no ulterior motive." At least not one he would share. "Despite our past, I've no desire to see her harmed."

"Her actions dragged you into a scandal that lasted for months and is still discussed today. You put on a good show, my friend, but you bear scars. And some festering wounds, perhaps?"

Remaining still as a statue, Marcus kept his face impassive and struggled against his gnawing resentment. His pain was his own and deeply personal. He disliked being asked about it. "Do you think me incapable of separating my personal life from my professional one?"

Eldridge sighed and shook his head. "Very well. I won't pry."

"And you won't refuse me?"

"You are the best man I have. It was only your history that gave me pause, but if you are comfortable with it, I have no objections. However, I will grant her request for reassignment, if it comes to that."

Nodding, Marcus hid his relief. Elizabeth would never ask for another agent; her pride wouldn't permit it.

Eldridge began to tap his fingertips together. "The journal Lady Hawthorne received was addressed to her late husband and is written in code. If the book was involved in his death . . ." He paused. "Viscount Hawthorne was investigating Christopher St. John when he met his reward."

Marcus stilled at the name of the popular pirate. There was no criminal he longed to apprehend more than St. John, and his enmity was personal. St. John's attacks against Ashford Shipping were the impetus to his joining the agency. "If Lord Hawthorne kept a journal of his assignments and St. John were to acquire the information—bloody hell!" His gut tightened at the thought of the pirate anywhere near Elizabeth.

"Exactly," Eldridge agreed. "In fact, Lady Hawthorne has already been contacted about the book since it was brought to my attention just a sennight ago. For her safety and ours, it should be removed from her care immediately, but that's impossible at the moment. She was instructed to personally deliver the journal, hence the need for our protection."

"Of course."

Eldridge slid a folder across the desk. "Here is the information I've gathered so far. Lady Hawthorne will apprise you of the rest during the Moreland ball."

Collecting the particulars of the assignment, Marcus stood and took his leave. Once in the hallway, he allowed a grim smile of satisfaction to curve his lips.

He'd been only days away from seeking Elizabeth out. The end of her mourning meant his interminable waiting was over. Although the matter of the journal was disturbing, it worked to his advantage, making it impossible for her to avoid him. After the scandalous way she'd jilted him four years ago she would not be pleased with his new appearance in her life. But she wouldn't turn to Eldridge either, of that he was certain.

Soon, very soon, all that she had once promised and then denied him would finally be his.

Sylvia Day's Georgian series continues with *Passion for the Game*.

"If all angels of death were as lovely as you, men would line up to die."

Maria, Lady Winter, shut the lid of her enameled patch box with a decisive snap. Her revulsion for the mirrored reflection of the man who sat behind her made her stomach roil. Taking a deep breath, she kept her gaze trained on the stage below, but her attention was riveted by the incomparably handsome man who sat in the shadows of her theater box.

"Your turn will come," she murmured, maintaining her regal façade for the benefit of the many lorgnettes pointed in her direction. She had worn crimson silk tonight, accented by delicate black lace frothing from elbow-length sleeves. It was her most-worn color. Not because it suited her Spanish heritage coloring so well—dark hair, dark eyes, olive skin—but because it was a silent warning. *Bloodshed. Stay away.*

The Wintry Widow, the voyeurs whispered. *Two husbands dead . . . and counting.*

Angel of death. How true that was. Everyone around her died, except for the man she cursed to Hades.

The low chuckle at her shoulder made her skin crawl. "It will take more than you, my dearest daughter, to see me to my reward."

"Your reward will be my blade in your heart," she hissed.

"Ah, but then you will never be reunited with your sister, and she almost of age."

"Do not think to threaten me, Welton. Once Amelia is wed, I will know her location and will have no further need for your life. Consider that before you think to do to her what you have done to me."

"I could sell her into the slave trade," he drawled.

"You assume, incorrectly, that I did not anticipate your threat." Fluffing the lace at her elbow, she managed a slight curve to her lips to hide her terror. "I will know. And then you will die."

She felt him stiffen and her smile turned genuine. Ten and six was her age when Welton had ended her life. Anticipation for the day when she would pay him in kind was all that moved her when despair for her sister threatened paralysis.

"St. John."

The name hung suspended in the air between them.

Maria's breath caught. "Christopher St. John?"

It was rare that anything surprised her anymore. At the age of six and twenty, she believed she had seen and done nearly everything. "He has coin aplenty, but marriage to him will ruin me, making me less effective for your aims."

"Marriage is not necessary this time. I've not yet depleted Lord Winter's settlement. This is simply a search for information. I believe they are engaging St. John in some business. I want you to discover what it is they want with him, and most importantly, who arranged his release from prison."

Maria smoothed the bloodred material that pooled around her legs. Her two unfortunate husbands had been agents of the Crown whose jobs made them highly useful to her stepfather. They had also been peers of great wealth, much of which they left to her for Welton's disposal upon their untimely demise.

Lifting her head, she looked around the theater, absently noting the curling smoke of candles and gilded scrollwork that shone in firelight. The soprano on the stage struggled for attention, for no one was here to see her. The peerage was here to see each other and be seen, nothing more.

"Interesting," Maria murmured, recalling a sketch of the popular pirate. Uncommon handsome he was, and as deadly as she. His exploits were widely bandied, some tales so outrageous she knew they could not possibly be true. St. John was discussed with intemperate eagerness, and there were wagers aplenty on how long he could escape the noose.

"They must be desperate indeed to spare him. All these years they have searched for the irrefutable proof of his villainy, and now that they have it, they bring him into the fold. I daresay neither side is pleased."

"I do not care how they feel," Welton dismissed curtly. "I simply wish to know who I can extort to keep quiet about it."

"Such faith in my charms," she drawled, hiding how her mouth filled with bile. To think of the deeds she had been forced into to protect and serve a man she detested . . . Her chin lifted. It was not her stepfather she protected and served. She merely needed him alive, for if he were killed, she would never find Amelia.

Welton ignored her jibe. "Have you any notion what that information would be worth?"

She gave a nearly imperceptible nod, aware of the avid scrutiny that followed her every movement. Society knew her husbands had not died natural deaths. But they lacked proof. Despite this morbid certainty of her guilt, she was welcomed into the finest homes eagerly. She was infamous. And nothing livened up a gathering like a touch of infamy.

"How do I find him?"

"You have your ways."

Enjoy more of Sylvia Day's Georgian series with *Don't Tempt Me.*

Paris, France—1757

With her fingers curled desperately around the edge of the table before her, Marguerite Piccard writhed in the grip of unalloyed arousal. Gooseflesh spread up her arms and she bit her lower lip to stem the moan of pleasure that longed to escape.

"Do not restrain your cries," her lover urged hoarsely. "It makes me wild to hear them."

Her blue eyes, heavy-lidded with passion, lifted within the mirrored reflection before her and met the gaze of the man who moved at her back. The vanity in her boudoir rocked with the thrusts of his hips, his breathing rough as he made love to her where they stood.

The Marquis de Saint-Martin's infamously sensual lips curved with masculine satisfaction at the sight of her flushed dishevelment. His hands cupped her swaying breasts, urging her body to move in tandem with his.

They strained together, their skin coated with sweat, their chests heaving from their exertions. Her blood thrummed in her veins, the experience of her lover's passion such that she had forsaken everything—family, friends, and esteemed future—to be with him. She knew he loved her similarly. He proved it with every touch, every glance.

"How beautiful you are," he gasped, watching her through the mirror.

When she had suggested the location of their tryst with timid eagerness, he'd laughed with delight.

"I am at your service," he purred, shrugging out of his garments as he stalked her into the boudoir. There was a sultriness to his stride and a predatory gleam in his dark eyes that caused her to shiver in heated awareness. Sex was innate to him. He exuded it from every pore, enunciated it with every syllable, displayed it with every movement. And he excelled at it.

From the moment she first saw him at the Fontinescu ball nearly a year ago, she had been smitten with his golden handsomeness. His attire of ruby red silk had attracted every eye without effort, but Marguerite had attended the event with the express aim of seeing him in the flesh. Her older sisters had whispered scandalous tales of his liaisons, occasions when he had been caught in flagrant displays of seduction. He was wed; yet discarded lovers pined for him openly, weeping outside his home for a brief moment of his attention. Her curiosity about what sort of shell would encase such wickedness was too powerful to be denied.

Saint-Martin did not disappoint her. In the simplest of terms, she did not expect him to be so . . . *male*. Those who were given to the pursuit of vice and excess were rarely virile, as he most definitely was.

Never had she met a man more devastating to a woman's equanimity. The marquis was magnificent, his physical form impressive and his aloofness an irresistible lure. Golden-haired and skinned, as she was, he was desired by every woman in France for good reason. There was an air about him that promised pleasure unparalleled. The decadence and forbidden delights intimated within his slumberous gaze lured one to forget themselves. The marquis had lived twice Marguerite's eight and ten years, and he possessed a wife as lovely as he was comely. Neither fact mitigated Marguerite's immediate, intense attraction to him. Or his returning attraction to her.

"Your beauty has enslaved me," he whispered that first night. He stood near to where she waited on the edge of the dance floor, his lanky frame propped against the opposite side of a large column. "I must follow you or ache from the distance between us."

Marguerite kept her gaze straight ahead, but every nerve ending tingled from his boldness. Her breath was short, her skin hot. Although she could not see him, she felt the weight of his regard and it affected her to an alarming degree. "You know of women more beautiful than I," she retorted.

"No." His husky, lowered voice stilled her heartbeat. Then, made it race. "I do not."

Introduction

ANGUS CLEGHORN, BETHANY HICOK,
AND THOMAS TRAVISANO

Elizabeth Bishop has emerged as one of the most important and widely discussed American poets of the twentieth century. However, Bishop published comparatively little in her lifetime, and our image of her as a writer and as a person has undergone a sea change over the past several years due to the publication of three major new editions of her work. The first of these editions, appearing in 2006, was *Edgar Allan Poe & the Juke-Box: Uncollected Poems, Drafts, and Fragments,* edited by Alice Quinn, a book that generated no little excitement and controversy through its publication of almost one hundred Bishop poems that had remained in manuscript at her death. This was followed in the spring of 2008 by the Library of America's *Elizabeth Bishop: Poems, Prose, and Letters,* edited by Robert Giroux and Lloyd Schwartz. This extensive volume made available hundreds of pages of previously unpublished or long out-of-print writings by Bishop, including poems, letters, stories, book reviews, critical essays, juvenilia, and even book-jacket blurbs. A few months later, in the fall of 2008, came *Words in Air: The Complete Correspondence between Elizabeth Bishop and Robert Lowell,* edited by Thomas Travisano with Saskia Hamilton. This collection, which includes almost nine hundred pages of intimate and revealing letters between two major American poets, suggested insights into many aspects of Bishop's life and world. These new editions, arriving in such quick succession, have expanded Bishop's published oeuvre by more than one thousand pages and have placed before the reading public a "new" Elizabeth Bishop whose complex dimensions were previously familiar only to a small circle of scholars and devoted readers. In February 2011, in time for the centennial of Bishop's birth, three further editions of Bishop's writing appeared from Farrar, Straus and Giroux: the succinctly titled pairing *Poems* and *Prose* (the latter edited by Lloyd Schwartz), and *Elizabeth Bishop and the "New Yorker,"* edited by Joelle Biele. These volumes demonstrated yet again the continuing interest in Bishop's steadily expanding body of published work.

When *Edgar Allan Poe & the Juke-Box* was first published in 2006, some readers and scholars, most notably Helen Vendler in an often-cited review in the *New Republic,* questioned the ethics of bringing into print the unpublished poetry of a deceased author. While, for some, a greatly enlarged understanding of the poet, of her work, and of her world is sufficient justification for this posthumous publication, others may prefer to defer to Elizabeth Bishop's perceived intentions, believing that her fastidious approach to editing her poems would be reason enough to keep the "discards" boxed up.

This book's essays demonstrate that many forces were at work that may have blocked or hindered the completion or publication of various Bishop poems: issues that might be textual, sexual, psychological, cultural, political, or social. The status of "a minor female Wordsworth" (*WIA* 122)—her own self-description to Robert Lowell—would be an easier reputation for Bishop to live with than would be, for example, that of a revolutionary lesbian poet. However, new information has materialized from Bishop's will indicating that she entrusted to others key decisions about the handling of her posthumous material. In his essay, Lloyd Schwartz notes that in her will Bishop gives her literary executors (her partner Alice Methfessel and the poet Frank Bidart) the "power to determine whether any of my unpublished manuscripts and papers shall be published and, if so, to see them through the press, and with power generally to administer my literary property." By extension, one could argue that the whole "Elizabeth Bishop Phenomenon," including the three volumes discussed here, is enabled by this provision of her will. In fact, the will's terms suggest that Bishop was by no means unwilling to have her unpublished papers see print and in fact seems to have anticipated that publication.

Perhaps readers who hold dear the traditional image of the author with a small, select, and carefully chosen oeuvre, and who reject the emergent posthumous one, may concede that in so constructing her will, Bishop might have been "the author, in a sense, of her own undoing," as Christina Pugh hints in this volume's concluding essay. In any case, the consistent support by executors Methfessel and Bidart for publishing Bishop's posthumous materials in essays, books, and periodicals in the decades leading up to the publication of *Edgar Allan Poe & the Juke-Box,* was sanctioned (and perhaps encouraged) by the author, who admitted to Robert Lowell in 1957: "But it is hell to realize that one has wasted half one's talent through timidity" (*WIA* 247), a remark noted by Richard Flynn in his essay for this volume. Bishop's work embodied a struggle of speech against silence, and this difficult articulation can be read throughout her traditional oeuvre through a predilection for the use of coded language, as well as through her lifelong tendency to suppress, or to leave uncompleted or unpublished, some of her most provocative and compelling writings.

This collection of critical essays on Bishop, *Elizabeth Bishop in the Twenty-First Century: Reading the New Editions,* features seventeen essays written by many of the leading—and several of the rising—figures in the field of Bishop studies, which explore a complex and interrelated series of issues that may be textual, bibliographical, political, critical, biographical, psychosexual, cultural, or literary historical. Through its multiplicity of informed perspectives, the volume aims to provide a timely, in-depth, and multifaceted exploration of the impact of these three major new editions on our understanding of Bishop as a writer, a person, and a cultural icon.

The essays are divided into four parts, reflecting an evolving and deepening response to the new Bishop. Part 1, "Textual Politics: Looking into the New Elizabeth Bishop," groups four essays that analyze how the controversial volume *Edgar Allan Poe & the Juke-Box* revises Bishop's canon in ways we cannot ignore. When an author's published work suddenly doubles in volume, as it has with Bishop twenty years after her death, that event prompts the key questions taken up in this first section. For example, in the lead essay, Jonathan Ellis asks: What are the aesthetics and ethics of Quinn's editorial decisions, and do Quinn's choices make her more of a coauthor than a mere editor? Moreover, asks Jeffrey Gray, on what criteria does Quinn base her decisions for the inclusion and exclusion of certain poems, and did she sometimes make unfortunate decisions as she chose to publish particular drafts? Gray suggests that some of Quinn's editorial choices regarding certain poems tend to obscure key thematic points or important aspects of Bishop's aesthetics. Helen Vendler was horrified by Quinn's volume and said so in a widely discussed review that appeared in the *New Republic.* According to Vendler, the poems, drafts, and fragments collected in Quinn's volume were the "maimed and stunted siblings" of the poems of Bishop's *Complete Poems.* But are they? Charles Berger argues here that some of these efforts were finished or nearly finished poems, featuring, to take just one example, a group of elegies that revise the tradition in such a way that they could be counted among the best of the twentieth century. Why did Bishop choose not to publish them? Was she saving them for a later volume? In some cases, her decision not to publish this or that poem may have had more to do with sexual politics at midcentury, a cultural climate that might have censured the more overtly sexual lyric poetry written by a lesbian poet. Or, at the very least, argues Lloyd Schwartz, that climate would have marginalized Bishop, who was then enjoying the status of a Pulitzer Prize–winning poet with a first-read contract with the distinguished but aesthetically conservative *New Yorker.* Schwartz suggests that Bishop's poetry can now be received in a different critical climate that welcomes her finished love poems to women as part of a more "complete" and inclusive oeuvre. Ultimately, as Ellis contends, this new body of work invites us to let go of the famous perfectionist that has dominated readings of Bishop and introduces us to new ways of reading her into the twenty-first century.

From "The Map" onward, it is clear that, for Bishop, geography is a prime determinant of knowledge. The two opening essays in part 2, "Crossing Continents: Self, Politics, Place," examine Bishop's travels from Europe to Florida—with stops in New York and Nova Scotia. The final three essays find her settling into a complex relationship with Brazil. While the poet's journeys are well known, these essays introduce readers to aspects of Bishop that were largely hidden from the public until the publication of Alice Quinn's *Edgar Allan Poe & the Juke-Box* and the subsequent twenty-first-century editions. These essays, which focus on Bishop's engagement with various points of rest in her long succession of travels, show how "different points of the compass" (*WIA* 540) affect her psychological, sexual, and political orientations together with her evolving poetics. Angus Cleghorn's essay investigates "Bone Key," a volume Bishop toyed with publishing during her years in Florida. Its poems speak directly to her erotic awakening in Florida and its continuity in Brazil. Cleghorn argues that "Bone Key" shows that Bishop's move to Florida prompted her to write less emotionally evasive and more frankly erotic poems—even if these poems remained unpublished. Heather Treseler sees Bishop's therapy and letter writing as contributing to these tropes in the unpublished poems, which offer a new psychic grammar through imagery that extends into well-known canonical poems that we can now better understand.

In Brazil, as Barbara Page and Carmen L. Oliveira suggest, Bishop matures into the ever-searching poet engaged with the politics of her lover, the architect Lota de Macedo Soares, while remaining fascinated with her position as an alien observer in a strange land who is nonetheless an observer blessed with an insider's vantage point into many aspects of Brazil's people and their politics, language, and culture. Lorrie Goldensohn, who considers Brazilian drafts that show "that sense of constant readjustment" Bishop found necessary for intense engagement there, argues that Bishop's eighteen years in Brazil offer a necessary distance from her roots, a distance that made it possible for her cathartically to reconstruct her past self in her work. In this section's final essay, Bethany Hicok traces Bishop's evolving response to Brazilian political challenges, particularly its urban poverty and the threatened lands and peoples of its interior, revealing a poet who was much more directly engaged in Brazilian politics than has previously been thought and who struggled to write this experience and find a poetic strategy that would constitute an effective form of protest. What our essayists read here is like a subterranean poetics and politics that alter the previously accepted master narrative of Bishop's life and poetry.

Part 3, "New Correspondences: The Poet with Her Peers," brings together essays on four of Bishop's most important colleagues in various fields of artistic endeavor: the sculptor Alexander Calder, the poets Ezra Pound and Robert Lowell, and the novelist and short-story writer Flannery O'Connor. Bishop was once considered to be a comparatively isolated figure, but each of these four essays, drawing on the prose, poems, and letters newly available in the twenty-first-century editions, makes clear the depth and intricacy of her relationships with figures of great cultural importance. Each essay shows how Bishop's relationship with one of these figures serves to reveal an aspect of Bishop's cultural engagement while providing insight into the way her artistic principles and poetic output evolved in dialogue with them. Peggy Samuels notes Calder's often-stated emphasis on such qualities as tentativeness and hesitation, spontaneity, playfulness, humor, buoyancy, and a sense of private celebration, and she shows how these characteristics found similar expression in Bishop's poetry. Samuels argues that Calder's experiments with what he termed "composing motions" helped Bishop to discover and develop the unique tempo and pacing of her own poetic lines and that her assimilation of the uniquely three-dimensional quality of Calder's art helped her to shape on the page a style that set her apart as a poet who managed to be subtly yet deeply experimental and at the same time spontaneous and completely natural. Francesco Rognoni explores Bishop's complex and ambivalent relationship with Ezra Pound. During her term as poetry consultant to the Library of Congress from 1949 to 1950, Bishop frequently visited Pound in St. Elizabeths Hospital, where he was being held on charges of treason for his radio broadcasts in support of Mussolini during World War II. In his study of Bishop's uneasy attitudes toward Pound, Rognoni brings together a wide range of sources, including in particular her dialogue with Robert Lowell (a close friend of Pound's) in *Words in Air*. And he shows how Bishop's evolving and conflicted response toward Pound slowly achieved crystallization in her remarkable 1957 "Visits to St. Elizabeths."

George S. Lensing's essay studies the many points of meeting between Bishop, a spiritually engaged religious skeptic, and her friend Flannery O'Connor, a devout yet searchingly inquisitive Roman Catholic. Lensing argues that—despite the inherent differences between verse and prose—Bishop's and O'Connor's literary styles are often uncannily similar. Lensing suggests further that through their keen observation of the cultural and spiritual incongruities of Bishop's adopted Brazil and O'Connor's lifelong home in the American South, each writer found the means to embody a kind of sacramental efficacy in the complex and problematic symbolic epiphanies that conclude their most compelling works. In the final essay of part 3, Richard Flynn looks closely at Bishop's relationship with Lowell as revealed in *Words in Air,* while drawing as well on the extensive representation of her juvenilia in the Library of America volume. Flynn argues that Bishop's mid-century aesthetic evolved in direct dialogue with Lowell through their lifelong colloquy over their troubled childhood experience and their parallel colloquy on the art of representing observation and feeling in verse. Through this dialogue, Flynn contends, each poet was able to find a style that avoided both blandness and sentimental excess, and each was thus able to create a body of autobiographical poetry that was self-exploratory without being confessional.

Our writers for part 4, "The New Elizabeth Bishop and Her Art," encourage us to look toward the future as we reconsider and revise our readings of Bishop in the years to come. What questions do we need to consider as we move forward? What possible new directions might Bishop studies take? As we see all this new material laid out before us, it is impossible not to speculate about the possible directions Bishop's career might have taken and what volumes might have emerged, or so Thomas Travisano suggests in his uniquely outlined "speculative bibliography," in which he sketches out a potential final book of Bishop's poems, a notional volume he calls *Geography IV.* Pulling together Bishop's poetry published after her last book, *Geography III* (1976), as well as the new material in Quinn's book and the Library of America edition, Travisano posits a volume wherein Bishop deepens the "powerfully introspective" cast of *Geography III* and further hones her social critique as she had developed it in later poems. Jacqueline Vaught Brogan, drawing on letters and drafts, shows how Bishop's subversion of conventional poetic form develops in several sestinas that Bishop wrote at different stages of her career. Brogan argues that the new editions deepen our understanding of Bishop as not only a consummate poet of her craft, but also one who was deeply engaged in the social, political, and cultural issues of her day. In turn, Gillian White sees enormous potential in the Lowell and Bishop correspondence for reading Bishop's poetry in new ways, specifically through the strong critique that Bishop launched against the United States in her letters to Lowell during the Brazil years. Finally, in a provocative comparative essay that ends our new volume, Christina Pugh offers a cautionary tale to Bishop's future readers, based on the case of Emily Dickinson scholarship. Variorum editions and facsimile reproductions of Dickinson's work have led some prominent readers to redomesticate Dickinson as a "woman poet" and thereby undermine some of the power of her lyric voice. Bishop, presented in facsimile form in the new editions, could experience the same fate. Pugh warns, too, that all the attention on Bishop's "life" in her drafts and letters, rather than on the completed work, may also lead us to rely too heavily on biography.

The essays brought together in this collection make clear that while Bishop is rightly valued for the few dozen exquisitely crafted lyric poems that she published in her lifetime, she was also a superb prose writer and an extraordinarily brilliant letter writer who maintained an active and prolific, if somewhat disorderly, writer's workshop out of which lively and revealing pages in many genres steadily poured, only a small percentage of which actually found their way into print before she died. Our essayists observe Bishop through a variety of lenses and read her poems, prose, and letters in a range of different ways. But taken together these essays suggest that Bishop was not only a poet of audacious yet masterly skills, and of considerable, if often latent, emotional power, but also a poet crucially engaged with such vital cultural and political issues as outsiderhood, gender, sexuality, national identity, social class, war, the environment, power relations, and family intimacy and conflict. The new editions also allow us to see more clearly Bishop's role as a deeply influential poet and as a cultural figure who was engaged in significant dialogue with an extraordinary spectrum of important writers, artists, and composers of many nations. Moreover, the new editions invite one to observe with surprising clarity the deep ambivalence and reluctance with which Bishop confronted the public role of "major poet" in midcentury American society. This was a role her talent may have entitled her to claim, but it was also a role from which she always shied away, her refusal in part revealed through her decisions about which poems to publish and which to suppress. In her unpublished poems, letters, and essays, as well as in the margins of her greatest published poems, we see the outlines of the public poet who might have been, a poet Bishop was never quite willing to become. In her correspondence with Robert Lowell, we see the price Lowell had to pay for assuming that public role even as we see the price that Bishop had to pay for refusing it. The essays in this collection, for all their diversity of subject, method, and opinion, push toward the conclusion that whatever one may think of the decisions made by editors and publishers in placing these new writings before the public, it is hard to dispute that in their various ways the appearance of this new body of work in many genres leads one toward a deeper and more complex understanding of Bishop's relationship to her art and to her world.

Textual Politics
Looking into the New Elizabeth Bishop

Alice in Wonderland

The Authoring and Editing of Elizabeth Bishop's Uncollected Poems

JONATHAN ELLIS

Edgar Allan Poe & the Juke-Box, edited by Alice Quinn, was marketed as a new book of poems by Elizabeth Bishop, or at least as a new book of "Uncollected Poems, Drafts, and Fragments." The book's subtitle was the first thing to attract Helen Vendler's scorn in her infamous *New Republic* review of the book: "This book should not have been issued with its present subtitle of 'Uncollected Poems, Drafts, and Fragments.' It should have been called 'Repudiated Poems.'... Students eagerly wanting to buy 'the new book by Elizabeth Bishop' should be told to go back and buy the old one, where the poet represents herself as she wished to be known. The eighty-odd poems that this famous perfectionist allowed to be printed over the years are 'Elizabeth Bishop' as a poet. This book is not" (33). Before assessing the merits of Vendler's criticisms of *Edgar Allan Poe,* it is worth remembering that Bishop could be guilty of misleading titles too. Her 1969 volume *The Complete Poems,* for example, was anything but "complete" since it left out all kinds of poems later to find a home in the "Uncollected" and "Poems Written in Youth" sections of the 1983 *Complete Poems: 1927–1979.*[1] As Charles Berger points out: "Now that we can easily see the other choices she might have made, as opposed to the comparatively lackluster poems that she included to round out the [1969] volume, it becomes all the more interesting to think about what message she intended to send about the shape of her oeuvre and her career. Was she saving better drafts for a later volume?" (4).

Bishop was always about to complete a new poem or story. One of the unfinished poems in *Edgar Allan Poe* is actually titled "Something I'd Meant to Write About for 30 Years." In 1957, for example, she told Robert Lowell about a poem she was working on called "Letter to Two Friends": "It began on a rainy day and since it has done nothing but rain since we've been back I took it up again and this time shall try to get it done. It is rather light, though. Oh heavens, when does one begin to write the *real* poems?" (*OA* 348). At the point of writing this letter,

Bishop had published two collections of poetry, the second of which had won the Pulitzer Prize. Yet even with this much "real" writing complete, she was still unsure whether she was a poet. Here is the opening section of "Letter to Two Friends":

> Heavens! It's raining again
> and the "view"
> is now two weeks overdue
> and the road is impassable
> and after shaking all four paws
> the cat retires in disgust
> to the highest closet shelf,
> and the dogs smell awfully like dogs,
> and I'm slightly sick of myself,
> and sometime during the night
> the poem I was trying to write
> has turned into prepositions:
> ins and aboves and upons
> [overs and unders and ups]—
>
> what am I trying to do?
> Change places in a canoe?
>   method of composition— (EAP 113)

The poem is remarkably similar to the letter, from the general complaints about rain and writing to her exclamation to the "Heavens!," "Letter to Two Friends," like Sylvia Plath's 1958 poem "Poems, Potatoes," is a great poem about not being able to write poetry. In Plath's case, the problem is caused by a gap between the imagined poem, which is "knobbly" and real, and the finished poem, in which words muzzle and murder the original idea (*CP* 106). Bishop's dilemma is both less philosophical—she always knows that poems are part unreal—and more practical. The poem she is "trying to write / has turned into prepositions: / ins and aboves and upons." It reads more like a letter. Reading *Edgar Allan Poe,* not just alongside *The Complete Poems* but also alongside *One Art: Letters* and *Words in Air: The Complete Correspondence between Elizabeth Bishop and Robert Lowell,* reveals how closely Bishop composed letters and poems and perhaps also how this closeness could sometimes mar her poetic gifts. The second stanza depicts the activity of changing genres (and perhaps changing her "method of composition") as akin to switching "places in a canoe." There is a lovely unwritten pun here that Bishop surely implies even if she never writes it down. If you attempt to change places in a canoe you are liable to tip the canoe and end up in the water. By trying to begin a poem like a letter she can muddy the poetic process. The "ins and aboves and upons" that are necessary to help narrative function successfully may affect the flow of a poem. In attempting to write a poem like a letter, therefore, Bishop is able to change artistic perspective, but, like changing places in a canoe, this switch involves a substantial risk, if not to her own body, then certainly to the body of her poetry.

Bishop's canoe analogy also fits in with her general habit of depicting travel as an activity that destabilizes and unsettles human identity. In her early poem about a great-uncle's "Large Bad Painting," for example, the speaker concludes her analysis of the painting still unsure what brought the ships there, "commerce or contemplation" (CP 12). In "Arrival at Santos," another boat trip leaves the speaker craving "bourbon and cigarettes" (CP 90). In her masterpiece "Questions of Travel," a foreign landscape contains too much to take in at first glance, leaving the speaker disoriented, as if observing the world "in soft slow-motion" (CP 93). In a typical Bishop inversion, the mountains "look like the hulls of capsized ships, / slime-hung and barnacled" (CP 93). The traveler who comes to see the other side of the world literally sees that world as if it were underwater or upside down. Everything foreign is blurred and out of focus, or perhaps too clear and too precise. The point is that the traveler never *sees* things as those at home see them. They are always objects of potential memory ready to be photographed or recorded in a notebook, never simply things with which one lives. The canoe about to tip in the unpublished poem can thus be seen as part of a sequence of poems in which Bishop depicted travel as an experience akin to being flooded, shipwrecked, or submerged underwater, an experience that obviously might lead to death and certainly to a reevaluation of selfhood. Changing places in a tipping canoe attests to the perhaps impossible task of seeing Brazil, or indeed anywhere, as if one lived there permanently and were not continually blinded by "barnacled" eyes.

To return to Berger's original question in relation to the 1969 *Complete Poems*— "Was she saving better drafts for a later volume?" Perhaps Bishop was always saving drafts for later, never-to-be-finished volumes. In addition to this, as *Edgar Allan Poe* demonstrates, she frequently saved other kinds of writing, such as letters, that might in time have shed enough prepositions to become poems. In fact, I wonder whether Bishop ever considered any poem or poetic statement complete. As numerous critics have observed, her poems never really conclude, particularly not about the relationship of the self to the world. Nevertheless, her nonconclusions do bring her poems to an end. In "The Bight," for example, Bishop depicts a world of "untidy activity" continuing well after the poem has finished, "awful but cheerful" (*CP* 61). The speaker's messy life remains as unruly as the seascape in view of her desk. Yet she can and does impose order on the poem. "Awful but cheerful" is tonally ambiguous but poetically right. It completes the poem even as it leaves the poem and perhaps the reader feeling at sea. How can we survive living in a world "awful but cheerful"? Bishop does not answer these questions. As Gary Fountain points out, "One wonders in what place, in what nation, might the authentic self, a real but not hidden Elizabeth Bishop, reside comfortably?" ("Maple Leaf" 293). Fountain is referring to Bishop's feeling of being at home both in and on the border between various Atlantic nations and regions, including Brazil, New England, and Nova Scotia, but one might equally apply this notion of her multiplying and at times contradictory identities to the books that have been published by her or in her name. Where is Bishop's body of work most at home: in individual collections of poetry she cleared for publication or in the different *Complete Poems* prepared by others?

Vendler asserts that the 1983 *Complete Poems* remains the book by Elizabeth Bishop that students should be told to buy and also the book "where the poet represents herself as she wished to be known." This is not strictly true. As the "Publisher's Note" to the 1983 *Complete Poems* makes clear, Bishop did not in fact authorize all of its contents:

> She would not have reprinted the seventeen poems written in her youth; she was too severe a critic of her own work. . . . She never reprinted "Exchanging Hats," a poem that belongs among her best. . . . The background of "Pleasure Seas," which appears here for the first time, is odd. Written in 1939, it was accepted by *Harper's Bazaar* but never printed; the sole surviving copy was found among her papers. In the group of occasional poems, there are four which she enclosed in letters to Marianne Moore in the mid-thirties. (xi)

Robert Giroux and other scholars presumably spent time at Vassar College looking through Bishop's letters and papers to locate these poems. Given the amount of new material in *Edgar Allan Poe,* itself a selection of 3,500 pages of Bishop's writing now held at Vassar, one can see why a proper assessment of the drafts and notebooks was not possible in the early 1980s. Bishop's estate must have thought it best to publish a *Complete Poems* as quickly as possible to maintain and strengthen her reputation. This volume led to important reassessments of her writing by poets like Eavan Boland, Seamus Heaney, Tom Paulin, and Adrienne Rich, not to mention critical essays by scholars like Vendler herself. But it is only a version of Bishop's *Complete Poems,* not the definitive one. The 1983 *Complete Poems* does not even reproduce the individual volumes of poetry as Bishop intended. *Questions of Travel* (1965), for example, was originally published with the short story "In the Village," but not here. *Geography III* (1976) also included Bishop's translation of Octavio Paz's poem "Objects & Apparitions," but *The Complete Poems* exiles it to a section titled "Translations" at the very back of the book. While *Edgar Allan Poe* may be the most obvious example of Bishop's wishes being ignored, it is thus not the first or only occasion of this happening.

Vendler's reference to Bishop as a "famous perfectionist" is not above criticism either. This idea took hold long ago and is now present in nearly every critical assessment of her work. For Adam Kirsch, her "insistence on perfection . . . makes Elizabeth Bishop not just a cherishable poet, but an exemplary one" (4). Gillian White thinks "perfectionism" to be "synonymous with her name" (8). But what does it mean to be a perfectionist, and do perfectionist poets, even ones as good as Bishop, always get it right?

Bishop is perhaps not always the best judge of her poetry. This is not the easiest thing to write. It is perhaps one of the last taboos among Bishop critics. In fact, most reviewers of *Edgar Allan Poe* begin by asserting the exact opposite. According to Charles Simic: "Unlike just about every other poet whose collected poems are bound to contain embarrassments, she never published a bad poem" (17). I do not believe this is true. I think critics ignore poems like "Wading at Wellfleet," "Varick Street," "Twelfth Morning; or What You Will," and "Night City," to give an example from each of the main four collections, because they appear imperfect in comparison with poems like "Roosters," "At the Fishhouses," "Sestina," and "One Art." For me, Bishop's poetry is complex and varied enough not to need perfection as its defining feature. In fact, I think comparing *Edgar Allan Poe* and *The Complete Poems* reveals how often Bishop kept back some remarkably innovative writing. Put simply, she did not always publish her best or most finished poems as has previously been assumed. Sometimes she kept such poems to herself. To give a few random examples, *North & South* (1946) would certainly have been enriched by the inclusion of the surrealist poem written in Spain, "In a Room," its treatment of love less negative had the literary climate and her own temperament permitted her to publish "It is marvellous to wake up together." *A Cold Spring* (1955), arguably Bishop's weakest collection, would also have benefited from the publication of some of the Key West poems as I have argued elsewhere ("Elizabeth Bishop's Bone Key Poems" 37–40).

Bishop was not alone in refusing to publish poems that now seem unarguably part, not just of her oeuvre, but of the twentieth-century poetic canon. As Alice Quinn's notes to *Edgar Allan Poe* show, poetry editors were just as culpable

(Quinn's own magazine, the *New Yorker,* rejected several stunning poems) and may even have strengthened Bishop's self-imposed ban on certain subjects for poetry. She appeared particularly vulnerable to adverse criticism at the beginning of her career in the late 1930s and the 1940s. The central section of *Edgar Allan Poe* covers little more than a decade of Bishop's writing life (1937–50) but almost one-third of the poetry collected here. As a general rule, Quinn appears to let very good poems speak for themselves without much or sometimes any editorial comment. The beautiful love poem "Close close all night," recently anthologized by James Fenton, is dated to the 1960s with a note on its origins as a wedding gift to a friend, but with little further critical commentary. "For Grandfather" and "A mother made of dress-goods" are equally important poems in regard to Bishop's Nova Scotian childhood, in particular her relationships with her maternal relatives, but again Quinn keeps her editorial notes to a minimum. Fragmentary drafts or slight poems, on the other hand, are normally supported by at least two or three pages of elaborate explanation. Quinn implicitly acknowledges that the former group can make their own way in the world; the latter require some apology and assistance. "Key West," "The Soldier and the Slot-Machine," "The walls went on for years & years . . ." and "In the golden early morning . . ." are some of the most intriguing drafts in the book but the notes provide very little information on them. "The walls went on for years & years," for instance, looks like a good first draft of a poem in the main section of the book, although the notes reveal that it is actually only a selection from "thirteen pages of closely related drafts" with "not one word . . . crossed out" (*EAP* 281). Quinn admits to having "no idea where the poem as represented fits on the spectrum of drafted material" (281). She could at least indicate why these lines have been chosen above others. My own transcription of the drafts suggests that they are not necessarily the most accomplished. As Frances Dickey points out in relation to Quinn's annotations to the poem "Villanelle," her notes are both "indispensable as context for the poems" while at the same time giving "one the sense of being at the editor's mercy: what did the next page after this poem in the notebook look like?" (81). If the aim of a book like this is to give readers an insight into the composition process—the unedited stage in a poem's creation—why edit out evidence of the poet's method of composition?

This brings me to what I think is one of the most important yet unacknowledged elements of *Edgar Allan Poe,* the presence not of Elizabeth Bishop but of Alice Quinn. Quinn is best known as poetry editor of the *New Yorker* (Paul Muldoon replaced her in 2007) and as executive director of the Poetry Society of America. I believe that in years to come she will be as known, if not better known, as the editor of this book. Quinn worked on *Edgar Allan Poe* for more than a decade, and she was also involved in editing and selecting material for other Bishop publications, including *One Art*. According to the acknowledgments at the back of the book, Robert Giroux first had the idea of asking Quinn "to assemble" the collection (*EAP* 365). Quinn in turn thanks William Logan for "preparing a manuscript" (365), various Bishop scholars for helping her date and describe the poems, and a number of archivists and librarians for guiding her through Bishop's papers. In the main notes, she also thanks many of Bishop's friends for safeguarding and in one case transcribing drafts and poems that do not exist elsewhere.

Quinn's language is like that of a curator introducing an exhibition of paintings or sculptures rather than an editor of a book. She has even commented elsewhere on the book's "miscellaneous quality" ("Interviewed" 78). Quinn implies that she is no more than an arranger of preexisting works of art, an assumption several critics and reviewers of the book, most famously Vendler, have disputed. What Vendler takes most issue with, of course, is the idea of these poems as either collectable or finished. She disagrees in principle with the very idea of publishing any new work by Bishop. There are, in her opinion, only one or two "poems worthy of anthologizing" (36). Vendler's extremely evaluative judgment of the book is motivated by a rather possessive sense of Bishop's reputation. One can argue all day about whether one poem is better than another. I have already had a mischievous go myself. This is surely one of the achievements of Quinn's edition, whether one agrees with her editorial decisions or not. In fact, I would argue that Quinn's own writing in this book, specifically the notes that accompany and frame almost every poem and form approximately a third of the book, are just as important as Bishop's writing. It is my contention that Quinn is more than simply the curator of Bishop's uncollected poems. In providing so much of the published text, she is at least the book's coauthor, the ghost writer by whom one cannot help being guided as we flick between Bishop's drafts and Quinn's explanations. Indeed, Quinn's notes are so expansive one wonders whether this part of the book might be another biography of Bishop's life in disguise or at least a miniature life study. Put another way, perhaps *Edgar Allan Poe* is misleading not so much in its title or subtitle, but in its attribution of authorship mainly to Elizabeth Bishop.

Quinn's prose provides a tantalizing glimpse of a second biography of Bishop, the first being Brett Millier's in 1993. It could be read as a narrative on its own terms, although this would be difficult without the poems. As Carol Rumens observed in her review of *Edgar Allan Poe:* "Quinn has actually written us a poem-led literary biography, modestly disguised as end-notes" (18). This is not necessarily a bad thing. There is something more than a little reminiscent of Paul Muldoon's recent book of criticism *The End of the Poem* (2006) about many of Quinn's flights of fancy. As poetry editor of the *New Yorker,* Quinn obviously helped introduce Muldoon's poetry to American readers. They clearly come from the same critical school of imaginative association. A word or phrase in one of Bishop's poems sends Quinn spinning through the archives to record every other mention of the same word or phrase in letters, poems, and notebooks. Some of her connections are convincing; others appear whimsical. All of them make the reader think. Quinn is particularly astute at contextualizing Bishop's prose writings, the majority of which remain tantalizingly hidden in handwritten notebooks. Bishop, like Coleridge, is a master at pithy prose statements, not just on other poets and writers (though there are many good examples of this) but also on art criticism, history, philosophy, and politics. Bishop scholars know much of this material by heart, but why should they be the only readers of it? Although Quinn can only give us a sample of Bishop's notebooks, travel journals, and unpublished letters, for a book aimed at a mainstream audience we are fortunate to be given so much. When these prose writings are fully available, they might have as big an impact on Bishop's reputation as her unpublished poems. Vassar College is housing the twentieth-century equivalent of Coleridge's *Table Talk* or Emerson's notebooks.

Quinn's choice of prose is motivated by her stated aim of allowing readers to make their own links between "both the finished and the unfinished poems" (*EAP* xv). Her model was the early editions of Emily Dickinson's poetry, which, in spite of their many flaws, helped create an audience for the work. Like many Bishop critics, Quinn defends a reading of Bishop's *Complete Poems* as "perfect" and the rest of her oeuvre as implicitly flawed. As she explained in an interview: "I felt I couldn't present these unfinished things without any context. I felt her reputation had so much to do with her own discrimination, and the fact that we had seen only perfect poems" ("Interviewed" 78). Quinn's image of *Edgar Allan Poe* as a book of "unfinished things" is thus not that different from Vendler's subtitling it "Repudiated Poems." Both statements depend on an assumption that "we had only seen perfect poems" prior to the publication of the new book. Quinn's clear anxiety about the artistic merits of many of Bishop's poems in *Edgar Allan Poe* is one of the untold stories of the volume's commissioning and publication. In lectures and public talks to promote the book, she often admitted to feeling nervous about leaving the poems on what she saw as "a clothesline" without context. The book's notes became important to her as a way of connecting the "unfinished things" to the published work, thus preventing the "imperfect" work being hung out to dry.

Although Quinn's notes take various forms, they tend to peg Bishop's writing to biographical rather than artistic origins. There are times when such biographical detail is relevant and illuminates the draft in question. But there are just as many examples of this not being the case. In Quinn's notes on "In a cheap hotel," for example, she manages to shoehorn in the following reference to an early lover's suicide: "The poet Elizabeth Spires, who interviewed Bishop for *The Vassar Quarterly* in 1979—an interview that was later expanded and published in *The Paris Review*—conveyed to me her sense that the line 'love chains me to the bed and he berates me' may reflect something of Bishop's abiding guilt over the suicide of Robert Seaver, the young man she dated in college" (*EAP* 290–91). Quinn's discomfort at bringing this information to bear on the poem may be apparent in her attribution of the link to Elizabeth Spires. "I have not brought up this guilty secret," she appears to say, "she told me." At moments like this, Quinn is no longer recognizable as the poetry editor of the *New Yorker*. I cannot help but sense an element of jealousy in such leaking of irrelevant biographical experiences. Stephen Yenser registers precisely these emotions in his review of *Edgar Allan Poe:* "If the editor's devotion to the poet is one reason for the existence of this book, the other must be her own aspiration" (186). To return to Quinn's analogy of the unfinished poem as a garment on a clothesline, continually in danger of flying away, her default response when faced by a poem that confuses her appears always to be to reintroduce the poet's dirty laundry. Sensational facts bring mysterious poems down to earth, but this may not help either Bishop's reputation or the reader's understanding.

Instances of Quinn's tactlessness are so numerous it is difficult to know where to begin. In *Life and the Memory of It,* Brett Millier employs a pseudonym to protect the identity of the young woman with whom Bishop lived in San Francisco, a practice that in the last fifteen or so years has become an informal convention among Bishop scholars. Quinn breaks it the moment she cites from an unpublished letter, casually publishing the woman's real first name (*EAP* 340). In another note, this time on "I had a bad dream," a further emotional secret is produced to entertain the reader: "This is a terribly prescient poem when one considers the death of Bishop's companion of fifteen years, Lota de Macedo Soares, who died after lingering in a coma for five days after taking an overdose of pills while visiting Bishop in New York in September 1967" (*EAP* 287). The poem this note accompanies was written in the 1940s, probably before Bishop had met Lota and certainly before she had fallen in love with her. In other words, while the poem may seem "prescient" to certain readers aware of the tragic circumstances of Lota's death, interpretations of this sort do not provide us with any of the artistic, historical, or personal contexts necessary to interpret Bishop's writing in the 1940s.

The strengths and weaknesses of Quinn's biographically inflected approach are particularly to the fore in her notes to Bishop's attempted elegy for Lota, "Aubade and Elegy," probably written in 1970. Quinn provides a facsimile of the poem in the main part of the book but exiles the equally fascinating notes for it to the appendix. The separation of draft from notes implies that the former is more finished and ready to be seen and the latter more sketchy and private. But this is not the case. The draft poem is painfully repetitive and short; the notes more developed and formal. Quinn has chosen the first draft as if it were the last and placed the more polished writing out of sight when surely it would have made more sense to present all of the drafts in one sequence as she does with "One Art." This is not to say that the first draft is not significant on its own, although Quinn never really engages with the form of the poem or, oddly enough, given her usual emphasis on the relationship between art and life, its deep connection to Bishop's actual memories of finding Lota's body. Instead, she employs the notes to correct her on dates—"Bishop mistakenly believed Soares arrived in New York on September 17 rather than the nineteenth" (*EAP* 342)—before providing a melodramatic two-page summary of the rise and fall of Bishop and Lota's relationship. Quinn's notes continually concentrate on the most sensational sections of Bishop's biography. She gives no space or time to the mundane moments that give these significant episodes context and poignancy. Nothing in the drafts is ever allowed to be half-true or even fictional.

Ironically enough, when a biographical reading is appropriate, the editor neglects to provide it. The draft of "Aubade and Elegy" included in the main section is perhaps one of the most autobiographical pieces of writing in the book, but Quinn gives us only a general outline of where the poem was probably composed (in Bishop's home in Ouro Prêto). Bishop continues to type out the same phrase, "No coffee can wake you," as if still reexperiencing "the black wave" of Lota's death (*EAP* 149). Bishop described the experience of finding Lota's unconscious body in several letters to friends. This is Bishop's longest account of what happened in a letter to U. T. and Joseph Summers while Lota was still in a coma in New York: "Well—sometime toward dawn she got up and tried to commit suicide—I heard her up in the kitchen about 6:30—she was already almost unconscious. I thought she had taken Nembutal since she had a bottle of it in her hand—but later blood tests showed only Valium, I think. I'll not go into details except that within about 20 minutes—I don't think it was much longer than that—we had her in the ambulance and off to St. Vincent's—and they were giving her oxygen on the way there" (*OA* 468). Bishop makes a point of not going "into details" in the letter. We can only speculate what must have gone through her mind in the twenty minutes between finding Lota and the ambulance arriving to take her to St. Vincent's Hospital. Yet I cannot help but think that the draft may be using her memories of this very morning. Bishop clearly addresses Lota as if she might be still alive: "No revolution can catch your attention / You are bored with us all. It is true we are boring" (*EAP* 149). At the same time, the poet is aware of the pointlessness of talking to her in this way. The coffee that can no longer wake her dead body is poignantly still present in the smell of the earth into which the body is to be laid: "the smell of the earth, the smell of the dark roasted coffee" (*EAP* 149). Could this be a very bleak representation of Lota's cremation? Is this why Bishop keeps painfully typing the same phrase but cannot move on? My point is not that this is the best or only autobiographical reading of the draft, or that one should read all drafts in relation to Bishop's life, but one does expect Quinn to be consistent in her methodology. Why does she suddenly stop here when she is so determined to read everything else in relation to biography?

Quinn's treatment of Bishop's aesthetic statements is equally biographically slanted. This is how she introduces Bishop's famous letter to Anne Stevenson on her experience of reading Darwin: "In a letter to Anne Stevenson, begun on January 8, 1964, and finished on 'January 20th — St. Sebastian's day,' Bishop formulates some ideas about art that Stevenson quotes directly in her book, ideas so apparently central to Bishop's thinking that the passage is reprinted in *Elizabeth Bishop and Her Art*, edited by Lloyd Schwartz and Sybil P. Estess, under the heading 'The "Darwin" Letter'" (*EAP* 320–21). If Quinn thinks the content of this letter insignificant, why does she simply not say so? And if it is insignificant, why mention it at all? To dismiss Bishop's most lyrical and lucid account of the role of observation and surrealism in her poetry as "some ideas about art" is to sound at best rather dismissive, at worst positively rude. Quinn further implies that critics have been mistaken in attaching significance to these ideas. They are "apparently central to Bishop's thinking," not self-evidently so.

Quinn cuts Bishop down to size in other ways, too. One of her favorite methods of attack is to cite without comment another critic's negative judgment of a poem. In her note to "A Baby Found in the Garbage," for example, she turns to Victoria Harrison's monograph on Bishop to dismiss how the poem "melodramatizes the ride to the dump" (*EAP* 317). Quinn's citation of Harrison's ideas implies that she also considers the poem melodramatic. If so, why collect the poem in the first place? "A Baby Found in the Garbage" is certainly less finished than Bishop's other Brazil poems, but Quinn never makes this point.

In my opinion, the poem's flaws relate not to its melodramatic tone but to a rather abrupt and unconvincing shift in perspective from the "apartment house built for the rich" to the garbage chute down which the baby's body has been thrown (*EAP* 111–12). The gaze in the poem moves literally and figuratively downward as elsewhere in her published work. Bishop often begins up there, on a balcony ("A Miracle for Breakfast"), on the top of a mast ("The Unbeliever"), or even on a ceiling ("Sleeping on the Ceiling"). In her best work, she comes down from her various lofty lookouts to challenge her own privileged experience of the world. Bonnie Costello reads Bishop's vertical movement downward as an engagement with and a rejection of the Romantic tradition, specifically its treatment of the sublime (91). Costello suggests that while Bishop is always attracted to "ideal absolutes," her "primary identification remains with the mutable world" (92). In "At the Fishhouses," for example, the poem moves gradually away from the recognizably human world of lobster pots and Lucky Strikes to the water's edge: "Cold dark deep and absolutely clear / element bearable to no mortal" (CP 65). Seamus Heaney is particularly eloquent on the poem's daring and unexpected imaginative leap: "What we have been offered, among other things, is the slow-motion spectacle of a well-disciplined poetic imagination being tempted to dare a big leap, hesitating, and then with powerful sureness actually taking the leap. . . . It is not that the poet breaks faith with the observed world, the world of human attachment, grandfathers, Lucky Strikes and Christmas trees. But it is a different, estranging and fearful element which ultimately fascinates her" (105–6). Perhaps Bishop was able "to dare a big leap" only one or two times during her poetic career. One gets the sense in unfinished poems like "A Baby Found in the Garbage," and perhaps in the majority of poems in *Edgar Allan Poe*, that the lift-off has not yet taken place. She is still keeping faith "with the observed world."

In this sense, a close reading of her drafts and unfinished poems can reveal some of the artistic strategies and tensions enacted elsewhere in her writing. As Charles Simic points out: "What these uncollected poems lay bare for me is how much emotion there was in Bishop's poems to start with, which her endless tinkering tended to obscure in the end. It has made me read her published work differently, discovering intimate elegies and love poems where previously I heard only an anonymous voice" (19). Quinn does not appear as interested as Simic in looking for this kind of emotion in the published work. Neither is she that interested in risking her own emotional, human judgments of the unfinished poems, a process that, as Simic argues, can frequently lead to the discovery of seemingly "new" work in the "old" *Complete Poems*.

A further danger is that readers might see *Edgar Allan Poe* as an accurate facsimile of the archive rather than a personal selection and commentary on it. While Quinn's book does mine most of the precious material, it hacks at it in peculiar ways. Rather than keeping to the tried-and-tested formula followed by most modern editors—first draft or last draft—Quinn goes for something in the middle.

"In all cases," she admits, "I present the most coherent, intact draft—the fullest and/or most legible available—rather than opt for a less decipherable or less complete version of a more advanced draft" (*EAP* xvii–xviii). This is understandable and may have made Quinn's job easier in the short term, but it cannot be justified on any other grounds. If the aim, as she confesses elsewhere, is "to preserve the feeling of the draft," one cannot pick and choose on the basis of legibility which draft to transcribe. Inevitably, some of the more intriguing or plain mysterious lines and stanzas are in the notes at the back of the book, or the reader has to make do with Quinn's summaries of them.

As a final example of Quinn's editorial intrusion, here she is actually inserting herself in the very middle of an unpublished section of Bishop's prose: "Two men, one is lame & they have a very dirty pet dog, are sieving the sand on the beach very slowly & thoroughly, a little strip about 2 ft. wide and 10 ft. long, at a time. [I'd love to know what they're finding.] The beach is almost deserted" (*EAP* 254). The effect of reading this passage is somewhat similar to the experience of watching Samuel Beckett's play *Krapp's Last Tape*, in which the main character continually comments on his past selves, particularly his writing selves. The significant difference in this case of course is that Quinn is commenting on somebody else's writing. She has stolen and written in another writer's notebook. In fact, she almost seems to be impersonating Bishop, who frequently revises initial impressions in her published poetry and prose through parenthesis in precisely this way. It is possible to see *Edgar Allan Poe* as a kind of double gift, both of a new book of Elizabeth Bishop's writings and a very knowledgeable critic's readings of them. I would prefer more Bishop and less Quinn, more clothes and less dirty washing.

In addition to this, not all the drafts are transcribed. On some occasions we are given a facsimile and a transcript. In the case of "In a Room," "It is marvellous to wake up together," "Miami," "The Blue Chairs (that dream)," "Dear, my compass," "Inventory," "Aubade and Elegy," and "Belated Dedication," all we are given is a facsimile. While there is a certain frisson in being able to study Bishop's composition process, it is actually extremely difficult to decipher all of her handwritten additions and corrections. In the case of "In a Room," for example, the paper is folded over at one point, totally obscuring three or four words. At other points on the typescript, Bishop has added or deleted words in handwriting. Some of her changes look final. Others are clearly only alternatives as indicated by the question mark. This suggests that the poem is *nearly* finished, but not quite. One suspects that many of the "uncollected poems" in the book are in a similar state, but this is one of the few occasions in which we can actually prove it. Most of the other facsimile poems look finished or at least are easier to read. One would not want to miss what looks like a drawing of an upturned bed in the top right-hand corner of "It is marvelous to wake up together" (the electrical storm's point of view looking downward?) or the artwork that frames "Dear, my compass." But as several reviewers of the book have pointed out, there is no editorial consistency here. As Vendler states, "A printed page renders a poem in a way that a photocopy of a transcript does not" (36). It gives authority to the printed poem and casts doubt on the facsimile. The printed poems look clean and cleared for publication. Poems in facsimile look messy and private. But this is a fiction created by editorial decisions rather than a reflection of the contents of Bishop's actual papers. This is all the more frustrating given the very real quality of at least three or four of the poems Quinn presents only in facsimile form. "In a Room," "It is marvellous to wake up together," and "Dear, my compass" are all wonderful poems that deserve an immediate place in the Bishop canon. But for them to be taught and studied properly, one needs to have the facsimile versions in *Edgar Allan Poe* alongside the newly printed versions in the Library of America edition of Bishop's *Poems, Prose, and Letters*. The aims of these two books are obviously different. Whereas *Edgar Allan Poe* gives us a crucial and illuminating insight into the creative process, the Library of America book is mainly an anthology. But in order to feel and literally *see* the journey from notebook to published poem, readers need the before and after in one place. Flicking between two books is, after all, something of a scholarly luxury.

At first, it appears impossible to guess what Bishop may or may not have felt on publication of this book. Vendler thinks she would have replied with "a horrified 'No'" (34). Michael Schmidt, on the other hand, "wonders whether she might have been persuaded" (2). John Palattella concludes that "publishing these works isn't wrong. But it is weird, since their very persistence seems to defy one of Bishop's key insights: 'so many things seem filled with the intent / to be lost that their loss is no disaster'" (46). I think Bishop would have been annoyed and dismayed by the book, not at its existence, but by the suggestion that she was its sole author. In 1962, Bishop experienced working on a book that was rearranged, reedited, and, in some cases, rewritten by somebody else, her prose book about Brazil. She spent the last fifteen years of her life repudiating it, and perhaps the same would have occurred on this occasion.

According to Quinn, "we're still in a very early stage of Bishop scholarship although there are at least a dozen books about her" (83). Similarly, I think we are still in a very early stage of making sense of *Edgar Allan Poe* though there are more than a dozen reviews of it. Vendler attempted to lay a curse on the book, stating categorically that "these newly published materials will be relegated to what Robert Lowell called the 'back stacks,' and this imperfect volume will be forgotten, except by scholars. The real poems will outlast these, their maimed and stunted siblings" (37). I disagree. I think this book is imperfect, but so, too, are *The Complete Poems, The Collected Prose,* and *One Art* (the briefest of comparisons between Bishop's letters to Lowell in *One Art* and those collected in *Words in Air* shows up the transcription errors in the earlier volume). The sooner we abandon the idea of Bishop as a perfect writer only to be found in these books, the sooner we will find other ways of reading her. Vendler attempts to reawaken a fairly tired analogy of the creative process as akin to childbirth. She places the "real" and explicitly mature poems of *The Complete Poems* against the "maimed and stunted siblings" in the new volume. *Edgar Allan Poe* can and should be criticized for the contexts in which the drafts and fragments are framed rather than for its existence.

There are at least three ways in which *Edgar Allan Poe* could be immediately improved in subsequent editions. First, and most importantly, there needs to be an index. Second, every poem in facsimile must be transcribed. Third, the dozen or so poems that Bishop crossed out in her notebooks and papers should be identified as such in the main section of the book rather than in the preface. As Susan Rosenbaum observes, "Surely this threshold between legibility and illegibility, perhaps indicating Bishop's desire to both preserve and erase the poems, is potentially an important frame for reading them" ("Collecting" 81). Much in the same way that Bishop had a "subliminal glimpse of the capital letter *M* multiplying" in her memoir of Marianne Moore (*CPr* 156), I cannot help but seeing the capital letters *Q* and *A* multiplying. For me, they stand in for the many questions the book tries to answer and for the text's various absences, accidents, additions, and authors, one of whom is clearly Alice Quinn.

NOTE

1. References to Bishop's *Complete Poems* are to the 1983 volume *The Complete Poems: 1927–1979* rather than to the 1969 volume *The Complete Poems*. See Brett Millier's *Life and the Memory of It* (410–11, 415–17) for detail on the publication and reception of the 1969 *Complete Poems*.

Postcards and Sunsets

Bishop's Revisions and the Problem of Excess

JEFFREY GRAY

T. S. Eliot thought that every important new work alters the existing canon. As numerous examples attest, the rule holds true also of individual author canons, where the belated addition of a lost novel, essay, or poem compels us to read the entire oeuvre in new and unexpected ways. Elizabeth Bishop's readers have long known that the poet's 1983 *Complete Poems* was not "complete." For some time after publication of that volume, through the efforts chiefly of Thomas Travisano, Lloyd Schwartz, and Lorrie Goldensohn, other poems began to see print.[1] This process of recovering Bishop's unpublished poetry culminated in 2006 with the publication—foreshadowed if not advertised by several poems in the pages of the *New Yorker* during the previous year—of *Edgar Allan Poe & the Juke-box,* Alice Quinn's selection of fragments, near-poems, and drafts from the Vassar archive, where Bishop's manuscripts are collected. If "complete" means the inclusion of every draft and every poem, then Bishop's published work remains incomplete, but Quinn's book, giving us numerous heretofore unpublished poems, constitutes a revision of the Bishop canon impossible to ignore.

In the present essay, I wish to address the question of why some poems are included in the Quinn volume and not others and, more particularly, why some drafts (in the many instances where the archive holds several drafts of the same poem) and not others were singled out for publication. Bishop's preferences in her work and even her guidelines for revision are known. Given her own criteria, an argument can be made for preferring, in some cases, alternative versions to those published in *Edgar Allan Poe & the Juke-box.*

As regards her selection of the poems, Quinn says surprisingly little in her introduction beyond the comment that she found some of the material "compelling" (xv). On the question of drafts, she says more, remarking that she "sought to present the most coherent, intact drafts" (xv), and, in "A Note on the Text," adding that she chose "the fullest and/or most legible available rather than opt for a less decipherable or less complete version of a more advanced draft" (xvii–xviii), and, finally, that she has not reproduced work "that is restrictively fragmentary . . . [and] that does not indicate to a certain degree something of [Bishop's] artistic ambition" (xvii). More than a hundred pages of notes follow the poems, offering histories of themes, tropes, and drafts, but the above comments constitute all the stated criteria.[2]

My argument will concern a particular poem, "Florida Revisited," or rather— in the version Quinn has chosen—more problematically, "(Florida Revisited)?" I will compare this latter version with other drafts and with the early poem "Florida" (from Bishop's first book, *North & South*), to which Bishop originally intended it to be a sequel.[3] I will finally argue for a version of "Florida Revisited" that shakes itself free of the early poem, free from the kind of rhetoric Bishop most distrusted, and ultimately from the poet's own state of "florida"—that is, her own youthful flowering, remembered in the revisiting of the geographical state of Florida almost four decades later. Bishop's struggle through several versions, each more spare and focused than the last, had moved "Florida Revisited" steadily toward completion, but, with her practice of waiting months or years for words to fill in the blanks of a poem, she did not live long enough to finish it. The poem is important for readers of Bishop as a late treatment of travel's disillusion, and, in what it reveals of the *direction* of Bishop's revision process, as an example of her evolving poetics of entropy.

"Florida Revisited," in all of its versions, is a travel poem. For a poet as shy of effusiveness as Bishop was, travel poems presented a particular problem, since encounters with the Other, the unknown, and the exotic are likely to elicit inflated rhetoric. In many of her poems of the Caribbean and South America, Bishop counters this danger of excess in part by creating unsentimental and even shallow narrators. That her poems often seem the opposite of pretentious or sublime—that they seem antivisionary, humble, diffident—is a measure of this effort to contain sentiment while not losing sight of the wonder that precipitates the poems and suffuses the best of them. Few of Bishop's travel poems dwell at the epiphanic end of the travel-poem spectrum, though we find representations of epiphany and/or celebration in Bishop's prose, in the early poem "Pleasure Seas" with its repetitions of "happy" and "happily," and in late poems such as "Santarém," a poem, however, that took her almost twenty years to complete.[4] The golden sunsets of "Santarém" were not possible for Bishop until her fear of sentiment (and sentimental language) surrendered to intimations of the transcendent and to a more expansive linguistic and emotional register.

Instead, for Bishop, Nature seemed to need saving from its own bad taste and excess. The surfeit of "Over 2,000 Illustrations and a Complete Concordance" is expressed in the tedium of catalogues and the triviality of travel experience—according to the speaker—connected "only by 'and' and 'and'" (*CP* 58). A similar excess nauseates the Crusoe of "Crusoe in England," who suffers from nightmares of endless repetition:

> infinities
> of islands, islands spawning islands,
> like frogs' eggs turning into polliwogs
> of islands, knowing that I had to live
> on each and every one, eventually,
> for ages. (*CP* 165)

One of Bishop's best-known poems, "Questions of Travel" is rife with complaints about nature's excess: "too many waterfalls," "crowded streams," "so many clouds" in the opening lines, and, later, trees that are "really exaggerated in their beauty" (*CP* 93). Similarly, in the still unpublished "Florida Revisited," the sunsets are "over-exaggerated," while "giant dews" mirror the hypertrophied vegetation of "Brazil, January 1, 1502," a poem in which both tourists and conquistadores find "every square inch filling in with foliage," "giant leaves," "monster ferns," and "giant water lilies" (*CP* 91). The drafts published in *Edgar Allan Poe* exhibit the same misgivings: In "Rainy Day, Rio," for example, Bishop writes, "Mountains should really not protrude / In city streets and brandish trees / at skyscrapers"; it is, she says, "so rude / Of Nature not to go away" (133).

The nausea of excess may reflect a cultural more than a literary reality—the disapproving reaction common in northern travelers' accounts of the South. Bishop is as candid as D. H. Lawrence was regarding her distaste for certain features of tropical life. The narrator of "Arrival at Santos" makes no apologies for her ignorance of the place she's visiting and complains about the inferior postage stamps and soap, among other things. She is a figure we find also in some of Bishop's unpublished prose, such as the (undated) "A Trip on the Rio São Francisco" (VC 55.4), where the writer sees the wash water, the laundry, the houses, and indeed the people themselves as "dingy, yellow brown"; and in early poem drafts such as "Travelling, a Love Poem (or just *Love Poem?*)," where she decides not to visit the church because "I can just smell the pee-pee" (*EAP* 162). She speaks of the fanatical personal cleanliness of the Brazilians but wonders why "Brazilian toilets are the filthiest I have ever encountered." As Lawrence once remarked—in his preface to Edward Dahlberg's *Bottom Dogs*—you can tell North Americans by their kitchens and their bathrooms, whose cleanliness projects the "secret physical repulsion between people" (xi). Perhaps the absence of that repulsion accounts for the South's plumbing, which, at any rate, neither Lawrence nor Bishop found to their liking.

It may be helpful to place Bishop's less celebratory mode in a particular conceptual context, that of existentialism, the chief philosophical current of the time, contemporary with Bishop's work of the 1940s, 1950s, and 1960s. In Sartre's *Nausée* (published in 1938 but popular through the late 1960s), the protagonist Roquentin suffers the oppressive fullness of the world and sees the cause of it in the sickening quality of his own existence. As much as he longs for something else, something distinct, Roquentin can't get away from the evidence of his own engagement with the world. (Compare, in Bishop, the lines "I need a virgin mirror / no one's ever looked at / that's never looked back at anyone," from "The Riverman" [*CP* 107], where that character apparently wishes for what Sartre called a prereflective consciousness, a world not limited by the solipsism that Sartre thought basic to the human condition.)

What happens when we consider this nausea at excess in the poetic rather than the natural sphere? My title invokes sunsets not only because they appear in the various versions of "Florida Revisited" (and in "Santarém" and in several of Bishop's prose works) but also because they are a handy metaphor for what Bishop deplored in poetry. Poems, she seems to say, resemble sunsets: they run the risk of becoming bad postcards; she describes Florida in 1938 as "the poorest / postcard of itself" (*CP* 33). Consider also the pictures of "corny waterfalls and lakes" (*EAP* 160) she sees in "Memory of Baltimore," and the lines I have quoted already from "Arrival at Santos," expressing the tourist's distaste for Brazilian waterfalls.

In spite of this frequent registering of nature's gauche and suffocating abundance, as the 1960s became the 1970s Bishop gradually migrated toward those sunsets in poems such as "On the Amazon" (in *EAP*) and "Santarém," in which the world is bathed in golden light: "gorgeous," "gilded," "burnished" (*CP* 185). In "Santarém," Bishop surrenders to the invitation to stasis that nature seems to offer: never to move again, never to go back, but to die there at the crosscurrent of the two rivers, as Mr. Swan is about to do, who "wanted to see the Amazon before he died" (187). Consider also how "Santarém" parallels in rhetoric and theme the unpublished "A Trip on the Rio São Francisco" (VC 55.4), from which I quote the following passage: "Women were still doing their laundry; odd pieces were still drying on the banks and nearer ledges while the gorgeous sunset went on and on. The sky grew richer and redder by the minute, and the water red and glazed. The remaining washing was stained pink, and the big tin basins, on the heads of the women walking home, caught the light. It was a peaceful, grand, but somehow sad, perhaps because almost completely silent, opening to our trip."

I want to keep this struggle in mind—between transcendence, on the one hand, and fear of sentiment and excess on the other—as I compare the draft of "(Florida Revisited)?" which Alice Quinn prints in *Edgar Allan Poe,* with the early "Florida" poem and with yet another version of "Florida Revisited" in the archive. In Bishop's efforts to bring "Florida Revisited" to completion, it is the sense of surfeit that, curiously, both gave her pause and guided her revision.

Quinn, in "A Note on the Text," after remarking that she has used the "most coherent, intact draft—the fullest and/or most legible available" (xvii), concedes that "there are a few extreme cases" (xviii), and that one of these is "(Florida Revisited)?"[5] By calling it an "extreme" case, Quinn refers to the fact that "(Florida Revisited)?"—which is reproduced in facsimile in *Edgar Allan Poe & the Jukebox*—is covered like a palimpsest with handwritten lines that revise and reorganize the typewritten ones (see fig. 1). Indeed, Quinn says that this draft was the most challenging poem of all in the book. But the case is "extreme" in other important regards as well, since several handwritten *and* typewritten versions of the poem exist in the archive, competing with the version Quinn has chosen. Quinn publishes as "(Florida Revisited)?" the first page of three pages in file 64.24 of the Vassar archive. Though the file is undated, Brett Millier dates the poem from August 1976 and quotes it in part in her biography (523–24). Perhaps this precedent—Millier having called attention to the poem already—prompted Quinn's choice. Quinn is using the first and longest draft of the three in this file; however, not only do others in that file seem more "finished," but there is another file, another set of drafts of this poem, numbered 73.9, out of a box (73 through 76) labeled "Notebooks of Drafts, Dreams, etc.," which is dated 1974–77.

Quinn does not mention this other file, which contains three more pages of drafts of the poem (and a title without the parentheses or question mark—indeed, the draft Quinn selects is the only one of all of the versions that has these typographical features). Quinn says she has used the most *intact* drafts, but the one she prints—"(Florida Revisited)?"—is not evidently more intact than others in that box, or than those of 73.9. Moreover, it is not evidently the "final" draft or even a later one: Quinn suggests that the handwritten words "2nd or 3rd" at the top of the first page of the version she prints mean the second or third *draft,* but the words more likely refer to the order of the stanzas.[6] In fact, the typewritten stanza at the bottom of "(Florida Revisited)?" is numbered "1"—that is, with the intention of moving it to the top. In what I take to be later drafts, that stanza has in fact been moved there and developed.

(FLORIDA REVISITED)?

The coconut palms still clatter;
and the pelicans still waddle, soar, and dive,
and the sickly-looking willets pick at their food.
The sunset doesn't color the sea; it stains
the water-glaze of the receding waves instead.
At night the "giant dew" drips on the roof
and the grass grows wet and the hibiscus drops
folded, sad and wet, in the morning.
And it still goes on and on, more or less the same,
as it has, apparently, for over half my life-time—!
Goes on, after, or over, how many deaths,
how many deaths and loves lost, lost forever.

The sun sets; a man is making a movie of it
(this is hard to believe, but true)
and directly opposite
the full moon rises, covered with tears.
It can't stop crying now but will, eventually,
one supposes, and look clearly down,
composedly, on all the earthly dew.

Change is what hurts worst; change alone can kill.
It kills us, finally — but not these earthly things.
One hates this immutability
one hates immutability.
Finally one hates the Florida one knows,
the Florida one knows.

Oh palms, oh birds, & over sunset
full and weeping moon
— oh unendurable

And the dead black bird, or the breast of one,
lying just at the foam's edge
that proved to be a piece of charred wood — just like feathers.

Just at the water's edge
a dead, black bird, or the breast of one,
coal-black, glistening, each wet feather distinct
that turned out to be a charred wood,
feather-light, feather marked
but not a bird at all — dead, delicately graven, dead wood
light as the breast of a bird in the hand —
feathers ///

FIG. 1. Facsimile of "Florida Revisited" from *Edgar Allan Poe & the Juke-Box* by Elizabeth Bishop, edited and annotated by Alice Quinn. (© 2006 by Alice Helen Methfessel. Introduction © 2006 by Alice Quinn. Reprinted by permission of Farrar, Straus and Giroux, LLC)

An alternative candidate, then, for the most intact or least fragmentary version is the other typewritten draft in 64.24 (see fig. 2). There are several significant differences: first, the title of the version Quinn prints, with its parentheses and question mark, gives us the compound doubts we recognize from some famous Bishop poems: the opening of "Santarém" ("Of course I may be remembering it all wrong / after, after—how many years?"); the catalogue of doubts that is "Questions of Travel"; the confused and depressed narrator of "Crusoe in England"; and the parenthetical return of the repressed at the end of "One Art," among other examples. The parentheses and question mark foreground, in other words, the diffidence and anxiety of the poem at this stage, a stage in which the title and topos weren't yet clear to the poet. Should this new Florida poem constitute a revisit, or a new poem? Bishop seems to ask. The doubt becomes the topic of the poem, the obstacle to shaping the poem, and finally the inability to complete it or publish it. But, interestingly, the other versions, which I take to be later, do *not* use that typography. Apparently written over a three-year period, these versions were all simply titled "Florida Revisited" and contain solutions—though perhaps not successful ones—to the formal problems of "(Florida Revisited)?"

The facsimile of "(Florida Revisited)?" in *Edgar Allan Poe* begins with direct references to the earlier poem "Florida." Bishop revisits not merely the place—Fort Myers, Florida, which she had first visited in 1936—but also the poem (written in 1938). She looks at the frame of mind, the deep ambivalence that was already there in "Florida." (Millier's date for the revisiting poem—1976—is about right, since Bishop briefly escaped to Fort Myers from Harvard in 1975 and probably began the poem in that period.)

Revisiting is in fact the whole problem. Bishop had already pondered the topic in "The Traveller to Rome" (*EAP* 75), a poem that concerns multiple visits to the same canonical cultural site:

> If [the traveler] should see it again,
> ....
> would he notice more detail,
> would it be more beautiful
> than it was then?

No, the poet says: "first the first fact is the fact." This declaration forestalls any effort to revise a place or experience: "first the first fact is the fact / galvanized / of being there" (75). Similarly, seeing it ("the mortal stare") that first time precludes

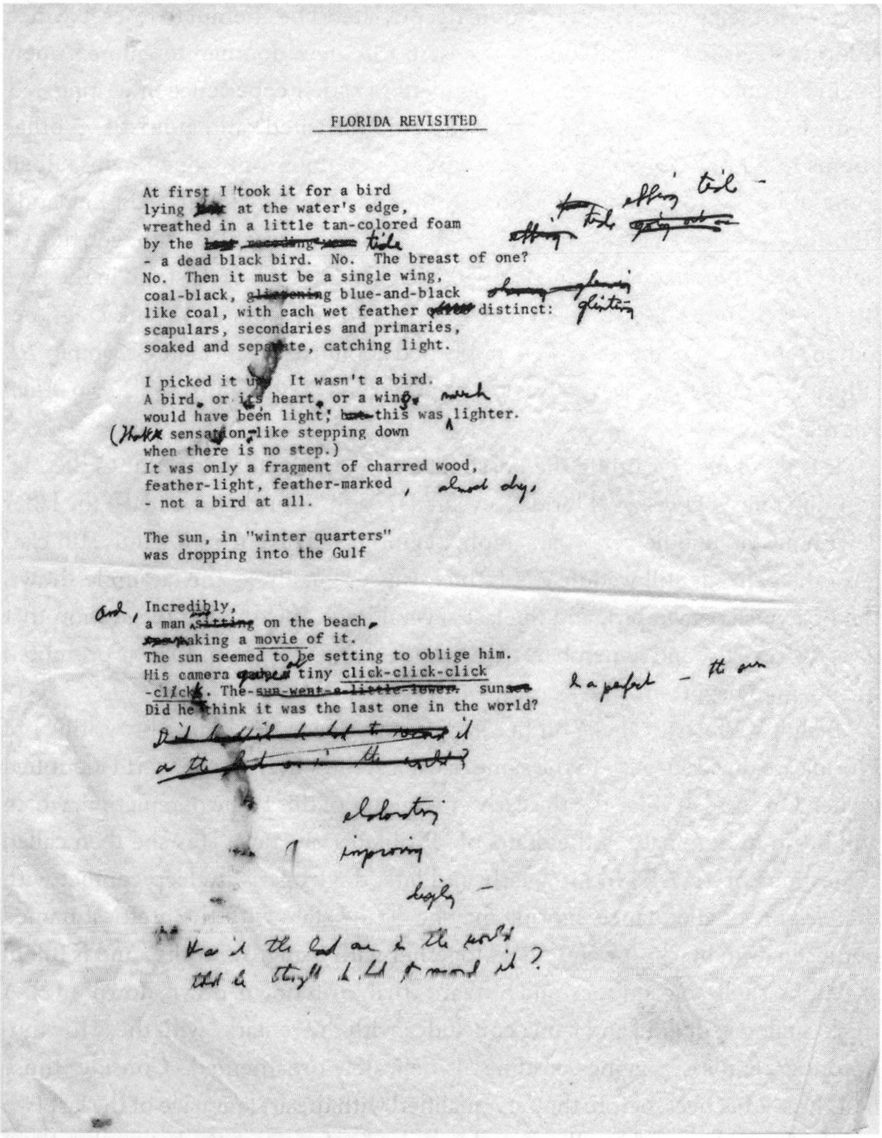

FLORIDA REVISITED

At first I took it for a bird
lying at the water's edge,
wreathed in a little tan-colored foam
by the tide
- a dead black bird. No. The breast of one?
No. Then it must be a single wing,
coal-black, glistening blue-and-black
like coal, with each wet feather distinct:
scapulars, secondaries and primaries,
soaked and separate, catching light.

I picked it up. It wasn't a bird.
A bird, or its heart, or a wing,
would have been light; but this was lighter.
(The sensation like stepping down
when there is no step.)
It was only a fragment of charred wood,
feather-light, feather-marked,
- not a bird at all.

The sun, in "winter quarters"
was dropping into the Gulf

Incredibly,
a man sitting on the beach,
making a movie of it.
The sun seemed to be setting to oblige him.
His camera tiny click-click-click
-click. The sun went a little lower. suns
Did he think it was the last one in the world?

FIG. 2. Unpublished draft of "Florida Revisited" by Elizabeth Bishop. (© 2009 Elizabeth Bishop Estate. Printed by permission of Farrar, Straus and Giroux, LLC)

reseeing it, seeing it differently or more deeply, later. The attempt to resee it, which "Florida Revisited" at first constitutes, is, in this view, doomed to failure. A new poem can only be a new seeing, independent of earlier experience or writing.

Bishop had been hoping to finish "Florida Revisited" and at least two other poems to fill out *Geography III* (1976), which contains only nine poems, albeit some of her best, including her longest, the much-praised "Crusoe in England." "Florida Revisited" is concerned, as the character Crusoe is also, with "get[ting] it right" (162). But the revisit couldn't be got right; that "first fact" stood in the way. Bishop had hoped also to finish "Santarém, begun in 1960, and "Pink Dog," begun in 1963. Both of the latter were published about two years after *Geography III*. "Florida Revisited," however, was never published at all by Bishop; *Edgar Allan Poe* marks its debut.

It is the doubt regarding the possibility of revisiting that constitutes the biggest difference between "(Florida Revisited)?" and "Florida Revisited": the latter is without the middle verse paragraph, beginning "The coconut palms still clatter; / the pelicans still waddle . . ." (which was originally, as the facsimile shows, the first verse paragraph), and the last several lines. It is the middle section that directly "revisits" and remembers the 1938 poem and that seems to have prompted the poem to begin with.[7]

Bishop's efforts to shake off her earlier experience (including its writing) of Florida are due, I suggest, to the same nausea at the surfeit of the world identified earlier. One sees in "Florida" the early emergence of this trope of repletion, which will begin to dominate in the drafts of "Problems of Travel" (as she then called "Questions of Travel") in 1955; early and late, the trope is in deep conflict with the *pleasure* of abundance. Florida may be "[t]he state with the prettiest name," but it "floats in brackish water / held together with mangrove roots," and is full of skeletons, skulls, mosquitoes, and buzzards that "drift down, down, down" (32). A thick catalogue of flora and fauna concludes with the remark "with these the monotonous, endless, sagging coastline / is delicately ornamented." Consider those first three adjectives, before they are qualified with the art language of the last two words: "monotonous," "endless," and "sagging" refer respectively to color, time, and physical weight—indeed, the last of the three adjectives spells out the awfulness of the first two: the burden of endlessness is so heavy that the land itself sags under its weight, the coastline doing what coastlines do in Bishop's earliest collected poem, "The Map."

Does this horror at repletion explain why the speaker in Quinn's draft, almost four decades later, concludes, "Finally one hates the Florida one knows, / the Florida one knew"? One should answer this while bearing in mind that Florida is not only a geographical state but also a state of being, that is, covered with flowers (Sp. *florida*)—thus, also, florid or ornate, but still with the sense of being in flower—which is why it has the "prettiest name," and why revisiting that state can be painful. Bishop in fact refers to all the activity of "Florida" as having been going "on and on"[8] for "half my lifetime," but it had been going on somewhat longer than that: it is the difference between the poet at twenty-seven and at sixty-five. Though there was something false, as Bishop saw it, in the glamour of 1930s Florida, "Florida" nevertheless luxuriates in its "wild" life; among the skulls and skeletons and brackish water, the place abounds with "unseen hysterical birds who rush up the scale / every time in a tantrum," "[t]anagers embarrassed by their flashiness," "pelicans whose delight it is to clown, / who coast for fun on the strong tidal currents" (32), and a dozen other exuberant sights and sounds. If that glamour is gone now, it may be the sixty-five-year-old subjectivity that has banished it. (But the bleakness, too, of the later attempt is presaged in the earlier poem in the entropic ending with its vision of a "careless, corrupt state" of "all black specks / too far apart, and ugly whites; the poorest / postcard of itself" [32].)

The direction that Bishop's revising usually took was *away* from effusiveness and sentiment. To return to Florida was to return to the poem "Florida" and to the uneasiness with excess (again, both linguistic and physical) that began to emerge in that poem. When we look at the unpublished version of "Florida Revisited" to which I've been referring (that is, the early draft in VC 64.24; fig. 2), we see the editing out of that effusiveness and excess; we see, indeed, that both the commentary *and* the perspective of "Florida" are absent. Without the middle section, and without the short closing sections, the poem is reduced to two small incidents, which in the end Bishop may have felt were not yet enough: (1) the finding of a piece of charred wood on the beach, which she'd thought was a bird or part of one; and (2) the man on the beach filming the sunset. In the versions of both archive boxes containing these drafts—leaving aside only Quinn's choice, "(Florida Revisited)?"—these two incidents constitute the poem entirely. These versions also reveal important developments of each incident, not found in the earlier "(Florida Revisited)?" version, tied as it is to the 1938 poem. Consider, regarding the first incident, these lines:

> Then it must be a single wing,
> coal-black, glinting blue-and-black
> like coal, with each wet feather distinct:
> scapulars, secondaries, and primaries,
> soaked and separate, catching light. (VC 64.24)

In their vivid development of the first incident, these lines are not material Bishop is likely to have dropped. The same is true of the line "wreathed in a little tan-colored foam," earlier in that stanza. The man on the beach, now that the other material has been dropped, is also fleshed out further:

> The sun seemed to be setting to oblige him.
> His camera gave out tiny click-click-click
> -clicks   the sun
> Did he think it was the last one in the world?[9]

It is as though, once the repetitive material with which the poem began—the material connecting "Florida Revisited" with "Florida"—was jettisoned, the poet was free to let these two incidents create a new poem, rather than a reprise of an earlier one.

Bishop also left out the last section of the Quinn version, with its hyperbole, moral commentary, and iambic pentameter:

> Change is what hurts worst; change alone can kill.
> Change kills us, finally—not these earthly things.
> One hates all this immutability.
> Finally one hates the Florida one knows,
> the Florida one knew.
>
> Oh palms, oh birds, and over-exaggerated sunsets—
> oh full and weeping moon   [why do you weep?]
> —oh unendurable [world]   [Well, loneliness is always
> an excuse.] (EAP 178)[10]

One sees immediately Bishop's motive for these latter deletions. First, though she did allow herself quite a few "Oh's" of exclamation, Bishop wasn't likely to allow herself the Shelleyan heights of "oh unendurable World"; she was equally likely to hesitate before "how many deaths by now" or "love lost, lost forever."

"Florida Revisited," then, in all its versions *except* the one chosen by Quinn, is largely antivisionary and antirhetorical, more so even than the earlier "Florida," which presents at least a qualified transcendence. "Florida Revisited" begins at a lower level of expectations even than that of the traveling alter ego of "Arrival at Santos." What the speaker thinks she sees—not with hope or anticipation—is a dead bird, a far cry from the lively pelicans, willets, and tanagers of 1938. What she really finds is a stick of wood. It is hardly a declension, since the two objects be-long equally to that dystopic fish-gut-strewn beach familiar from Derek Walcott's poems. The incident acts out the misprision so characteristic of Bishop's poems, a misprision that leads her to the kinetic mismatch of body and object when she picks up the stick, "like stepping down / when there is no step," too late for the body to correct itself, the familiar doubts (getting it wrong) now somatized.

The second incident sets up the supposed natural grandeur of the sunset—although certainly the sun "dropping into the Gulf" could be read as already en-tropic—and then reduces it to a tourist's pathetic attempt to capture it on film. The atrophy and enervation of both incidents can be seen as reactions to that surfeit that, as I have suggested, runs through Bishop's work.

From here, Bishop found nowhere to go. The poem tries to rise from the status of a sketch, but the connections that provided its reason for being in the Quinn version—that is, its dependence on the initial visit and earlier poem—had to be discarded: the remembered pelicans, willets, and sunset; the reflections on change that seem to rise out of nowhere, prompted neither by the charred stick nor by the hapless photographer; and most of all the inflated rhetoric of the moon weep-ing, the poet weeping for lost love, and the apostrophes—"oh full and weeping moon! / —oh unendurable [world]."

I would nevertheless argue that when we reduce the poem to the two incidents, removing the catalogues, the linguistic *and* natural excess, along with all evidence of a revisit, the poem clears a space for itself within Bishop's oeuvre. Both the beachcomber searching through flotsam on the tide flats *and* the naive photogra-pher who holds a camera ineffectually up to nature are figures for "failed" poetry, which for Bishop at this point was the only kind of poetry—here I mean not that Bishop was depressed at not having finished certain poems for *Geography III* but that in her poetry she resisted the pretense of understanding what she sees; she strove to achieve that kind of neutral being in the world that Gide associated with great writing and that François Jullien discusses in *In Praise of Blandness,* a writing that allows for an indeterminate world and a quietism of the senses.[11] The poem suggests that neither one's own judgment and perception, which one must rely on and yet cannot (since one mistakes what one sees), nor one's technique as an art-ist (the pitiful cameraman figure, recalling Lowell's "Epilogue") can save the day. Judgment is practically worthless in the first section; technique, in the second, is reduced to an effort to capture "reality," as if it were out there to be captured. Both facets of the artistic subjectivity, then, are revealed as dead ends. But both raise the question of what to make, as Frost's oven bird asked, of a diminished thing.

This is where the struggle against fullness and excess led Bishop at that time:

to the linguistic and affective flattening of "Florida Revisited." And yet, as I have noted, in the case of remembering Santarém, Bishop could produce the opposite kind of poem: celebratory, ecstatic, suffused with light, and, notably, replete with catalogues of things joyfully going wild, that is, *not* making sense. (Her explicit rejection of binary sense-making in that poem is immediately followed by her catalogue of mongrelism and mixtures of various kinds.)

How do we account for the contrast? On the one hand, there is the nausea and suffocation from the surfeit of nature—the sense that nature, like one's own effusions about it, *should* be more restrained, less incursive (I take this to be Bishop's default poetic mode)—and on the other hand, the sense that nature, like one's travels through it, offers aesthetic and spiritual epiphanies, particularly in moments of subject-object collapse, in the dissolving of distinctions that we find in "Santarém," moments duplicated in "On the Amazon," where "everywhere smudges / of rainbow and shafts / of soft sun backwards . . . / the world, all pink, / has dissolved at last" (*EAP* 124). Indeed both of these poems, as well as the curious "Crossing the Equator," remind one of Rimbaud's lines: "Elle est retrouvée! / —Quoi? L'éternité. / C'est la mer melée au soleil," in which eternity is recovered in the indistinguishable joining of the sea and the sky, those two bodies acting like the two rivers that touch yet do not merge in "Santarém."

In the short draft of "Florida Revisited," Bishop edited out the worry over the excess of nature that had oppressed her for decades, and edited out, along with it, her memory of Florida in the 1930s. She wrote in another context—but at almost the same time as her writing of "Florida Revisited"—that she was "superstitious about going 'back' to places, anyway: they have changed; you have changed; even the weather may have changed."[12] The transcendence that she imagined might save the poem, and that characterizes the examples just quoted, was, at this stage, either unavailable or unacceptable to her. But "Florida Revisited" refuses to settle for anything less, and this is what makes it significant in Bishop's oeuvre. The fullness of Quinn's draft gives us only the revisit, which is not what Bishop wanted. She was looking, as always, for something new: for freshness, for "first facts."

NOTES

1. I am grateful to Farrar, Straus and Giroux, and to Special Collections, Vassar College, for permission to reprint draft pages from the Elizabeth Bishop archive.

2. As regards these criteria, I note that numerous fragmentary poems *are* included in Quinn's book ("Inventory" [143], "Don't You Call Me That Word, Honey" [68], "Crossing the Equator" [95], "Travelling, a Love Poem" [162], "Syllables" [101], "Homesickness" [87], and others) while other poems in the archive, arguably more complete and/or of greater interest, are not. Consider,

for example, "How to Detect a Moderate Rain" (64.2) or "A Trip to the Mines" (67.20), neither of which is included in Quinn's volume. Of these two, the former is more complete than many of Quinn's included drafts, even though it is not one of Bishop's most ambitious or important poems, while the longer poem ("A Trip to the Mines"), though unfinished, is not more so than most of the poems Quinn includes; moreover, it is one of those Bishop poems that (like "Brazil, January 1, 1502") treats global, colonial, historical issues. It begins, "The slaves, the slaves have disappeared, / In all their thousands, millions even . . ." and asks later, "Where are they now, these two million slaves"; it also foreshadows the metonymic golds of "Santarém," and offers biographical insight in its apparent reference to Mina Velha, the oldest mine in Ouro Prêto, not far from Bishop's home there. Another poem that seems worthy of inclusion for its interest, and relative completeness, is "Antibes and Antibes Way" (to which, however, someone has added the handwritten note "Elizabeth says this is not for publication").

3. Another poem titled "Florida" remains unpublished in the archive; my references will be only to the published poem, which appeared in 1946 in *North & South* (in *CP* 32).

4. "Pleasure Seas," though written in 1939 and intended for publication, was not published until after Bishop's death.

5. Quinn writes, in full: "There are a few extreme cases. The extensive revisions visible in the facsimile for 'Florida Revisited' show just how difficult it is to reliably set forth any single version of this poem—the stanza at the top of the facsimile is accompanied by the notation '2nd or 3rd'—but the draft as printed does give us a sense of the arc of the poem as Bishop envisioned it, and I've followed her instructions on the page in ordering the legible parts" (xviii).

6. In many or perhaps most cases, no one is sure which version should take precedence. Quinn opts for whichever seems most "coherent," "intact," "fullest," or "most legible," as her "Note on the Text" explains. Dean Rogers, the archivist at Vassar, explains that the last page will usually be the last or latest draft, though, in fact, as he concedes, it sometimes seems to be the opposite. Then again, the pages may have been shuffled by the many scholars who have perused the archives.

7. Omitting the stanza of "The coconut palms" means that the first mention of the sunset is also left out, though it was a rather washed-out affair, given the forlorn subject position of the observer:

> The sunset doesn't color the sea; it stains
> the glaze of wet receding waves instead.

8. Where, in "A Trip on the Rio São Francisco," the phrase "on and on" is used to describe endless beauty, in "(Florida Revisited)?" it is used to describe endless, monotonous surfeit, a world of things imprinted with and yet indifferent to oneself.

9. The lines I have quoted cannot fully represent the draft since there are other notes not only on this page, but also on the back of it, and on additional pages. The reader can see at the bottom of the main page Bishop's handwritten alternative lines regarding the man filming the sunset: "Was it the last one in the world / that he thought he had to record it?" Note also that the "click-click" of "Florida Revisited" revisits "The Bight"; indeed, the whole poem does in the sense that it describes a stretch of littered coastline, as did "Florida" also:

> The bight is littered with old correspondences.
> Click. Click. Goes the dredge,
> And brings up a dripping jawful of marl.

10. Brackets here indicate handwritten interpolations by Bishop.

11. One could add to the French examples an important Spanish Caribbean one: Antonio Benítez-Rojo, who, in *The Repeating Island,* argues for a nonapocalyptical poetics: "The Caribbean

is not an apocalyptic world; it is not a phallic world in pursuit of the vertical desires of ejaculation and castration" (10). It seems to me that Bishop subscribed to what Benítez-Rojo called an "aquatic poetics," not an apocalyptic one.

12. Bishop made this remark in the 1977 edition of her translation of *The Diary of Helena Morley*, to explain why she had not gone back to the Brazilian village of Diamantina, where Morley had lived.

Bishop's Buried Elegies

CHARLES BERGER

The arrival of Alice Quinn's edition of uncollected Bishop texts makes available to a public readership these tantalizing uncollected pieces—hard to describe as a group—which only Bishop scholars have been familiar with up to now. It will be fascinating to follow the long-term influence of this volume on Bishop criticism. Once the book goes into paperback, it will surely be used by some teachers in advanced undergraduate or graduate classes. Many more quotations from uncollected material will start appearing in scholarly articles, for there's hardly a poem in this book, in whatever state of completion, lacking in quotable moments. It's also the case, I think, that only a few of these poems strike the reader as strong enough to stand up against the published poems in the Bishop "canon," though even as I write these lines I find myself rebelling against overly narrow criteria of inclusion.

Bishop worked on poems, as we know, over long periods of time, observing how loosely gathered files of experience could be magnetically drawn into the orbit of the slowly composing poem. The phrase "God's spreading fingerprint," from "Over 2,000 Illustrations and a Complete Concordance," encapsulates her technique. Playing against E. M. Forster's "only connect," Bishop writes: "Everything only connected by 'and' and 'and.'" This ritual plaint against the arbitrariness of parataxis is belied by the connections she ignites in that poem between lines of experience. That Bishop was able to draw so much in, so much together, gives added interest to what she chose to leave out. The intensity of her fused materials, giving off that famous Bishop "polish," can be exhausting, and some readers may find relief in these less finished pieces, though to hope for deeper layers of revelation would be a mistake. Bishop layered plenty of revelation into her published work. Still, a rougher Bishop promises novelty, and learning to look at her in new ways will invigorate criticism of all her work. There are plenty of partial "finds" in *Edgar Allan Poe & the Juke-Box* and even when the draft or fragment is slight, an astute reader can learn a good deal about how Bishop's poetic economy worked. If this volume does not often expose the foul rag and bone shop of Bishop's heart, it does illuminate, especially in borderline cases, her own implicit ground rules for self-presentation.

In "A Note on the Text," Quinn briefly describes her editorial method. *Edgar Allan Poe & the Juke-Box* is, first of all, "a thoroughly representative selection of the draft material in the archive. I have not reproduced all of Bishop's uncollected juvenilia or work that is restrictively fragmentary, that does not indicate to a certain degree something of her artistic ambition for it or otherwise command interest because of its biographical significance" (*EAP* xvii). In a section titled the "State of the Manuscripts," Quinn explains that since this book "is not a facsimile edition," she has employed the following criteria of textual presentation: "In all cases, I present the most coherent, intact draft—the fullest and/or most legible available—rather than opt for a less decipherable or less complete version of a more advanced draft. In the notes to the individual poems, I have reproduced many of the revisions and variants I found" (*EAP* xvii–xviii). Inevitably, questions will arise as to what counts as the most coherent, intact draft, or why the goal of a volume such as this should be to present whole drafts, as opposed to examples that are more frankly fragmentary. Only if one is intent on producing a reader's edition would textual coherence matter. *Edgar Allan Poe & the Juke-Box* is indeed a reader's edition, but Quinn has also done a good job of indicating the difficulties involved in selecting versions of Bishop's many drafts. She points the way to further textual scholarship on these matters, but also makes the poetry legible enough to inspire interest and fascination in the general reader.

Perhaps the most intriguing question that can be asked of this volume is: What have we missed all along by not having at least some of these poems either published, or worked on until ready to be published? (I realize how comically presumptuous it is to question Bishop in this fashion, but can one avoid such trespass, given the fact of these draft/fragments?) After all, it isn't as if Bishop's reputation needs boosting, especially now that she has been inducted into the Library of America. The very assumption of a market for unpublished extracanonical work argues in and of itself for the existence of a canonical body of familiar poetry—and hunger on the part of readers for even more material. But novelty counts, too. Rather than feeding that hunger by obsessive rereadings of the already, but always imperfectly, known poem, there is a natural urge to absorb new avatars of the familiar spirit. These drafts, or unpublished poems—call them what you will—might pull some readers away from Bishop's published body of poetry, for a while at least, as we all try to understand the poet's guiding assumptions about what belonged in her public portfolio.

A small grouping of elegiac, epigrammatic poems, mostly from the early 1950s, taken together with Quinn's excellent notes, deepens the puzzlement surrounding some of Bishop's decisions about what to publish and what to hold back (or suppress). How does one account for the poet's reluctance to add "For M.B.S., buried in Nova Scotia," "Where are the dolls who loved me so . . . ," "A Short, Slow Life," and perhaps the somewhat less finished "Syllables," to the roster of poems she was eager to flesh out into a second book of poems? By highlighting the chronological clustering of these poems in the early 1950s, just after Bishop left Key West for Brazil, and prior to the appearance of *A Cold Spring,* Quinn prompts us to ask whether the crises in Bishop's life at this time, coupled with her isolation from publishing centers and poetry circles, made her less willing to release certain poems. "For M.B.S.," an epitaphic elegy for Bishop's aunt, and "A Short, Slow Life" supplement "Sestina" and "First Death in Nova Scotia," providing even further proof of Bishop's mastery in the realms of strict, heartbreaking elegiac ethos.

These buried elegies, as I like to call them, seem to have been worked on by Bishop over many years, as she was accustomed to do, but they also seem to have been typed up in final, or quasi-final, draft form in the early 1950s, when Bishop was first in Brazil. They exist in a grouping of three or four, depending on one's criteria for the elegiac poem. They were thus available for inclusion in *A Cold Spring,* when it was published, along with the reissued *North & South,* in 1955. For whatever reason, Bishop chose not to publish this cluster of striking elegies and ubi sunt lyrics at that time, nor did she choose to include them in the "Elsewhere" section of *Questions of Travel,* where they could have joined the other Nova Scotia poems, "Sestina" and "First Death in Nova Scotia." Unlike those two published elegies, or elegy-inflected poems, the short pieces I discuss here are less aesthetically annealed against the display of affect, less enameled in defense against what the poet was enamored of. Bishop's strategic presentation of herself as "another armored animal," to borrow a phrase from Marianne Moore, is something of a long-willed pose meant to position her among the Stoics and to ensure a more lasting preference for her style of elegy. But these unpublished, "buried" elegies deserve to be "said"—I am using a key word from one of them—and thereby unsilenced. All praise to Alice Quinn for making them so public.

"Syllables" is the first of these poems that I will discuss. The poem, as Quinn tells us, exists in four pages of drafts, and a single typed copy, which she prints in her edition. (Victoria Harrison, as Quinn notes, made a careful study of the typewriters Bishop used over the years; she dates the poems I am discussing from the early 1950s, at least in their final typed versions.)

> Whatever there was, or is, of love let it be obeyed:
> —so that the grandfather mightn't have been blinded,
> the river never dwindled to what it is now,
> nor the leaning big willows above it been blighted,
> nor its trout been fished out;
> nor, by the naked boys, the swimming hole been abandoned,
> dissolved, abandoned, its terra cottas and gilt.
> (—the boys who dove for white china doorknobs
> stolen from the hens' nests;)
> Whatever there is, or was, of affection
> may it be said.
>
> The barn swallows belonged to
> the barns, they went with the church's wooden steeple.
> & they flew as fast as they did because the air was so still—
>
> That steeple—I can't remember—wasn't it struck by lightning? (EAP 101)

Robert Frost might have turned the opening eleven-line verse paragraph into a rhymed sonnet and included it in *West-Running Brook*. I cannot imagine a sense of "finished" that does not apply to that opening section, with its gnomic, faintly accusatory self-injunction to openly declare one's affections, as if in obedience to love's dark dicta. The poem implies that the act of speaking one's love can in some fashion bring about the preservation of those things that constitute the heart's deep affections. Indeed, the firm but gentle imperative to speak—"may it be said"—constitutes an imperative toward utterance. That this line should appear in a poem that Bishop chose not to publish—and she was no Emily Dickinson when it came to the marketplace—is a profound irony. "Syllables" will thus take the form of an elegiac, ubi sunt prayer, with the formulaic "so that" operating as a kind of verbal charm fashioned to ward off abandonment. This is how the memory machine of poetry can indeed work—but It Must Be Said. Bishop says it in draft form, but she will then abandon the draft, disobey the imperatives of love, by refusing to make the poem, and the things it carries, public. By withholding the full saying of these emblems of affection, Bishop almost seems to conspire in the slow lapse of time, and the gain of decay and dissolution. To think that the poem was alternatively titled "Autobiography" is sobering.

"For M.B.S., buried in Nova Scotia," has the look of a classical elegiac epigram, or a Jonsonian seventeenth-century version of that form. The poem is a sinuous single sentence, reproducing the effect of breathing by sharply indenting two of its six lines. And the poem has a certain formal austerity to it, balanced by the knowing intimacy of the second-person address.

> Yes, you are dead now and live
> only there, in a little, slightly tip-tilted graveyard
> where all of your childhood's Christmas trees are forgathered
> with the present they meant to give,
> and your childhood's river quietly curls at your side
> and breathes deep with each tide. (EAP 98)

I can hardly think of a more quietly moving twentieth-century elegy, one that so masterfully backgathers so many elements of the elegiac tradition—but then refuses to bequeath itself to the reader as a present, by remaining unpublished. Bishop addresses the poem to her aunt, her surrogate mother. She can lay claim to knowledge of her aunt's desires by the exercise of memory, both her own memory and the memory of her aunt's memories. Her reading of her aunt remains hypernaturalistic, so the poem situates itself in a spot of time: "only *there,* in a little, slightly tip-tilted graveyard." But this "now," this "present," tip-tilts seamlessly into an eerie, *unheimlich* fusion of past and future. To be dead now is to live in a fulfillment of womb-like repose, curled against the river and breathing along with it, as Wordsworth imagined himself breathing in his native Derwent. The most mysterious word in the poem is "forgathered": "all of your childhood Christmas trees are forgathered / with the present they meant to give." We all remember the line that haunted Bishop for years, before finally settling in "At the Fishhouses"—"A million Christmas trees stand / waiting for Christmas"—where the slash of the line break works to prefigure the fate of those trees. As Bishop wrote in an early journal entry: "I know how they feel." The vision of those trees in this elegy, however, is different. The trees are "forgathered," but there is no sense that they will be cut down. Most crucially, they are not simply gathered, they are forgathered, massed, as if in anticipation of the dreamer's desire. They come, magus-like, with the "present they meant to give," as if to make reparation for something lacking; but they do not actually bestow that present, for they remain poised in the state of meaning to give. Even forgathered by poetry's power to inhabit the dead dreamer's desire, these trees and their perpetual presents are situated at the near verge of death, as close to the knowing edge of gnosis as Stevens takes us in poems such as "Not Ideas about the Thing but the Thing Itself," or "Of Mere Being." It is intriguing to think that Bishop might have been working on this elegy when Stevens's *Collected* appeared in late 1954, with "Not Ideas" as its last poem; perhaps she worked on it late enough to become aware of "Of Mere Being," first published in *Opus Posthumous* in 1957.

"A Short, Slow Life" also reads like an epigrammatic elegy, mourning the loss of a pocket of time, a pocket in time, much as Frost in "Directive" mourned the slowly closing hole in dough that marked the disappearance of his own lost house. "A Short, Slow Life," a deeply Wordsworthian lyric, compresses and abstracts "The Ruined Cottage," seeing Time as the inevitable enemy:

> We lived in a pocket of Time.
> It was close, it was warm.
> Along the dark seam of the river
> the houses, the barns, the two churches,
> hid like white crumbs
> in a fluff of gray willows and elms,
> till Time made one of his gestures;
> his nails scratched the shingled roof.
> Roughly his hand reached in,
> and tumbled us out. (*EAP* 103)

This vision of time as the rough beast whose nails scratch the roof, and whose hands or paws reach in and evict the huddled tenants, predicts the lion-sun in "The End of March" who walked the beach, and "batted a kite out of the sky to play with." The phrase "dark seam of the river" is unforgettable, one of Bishop's most gnomic fusings. The comforts of domesticity are stitched precariously to the dark seam of that which connects and separates home from the *unheimlich*. "This side" is sutured to the "other side," kept apart from it only by a dark seam. When Time shifts, in one of his periodic adjustments, the seam gives way and boundary lines are erased. The gothic domesticity of "A Short, Slow Life" has a Dickinsonian chill to it.

The final elegiac piece in this particular grouping from the early 1950s is "Where are the dolls who loved me so . . . ," a masterpiece of psychosexual identity formation and counterformation. One might imagine this poem as being spoken by "the child" of "Sestina," with a focus this time not on the grandmother, but on the child's quasi-human playmates. One wishes that Sylvia Plath and Adrienne Rich could have seen this poem in *A Cold Spring,* which might have been issued as a single volume, instead of being coupled with *North & South,* had the book included more poems, especially in this mode:

> Where are the dolls who loved me so
> when I was young?
> Who cared for me with hands of bisque,
> poked breadcrumbs in between my lips,
>
> Where are the early nurses,
> Gertrude, Zilpha, and Nokomis?
>
> Through their real eyes
>
> blank crotches,
> and / play / wrist-watches,
> whose hands moved only when they wanted—
>
> Their stoicism I never mastered
> their smiling phrase for every occasion—
> They went their rigid little ways
>
> To meditate in trunks or closets
> To let [life and] unforeseen emotions
> glance off their glazed complexions (EAP 102)

This eerie addition to the permanent corps of ubi sunt lyrics plays with gendered and eroticized acts of identification in ways predictive of "In the Waiting Room." As with several other poems in this grouping, there is more than a touch of gothic frisson present in the poem's elegiac workings. Dread and desire commingle in this doll's house. The poem shows striking signs of playing with Freud's own essay about dolls, otherwise known as *The Uncanny.* In a letter written in December 1953, from the period when these poems were apparently composed, Bishop tells her correspondent that she read "all of Dickens, Trollope, Freud (Lota has a large psychological library)" (*OA* 283). I note in passing how interesting it is that Bishop seems to place Freud among the Victorians in this grouping. What Bishop exactly meant by "all" in the case of these voluminous authors is less important than registering her accomplishment of the desire announced later on in "The End of March," to find a "crypto-dream-house" (which she seems to have found chez Lota), where she might do "*nothing*" all day long but read "old, long, long books," only some of which might prove, alas, "boring." More to the point, it seems to me that Bishop must have returned with a vengeance to *The Uncanny*, based on the ways in which her doll poem echoes and revises Freud's most literary of essays.

The Uncanny has enduring appeal largely because it locates a perdurable sub-genre of imaginative literature and film: works that evoke feelings of fear, horror, distress, or unease. But Freud is interested in what might be called a sub-subgenre: "The uncanny is that species of the frightening that goes back to what was once well known and had long been familiar" (124). Freud acknowledges only one serious precursor to his investigation, E. Jentsch, whose work Freud praises for being rich in content, while also pointing out that it is not "exhaustive"—in other words, Jentsch is provocative enough, but in the end leaves room for Freudian supplementation. Veteran readers of the *The Uncanny* will recall that Freud has some trouble dismissing Jentsch's central definition of the *unheimlich* as involving an elemental confusion between the living and the dead, the animate and the in-animate, the human and the inhuman. For Jentsch, the frisson associated with the uncanny arises whenever we are unsure as to whether something is alive or dead, human or artificial. Freud wants to reject that notion as not cutting deep enough into the complex of feelings surrounding the *unheimlich*, but it lingers throughout his own essay. And how can it not, considering that the central text Freud focuses on in his essay, Hoffmann's "The Sand-Man," features an automaton, a doll, an artificial woman? But Freud wagers that his essay will persuade readers that what truly accounts for feelings of the uncanny involves a deeper sense of dread than that invoked by a state of confusion over ontological status, however unsettling that condition of doubt may be. For the most penetrating aspect of Hoffmann's tale, for Freud, centers on the feeling of horror evoked by the "motif of the Sand-Man, who tears out children's eyes" (136). And that horror can be traced, according to Freud, to the "substitutive relation between the eye and the male member that is manifested in dreams, fantasies, and myths" (140). In other words, what generates the dread of the *unheimlich* is not species anxiety, but castration anxiety.

Bishop's poem delights in the dismissal of any concerns on the child's part as to whether the dolls are alive or dead, as if the question itself was an artificial one. Of course their love for her is a returned projection (she manipulates them so that they mother her), but what matters finally is that love was being issued and transferred. For this child, the dolls are comforting, not unsettling; in retrospect, they prove to be role models, due to their "stoicism" and their ability to "meditate in trunks or closets." From the adult's perspective, of course, the animation of the dolls, driven by the child's need, is both poignant and a little eerie, or uncanny, since Bishop succeeds at naturalizing the child's perspective, so that for a moment or two it seems not at all unlikely that the dolls might indeed serve as emblems of meditation. But where Bishop most engages the core of Freud's argument, intentionally or not, is when she zeroes in on the castration complex itself, fixing on the all-purpose genital "lack" of dolls, their "blank crotches." The blunt phrase, assigned a line to itself, stops one cold, and induces a chill, coming close to capturing that infantile element that Freud wishes to locate, since Bishop is working back to the pregenital stage when the slate is blank for both sexes and the absence of specific genitalia is ascribed not to a symbolic castration, but to the polymorphous possibilities of unfixed eros. In a sense, then, Bishop is parodying and revising the Freudian narrative of castration. As if to drive the point home, she unblinds the eyes of her dolls, who have "real eyes." For the Bishop of "Where are the dolls who loved me so . . ." and the late "In the Waiting Room," the anxiety of the uncanny does not arise from "losing" the phallus, but from losing the generative space of a counterbiological blankness.

Another product of this "elegiac" period in Bishop's career is less of an elegy proper than a meditation on the death drive in the form of the compulsion to repeat. In this case, what gets repeated are verbal talismans, leitmotifs that people use and abuse throughout their lives. The draft is entitled "The Grandmothers," and it exemplifies the strength of Quinn's volume, because it raises to the foreground an unfinished text that contains striking moments of self-clarity. The poem is perhaps less a portrait of Bishop's trio of grandmothers (one is a great-grandmother) than an anatomy of how people close to us can dwindle or grow into one signature word or phrase. Here is the opening stanza:

> I had three grandmothers, (one "great" one, understood)
> three average Christian ladies of their day,
> predominantly good;
> they had their faults, but nothing serious.
> But each one had one phrase she used to say,
> so awful, so mysterious,
> [it haunts their grandchild to this very day.] (EAP 107–8)

These quotidian verbal amulets, worn and repeated by the grandmothers, strike the poet as both arbitrary, yet uncannily prophetic, especially when chanted as a kind of litany: *"My day will come"*; *"Nobody knows"*; and, what frightened her most of all, *"Ho-hum, Ho-hum, hum-a-day."* It takes all too little, as the poem tells us, for these hackneyed expressions to break free from context and become incantatory, stirring a cauldron of inherited fears, fears over what might be inherited.

Indeed, the poem presents as spur to its own formation the frightening (but also slightly humorous) realization that the poet herself is beginning to crystallize into a repeater: "without my realizing / a phrase is crystallizing / I've / started to employ it —" (*EAP* 107). Even a poem devoted to utterance strays slightly into the precincts of the gothic, as the poet realizes that something is growing on and in her—the dreaded, obsessional word or phrase. The closing lines of this unfinished poem have that chill that we find in the cluster of elegies from this period. And it predicts a fate whose permutations are spelled out and traced in later Bishop poems: "Give me thirty years, give & take a year, / What [terrible] phrase . . . // will my old lips have kept repeating, repeating?" (*EAP* 108). This final question can take its place, for poetic charge, alongside any number of Bishop's more famous interrogatives.

Reading through Quinn's chronological collection highlights another oddity of Bishop's publishing procedures: the strange assortment titled "New and Uncollected Work" that she affixed to the end of the 1969 *Complete Poems*. Now that we can easily see the other choices she might have made, as opposed to the comparatively lackluster poems that she included to round out the volume, it becomes all the more interesting to think about what message she intended to send about the shape of her oeuvre and her career. Was she saving better drafts for a later volume? Nobody can fail to notice the tame, occasional quality of that final section of *The Complete Poems,* especially when juxtaposed with a number of the poems that I have been discussing. It seems as if Bishop was obscuring some of the reasons that lay behind her resistance to finishing certain poems by publishing less vexed (but much less interesting) poems in their place.

We do not find many "buried elegies" after the mid-1950s or so, since Bishop seems to have completed and published her ventures into the genre: "Sestina," "First Death in Nova Scotia," "One Art," "The End of March," "Five Flights Up." (As readers will note, my definition of what counts toward elegy in Bishop is an expansive one.) A poem that Quinn places in the mid-1970s, "For Grandfather" (*EAP* 154), bears a close resemblance to the family elegies from twenty years before. The poem strikes me as finished, and powerful, so it makes little sense to think of it as a draft. It is likely to have been one of the poems Bishop intended for inclusion in the projected volume entitled "Grandmother's Glass Eye," which she listed in her Guggenheim application dated October 1, 1977 (Millier 538).

Bishop's maternal grandfather, William Bulmer, died in 1927, so the poem's opening, hushed question to him—"How far north are you by now?"—balances a sense of intimate proximity to the near dead with a chilled recognition of the distance traversed by them across a half century of death. And yet, as the second line immediately reminds us, the living, too, are in motion toward death, following the tracks of the departed: "—But I'm almost close enough to see you" (*EAP* 154). Bishop fashions this elegy as a polar journey, but one outfitted with her trademark signs of dislocated domesticity. The grandfather is "trudging on splaying snow-shoes," and in a role reversal, the granddaughter wants to make sure he is warm enough, so she inquires if he is dressed for the journey: "Where is your sealskin cap with ear-lugs? / That old fur coat with the black frogs?" (*EAP* 154). As with a number of these buried elegies, the poem betrays notes of tenderness and intimacy not often found in Bishop's published material: "If I should overtake you, kiss your cheek" (Is there another kiss bestowed anywhere else in Bishop?) And she imagines the texture of his face: "its silver stubble would feel like hoar-frost / and your old-fashioned, walrus moustache / be hung with icicles" (*EAP* 154).

For all the winning personalism of "For Grandfather," the poem also fulfills the elegiac imperative to place itself within the constellation of other elegies, other poets, as a way of immortalizing itself and its subject. For this northern elegy, the lodestar is Wallace Stevens, who infuses the poem by means of several signature tropes. Following in the wake of her grandfather, the poet observes that overhead, "Aurora Borealis burns in silence." And "The Snow Man" predominates as well, as the poem's last line makes clear: "Grandfather, please stop! I haven't been this cold in years." One must have a mind of winter and have been cold a long time to persevere on this trek. But perhaps the poem's deepest and most subtle allusion is to another poem in the Bishop oeuvre, "The Imaginary Iceberg," thus constituting a necessitous, semi-conscious acknowledgment of the poet's own claim to canonical stature. The snowscape of "For Grandfather" induces this reflection: "These drifts are endless, I think; as far as the Pole / they hold no shadows but their own, and ours" (*EAP* 154). This scenario of rich solipsistic reflection, with room enough only for a close relative and a close poetic relation such as Stevens, brings Bishop back to a poem at the beginning of her career, thus tying together origins and ends. The extraordinary paean to the iconic figure of the iceberg reads as follows:

> This iceberg cuts its facets from within.
> Like jewelry from a grave
> it saves itself perpetually and adorns
> only itself . . . (*CP* 4)

Within "For Grandfather," poetic solipsism melts to the extent that the polar land-scape can now include a pair of shadows: "ours."

Thus far, I have been treating poems that a certain number of inveterate Bishop readers might be happy to regard as finished or nearly ready for publication. In such cases, I would argue, we cannot know whether Bishop "rejected" these po-ems definitively, or withheld them for later placement, even decades down the road. She might well have included these family elegies, given a final polishing, in "Grandmother's Glass Eye." Other texts in *Edgar Allan Poe & the Juke-Box* exist in more larval form and certainly qualify as "drafts" moving toward further stages of completion. A certain glamour has always accrued to the fragments of great poets or artists, even to the extent that in many cases we are satisfied by the sugges-tively unfinished, getting enough charge from the glittering shards in hand. This is true, I think, of "A mother made of dress-goods . . ." (*EAP* 156–57), an emergent family elegy from near the end of Bishop's life. The poem handles maternal me-tonymies, as its title indicates, cataloguing items of clothing associated with the long-lost mother and invoking a feeling of "women feeling for the smoothness of yard-goods," to invoke that memorable line from the inaugural poem of Bishop's inaugural volume. As is true for "In the Waiting Room" as well, voice soon be-comes the core issue:

> A voice heard still
> echoing
> far at the bottom somewhere
> of my aunt's on the telephone—
> coming out of blackness—the blackness all voices come from (*EAP* 156)

Would Bishop have regarded "In the Waiting Room" as rendering this draft-poem redundant, or would she have found ways to move this meditation on the mother's trace—"A mother is a hat" (a phrase reminiscent of the line in "The Man-Moth," "the whole shadow of Man is only as big as his hat")—forward into regions not yet broached by her?

In her letter of application to the Guggenheim Foundation, Bishop proposed a second new project, a book-length elegy for her partner Lota de Macedo Soares, who had committed suicide in September 1967, almost exactly a decade earlier. Her working title for the volume was, simply enough, "Elegy" (Millier 538). What Quinn rightly calls "Bishop's first attempt at the poem" (*EAP* 219), "Aubade and Elegy" (*EAP* 149), is presented to us in facsimile form, which Quinn occasionally uses in order "to illustrate the range of manuscript material" (*EAP* xvii). Quinn goes on to include three facsimile pages of notes for the poem in the appendix (*EAP* 219–22), yet another feature that makes her volume essential as a supplement to the new Library of America edition. "Roosters" was an aubade, and it was also an elegy for a dying love affair. In this early draft, Bishop is using the three-line stanza of "Roosters" and "One Art," though unrhymed in this instance, though it is certainly possible that a rhyme-scheme might have formed over prolonged drafts. Once again, Bishop seems to be returning to her earlier poetic topoi in these late poems of love and loss. "Aubade and Elegy" opens on a strong note of habitual mourning, mourning (and morning) as a kind of habit:

> No coffee can wake you no coffee can wake you no coffee
> No revolution can catch your attention
> You are bored with us all. It is true we are boring.
>
> For perhaps the tenth time the tenth time the tenth time today
> and still early morning I go under the crashing wave
> of death
> > I go under the wave the black wave of death. (*EAP* 149)

Rolled round in earth's diurnal course, like Wordsworth's Lucy, no earthly revolution can snare the arch-political Lota now. That big black wave from "In the Waiting Room" is back, but whereas in the published poem it transported the young Elizabeth to a second birth into the world of poetic meanings, this time the wave seems to extinguish the poet. The hammering negativity of the poem's opening lines set up a severe obstacle for the elegy to overcome. A way out, perhaps, emerges with the memory of Lota busy in her garden, "transplanting sweet williams"—doing the poet's work of elegiac mourning, which is always a form of transplantation. Alice Quinn's volume is filled with these sorts of cuttings, some of which would surely have blossomed over time, in other settings.

Elizabeth Bishop's "Finished" Unpublished Poems

LLOYD SCHWARTZ

One of the major controversies over Elizabeth Bishop's posthumous publications has been the ethical issue about bringing into print poems she either regarded as unfinished or chose not to publish. Some critics have rushed in to "save" Bishop's reputation for perfection, complaining that these poems that she left unpublished at the time of her death compromise the high standards she maintained with her published poems. But in Helen Vendler's 2006 *New Republic* review of *Edgar Allan Poe & the Juke-Box,* her anger at the *New Yorker* for publishing unfinished drafts of poems without indicating that they were in fact only drafts seems more justified than her dismay over the appearance of these posthumously published poems in a volume subtitled *Uncollected Poems, Drafts, and Fragments.* Vendler suggests that it would have been more accurate to call these "repudiated" rather than "uncollected" poems. But Bishop habitually returned to poems that she hadn't completed, often years later, and among them are some of her masterpieces: "Crusoe in England," "The Moose," "Pink Dog."

Bishop never really "repudiated" most of her drafts. If anything, she was quite prepared for their posthumous publication, since her will actually gives her literary executors "the power to determine whether any of my unpublished manuscripts and papers shall be published, and if so, to see them through the press." And rather than diminish Bishop's reputation, as Vendler feared, these poems—sometimes "imperfect" but sometimes as polished and deeply felt as her published work and often remarkably ambitious, dealing with subjects she never or only barely touched on in her published work (politics, sexuality, death, her own alcoholism)—significantly expand what we've tended to accept as her relatively narrow range.

So there's probably less ethical conflict in Bishop's posthumous publications than with, say, the *Aeneid* or the posthumous works of Kafka, and the controversy distracts us from a greater mystery. Bishop left numerous drafts of poems that she came very close to completing, or completed without publishing, even though she was desperate to publish more poems.

We can, of course, speculate about the reasons she didn't publish these, ranging from her sense that they were just not ready, to her more general distrust of personal, "confessional" poetry and her deeper fears of self-exposure ("I want closets, closets, and more closets," she told Richard Howard, jokingly, about her new apartment)—though those fears she overcame in her later, more open work (Fountain 293). None of these explanations really takes us very far. However, among the most thoroughly finished of those poems she could not bring herself to publish before her sudden and untimely death are poems sexual in nature.[1] And although she published and republished a handful of love poems during her lifetime, they are relatively abstract, indirect, or downright obscure. (Her most explicit published indication of love for another woman, the dedicatory epigraph to her book *Questions of Travel,* is a quotation from Camões in Portuguese.) When I was working on my dissertation on Bishop, I asked her about the bewildering syntax at the end of "Rain Towards Morning" ("an unexpected kiss / whose freckled unsuspected hands alit") (*PPL* 59), and her reply was, "But it's obvious"! I suspect that the poem that begins, "It is marvellous to wake up together" (*PPL* 217) is actually an earlier (and far more explicitly narrative) version of what became "Rain Towards Morning"—are there two other Bishop poems with such unusual yet closely overlapping imagery (especially the image of the "cage" of rain)? Yet many Bishop readers today seem to be more touched by "It is marvellous" and prefer its colloquial, almost prosy openness. "Rain Towards Morning" is a refined, prismatic gem, but seems emotionally evasive in comparison. Its absence from the anthologies should surprise no one.

Perhaps the best-known poem Bishop published in a magazine but never collected is the labor-intensively witty, slippery-rhymed, and trickily gender-bending "Exchanging Hats," one of James Merrill's favorite Bishop poems and one he loved to read aloud. Did Bishop regard it as too playful, too much like light verse? Yet she published it in a serious journal, *New World Writing,* and the ending of the poem, with its funereal allusions, turns darkly chilling:

> Unfunny uncle, you who wore a
> hat too big, or one too many,
> tell us, can't you, are there any
> stars inside your black fedora?
>
> Aunt exemplary and slim,
> with avernal eyes, we wonder
> what slow changes they see under
> their vast, shady, turned-down brim. (*PPL* 199)

She put a lot of work into "Exchanging Hats." Was she ultimately wary about keeping before the public a poem dealing so directly with the dangerous issue of sexual identity?

Always self-critical, she could be right on target about the quality of some of the poems she published. She included "The Mountain" in *A Cold Spring* (1955), after publishing it in *Poetry* (October 1952), yet dropped it from the paperback version (1965) and didn't include it in the first edition of *Complete Poems* (1969). "I don't think much of it," she wrote to Marianne Moore in 1953. She published "A Norther—Key West" in the *New Yorker* (January 20, 1962), but never included it in any of her collections. Most readers wouldn't disagree with these decisions. Neither of these poems, however, concerns a subject about which Bishop could be in any way uneasy.

But sometimes Bishop could also be too self-critical, and I'm not sure that she was unfailingly right about all her literary decisions. On occasion, she was perhaps too easily intimidated by editors' opinions, though some of her capitulations she came to regret.[2] She was confident enough about her unnerving, vividly imagined Key West poem "The Street by the Cemetery" to send it to the *New Yorker*. The poem depicts poor people sitting on a verandah in the moonlight looking out on a graveyard, "like passengers on ship-board"—"steerage" passengers, yet sitting on deck-chairs—with "nothing much to say / to the neighbors three feet away" (*PPL* 216). It's a haunting image, in three elegantly rhymed six-line stanzas, of the living literally facing—"hypnotized" by—incomprehensible death. But the *New Yorker* (which certainly wasn't always right either) turned it down, and Bishop never included it in a book. The finished draft exists in a single vigorously crossed-out copy. I wish she had persisted either in continuing to revise it or sending it elsewhere. I'm glad it's been made available for us to read.

There are memorable, moving poems that seem only a hairbreadth away from being finished. "For M.B.S., Buried in Nova Scotia" (*PPL* 234)—a memorial for Bishop's beloved aunt Maud Bulmer Shepherdson, who took the young orphan in when it became clear that her wealthier paternal grandparents were unable to keep her healthy or make her happy. That cemetery, as Alice Quinn traces in her notes to this poem, was for Bishop an idyllic spot, and the poem, with its distant echo of the fir trees in "At the Fishhouses" that stand "waiting for Christmas," and its tellingly enjambed opening line ("Yes, you are dead now and live") is a sort of pastoral elegy, a Wordsworthian image of final peace and a comforting, protecting, living Nature ("and your childhood's river quietly curls at your side / and breathes deep with each tide").

"A Short, Slow Life," which Alice Quinn describes as having "innumerable drafts . . . in only slightly different versions" (*EAP* 310), is Bishop's image of being expelled from that pastoral childhood Eden, the fairy-tale life in Nova Scotia (with its houses, barns, and churches hidden like Hansel-and-Gretel "white crumbs" among the willows and elms). This poem is set, like Aunt Maud's cemetery, close to "the dark seam" of a riverbank:

> till Time made one of his gestures;
> his nails scratched the shingled roof.
> Roughly his hand reached in,
> and tumbled us out. (*PPL* 235)

(I'm reminded of the scene in Walt Disney's *Mickey and the Beanstalk* in which the galumphing giant lifts the roof off the house and threateningly reaches in.)

Two later poems of childhood and family also seem essentially finished. Bishop worked hard on "Salem Willows" (the title refers to a park in Salem, Massachusetts) (*PPL* 257), which survives in fourteen pages of drafts. This is another poem in which her Aunt Maud figures, as a kind of Fate, knitting and waiting while her young niece rides the magical carousel "around and around and around"—like the mechanical motions of the elegant toy horse in "Cirque d'Hiver" (*PPL* 23), with whom Bishop so explicitly identifies (and here she's also surrounded by life-like mechanical animals). Precise, vivid, haunting, "Salem Willows" captures the qualities Bishop said, in her unfinished essay "Writing Poetry Is an Unnatural Act" (*PPL* 703), that she admired most in the poems she loved best: "*Accuracy, Spontaneity, Mystery.*" It's so piercing because it so fully relives that childhood experience.

"A Drunkard" tries to recapture yet another childhood incident that also took place in Salem, one of the few pieces she wrote that deal directly with her mother. But the seams still show in her effort to stitch the poem together, and parts of the poem seem more like prose than verse: "I felt amazement not fear / but amazement may be / my infancy's chief emotion" (*PPL* 252). It's one of Bishop's most revealing efforts—an etiology of her alcoholism, stemming from her memory of being with her mother during the "Great Salem Fire"—but it's still steps away from a satisfying poetic solution.

"For Grandfather" is much more successful. It's about the long-ago death of William Bulmer, Bishop's mother's father, who died in 1927 and is also the subject of the charming "Manners." The images of snow and cold here recall another Nova Scotia elegy, "First Death in Nova Scotia," about Bishop's young cousin. This dream poem, with its detailed description of her grandfather, is a poignant outcry of feelings—feelings she still has of terrible loss and abandonment—that are reflected in the chill nightmare landscape:

> Where is your sealskin cap with ear-lugs?
> That old fur coat with the black frogs?
> You'll catch your death again.
> . . . .
> These drifts are endless, I think; as far as the Pole
> they hold no shadows but their own, and ours.
> Grandfather, please stop! I haven't been this cold in years. (*PPL* 256)

Equally extraordinary, but taking a very different direction, is the touching yet tough, and indirectly autobiographical monologue "Keaton," which exists in a single draft. If you had to choose any celebrity you thought Bishop might identify with, it would surely be Buster Keaton, the most inward and understated, the most inventive and gravest, of the silent-movie comedians: "The Great Stone Face," as he was called. With his flat porkpie hat "—witness the diameter of my hatband / and the depth of the crown of my hat" (*PPL* 243)—and his unbudgeable determination ("I have set my small jaw for the ages / and nothing can distract me from / solving the appointed emergencies / even with my small brain"), he is a direct descendent of another artist / creature with whom Bishop identifies, "The Man-Moth"—"The whole shadow of Man is only as big as his hat . . . what the Man-Moth fears most, he must do, although / he fails, of course" (*PPL* 10). Fearing his rigid spine will break, everyone advises Keaton to "Bend, bend." But he refuses to take this advice. Can't take it. His summary conclusion: "I am not sentimental" (*PPL* 243). I would add "Keaton" to the list that includes "The Man-Moth," "Cirque d'Hiver," "The Gentleman of Shalott," "The Sandpiper," "Crusoe in England," and the prose monologues of the discomfited creatures in "Rainy Season; Sub-Tropics" ("Giant Toad," "Strayed Crab," and "Giant Snail") as among Bishop's most obliquely revealing self-portraits.

"Mr. and Mrs. Carlyle" is one of the last poems Bishop was working on and one she had been revising for years. She loved Mrs. Carlyle's letters and included them on the syllabus of the course in letters she taught at Harvard. The anecdote in this poem involves a misconnection between the couple, who probably spent more time apart, given Thomas's busy lecture schedule, than together. They were supposed to meet at an inn called "The Swan with Two Necks." So Jane, even though she had a headache, was forced to deliver her own luggage by public transportation, to avoid "a fuss" ("She lived not to vex / Mr. Carlyle"). It's one of Bishop's rare poems that deal directly with marriage (even among her prose pieces, only "Memories of Uncle Neddy" comes to mind as a story about a married couple). One version of the last stanza is a chilling image of conjugal inextricability, with one of the most violent words in all of Bishop:

> One flesh and two heads
>   engaged in kisses or in pecks.
> Oh white seething marriage!
>   Oh Swan with Two Necks! (*PPL* 264)

It's sad that Bishop couldn't come up with what Robert Lowell called "the un-imaginable phrase" ("unerring Muse who makes the casual perfect")[3] that might have given her the confidence she needed to make these poems public.

Two ambitious poems centering on erotic encounters expand even further what we know of Bishop's work, and are in different stages of incompleteness. One seems clearly unfinished, the explicitly lesbian "Vague Poem (Vaguely love poem)," which veers from startlingly flat prose statements, as if she were writing a letter—"They talked a lot about 'rose rocks' / or maybe 'rock roses' /—I'm not sure now, but someone tried to get me some. / (And two or three students had)"—to a remarkable rhapsodic conclusion:

> Just now, when I saw you naked again,
> I thought the same words: rose-rock, rock-rose . . .
> Rose, trying, working, to show itself,
> forming, folding over,
> unimaginable connections, unseen, shining edges.
> Rose-rock, unformed, flesh beginning, crystal by crystal,
> clear pink breasts and darker, crystalline nipples,
> rose-rock, rose-quartz, roses, roses, roses,
> exacting roses from the body,
> and the even darker, accurate, rose of sex— (*PPL* 255)

The other poem is the brilliant, daring, and bewildering "Edgar Allan Poe & the Juke-Box" (*PPL* 221), which Bishop intended to be the last poem in *A Cold Spring*—"that last impossible poem," as she calls it in a letter to Robert Lowell. A few passages are clearly not finished, with possible additions or substitutions written in the margin, but most of the poem seems fully worked out. Yet she never published it. Bishop describes a scene of people—only women?—cruising in a Key West bar. The language ranges from the painterly ("bottles and blue lights / and silvered coconuts and conches") to the metaphorical ("the drinks like lonely water-falls / in night descend the separate throats") to double entendre, where the juke-box becomes virtually genital ("the nickels fall into the slots"; "the burning box"), to some strange combination of archetypal myth and suggestive euphemism ("the hands fall on one another / [down] darker darkness under / tablecloths, and all descends, / descends, falls . . . the earthward fall of love / descending from the head and eye / down to the hands, and heart, and down") (221). All these "down"-ward glances and movements descend even to a pun on the musical "down-beat" on the jukebox, the strict, steady "measure" of pop songs with their melodramatic depictions of "drink and murder" (was someone playing "Frankie and Johnny"?).

Then Bishop makes one of her most startling leaps, an unpredictable transition to a reference to Poe's theory of "exactness" in poetry, which she compares to the nature of desire itself: "pleasures are mechanical / and know beforehand what they want / and know exactly what they want" (221). She concludes with the question of whether Poe (or is she suddenly asking him directly?) or poetry "obtain that single effect" nearly half as successfully as "horror here," the nightmarish search for satisfied desire in the Starlight or La Conga dance halls. Bishop never seems to have felt fully resolved about this connection she's trying to make between the obsessive search for pleasure and the "single effect" of poetry. The surviving draft has a long diagonal slash drawn through it.

It's illuminating to discover how hard Bishop struggled with challenging subject matter. But she also completed (without any trace of effort or dissatisfaction) three remarkable poems all dealing explicitly with lovers sleeping together, poems that she never chose to publish. Two of them she wrote in Brazil and (as far as we know) never even kept her drafts when she returned to the United States.

One was used by her young artist friend José Alberto Nemer (now quite a distinguished national figure in Brazil) as part of an engraving depicting an entwined couple:

> Close close all night
> the lovers keep.
> They turn together
> in their sleep,
>
> close as two pages
> in a book
> that read each other
> in the dark.

> Each knows all
> the other knows,
> learned by heart
> from head to toes. (EAP 141)

The second stanza, with the poem's one—heart-stopping—slant rhyme (book/dark), has one of Bishop's most eloquent and suggestive images, in which she turns the literary into the erotic. This largely monosyllabic poem is very simple in its language, yet it's also very tightly knit and teases playful new meaning out of its old clichés ("learned by heart"; "head to toes").

The other poem she left in Brazil is more complex, her only surviving poem that deals with her persistent theme of *North & South*—North *versus* South—that directly, explicitly discusses her awareness of her inescapable rootedness in the North, and that looks back at her northern origins from the point of view of living below the equator, in the opposite hemisphere (which is also the subject of her fictionalized memoir "Memories of Uncle Neddy"):

> Dear, my compass
> still points north
> to wooden houses
> and blue eyes,
>
> fairy-tales where
> flaxen-headed
> younger sons
> bring home the goose,
>
> love in hay-lofts,
> Protestants, and
> heavy drinkers . . .
> Springs are backward,
>
> but crab-apples
> ripen to rubies,
> cranberries
> to drops of blood,
>
> and swans can paddle
> icy water,

> so hot the blood
> in those webbed feet.
>
> —Cold as it is, we'd
> go to bed, dear,
> early, but never
> to keep warm. (PPL 251)

The better I get to know this poem, the more bewitching I find it, with its primal, primary colors (blue eyes, yellow hair, red apples and cranberries, rubies and blood) and opposing temperatures (including body temperatures), its language and imagery pervasively drawn from the more sinister, violent, sexual side of fairy tales—a kind of corollary to the more domestic and child-oriented fantasy of "Sestina," with its animated almanac and teakettle. There are two original manuscripts, one handwritten, one typed, and to continue the fairy-tale motif, both are "illuminated" with picture-book watercolor illustrations in the margins.

At the same time, it's also a love poem addressed to a "dear" beloved, and in a dramatic coup, triggered by the characteristic Bishop dash at the beginning of the first line of the last stanza of the handwritten version (the only textual difference between the two manuscripts), Bishop wrenches the fairy tale back to the real-life possibility of an insatiable and probably doomed sexual liaison, their cold bed the only place these lovers from opposing hemispheres and of opposing temperaments can ever hope to meet.

The third finished—and titled—love poem, "Breakfast Song," is even more powerful. In January 1974, I saw it in Bishop's notebook (which she had asked me to bring to her while she was at the Harvard infirmary and I snuck a peek while she was out of the room for some medical procedure, probably an X-ray). I was so astonished I was desperate to make a copy for myself, partly fearing that I might never see the poem again. (That notebook seems to have mysteriously disappeared, and, as far as I know, the copy I made is the only complete extant version of this poem.)

BREAKFAST SONG

My love, my saving grace,
your eyes are awfully blue.
I kiss your funny face,
your coffee-flavored mouth.
Last night I slept with you.

Today I love you so
how can I bear to go
(as soon I must, I know)
to bed with ugly death
in that cold, filthy place,
to sleep there without you,
without the easy breath
and nightlong, limblong warmth
I've grown accustomed to?
—Nobody wants to die;
tell me it is a lie!
But no, I know it's true.
It's just the common case;
there's nothing one can do.
My love, my saving grace,
your eyes are awfully blue
early and instant blue. (PPL 256–57)

A version of the opening two lines of this poem have been found in another note-book under the title "SIMPLE-MINDED MORNING SONG."[4] Again, the language here is simple and conversational ("funny face," "awfully blue"), though with at least one Bishop-like Hopkinsian exception ("nightlong, limblong"). The "funny face" and "coffee-flavored mouth" anticipate the equally real though slightly less specific "joking voice" and "gesture I love" in "One Art" (both descend from Shake-speare's "My mistress's eyes are nothing like the sun"). Bishop's rejected earlier title seems to want to apologize for her unusual straightforwardness.

But it's just that straightforward candor, the directness and candor that startled readers of "In the Waiting Room" only three years earlier, that gives this poem such poignant Shakespearean resonance. Here I'm reminded of Sonnet 73:

That time of year thou may'st in me behold
When yellow leaves, or none, or few do hang
Upon the boughs which shake against the cold,
Bare ruined choirs where late the sweet birds sang.

"Breakfast Song" is equally autumnal, a poem about a relationship between a younger person and an older lover, for whom approaching winter, darkness, and cold "make more strong" a love whose days (and nights) are inevitably numbered.

Bishop was never more naked about her helplessness facing death, the horror of having to "go . . . to bed" (she's virtually describing a rape) "with ugly death" in— she can't even bear to name it, though we all know what it is—"that cold, filthy place." Yet she is wise enough to acknowledge that "It's just the common case." There's no fighting a universal condition. This is less "[r]age, rage against the dying of the light" than "[r]ipeness is all," a resigned acceptance of her—of *our*— mortality. And there is beauty, *music* in that resignation, as in Keats's "To Autumn" ("Where are then songs of Spring? . . . Think not of them, thou hast thy music too—"). This is, after all, a "Song." We can face mortality with grace as long as there is the "saving grace" of love and beauty.

Like a number of other Bishop poems, "Breakfast Song" plays with a traditional genre, here the aubade. But instead of the expected lark waking us at dawn, we have breakfast, the morning (morning *after*) coffee and kisses following a night of lovemaking. Like the ironic joke about "the art of losing" in "One Art," the jokey references to breakfast ("coffee-flavored mouth," "instant" blue eyes) keep the poem from falling into sentimentality ("I am not sentimental," "Keaton" concludes) yet heighten its poignance.[5]

It's almost impossible not to speculate on why Bishop never published these masterly poems. Yet I want to encourage us not to. We don't know and she can't (and probably wouldn't) tell us. No answer will be truly satisfying. It would be more fruitful to see how these poems fit into the larger context of Bishop's achievement, and to consider how much they contribute to and expand our sense of that achievement.

NOTES

1. In a telling letter to me (October 21, 1974), Bishop worries about my use of the phrase "have sex" in my dialogue poem "Who's on First?": "One phrase I can't abide—it may be what everyone says at present, but it always offends me—that is 'to have sex.' (Even Isherwood has used it.) If it isn't 'making *love*'—what other way can it be put? (I first heard it years ago when the famous fan dancer ???? was talking about her pet snake—maybe that prejudiced me.) Oh—*Sally Rand!* It seems like such an ugly, generalized sort of expression for something—love, lust, or what have you—always unique, and so much more complex than 'having sex'" (*PPL* 895–96). The phrase "To have sex" appears on the sheet she handed out to her Harvard poetry writing students in 1975: "IF YOU WANT TO WRITE *WELL* ALWAYS AVOID THESE WORDS" (Bishop, *Prose* 252).

2. Bishop frequently revised poems after they appeared in magazines and before their book publication. When the *New Yorker* urged her to take out the capital letters in the list of flowers in "North Haven," which undermined the allusion she wanted to Shakespeare's "When Daisies Pied," she was so upset when she saw the printed version in the magazine that she wanted to publish a corrected version as soon as possible, hence the rare broadside version of this poem, with Kit

Barker's illustration, and the quick appearance of the poem in the Robert Lowell memorial issue of the *Harvard Advocate*. (It is that version that was used in Bishop's posthumous *Complete Poems*.) But some editorial changes she kept or simply ignored. In every one of Bishop's drafts of the famous first line of "One Art," the line ends with a colon:

> The art of losing isn't hard to master:

But on her final draft, which has the *New Yorker* copy-editor's indications for the typesetter, Bishop's typed colon is changed to a semicolon, which is how it was published. Bishop retained that emendation in *Geography III*. Of course, it's possible that she herself liked this change, or that she felt the *New Yorker*'s punctuation was more authoritative than her own (she often apologized for her punctuation). Perhaps she just never noticed the change, or forgot about it. But I think she was right in all her own drafts, and that the colon is a sharper way of connecting the opening line with the explanation that follows. (Photographs of Bishop's drafts of "One Art" are included in *EAP* 223–40.)

3. "For Elizabeth Bishop 4" from *History* (Lowell, *Collected Poems* 595).

4. See Alice Quinn's note in *EAP* 348.

5. "Breakfast Song" and "Dear, my compass" were set to music by the American composer John Harbison, who used them as the concluding poems to each of the two parts of his Bishop song cycle, *North and South* (1999) — "Breakfast Song" as a nostalgic waltz, "Dear, my compass" as an agitated chaconne. The other poems in the cycle are the first two "Songs for a Colored Singer" (which Harbison calls "Ballads for Billie"), "Late Air," and "Song." On September 26, 2006, Naxos released a CD of this cycle recorded at a live concert performance at the Museum of Contemporary Art, Chicago, with the Chicago Chamber Musicians accompanying the late mezzo-soprano Lorraine Hunt Lieberson, May 13, 2001 (*John Harbison: Chamber Music*, Naxos 8.559188).

Part II

Crossing Continents
Self, Politics, Place

Bishop's "Wiring Fused"

"Bone Key" and "Pleasure Seas"

ANGUS CLEGHORN

Elizabeth Bishop's *Edgar Allan Poe & the Juke-Box* and the Library of America edition of Bishop's poetry and prose provide readers with additional context enabling a richer understanding of her poetic project. Alice Quinn's compelling tour of previously unpublished archival material and her strong interpretive directions in the heavily annotated notes let us color in, highlight, and extend lines drawn in *The Complete Poems*. Some of those poetic lines include wires and cables, which are visible in Bishop's paintings, as published in William Benton's *Exchanging Hats*. If we consider the extensive presence of wires in the artwork alongside the copious, recently published poetic images of wires, we can observe vibrant innovation, especially in the material Bishop had planned for a Florida volume entitled "Bone Key." The wires conduct electricity, as does *The Juke-Box*, both heating up her place. Florida warms Bishop after Europe: in this geographical shift, we can see Bishop relinquish stiff European statuary forms and begin to radiate in hotbeds of electric light. Also existing in this erotic awakening is a new approach to nature in the modern world. Instead of wires representing something antinatural (modernity is often this sort of presence in her Nova Scotian poems, for example, when the moose stares down the bus), the wires conduct energy into a future charged with potential where "It is marvellous to wake up together" after an "Electrical Storm." This current brings Bishop into alien territory where lesbian eroticism is illuminated by green light, vines, wires, and music. "Pleasure Seas," an uncollected poem that stood alone in *The Complete Poems*, is amplified by the previously unpublished Florida draft-poems, many of which include the words "Bone Key" in the margins or under poem titles; this planned volume is visible in the recent editions and is prominent in Bishop's developing sexual-geographic poetics.

In *The Complete Poems*, "Pleasure Seas" is first of the "Uncollected Poems" section. As written in the "Publisher's Note," *Harper's Bazaar* accepted the poem but did not print it as promised in 1939. This editorial decision cut "Pleasure Seas" out of Bishop's public oeuvre until 1983, when Robert Giroux resuscitated it in the "Uncollected" section. Thus it is read as a marginal poem and has received relatively little critical attention—far less than "It is marvellous to wake up together," a previously unpublished poem found by Lorrie Goldensohn in Brazil that has been considered integral to understanding Bishop's hidden potential as an erotic poet since Goldensohn discussed it in her *Elizabeth Bishop: The Biography of a Poetry* (1992). Perhaps because "Pleasure Seas" has been widely available since 1983 in *The Complete Poems,* this poem does not appear to critics as a found gem like "It is marvellous. . . ." Now, however, we can read these previously disparate poems together in the Library of America *Bishop: Poems, Prose, and Letters* volume, in which "Pleasure Seas" was placed accurately by the editors Lloyd Schwartz and Robert Giroux in the "Unpublished Poems" section. As such, it accompanies numerous unpublished poems, many of them first published by Quinn in *Edgar Allan Poe & the Juke-Box.*

"Pleasure Seas" is a tour de force, and its rejection in 1939 likely indicated to Bishop that the public world was not ready for such a poem. I speculate that had that poem been published as promised, Bishop would have had more confidence in developing the publication of "Bone Key," a volume which would have followed, or replaced *A Cold Spring* and preceded *Questions of Travel;* she might have re-formed *A Cold Spring* into a warmer, more ample volume as "Bone Key." *A Cold Spring* ends with the lesbian mystique of "The Shampoo," the bubbles and "concentric shocks" of which make a lot more sense when accompanied, not by the preceding poem, "Invitation to Miss Marianne Moore," but by erotic poems such as "Pleasure Seas," "Full Moon, Key West," "The walls went on for years & years . . . ," "It is marvellous to wake up together," and "Edgar Allan Poe & the Juke-Box."

Bishop's writing in Florida involves tremendous struggle to express sexual desire and experience. Automatic bodily impulses contend with traditional strictures. Since in Florida "pleasures are mechanical" (*EAP* 49) and, for Bishop, counter the norms of heterosexual culture, her tentative imagination treads "the narrow sidewalks / of cement / that carry sounds / like tampered wires" in "Full Moon, Key West" (*EAP* 60). She fears the touch of her feet may detonate bombs. Bishop's recently published material offers explosive amplitudes measured against the constraints of traditional poetic architecture. "Full Moon, Key West" and "The walls went on for years & years . . ." in *Edgar Allan Poe & the Juke-Box* are dated circa 1943. In "The walls . . . ," Bishop envisions nature merging with technology to provide an extension of space in her environment:

> The morning light on the patches of raw plaster
> > was beautiful.
> It was crumbled & fine like insects' eggs
> or walls of coral, something *natural.*
> Up the bricks outside
> climbed little grill-work balconies
> all green, the wires were like vines.
> And the beds, too, one could study them,
> white, but with crudely copied
> plant formations, with pleasure. (EAP 61)

Teresa De Lauretis writes in *Technologies of Gender* about how innovative language and technology (in film) represent gender and sexuality in new formal expressions of life previously considered impossible. The new poetic material from Bishop similarly reformulates human living spaces. In the above poem, the man-made room's construction breaks down into *natural* similes. A dialectic between nature and architecture has nature grow into walls, balconies, and rooms. This poetic process is found in later poems such as "Song for the Rainy Season," in which the mist enters the house to make "the mildew's / ignorant map" on the wall. Typical human divisions between construction and organicism are made fluid. In "The walls . . . ," divisions between inner and outer worlds crumble; for instance, white beds are studied, but are they beds to lie in, or plant beds on the balconies? Bishop writes that they are "with crudely copied / plant formations," suggesting both flowers and perhaps a patterned bedspread. The phrase "walls of coral" itself merges architecture with nature, also echoing Stevens's 1935 image of "sunken coral water-walled" in "The Idea of Order at Key West," which Bishop had been reading and discussing in letters with Marianne Moore. Stevens and Bishop draw attention to artifices of nature, and nature overpowering artifice. The dichotomy of the natural versus the manufactured world is deconstructed through innovative crossover imagery, continuing in these lines:

> Up the bricks outside
> climbed little grill-work balconies
> all green, the wires were like vines. (EAP 61)

Vines simply grow up buildings, so we have a precedent for nature's encroachment on man-made constructions. Here, Bishop replicates natural vines with "little grill-work balconies / all green," a man-made architecture that looks as if it grows on its own. Then the poet surprises us again with another simile, "the wires were like vines." The imagery of the wires blackly echoes that of the balconies; again this accretion lends the physical man-made constructions a fluid, surreal life of their own, which is empowered naturally by the simile that has them acting like vines. Vine-wires extend nature through technology into potential domains far from this balconied room. However, despite the revolutionary "Building, Dwelling, Thinking," to use the title of the well-known Heidegger essay, this is a poem of walls, which offers temporary extensions of nature, only to be shut down when

> One day a sad view came to the window
> > to look in,
> little fields & fences & trees, tilted, tan & gray.
> Then it went away.
> Bigger than anything else the large bright clouds
> moved by rapidly every evening,
> rapt, on their way to some festivity.
> How dark it grew, no,
> but life was not deprived of all that sense
> of motion in which so much of it consists. (EAP 62)

With a last line again sounding like Stevens, and yet the rest of the poem very much Bishop, "The walls . . ." concludes with walls between the poet's human nature and nature's indifferent "festivity." The muted colors of traditional human habitation infiltrate her window, so Bishop will have to wait, as her wishful thinking indicates earlier in the poem, for a "future holding up those words / as something actually important / for everyone to see, like billboards" (61). My essay hoists up these formerly scrapped images of alien technology, held back in Bishop's time, "like billboards."

Those diminutive "little fields & fences & trees, tilted, tan & gray" are found in an earlier poem, "A Warning to Salesmen," written between 1935 and 1937. Earlier poems, especially from Bishop's years in Europe, lack wires as conduits of energy and transformation. "A Warning to Salesmen" offers a static portrait of marital doldrums; it speaks of a lost friend, dry landscape, and a farmer at home

> . . . putting away vegetables in sand
> In his cellar, or talking to the back
> Of his wife as she leaned over the stove. The farmer's land

Lay like a ship that has rounded the world
And rests in a sluggish river, the cables slack. (EAP 16)

Alice Quinn found this poem in Bishop's notebook, written when she took a "trip
to France with Hallie Tompkins in July 1935" (251). Even if it is a poem of loss, it
also anticipates gain. The slack cables await tightening. The lack of desire in the
poem begs for it; Quinn notes this through Bishop's scrawling revisions:

> Lines scribbled at the top of the page to the right of the title: "Let us in confused, but
> common, voice / Congratulate th'occasion, and rejoice, rejoice, rejoice / The thing
> love shies at / And the time when love shows confidence." To the right at the bottom
> of the draft, Bishop writes, "OK," but the whole poem is crossed out. And below, on
> the left: "My Love / Wonderful is this machine / One gesture started it." (251)

This machine anticipates the mechanical sexual pleasures found in the Florida bars
written into "Edgar Allan Poe & the Juke-Box." "A Warning to Salesman" shows she
had long been waiting for Florida.

Before she slots nickels into the Floridian jukebox, Bishop's trip to France
includes time spent residing by Luxembourg Gardens in fall 1935. "Luxembourg
Gardens" is a poem indicating Bishop's relationship with European traditional architecture, which begins:

> Doves on architecture, architecture
> Color of doves, and doves in air—
> The towers are so much the color of air,
> They could be anywhere. (EAP 27)

While the deadpan-glorious tone might resemble Stevens, we might also think of
Bishop's "The Monument," which was written earlier and first published in 1940; it
also ambiguously provokes present explorations of art, thought, and place, rather
than fixing memories of the past. Barbara Page's essay "Off-Beat Claves, Oblique
Realities: The Key West Notebooks of Elizabeth Bishop" clearly demonstrates that
Bishop's "The Monument" is a response to Stevens's statues in *Owl's Clover*, one
of which was located in Luxembourg Gardens, as Michael North demonstrates
in *The Final Sculpture: Public Monuments and Modern Poetry*. Similar to Stevens's
rhetorical parody of monuments, in Bishop's "Luxembourg Gardens," "histories,
cities, politics, and people / Are made presentable / For the children playing below the Pantheon" (27), and on goes a list of history's prim pomp. Then a puff

of wind sprays the fountain's water, mocking "the Pantheon," the jet of water first drooping, then scattering itself like William Carlos Williams's phallic fountain in "Spouts." Finally, the poem ends with a balloon flitting away, as children watching it exclaim, "It will get to the moon." By employing the fluid play of kids, wind, water, and dispersal, Bishop builds a conglomerate antithesis to traditional Parisian monumentality. With even more Stevensian flux than "The Monument," this poem situates Bishop's critique of monuments in Europe, unlike the well-known "Monument" poem, which could be anywhere, and thus speaks of a more liberating and expansive American perspective, drifting from European classical culture possibly all the way to Asia Minor or Mongolia.

Also from her 1935 notebook is "Three Poems," which works well to explain Bishop's transition from studying the architecture of Europe to recognizing its sterile limitations and then finding her own perspective. Section 3 develops an emotional movement away from stultifying monumentality:

> The mind goes on to say: "Fortunate affection
> Still young enough to raise a monument
> To the first look lost beyond the eyelashes."
> But the heart sees fields cluttered with statues
> And does not want to look. (EAP 19)

In the final stanza a future is foretold by the promise of a fortunate traveler:

> Younger than the mind and less intelligent,
> He refuses all food, all communications;
> Only at night, in dreams seeking his fortune,
> Sees travel, and turns up strange face-cards. (EAP 19)

Starving (a word Susan Howe uses to describe American women poets before Dickinson), this speaker is impoverished by statues and has, as the lone alternative, future fortune in surreal night visions of travel. Bishop's travels will fill her gypsy-heart's desire as it expands its vocabulary in the roaming poetic technologies found in Florida and Brazil, but Paris itself does not illuminate love.

In the Paris of "Three Poems," "The heart sits in his echoing house / And would not speak at all" (19). This inarticulate "prison-house" enables us to see why Bishop needed to travel in search of home as an idea, but not a physical settlement, as her use of Pascal illustrates in "Questions of Travel." Her jaunt to Brazil inadvertently became an eighteen-year residence with Lota de Macedo Soares, but their home was not fully expressed in the volume *Questions of Travel*. Florida was the source of sexual-poetic experimentation; Bishop's work from there proliferates with freedom not yet found in Europe, and not written into the published poems from Brazil. The reticent Bishop did not want to be known as a lesbian poet; it would limit her reputation and her private life in the public sphere, and she likely feared that sexual expression would not be accepted in print. A poem from *Questions of Travel*, "Electrical Storm" (1960), strikingly indicates excitement with Lota in Brazil. Just as striking, though, is the repressive prison-house in this poetry. It reveals as much repression as it does desire:

> Dawn an unsympathetic yellow.
> *Cra-aack!*—dry and light.
> The house was really struck.
> *Crack!* A tinny sound, like a dropped tumbler.
> . . . .
> then hail, the biggest size of artificial pearls.
> Dead-white, wax-white, cold—
> diplomats' wives favors
> from an old moon party—
> they lay in melting windrows
> on the red ground until well after sunrise.
> We got up to find the wiring fused,
> no lights, a smell of saltpetre,
> and the telephone dead.
>
> The cat stayed in the warm sheets.
> The Lent trees had shed all their petals:
> wet, stuck, purple, among the dead-eye pearls. (PPL 81)

While the electrical storm is substantial, the poem narrates it after the fact, and the storm cuts off communication with a dead telephone and "wiring fused." So the electricity certainly was there, but the lightning is pejoratively "like a dropped tumbler." And the only animal in bed is Tobias the cat, "Personal and spiteful as a neighbor's child." Personal electricity is not expressed, certainly not through Lent; it is spited in the society of neighbors and "diplomats' wives," whose nature is described as "dead-white," their hail like "artificial pearls." Unlike the earlier poem of desire "The walls went on for years & years . . . ," in which balconies are transformed by vines into wired energy, "Electrical Storm" displays the reverse action.

Nature is hardened into artifice. Social civilization, like Bishop's monuments, is a restrictive agent, part of the past in conflict with the newfound energy of Bishop's tropical present.

In Brazil, the poet constantly observes the natural world as vulnerable to civilization. Sometimes Bishop presents an alternative harmony, as in "Song for the Rainy Season," which moistly answers to the repressive short-circuiting of "The Electrical Storm" by opening the door of an "open house" to the mist infiltrating the house and causing "mildew's / ignorant map" on a wall. This poem's erotica is played out as the house receives nature's water. The house, with its opening to the outer environment, suggests Lota de Macedo Soares's property, Samambaia (a giant Brazilian fern), in the mountains above Petrópolis where Macedo Soares built Bishop a studio (*PPL* 911). The progressive architecture of their house lends itself to the way in which Bishop's poem has the outer environment flow indoors. More often, however, *Questions of Travel* traces aggressive conquests, as Bishop works through history's impact on the country. Natural power has been contained— harnessed, mined, and packaged throughout history. Take "Brazil, January 1, 1502," for example, and note how Bishop's natural images dialectically break down, then reach forward technologically. The branches of palm are broken, pale-green wheels; symbolic birds keep quiet; the lizards are dragon-like and sinful; the lichens are moonbursts; moss is hell-green; the vines are described as attacking, as "scaling-ladder vines," and as "'one leaf yes and one leaf no' (in Portuguese)"; and while the "lizards scarcely breathe," the "smaller, female" lizard's tail is "red as a red-hot wire." That beacon beckons from the poem's forms of colonial imprisonment. Breathlessness will find breath in *Edgar Allan Poe & the Juke-Box*.

William Benton's words from *Exchanging Hats: Elizabeth Bishop Paintings* accurately convey the benefit of studying two of Bishop's art forms to gain greater compositional insight into her "One Art." In his introduction, he writes, "If Elizabeth Bishop wrote like a painter, she painted like a writer" (xviii). Wires, cables, and electrical technology are strewn abundantly through the paintings. Observed in sequence, Bishop's black lines powerfully extend this emergent narrative of Bishop as an electric writer. The paintings *Olivia, Harris School, County Courthouse, Tombstones for Sale, Graveyard with Fenced Graves, Interior with Extension Cord, Cabin with Porthole,* and *E. Bishop's Patented Slot-Machine* are marked with black lines that technically disturb nature. The bold presence of Bishop's lines factor in virtually every painting to infringe upon nature (with the exception of the explicitly pretty watercolor odes to nature, such as the arrangement on the cover of *One Art*).

When we align the Florida paintings with "Bone Key" and other published poems from Florida, we can chart the artist's development in accord with the technological presence of wires. As with the early poems in *Edgar Allan Poe & the Juke-Box,* her often-undated Florida paintings, circa 1937–39, when Bishop had returned from Europe, depict square architecture set off by wires askew. In *Olivia,* a painting of a weathered wood house on Olivia Street in Key West, the modest brown house is fronted by two contrasting white porch pillars, and to the left, "like a cosmic aspect, the telephone lines form a tilted steeple" (Benton 18) connected to the proximate telephone pole. The painting comes across as a satiric "Monument." Likewise, the next painting, *Harris School* (21), is topped with battlements contrasted by wispy kites flying freely in the orange sunlight. Bishop's painterly contrasts invoke satire, rather like the parody of old Parisian architecture in "Luxembourg Gardens." *County Courthouse* (23) is extremely dramatic—a transitional painting in the evolution of Bishop's transgressive art. Benton describes it well: "A view composed of what obstructs it. The central triangle [courthouse structure] that leads the eye into the painting is at once overwhelmed by foliage. Downed power lines contribute to the sense of disorder. The scene is the exact opposite of what a Sunday watercolorist might select. It is, in fact, a picture whose wit transforms it from a 'scene' into an image of impasse" (22). The palms in the foreground overpower the courthouse of similar size in the center. Nature's supremacy over the architecture of man-made legal institution is accentuated by downed power lines, symbolizing, as often for Bishop, that our efforts to transmit information over and above nature depend on the cooperation of nature, the winds of which can knock down our voices.

Tombstones for Sale, which appears on the cover of *The Collected Prose,* and *Graveyard with Fenced Graves* (31, 33) are filled with iron bars in harsh but beautiful contrast with flowering trees. Recall the ironwork balconies "growing" up buildings in "The walls went on for years & years. . . ." These wonky walls are evident in *Interior with Extension Cord,* a painting of undetermined year with "the dramatic focus on the extension cord crossing the planes of the white room" (42). In here, the barren walls out-space the open door with view of the garden. The painting yearns for nature to be let in the door. *Cabin with Porthole,* the next painting (45), provides compositional relief. Bare but cheerful yellow walls surround the open porthole with blue ocean view; the painter's travel bags are casually set in order beside a neat flowerpot on the table. Travel looks homey here, made additionally comfortable by the fan plugged into the wall with electrical cord in the top-right corner. The next undated painting, *Gray Church* (47), is set by Benton in contrast to the lightness of *Cabin with Porthole.* The editor's placement of *Gray Church,* the painting's mood nearly as dark as van Gogh's *The Prison Courtyard,* suggests that

Benton, like Quinn in *Edgar Allan Poe & the Juke-Box,* ordered a dramatic narrative sequence so observers could follow an interpretive trail of artistic development.

Although *E. Bishop's Patented Slot-Machine* (77) appears later in the book's sequence, perhaps because it is more of a sketch than a painting, it would have likely been created near the time she wrote "The Soldier and the Slot-Machine" in Florida, as Quinn documents it with a rejection letter from the *New Yorker,* dated October 28, 1942 (*EAP* 279). These amateur works of art evince the crucial importance of publishing flawed poems, scrawl, sketches, and paintings, which are incredibly useful tools to instruct us about their masters; in this case we see projection of the artist's techno-dreams. Of *E. Bishop's Patented Slot-Machine,* Benton writes, "The rainbow arc at the top of the picture—resembling the handle of a suitcase—bears the legend "The 'DREAM'" (76). This dream, rainbow-shaped, carries technology in the form of the slot-machine. Whether or not observers want to view the rainbow dream as lesbian codification, as some students of "The Fish" do with that poem's victorious rainbow of otherness, the undeniable fact is that Bishop has painted "The 'DREAM'" onto the handle of her slot machine. This slot machine is dependent upon currency for the dream of a fortunate future. Although an amateur painting, it is far more developed in terms of the progress of artistic, hopeful vision than earlier works, such as 1935's "Three Poems," in which Bishop is desperately scanning seas from France, and the fortuneteller turns up strange face cards as the only potential currency, so the poet dreams of travel.

The 1942 sketch and poem "The Soldier and the Slot-Machine" (*EAP* 56–57), not to be confused with the painting just discussed, appears like an adult-version Dr. Seuss parody of *E. Bishop's Patented Slot-Machine* complete with fearful alien beast atop machine in the sketch. In the poem, Bishop uses the soldier persona to depersonalize her dream, destroyed by a third-person other. Still, the persona employs first person: "I will not play the slot-machine" bookends the poem as a mantra of abstinence from the drunken slot machine. Nevertheless, it consumes coins until they melt surreally into "a pool beneath the floor . . . / It should be flung into the sea. / / Its pleasures I cannot afford" (*EAP* 58). This denial and apparent dismissal through the otherness of the soldier stays with Bishop, who cannot trash her desires in the sea; they pulled on her for years even if their expression remained unpublished. After the *New Yorker's* Charles Pearce rejected "The Soldier and the Slot-Machine," Bishop recalled this event twenty-two years later in a letter to Robert Lowell: "Once I wrote an ironic poem about a drunken sailor and a slot-machine—*not* a success—and the sailor said he was going to throw the machine into the sea, etc., and M[oore] congratulated me on being so morally courageous and outspoken" (*EAP* 279). Moore in 1964 was at that time congratulating Bishop on a moral lesson to be learned about Brazilian crime and punishment in "The Burglar of Babylon." However, the point that Bishop makes with quiet sarcasm in her letter to Lowell is that Moore missed the irony so crucial to understanding "The Soldier and the Slot-Machine." Moore reads moral courage in Bishop's condemnations; actually, Bishop's morally courageous core, the one of social conformity that Moore applauds, melts in the machine. The soldier's denial to play it is weaker than the power of the machine itself, which melts and breaks into subterranean pieces—unacceptable mercurial junk that will be "taken away," a disposal of natural, illicit desire. Travel in Florida and Brazil offers many cabins with portholes for Bishop to view the sea far away from stultifying northwestern culture.

Sometimes Bishop allows the establishment to triumph, as in the balanced yellow painting of *The Armory, Key West.* Even here, though, wires dangle from the flagpole to create slight asymmetry. *Merida from the Roof* (27), the well-known cover art for *The Complete Poems,* while a bit chaotic with copious windmills outnumbering church steeples, nevertheless illustrates an intoxicating tropical harmony. The dominant palm, telephone wires, city streets, and buildings hang together nicely from the painter's balcony view. This Mexican painting from 1942 anticipates work Bishop would do in Brazil over the next two decades, such as "The Burglar of Babylon," which ends with the poet looking down on Rio's crime ridden poverty with binoculars.

When we contrast *The Complete Poems* with *Edgar Allan Poe & the Juke-Box,* we can see just how much further Bishop's unpublished poems went in configuring her relation with the world through nature and technology's extensions of it; natural growth is given additional electrical currency to express sexual awakening, and I argue, a potentially full realization of her poetic power. Lorrie Goldensohn in *The Biography of a Poetry* discusses her discovery of "It is marvellous to wake up together" in a box from Linda Nemer in Brazil. This discovery and "Edgar Allan Poe & the Juke-Box" best exemplify Bishop's rewired sexuality. Quinn cannot be certain which of these poems was written first. In terms of the arc of the poetics I'm tracing here, it makes sense for "Poe's Box" to come first because it works to loosen up the sexual expression of "It is marvellous. . . ." However, Quinn notes work on "Edgar Allan Poe & the Juke-Box" as late as 1953, and narrates its intended place as the closing poem of *A Cold Spring,* which Bishop considered calling "Bone Key." It may have been written as early as 1938, when Bishop wrote to "classmate Frani Blough from Key West about her immersion in Poe" (*EAP* 271). Lloyd Schwartz and Robert Giroux date it in the late 1930s to early 1940s period. As *A Cold Spring* stands, it concludes with the rapture of "The Shampoo"—a thinly veiled poem of lesbian eroticism in nature's guise. And yet when I teach this poem to students, I often have to explain the "concentric shocks." "The Shampoo" is a wonderful climax, but it abruptly follows "Invitation to Miss Marianne Moore." This sequence repeats the juxtaposition evident in Bishop's letters between her lush tropical experience and her polite correspondence with Moore. Now we can envision an enlarged not so cold spring in the key of human bone warming up with "Edgar Allan Poe & the Juke-Box."

This poem is filled by emanations of light and sound from the jukebox. *Starlight* and *La Conga* are the Floridian dance halls described as "cavities in our waning moon, / strung with bottles and blue lights / and silvered coconuts and conches" (49). This erotic-tropical electric fulfillment sounds more like Walcott than Bishop. The poem has "nickels fall into the slots," drinks drop down throats, hands grope under tablecloths while "[t]he burning box can keep the measure." Perhaps to ruin the party, Edgar Allan enters the last stanza, in which Bishop writes, "Poe said that poetry was *exact*." This poem, though, is a corrective to Poe's poetics, for Bishop knows for herself and Poe in the drinking establishment of poetry that "pleasures are mechanical / and know beforehand what they want / and know exactly what they want." Bishop focuses on "The *Motive* for Metaphor," like Stevens, or like Baudelaire whom she was also reading at the time, knowing and tracing her desire for expression as expression. Conversely, Poe in the nineteenth century tried to unite his metrical poetic exactitude with ideals of beauty while explaining his technique in "The Philosophy of Composition." While the mechanics of meter involve precise measures, Bishop suggests that seeking pleasures is comprised of a more powerful mechanics. "Lately I've been doing nothing much but reread Poe, and evolve from Poe . . . a new Theory-of-the-Story-All-My-Own. It's the 'proliferal' style, I believe, and you will see some of the results . . . [a reference to her prize-winning *Partisan Review* story 'In Prison']" (*OA* 71; *EAP* 271). Bishop's use of Poe illustrates her gripe with tradition as a source of monumental fixture, thus limited understanding, which has taught her well but prevents the poet from dancing at La Conga and telling that Floridian tale in *A Cold Spring*. Bishop wanted this poem near the end of *A Cold Spring* but didn't quite get it done. The final lines of the poem deal a further blow to Poe, and by extension to Bishop herself, when she asks: "how long does your music burn? / like poetry or all your horror / half as exact as horror here?" (50). Poe's horror stories (see Bishop's notes on "The Tell-Tale Heart" on the upper-right corner of the draft of this poem) and, I would suggest, her writing in *The Complete Poems* (as wonderful as it is) articulate a fictional horror that comes only halfway to expressing the full pleasure of horrific catharsis available in the experience and writing of Florida honky-tonks. Who would have thought Elizabeth Bishop a "honky-tonk woman"? Bethany Hicok traces Bishop's florid nightlife in her *Degrees of Freedom: American Women Poets and the Women's College, 1905–1955* (2008), and thanks to Quinn we have the poetic evidence in print.

"It is marvellous to wake up together" is a full and complete rendering of Bishop's eroticism. We might give Bishop latitude for not publishing this one in the Second World War period; Quinn estimates the date between 1941 and 1946 when Bishop lived with Marjorie Stevens in Key West (267). Perhaps in the twenty-first century readers are comfortably relieved to hear Bishop express her lesbian sexuality, but in her time she did not want to be publicly scrutinized as a lesbian poet. In some respects, "It is marvellous to wake up together" is like "Electrical Storm" since the poem speaks of sex after it has happened. Here, though, the stormy clearing is less anxious and repressive. Instead of diplomats' wives and spiteful neighbors' children, Bishop feels

> . . . the air suddenly clear
> As if electricity had passed through it
> From a black mesh of wires in the sky.
> All over the roof the rain hisses,
> And below, the light falling of kisses. (EAP 44)

Technology is godlike, hovering over their chosen house, and yet it is not alien, for the lightning storm's electrical current of rain follows in hisses rhymed with kisses. Bishop is fully in the arena now—with the powers above electrically charging the nature that conducts itself harmoniously in the bedroom.

In the second stanza, electricity frames the house so readers can imagine it being sketched artistically. Remnants of past prison-houses exist, and yet the past constraints of an inarticulate heart are transformed in this reality where "we imagine dreamily / Now the whole house caught in a bird-cage of lightning / Would be delightful rather than frightening"; the pleasure of this reality is also a dream, and it remains a dream in the last stanza. My point is not simply that dreams can come true, but that this true dream is limited to this house's electrical currents. The speaker is "lying flat on [her] back," which is an interesting line because it suggests sex, and yet it is from this position, this "same simplified point of view" that the speaker emphasizes inquiry:

> All things might change equally easily,
> Since always to warn us there might be these black
> Electrical wires dangling. Without surprise
> The world might change to something quite different. . . .

What sort of change is envisioned? The poem vaguely considers open futures; "something quite different" could be horrific or promising. Whatever change may come, these wires hang over the house, through Bishop's poem and art as charged presences connected to future advancement.

"Dear Dr.——" was written in 1946, around the same time Bishop might have finished "It is marvellous to wake up together." It continues to wire her present into the future:

> Yes, dreams come in colors
> and memories come in colors
> but those in dreams are more remarkable.
> Particular & bright   (at night)
> like that intelligent green light in the harbor
> which must belong to some society of its own,
> & watches this one now unenviously. (EAP 77)

These seven lines pull together a lot. Bishop's dreams in Paris were quite alienated from her art-culture milieu; in Florida, dreams are amplified by jukeboxes, liquor, and dancing. There she finds physical lushness to match the dream currents that will sizzle in Brazilian experience. And yet in "Dear Dr.——," Bishop, near the end of her relationship with Marjorie Stevens, is writing from Nova Scotia to her very helpful psychiatrist, Ruth Foster (286), expressing this foreign glow as an alien perspective: "that intelligent green light in the harbor / which must belong to some society of its own," suggesting some alien technological prophesy, which "watches this one now unenviously" (77). Goldensohn writes of electrical impasse in *The Biography of a Poetry:* "But still the wires connect to dreams, to nerve circuits that carry out our dreams of rescue and connection, or that fail to: in "The Farmer's Children," a story written in 1948 shortly before Bishop went to Brazil, the wires also appear, telephone wires humming with subanimal noise eerily irrelevant to the damned and helpless children of the story" (33). This story, written late in the Florida years, is further evidence of Bishop's "proliferal" style, the multigeneric "One Art" developed in response to family, northern traditions, Poe, and Europe. Bishop's evolving art comprised of poetry, fiction, letters, and painting demonstrates psychosexual evolution found in southern tropical harbors, far from the northern remoteness of her mother's Nova Scotia.

These poems from *Edgar Allan Poe & the Juke-Box* register extensively the alien vision so far ahead of what was admitted in Bishop's present. By contrasting the reserved perfections from *The Complete Poems,* such as "Electrical Storm," and the limits of history as in "Brazil, January 1, 1502," we can see what is held back there, waiting for the more fully expressed imperfect transgressions of *Edgar Allan Poe & the Juke-Box. The Complete Poems* provides intricately innovative poems that point out limited perspectives while expanding ethical imaginations of the future, whereas Quinn's book enables readers to thoroughly explore the dream workings of a poet bursting from the libidinal confines of her time, swinging by green vines through wires of sound and light to transmit electricity for an erotically ample future.

Bishop's anxiety and longing for a more tolerant future society, as expressed in "Dear Dr.—," can also be traced back to her thwarted effort at publishing "Pleasure Seas." This powerful erotic poem sits chronologically in the middle of her poetic development away from Europe (signaled by "Luxembourg Gardens" and "Three Poems" circa 1935), and stimulated by Florida in the late 1930s. "Pleasure Seas" illustrates the new powerful range of Bishop to be discovered when reading *Edgar Allan Poe & the Juke-Box* and the Library of American edition next to *The Complete Poems*. As an "Uncollected Poem" in *The Complete Poems,* "Pleasure Seas" would perhaps sit more easily in the *Poe & the Juke-Box.* The aberration of "Pleasure Seas" in *The Complete Poems* may explain why only a handful of critics have discussed its significance. Bonnie Costello, Barbara Comins, Marilyn May Lombardi, and Jeredith Merrin have published helpful interpretations of "Pleasure Seas." Each critic picks up on the poem as an indication of developments that Bishop makes, or does not quite make, in other published poems. Bonnie Costello, for example, writes in *Questions of Mastery:* "'Seascape' and 'Pleasure Seas' . . . anticipate the perspectival shifts in 'Twelfth Morning; or What You Will,' 'Filling Station,' and 'Invitation to Miss Marianne Moore,' in all of which the poet's pessimism is countered. In these later poems she achieves a vision at once immediate, even intimate, and yet directed at the world and questioning a single perspective of selfhood" (15–16). Costello also makes an important observation in a note: "'Song' may be a rewriting of 'Pleasure Seas'" (249 n. 16). However, according to Schwartz and Giroux, "Song" was written in 1937, two years before "Pleasure Seas," which then reads as an amplified fulfillment of the sad song from two years earlier. The latter ocean poem swells with pleasure in the face of forces that threaten that very pleasure. Now that we can read "Pleasure Seas" in the larger context of Bishop's struggle to write sexual poetics, the poem makes more sense and gathers like-minded poems into its vortex of desire.

"Pleasure Seas" is a study of water—contained, distorted and freed. It begins with still water "in a walled off swimming-pool" (195)—another wall like the ones that go on "for years and years" in the poem from 1943. This man-made pool contains "pink Seurat bathers," like the publicly acceptable automatons in his famous paintings *Bathers* and *La grande jatte*. This viewer, though, is a surrealist who observes this scene through "a pane of bluish glass." Seurat's bathers have "beds of bathing caps," again resembling and anticipating the beds inside and outside the balconied rooms of "The walls go on for years and years." Are these bathers' heads in or out of it? Contained within a pool, they are willing prisoners of public space in chemically treated water. At the close of the poem, they are "Happy . . . likely or not—" in their floral "white, lavender, and blue" caps, which are susceptible to greater weather forcing the water "opaque, / Pistachio green and Mermaid Milk." The floral garden colors of their caps contrast with disarming shades. That awfully bright green is "like that intelligent green light in the harbor" of "Dear Dr.—," belonging to the alien society unenvious of the contemporaneous one. Jeredith Merrin, in "Gaiety, Gayness and Change," asks how "Pleasure Seas" moves "from entrapment to freedom, from (to borrow from Bishop's own phrasing from other poems) Despair to Espoir, from the 'awful' to the 'cheerful'"? (Merrin 154).

The next sentence of "Pleasure Seas" envisions free ocean water "out among the keys" of Florida mingling, interestingly, with multichromatic "soap bubbles, poisonous and fabulous," suggesting both "The Shampoo" to come, and the poisonous rainbow of oil in "The Fish"—another natural being that should exist freely in nature, which is caught in a rented boat. Even "the keys float lightly like rolls of green dust" connotes geological formations that are susceptible to erosion. Everything green and natural is made alien. The threat is intensified by an airplane, a form of human technological height that flattens the water to a "heavy sheet." The sky view is dangerous in Bishop's poems; consider "12 O'Clock News" in which the view from the media plane ethnocentrically objectifies the dying indigenes below. In "Pleasure Seas," the poet says the plane's "wide shadow pulses" above the surface, and down to the yellow and purple submerged marine life. The water's surface even becomes "a burning-glass" for the sun—the supreme force of nature is harnessed as destructive technology, as with the high airplane, which, as Barbara Comins notes in "That Queer Sea," is "casting a 'wide shadow' upon the water . . . suggesting some inherent anguish in going one's 'own way'" (191). Comins and Merrin see Bishop here pushing the poetic limits of her sexual expression.

Even though the sun turns the water into "a burning glass," the sun naturally cools "as the afternoon wears on." Nature and technology dance in a somewhat vexed but "dazzling dialectic" here. Brightest of all in this poem is the "violently red bell-buoy / Whose neon-color vibrates over it, whose bells vibrate // To shock after shock of electricity." Neon is the most alien of lights. As with the jukebox charging its place, this buoy electrifies its environment. Its otherly transgression "rhythmically" shocks pulses through the sea. "The sea is delight. The sea means *room.* / It is a dance floor, a well ventilated ballroom." These lines from "Pleasure Seas" contain the charge picked up in "the dance-halls" of "Edgar Allan Poe & the Juke-Box." That poem has seedy, drunken desire releasing the inner alien; in "Pleasure Seas" it is potentially transgendered here in the homonym of the "red bell-buoy," the color of passion also found in "the red-hot wire" of the lizard tail in "Brazil, January 1, 1502." That lizard is notably female. Both poems vibrate outward into larger spaces.

From paradisal waters, the poem retreats to the "tinsel surface" of swimming pool or ship deck where "Grief floats off / Spreading out thin like oil." Natural poison spills, damages, and disperses. "And love / Sets out determinedly in a straight line . . . But shatters" and refracts "in shoals of distraction" (196). These shoals receding around the keys anticipate the homosexual vertigo of Crusoe's surreal islands in the late, great semi-autobiographical poems of *Geography III,* the 1976 volume beginning with young Elizabeth Bishop's formative experience of inversion depicted "In the Waiting Room"—"falling off / the round, turning world" (160). "Pleasure Seas" ends with water crashing into the coral reef shelf—at the surface of nature, half in, half out—"An acre of cold white spray is there / Dancing happily by itself." Out there in the sea, as land gives way to coral reef, the poet creates a "well ventilated ballroom" to be free and ecstatic. Unlike the public spaces of the Florida honky-tonks, these pleasure seas are solitary. They are, however, natural—and thus contrast the ironic happiness of "the people in the swimming-pool and on the yacht, / Happy the man in that airplane, likely as not—" (196). This pleasure of 1939 holds the promise of liberation, momentarily.

While explorations in the late 1930s lead to joyful poems such as "It is marvellous to wake up together," and the thirsty "Edgar Allan Poe & the Juke-Box," another Florida poem bids farewell, circa 1946. "In the golden early morning . . ." contains many of the Floridian tropes merging nature with technology. About a trip to the airport, it indicates a breakup with Marjorie Stevens ("M" in the poem). As the speaker is being driven to the airport in the early morning, she reads the newspaper stories of human horror:

> I kept wondering
> *why* we expose ourselves to these farewells & dangers—
> Finally you got there & we started.
> It was very cold & so much dew!
> Every leaf was wet & glistened.
> The Navy buildings & wires & towers, etc.

> looked almost like glass & so frail & harmless.
> The water on either side was perfectly flat
> like mirrors — or rather breathed-on mirrors. (*EAP* 80)

The water as foggy mirror is an example of how technology (a mirror in this case) extends nature to reflect for Bishop an extension of herself that can't quite exist freely on its own, or in the social world.

More dramatically, an airplane descends this early morning: "Then we *heard* the plane or felt it." She feels the sublime vehicle "as if it were made out of / the dew coming together, very shiny." The plane is similar to the aircraft's technological transgression in "Pleasure Seas," but in "In the golden early morning . . . ," it is also like a product of nature made from the dew. This simile resembles the fusion of technology and nature in "Pleasure Seas," where the red bell-buoy charges the sea, or in "The walls . . . ," where the "wires were like vines." These images express Bishop's longing to extend but not quite transcend the provocative desires of the physical world. Her projections are made possible by poetic language's explicit tropic function: it is a technological extension of reality. Bishop's technologies blatantly transgress nature by pointing to her exclusion from it when it participates in traditional symbolic order. She comments, as the flight crew in the poem gets out of the plane, "I said to you that it was like the procession / at the beginning of a bullfight" (*EAP* 81). Somebody's going to die. From the outside looking in, Bishop is neither inside the plane nor remaining part of the natural morning. Always liminal, always on the move, she and her poetry are the technological current transmitting nature. Bishop's speaker "In the golden early morning . . ." says good-bye to "M" and the third-party driver, prepares for departure, and questions why she travels.

Technology is a menace and a liberator. In Florida, Bishop's multigeneric poetic innovations wired bodily desires with machines that tampered with nature, extending its growth into human domestic abodes. In Brazil, Bishop would experience such domestic electricity with Lota de Macedo Soares, but only rarely write about it in the odd letter. Goldensohn describes a letter to Ilse and Kit Barker in late 1959: "Both danger and power course along a field of connections that two loving women, one grounded, and one mounting precariously into the air, complete between them; as in a body of poetry, the properly twiddled wires secure both speech, sight. This image, perhaps too exotic and special in reference, was never used in a poem; but both telephone and wires did make their appearance in 'Electrical Storm,' written at roughly the same time as the Barker letter" (33).

With the "wiring fused, / no lights, . . . and the telephone dead," "Electrical Storm" is about power outage — unlike the active charges running through the

Floridian poems that never saw print in her lifetime. While Goldensohn sharply perceived shared electricity in the letter and in "It is marvellous to wake up together," the rejection of 1939's "Pleasure Seas" and related ecstatic developments in "Bone Key" would likely have made it to print had "Pleasure Seas" and other uncollected poems reached readers, and given Bishop confidence to wire her bodily desires into an uncharted poetics of alien seas. Now we have it. *E. Bishop's Patented Slot-Machine* has finally been approved.

Dreaming in Color

Bishop's Notebook Letter-Poems

HEATHER TRESELER

In an interview with Elizabeth Spires about a year before her death, Elizabeth Bishop spoke with unprecedented openness about her experience of psychoanalysis, letter writing, and the composition of poems. When Spires asked Bishop if she ever had a poem come to her as *donnée,* Bishop claimed that she had written her summa of elegies, "One Art," with remarkable ease; it was, she stated, "like writing a letter" ("Art of Poetry, XXVII" 118). Bishop's alliance of her villanelle with the narrative praxis of letter writing reflects the definitive turn that her poetry took in the late 1940s. It was in the latter part of this troubling and alcoholic decade that Bishop found a means of transmuting the pain of maternal loss and early deprivation into a poetics that avoided the pitfalls of too much "personality" or "impersonality," a division heightened by the New Critics' denunciation of women poets' so-called "baroque," or emotional, tendencies in the postwar era (Brunner 74–75). The epistolary poem, and the conceit of privacy invoked by the letter's form, provided Bishop with a means of skirting this gendered binary and a way of achieving the psychological lyricism that constitutes her poetic legacy.

This essay reads several previously unpublished letter poems from one of Bishop's "Key West" notebooks (VC 75.3b): "I see you far away, unhappy" and two poems from a series entitled "Dear Dr.—." These epistolary poems indicate the significance of Bishop's relationship with her psychoanalyst, Ruth Foster; her sustained interest in Klein, Freud, and psychological models of psychic life; and, most importantly, Bishop's use of the letter to foreground the lyric's capacity for intimate, intersubjective address. Tellingly, these notebook letter-poems contain images and narrative features that reappear in two of Bishop's most well-known poems, "One Art" and "At the Fishhouses," suggesting the importance of the lyric letter in Bishop's evolving "narrative postmodernism": a distinctly relational aesthetic that appears in the epistolary poems of *A Cold Spring* (1955) and in the "alluvial dialect" of her mature voice (Travisano, *Midcentury* 182; Gray 57).

The tropes of epistolarity in *A Cold Spring* (1955) and in the autobiographical story "In the Village" (1953) have often been read within the context of Bishop's expatriate residence in Brazil, during which time she came to understand letter writing as an extension of her poetic labors or, as she wrote to Kit and Ilse Baker in 1953, "like working without really doing it" (*OA* 273).[1] Critics have also intuitively linked the seemingly playful epistolarity in *A Cold Spring* with the gravely casual, self-interrogatory narratives in the free verse poems of Bishop's last decade.[2] Langdon Hammer, for example, argues that poems such as "The End of March" and "Poem" evince the poet's sustained fascination with the "rhetorical gestures" and tonality of letters (164, 177). Hammer conjectures that the letter-poem enabled Bishop to develop a "trope of thirdness": a Winnicottian dimension in which the anonymous reader is the privileged participant in the reciprocal play of correspondents (164). Bishop's notebook letter-poems also accord with Joanne Feit Diehl's observation that much of Bishop's oeuvre seems informed by a desire to "make reparation to the abandoning mother"—to give a poetic gift that will simultaneously "replenish" the author, the proverbial "wounded surgeon" of the lyric voice (Diehl 8, 108; Eliot, *Complete Poems* 127).

In Bishop's two explicit, gift-like, and "subversively celebratory" letter-poems, "Letter to N. Y." (dedicated to Louise Crane) and "Invitation to Miss Marianne Moore," it is the narrowed address of a specified recipient that, ironically, enhances the reader's sense of the letter-poems' tacit *communiqués* (Gilbert and Gubar, *No Man's Land* 211; *PPL* 61, 63–64). Bishop's unpublished notebook letter-poems, however, in voicing the psychoanalytic material of dreams, screen memories, and the garrulous ghosts of regret, appear to grant the reader full warrant to the literary artifact's revelation of selfhood. In these lyric letters, the poet's polyphony of voices, Freudian symbology, and Kleinian exploration of the mother-daughter dyad further establish Bishop's position as a precocious "postmodernist" among her midcentury peers (Longenbach, *Modern Poetry* 22; Travisano, "Bishop Phenomenon" 229). In these letter-poems' play of multiple authoring selves and *destinataires*, in their especial (but necessarily trespassed) *confiance*, Bishop emphasizes the constitutive "triangulation" of the lyric poem in which a third, unnamed reader is required to complete the circuit of its intersubjectivity, its rendering of individuation into a rhetorically social form (Miller 140; Altman 186; Stewart 13).

Given these letter-poems' similarity to psychoanalytic dialogue, with the patient (or poet) narrating biographic stories to a specific other, it is not surprising that Bishop turned to the epistolary mode in the late 1940s following a second stint of psychoanalysis with Dr. Ruth Foster, a New York clinician. By all accounts, Bishop's work with Dr. Foster was a great solace to her during an uncertain and often turbulent phase of her life. Millier reports that Bishop and Dr. Foster "spent two years . . . [investigating] the origins of [Bishop's] depression and alcoholism," and that she had assured Bishop that she was "lucky to have survived" the grievous losses of her childhood (180, 194).

Shortly after Dr. Foster's death in 1950, Bishop would write to Marianne Moore that Dr. Foster had been "so good and kind" and had "certainly helped [her] more than anyone in the world" (Millier 180; *OA* 206). Bishop's superlative praise may have been an intentional snub of Moore, who could be overweening in her concern for the younger poet's health, ambition, and grammatical specificity; it is clear, however, that Dr. Foster was a major influence on Bishop's reckoning of her early losses (Diehl 36–38).

Throughout the spring of 1946, Bishop struggled to maintain some modicum of sobriety while she did analytic work with Dr. Foster, negotiated with Houghton Mifflin about the belated appearance of *North & South,* and wavered about whether to abandon Key West and her tempestuous relationship with Marjorie Stevens (Millier 180–87). By the fall of 1946, however, Bishop's *North & South* had been published to admiring reviews and she had signed a first-reader's contract with the *New Yorker.* Bishop's poetic career, as Millier notes, had finally earned its "proper beginning," and despite the profound suffering in her private life that year (188).

Bishop's notebook letter-poems appear to have been written in the intermediary months between her work with Dr. Foster and her book's generally positive critical appraisal in the fall of 1946. And they may have been composed during the pilgrimage that Bishop made to Nova Scotia in July, which was her first trip to Canada since her mother's death in 1934 (Millier 180). These notebook letter-poems to Dr. Foster and to an incarcerated beloved reveal Bishop's ingenious use of the letter's anticipated "encounter" with a specified addressee, its related attempt to "revise both self and other," and its *fort/da* tropes of rejection and redress (Bower 5; McCabe 26–27). Like a psychoanalytic dialogue, the personal letter served Bishop as a narrative epistemological frame in which to explore the phantasmagoria of dreams, the residual injury of maternal loss, and the unstable nature of memory itself.

Finally, while the poem "I see you far away, unhappy" and the poetic series "Dear Dr.—" are of certain literary value in themselves, they also supply some of the imagery and underlying psychic grammar for a few of Bishop's most admired poems. These include the "rocky breasts" of "historical, flowing and flown" knowledge in "At the Fishhouses" and the lost "mother's watch" in "One Art" (*PPL* 52, 167). The latter, when juxtaposed with the tropes of surveillance (or who "sees," "watches," and "looks") in Bishop's letter-poems, seems assuredly a pun on both a lost timepiece and the traumatic loss of maternal "watch" or care.

Millier notes that Bishop left for Nova Scotia on July 1, 1946, and made the somewhat unlikely decision to stay alone at the Nova Scotia Hotel directly "across the bay" from the Nova Scotia Hospital where her late mother, Gertrude Bulmer Bishop, spent the last eighteen years of her life (180). In a notebook passage that Quinn quotes and dates from Bishop's 1951 trip to Canada, Bishop reports catching a glimpse of the Nova Scotia Hospital in a taxicab ride from the Dartmouth airport (*EAP* 300–301). Within her diary's letter-to-the-self, Bishop narrowly contains the shock of this surprise.

> N. S. looked lovely from the air — fresh dark greens, red outline, glittering lines of rivers — more animated than Maine looked, & that amazing cleanness that strikes me every time. We landed in Dartmouth — a clearing in the fir woods — the taxi comes across on a little ferry — 1st driving right by the Insane Asylum (I was quite unprepared for this.) A beautiful, dazzling day, & the unparalleled dullness of everything — I feel it in everything here, shop-windows, food, — the smallest trifles. Depression here must be worse than anywhere — only fortunately I'm not depressed. (VC 43.6, qtd. in *EAP* 300–301)

Depicting this scene with her proverbial map-makers' "[m]ore delicate . . . colors," Bishop contrasts the vividness of the natural landscape with the "unparalleled dullness" of the human culture, the lack of flavor in the local storefronts and cuisine ("The Map," *PPL* 3; *EAP* 300). But she appears to take some comfort in travel's headlong parataxis or "Everything only connected by 'and' and 'and'": an equalizing logic by which she gives as much narrative attention to the topography of Nova Scotia as to the typographically accentuated "Insane Asylum" ("Over 2000 Illustrations and a Complete Concordance," *PPL* 46). As if to distance herself from the latter, Bishop adopts a mock-clinical posture, noting that a stay in Dartmouth would be sure to worsen one's "depression." In a line of almost comic self-defense, she notes that she is "fortunately . . . *not* depressed" (*EAP* 301, emphasis added).

Aside from this clinically toned assessment, Bishop allows but one parenthetical admission of emotion in this passage: "(I was quite unprepared for this)" (*EAP* 300). This line is strikingly similar to the tense imperative in "One Art," in which the narrator likewise embeds a stern note, or letter-to-self, within protective parentheses: "though it may look like (*Write* it!) like disaster" (*PPL* 167). If the task of "writing it" is essentially the task of authoring a recognition — one akin to an epiphany coached by an analyst or enabled by the biographic narrative of a letter—Bishop appears to strain against her repressive instincts although she presumably addresses only herself in this journal entry, acting as her own audience and clinician (*PPL* 167).

The dueling voices in this entry suggest the tensions of psychoanalytic anagno-risis and echo the polyphony in Bishop's letter-poems to her analyst. In "I see you far away, unhappy" and in the "Dear Dr.—" series, Bishop works from the conceit of psychoanalysis as a constructed narrative in which "a person's life unfolds back-wards, like a Greek tragedy, from effect to cause" (Feirstein 179). Hence, Bishop uses the letter's "intercourse with ghosts" (or the epistolary imagoes of self-and-other) to trace the etiology of loss; to explore the borderland between actual and screen memories; and to make poetic reparations for the primary and defining loss of the abandoning mother (Kafka qtd. in Miller 135; Diehl 109).[3]

Bishop's handwritten notation, "from Halifax," at the top of page 153 in her Key West notebook strongly suggests that she composed her letter-poems during or proximate to her two- to three-week stay in Nova Scotia (VC 75.3b).[4] The first of these letter-like poems, "I see you far away, unhappy," appears in the legible, but agitated-looking script on page 152 of the Key West notebook (VC 75.3b). Despite its textual clarity, this poem was not included in either Quinn's or Schwartz and Giroux's recent anthologies. Yet this thirteen-line *cri de coeur* has keen literary and biographic import. It also provides an invigorating context for the "Dear Dr.—" series, which directly follows it. Given the poem's likely geographic locale of com-position, the narrator might be addressing the ghost of Bishop's institutionalized mother and, by extension, the mortmain of the past on the psyche's present tense.

> I see you far away, unhappy,
>   small
> behind those horrible little green
>   grilles
> like an animal at Bronx Park
> & I want to do something about it
>   but [of course] I can't[5]
> because time (capitalized)[6] for
> some reason or other
> has put his big hands
>   in between us.

Otherwise you know perfectly
well I'd do everything I could. (VC 73.5b 152)

Bishop's poem works from the rhetorical premises of a personal letter in its par-
ticularized address, its simultaneous invocation of distance and intimacy, and
its attempt to reconcile a shared traumatic memory. The narrator, in addressing
someone "far away," implicates the poem's tacit epistolarity: only a letter-like poem
could convey intimate speech across such a surreal distance, rendering the force
of its tenderness.[7] As Gerald MacLean observes, letters are always "directed from
here to there, across a space between, the abode of the never entirely absent other,"
and Bishop's addressee, while seemingly "far away," becomes eerily present within
this letter-poem's rhetorical, displaced "abode" (177).

It is the conjured visual presence of the addressee that catalyzes the narrator's
speech, "I *see* you far away, unhappy," and the telegrammatic missive that follows
depends upon this operative distance between correspondents as well as the conceit of the letter as an enabling "bridge" (VC 75.3b 152; Altman 13). In the poem's
opening mise-en-scène, the narrator envisions the addressee imprisoned behind
"horrible little green / grilles," an image that suggests the barred windows of an
institution, backlit with the green fluorescence characteristic of clinical settings.
The addressee also appears "small" (152). Fittingly, both this word and "grilles"
sit independently on the second and fourth lines, spatially overshadowed by the
full-length lines above and below them. This lineation typographically mimics the
addressee's circumstance as a kind of zoo specimen, someone forced to live "like
an animal in Bronx Park" (152).

Within five compressed lines, Bishop re-creates the uncomfortable exposure
of institutional life: the addressee is visibly "unhappy" and "small" in her human
menagerie. Indeed, the loved one essentially lives in a Foucault-like institution
that cages (and displays) its occupants' unprivate lives, a circumstance that the
letter-poem—with its own public/private tension—uniquely memorializes. Altman observes that "as a reflection of the self, or the self's relationships, the letter
connotes privacy and intimacy; yet as a document addressed to another, the letter
reflects the need for an audience, an audience that may suddenly expand when
that document is confiscated, shared or published" (186–87). While Bishop did
not choose to publish this poem, with its likely reflection of a troubling maternal
relationship, she did bequeath her notebook to Linda Nemer with the understanding that Nemer might later sell Bishop's materials for a "good price" (*EAP* xii).
Hence, true to Altman's supposition, the ultimate privacy of this letter-poem has

at last come into public purview, attaining its "third" audience well over sixty years after its inscription.

Witnessing the addressee's miserable captivity, the narrator expresses an immediate desire "to do something" (152). The narrator's ability to effect change, however, is summarily foreclosed in the seventh line—the poem's midpoint and subjective hinge—wherein the narrator's eagerness to help is abruptly thwarted by the real-world constraints of "time" (152). The latter is synecdochically (and somewhat frighteningly) featured in the disembodied "big hands" of a clock or a watch: a decidedly childlike aperçu. Indeed, visual echoes of this image recur in the "watch" of a mother in "One Art" and in the wristwatch of an addled psychiatric patient in "Visits to St. Elizabeths," extending Bishop's associative matrix between the caprice of temporality, madness, and the abandoning mother (PPL 167, 127–29).[8]

To better understand her own psychic troubles and those of her friends, to explore the wellsprings of the imagination, and to reckon the trauma of her early years, Bishop was an avid student of psychology for most of her adult life. Her postcollegiate notebooks are peppered with notes on Freud and psychoanalysis as well as reading lists for articles in academic journals such as *Psychological Review* and the *American Journal of Psychology*. One such list contains the following article titles: "Absolute judgments of character & traits in self and others," "A study of revised emotions," and, perhaps most tellingly, "Affective sensitivities in poets & scientific students" (VC 74.11, 61). Once she settled in Brazil, Bishop reported to friends that she was reading Lota's "large psychological library," Ernest Jones's "wonderful and fearful" biography of Freud, and Klein's *Envy and Gratitude* ("superb in its horrid way"), as well as the popular child development theories of Benjamin Spock and Arnold Gesell (OA 283; WIA 173; OA 462; Millier 267). Most revealingly, when Bishop's companion, Lota de Macedo Soares, began to show signs of mental strain in 1967, Bishop commuted to Rio de Janeiro twice weekly so that Soares could see an analyst there who had trained with Klein (OA 462). Bishop saw this Kleinian analyst too, during this interval.[9] Hence, it seems apropos and even necessary to read Bishop's post-1946 poetry in the context of her early experiences with psychoanalysis, her ongoing study of psychology, and her subsequent interest in Kleinian therapy.

Bishop's "I see you far away, unhappy" poem essentially operates as a mechanism of sublimation, a "memento" in its displacement of desire for the beloved into a narrative lyric wish that can be sent imaginatively across geographic, temporal, and mortal divides (Lombardi 192). The poem also partakes of the reality-testing that Freud believed was essential to the mourning process: although the narrator initially regards the addressee as if she were alive and able to receive this missive, she eventually concedes that "time" has intervened, rendering any amelioration of the circumstance impossible ("Mourning" 244). An inability to revise the past or to live fully within the present persists as a motif in Bishop's oeuvre; this recurrent impasse might reflect Bishop's own struggles to introject the lost mother, to redirect the libido of a thwarted primary investment (Lombardi 192–93).

Bishop's postanalytic attempts to reckon with maternal loss and early traumatic memories might also help to account for the decided psychological thickening in her later work, its "almost exaggerated awareness of subjectivity" (Gray 60). In her last three volumes—*A Cold Spring* (1955), *Questions of Travel* (1965), and *Geography III* (1976)—Bishop utilizes a range of narrative forms to answer the "old correspondences" mentioned in "The Bight," a poem composed on her birthday (*PPL* 47). Indeed, Bishop's use of the letter-poem in the late 1940s suggests her effort to reply to the "torn open, unanswered letters" of unearthed psychoanalytic material and to maintain—in the form of the letter-gift—the ongoing work of relationality. In this way, letters appear to complement and extend the activity of the Freudian dredge in "The Bight," which plumbs the harbor's depths and lifts to the surface a "dripping jawful of marl" (*PPL* 47).

In the "awful but cheerful," decidedly "untidy activity" of psychoanalysis and of narrative poetry, Bishop evolved an aesthetic governed by an elegiac selfhood, one that accords with Freud's notion of the ego as a "precipitate of abandoned object-cathexes" (*PPL* 47; "Ego" 29). Like her survivalist animals—the hooked fish, the blood-spattered armadillo, the darting sandpiper—Bishop's poetic "self" often appears to be a reliquary of loss and yearning, a persona of storied scars (*PPL* 33, 83–84, 125). The letter-poem, in its narrative capaciousness, lent Bishop a model for admixing psychoanalytic insight, natural description, and casual parable into an other-directed missive, an interiority that invites a response from its long-distance interlocutor.

While it is possible that Bishop had her then-estranged lover, Marjorie Stevens, or some other amorous addressee in mind in writing "I see you far away, unhappy," it seems likely that Bishop was ruing a more primary genre of love-loss. The poem's final, chastising lines, "Otherwise you know perfectly / well I'd do everything I could," have the unmistakable air of a child imitating a parental tone of voice, chiding a wish for the impossible (VC 152). Bishop's tonal shift—from the pitying sympathy of the poem's first six lines to the childlike bargain at the conclusion—accords with Melanie Klein's observation that in mature relationships of any complexity, individuals continue to enact (and negotiate) the structure of their earliest relations;

as such, they may play the role of "parent" or "child" interchangeably, a protean dynamic Bishop manages to inflect within the brevity of thirteen lines (324–25).

Given Bishop's decided interest in Klein's work and her later work with a Kleinian analyst, it seems likely that Bishop composed her notebook letter-poems having some familiarity with Klein's theories. In her landmark essay "Infantile Anxiety Situations Reflected in a Work of Art and in the Creative Impulse" (1929), Klein asserts that daughters suffer an anxiety similar to sons' Oedipal conflict. It involves the daughter's desire to "rob" the mother's body; a subsequent fear of maternal aggression; and, ultimately, the daughter's overriding worry that the mother's actual presence and affection will be lost (217). As in Bishop's letter-poem, the child's anxiety in Klein's model is initially generated by "seeing" or "not seeing" the mother: "When the little girl who fears the mother's assault upon her body cannot *see* her mother, this intensifies the anxiety. . . . At a later stage of development the content of the dread changes from that of an attacking mother to the dread that the real, loving mother may be lost and that the girl will be left solitary and forsaken" (217, original emphasis). A Kleinian mother-daughter dyad seems to be at work in "I see you far away, unhappy," in which the speaker conjures the addressee from her "far away" place in order to "see" her and, perhaps, to relieve the intense anxiety about maternal attack and abandonment that Klein identifies. Such an "attack" and maternal disappearance are subsequently the subjects of Bishop's short story "In the Village," wherein the mother—unmoored by excessive grief—frightens the child with her erratic behavior, verbal attacks, and sudden disappearance. As McCabe notes: "The dead still participate in our imagination of them. . . . Poems become ceremonies to mourn departure through repetition" (214). Bishop makes her cyclical returns in this letter-poem, in several published poems, and in many of her prose stories, revisiting the alarming disappearance and sharply felt absence of a mother in a young child's life.

The separation between the speaker and the addressee in the letter-poem, enacted by the "big hands" of "time," invokes a child's distinct sense of arbitrary loss and, perhaps, the fear that "some reason or other"—including *unreason*—could reunite them in death or in the institutionalized world of the mad (VC 75.3b, 152). As Millier and Lombardi note, during the crisis moments of her alcoholic and depressive troubles in the 1940s, Bishop was haunted by the real possibility that she could slide into alcoholic decline and, like her mother, lose her mind. Writing from the Yaddo Writers' Colony in 1949 to her physician, Anny Baumann, Bishop expressed her renewed determination to abstain from drink, mentioning the stern advice she had once received from Dr. Foster: "I suddenly made up my mind. I will *not* drink. I've been stalling now for years & it is absolutely absurd. Dr. Foster once said: 'Well, go ahead, then—ruin your life'—and I almost have. I also know I'll go insane if I keep it up. I cannot drink and I know it" (*OA* 210). Hence, when the poet-speaker in "I see you far away, unhappy" writes in her letter-poem that she cannot counter time's "big hands," nor can she trespass the "horrible little green / grilles" separating herself from her addressee, it may have been with the tacit understanding that to do so would be, in effect, to renounce a sane life (VC 75.3b, 152). The mother must remain a ghostly conjured presence, someone the speaker can address only across the impossible postal distances of mental dissolution and death.

While "I see you far away, unhappy" re-creates the narrative circuit that Bishop was constructing in the late 1940s among psychoanalytic themes and epistolary conceits, it also shares an economy of symbols with the "Dear Dr.—" sequence that directly follows it in the poet's notebook, a sequence that makes the poet's overlay of analytic narratives, letter writing, and dreamwork even more explicit. Bishop's description, for example, of her addressee being trapped behind "those horrible little green grilles" in "I see you far away, unhappy" would seem to share some connection with the "green light" that recurs in the letter-poems to her analyst, where it alternately represents the extreme isolation of madness, the benign watchfulness of a mother, and the "particular & brighter" color of dreams themselves (VC 75.3b, 157).

This "green light" appears in what seems to be the very earliest draft of the "Dear Dr.—" sequence. Quinn, in making her selections for *Edgar Allan Poe & the Juke-Box,* may not have considered all of the poem's drafts as she does not refer to three unnumbered versions, each written on unbound scraps of paper that were found inside of the Key West notebook near the other "Dear Dr.—" poems (VC 75.3b). When Vassar College acquired some of Bishop's Brazilian materials in 1986, these three poems were removed and stored separately in order to prevent their loss or damage (Rogers).

Quinn cites only "four copies with just slight variations" of the "Dear Dr.—" poem, when in fact there are at least seven copies and several with significant variations (*EAP* 286). This poetic septet includes a version on notebook page 153, a version on page 155, three unnumbered versions beginning "Dear Dr. Foster," "Dear Doctor Foster," and "For Dr. F." (stored in Folder 75.1), and the two versions on notebook page 157. One of the three unnumbered drafts appears to be the original version; it captures the poet in an almost undressed state of *homo faber,* an early moment of poetic making. Like the initial drafts of "One Art," this page (with its two miniature "Dear Dr. Foster" and "Dear Doctor Foster" drafts) contains the seedling essence of the full poem.

are in color

Dear Dr. Foster, yes dreams do have color

&   memories have colors.   are in

in time? [this phrase is circled]

gas tank

1 gregarious like loaves of bread rising [latter phrase written on a steep
upward slant]

1 greg [crossed out]
  gregarious green light

Dear Doctor Foster,
yes dreams are in color
& memories are in color   too [word is circled]
           harbor (VC 75.1)

Bishop's epistolary address of her psychiatrist seems to direct and sustain the activity of her dream-reportage. In a December 1947 letter to Robert Lowell, Bishop
praised his dream poem "Falling Asleep over the Aeneid" and mentioned that her
own "psychiatrist friend" was writing an article on color in dreams, a phrase that
intimates the warmth and alliance she felt with Dr. Foster (OA 151).

"I've heard quite a lot about it," Bishop added, as if her "friendship" with Dr.
Foster placed her in the psychoanalytic know. "I gather from it [Lowell's poem] that
when you dream you dream in colors all right" (OA 151). Bishop's exchange with
Lowell elucidates the interplay of letters, analytic insights, and the back rooms (or
dream rooms) of poesis. It seems to be understood, in Bishop's remarks, that Lowell has drawn upon his own dreamwork—the Freudian task of translating latent
thoughts into visual images—to create what Bishop admiringly calls a "*stirring*"
poem (OA 151; Freud, "Introductory Lectures" 170). For Bishop and for many in
her post-Freudian generation, dreams were understood to be idiosyncratic in their
"residue" from an individual's life, but also to serve as a key to a common symbolic
language: one inflected, as Freud had argued, with the particular concerns of the
dreamer's historical age ("Introductory Lectures" 98–99).

Bishop's letter-poem figuratively extends an analytic conversation as she gives
Dr. Foster an impressionistic description of a recent dream or, perhaps, an associative survey of the objects near the bay in Dartmouth. When Bishop begins the draft
anew, at the bottom of the page, she adds the word "harbor," which anchors her

conjuring to a specific place. The poem's intermediary images—the "gregarious" or friendly, outgoing "gas tank" and "green light"—suggest sociality and relationship or, in the Latinate sense of the word, a "group-seeking" nature. If, however, these images stand in metonymically for the desired mother, "gregarious" might have the connotation of disturbed extroversion as in the outward, talkative anxiety of the unhinging mother in Bishop's short story "In the Village."

The phrase "loaves of bread rising," which Bishop abandoned in subsequent drafts, might have seemed too obvious an association with nurture, domestic life, and the maternal body. In Klein's original essay "Love, Guilt and Reparation" (1937), the analyst specifically allies poets' interest in nature and natural scenes with the warmth of feeling that the child retains for the mother's breast (336–37). In describing a harbor view with the vaguely mammary images of a "gas tank" and of "loaves of bread rising," Bishop may have been consciously or unconsciously re-creating a Kleinian rubric in which the poet projects his or her benign imagoes onto a landscape. In fact, when Bishop published "At the Fishhouses," a poem closely allied with the aqueous feminine images in the "Dear Dr.—" series in 1947, Lowell told Bishop that he thought it was one of her best. But he also admitted that he found the breast imagery in the last stanza to be "too much" (qtd. in Millier 192). Perhaps Lowell, having written in "The Quaker Graveyard in Nantucket" a "piscatory ecologue" and an homage to masculine violence, could not envision his native Atlantic as a source of maternal succor (Dubrow 48).

Less speculatively, the "gregarious green light" in this version of the "Dear Dr.—" sequence seems an obvious parallel to the "green grilles" that restrict the addressee in "I see you far away, unhappy." The green light in the latter, possibly from a mental institution's windows, and the "gregarious" green nautical light in the harbor of the "Dear Dr.—" poem appear to play with notions of parental surveillance, a trope that recurs in "Squatter's Children," "Manners," "Sestina," and, perhaps most memorably, in "One Art." If the "green grilles" in "I see you far away, unhappy" signify the mother's institution, where she is carefully watched and monitored, the green light in the "Dear Dr.—" poems might represent the monitory gaze of the mother herself, stationed across the bay, or that of the psychiatrist, stationed across the room from the analysand.[10]

In the draft that appears on page 153 of her notebook, Bishop writes that the green light "comes to look," a phrase that she subsequently replaces with "watches this one now unenviously" (in the drafts on pages 155 and 157). The changed predicate intensifies the action of the "green light" from that of a casual spectator to that of a parental figure or guardian. This reinstatement of the parental gaze in an inanimate object fits the interpretative schema that Diehl proposes for the surfeit of visual detail and natural imagery in Bishop's oeuvre: namely, that the poet

regularly compensates for the abandoning mother's inattention with attachment
to "transferential objects . . . a world that is reinvested with a displaced domesticity" (8). In the evolving process of the "Dear Dr." sequence, Bishop complicates
(or removes) some of the more apparent maternal images and expands her frame
of reference considerably, linking conjectural ratiocinations to concrete, ungendered objects.

The expanded version of "Dear Dr.—" that appears on notebook page 157,
for example, considers the influence of emotions on memories in a fragmentary
syntax of psychic life, one that suggests Bishop's engagement with Freud's notion
of the screen memory. (This draft does not appear in Quinn's or in Schwartz and
Giroux's anthologies.)

> Dear Dr. Foster
> yes, dreams are in colors
> and memories come in color
> though that in dreams is more remarkable.
>   particular   & brighter,
> at their first like that   green light in the harbor
>   which must belong to a [scratched out word] society
>   just itself   of its own
> & watches this one just for now unenviously.
>
> The past are from
>
> memories
>
> all those photographs waters
>   con
> manufacture, their fluences
> [indecipherable line]
>
> with all the photographs & notes
>   manufacturing fluences every minute
>
>   rotogravure
> with the photographs water
>   manufacturing fluences every minute—
>
>   insidious (vc 75.3b, 155)

Describing the "green light" as belonging to a "society / just itself . . . of its own" intimates the isolation and frightening singularity of madness, especially if the "green light" in this poem is aligned with the "green / grilles" in "I see you far away, unhappy," where it seems to represent the barred windows of a hospital or psychiatric ward. Despite the green light's isolation, however, it "watches this one just for now unenviously." Hence, the green light gazes without jealousy at the dreaming narrator, who has suddenly (and perhaps very alarmingly) discovered her dreams to be far "more remarkable / particular & brighter" than her memories' more sedate hues.

In his work on screen memories, Freud theorized that individuals create self-protective memories "relating to" and not "from" childhood ("Screen" 322). As instinctual autobiographers, individuals renarrativize stories of their early years: a process that allows the subject a psychically guarded, if somewhat distorted, access to his or her past ("Screen" 322). Bishop may have believed in this defensive mechanism, as Freud had described it. In her late-life interview with Spires, Bishop mentioned that her psychoanalyst was impressed with her ability to remember events from a very early age: "I went to an analyst for a couple of years off and on in the forties, a very nice woman who was especially interested in writers, writers and blacks. She said it was amazing that I would remember things that happened to me when I was two. It's very rare, but apparently writers often do" (126). Although Bishop may have been able to recollect memories from an age that impressed Dr. Foster, in her analytic poem she questions the strength and validity of those recollections. Memories, she asserts, are subject to the false "photographs" that "waters / manufacture," or the false screen memories generated by emotion. Bishop grants "the past" plurality in stating that it comes from "memories," which implies a multiplicity of sources and competing versions of "fact."

Hence, even "rotogravure . . . photographs" are subject to the "insidious" force of "fluences," a truncated aphaeretic version of "influences" that suggests a range of connotations. Bishop, as a student of classical languages, may have had in mind the Latin *fluentem*, "a flowing, a stream," or the contemporary English version of "fluence" as the application of a "mysterious, magical, or hypnotic power to a person" (*OED*). The *in*-fluence of tears, the *con*-fluence of harbor waters, and the black-magic force of false memories are all valences of meaning in Bishop's fragmentary verse.

If mental images from the past are shaped by the "manufacture" of emotions, then "the past" in this letter-poem is arguably as destabilized as "knowledge" is in the concluding lines of "At the Fishhouses." In that poem's crescendo, human knowledge is portrayed as a radically unfixed entity: not an inert store of *sapientia*, but a process at once sempiternal and transient, fluid and already "flown" (*PPL* 52). Like the powerfully "dark, salt, clear" waters in "At the Fishhouses," the "fluences" of "photographs & notes" are forces of mutability, inducing an "insidious" change of memory, of fact.

Metapoetically, Bishop questions the role of "notes" as she is, presumably, making them, writing another poem that might serve to aestheticize her sorrow or to induce uncanny metamorphoses of memory. This anxiety swirls in her letter-poem's last lines: "rotogravure / with the photographs water / manufacturing fluences every minute / insidious" (VC 75.3b, 155). In a juggling match of subjects, predicates, and objects, Bishop mimics the enmeshed circuitry of memory, emotion, and the distortions attendant in high feeling. All is mixed to an ongoing "insidious" amalgam, resistant to linear narrative, but one seemingly permitted in the exploratory letter-poem, modeled on the intrapsychic "play" of the analytic hour. In the "Dear Dr.—" sequence, Bishop returns ritualistically to the epistolary address of her psychiatrist. The letter, with its air of especial confidence, its guarded invocation of an absent presence, and its conceit of reciprocity, seems to have been an inviting form for Bishop's explication of the subterranean forces of the mind and the unwieldy life of feeling.

In choosing to feature only one, neatened version of the "Dear Dr.—" sequence and not to publish "I see you far away, unhappy," Quinn overlooked the fascinating qualities of these letter-poems, which are critical to assessing the influence of psychoanalysis and filial grief in Bishop's psychic cartography. As a poet who frequently rejected the strictures of linear narrativity, of "historians' . . . colors," Bishop would borrow both from the modernists' legacy of open forms and from emergent models of narrativity in her postwar, post-Freudian period to depict the mutability of an historical selfhood (PPL 3). Or, as she wrote in "Dimensions for a Novel": "A constant process of adjustment is going on about the past—every ingredient dropped into it from the present must affect the whole" (PPL 673). Bishop's associative letter-poems experiment with the extent to which these dynamic processes of subjectivity, half-culled from the unconscious, might be effectively "sent" to an interlocutor.

The quotidian thickness and psychological verisimilitude that mark Bishop's mature aesthetic may owe more to the crisis years during and after her psychoanalysis than has been previously acknowledged. As she composed the poems of *A Cold Spring* (1955), Bishop was steadily attaining the difficult grace of the "water-spider," the creature she cited in her admiring review of Emily Dickinson's correspondence in 1951 (PPL 689–90). In a psychoanalytic update to Keats's Negative Capability, Bishop lauds Dickinson's late letters for their enhanced "structure and strength," their ability to hold an "upstream position by means of the faintest ripples, while making one aware of the current of death and darkness below"

(*PPL* 690). Bishop, in these notebook letter-poems, skates across the dark waters of the bight, noting the wreckage on the littoral and literal shores of her early life's symbology, progressing by means of her own generative action: that of the continually redressing, addressed letter.

NOTES

1. Epistolary mourning is a leitmotif in Bishop's "In the Village," a story she composed during her first year in Brazil, and that she published both in the *New Yorker* (1953) and between two sections of poetry in *Questions of Travel* (1965).

2. Susan McCabe notes that *A Cold Spring* reads as "a series of correspondences with significant others" (135). Of the eighteen poems in this modest volume, at least three are explicitly epistolary: "Letter to N. Y.," "Invitation to Miss Marianne Moore," and, as a verbalist postcard, "View of the Capitol from the Library of Congress" (*PPL* 61, 63–64, 52–53).

3. Describing the uncanny involvement of the reader in Thomas Hardy's "Torn Letter," J. Hillis Miller cites Kafka's theory of letter writing in *Letters to Milena* (1954): "It [letter writing] is, in fact, an intercourse with ghosts, and not only with the ghost of the recipient but with one's own ghost which develops between the lines of the letter one is writing" (135).

4. The "from Halifax" notation, positioned in the top left-hand corner of notebook page 153, above one of the first "Dear Dr.—" poems, effectively mimics the placement of a letter's return address, a subtle gesture that Bishop, with her usual attention to visual and typographical detail, may have playfully intended.

5. "Of course," while legible, is crossed out in Bishop's draft.

6. Bishop's own notation, presumably a reminder to capitalize "time" in another draft.

7. Altman defines "epistolarity" as "the use of the letter's formal properties to create meaning" (4).

8. "A Short, Slow Life," a notebook poem that Lloyd Schwartz dates to the "mid to late 1950s," also features "Time" as the villainous agent. In this ten-line lyric, Time's "hand [has] reached in" and "tumbled" the speaker from her surroundings, fracturing a bucolic, Great Village–like scene where "[the] houses, the barns, the two churches, / [were] hid like white crumbs" (*PPL* 235).

9. In a letter to her New York physician, Anny Baumann, Bishop mentions her intermittent work with a Kleinian analyst in Rio de Janeiro: "I am telling you all my troubles again—I have no one else to tell them to!—except once and a while I see the analyst, too—but he is not of much practical help to me, much as I like him" (*OA* 462). Since Bishop could not expect immediate psychological advice from Baumann through the international mail, it seems more likely that Bishop continued to find epistolary composition therapeutic, a "home-made" version of the analytic hour ("Crusoe in England," *PPL* 154).

10. Bishop may have also been alluding to the iconic green light in F. Scott Fitzgerald's *Great Gatsby,* which she taught in a course at Harvard University. In Fitzgerald's tale, the protagonist harkens after an elusive "green light" at the end of a dock in East Egg, which symbolizes his wish to reclaim the past, to capture the affections of his beloved, and to revise history's sharp delineation of possibility (182). In Bishop's letter-poem, the narrator similarly wishes to break the literal stronghold of time: to elude its "big hands" and to rescue a symbolic female figure from the disciplinary "green / grilles" of an intractable past.

Elizabeth Bishop's Drafts

"That Sense of Constant Readjustment"

LORRIE GOLDENSOHN

In a much-noticed review of Alice Quinn's *Edgar Allan Poe & the Juke-Box,* Helen Vendler steadied the troops against any eager embrace of these uncollected and previously unpublished poems and fragments. Back into their archival lairs the whole lot should go: against "the real poems," these are only "their maimed and stunted siblings" (33). And indeed it is true that only a small handful of the poems rise to the level that the best of *The Complete Poems: 1927–1979* offer us. Those on the lookout for a new collection of poems to rival *Geography III* or any other of Bishop's previous books must surely be disappointed. If we are fair, a match-up between the splendors of the new collection and of the old *Complete Poems* would be lopsided in favor of the old. In *Edgar Allan Poe & the Juke-Box,* what is of interest is usually not finished, and nearly all of what is newly given as finished is not of great interest. But finally, one must ask, why should these books match each other anyway? They are quite different entities illustrating legitimately different perspectives on the poetry of Elizabeth Bishop. The new collection could not have been done except posthumously, at a moment when the live career had ceased, and the completed curvature of the whole is newly in evidence. Against what we make of the achieved Bishop, *Edgar Allan Poe & the Juke-Box* makes more fully possible an expedition into what might have been. It provides us with the best look yet at Bishop's actual working habits, and baits our further interest with the judgments she made along the way.

One of the most intriguing of the unfinished poems that Alice Quinn includes is "Apartment in Leme," which went through approximately thirty pages of draft revisions and could have been as arresting a poem about Brazil as any of the dozen that Bishop left completed. Quinn presents the poem in what looks to have been the last draft: the poem split fairly late into four sections, the first three typed out, and then the fourth scratched in by hand. Ordering the drafts could not have been easy. As I review the thirty scrambled pages that Bishop left (now at Vassar

College), I see how the figure that she took up for the surface of the sea—"those corroded old bronze mirrors" eventually becomes "an old bronze mirror black but shiny," and then appears to settle, with increasing determination into this invocation of that watery face:

> Oh, slightly roughened,
> greeny-black, scaly
>
> as one of those corroded old bronze mirrors
> in all the world's museums (How did the ancients
> ever see *anything* in them?),
>
> incapable of reflecting even the biggest stars. (EAP 135)

And another evolution brought the coffeepot on the breakfast table into its final form: "—regularly the silver coffee-pot goes into / dark, rainbow-edged eclipse"; with this phrase, Bishop neatly landed the pot itself in the realm of the iridescent and liminal so familiar to her readers (134). The surface of the pot is silver, but like all surfaces exposed to the corrosive breath of salt air, its reflectiveness dims, then breaks and refracts, and must be periodically polished and brought back to its elusive silver self.

I was struck by this poem when I first encountered it. Looking over the drafts, you can see how Bishop carefully and incrementally layered over and built up each incoming draft stanza with a few alternating modifiers and some alternating tenses and modes as she prodded the possibilities. The last in a trial series often contains the final form of a line or phrase, or repeats and strengthens the syntactical members of a sequence. To illustrate from the unpublished drafts this little stutter of the poet's mind at work:

> white candles, dead white candles, snuffed out in dried surf
> snuffed out in dried surf, dead white candles,
> dead white candles, snuffed [in last night's surf] [*cancelled*] dead white candles
> and the green glass bottles of white alcohol
> meant for the goddess meant to come last night (VC, Folder 64.19)

In "Apartment in Leme," a line full of Bishop's characteristic invention evolved from "A great grouping of stars," and modulated to "A spray of fiery white cur-

rants"; then she fixed the stars into "One cluster, bright, astringent as white currants / hung from the Magellanic Clouds" (135). A previous phrasing, "A great
grouping of stars" sounds pretty good; but the stars seen as bright, astringent currants makes one of those startling fusions of the senses at work, leading into a precise and unarguable juxtaposition of near and far where the brightness of the stars
turns to a lusciousness of fire and acidity which from our position at the window
or on the beach we long to reach up and touch.

Bishop's drafts show that her poems anchored early, with fairly certain lines of
convergence between place, time, and meaning; completion was a patient exercise
of waiting for vision to clear, in Lowell's phrase, to let the "gaps or empties" fill up.
In drafts, she adjusts for precision, and cuts here and there for focus, but admits no
major change of direction once the poem is securely under way, which usually occurs by the second or third draft. "Apartment in Leme" had nearly all of its events,
objects, and characters from the beginning drafts, but it took a while longer for
the ending to come, and for the lines to fall into four sections. Steadily, however,
the mainframe is sea and sky with two niches for human habitation, one for the
watcher up in the high-rise apartment, and another for the people below on the
sand. Controlling the diaphragm of the poem is the sea's animal breath, "your cold
breath blowing warm, your warm breath cold" (*EAP* 134):

> Wisps of fresh green stick to your foamy lips
> like those on horses' lips. The sand's bestrewn:
> white lilies, broken stalks,
>
> white candles with wet, blackened wicks,
> and green glass bottles for white alcohol
> meant for that goddess meant to come last night.
>
> (But you've emptied them all.) (135)

In this wry, playful passage with its rocking, incantatory repetitions, the sea
mingles the breath of both wayward deity and hungover poet, bringing on the
implements of the cult of the goddess Iémanja, whose followers dunk in the sea in
white dresses early in the morning of the New Year.

The domesticated envelope of the poem is disarmingly casual, and the way
that we can flirt with the ocean's open mouth carries even a touch of cheerful
insolence:

> Sometimes you embolden, sometimes bore.
> You smell of codfish and old rain. Homesick, the salt
> weeps in the salt-cellars. (EAP 134)

The effects of the salt sea are everywhere. When the white-clad worshippers hold hands and walk waist-deep into the water, the goddess may well have come, or may be coming. Yet this possibility is about co-equal with the earlier facts of the poem's setting in section 2:

> It's growing lighter. On the beach two men
> get up from shallow-newspaper-lined graves.
> A third sleeps on. His coverlet
> is corrugated paper, a flattened box." (EAP 135)

The men who get up, the one who sleeps on, a running dog, and two early bathers have as much impact on the scene as the worshippers. Like the children skating on a pond alongside a wood in W. H. Auden's "Musée des Beaux Arts" who do not especially want "the miraculous birth" to happen, or like the torturer's horse who scratches his innocent behind oblivious of "the dreadful martyrdom" (179), Bishop's people, worshippers and passersby, exist with equal right and weight. What is, *is*, as it fills the canvas of a multilevel reality.

These are the final lines that Alice Quinn transcribes:

> . . . We live at your open mouth,
> with your cold breath blowing warm, your warm breath cold
> like in the fairy tale
>
> no — the legend." (EAP 136)

It is not possible to determine whether Bishop would ultimately have teased out the distinction between "fairy tale" and "legend" further — or whether she would have been satisfied to leave this somewhat blurry apposition of qualities as the poem's culmination. Nevertheless, enough is happening in the poem as it exists, both emotively and descriptively, to earn its right to our close attention. It is not "maimed"; it is not "stunted"; it is merely unfinished. Even so, much can be made of its oceanic theme, of its use of perspective in relation to other Bishop poems. Like "Five Flights Up" (CP 181), this poem leans from a high window in an apartment building at dawn. It's almost playfully suggestive reference to the rites of Macumba, and of the appearance of the goddess Iémanja, is close to the way that Bishop introduced us to the serpent goddess Luandinha in "The Riverman" (*CP* 105–9). Both poems mix the sacred and the credible ordinary. For the Riverman, "the moon burns white / and the river makes that sound / like a primus pumped up high— / that fast, high whispering / like a hundred people at once—" (108), and for the elevated lookout in the city apartment by the beach, the atmosphere is no less intense and sensuous, wrapped as it is, living "at your open mouth, oh Sea" (*EAP* 134).

Both "The Riverman" and "Apartment in Leme" balance the presentation of their local deities so that the voice of the poem neither presumes a devotee's familiarity nor distances or stiffens with condescension or an unwarranted assumption of "objectivity." The themes are treated in a way that is serious, curious, respectful. The sacaca in "The Riverman" offers him the way to a self-improving education and mastery:

> When the moon shines and the river
> lies across the earth
> and sucks it like a child,
> then I will go to work
> to get you health and money. (*CP* 109)

"Apartment in Leme" greets the New Year with celebratory ablutions and offerings, which either the sea or the goddess may or may not accept. But the large, animate breathing of the sea matrix in which even the observer is held lightly suffuses the poem with intimations of redemptive and transformative power. Each water-bound poem is saturated in the magical. Both the downward telescoping of this draft, as well as its seizure by that large sea breath, become Bishop's quintessential moves of altered perspective, of a piece with the Riverman who dives to an underwater rendezvous, or of the spectator who watches the death of Micuçú through binoculars from the terrace, or even of Marianne Moore flying across the Brooklyn Bridge, or of the Man-Moth, who plunges from the top of his building to the subway below, or the Unbeliever, who sleeps at the top of the mast. "Apartment in Leme" is one more congenial instance of Bishop's extraordinary mobility of vantage point, and of her deft distortions of scale and distance within a dizzying but consistent emotional universe. The world of the poem is also simultaneously shrunken, as the eye of the observer swoops down or up, and enlarged, as the distant member is brought close to the subjective eye through crystalline description.

Bishop's poem unfolds organically, where you see in each successive draft how she tried to make the initiating thought more precise and more telling. She wasted nothing, and chose to refine her ideas within a narrow field of elements. Her approach resembles a softer, more pliant version of Michelangelo's, who saw the finished statue in the block of marble: all that needs to be done is to carve away the excrescent stone. The poem seems largely there from the start: there may have been hesitations in composition—some of them very long-term indeed—but her task was to probe, pare, and gradually unwrap the fresh, wet poem from its matrix of dream and memory.

"Apartment in Leme" is a steady excavation of personal experience and relies on exact observation of a chosen scene. This unfinished poem affords a particularly tantalizing glimpse of how and why this poet moves words along from phrases into lines, and then from lines into poems. But whether Bishop's draft is read by itself or in the company of other poems by her or anyone else, it is distinctly a service to readers to make what we have available to those who have not yet or do not usually enter archives.

Above all, in the assembling of this unfinished work, there is a hovering sense of the live act of composition. All of the drafts, with Alice Quinn's perceptive notes alongside, ignite our awareness of what the unfinished but capaciously suggested future poem might have been; a static set of material scraps is made to vibrate with possibility. Many of the murkier bits and pieces seem destined for obscurity. And yet, over time, inquisitive readers can never tell from which direction a heightened and enlivened signal might still flare, should we be lucky or clever or industrious enough to set the right scrap next to the right work. This *was* a poet after all whose work evinced such a visceral integrity. While fragments of the work may provide further ideas about what Bishop was writing, thinking, or experiencing, I do not know of any instances where the fragments are deeply conflicted; the new bits here may confirm or qualify what Bishop says elsewhere, but nowhere do her beliefs or principles appear contradicted. Because of this consistency, or harmony in Bishop's work, all of the new writing with which Alice Quinn supplies us has a notably trustworthy element of witness, a witness only amplified by the fullness of interpretive context that her annotations offer.

Some of the completed specimens that Alice Quinn has included, such as "Money," or "For Grandfather," however, yield less of aesthetic value than the unfinished poems. Both of these pieces seem meagerly equipped with insight, and the latter skates too close to pathos, as with "A Baby Found in the Garbage." Short of writing a novel or a piece of journalism, what more could a writer really have made of this last poem whose title says everything to be said on the subject? The

rigorously antipathetic tone of a poem such as "Pink Dog" is a much better register
of what Bishop could or might do in the way of savage social commentary. At the
other end of the scale of feeling, even undeniable charmers like "Close, Close All
Night" edge into light verse. And at least a few more poems like "To Manuel Bandeira, with Jam and Jelly" possess undeniable ebullience and charm, but seem too
narrowly occasional verse. Maybe in a spirit of editorial thoroughness one adds
such poems, safe in the knowledge that someone will take to one or the other. De
gustibus. On the other hand, poems like "It is marvellous to wake up together . . . ,"
"In a cheap hotel . . . ," "St. John's Day," "Gypsophila," "Breakfast Song," and "Vague
Poem" are sure to be found in any new and complete edition of Bishop's poems,
and it is fine to have them here.

   "The Drunkard," or even "For Grandfather," look at least as finished as "Apartment in Leme." Here we can only say helplessly that neither of these efforts approaches "The Prodigal" or "In the Waiting Room" with anything of their power
or beauty. But now we come to the strongest part of Alice Quinn's rationale for
putting these bare, plain, but biographically suggestive poems in the collection:
They do manage to tell us about the poet's life in words that are still stronger and
more authoritative than anything a biographer might put forth. This is not a minor contribution. They fatten the record, they provide a broader gauge of feeling,
and situate what we have come to know in an imaginatively widened context of
personal history. "In the golden early morning . . . ," which never got to a real title,
is an amazing condensation of grief and panic, mysteriously coalescing around an
early-morning flight with two persons seeing off a third; the prosaic four lines first
cited build into the poem's devastating conclusion:

> M gave me a few last minute instructions & said
> "Call me from Miami." You to my surprise
> gave me a violent hug & a kiss on the cheek.
> M kissed me on both cheeks & I knew she was about to cry.
> So off I went & why do we undertake
> these terrifying & cruel trips & why did I come here (EAP 80)

We can perhaps assign names to two of the people—Marjorie Stevens might be
"M," and surely Bishop is the traveler. Several of the poems in North & South, such
as "Letter to N. Y.," are far more elegantly finished, but the raw close-up of feelings
in this little scene are bitterly and vividly coherent. Even in their refusal of more
expansive detail, they support a graphic idea of Bishop's life in the 1940s, shuttling
back and forth between Key West, Miami, and New York. Similarly haunting in

quality is the poem that precedes this in the collection, "I had a bad dream . . . ," where the shame and terror of exposure menace the lovers lying together in bed, cheek to cheek.

If we take the old New Criticism seriously, the inclusion of biographical data in a poem will not shoulder the poem's way into greatness: a poem is said to be a good poem only if it can stand on its own two feet, without external reference to the poet's life, because it is then more "universal," more "ours." But why should we straitjacket our motives for reading poems in this way? And why should we confine our reading of a great poet to only those poems certifiably signed off on for posterity? In other arts, sketches and plans are not only permissible, but honored. These poems are certainly incomplete and fragmentary; we are not even convinced that were they all finished, that they would be "as good" as others of Bishop's published work, and in several poignant instances, without their connection to Bishop, they would indeed be lacking in resonance for many readers. But why should we ignore what they tell us of a life and of working methods of so much interest to us?

Of her methods and intentions, Alice Quinn writes emphatically: "It must be explicitly stated that the ordering of this material is in no manner definitive" (*EAP* xv). She says further: "I have not reproduced all of Bishop's uncollected juvenilia or work that is restrictively fragmentary, that does not indicate to a certain degree something of her artistic ambition for it or otherwise command interest because of its biographical significance" (*EAP* xvii). Both of the final clauses here become quite important.

A charge against *Edgar Allan Poe & the Juke-Box* by Helen Vendler represents Quinn's effort as a violation of Elizabeth Bishop's wishes, and as an affront to the canon of her work. Would Bishop have uttered a "horrified NO" to the idea of its publication? To the first question, Quinn answers that these Bishop papers are drawn from work that "for one reason or another she chose not to publish but did not destroy" (*EAP* x). This becomes critical: in other words, there is no express commandment that we are contravening. The second question I do not believe we can answer; the poet is dead, and the era in which she lived has also departed or significantly altered its disposition of textual remains in ways whose technology Bishop could not imagine or did not care to think about. Counterfactual suppositions about what she might have done or wished remain suppositions in the face of the great fact that she did not burn, or ask anyone else to burn, what is now contained in Quinn's book.

Elizabeth Bishop expressed horror on one occasion at what had happened to Marianne Moore's unpublished papers, but she also vigorously coached her heirs to get a good price for her own papers, and to see them shepherded into literary archives. She was herself an avid reader of biographies, letters, and journals, and nowhere displays a purist indifference to a contextualizing of other artists' and writers' work. Quinn cites a letter written on July 8, 1971, in which Bishop describes a seminar she intends to teach on "'Letters'! . . . Just *letters*—as an art form or something. I'm hoping to select a nicely incongruous assortment of people— Mrs. Carlyle, Chekhov, my Aunt Grace, Keats, a letter found in the street, etc., etc." (*EAP* 359). She certainly knew the value of documents as witnesses for an analysis of style and a deeper understanding of literary form: letters are "an art form or something." She must have known that her own papers, kept so carefully for so many years, would serve for others much as a thumbprint acts to identify a person: these drafts were testimony or artifact that might indicate a cast of mind, the contours of a dominant idea, or the ongoing struggle with the meaning of a pervasive image.

One of Quinn's more interesting choices with respect to such an unresolved struggle was her inclusion of a draft for a late poem entitled "Mr. and Mrs. Carlyle." Quinn notes that eight pages of drafts were left of this poem, a poem not terribly interesting in the one version set out as the last Bishop poem before the appendix—but her notes include these lines:

> she saw him
> against the light
> wearing a new white beaver with a broad brim

A few more lines, not entirely coherent, and then Bishop writes:

> on the dry hot haze at the end of the street
>   he superimposed on the scene
>   blood and the guillotine (*EAP* 358)

Strong summer light and heat in her tidy, conjugal scene, also the marvelous hat: and then the violent incongruities. The poem would have been wonderful.

But it is an imperfect business so to rummage: back and forth we go, shuttling between facsimile reproductions, copious notes, and official addenda. Any reading of such a collection does not unfairly seem to require a certain imaginative dexterity and a high tolerance of the indeterminate.

This is a book about process—and it is a selection legitimately tailored to the taste of a single critic; Alice Quinn's generally illuminating notes make a persuasive case for her choices. As we know from scholarly response to *Edgar Allan Poe & the*

Juke-Box, other poets or scholars may have assembled a different book. I hope they do—and after much effort of this kind, we should be able to come to some working consensus as to which papers merit repeated circulation. Alice Quinn makes no claim to comprehensiveness, and from this large store others will very likely choose differently in the future. It seems to me, however, that Quinn has been faithful to her intentions. The somewhat arbitrary decision to add facsimile copies of poems that are not printed out simultaneously as text, and the only occasional illustration of all the drafts, may continue to be bothersome to many who would welcome a more consistent policy of duplication. It is not clear, for instance, why all of the drafts of a published poem, "One Art," are given, with no complete set of drafts for any of the previously unpublished or unfinished poems. But what these inclusions do add is a sense of the actual difficulties of decipherment, and we are furnished with the incidental photocopy of what caused editorial indecision. We see with our own eyes here and there how hard, but also how eventually rewarding, it is to pull clean copy out of many pages that are fascinatingly hen-tracked with both typescript and handwriting. A page reproducing a draft of "Florida Deserta" is exasperatingly hard to make out, but that seems the point: we may rest assured that in the flesh, in fact even enlarged by a hand magnifying glass, these pages are in spots well-nigh impenetrable.

The great gift of *Edgar Allan Poe & the Juke-Box,* however, consists of the unfinished and fragmentary poems on love and politics. A large number of selections on the former topic seem especially valuable. But in "Suicide of a Moderate Dictator," both its prose and poetic forms testify to Bishop's continually expanding interest in a political subject; this poem is more committed to making a frontal assault on politics than a brilliant, but less explicitly targeted poem like "The Armadillo." In a finished state, "Suicide of a Moderate Dictator" might have rivaled the keen observation of a poem like "Going to the Bakery." One reason for "Suicide of a Moderate Dictator" to be laid aside may have been that there was no entry point within this poem as sketched for the position of the outsider, which Bishop manipulated so successfully and astutely in "The Burglar of Babylon" and "Going to the Bakery." It is illuminating, though, to see how she sought to stretch her range.

I'm also grateful for poems like "The Soldier and the Slot-Machine," or for the sour, almost squalid desperation of "In a Room." These poems not only deal death blows to the prevailing image of Elizabeth Bishop as a Genteel Poetess who would never toss and turn in a cheap hotel or be seen in a dubious bar, but their raw edginess tests Bishop's capacity for a darker, saltier and more adventurous series of selves and moods. On the whole, the blacker moods are offset by the slyly effervescent comedy that bubbles through the great poems like "At the Fishhouses" and "The Bight"—yet it seems worth it to me to be shown how many-minded and variegated the temper of this poet was in her command of both the awful and the cheerful. Although Bishop wrote a beguiling poem called "Manners," her famous mastery of form does *not* make her an avatar of the ladylike or of the precious.

In this direction, Alice Quinn's inclusion of "Vague Poem (Vaguely Love Poem)," as well as her facsimile reproduction of "It is marvelous to wake up together . . . " (*EAP* 44), demonstrate for us what sort of love poems Bishop may have published as well as written had her era coincided with freer "manners & morals, morals & manners" about same-sex partnering. "Vague Poem," with its loving evocation of female genitalia, is decisively unsentimental. In this poem, the poet gives herself permission to look inquisitively at her naked lover—even to stare as hard as Gustave Courbet did in "The Source of the World"—at what even now we rarely picture with any exactitude in words. The connections that Bishop traces have as much originality and descriptive accuracy as any words she picked out for more conventional objects:

> Rose, trying, working, to show itself,
> forming, folding over,
> unimaginable connections, unseen, shining edges.
> Rose-rock, unformed, flesh beginning, crystal by crystal,
> clear pink breasts and darker, crystalline nipples,
> rose-rock, rose-quartz, roses, roses, roses,
> exacting roses from the body,
> and the even darker, accurate, rose of sex— (*EAP* 152)

This is not only a loving poem, but a fearless one.

Quinn's facsimile reproduction of "Belated Dedication" shows an incisive boundary-breaking in Bishop's vision that little else other than "Pink Dog" seems to support. As you peer at the scattered, cluttered typescript of this poem, which Quinn did not even try to copy out in lines, you realize that Bishop is juxtaposing a view "down through two open stove lids" with another look down from a stone churchyard angel's eyes "as in the past I'd stared // down through the identical eyes / of the privy shameful muck." And then there's more fiddling:

> The blue tides had withdrawn
> and left the red-veined mud carved into flames
> The gusts of rain lifted only to show
> Avernus

> all apertures . . .
> lay below broken . . .
> in "classic fragment." (EAP 159)

Hmm: apertures leading through the fire in the stove, through the graveyard, through the privy. Where would this poem have gone? It is dedicated to Bishop's beloved doctor and friend Anny Baumann, whose clear eyes had helped Bishop see through a variety of the deeper layers of consciousness. Is she saying that any aperture of the world or the body could be looked at attentively, and probed for an almost mystical correspondence? It looks like a Blakean Romantic binary, as if the hell that she is finding could be flipped to show the underside of heaven.

Since Bishop's perfectionism is also alleged as reason for not including these provocative fragments and unfinished drafts, or work that she set aside as not worthy of publication, this perfectionism is worth a thought. And yet I do not believe that 'perfectionism' is the right word to describe her patient process, of which Lowell wrote:

> Do
> you still hang your words in air, ten years
> unfinished, glued to your notice board, with gaps
> or empties for the unimaginable phrase—
> unerring Muse who makes the casual perfect? (Lowell, *History* 198)

Her own description of her process as one of waiting for the well to fill up feels right; we could say that the years in which these poems might be finished just ran out on her. But some of them could have been finished, as "The Moose" in its plus twenty years of gestation proved.

If Alice Quinn's *Edgar Allan Poe & the Juke-Box* distresses some readers by its compilation of drafts and fragments, it should deeply satisfy others with its large display of Bishop's intensifying ambition as a mature poet, and for Quinn's efforts to set poems and ambitions in contexts both provocative and informative. It also might be a good idea to acknowledge the not unmixed quality of *The Complete Poems: 1927–1979*. While this book gave us the poems which have established the reputation that this poet deserves, it also contained, alongside gorgeous translations and gleeful occasional work, its own lesser poems, more than a few falling short of perfection. The 1983 edition of Elizabeth Bishop's work includes all of the poems of *North & South*, several of which such as "Casabianca," "The Colder the Air," and "Late Air," seem too clever and cool by half. I do not think that many readers would have missed much of the tedious juvenilia, either, had some hand removed them. This book, too, which appeared in 1983 four years after Bishop's death, could not have been compiled with her detailed assistance. Did Bishop leave a table of contents that included every one of the juvenile poems? It should be noted that some of the early clowning in verse that Quinn puts in print might also have been trimmed—but "Valentine V" is a strange and welcome little addition. These poems also demonstrate how much poetry a young Elizabeth Bishop was reading carefully enough to imitate, from Richard Crashaw to W. H. Auden. But did Robert Giroux put the collection in order? Who decided on the work in the "Uncollected Poems" section, some of whose treasures lead straight to the poems of *Edgar Allan Poe & the Juke-Box*?

It seems to me that the idea of Bishop's publication of only the perfect could be somewhat amended, and that we should welcome the continuing upward adjustment of her reputation that this collection actually advances. Finally, we could profitably reflect on what Robert Lowell wrote to Elizabeth Bishop on August 12, 1963: "You *never* write junk, seldom write anything that isn't a kind of landmark, so your slow pace must be the one that wins the race. Still I brood about all those rich unfinished fragments, such a fortune in the bank, but you have done so much better than I could advise you, that I won't prod. You mustn't waver in knowing how much you have" (*WIA* 489).

Foreign-Domestic

Elizabeth Bishop at Home/
Not at Home in Brazil

BARBARA PAGE AND CARMEN L. OLIVEIRA

The orienting metaphor for Elizabeth Bishop's life and work is North and South, the poles of her travels and dialectical sources of her art. From earliest childhood to the last years of her life, with remarkable persistence, she carried core material wherever she traveled—a carapace of memory and sensibility to substitute, or compensate, perhaps, for the missing home. Some poems she began early were completed only in her last decade. Some kernels of poems traveled with her from North to South and back again, but never found resolution. As she traveled, however, certain of her core concerns reached new articulations within her growing realms of language and experience. In "The Bight," she had bemoaned the "old correspondences" of unfinished work, but in her long life in Brazil, she found new correspondences to early preoccupations, along with the simply new. It has been remarked that Bishop found herself able to address early—often painful— childhood memories from the geographical and emotional distance of Brazil. As Lorrie Goldensohn has argued in *Elizabeth Bishop: The Biography of a Poetry,* for example: "The dislocations of exile took her out of the linear, forward march of her life, and back through memory into a simultaneous recognition linking a primitive, childlike Brazil and Bishop herself as a child" (xi). Bishop remarked, "It is funny to come to Brazil to experience total recall about Nova Scotia" (*OA* 249), and quite early in her residence in Brazil, Bishop composed her finest story of her northern childhood, "In the Village." It may be doubted, however, that Bishop ever considered her life a "forward march." As she famously remarked to an interviewer: "I never meant to go to Brazil. I never meant doing any of these things. I'm afraid in my life everything has just *happened*" (Monteiro 128). In her writing life, however, feeling and thought circled round persistent themes, often for years, subject to reconsideration as new experience augmented and altered her imaginative carapace. And though Bishop retained a capacity for childlike wonder represented in poems throughout her career, she inevitably aged, not simply in years, but in attitude, as decidedly un-innocent aspects of her experience in Brazil bore in on her. In her discussion of Bishop's prose, Goldensohn writes that, in the warmer embrace of her new life in Brazil, she was able to articulate the "estranging effects" of her Nova Scotian childhood (174). Soon enough, estrangement also entered and complicated her life in Brazil. Although her move to Brazil released childhood recollections and brought fresh experience into her work, finally, Bishop's South, as surely as her North, not only inspired but also troubled her art.

Bishop's papers range from juvenilia, in her elongated schoolgirl handwriting, to drafts of late poems recollecting her life in Brazil, stained with tropical damp and overwritten in a spidery scrawl. Alice Quinn's publication of a large selection of drafts and fragments from these papers, in *Edgar Allan Poe & the Juke-Box*, illustrates the degree to which Bishop retained material over years and decades. It also reveals just how much of her writing she never would or could bring to light. Lloyd Schwartz argues elsewhere in this volume that Bishop completed a number of draft poems but never published them, evidence that Brazilian warmth never entirely thawed Bishop's northern reticence. Bishop took pains, however, to preserve these drafts and fragments that now give us glimpses into possible poems and prose despite her chronic despair of finishing them. In this essay, we concentrate on unpublished pieces on Brazilian subjects as they shed light on Bishop's lifelong sense of being never quite at home—a feeling that was for a time alleviated by newfound happiness in Brazil, but finally returned with haunting, estranging force.

Bishop wanted to write about her travels and observations of local people in Brazil, although she sometimes considered it a distraction from poems, and she feared becoming merely picturesque. Kim Fortuny argues that Bishop's very reluctance before her "foreign" subject made her a fine travel writer (25). In poems about Brazil, Bishop's acute awareness of herself as an outsider sets perspective but also limits on understanding. The traveler of "Questions of Travel" entertains serious doubts about her capacity to bridge cultural distance when she asks: "Is it right to be watching strangers in a play / in this strangest of theatres?" (*CP* 93). Fortuny reflects on the disturbing ethics of distanced observation, but argues that "Bishop understood the hazards of foreign travel; she knew firsthand about the dangers of privileged observation. The risk was not to the observer, as many adventure writers would have us believe. Rather, the real risk was always to the observed" (26). In time, Bishop grew accustomed to her life in Brazil and began to write about it with growing confidence, although she remained aware of her standing as a foreigner. Trying to entice Robert Lowell to visit, she became acutely conscious of its difference—from his and her northern perspective—and worries to him that

Brazil "really is much more 'foreign' than Europe" (*OA* 340). The overwhelming presence of poverty in Brazil naturally troubled Bishop and also caused particular difficulties in her work as she tried to address conditions of "the poor." Armed with irony, her stock in trade as she called it, occasionally she succeeded, most notably in "Pink Dog" (*WIA* 758). Often, she failed, though not for lack of trying. In her *Life* World Library *Brazil,* she attacks at the very outset "one of Brazil's worst, and certainly most shocking, problems: that of infant mortality" (10). As a poet, however, she could not control this subject, as evidenced in the draft of "A Baby Found in the Garbage," which Victoria Harrison rightly describes as melodramatic (166). Viewed at a careful distance, and treated with tender irony, the *favela*'s speck-like "Squatter's Children" claim their rights in heaven if not on earth, and the black boy Balthazár of "Twelfth Morning; or What You Will" celebrates his wishful anniversary, "the Day of Kings." In "Manuelzinho," spoken through Lota's voice, Bishop achieves intimacy and complexity of tone, a mixture of affection and exasperation. Harrison argues that the poem requires readers to be "of two minds," engaging with the loving intimacy of the speaker while reproving her condescension (154). Bishop was of two minds about much of her experience, never more so than in her efforts to write about Brazil. Becoming aware of readers' objections to "Manuelzinho," however, she defended it as faithful to reality, quoting Brazilian friends saying, "My God (or Our Lady), it's *exactly* like that" (*OA* 479).

In her 1977 review essay of *Geography III,* "Domestication, Domesticity, and the Otherworldly," Helen Vendler outlines what she sees as the framing dialectic of Bishop's work. She describes this as the "continuing vibration of her work between two frequencies—the domestic and the strange. In another poet the alternation might seem a debate, but Bishop drifts rather than divides, gazes rather than chooses. Though the exotic is frequent in her poems of travel, it is not only the exotic that is strange and not only the local that is domestic" (32).

This is apt in broad outline, but Bishop's long residence in Brazil complicates and sometimes jars the "vibration." As Bishop immersed herself in Brazilian culture, reading extensively and traveling widely in the country, she translated Portuguese poems and prose and struck up friendships with Brazilian writers, artists, and architects. But as her initial exhilaration with new love and a new life gradually gave way to sober second thoughts about herself in Brazil, the sense of being foreign, not quite at ease on her new continent, grew. Despite her skill and success as a translator, Bishop never mastered written or spoken Portuguese and insisted that, although she had been influenced by Brazil, she remained "a completely American poet" (Monteiro 19). In an important way, Brazil not only was, but needed to be, strange to her. That strangeness, though often unnerving, touched a substrate of her own psychic otherworld, in dreams she took pains to record, in touches of surrealism in poems, in an embrace of unintentional actions and verbal gestures.

As she settled into her life in Brazil with Lota de Macedo Soares, Bishop did attempt to domesticate the strange and did rediscover the strange in domestic settings, as was her habit. Many drafts and fragments in *Edgar Allan Poe & the Juke-Box* exhibit this informal dialectic between the domestic and the strange. In other drafts and poems we see Bishop lending herself in sympathy to her extended South, in what might be called "efforts of affection," to borrow her words from a different context. The added twist here is of a world seen "the other way around," as she writes in "Questions of Travel." In Brazil, Bishop establishes outposts of the domestic, never quite forgetting her own strangeness as tourist, traveler, or outsider. Some "efforts of affection" prove exhausting, leaving her baffled and defeated. Many unfinished poems attest to these defeats. Some of her finest poems, however, arise from the very depths of this estrangement.

Vendler writes, "Domesticity is frail," and notes that in "First Death in Nova Scotia," efforts "to encompass [Bishop's cousin] Arthur's death in the domestic scene" fail: "the strain is too great" (36). Likewise, in "In the Waiting Room," the child's effort "to include in her world even the most unfamiliar data" and to gather her separate identity together with "the family voice" collapses as the waiting room slides "beneath a big black wave" (38). In the lines, "you are an *Elizabeth,* / you are one of *them,*" Vendler sees a connection to Carlos Drummond de Andrade's "Poema de Sete Faces," translated by Bishop as "Seven-Sided Poem."

> Mundo mundo vasto mundo,
> se eu me chamasse Raimundo,
> seria uma rima, não seria uma solução.

Bishop translates this nonliterally:

> Universe, vast universe,
> if I had been named Eugene
> that would not be what I mean
> but it would go into verse
> faster. (Bishop and Brasil 62, 63)

Vendler remarks, "If one's name rhymed with the name of the cosmos, . . . there would appear to be a congruence between self and world." What Drummond actually writes is, "it would be a rhyme, not a solution." And in "In the Waiting Room," what Bishop writes of the apparent congruence between herself and the world is: "how 'unlikely.'" Bishop understood that, whether at home or abroad, likeness and unlikeness stood close together, and whether "here, or there," as she writes in "Questions of Travel," estrangement was never far.

In Brazil, Bishop did, however, try out a more revealing rhyme with her own name, in the draft, "New Year's Letter as Auden Says—" (*EAP* 115). Its unincorporated first line, "where the shoes don't fit my feet," recalls her wry comment on translation: "Translating poetry is like trying to put your feet into gloves—" (314). In "New Year's Letter," the immediate object of her domesticating affection is a parrot that speaks English "[Lota!] Get out of the sun!"—and calls for "A Coffee!" Immediately following, though, the lines "The small black birds that dance / like spots before the eyes" (115) call up a familiar sight high in the sky of *urubus*—buzzards—that Brazilian children consult for weather information. In Bishop's northern eyes, however, the birds suggest the experience of dizziness, rather like the near-faint of the child in "In the Waiting Room."

Bishop signs off her "New Year's Letter" confessing to be

> confusing ends and means
> in the country of coffee beans
>
>> If I cannot speak Portuguese
>> shall I ever say Shibboleth?
>> —But
>>> With love, Elizabeth. (*EAP* 116)

"Shibboleth," a Hebrew word chosen to detect members of an enemy tribe because they could not pronounce one of its syllables, is a term for a test to detect foreigners, a test Bishop here in Brazil expects to fail.

Anxiety hovers over Bishop's attempts to domesticate the strange, as in the fragment "Foreign-Domestic," dating from around 1957, soon after she and Lota obtained a phonograph. As it opens (at Samambaia), she is listening to Vivaldi on "the sweet 'eye-fee'"—a Brazilian pronunciation of "hi-fi." Elsewhere she spells the term more accurately as "eee-fee," but this loses a desired musical interplay of eye and ear, as she composes a domestic scene troubled by discordant notes. In the next room, "you" (in life, Lota) can be seen only partially:

> just two bare feet upon the bed
> arranged as if someone were dead . . . (*EAP* 117)

The poet interrupts her listening to reassure herself that Lota is alive. She is. "So that's all right. I settle back." For the balance of the lines, Bishop noodles with a notion of musical (and by extension, poetic) form as restraint against an instrument's attempt to escape its musical confines. Below her lighthearted lines she cites an ominously different couplet, by William Blake:

> (Said Blake, "And mutual fear brings peace,
> Till the selfish loves increase . . .")

Impossible to say where Bishop was headed with these lines, from "The Human Abstract," in Blake's *Songs of Experience*. But the "sweet" simplicity of "Foreign-Domestic" remains laced with anxiety of the eye (the "two bare feet upon the bed / arranged as if someone were dead") and of the ear hearing Vivaldi pulling down the oboe as it "starts to celebrate / escaping from the violin's traps, / a bit too easily, perhaps." In Blake's "Human Abstract," the next couplet reads: "Then Cruelty knits a snare, / And spreads his baits with care" (Blake 27). These lines invite comparison to the disturbing note in Bishop's "Song for a Rainy Season," from 1960, which presents another scene of domestic intimacy, set at Samambaia, about a house open to tropical dampness:

> darkened and tarnished
> by the warm touch
> of the warm breath,
> maculate, cherished,
> rejoice! For a later
> era will differ,
> (O difference that kills,
> or intimidates, much
> of all our small shadowy
> life!) . . . (*CP* 102)

In another draft poem of partially discomfited intimacy, "Letter to Two Friends," Bishop confesses with partial truth to having "no gift for languages" (*EAP* 114). Remarkable, then, is the extent to which she devoted herself to translation. Most poets do make translations, and Bishop rendered poems not only from Portuguese but also French and Spanish. She also translated prose, including *The Diary of Helena Morley* and stories by Clarice Lispector. Still, her library attests to the depth of her attention to Portuguese-language poets, and she continued translating and introducing Brazilian poets to English-speaking readers long after she left Brazil.

In 1953, Bishop struck up a friendship with Manuel Bandeira, a much-honored and popular poet then in his sixties: "*The* Brazilian poet," she wrote to Robert Lowell, a little dazzled (*WIA* 142). Neither was fluent in the other's spoken language, but their easy familiarity—unusual for Bishop—was facilitated by Bandeira's long friendship with Macedo Soares, a noted conversationalist, who often entertained intellectuals and artists at her home. In August, Bandeira published in Rio's *Tribuna da Imprensa* a translation of part 3 of Bishop's "Songs for a Colored Singer":

> Nana nana
> nana. Dorme o adulto,
> e a criança dorme.
> Ao largo, ferido de morte, naufraga
> o navio enorme.
>
> Lullaby.
> Adult and child
> sink to their rest.
> At sea the big ship sinks and dies,
> lead in its breast. (*CP* 49)

Bishop was delighted with his rendering, remarking to Robert Lowell, "Manuel Bandeira . . . is doing them and doing them extremely well, I think. I have been trying to return the compliment" (*EAP* 313). In fact, this lullaby was the only poem by Bishop Bandeira published in Portuguese translation. She, however, translated four of Bandeira's poems that would ultimately lead off her coedited *Anthology of Twentieth-Century Brazilian Poetry.*

In a sort of potlatch exchange of courtesies, Bishop gave Bandeira a jar of jam and a copy of e. e. cummings's *Xaipe: 71 Poems,* and Bandeira sent her a hammock and a cummings-esque note of thanks:

> Th
> an
> k you
> tooooooo
>)or also?(

for the

71

Cumm

ings'

po?e!ms!!

An

d now

Get into this Brazilian hammock

and let me sing for you:

"Lullaby.

Sleep on and on."

Xaipe, Elizabeth. (vc 1.8)

"Xaipe," in Greek, means "Rejoice," and this happy exchange prompted further exuberant correspondence between Bandeira and Bishop, of the sort she usually reserved only for intimate friends. In return for further jars of sweets, including one rendered from the native jabuticaba fruit, Bandeira wrote:

> I wish I had two bellies
> because of your good jellies. (EAP 313)

Hoping to match his wit, Bishop fired off a pseudoscholarly tribute to Bandeira's fame, complete with footnotes, showing off her awareness of Brazilian current affairs. It begins:

> Your books are here; the pages cut.
> Of course I want to thank you, but
> how can I possibly forget
> that we have scarcely spoken yet?
>
> Two mighty poets at a loss,
> Unable to exchange a word,
> —to quote McCarthy, "It's the most
> unheard-of thing I've ever heard!" (EAP 105)[1]

Bishop's footnotes display her familiarity with both U.S. current events (Senator Joseph McCarthy's latest howler) and Brazilian current events featuring Bandeira (honored in bronze; kissing the latest beauty queen). Bandeira's translations into

Portuguese of popular subjects in English—Elinor Glyn, Tarzan—bespoke an affinity with her own attempt to write blues lyrics. Bishop's growing interest in Brazilian popular poetry would lead eventually to "The Burglar of Babylon."

As early as 1953, Bishop began to think of writing a poem about St. John's Day, one of Brazil's most popular holidays, marking the Southern Hemisphere's winter solstice. By then, she had begun her gingerly immersion into Portuguese—writing in a notebook, under "St. John's Day," "São João," followed by the couplet that probably inspired her draft poem:

> São João se soubera que hoje e seu dia,
> Do Céu desceria com alegria e prazer (Old Song).

She misquotes slightly: to complete the couplet "prazer" precedes "alegria." On the facing page, she writes:

> *If St. John only knew it is his day*
> *He would descend from Heaven & be gay.*

Immediately below, she has written, "But he's supposed to be asleep throughout the festivities . . ." (VC 76.2).

Framing meditations around saints' names was not new to Bishop; the place-names St. Peter's (Cathedral, in Rome) and St. John's (Newfoundland) figure in her poem "Over 2,000 Illustrations and a Complete Concordance." Although St. John's Day is recognized in parts of Canada, the exuberance and display in Brazil's celebration of this sacred holiday were striking to her, prompting comments in letters to friends: "This is Saint John's Day—our shortest, your longest, and the biggest holiday here, of the *sanctificado* kind, that is. . . . Fire balloons are supposed to be illegal but everyone sends them up anyway and we usually spend St. John's night . . . watching the balloons drift right up the mountain towards the house. . . . Lota has a sprinkling system on the roof just because of them. They are so pretty—one's of two minds about them" (Baumann, VC June 24, 1955). "St. John's Day" sustains a playful lightness of tone, at least until the final stanza, when some odd reservations appear:

> But no, no prayer
> can wake him. Is it cowardice?
> He sleeps, he always sleeps away the solstice.
> If he didn't his party might be gayer. (EAP 109)

In the early draft, another more surprising and personal thought about religious belief pops up, carrying her back to her reading of Pascal in Key West: "Maybe if Pascal had not stopped thinking, I might have been converted."

As with so many of her Brazilian poems and drafts, the events of "St. John's Day" are observed from a distance—a remove that seems, in this case, to provoke remarkably fanciful figures. The lights twinkling in the streets below are "cat's whiskers," a tender if rather technical reference to the gold or copper wire in crystal wireless receivers, and the firecrackers' smoke is seen as demiurges' cracking "puff-ball knuckles," a puffball being literally a round fungus that bursts when dried, spraying powdery spores. The core figures of the draft poem, though, gently articulate persistent self-impressions of the traveler-tourist poet. The personified sun has swerved "as far out of his course as he could get, // taking the opportunity / to see things that he might not see again" (109), lines that lead straight to Bishop's "Questions of Travel," her searching meditation on travel as displacement, as voyeuristic embarrassment and as joyful exercise of the "childish" desire to "rush / to see the sun the other way round" (*CP* 93). Unwilling to claim a right to see dreamed-of places, the traveler nonetheless cautiously questions the philosopher: "could Pascal have been not entirely right / about just sitting quietly in one's room?" "St. John's Day" noisily repudiates Pascal with a cheerful innocence devoid of the troubling allegorical import of her later "Armadillo."

As celebrated in Brazil, St. John's Day suited Bishop's disposition to dwell in the sensibility of childhood. The saint is popularly represented, not as the adult prophet and martyr, but as a child bearing a lamb in arms, a figure of pastoral innocence who is the intended recipient of prayers sent heavenward in those dangerous, illegal fire-balloons of Bishop's "Armadillo." But, perhaps to justify the hullabaloo of Roman candles and firecrackers that marks the holiday, as we see in Bishop's draft, the child St. John always "sleeps away the solstice." Or, as a popular Brazilian *junina* (June celebration) song has it: "St. John is sleeping, / he won't wake up. / AWAKE, AWAKE, AWAKE, John!"[2]

In "St. John's Day," Bishop evidently intended a comparison between the cosmic power of the sun, now at its weakest, and the bumptious but diminutive claims of the world below, where, in "the small tip-tilted town" the lights "shake, almost, to prove / to that withdrawing, orange presence above / the power of *their* electricity" (*EAP* 109, emphasis added). In "Gypsophilia," dating from the early 1960s, the poet, again at Samambaia, casts one eye down into the affairs of "an ordinary evening" (as Wallace Stevens would have it) around Petrópolis and the other up and out to the planetary realm. Again, the mundane occupants are viewed tenderly, as the title figure, Gypsophilia—"baby's breath"—suggests.[3] It is tenderness, however, tinged with melancholy. In the fading light, the poet muses: "I like the few sad noises / left over in this smokey sunset." In "Gypsophilia," in the noise drifting up from below, we can hear a lingering echo of Bishop's Nova Scotian memories from "In the Village":

> At Altenberg's, the orchid nursery,
> somebody beats the hanging iron bar
> until it sounds like farriers
> down there, instead of flowers.
> But the last clangs are
> the last words of a bell-buoy out at sea. (EAP 128)

The clangs on the iron bar, as if from blacksmiths, and their likeness to a buoy, eerily replicate the language from the close of "In the Village":

> Clang.
> *Clang.*
> Nate is shaping a horseshoe.
> Oh, beautiful pure sound!
> It turns everything else to silence.
> . . . .
> Now there is no scream. Once there was one and it settled slowly down to earth one hot summer afternoon; or did it float up, into that dark, too dark, blue sky? But surely it has gone away, forever. It sounds like a bell buoy out at sea. (CPR 274)

In "Gypsophilia," the idiot dog's *oblique* barks recall Bishop's preoccupation with what she called in a notebook entry from the 1940s an "interstitial situation": those "oblique realities that give one pause[,] that glance off a larger reality. . . . I see the man, over at Toppino's [near Key West] (or saw him chopping wood at Lockeport) [in Nova Scotia] then hear the sound, see him, then hear him, etc. The eye and ear compete, trying to draw them together, to a 'photo finish' so to speak. . . . Nothing comes out quite right" (VC 75.3b, 189, 193). Much of Bishop's life in Brazil gave scope to such "interstitial situations." As she writes, in "Gypsophilia," "We live aslant / here on our iron mountain," where, for her, incongruities are welcome, if sometimes unnerving, daily fare. Bishop's description of the dog "chop-chopping at the mountains with a hatchet," though, is curiously violent in the moody scene of the "smokey sunset" (EAP 128). Such metaphors mix casually with the workaday reality of the scene: Altenberg's was in fact an orchid nursery near Petrópolis, and moisture retained by the foliage of the Atlantic forest near Samambaia does produce what botanists call a "sub-stratum of dew."

The six pages of handwritten and typed drafts of "Gypsophilia" reveal a difficulty with the transition Bishop evidently intended, from the mundane to a cosmic perspective. In each draft, she sets off her concluding stanza of cosmic meditation from the sensory impressions that precede it:

> We live aslant
> here on our iron mountain. Venus
> already's set.
> Something I'm never sure of, even yet—
> do we shine, too? Is this world luminous?
> I try to recollect but can't. (*EAP* 129)

In the early drafts, Bishop's thought leaps directly from the clanging iron at Altenberg's nursery to "We live aslant / here on our iron mountain." Later, she makes a transition by way of an appearance of Manuelzinho's family—Jovelina, Nelson, Nina—part of the extended household at Samambaia. As she remarked to Pearl Kazin, "that family certainly is important in my life. I have just written my fourth poem about them" (*OA* 397). Evidently, there was more to say than had appeared in her published poem "Manuelzinho." There the title figure is "a gardener in a fairy tale"; his accounts are "Dream Books." And here his wife, Jovelina, hair hanging down under her husband's old hat, is "a figure like a young witch," as if in a fairy tale. Each child carries an "enormous sheaf" of daintily flowered baby's breath, a double emblem of innocence.

Although unfinished, "Gypsophilia" draws together sense and memory, as well as a vague aspiration toward cosmic illumination. But the connections between them remain oblique, only half-recalled from the poet's own childhood. In the dying light, though Venus has already set, it calls up a teasing set of associations. The goddess of erotic love retires, leaving a scene alive with wistful figures of tenderness: the orchid nursery and baby's breath borne in children's arms. Beneath, however, lies an older, harder condition of life under the planets, "here on our iron mountain." In the plangent moment of dying day, Bishop places in the scene those "oblique realities that give one pause" and "that glance off a larger reality." Once again, the poet is left in a state of doubt: "Is this world luminous? I try to recollect but can't" (*EAP* 129).

By 1963, when Bishop began composing "Apartment in Leme" (*EAP* 134), she thought she was on the verge of completing her book *Questions of Travel,* although it would not appear for two more years (*OA* 415). The relative ease and happiness of her life in Samambaia had been disturbed, first by worsening political and economic conditions in Brazil, and second by Macedo Soares's appointment as director of the project to build Flamengo Parque in Rio, a job that devoured her time and strength, leaving her distracted and increasingly irritable. Reluctantly, Bishop moved with her to Rio, although she much preferred country life and felt more and more neglected. By now, she believed that she understood enough of Brazil to interpret conditions and events to northerners, while she continued gathering memories from her past to compose poems and stories of her childhood. She wrote to Lowell: "All this nostalgia and homesickness and burrowing in the past running alongside trying to write articles about the Brazilian political situation—I can't—translating some Portuguese poems, etc. Are other writers as confused & 'contradictory'? Or do they stick to one thing at a time?" (*OA* 409). Still, Brazilian popular culture and lore continued to charm and stir her imagination, despite growing unhappiness with her situation. In this period, Bishop located a number of texts in Rio, voicing her dismay at contemporary conditions and her mood of confusion and discouragement. She completed "The Burglar of Babylon" in a burst of inspiration. Its deceptively childlike ballad stanzas enfold the plain truth of the stain of poverty on "the fair green hills of Rio," where "Rich people in apartments / Watch through binoculars"—among them, Bishop herself—as soldiers track down and kill the desperate criminal Micuçú (Schwartz and Estess 301). The twenty-nine draft pages of "Apartment in Leme" indicate a concerted effort to finish the poem. In it, Bishop's childlike love of fantasy and cosmic mysteries collides with a jaded recognition of grim conditions in the city and her own waning happiness, as she looks down on the unfolding scene.

Unlike "St. John's Day" and "The Armadillo," which open with sunset and the onset of festivities, "Apartment in Leme" opens in a tired aftermath, the dawn (6:00 a.m., in one draft) of January 1, following a New Year's Eve celebration. As in her St. John's Day poems, though, the poet once again looks down from above and at a distance. The scene she composes takes impressions from her mood.[4] The islands are sleeping; the pale rods of light, like "our knives and forks," are tarnishing. The Sea, personified, is intensely embodied and at the same moment referred to an otherworld of fantasy:

> Because we live at your open mouth, oh Sea,
> with your cold breath blowing warm, your warm breath cold,
> like in the fairy tale. (*EAP* 134)

The sea's moisture touches everything—"Breathe in. Breathe out"—and it alters the instruments of sight: "the windows blur and mirrors are wet to touch." The sea's breath almost seems one with the speaker's, yet she says to the sea, "you keep your distance." Much is in retreat, done with, receding into the past. In another draft, Bishop writes, but crosses out: "On the defensive, I think 'it's not exactly *sad* . . . '" (VC 64.19). Her gaze shifts downward to the homeless men who have slept on the beach, two early bathers, a dog—and the remnants of celebration: lilies with broken stalks floating in the surf, candles with blackened wicks, empty cachaça bottles. Bishop—who ever loved the sea and daily bathed at Leme beach—remarks tiredly, but with one flare of wit:

> Sometimes you embolden, sometimes bore.
> You smell of codfish and old rain. Homesick, the salt
> weeps in the salt-cellars. (EAP 134)

The leftovers of celebration—lilies, candles, empty cachaça bottles—unexpectedly arouse the poet's speculative imagination. All of these were "meant for the goddess meant to come last night" (*EAP* 135).

The poet's capacity for childlike wonder revives: "Perhaps she came, at that." Iemanjá, goddess of the sea, familiar to coastal Brazilians, and, for practitioners of candomblé, the feminine principle of creation and patron of fishermen, *may* have appeared. The sea takes on a fantastic appearance—"roughened, / greeny-black, scaly"—opaque like a "corroded old bronze" mirror. In another draft, though corroded, the sea was "capable, still, of reflecting the biggest stars," but here not. Much in this poem turns on what can or cannot be seen, what might once have been seen—"(How did the ancients / ever see *anything* in [those mirrors]?)" What could be seen, by lovers and worshippers on the beach, "if they had noticed"? Imagination enticed, the mind's eye calls up the enchanted night. Although the sea does not reflect them, the stars were bright, and a cluster, "astringent as white currants . . . hung from the Magellanic Clouds" (a galaxy seen from the Southern Hemisphere). On the beach,

> The candles flickered. Worshippers, in white,
> holding hands, singing, walked into you waist-deep.
> The lovers lay in the sand, embraced. (EAP 135)

Then the poet's attention shifts to a final, farther vision of fishing boats at sea, invisible but for their five "saffron flares." Mysteriously, these pitiable rival illuminations are "farther [out] than the stars, // weaker, and older." Thus ends the night of Iemanjá, the stars and the sea.

The conclusion of "Apartment in Leme" breaks into two stanzas, reflecting the poet's movement between a flat, heavy mood embodied in the reluctantly rising sun and another, catching the deep rhythmic breathing of the storied sea. The sun rises "metallic; two-dimensional" (*EAP* 136). The sea, still exerting its sensual, transformative influence, sighs and breathes, warm and cold. To the poet—"weaker, and older," like the fishermen forever at sea, wobbling and hitching along—the goddess is not simply believed in, as a child believes a fairy tale. We age, tarnish, corrode in the sea's breath. On this New Year's morning, from an eleventh-floor balcony overlooking Copacabana Bay, the sea, Bishop's sea, does not belong to children, but rather arises from knowledge and profound feeling. As Bishop writes, in "At the Fishhouses," "our knowledge is historical" (*CP* 66). However it may be that Iemanjá appears to worshippers and lovers, whatever enlightenment she imparts, Bishop's knowledge from the sea is more difficult: "drawn from the cold hard mouth / of the world, derived from the rocky breasts." Much inspiration in her work has stemmed from Bishop's capacity for childlike wonder, but at this moment of suppressed sadness, sighs felt with every breath, an imperfect memory of her source resolves itself: the warm-cold breathing of the sea is not, for her, the stuff of fairy tale, but legend, the deep memory of the ages—a lesson, if it can be read.

Bishop lived in Brazil for nearly two decades and returned for stays some years after. For a surprisingly long time—ten years, at least—she had been happier in her life with Lota in Brazil than at any other time, and Brazil inspired some of her finest work. Over time, though, her translation to Brazil proved, in Drummond's words, "a rhyme, not a solution." She remained, not a tourist, not a visitor, but still ineluctably foreign. Her inability to master Portuguese aggravated her sense of persistent foreignness in Brazil, as she had confessed in letters and her attempts at verse epistles, "Letter to Two Friends" and "New Year's Letter as Auden Says—." If anything, Bishop's life in Brazil intensified her intuition that each language, each culture, remained stubbornly foreign to the other. Yet she became a distinguished translator of Brazilian poetry as well as a recognized interpreter of one country to the other. Once, unusually, she composed and delivered an introduction of Robert Lowell in Portuguese to a Brazilian audience. When Lowell published *Imitations*, Bishop had objected to liberties he took with the original language of the poems he rendered into English (*WIA* 354–55, 356–58). In her Brazilian introduction, she had the last word on the subject, describing his *Imitations* as "in reality, new poems" (*PPL* 712). Bishop's "efforts of affection" succeeded in many poems and stories of Brazil, but some attempts to make new poems from deep-rooted Brazilian life lay stillborn, as *Edgar Allan Poe* testifies. Those, like the goddess Iemanjá, and her scene, might be glimpsed but never fully known or translated.

NOTES

1. The Brazilian scholar Flora Sussekind discovered Bishop's poem in tribute to Manuel Bandeira in his archive at the Fundação Casa de Rui Barbosa. She cites Bishop's "To Manuel Bandeira, With Jam and Jelly" in her essay entitled "A geléia e o engenho." Her title playfully remarks on Bishop's wit, as "engenho" can mean both ingenuity and what Brazilians call a sugar mill. In her view, Bishop's hard grinding to bridge a language gap by sheer ingenuity brings forth this poem that speaks sweetly to her fellow "poet's belly."

2. In Portuguese, the title is "Capelinha de Melão" (Little Melon Chapel). In Portuguese, the words are:

São João está dormindo
Não acorda não!
Acordai, acordai, acordai, João!

3. In Brazil, "Gypsophila" (the correct botanical spelling) is commonly called *mosquitinho* (little mosquito), but this is not to Bishop's purpose, so she imports the northern common name.

4. "Twelfth Morning; or What You Will," published in 1964, bears comparison:

The sea's off somewhere, doing nothing. Listen.
An expelled breath. And faint, faint, faint
(or are you hearing things), the sandpipers'
heart-broken cries. (CP 110)

Bishop's Brazilian Politics

BETHANY HICOK

Among the major contributions of the new Library of America edition of Elizabeth Bishop's *Poems, Prose, and Letters* are not only more poems, a handful of which are finished or nearly so, but a great deal of Bishop's exceptional prose, most of which was published only in magazines and literary journals throughout her career, such as her wonderful essays written at Vassar in the 1930s. But some of the best pieces were not published at all. Among these is an account of a trip she took to Brasília, the new capital of Brazil, and the surrounding indigenous people. She traveled with Aldous Huxley and his wife, as well as others, in 1958. The essay is obviously finished and polished, and Bishop sent it to the *New Yorker*. The magazine rejected it, apparently because Huxley did not say enough in it (Fountain and Brazeau 163). The trip most certainly inspired one of Bishop's great poems, "Brazil, January 1, 1502." And the essay can be seen as a kind of companion piece to that poem, revealing—along with other newly published material in Alice Quinn's *Edgar Allan Poe & the Juke-Box*, the Library of America edition, and the complete Lowell and Bishop correspondence—Bishop's increasingly involved dialogue with Brazilian politics.

We can now see that her exposure to the epicenter of this discussion, through her long relationship with Lota de Macedo Soares, a member of Rio's intellectual and cultural elite, and her immersion in Brazilian cultural and political life, allowed her to make important links to social, cultural, and political issues that had concerned her since college. The story of Bishop's Brazilian politics emerges from these new editions in recently published poems, such as "Suicide of a Moderate Dictator," and reveals itself most strikingly in the Brasília essay and another poem of this period "Brasil, 1959."[1] *Words in Air*, the complete correspondence between Bishop and Lowell, in turn, shows us a Bishop struggling with how to find a suitable "form" of protest that could address the gathering revolutionary crisis in Brazil that eventually led to the fall of democracy in that country. I take up several key moments in Bishop's evolving poetics of this period—the fall of the Brazilian dictator Getúlio Vargas in 1954 that inspired Bishop to make several attempts to write a more overtly "political" poetry; the trip she took to Brasília with Huxley; and, finally, the deepening revolutionary crisis in Brazil between 1961 and 1964 out of which emerged one of Bishop's great but neglected ballads, "The Burglar of Babylon." This newly published material allows us to establish an important link between Brazilian politics, social policy, poverty, race, and gender—issues that Bishop was able to finally bring together in some of the most powerful poetry emerging from her Brazilian years.

The story of how Bishop ended up in Brazil is well known. In November 1951, Elizabeth Bishop boarded the SS *Bowplate* in New York harbor for the beginning of a planned trip around the world. Her first stop was Rio de Janeiro to visit Pearl Kazin and Kazin's new husband, Victor Kraft, who were staying with a friend, Mary Morse, and Lota de Macedo Soares (Millier 235). While there, Bishop ate the fruit of the cashew plant, became violently ill, and Macedo Soares nursed her back to health, then invited her to stay, and Bishop did—for nearly two decades. We know that much of this time (at least the first decade) was a relatively happy and productive period for Bishop, and within the safety, distance, and love created in Brazil with the life she made with Macedo Soares, she was able to return to the traumatic events of her childhood and come to terms in powerful poetry with the loss and suffering she had experienced. This story of childhood loss and new love found is a familiar one to Bishop's readers.

But there is another story about Bishop's years in Brazil with Macedo Soares, a story that has not yet been told, a tale of Brazilian politics that can be more clearly seen through the newly published poetry and prose of the new editions. To begin with a brief outline: Macedo Soares was not only a Brazilian aristocrat, but a self-taught architect with political ambitions who came from a prominent political and journalistic family in Rio de Janeiro (Fountain and Brazeau 129–33). She was a close friend of Carlos Lacerda, a well-known journalist and political agitator who founded the right-wing newspaper *Tribuna da Imprensa* for the purpose of bringing down the Brazilian dictator Getúlio Vargas (Skidmore 124). Lacerda was, as the historian Thomas Skidmore has written, a "master of political invective" and "destroyer of presidents" (124, 200). After Vargas committed suicide in 1954, Lacerda, who had presidential ambitions, aimed his attack at his successor, Juscelino Kubitschek, and then Jânio Quadros, who resigned in 1961 after only seven months in office; and then finally, in 1963, he worked to oust João Goulart, whose presidency fell in 1964 after a military coup that ended democracy in Brazil and plunged the country into a long period of military rule until 1985. This colorful history features Lacerda in a series of operatic incidents surrounding the demise of these presidencies. For instance, during the coup, which Lacerda had helped to support, Lacerda was barricaded in his palace "dressed in a leather jacket and armed with two submachine guns and a pistol" (Skidmore 301).

Bishop came very close to the action in 1961. When Lacerda became governor of Guanabara (greater Rio de Janeiro) in 1960, he hired Macedo Soares to be chief coordinator of a complicated project to build an elaborate park along a three-mile piece of land on the southern shore of Guanabara Bay, and the two women moved to an apartment in Rio (Millier 319). And, at least early on, both Bishop and Macedo Soares had great admiration for Lacerda. Moreover, despite his reputation as a destroyer of presidents, he was a good governor. Skidmore calls his administration as governor of the State of Guanabara "efficient and progressive" (232). Bishop's letters to Lowell are full of praise for him, but as early as 1954, Bishop tempered her praise in a letter to her friend Pearl Kazin. She wrote that she found Lacerda "honest" but worried that "he's got too much ego and will probably end up in about ten years as a cynical politician" (OA 288). Bishop's move to Rio placed her much closer to the action, the details of which I will take up in the last part of this essay. While Bishop seemed to prefer the quiet, rural life at Samambaia, she nevertheless capitalized on the drama in her letters to Lowell, and they most certainly fed her art.

Bishop wrote her first "political" poem, "Suicide of a Moderate Dictator," which appears in both Edgar Allan Poe and the Library of America edition, in the mid-1950s. In 1992, when the Georgia Review first published the poem, Thomas Travisano, who discovered it in the archives, noted that it "represents a category for which examples exist only in Bishop's unpublished oeuvre: the political poem" (qtd. in Quinn 310). Now we have several further examples of her Brazilian political poems before us in the new editions. Bishop was closely connected to the events that surrounded the composition of "Suicide of a Moderate Dictator," which is based on the suicide in August 1954 of the "moderate dictator" of the title, Getúlio Vargas, president of Brazil from 1930 to 1945, and from 1951 until his suicide in 1954. It is dedicated to her friend Lacerda, perhaps Vargas's most outspoken critic. Lacerda's accusations of corruption against the Vargas family led to an assassination attempt on Lacerda. This was followed by a call from the Brazilian military for Vargas's resignation, which resulted in his suicide (WIA 164n). Vargas had a reputation for reform and so was popular with the "Brazilian masses," as Bishop put it in her account of the Vargas government in her Life World Library book on Brazil (130). His opponents described his regime as "'Fascism Brazilian-Style,' or

'Fascism with Sugar,'" according to Bishop's account of him (130). She explains that under the Vargas regime, "individual rights were curtailed, there were arbitrary arrests and the press was controlled. But there were no public executions, no shootings, no concentration camps" (130). Hence, the "moderate" modifier in Bishop's title.

Bishop's poem begins by imagining how the news will reach the people:

> This is a day when truths will out, perhaps;
> leak from the dangling telephone ear-phones
> sapping the festooned switchboards' strength;
> fall from the windows, blow from off the sills,
> —the vague, slight unremarkable contents
> of emptying ash-trays; rub off on our fingers
> like ink from the un-proof-read newspapers[.] (PPL 236)

Each of the poem's three stanzas begins with a variation on that opening line: "This is the day . . . ," "Today's the day . . . ," "This is the day. . . ." The repetition alone works against the wish-fulfillment fantasy that some kind of "truth" will emerge from *this* story. Bishop's leaking and dangling telephones, pollinating, "un-proof-read newspapers," ashtray contents, and the "sapping" of strength all suggest that getting at the truth is highly unlikely. We are literally dusted with the political fallout. The poem exists in five drafts, according to Quinn's notes (*EAP* 310), and this version is the final typed draft with only a few corrections. It seems finished, or nearly so. Bishop composed this poem at about the same time as her Pound poem, "Visits to St. Elizabeths," and it shares some of that poem's use of the lulling cadences of the nursery rhyme as ironic political commentary, although "Suicide of a Moderate Dictator" lacks the cumulative power of the Pound poem.

It was in the late 1950s, after Bishop's trip to Brasília with the Huxleys, that she was able to develop a method that could turn her concern with the political and social into powerful poetry focused on the political problems of Brazil. It begins with her 1958 essay "A New Capital, Aldous Huxley, and Some Indians." In her essays of the 1930s and 1940s, many of which were published when she was still in college, Bishop had developed a sophisticated theory of poetry, but it took her some time to make these theories work as poetry.[2] I have a hunch that her Brasília essay serves the same purpose. Inspired, as Jeffrey Gray has argued (26), by her readings in anthropology, particularly Levi-Strauss's *Tristes tropiques*, Bishop seems to modify her theory of poetry in relation to a Brazilian context by focusing on the themes of the traveler and his or her encounter with the other, staging intimate, sometimes uncomfortable encounters for the reader with other cultures and ways of knowing.

The trip to Brazil's new capital and the utopian discourse surrounding the founding of Brasília provide Bishop with rich material for irony. Bishop begins her essay by highlighting geographical points that serve to define the essay's major themes. She writes: "One could graph modern Brasilian history . . . on the three points connected by the Huxley trip: by way of Itamarati [in Rio de Janeiro, former capital of Brazil]; to the safe, democratic insipidity of the name 'Brasília,' and then beyond, to the dwindling tribes along the Xingu River, Indian again, for here as in the United States, many geographical names have held to their originals, or approximations of them" (*PPL* 365). Bishop maps the following points on her rhetorical compass. First is Rio de Janeiro, River of January, original site of the Portuguese "discovery" of Brazil and subsequent "colonization"; it is Brazil's old capital; next, Brasília, the bland, new center of Brazil; and, finally, the "dwindling" Indian tribes whose numbers will become even more endangered as a result of the move to the interior. Bishop's adjectives — "insipidity," "dwindling" — make her own attitude and the direction of the essay clear. Although Bishop attempts journalistic balance — she states both the pros and cons of locating the country's new capital in such a remote location — her use of irony slants her readers toward the view that Bishop shared with Macedo Soares and their political friends. They, like most of their fellow denizens of Rio, thought the whole idea of Brasília was a disaster: here was a remote city built in the middle of the jungle, inaccessible except by plane, while people in Brazil's former capital, Rio de Janeiro, lacked such basic amenities as water and electricity.

As Bishop noted in her essay, opponents thought that the "attempt to build a city before building a railroad to its site" was ludicrous (366): "Brasil needs schools, roads, railroads . . . medical care, improved methods of agriculture, and dams and electric power," Bishop wrote (367). Brasília itself is flat, uninteresting, "remarkably unattractive and unpromising" (368), and full of dust. Bishop notes that "in the late summer of 1958 one's first and last impression of Brasília was of miles and miles and miles of blowing red dust" (367). Bishop's description of Brasília is in direct opposition to the utopian discourse surrounding the idea of Brasília. Brasília is based on an old dream, as Bishop had written in her *Life* World Library book, *Brazil*. While plans had begun in 1956, the idea could be dated more than a century earlier. As Bishop wrote in *Brazil:* "The move was thought of as a sort of exodus to a land of Canaan, a great stroke that would solve the country's problems as if by magic. A capital in the interior would be a romantic repetition of the long marches of the *bandeirantes* through the wilderness, bringing civilization to the remotest areas, as far away as the western frontier. It was the myth of the city of gold, with the possibility of wealth and opportunity for all" (56).

Bishop's essay is an attempt to puncture this inflated dream. Take, for instance, her description of President Kubitschek, the mastermind behind Brasília, who appears early in the essay like some postmodern Kurtz, a commodity fetish in among the "sunglasses," "sardines," "ropes of dry red sausages," "bottles of *cachaça*," and "headache remedies" (*PPL* 368). His head—Bishop describes it as "the head from which all this has sprung"—appears in profile "in a blur of gold" on "plastic plaques embossed in gold" with the "magic word BRASILIA" (368). Brasília was the visible symbol, according to Skidmore, of Juscelino Kubitschek's successful economic development program (167–68). Kubitschek had an enormous populist appeal, and his presidency, which began in 1956, was a time of unprecedented economic growth and political stability for Brazil, as Brazil experienced growth "three times that of the rest of Latin America" (Skidmore 164). Kubitschek was able to exploit Vargas's alliances but "without the authoritarianism" (Skidmore 167). The building of Brasília, Skidmore notes, "generated a sense of excitement among all classes of Brazilians, who looked upon the construction of a new capital in the neglected interior as the sign of Brazil's coming of age" (167–68). But it also, as Skidmore points out, "diverted attention from many difficult social and economic problems, such as reform of the agrarian system and the universities" (168). Bishop's essay refocuses our attention on the problems that the utopian myth of Brasília hides.

Take Brasília's "visionary architect," for instance, the celebrated Oscar Niemeyer. It is not that Bishop does not appreciate the power of Niemeyer's design, but she is quick to point out that it reflects the old prejudices: "It might strike a critical visitor as ironical that for over two years thousands of workers have been left to build wooden houses or shacks and shift for themselves, while the first two buildings to be completed should both be called 'Palace'" (*PPL* 371). Of Niemeyer's design for the "Palace of the Dawn," Bishop notes that it is "certainly one of the most beautiful of all Oscar Niemeyer's buildings. The pillars in particular, are an architectural triumph," but then she adds, in an aside that fairly drips with sarcasm, "it is, after all, no mean feat to invent a new 'order'" (376). But the coup de grâce in Bishop's commentary on Niemeyer's design is the "sunken wing" he built for the "servants quarters," which is "connected with the Palace by a subterranean passage" (379). Bishop calls it a "feeble, not to say depressing, solution" (379–80). "Surely," she writes, "in Brasília, sometimes referred to as 'the most modern city in the world,' Niemeyer, of all architects, should not have found it necessary to put them underground" (380). It turns out that Niemeyer used the same design for his own house outside Rio, a move that had been criticized, Bishop noted, by Henry

Russell-Hitchcock in the magazine *Latin American Architecture*. Bishop writes: "In both cases his solution of practical problems seems to have been the same: put them underneath, or underground, like a lazy housewife shoving household gear out of sight under a deceptively well-made bed" (380).

When we finally reach the Uialapiti Indians, we are predisposed to dismiss Brasília as folly, and its costs become more evident when Bishop points out the connection between their "dwindling" tribes and the erection of the utopian city. Huxley's role in all this also becomes abundantly clear: he has been brought in as a propagandist for the government. During the trip, an "exuberant" man shows up to ask Huxley to write a message for a collection to be put "in a future Brasília museum" from "visiting celebrities." Huxley dutifully "produced a few phrases," as Bishop puts it, "about the interesting experience of flying from the past (the colonial towns in Minas) to the future, the brand-new city of Brasília" (388–89). Bishop adds dryly that Huxley's missive was published in the Rio papers "as a telegram Huxley had sent to President Kubitschek, giving a rather odd impression of the Huxley telegram style" (389). Like a characteristic Bishop poem, the description of the endangered Indian reality that follows this duplicitous public fawning after celebrity forces us to reevaluate and reconsider Brasília's potentially sinister ramifications.

Bishop meets Claudio Villas Boas, who has lived and worked among the Indians for many years for the Brazilian Indian service, who speaks of "how hard it is to help the Indians, a losing battle against disease and corruption" (392). "Brasília," he tells Bishop, "has brought the possibility nearer by six hundred miles" that the land on which the Indians live will be sold, and they will be left with nowhere to go: "The Indians own no land; there are no reservations for them to retreat to if the lands where they live should ever be sold" (392). Those "retreating" Indians who withdraw always farther back behind the jungle canvas in Bishop's "Brazil, January 1, 1502" acquire further poignancy next to this comment.

Huxley really does not come off well in this account. Perhaps that is the true reason the *New Yorker* rejected this piece. Indeed, as Bishop reports it, the Indians call him "homely." Bishop herself observes, "And under the circumstances Huxley did appear, not homely, but exceedingly long, white, refined, and misplaced" (393). Bishop enhances the difference between the two of them by relating the anecdote, which she also told in a number of letters, that one of the indigenous men asked her to stay behind to be his wife, resulting in much merriment. But the story suggests that Bishop achieved a level of acceptance that the remote Huxley could not. Toward the end, Bishop definitively links Huxley to the utopian folly of Brasília through his own more recent work. Huxley, author of one of the most famous dystopian novels of the twentieth century, *Brave New World* (1932), spoke to Bishop about his new book, which he referred to by the working title "Utopia," but which was published as *Island* in 1962. Bishop quotes what Huxley told her about the novel: "It is a society 'where men are able to realize their potentialities as they have never been able to in any past or present civilization,'" to which Bishop adds with keen dramatic irony: "It seemed quite natural to be hearing about it five thousand feet up in the air, deserting one of the most primitive societies left on earth, rushing towards still another attempt at 'the most modern city in the world'" (398).

Bishop's criticism of Brasília is underscored by Antônio Callado's account of the same trip in *Correio da Manhã*, the Brazilian newspaper that Bishop quotes in her essay: "It is a city of consumers, set down in a desert where not even a cabbage plant can be seen. For a long time to come, its red dust will absorb, like blotting paper, the energies of the country" (400). Callado's remarks are shared by "all intelligent Brasilians I know," Bishop writes at the end of the essay, but, nevertheless, "rather desperately and resignedly, they are hoping for the best" (401). She ends with this sentence: "Perhaps we should also spare a little hope for the Indians" (401).

Bishop's poem "Brasil, 1959," unpublished in her lifetime, was her first attempt to put the nexus of ideas generated by the Brazil trip into poetry. She begins by describing the dire economic situation in Brazil and its endemic problem of runaway inflation: "The radio says black beans are up again." Disasters accumulate. The beans are full of worms; "a woman [is] drowned right in the city's heart"; floods are common: "Why doesn't the army send us trucks?" the speaker asks. Against this stark economic reality, Brasília rises in the middle of the poem, "a fairy palace small, impractical"; it "rises upon a barren field of mud / a lovely bauble, expensive as a jewel" (*PPL* 244). The poem also notes Brazil's corruption in a raw line that, nonetheless, I rather like: "crooks, crooks, stupid stupid stupid crooks" (244). Ultimately, this early poetic attempt falls far short of the essay, however.

Just a year later, though, the *New Yorker* published "Brazil, January 1, 1502." As I have suggested, this poem shares some of the same language as the essay in its staging of alienating first encounters. When she stepped off the plane in Brasília, Bishop writes in her essay, "the first thing that greeted my eyes . . . was a three-throned shoe-shine stand against the wall of the small airport building" (367). In "Brazil, January 1, 1502," she begins with lines that faintly echo the essay's moment of first encounter: "Januaries, Nature greets our eyes / exactly as she must have greeted theirs" (*PPL* 72). Several critics have already noted how these lines establish a connection between the twentieth-century traveler (and reader) — "our eyes" —

and the Portuguese conquistadores of the poem. James Longenbach argues that in addition to exposing Portuguese colonialism, the poem also raises "the possibility of Bishop's—or anyone's—complicity in the continuing imposition of those values" (30). Jeffrey Gray notes that in "Brazil, January 1," Bishop brings together "two experiences of discovery: the classical moment of the conquistador and the modern arrival of the tourist," providing a crucial decentering of both (36). With these poems, Gray argues, "Bishop helps us understand travel in postmodernity—neither as conquest, nor as pilgrimage, nor even as immersion in societies necessarily less spoiled and more grounded than one's own but rather as decentered, travel in which neither the traveling subject nor the visited site are stable entities" (25). This close affiliation creates discomfort for the reader and allows Bishop to lead us to a kind of critical awareness of the poem's multilayered critique: the violence of the Portuguese exploitation of the Indians, as well as our own potential to continue the violence. It is a question of sight, of how we *see* the world. In Brasília it is important to describe what "greeted my eyes." It is not fairy palaces but the "shoe-shine stand," representing some poor laborer, probably, that cleans the shoes of the traveler, which will be covered with the RED dust of Brasília.

And we realize, too, that it was what the Portuguese saw that led them to find their own utopian dream in Brazil. Like the utopian dream of Brasília, the Portuguese turned the Brazil they found into something

> not unfamiliar . . .
> . . . corresponding . . .
> to an old dream of wealth and luxury
> already out of style when they left home—
> wealth, plus a brand-new pleasure. (PPL 73)

Thus, "directly after Mass," the Portuguese "ripped away into the hanging fabric, / each out to catch an Indian for himself" (73). Bishop's poem dramatizes the exploitation of the Indians as part of Brazil's colonial past, but the opening lines link the poem to the present, placing "our eyes" uncomfortably in line with "theirs." As travelers to this country, we also bring with us a set of prejudices and desires. Those desires, in this case that "old dream," as Gray argues, "is important to Bishop's theme of travel projection. . . . Because the Portuguese are primed with Edenic texts and dreams, they find Brazil 'not unfamiliar'" (39). If we think about this poem in connection with Bishop's essay about Brasília, we see some of the same significant points. Treating Bishop's essay and her poem as companion pieces shows how closely the ideas of both overlap and how each shares a utopian dream of a city of gold that is catastrophic for the poor and disenfranchised. Bishop's message is consistent in her political poetics of this period, developing as it does a method of critique that allows her (and us) to "spare a little hope."

It is Robert Lowell who is generally considered the more overtly political poet, but extensive correspondence between Bishop and Lowell during Bishop's almost two decades in Brazil reveals just how deeply politics became personal for Bishop in a way that it never had before, and particularly after 1961, when Bishop and Macedo Soares moved from their quiet retreat in Samambaia to the apartment in Rio de Janeiro so that Macedo Soares could be closer to her work as chief coordinator of the Rio park project. The move put Bishop into closer proximity to the profound political turmoil of this period, which began with the sudden exodus from office of President Jânio Quadros in 1961. Quadros's election was originally a source of renewed hope for many Brazilians. He had campaigned on a platform of reform, promising to deal with runaway inflation and corruption. Instead, what followed was a period of tremendous instability, political turmoil, and the constant threat of revolution. Yet just seven months after Quadros took office, he was "leaving the country without a tie," as Lowell, who was reading the unfolding news in the *New York Times,* put it in one panicky letter to Bishop (*WIA* 374). In response to the unfolding crisis, Lowell offered to send Bishop money, in case she and Macedo Soares had been unable to get their money out before the banks closed (376). Bishop assured Lowell in a September 25, 1961, letter that they and their money were safe. But her description shows how closely connected Bishop was to the events that precipitated Quadros's resignation.

Once again, their friend Carlos Lacerda was at the forefront of the attack that brought down Quadros. Lacerda was a member of the Democratic National Union Party, União Democrática Nacional, or UDN, which "drew support from upwardly mobile middle class groups, especially in larger towns and urban centers" (Levine 214). The party's members were by no means unified in their views, but generally speaking they were anticommunist, prodemocracy and prodevelopment. Lacerda was nominated as the party's presidential candidate just before the military coup that unseated Goulart in 1964. Lacerda's attack against Quadros ostensibly had to do with Quadros's "independent" foreign policy. Quadros "had begun to identify himself with the 'nationalist' position, which contradicted the views of most of the UDN, as well as the 'anti-Communist' officers among the military" (Skidmore 201). Lacerda's strategy of attack was similar to the one he had used against Vargas and then Kubitschek, except that there he had focused on corruption instead of foreign policy. At any rate, it was Lacerda's "access to mass media" that made his attacks so successful (Skidmore 201). The event in August that Bishop mentions in her letter to Lowell "began over Quadros's sudden award of the Cruzeiro do Sul Order to Cuba's Che Guevara," a sign that Quadros had moved to the left (Skidmore 201). Skidmore describes "a comic-opera incident, involving a mix-up with Lacerda's baggage," where Quadros refused to see Lacerda, and on the night of August 24, "Lacerda delivered a blistering radio attack" (Skidmore 201). Bishop told Lowell in her letter that Lota

> was very much involved in everything and stayed at the Governor's Palace all night long several nights, arriving home for breakfast. You know that the Governor of the State of Guanabara is an old friend of ours, Carlos Lacerda—and he is the man who set the whole thing off—more or less. It is extremely complicated, of course. I even wrote a note to the *NY Times* about ten days ago—maybe you'll see it—maybe they won't print it. But really—the US papers I've seen, or what's been quoted from them here—have everything entirely wrong. My one point was that the US doesn't believe a word of what Russia says—but when it comes to S.A. anything anyone says—dictators or would-be dic. of the right or of the left (as now) they take on faith. Things look very bad. I think I'll give after-dinner speeches on the Brazilian Situation when I get to N.Y. I seem to know quite a lot about it. The Navy steamed up and down right in front of our apartment here and I watched through binoculars. But Rio itself was pretty quiet—thanks to Carlos—(whom the *NY Times* calls "feudal and reactionary" etc., etc. The army actually is so *un*-warlike that they backed down—and really behaved very well!) (*WIA* 376)

While Bishop's political discourse strikes one, in retrospect, as rather naïve, even reactionary, this letter to Lowell reflects Bishop's increasingly personal involvement. She was both in the middle of it through her relationship with Macedo Soares, as it were, and somewhat outside of it. After all, she was an American living in Brazil, and so she might have remained an observer, although an involved one.

But in 1962, when Bishop defended Lacerda in public in an angry letter to the *New Republic,* she does not seem naïve at all, or, indeed, distanced. She is responding to an article by the Brazilian correspondent, Louis Wiznitzer, that had appeared in the *New Republic* a month earlier: "I want to register strong protest," Bishop begins, uncharacteristically (22). Her famous reticence is nowhere in evidence in this letter. She is forceful and knowledgeable in her opinions. Wiznitzer claimed that Lacerda was responsible for "a wave of rightwing terrorism [that] has been spreading throughout Brazil" (19). He also accused Lacerda of "blackmailing" Quadros and, as Bishop puts it, "selling government property as real estate" (22).

Bishop calls these accusations groundless, and, in the case of the latter, one that "exactly follow[s] the line of Communist propaganda here" (22). Wiznitzer argued that the majority of Brazilians wanted Quadros to return to the presidency. Bishop disagrees: "During the past year I have been working on a book about Brazil and I have had talks with reputable journalists, economists, and international lawyers in Rio de Janeiro. These people and all my Brazilian friends are pro-democracy and pro-United States" (22). She calls Wiznitzer's article "malicious" and "distorted" (22). Apart from his views about Lacerda, Wiznitzer's views are not really malicious, but my point here is that Bishop's opinion on the subject of Brazil reflects a very well-defined and particular view of the subject, a view closely aligned with that of Macedo Soares.[3] Both Bishop and Macedo Soares became more critical of Lacerda as the situation worsened in Brazil from 1961 to 1963, and as Macedo Soares became increasingly embroiled in governmental bureaucracy in the building of the park. By 1963, in a letter to Lowell, Bishop was calling Lacerda "dangerous" (WIA 436), a view not so far from that of Wiznitzer, which she had previously criticized. In another letter from October 1963, she worries about Lacerda using their Samambaia house as a "hide-out" (WIA 506).

The situation in Brazil and in the world (Lowell wrote to her repeatedly during this period about his fear of nuclear annihilation) prompted Bishop to seriously consider what would be a suitable form of protest, given the political situation. In a June 1961 letter to Lowell, Bishop tries to put it into words. Referring to a comment Lowell had made in an interview that appeared in the *Paris Review* in the winter–spring issue, she writes:

> What you are saying about Marianne [Moore] is fine: "terrible, private, and strange revolutionary poetry. There isn't the motive to do that now." But I wonder—isn't there? Isn't there even more—only it's terribly hard to find the exact and right and surprising enough, or un-surprising enough, point at which to revolt now? The Beats have just fallen back on an old corpse-strewn or monument-strewn battle-field—the real protest I suspect is something quite different (If only I could find it. Klee's picture called FEAR seems close to it, I think . . .). (WIA 364)

There is some dispute over which Klee painting Bishop meant. The editors of *Words in Air* identify it as Klee's 1932 *Mask of Fear,* which in hindsight strikes me as the perfect condensation in visual form of one of Bishop's most famous lines from "The Bight": "All the untidy activity continues / awful but cheerful" (PPL 47). Klee's large blob-like mask that moves across his canvas on tiny feet embodies the "awful but cheerful." But in her recent essay on Bishop and Klee, Peggy Samuels identifies the painting as Klee's 1934 *Angst*, which Bishop had seen exhibited at the Buchholz gallery (547). Whatever the case, Klee's art provided Bishop with "an aesthetic model," as Samuels puts it, for what was at present "difficult to invent" in poetry (547). Form, as Bishop suggests in this letter, certainly plays a role in how Bishop formulates a "real protest" to political and social crisis in her own work.

I think we can now see that Bishop achieves this "form" of protest in a variety of ways, but especially in 1964 in her neglected but brilliant ballad "The Burglar of Babylon," a poem that grows directly out of the political chaos and concerns of these years. The seeds for "The Burglar of Babylon" seem to have been planted around the time of political upheaval in Rio and Bishop's move there with Macedo Soares. Bishop wrote to Lowell that Elizabeth Hardwick's August 1961 review of Oscar Lewis's *The Children of Sanchez* in the *New York Times Book Review*, "Some Chapters of Personal History: A Brilliant Study of a Mexican Family Probes the Lives of the Unknown Poor," inspired her "to tackle the *favela* business here — (The Rio slums—if anyone doesn't know by now)" (*WIA* 379), which she did in her *Brazil* and then in 1964 in what Marianne Moore called her "finest poem" (*WIA* 560), her ballad "The Burglar of Babylon."

From 1961 to 1964 the political situation worsened in Brazil, leading finally in 1964 to the fall of Goulart and the end of democracy in Brazil. After Quadros resigned in 1961, Goulart, his vice president, became president, but not before the country went from a presidential to a parliamentary system in an effort to minimize Goulart's power. Goulart's policies of land reform and nationalization of parts of the oil industry that had been privately owned were unpopular with Brazil's middle class. In a letter to Lowell from April 1962 that she mistakenly dated April 26, 1928—a mistake that Bishop attributed, in a humorous aside to Lowell, to the current state of chaos in Brazil—she wrote: "There are rumors, rumors of revolution; things have never been such a mess. . . . The thieving is beyond belief" (*WIA* 408). By late 1963, the widespread fear was "that all of Goulart's moves had no further purpose than to create a revolutionary situation in which the president would emerge as the Brazilian Perón" (Skidmore 295). In a 1964 letter to Bishop, Lowell addressed the question of how to put all this into poetry:

I think everyone here feels that Brazil was rapidly dropping into chaos, more rapidly than even Brazilians knew or anticipated till lately. . . . This is a very confusing time. The big wars may be over, but when have so many governments toppled, so many changes, good and bad, come by violence. The radical business has brought us a little nearer to the turbulence. The issue is clear, but the working out is all uncertain, and wrung with twisted lines.

You speak of the artistic temperament, unsuited to this stuff. But you grasp strongly, and come up with full hands. . . . I wish you could find forms, narrative, description, fiction, poems—to get it out. . . . No eye in the world has seen what yours has. I have a vague image of a sequence of poems through which the Revolution moves. . . . I am thinking really that the Revolution might give a thread for you to draw together the gathering impressions of your ten years' stay. (WIA 533–34)

Despite Lowell's encouragement, Bishop, ultimately, knew that her poetic gifts did not rest in writing overtly political lyrics, and writing such a sequence of poems was beyond her grasp to shape into art, as Lowell might have done. But Bishop had gathered her impressions in ways that were more suited to her poetic skills, and that was in her recently completed ballad, one of several ballads that Bishop wrote at various points during her poetic career. And Lowell was clearly pleased with the results. As he said in a letter to Bishop when the ballad appeared, "it's surely one of the great ballads in the language, and oddly enough gives more of Brazil somehow than your whole Life book" (*WIA* 560). Lowell compared it to Bishop's poem on Pound, "Visits to St. Elizabeths," calling it one of Bishop's "peculiar triumphs like the Pound" (*WIA* 560).

Set in the *favelas* of Rio, "The Burglar of Babylon" tells the story of the hunt for and eventual death of the thief Micuçú on the hills of Rio where the poor live as "a fearful stain" on the hillside: "The poor who come to Rio / And can't go home again" (*PPL* 90). In her *Life* World Library *Brazil,* Bishop's first attempt two years previously to take on the *favelas,* she had noted the terrible conditions and fragile houses of the *favelas,* "without running water or sewers" and "literally a stone's throw from Rio's luxury apartment houses" (140). Bishop wrote many of her most subversive poems using conventional meter and rhyme, and this ballad is no exception. Here Bishop resists the convention of the traditional folk ballad. Rather than eliciting our pity for the poor unfortunates, as W. B. Yeats does in "The Ballad of Moll Magee," Bishop uses the occasion to slide both the speaker of her poems and her readers into a series of (sometimes uncomfortable) subject positions that force us to confront questions about gender, power, and even, in the case of the Burglar, the very question raised by the title poem of Bishop's 1965 volume *Questions of Travel:* "Is it right to be watching strangers in a play / in this strangest of theatres?" (*PPL* 74). It is a technique that I have argued owes much to her Brazil years and her prose renditions of that experience. The ballad's shifting perspectives and framing devices and forms of surveillance make it very much a

Cold War document, as well as a political commentary on Brazil. It was published in the *New Yorker* in 1964, the same year that the military coup ended democracy in Brazil and turned the country into a police state. The rich (and Bishop includes herself among these in a letter she wrote about the incident) watch the unfolding story of the hunt for Micuçú "with their binoculars," providing just one of the many layers of voyeurism and surveillance noted in the ballad, which also includes "a buzzard," "an army helicopter," "hysteric[al] soldiers" who end up shooting the officer in command by mistake, and "the yellow sun" itself.

Jacqueline Vaught Brogan has pointed out—in the most substantive previous reading of this ballad—that it may have taken as its model the "good-night ballad," which emerged in the late nineteenth century and consisted of a criminal's last words and his warning to society before his execution (515). Brogan argues that the ballad turns the "narrative line of the good-night ballad . . . inside out, revealing it to be society and its scripting of situations that is the actual 'criminal'" (522).

In its detailing of gross governmental incompetence and blind devotion to authority contained in the dying words of the mistakenly shot officer, who "committed his soul to God / And his sons to the Governor" (*PPL* 93), Bishop's ballad has other models as well, most notably the political *sambas* composed for Carnival, a selection of which Bishop translated in 1965. Moreover, the line appears to be a fairly direct criticism of Lacerda, who was still governor of Rio at the time. It was Lacerda's popularity with the military, along with his access to the mass media, that made him so successful in bringing down presidents. Bishop may have once been partial to Lacerda as a result of her relationship with Macedo Soares, but that changed as Lacerda seemed to Bishop to become more like the dictators he was fighting against, demanding the ultimate sacrifice from his soldiers (and their sons), not for freedom or justice, but for him alone. Perhaps Bishop also had in mind the sacrifice that Macedo Soares had made for Lacerda—of her time and of her health.

As in "Brazil, January 1, 1502," Bishop's ballad links contemporary Brazil to its history of colonial conflict in an early quatrain:

> There are caves up there, and hideouts,
> And an old fort, falling down.
> They used to watch for Frenchmen
> From the hill of Babylon. (92)

These lines with their historical references serve to deepen the layers of social persecution. She may have hated working on the Brazil book—that "awful" book, as she called it in a 1962 letter to Lowell (*WIA* 397)—but the work she did there, the lines of historical and contemporary political conflict she traced, gave her the foundation for this skillful and subversive ballad.

But there is another way that Bishop subverts the convention of the ballad form, and that is in the *breaking down* of the distance that is so much a part of the convention. The form, in other words, gave her the distance she needed to contain the chaos swirling around her, while at the same time allowing her to break the conventions that also worked to create more intimacy with the thief at the heart of the story. For most of this ballad, we feel we are perched outside looking into Micuçú's world; essentially we are in the position of the rich people. But there is a moment in the ballad when Bishop closes that distance in these three quatrains in the middle of the ballad:

> Rich people in apartments
>   Watched through binoculars
> As long as the daylight lasted.
>   And all night, under the stars,
>
> Micuçú hid in the grasses
>   Or sat in a little tree,
> Listening for sounds, and staring
>   At the lighthouse out at sea.
>
> And the lighthouse stared back at him,
>   Till finally it was dawn.
> He was soaked with dew, and hungry,
>   On the hill of Babylon. (*PPL* 93)

At the beginning of the quatrain, the rich people are watching, but there's a full stop at the end of the third line and a shift in perspective. Night has fallen, and Micuçú is alone on the hillside. He "hid in the grasses / Or sat in a little tree, / Listening for sounds, and staring / At the lighthouse out at sea." This quiet moment with Micuçú alone lasts for only one quatrain before the surveillance frame closes in again, but in the intimacy it conveys, it shares much with other moments in Bishop's work—Crusoe dangling his feet over the side of the volcano, the hermit in "Chemin de Fer," and even the confused child of "In the Waiting Room." In breaking down this distance, if only very briefly, Bishop perhaps offers her greatest challenge to not only the ballad form itself but to authoritarian political systems, such as those she was increasingly recognizing in Lacerda's Rio.

James Merrill suggests what is perhaps at the heart of why Bishop turned to the ballad at certain times in her career in a comment he made in 1988 in a talk titled "The Education of the Poet." Here, Merrill joined the debate over politics and poetic form. When he was growing up, Merrill told his audience, what was "very much in the air . . . was the injunction to forge a 'new measure'" (*Collected Prose* 11). Merrill cites both modernist poets—Pound and Williams—as well as his contemporaries—Ginsberg and Ashbery—as a source for this injunction, which suggests that formal innovation should follow a change in world. The question goes something like this, as Merrill puts it: "Doesn't our world, with all its terrifying fragmentations and new frontiers, call for equivalent formal breakthroughs? Who would dream of coping with today in heroic couplets or terza rima?" (11). And yet, in the end, Merrill defends his use of traditional form and points to his "need for a rhyme or an amphibrach," traditional elements that he "found most conducive to surprise" (11). These moments of intimacy in Bishop's work—the moment when the "Man-Moth" hands over his tear "if you're paying attention" or the moment when we sit quietly with Micuçú on the hillside—are, for me, central to Bishop's challenge to the world. The use she makes of traditional forms, and the transformations of perspective that she achieves through them, can only deepen our sense of sudden surprise.

One of the great contributions of all these new collections of Bishop's work is that they demonstrate beyond a doubt that Bishop's artistic life was all of a piece. It was indeed "one art." She used prose—letters, political commentary, stories—to work through and elaborate a theory of poetics that she laid out in three essays she wrote in college. And she continued to rely on this method of composition throughout her career. During college, in the politically fraught 1930s, she did not yet have the skill as a poet to bring together that complex nexus of social commentary that would one day become a feature of some of her best poetry. But Brazil changed that for her—the influx of new experience, the direct access to political upheaval, her relationship with Lowell, the writing of the Brazil book for the *Life* World Library, the travel—all contributed to a perspective that allowed her to put herself in the picture and find "the right point of protest now."

NOTES

1. Bishop spells "Brazil" with an *s* consistently in this poem and in her letters, and I have kept her spelling in cases of direct quotation. In other references to "Brazil" and "Brazilian," I have kept

the z, which is the preferred American spelling. The capital of Brazil, Brasília, is always spelled with an s.

2. In *Elizabeth Bishop: Her Artistic Development,* Thomas Travisano notes that Bishop's "early phase provided training for the later one" (18). James Longenbach argues, in "Elizabeth Bishop's Bramble Bushes," that Bishop, as early as her college writing, began developing a theory of poetry that valued "hermeneutic indeterminacy" (*Modern Poetry* 24). See also my discussion of Bishop's college essays and poetic development in "*Con Spirito,* Improvisation, and the Poetry of the 1930s," in *Degrees of Freedom: American Women Poets and the Women's College, 1905–1955.* I argue that Bishop developed sophisticated ideas of writing in prose essays first and then put those ideas into practice as she developed her art.

3. In an interesting footnote to this story, the *New Republic* published a review of Huxley's novel *Island* in the same issue in which Bishop's letter to the editor appeared. The reviewer called Huxley's *Island* "a curiously distasteful book. The paradise is unreal, uninviting and a bit too much like an experimental clinic with imported Indian overtones in Southern California. . . . You are left with a mysticism without God, a love without understanding and a compassion without heart" (18) (see Patrick O'Donovan, "Aldous Huxley's Island Paradise").

Part III

New Correspondences
The Poet with Her Peers

"Composing Motions"

Elizabeth Bishop and Alexander Calder

PEGGY SAMUELS

Bishop's lifelong interest in visual art and her offhand remarks that she would rather have been a painter suggest the depth of her attraction to poetry's sister discipline (Brown, "Interview" 24; A. Johnson 100).[1] Yet, the scarcity of extended descriptions about the visual arts in her letters and notebooks, combined with the rather daunting range of artists whom she mentions, make it difficult to tell any cohesive story about her response to particular features in the art that she saw. The discourse about artists at midcentury—the reception of painters of interest to the poet—provides a mediating context for Bishop's own understanding and can help to establish the ways that she drew on experiments in the visual arts to fashion her own distinctive poetics. With the help of this reception history, as well as manuscripts in the Vassar Collection and the volume edited by Alice Quinn, it is possible to see Bishop creatively transforming the work of Alexander Calder to conceptualize lyric structure and orient the lyric speaker.

In a 1959 letter to Ilse Barker, Bishop claimed that she could visualize "almost every" Calder that she had seen exhibited in Pittsfield, Massachusetts, almost thirty years before, in 1933.[2] She also stressed the vividness of her long-term memory of that exhibition when writing to Anne Stevenson in 1964.[3] From 1934 on, Bishop continued to have access to Calder's work, which was exhibited in New York City at the Pierre Matisse Gallery (the gallery that represented Loren Mac-Iver) and later at the Buchholz Gallery, which represented Calder in the 1940s.[4] Some of Bishop's knowledge of Calder likely would have come from her close friend and former college roommate Margaret Miller, who worked for James Johnson Sweeney, the most important early advocate for Calder's work in the United States. In 1943, Sweeney arranged for the sculptor to hold a one-man show at the Museum of Modern Art, and Miller worked with Sweeney on the catalogue of the exhibition. Given Bishop's interest in Calder and her friendship with Miller (to whom, in this period, Bishop still sent all of her poem drafts [*WIA* 73]), we can assume that Bishop would have been quite familiar both with Sweeney's remarks in the catalogue of the MoMA exhibition and with the midcentury critical reception of Calder. Later, Bishop would likely have had access to the writings of the most influential Brazilian critics of Calder, Henrique Mindlin and Mário Pedrosa. Even their commentary that preceded Bishop's arrival in Brazil would likely have been available to Bishop because Lota had played a prominent role in Calder's reception in Brazil (Saraiva 84).[5]

The pieces that Bishop remembered so vividly from Pittsfield were Calder's early small mobile sculptures: "some of the constructions were driven by small electric motors, others were moved by tiny hand cranks" (Sweeney 33). In the catalogue for that show, Calder announced his program: "Why not plastic forms in motion? Not a simple translatory or rotary motion but several motions of different types, speeds and amplitudes composing to make a resultant whole. Just as one can compose colors, or forms, so one can compose motions" (Calder, *Modern*). Explicating his work in 1932, Calder had emphasized that he was composing by setting the disparate kinds of motions in changing relation to one another: "Each element can move, shift, or sway back and forth in a changing relation to each of the other elements in this universe. Thus they reveal not only isolated moments, but a physical law of variation among the events of life" (qtd. in Giménez and Rower 47). Calder's remark makes clear that although the mobiles drew on the motion of planets and constellations, they had a wider relevance, illustrative of the intersecting trajectories and shifting relations between objects, motions, and events of lived realities. The Brazilian critics Mário Pedrosa and Pietro Maria Bardi emphasized the insertion of the mobiles in architectural and natural environments, the sculptures becoming part of lived realities (Saraiva 33, 74).

In her watercolor of the room in Samambaia that held one of Lota de Macedo Soares's Calder mobiles, Bishop slips the mobile into the environment in such a way that she reinforces Calder's view that his mobiles captured the cross-rhythms and disparate shapes of parts of the environment.[6] Bishop draws attention to the "play" of shapes in the room that "answer" the mobile's shapes. The closed rectangular stove, with its filled-in volume of heavy black, is poised against the lightness and openness of the mobile. With its closed shapes arranged in a "spray," the Calder mobile occupies a middle realm between a series of pictures on the back wall of the room, each enclosed by a prominently outlined rectangular frame, and a spangle of dotted flowers, an open spray, in a vase in front of the wall. Bishop situates the little stove door opener next to the Calder mobile so that it hangs at the same height as the center of gravity of the mobile. This little tool is composed of line, curve, and circle with a blank middle resembling the open-holed sphere of the

Calder shape closest to it. Positioned so that it is at the same height as the middle of the Calder, the mechanism of the stovepipe, which can move and open, draws attention to the qualities that the stove and the mobile share across their immense differences. The arrangement of shapes in the painting conveys Bishop's sense that any environment could be experienced as a Calder.

The reception of Calder at midcentury helps to characterize the nature of that aesthetic and lived experience. Midway between closed geometric shape and "open" organic biomorphic form, the Calder mobile, according to midcentury art criticism, acted as conciliator in the split between the geometric and the biomorphic that prominently structured the art scene at midcentury (or, as Alfred H. Barr famously articulated the conflict: "the silhouette of the square confronts the shape of the amoeba" [19]).[7] To see Calder as associated with but deviating from the school of geometric abstraction was a commonplace in the 1940s, especially after Robert Motherwell's recapping of the famous report of Calder's visit to Mondrian's studio, which appeared in the winter 1944 *Partisan Review:* "I was very much moved by Mondrian's studio, large beautiful, and irregular as it was, with the walls painted white, and divided by black lines and rectangles of bright color . . . like his paintings . . . and I thought at the time how fine it would be if everything MOVED" (97). Like Paul Klee, Calder was seen as inventing an alternative aesthetic to Mondrian, partly from the use of the "wandering line" that broke loose from Mondrian's straight-lined geometric forms. The sketchiness of Calder's line in his early wire sculptures, like Klee's wandering line, became associated with the human qualities of tentativeness and hesitation.[8] These qualities continued to be linked to Calder, even in the later mobiles, because of the hesitation and "waiting" as one element hovered before taking on speed and direction when impelled by a neighboring element. In a 1947 catalogue for Buchholz, later reproduced in multiple locales, Jean-Paul Sartre wrote: "The 'mobile' . . . weaves uncertainly, hesitates, and at times appears to begin its movement anew, as if it had caught itself in a mistake" (qtd. in Giménez and Rower 70).[9] Calder's work seemed to gather the qualities of improvisation and human frailty, partly in opposition to the coldness and certainty implied in the straight-edged, geometric abstractions of the followers of Mondrian. Yet, in that hesitation and improvisation, there is a sense of freedom from constraint in opposing the straight-lined tradition.

Calder set the observer inside a three-dimensional deep space to experience the disparate relations among objects that ascended and descended, moved out and in, curved around in different directions, much like Paul Klee's "fish swimming in all directions" (Hayter 130). Like Klee, Calder placed the observer among "floating motifs." The "motifs," Calder's orbiting shapes, literally floated above the observer's head. Sweeney asserted that "the organization of contrasting movements and changing relations of form[s] in space . . . was the first feature of his new approach" in creating the later mobiles (33). Gabrielle Buffet-Picabia emphasized Calder's "extraordinary command of the interaction between weight and motion" and described the way that the sculptor arranged elements' responsiveness to other elements (qtd. in Giménez and Rower 68).[10] In his own writing, Calder emphasized that he composed by arranging disparities: "Disparity in form, color, size, weight, motion, is what makes a composition" (qtd. in Giménez and Rower 59). Some commentators included sound as one of the elements ("sounds of a thin metallic nature emerging from the scarcely touching forms" [Janis 28]). Amidst these disparities, Calder managed to create a place for the observer, a position inside the mobile structure so that the viewer imagined himself set inside this space of changing relations. The observer had a place in the "field" without himself having given rise to the motions. There was a sense of the observer suspended and gently moving among objects with different weights and trajectories, part of a system in which these elements impacted one another. The system allowed one to sense the disparities between the elements so that the randomness and "accidents" felt peaceful, gentle, and orderly without becoming fixed or rigid.

Partly because of that gentleness, freshness, and surprise, in the 1940s Calder began to be associated with pleasure and buoyancy at a time when the country struggled with the experience of the war. Almost as though he himself were an element in one of his mobiles, Calder was seen as a counterweight to that grief (Marter 202). Sweeney and others spoke of Calder's humor, playfulness, and vitality (again, this feature became prominent particularly in contrast to Mondrian's emphasis on formal relations as geometric). Sartre declared, "A 'mobile,' one might say, is a little private celebration" (qtd. in Giménez and Rower 69). In 1950, Marcel Duchamp paid tribute to this pleasure and characterized it more precisely: "Through their way of counteracting gravity by gentle movements, they seem to 'carry their own particular pleasures'" (qtd. in Giménez and Rower 77). The sensation of pleasure arose partly because of the weightlessness and mobility of these floating elements but also in response to the freshness and surprise of not being able to predict the events that occurred. The most prominent Brazilian commentator, Henrique Mindlin, also characterized Calder's mobiles as "contain[ing] a human, unexpected and joyful element that is Calder's own" (Mindlin, "Alexander" 55). This system, harboring spontaneity, playfulness, pleasure, humor, buoyancy, and a sense of private celebration, counteracted and replaced the more frightening characteristics of the "system" of a world that had moved to a scale too large to accommodate individual desire or defiance.[11] Hesitation, then, had a humanist quality, and gathered the sensation of freedom (one was not locked inside a rigid system; there was space for "wandering" and for surprise) as well as a sensation of gentleness and privacy. Suspension in space became expressive of a suspension in time, with its rich human variation of directions and speeds and openness to a (pleasantly) unpredictable future.

With the help of manuscripts in the Vassar Collection and the recently published volume edited by Alice Quinn, we can see Bishop's invention of a lyric structure and reliance on a method that resembles Calder's "composing motions." The poem "Gypsophilia," set in Samambaia after Bishop moved to Brazil in 1951, carries the title of Calder mobiles from 1949 and 1950.[12] Calder's *Gypsophilia II* is extremely delicate. There's a sense of large spaces between small white circles and then a kind of spray of smaller circles, clusters of which would move somewhat independently or in pairs. From the movement emerges a sense of gentleness, balance, ascension, and descent. Because of the asymmetrical arrangement, the center is off-balance. Some of the upward-tending wires look slanted or veering.

The poem draft "Gypsophilia" suspends the speaker (as "we") on top of a mountainside, in a field of shapes, sounds, and events above and below her that float toward and away in trajectories of varying speeds and directions. A dog's "oblique barks" float upward and sideways, as if "chop-chopping at the mountains with a hatchet" and then "flake off in yellow sparks" (*EAP* 128–29). Far below, the "last clangs" of "somebody beat[ing] the hanging iron bar" at the orchid nursery float away, as if off to sea. Floating upward, a "lighter" variant on that clanging, "A child's voice rises, hard and thin." Below the speaker, Manuelzinho's family is crossing, at a "half-trot"; each of the parents carries branches that make a variety of series of horizontals, moving in a swath. A "spray" appears: "each child with an enormous sheaf / Of 'Gypsophilia,' 'baby's breath.'" In another draft of the poem not published by Quinn, Bishop arranges above the speaker a weightless "spray" of white stars balanced high above the gypsophilia carried by the children: "one can just make out / the tiny blossoms [of stars] glimmering white. . . . Now it is so dark / the tiny blossoms glimmering white / in systems of their own" (VC 66.5). The poem ends with descending and ascending motions: Venus setting and a question rising.

Amidst these "motions of different types, speeds, and amplitudes," the speaker herself is suspended but not motionless. She floats in a kind of weightless three-dimensional field. The repeated but incrementally softer sounds from a bell-buoy's clang on water give off the sensation of the presumably sedentary speaker traveling, floating farther away while standing still. Each object of attention resituates the consciousness of the speaker so that the "center" where the speaker is located "tips" in relation to another object or "moves off." The use of the word "sub-stratum" ("we're in / some cold sub-stratum of dew") repositions the speaker so that she appears to be at the bottom of a space while still above, high on the mountain. In another draft, she is suspended and borne: "in those minutely-blossoming sprays all about us, [we are] [c]aught up, somehow, and carried, carried" (VC 66.5). In this version, Bishop invents an image of condensation for the "we": she imagines the "we" (the couple on the mountain or the earth itself) as a small, dark, condensed black seed:

> a dead black seed
> caught somewhere
> caught, somehow, and carried, carried
> in those glimmering sprays about us.

Another variant ends:

> we live aslant
> an invisible round seed
> caught up somehow, and carried, carried
> fascicles
> about us
> borne in the fascicle." (vc 66.5)

"Fascicle," the exfoliated, bursting shape of flowers' stamens, characterizes our space: invisible at the center of a circle of a white spray of stars, we are suspended, borne along, "carried." In this unpublished poem, Bishop seems to be experimenting with setting the lyric speaker as if the viewer could become one of the elements in a Calder hanging mobile. The speaker is held and carried as a moving element among gently ascending, descending, and circling shape motifs, that condensing and unfurling, poising their disparate weights and motions, carry the timbre of gentleness, accident, and pleasure.

This method of composing allows Bishop to address a problem inherent in her fondness for description—the problem of an overly passive speaker. By setting her thoughts in disparate relations to the motions in the landscape, she orchestrates the gentle release of the motion of her own thoughts as one of the elements moving among other elements in the landscape. Her thought rises up as an object among other objects, with its own direction and lightness. Lyrics are systems for orchestrating the drift and weight of one thought or emotion as it arises from, is weighed against, or replaces another, and Calder's work gave Bishop one way of imagining the dynamics of poems.

To be "borne" or carried, subjected to motions and set in a world of motions, does not always occur in the key of pleasure and balance. Calder's mobiles also involved a more robust "bump" as one element met another, in midtrajectory. In Bishop's "Arrival at Santos," the speaker inhabits a Calder-like system where disparate elements appear seemingly out of nowhere and knock or move into other elements, sometimes with the humor that commentators mentioned frequently in their characterizations of Calder's work. The speaker and Miss Breen, climbing down the ladder backward, cross into the orbit of another, more determined motion—the boat hook that has suddenly swung into view as if from another part of the "mobile," and that then produces its effect (lifting Miss Breen from shipside to land). As in a Calder mobile, objects appear on the horizon, their sources not seen: while the speaker and her friend are eating breakfast, from the margins of experience, from the periphery, floats in another element ("Finish your breakfast. The tender is coming, / A strange and ancient craft, flying a strange and brilliant rag" [CP 89]). Like Calder, Bishop links suspense in time (the always being poised in one's own mental motion for the next event that will enter the "scene") with suspense in space (traveling on a trajectory that will "hit" or "be hit"):

> Oh, tourist,
> Is this how this country is going to answer you
>
> And your immodest demands for a different world,
> And a better life, and complete comprehension
> Of both at last, and immediately,
> After eighteen days of suspension? (CP 89)

The lyric speaker moves on her own trajectory—of travel, of desire (expressed in that suspension of the syntax)—toward other elements that have their own independent motions.

The speaker's thoughts enter as part of the set of objects acting on one another. Her thoughts "slip off" or away, set off in a little chain of one thing "knocking" another, from ports to other necessities like postage stamps or soap. Bishop calls our attention to the way that the elements participate in the "hesitation" or "uncertainty," which Sartre said characterized the motion in Calder's work. The objects themselves and the lyric speaker's thoughts about them are so unassertive that they cannot hold in place but move off ("slip," "waste"):

the unassertive colors of soap, or postage stamps—
wasting away like the former, slipping the way the latter

do when we mail the letters we wrote on the boat. (90)

This desultory sentence, although it is about objects, captures as well the speaker's "cascading" from one thought to another, slipping jerkily across the divide
between stanzas. The two motions—the long, suspended syntax of a sentence
that "closes" in hesitation and this more ungainly slipping sentence—run into
each other like the vastly differing movements in Calder's hanging mobiles: large
motions—the trajectory of the ship moving south, the crane, the tender—set off
a frisson of smaller shakes and shivers: the little quotidian items that can't stay in
place and the speaker's "cascading" from one thought to another. Postage stamps,
soap, glue, thoughts ricochet off one another without actually "taking" or sticking. The little rustling movement of this cascade then ceases abruptly when a new
trajectory "bumps" into it in midline: "We leave Santos at once; / we are driving
to the interior" (CP 90). A new kind of motion enters the "picture" at the end, one
with more initiative, less gentle, more in a straight line. It is as if Bishop is "composing" by setting motions in relation to other motions, setting disparate levels of
certainty and hesitation in the speaker's mind in a field of objects that move with
varying degrees of certainty. This concept of lyric imagines a poem as the site
where the orchestrating of syntactical variations can insert the mind's movements
in a nonmimetic relationship to a "moving" nature. The poem becomes a kind of
interface in which the movements of mind and the movements of nature can be
set next to or within one another.

In "The Armadillo," Bishop is clearly "composing motions," including even the
breeze that "disturbs [the mobile and] configures it differently at each moment"
(Mindlin, "Calder, Smith" 123). Bishop may have been responding to a small bro-
chure from the 1948 exhibit in which Pietro Maria Bardi had announced: "In a few
days, Alexander Calder will be planting his superlative equations of color, shape
and balance in our halls; in some countries where the curiously-shaped colored
paper balloons of St. John's day represent 'abstractionist release and aspiration'
for the majority of the population, the mobiles will be warmly, or even enthusias-
tically received" (148). Delicately composing the vagaries of movement in verse
lines that lift, drift, and hover, Bishop arranges for the "frail, illegal fire balloons"
to appear and rise, "flush and fill with light / that comes and goes," and "with a
wind, / . . . flare and falter, wobble and toss" (CP 103). The "Venus going down"
arranged against the balloons that, when the wind disappears, "steer [straight] be-

tween / the kite sticks of the Southern Cross," orchestrate man-made shapes balancing against or moving among the cosmic ones (*CP* 103). Each action releases a corresponding but disparate motion, varying by speed, direction, weight: a flame runs down, a pair of owls fly up; when the armadillo "left the scene," "a baby rabbit jumped out, / *short*-eared, to our surprise" (*CP* 103–4). Bishop arranges the shapes and motions with the lyric speaker oriented in the midst of these disparate trajectories: fire balloons "receding, dwindling, solemnly / and steadily forsaking *us*" (*CP* 103, emphasis added). The motion is felt as a moving away from a (tipped) center. The orientation produces a sense of potential (unrealized) threat to the speaker from the sudden and "dangerous" "downdraft from a peak" (*CP* 103). The rising up of objects from other motions ("owls who nest there flying up / and up, their whirling black-and-white" visible "until they shrieked up out of sight") creates a structure that "prepares" for the surprise emergence of an even fiercer movement at the end of the poem, "weak mailed fist clenched ignorant against the sky" (*CP* 103–4). As is true of most of the other objects in the poem, we did not know previously of the existence of this creature who "speaks" in motions at the end.

Bishop began to use Calder's aesthetic as her own method of composition, even before she came to Brazil. With the title poem, "A Cold Spring," Bishop opened her second volume of poems in the "space" of one of the later Calder mobiles. Although there are moments in this poem when a small motor or spring generates movement, the atmosphere of the poem more often contains the gentler trajectories and sense of suspension characteristic of Calder's mature hanging mobiles from the 1940s. After hesitation and delay, elements rise freely and spontaneously out of other sets of relations, and the whole "constellation" is associated with pleasure and offers Sartre's sense of a "private celebration."[13] The characteristics of freshness and surprise are prominently allied with pleasure. The lyric speaker is situated within this constellation not just as observer but as one moved by the unequally weighted shifting elements.

"A Cold Spring" orients the lyric speaker within the curving, ascending, and descending, shifting relations of shapes and motions of the landscape. There is an amplitude and ease in the massing of large shapes ("your big and aimless hills" [*CP* 55]). Ease is associated with extent, with a curving line, with volume, but also with the leisurely pace of movement. The expanse and aimlessness of those shapes seem connected to the length of time that is leisurely passing in a state of "waiting" (the hesitating of trees, flowers, leaves, the length of time that the mother takes to eat the afterbirth). At times, Bishop composes by setting one motion against another of unequal weight or activity. The first stanza's long, aimless, seemingly passive drift erupts at the close in a little explosion of activity and initiative: "the calf got up promptly / and seemed inclined to feel gay" (*CP* 55). Two disparate objects are poised: "the after-birth, / a wretched flag," remains lying on the hillside, while the calf rises up and carries the "gay" movement that is ordinarily associated with a flag (*CP* 55).

Each element wavers between receiving motion and initiating it. These are elements that, as Sartre said, "are halfway between . . . servility. . . . and independence" (70). The mother cow does not so much give birth to the calf as have the birth happen to her. "The little leaves" hover between active and passive. Passively, they are waiting and must be impelled from inside. Actively, they are engaged in "carefully indicating their characteristics" (*CP* 55). Elements shift or swing from passivity to activity: "a calf was born" to "the calf got up promptly / and seemed inclined to feel gay" (*CP* 55). Green limbs on a hillside receive rather than cause the emergence of lilacs, "whitening" in their tops.

Bishop's close of that first stanza with the verb "inclined" captures the sense of a landscape inclining toward spring. This event in time has its correlative in the sense of physical "tipping" or incline (the calf born "on the side of one" of the big hills). As the atmosphere warms up ("The next day / was much warmer"), the sense of one element leaning on another or tipping into one another becomes energized; there is more infiltration and diffusion (*CP* 55). The shape of a form seems so "open" that it becomes a blur, "like movement." As in a Calder, the shapes are seen in their double identity between objecthood and movement. The "inclining" or drifting of elements from one arena into another includes the activity of the human mind as one element among others in the whole of the composition. Bishop inclines human metaphor-making so that it crosses over into the register of the natural. She humorously marks the drifting over as "like" a physical touch: the dogwood petals' ragged edges are "burned apparently, by a cigarette butt," as if the human activity of thought, its special kind of motion, could lean over and into nature (*CP* 55). These linguistic qualities (the crossing from description into metaphor, the mind and its words crossing into nature) are set inside a natural world that has the same qualities of trajectories crossing, passivity / activity, receiving, inclining, leaning toward certainty, speeding up. Human metaphor-making, which can vary from heavy-handed imposition to a softer, less obtrusive, figurative turn, becomes integrated as one of the many kinds of movement in nature.

As in a Calder mobile, the movement of elements begins "hesitatingly" and speeds up after one object or "line" has leaned into the other. Now, "deer practiced leaping over your fences" and "the infant oak-leaves swing through the sober oak" (*CP* 55). Calder's characteristics of liveliness, youthfulness, gaiety ("swinging through") appear. In this section of the poem, the mechanism of action resembles the little Calder mobiles with their springs, each piece acting on the other and sending it into complementary but different motion. "Song-sparrows were wound up for the summer"; their "spring" causes the cardinal to sing, and in motion re-layed to other elements, the cardinal wakes the landscape (*CP* 55). The pun on "spring" not only recalls the early Calder mobiles but humorously plays on the most traditional of poetic topoi, the complementary relations between the sea-sonal moment of the awakening landscape in spring and the feeling of movement, initiative, that, passively received from the interior by the mind and heart, prompts desire and action. Living creatures having been "woken" up and touched—set into motion by other motions—themselves set in motion human love. This love that rises up from the human soul is set in relation to other gentle movements, such as the "spray" that first appears optically (in the "cap" of the hills) and begins to move, drift, and fall, or fireflies that begin to rise from "thick grass." New objects arrive unexpectedly from a previously unseen periphery. A new moon arises in the midst of, around the corner of, in relation to, other objects. The emergence of a new ob-ject is not something that the frame in which the speaker stands had centered on until the object appears and creates a new center. So, as each new object appears, the place of the observer is reset. Subjectivity is pulled toward but also stands as counterweight to each new shape or object that emerges.

As each event occurs, the positioning of the speaker alters. The moon rising makes space expand in relation to the speaker; the bullfrogs deepen space, their heavy and low sounds setting a boundary at another distance, as do the fireflies when they appear.

> Now, from the thick grass, the fireflies
> Begin to rise:
> Up, then down, then up again:
> Lit on the ascending flight,
> Drifting simultaneously to the same height,
> —exactly like the bubbles in champagne.
> —Later on they rise much higher.
> And your shadowy pastures will be able to offer
> These particular glowing tributes
> Every evening now throughout the summer. (*CP* 56)

Without losing their own position, the stationary observers here are pulled out into that experience of depth where elements float. The celebratory mood arises gently as one element responding to the drifting of others. The passivity itself, the allowing oneself to be opened and moved, has also its counterweight of stability or location. The lyric speaker is "held" in a mobile container with disparate textures and movements, located among them, "re-arranged" as they coalesce and part, open, close, shift. The fireflies that "later on . . . rise much higher," tipping upward, after some delay, alter the relative positions of the (comparatively) heavy, stable speaker and the now "higher," lightly floating objects. The poem "A Cold Spring" feels like a giant "warm" Calder.[14]

Bishop took advantage of possibilities in her own linguistic medium and re-vised Calder's aesthetic while adapting it for the lyric. She expanded the materials that could be used, beyond even those deployed by a sculptor known for democ-ratizing the range of sculptural materials. Bishop's expansive range of materials and textures becomes prominent in a draft poem from the mid-1960s titled "the first color." Again Bishop places the lyric speaker among a set of shifting motions, "tipped" and suspended in the midst of the inclining, tilting landscape of the town of Ouro Prêto:

> the town unshadows   unshadows
>   church by church falling   church by church,
>   from th[ei]r sheer coco[o]ns
>   and ope[n]ing, shini[n]g, half-opening glisten
>
>   half-open moths
>   stuck sleeping to the hillg[r]een hill
>
>   the streets go down
>   the three or four red veins
>   the purity   pure pink
>
>   the first color see[n] is blue baby blue
>   Pity pity pity the
>   quaresma blossoms grieve and allig[a]tor pears
>   glazed green and rotten—purple—
>
>   cabbag[e] moths invade the gauze
>
>   St Iph[i]genia
>   in fresh blue and white

> her sweet black face with lowered eyes
> and silver

> holds her toy church tight and bright f[la]mes peep
>   the bright flames peep, and leap
> from the closed windows, in the dawn— (vc 68.3)

Here in the baroque movements of rising and falling, furling and unfurling, texture after texture is presented as opening out into one another. The town "unshadows" as if a robe or cloth has been pulled open or away. While the speaker is looking down onto the town from above, the churches appear to be both falling farther down ("church by church falling") while simultaneously "opening" up to reveal their "glistening." While "the streets go down," the lifting of the shadows and the glistening makes the town seem to float upward. Here, emotions emerge or rise up from the landscape as merely another kind of unfurling: the blossoms give rise to grief ("quaresma blossoms grieve") and unfurl a soft immense gentleness ("Pity pity pity"). The emotion seems to drift over and take up residence in the visual icon of the saint: the "sweet black face with lowered eyes" of the St. Iphigenia, whose hugeness emerges from contrast with another object (she "holds her toy church tight") and serves to magnify her tenderness. Surfaces open toward one another with different kinds of "touch" at the end of the poem as the reflection of the dawn light from the church windows now shifts from the mere "glistening" of the opening stanza and the gentler action of "opening" to the energetic mobility (they "peep, and leap") of "bright flames." In this fragment we have no speaker emerge as subject, yet the implied observer of this dawn is set amidst these shifting materials and objects, elements that have their own trajectories and whose surfaces can accommodate the leaning of one on another or the unfurling of one into the other. This action of unfurling in Calder's hanging mobiles had been emphasized by Mário Pedrosa in one of the major pieces of Brazilian criticism on Calder ("Tension" 132).

Although space does not permit an extensive discussion and although the poem also owes much to Bishop's response to the aesthetic of Kurt Schwitters, in "The Moose" one can sense the presence of Calder's "composing by motions" and Bishop's extension of Calder's method to the dynamics of materials touching, crossing, or opening toward one another. Each object is given its own independence and its own motion, granting each a measure of dignity and almost its own freedom:

> A pale flickering. Gone.
> The Tantramar marshes
> and the smell of salt hay.
> An iron bridge trembles
> and a loose plank rattles
> but doesn't give way.
>
> On the left, a red light
> Swims through the dark:
> A ship's port lantern.
> Two rubber boots show,
> Illuminated, solemn.
> A dog gives one bark. (CP 170–71)

Each object has its own stability or independent motion. Yet each is sensed in rela-tion to the observer moving in her own steadier but winding "line." Around the reticent observer, Bishop arranges drifting disparate forms, colors, weights, and motions. Human language is one of the elements that drifts, with its own trajec-tory, across the speaker's space and can infiltrate:

> The passengers lie back.
> Snores. Some long sighs.
> A dreamy divigation
> begins in the night,
> a gentle, auditory
> slow hallucination. (CP 171)

The moose has its own independent existence and its own distinctive motion:

> A moose has come out of
> the impenetrable wood
> stands there, looms rather,
> . . . .
> . . . approaches . . . sniffs. (CP 172)

It wanders across the trajectory of the moving bus.

Two early memories of Bishop's maternal grandparents' house at night—one published recently by Jonathan Ellis and the other published by Alice Quinn—

offer models in autobiographical prose that may partially explain Bishop's attraction to Calder's aesthetic. The poet's reconstruction of two early memories render a child suspended and sealed between layers of unlike materials. Disparate sizes and weights of objects and materials, with disparate trajectories, open, coalesce, and expand, shifting the boundaries of the field in relation to the speaker:

> The starlight [viewed through a skylight] made the silence of the house separated, there was silence, itself, and then sleep, as illustrated by an occasional snore from my grandfather—or the other noises I was waiting for. But on dark nights the sky and the silence and the house full of sleep merged all together. (qtd. in Ellis, *Art* 37)

> [In the parlor, with grandparents] I sat silent and made the wallpaper come off the wall. Small bouquets of red-gray roses, thin trellaces of golden wires, swayed, retreated and advanced, in space out from their background of wide white and faint silver stripes—up & down—Where a lot of wallpaper showed . . . the gilt and rose skimpy summer house advanced as far as the lamplit blur of Gammie's white hair. . . . [and upstairs in bed][.] That arbor, bower—summer house—I had not words for it—I didn't know where I'd go—where I'd be—anything—sealed between downstairs and upstairs dark, warm, smelling a little of dog, kerosene, geranium blooms. (*EAP* 213–14)

These passages situate the self in relation to both intimate and vast spaces, not by grounding the self but by suspending it in layers of materials composed of varying kinds of substances—sleep, silence, and the night sky; lamplight and wallpaper, the unfolding odor of geraniums held against an enveloping extensive darkness. To grasp the primary feeling of subjectivity here, one must note that the "I" hangs suspended, enveloped, and almost tilting as different kinds of materials and shapes appear to sway forward, emerge into distinctness and subside, touch each other along long and shifting edges. In the memoir fragments, the child takes up a home within the tilting, swaying in and out, opening and closing, and drifting materials of the interior and exterior of room, home, yard, and world. In such scenes, we can sense the countermemory of the experiences that Quinn notes Bishop repeatedly imagined as a scenario of "falling into loneliness."[15] The usual scholarly rehearsal of primal psychological moments from Bishop's early childhood leans heavily on moments of dropping into a dangerous depth—the floating on the swan boat, from which the swan emerges to bite the mother's hand, the young child standing precariously on the "crust" of snow, as her mother "fell through it" and disappeared back into the house to retrieve the snowshoes (*EAP* 155–57). These moments' resonance with "the sensation of falling off / the round, turning world / into cold, blue-black space" that appears many years later in "In the Waiting Room" indicate that depth was associated with a fall into the immensity of loss and disconnection. David Kalstone first suggested the means by which writing could serve to prevent such a fall. Focusing on the prose memoir "In the Village," Kalstone worked out a compelling explanation for the relationship between the radiant surface of objects in Bishop's work and the psychological depth of her early loss of connection to her mother, explaining that the objects become radiant because they serve as distractions holding off the child's grief (220).[16] Suspended and arrayed around the child, the objects tentatively, precariously hold the child from collapsing into herself, into knowledge of sorrow and into a state of being overwhelmed by sorrow. The child, with the intensity of her attentiveness, holds onto the objects like life rafts; and, for Kalstone, the speaker of the poetry likewise arrays objects in balanced arrangements around herself. In his description, we can sense the foundation of her attraction to the orientation of the subject in the work of Alexander Calder. In the memoir fragments quoted above, we see her revision of Calder's aesthetic to include the arrangement of shifting, swaying, ascending and descending, unfurling, and coalescing disparate materials. Although Bishop used her mature aesthetics to compose these early memories, we seem to have access here to what one could call aesthetic ur-memories, ones that often structure Bishop's positioning of the lyric speaker in both published and unpublished poems from the mid-1940s onward.

NOTES

1. Bishop to Kit and Ilse Barker, July 28, 1968, Barker Correspondence, C0270, Manuscripts Division, Department of Rare Books and Special Collections, Princeton University Library.

2. Bishop to Ilse Barker, September 30, 1959, Barker Correspondence. Bishop mistakenly gives the date of the exhibition as 1931 to Stevenson and 1932 to Barker.

3. Bishop to Anne Stevenson, March 6, 1964, Washington University Libraries.

4. Bishop mentions going to the Buchholz Gallery (*OA* 96–97).

5. Lota also owned three of Calder's mobiles (March 12, 1960, Barker Correspondence). Bishop came to know Alexander Calder personally when he visited the house at Samambaia in 1959.

6. The watercolor is reproduced in Benton (65). The mobile represented in the painting is a composite of several mobiles and does not accurately represent any actual Calder work (conversation with S. C. Rower, Calder Foundation, 2008).

7. One can see Bishop thematizing that remark in the opening stanza of "Pleasure Seas" (*CP* 195).

8. Midcentury criticism linked Klee to Calder, and they were exhibited together in two exhibits in 1944. For Klee's influence on Calder, see Turner 229.

9. Beginning as catalogue copy for a 1946 show at the Louis Carré Gallery in Paris, the brief commentary on Calder by Sartre was widely translated and reproduced.

10. Buffet-Picabia's article was originally published in the same issue of *Cahiers d'Art* (1945–46) that extensively covered the work of Paul Klee about which Margaret Miller expressed enthusiasm (Registrar Exhibition files, Exhibition #385, Museum of Modern Art, New York), so it is likely that Bishop saw this article.

11. Thomas Travisano discusses midcentury poets' responses to this sense of the tiny scale of the individual (*Midcentury* 175–76).

12. Drafts of the poem can be found in *EAP* (128–29) and VC 66.5. The titles of Calder's works are sometimes used for several works. Bishop's poem seems closest to either 49.MO.019 (A07525), which was labeled *Gypsophilia* at a Buchholz exhibit in 1949, or 50.MO.003 (A00529), which was sold by Buchholz in 1950, and so probably was on display in the gallery. A reproduction of the latter mobile also appeared in the reissue of Sweeney's catalogue *Alexander Calder* (MoMA, 1951).

13. In a notebook that seems more often marked by the inability to get going and by despair, passages from which the poem arises have a distinct timbre of pleasure and surprise (VC 77.4, 17, 19).

14. In "The Mountain," originally part of "A Cold Spring" but deleted in the *Collected Poems*, Bishop experimented with the appearance and ascension of objects drifting upward and downward across an inanimate subject, each event unwilled by that subject (*CP* 197–98).

15. See notes by Alice Quinn (*EAP* 287). This fragment perhaps functions as an antidote to the more frightening complex of images—crib, wallpaper, fire, lines—traced by Goldensohn (*Elizabeth Bishop* 50–51). See Zimmerman for a more general discussion of Bishop and containment.

16. See also Keller 117–18; and Page 199.

"A World of Books Gone Flat"

Elizabeth Bishop's Visits to St. Elizabeths

FRANCESCO ROGNONI

"I've seen Pound some more and won his heart by telling him that I was a collateral descendent of Aaron Burr, whose only mistake was [in Pound's words] not having shot Hamilton twenty years earlier," Robert Lowell writes Elizabeth Bishop on November 20, 1947. And he goes on: "He remembers your work before the war as having more 'address' [again Pound's word, whatever it means] than Mary Barnard and some New Directions' woman whose name he can't recall" (*WIA* 15).

In the tenure of his poetry consultantship at the Library of Congress, Robert Lowell would quite certainly "win" Pound's heart, while conversely, his own heart was "won" by the older poet and inmate of St. Elizabeths mental hospital. Lowell would strongly support Pound's *Pisan Cantos* during the controversy surrounding the assignation of the first Bollingen Prize in 1949. It was also very typical of Lowell, and perhaps it went beyond the poetry consultant's "unwritten duty" to pay regular visits to Pound, to invite his friends and fellow poets to share in his growing affection for the author of the *Cantos.* And it was also typical for him to promote their verse with the older poet, perhaps fostering the kind of list making and ranking of poets—the game of who's best, who's second-best, and so on—for which he was so competitively keen.

Lowell and Bishop's friendship—recently brought into sharper focus by the publication of *Words in Air,* their complete correspondence—was soon to develop into what is perhaps the most complex and significant literary relationship of the second half of the twentieth century. It had begun only a few months before, with the exchange of some letters and two meetings. The second of these meetings, in Washington, took place on the very weekend (October 14–17, 1947) that Lowell had arranged for William Carlos Williams to visit Pound. On that occasion Bishop had lunch with Lowell and Williams, but did not follow a very nervous Williams in the taxi to St. Elizabeths; nor did Lowell, who spent the afternoon with Bishop in the National Gallery, gallantly carrying her shoes for her when she changed into a pair of flat ones (*WIA* 810).

Poised between compassion and revulsion, amusement and unease, Bishop's memories of visiting Pound, scattered throughout her letters and prose, and shaped into her nursery-rhyme poem "Visits to St. Elizabeths," are perhaps the most complex example of what may almost amount to a midcentury literary subgenre of "resolution and guarded independence." This would include at least Lowell's own reminiscences of and two sonnets on Pound, Berryman's striking description of his November 3, 1948, visit to St. Elizabeths[1] and his uncollected poem "The Cage" (*Poetry* 1950), Williams Carlos Williams's quite unfriendly "To My Friend Ezra Pound" (in his *Pictures from Brueghel*), and Louis Zukofsky's cryptic third poem in the sequence *Song of Degrees* (1950); but also, among many others, H. D.'s memoir of Pound, *End to Torment* (written in 1958 but published only in 1979), David Rattay's article "Weekend with Ezra Pound" (1957), and the pages on Pound in Mary Barnard's, Diane Di Prima's, and Al Alvarez's respective autobiographies, *Assault on Mount Helicon* (1984), *Recollections of My Life as a Woman* (1988), and *Where Did It All Go Right?* (1999).

Bishop's first visit to Pound would take place in May 1948, when she stopped by the capital on her way back from Key West to New York. A few weeks before, perhaps in preparation for this encounter, she was reading, as she writes to Lowell on April 8, "Pound's collected poems, 1926. I just noticed they are dedicated to Miss Moore's mother. It's really hard to see how important a lot of them were, now—" (*WIA* 32). This is a surprising aside, which may be unconsciously addressed less to Pound than to Marianne Moore, her poetic mentor, whose authority over her was now on the wane: since, of course, Pound's *Personae* is not dedicated to Marianne Moore's mother (as Bishop seems to believe), but to the homonymous but unrelated "Mary Moore of Trenton, if she wants it" (as Pound's dedication reads in both the 1909 and 1926 editions of that book).

No certain record is left of Bishop and Lowell visiting Pound together. "I don't know whether it was the time I went to see him with you or later," Bishop would write on May 20, 1955—when Pound gave an imitation "of Yeats' singing, to show how tone-deaf he was. The imitation was so strange & bad, too, that I decided they were *both* tone-deaf" (*WIA* 182). The comic side of this first visit (if indeed it is the same visit) goes unmentioned in the brief acknowledgment of it in her letter of May 18, 1948—"And thank you for taking me to see Pound. I am really endlessly grateful for that experience" (*WIA* 80)—a comment uncharacteristically hyperbolical in its curtness: as if she were mostly thankful that the "experience" was past and done, never to be repeated. Ironically, Bishop's own one-year appointment as poetry consultant from September 1949 would make visiting St. Elizabeths an almost unavoidable matter of fact.

In June 1949, Pound was visited by his old friend Marianne Moore, who is likely to have brought him advance notice of Bishop's visit. In March and again in October, he was also visited by Mary Barnard, one of the two women poets of weaker "address" Pound had mentioned to Lowell. In the 1930s, Pound had urged upon Barnard the discipline of translation and the composition of Sapphics (indeed, though she lived to be ninety-two and publish a respectable amount of original poetry, Mary Barnard is now mostly remembered for her 1959, often reprinted translation of Sappho). During her October visit, Pound suggested (he "ordered me," Barnard would write in her memoir, 268) that she go see Moore in Brooklyn, but no intimate spark was struck between the two women.

> To get along with Miss Moore [Barnard wrote to Pound on November 11, 1949] I think you have to be a man (she doesn't expect a man to be a lady in her mother's sense of the word) or if you are female, you have to be Elizabeth Bishop, who is a whiz at mathematics, plays the clavichord, and takes a *serious* interest in religion — that's the way she described E. B. to me, with real warmth in her voice. (She didn't use the word "whiz" however.)[2]

This is rather a portrait of Bishop as Bishop wanted to appear to Marianne Moore, and — perhaps even more — as Moore wanted to see her: with that "*serious* [underlined] interest in religion" (as opposed, perhaps, to Barnard's own studies in pagan mythology) that Bishop herself would quite certainly deny. (Incidentally, it is worth remarking that, as Bishop acknowledged, her interest in the clavichord had been fostered by Pound's writings on ancient music.) Indeed, Barnard's visit to Moore appears to have been a real trial (almost like Bishop's to Pound). Nor could anyone blame Pound for forgetting that, almost fifteen years before, Marianne Moore had written to him that "[Bishop's] and T. C. Wilson's are the best letters from young people that I have ever seen. If I had only letters to go by, I would take a long leap away from Miss Barnard."[3] In the same letter of November 11, 1949, Barnard goes on: "Is Elizabeth Bishop a perfect lady? I'm just curious. She seems to have one thing in common with M. M., anyhow. It's just as hard to meet her."

Whether Pound ever replied to Barnard to satisfy her piqued curiosity, we do not know. By the time Barnard's letter was written, Bishop must have begun her reluctantly regular visits to St. Elizabeths, either out of courtesy, to accompany other visitors, or to take Pound books from the Library of Congress. Recorded in her journal and letters (a charming anecdote is encapsulated in her memoir of Marianne Moore), these visits betray mostly annoyance and unease, together with typical self-irony, amusement, and perhaps a shade of regret for her own lack of charity: as in that journal entry where she diagnoses as "the perfect slip" the fact that, quite intentionally forgetting the visiting schedule, she had accompanied Weldon Kees to see Pound only a half hour before closing time.

In a March 18, 1950, letter to Norris Gerry, Weldon Kees wrote of his visit to Pound that he "found the experience somewhat inhuman, rather like visiting a museum, but certainly not an experience to have missed." He goes on, "[Pound] 'receives' at the end of a corridor in the hospital, which is a pretty gloomy affair, with catatonics and dementia praecox cases slithering about; but he certainly keeps up a spirit. Very lively and brisk, and his eyes go through like knives. . . . (Pound calls [Elizabeth Bishop] 'Liz Bish,' which she doesn't care for; nor does she care much for Pound, regarding him as a pretty dangerous character, through his influence— particularly the anti-Semitism—on the young)" (qtd. in Millier 221). And William Carlos Williams, for whom "the disturbed mind ha[d] always been a territory from which [he] shrunk instinctively as before the unknown," adds to the Gothic gloom of the hospital atmosphere when he tells how, while "taking a short cut to the exit" after a later visit to Pound, a "regularly spaced scream coming from somewhere in the building [he] was passing caught [his] ear . . . [and he] saw a figure from which [he] could not remove his eyes . . . [a] man, naked, full-on and immobile, his arms up as though climbing a wall, plastered against one of the high windows of the old building like a great sea slug against the inside of a glass aquarium, his belly as though stuck to the glass that looked dull and splattered from the bad weather" (Williams, *Autobiography* 335, 343).

In a different, much lighter vein is what is perhaps the longest and most detailed (though perhaps not entirely reliable) account of Bishop's visits to St. Elizabeths. I find it in Eustace Mullins's memoir, *This Difficult Individual: Ezra Pound* (1961), a book well known by Pound students, but—to the best of my knowledge—ignored by Bishop scholars. A fairly unsavory political character, Mullins (1923–2010) went to Washington as an aficionado of Pound, his disciple and self-appointed "butler" for some three or four years in the early 1950s. In his memoir, he tells us, with legitimate pride, how he managed "to bestow an additional privilege upon Ezra Pound while he was in the hospital—that is the privilege of drinking wine." He explains that, although

the rules at St. Elizabeths, as at all mental institutions, strictly forbid giving any alcoholic beverage to a patient[,] I thought this was an uncivilized situation, and on my third or fourth visit to Pound, I brought him a bottle of white Graves, 1945. It was the first wine he had been offered since his arrest almost five years before, as none of his other visitors had wished to defy the regulations. He insisted on uncorking the bottle himself (this was in the gloom of a ward afternoon), and after the corkscrew had done its work, he jerked it out with a tremendous "Pop!" while Dorothy Pound and I looked on aghast. We were sure that the noise would summon an attendant, but none appeared. . . . We had nothing to drink from but little paper cups, which did not interfere materially with the flavor. After several quaffs, Ezra became quite mellow. (298)

Pound was never a hard drinker, and "generally, there was but one bottle of twelve per cent wine for three or four of us, which was consumed over a period of three hours. . . . It is pleasant to think that some of the later *Cantos* were penned in the afterglow of a few paper cups of Graves." And Mullins continues telling how, in order to celebrate the publication of the *Classical Anthology Defined by Confucius*, the Australian poet William Fleming and his wife "decided to risk a libation," but "took the precaution of decanting the wine into a thermos bottle before leaving home so that the guards would suppose they were bringing their usual tea; but since half the fun was to uncork the bottle on the premises, it was not such an exciting afternoon. It is the only time I can recall having drunk wine from a thermos bottle" (298–99). It is, very aptly, in the midst of these convivial reminiscences that Bishop walks into Mullins's book:

It was early in 1950 that I made the acquaintance of Elizabeth Bishop, who was then Consultant in Poetry at the Library of Congress. This post is held for one-year periods by various poets who are in good standing with the current administration. No revolutionaries need apply.

Elizabeth was a lady, from the Back Bay of Boston. There was a fortune somewhere in the background (Eaton paper or something of that order), and she dressed with excellent taste. She had a mellifluous voice, and it was always a delight to hear her read her poetry. Some of these readings are now available on records. Also, she kept an excellent sherry on hand at the Library, the only Consultant who has shown such consideration for visitors.

Elizabeth wished to go out and see Ezra, but she needed moral support. At any rate, she would never go out unless I accompanied her. I mentioned the wine problem, but did not enlarge upon the attitude of the hospital authorities. Whenever Elizabeth went out with me, she brought not one but two bottles. Furthermore, these were more costly than those I had been able to provide. Usually she brought one

German and one French variety, a good Moselle or a Liebfraumilch, and perhaps an Haut Sauterne.

Despite the reinforcement of the wine, Elizabeth was never comfortable in Ezra's presence. I think that she looked upon him as a sort of naughty old grandfather whose habits are somewhat questionable, but who, after all, is one's ancestor. She insisted that the way in which he twisted the ends of his beard gave him a quite diabolical appearance. One afternoon, when the conversation lagged, Elizabeth volunteered the information that she was studying German. Ezra looked up and said, "Humph! That won't be much help to you!" The inference was that Elizabeth was beyond any sort of assistance, and she sank into a glum silence. (299)

Nothing in this recollection is entirely new, and most of it is perhaps more revealing of the author than of either Bishop or Pound. Mullins may be the only person who ever claimed that Bishop had "a mellifluous voice" (notice that the wines she brings to Pound are very "mellifluous," too!), and that "it was always a delight to hear her read her poetry." Obviously, he never bothered to refresh his memory by listening to her notoriously flat recordings! It is more significant that he stresses so strongly her ladylike appearance, assuming that she had "a fortune somewhere in the background." Possibly Bishop and Mullins are being snobbish to each other here, but it might have been Bishop's extreme unease in Washington, and particularly at St. Elizabeths, that made her heighten her natural aura of correctness (remember Mary Barnard: "Is Elizabeth Bishop a perfect lady?"), as if to make clear that she *belonged* somewhere else, that—if she had only wanted it—she could have *stayed at home* (*"wherever that may be!"*).

However, in spite of its condescension and its air of unreliability, Mullins's portrait of Bishop is charming, in part because of its almost lighthearted picture of her drinking habits, which strikes one almost as refreshing after so much recent insistence on her alcoholism.[4] Mullins's claim that Bishop "needed moral support" and "would never go out unless I accompanied her" finds confirmation in Bishop's own account, in an August 1950 letter to Lowell, of how "Pound is very forgiving about my not coming oftener, although he sees right through me—tells everyone how I always 'have to bring someone else along,' etc." (*WIA* 105).

Indeed, Bishop's response to Pound may be the ultimate example of her more general attitude toward life, reality, or whatever one wants to call the ultimate subject of any artist. "Surely she is a poet of Terror,"[5] Mary McCarthy would later say of her former Vassar school friend (perhaps recalling Trilling's famous 1959 speech on Frost)—a straightforward statement that would much impress Lowell, surprising him with its abrupt insight in spite of his twenty-year-long friendship with Bishop.[6] Robert Duncan, one of those poets "in the Pound tradition" (as she called them) that Bishop met, with some suspicion, on the West Coast in the late 1960s, remembers her liveliness: "She was the sort of person who had the twinkle of humor always in her eyes and [loved] an amusing situation. Even telling about her visits in St. Elizabeths, she was amused where lots of other people were outraged" (Fountain and Brazeau 248). Nothing better than "amusement" would keep Terror at bay. Responding to one of Lowell's most vivid vignettes of life in St. Elizabeths, she acknowledges that "one has to admire Pound's stoic cheerfulness" (September 11, 1948), but I doubt she would see that as an effective compensation for the "awfulness" of the situation. "Awful but cheerful"—the famous last line of her birthday poem "The Bight," that Bishop would ask to have engraved on her tombstone—would hardly describe the ambience of Pound's hospitalization: "cheerful but awful," perhaps.

Bishop would always claim to admire "Pound's courage" (MacMahon 28), but she never developed any affection for him. This may be due to the fact that Pound's poetic project and epic scope (whose "diffuseness" she found "exhausting") (PPL 862) and his pedagogical program were as alien to her as they were attractive to Lowell—who, on the contrary, often seemed to shape his career on Pound's (for example, when he saw his own Imitations "as a complement to Life Studies, sort of like Pound's Mauberley and Propertius,"[7] or in the Cantos-like inclusiveness of History) and, at least once, singled him out (with Hardy) as his favorite modern poet: "Because of the heartbreak."[8] But, apart from their very different poetics, the actual circumstances of Bishop's acquaintance with Pound may have played an even larger role in her uneasiness toward him. Bishop never saw her mother during her lifelong confinement in a Nova Scotian mental institution, though she must have "visited" her frequently in her imagination, and, possibly, she had never actually walked in a mental hospital before she entered St. Elizabeths. The fact of madness—and even if Pound's "madness" had much "method" in it, there were plenty of St. Elizabeths inmates who were mad enough and could not be avoided—was always a taboo with her. She always managed to be safely away when Lowell's manic attacks would reach their peak, while her mother's history of mental instability, depicted in a distanced way in the magical prose of "In the Village," is conspicuously absent from her poetry, until it is perhaps gently and very indirectly alluded to in the very late poem "The Moose" ("and / finally the family had / to put him away" [PPL 161]).

Having published, in 1953, a well-received translation of the Pisan Cantos, the first in any language (the effort was praised by Montale in the Corriere della sera),[9] the young Italian poet and scholar Alfredo Rizzardi set out to edit an issue of the Genoa journal *Nuova Corrente* entirely devoted to Pound, and wrote letters asking for contributions from a number of prominent American authors and critics (including Robert Fitzgerald, Hugh Kenner, Leslie Fiedler, and others).

It is quite surprising that Bishop so casually agreed to write an essay—not a poem—for Rizzardi: in a 1976 interview, she would remember: "I've been asked to write a piece of prose about Ezra Pound and I tried and tried and I couldn't" (MacMahon 58). Lowell twice said he felt *"naked* without [his] line-ends,"[10] and one would guess Elizabeth Bishop felt the same. Prose writing may require more "exposure," and clearly Bishop would not want to be exposed any longer to Pound's piercing gaze ("he sees right through me") (*WIA* 105), all the more so in the tranquillity of her first Brazilian years. Thus it was a poem, the first version of her "Visits to St. Elizabeths," that Bishop produced for Rizzardi's Pound issue of *Nuova Corrente.*

Similarly, Bishop's poetic tribute to Marianne Moore, "Invitation to Miss Marianne Moore," which she composed in 1948 for a special Moore edition of the *Quarterly Review of Literature,* took much less time to write than her prose memoir, "Efforts of Affection." The case of this poem comes in handy since it is, with "Visits to St. Elizabeths," the only other Bishop poem recognizably modelled on a previous text (Pablo Neruda's "Alberto Rojas Jimenez vienes volando"): almost as if, while writing to another poet—thus, somehow, in a more public mode than her voice was attuned to—Bishop needed an accepted pattern to rely on, a pre-text. ("North Haven," her poem in memory of Robert Lowell, could perhaps be seen in similar terms, being written in the tradition of the English elegy, yet it lacks the pre-set pattern Bishop followed in her poems about Moore and Pound.)

The Pound poem is modelled on "The House that Jack Built," "a nursery accumulative tale of great antiquity," the *Oxford Companion to English Literature* informs us, "possibly based on an old Hebrew original, a hymn in Sepher Haggadah" (5th ed., 1985). And if Bishop knew of its likely origins, as I do not think she did (one has to be a bookish foreign scholar to look up such a rhyme in the *Oxford Companion*!), this would add an ironic twist to her critique of Pound's anti-Semitism. But if it seems improbable that this irony was intentional, evidence can be found that she was deliberately exploiting the intricacy of the nursery rhyme almost as a parody, or infantile regression, of Pound's early metrical experiments. One can point to a letter written to Marianne Moore on September 10, 1938: "My friend Frani Blough brought me a whole collection of little books of Provençal poetry. I had never read any except the quotations in Pound's essay, and I have been reading it a great deal, and also 'Mother Goose,' which I brought along too. Between Pierre Vidal and

'The House That Jack Built,' I have enclosed some rhyme schemes that I hope will impress you—or *amaze,* anyway" (*OA* 78).

There is no way to ascertain when Bishop wrote "Visits," but the poem is very unlikely to have already been completed by 1951, as has recently been claimed.[11] My own guess is that the poem—of which, to the best of my knowledge, no mention is made in Bishop's published or unpublished correspondence before the Rizzardi-sponsored publication—was either written very quickly, after she had given up on the prose essay, or perhaps sketched before Rizzardi's request sometime in 1954 and then dressed up for the occasion. The self-generating form seems to require that the poem was written in a hurry, almost unthinkingly: almost in the same way in which Bishop must have walked the long and noisy corridor to Pound's St. Elizabeths quarters.

I know of only one surviving manuscript of the poem at Vassar College,[12] where the title is simply "St. Elizabeth's [*sic*] (1950)," a draft quite revealing in its few doubts and corrections. It appears that at first Bishop was attempting to vary the pattern of her model, almost writing against the grain of the nursery-rhyme scheme. Surprisingly, she first wrote: "This is the man / who lies" etc.; and she had some trouble with the crucial line, "This is a world of books gone flat." This first read: "The world of letters is stale and flat" (referring, perhaps, not only to "literature" in general, but also to Pound's hectic correspondence; during his stay at St. Elizabeths he sent at least one thousand letters a year). In an intermediate state, the line became, "The world of books is cold and flat," and it regained the nursery-rhyme refrain—where each stanza begins with the demonstrative "This"—only in the typed version of the manuscript, which corresponds exactly to the *Nuova Corrente* text. Again, it is almost as if Bishop had wanted to get free from the "cage" of the "House that Jack Built" and then thought better of it: that the repetitive form was not so much a cage as a protection, a shelter, and could be trusted as such to the end.

As Bishop explained to Anne Stevenson: "The characters [of the poem] are based on the other inmates of the St. Elizabeth's. . . . During the day Pound was in the open ward, and so one's visits to him were often interrupted. One boy used to show us his watch, another patted the floor, etc.—but naturally it is a mixture of fact and fancy" (*PPL* 853). In place of the pastoral ambience of the "House That Jack Built," the "house of Bedlam" substitutes a strangely maritime décor: a sea made of boards, where the winds blow against closed walls, the voyage is stalled and the crew go nuts. And the sequence of adjectives for the character of the "sailor"—"batty," "silent," "staring," "crazy"—is almost as significant and perhaps complementary to the sequence for Pound: the poet of the uncompleted *Cantos,* which opened with the full-sailed voyage of a new and ancient Odysseus (quite appropriately, this poem of restless paralysis will come last in *Questions of Travel*).

Lines that seemed to have proven problematic are, in the final stanzas, the ones devoted to the Jew's dance. The suggestion could be one of a Yeatsian "tragic joy" if it weren't for the nursery-rhyme rhythms that undercut the tragic and evoke a much more hysterical and spectral image. Both in the eleventh stanza, with its allusion to the Red Sea that opens up before the Children of Israel, and in the twelfth and last, where the biblical prodigy seems suddenly forgotten, the manuscript has several blank spaces and dangling lines, marked only by possible rhyme words. The Jew, who was dancing "joyfully," is now dancing "carefully" (but in the manuscript the word, which is quite hard to read, may be "brilliantly"); he is "walking the plank," like a victim put to death (in jest?) by an incongruous crew of pirates (as Bishop explained to Rizzardi).[13] And just what are they doing, the pirates, in this Bedlamic poem? One wonders whether the Disney version of *Peter Pan*, which came out just around that time, in 1953, and has been keeping children in suspense ever since over the fate of Wendy on the trembling plank, might not have made an impression on Bishop as well. It is almost as if Ezra Pound, self-styled Ulysses in the opening *Canto*, were downgraded to Captain Hook: a painful, deeply distressing regression, from the epic "poem containing history" (in Pound's famous definition) to Disney cartoon.

But the most interesting textual uncertainty comes at the very end of the poem, where—after calling Pound "tragic," "talkative," "honored," "old and brave," "cranky," "cruel," "busy," "tedious"—the double qualifier, "the poet, the man" and "the tragic man" (as in the first occurrence) compete for the climax of the final stanza, until she hastily made up her mind in favor of the latter. Thus the poem ends "of the tragic man / that lies in the house of Bedlam."[14]

One may speculate that Bishop decided only in the nick of time and, perhaps pressed by Rizzardi, sent a version of the poem that was still unsatisfactory and on which she would work again before publishing the poem in *Partisan Review* some six months later. Here, Pound at the end is not called again "the tragic man" as in the *Nuova Corrente* text, but, more poignantly, "the wretched man." Perhaps significantly, when asking Lowell if he had read her "Pound poem" (in an earlier letter, she had typically dismissed it as "a kind of poem, not much"), she mentions only the *Partisan Review* version (*WIA* 232).

Candice MacMahon's usually very accurate bibliography is slightly incorrect in the case of "Visits to St. Elizabeths," specifying that *Nuova Corrente* published the Italian version with facing original text, but listing it only among the "Translations" and not also in the "Contributions to Periodicals," where it would more rightly belong, and this may account for the fact that nobody has commented on the different texts.

The one exception is Randall Jarrell, who must have read both versions of the poem, since in a letter penned around April 7, 1957 (not February, as indicated in both the first and the expanded reprint editions of Jarrell's *Letters*),[15] he congratulated Bishop for the change she had made at the end of the *Partisan Review* text: "I like the Pound poem; it gets all the ways one feels about him and the poor contradictory awful and nice ways he is, and it's more varied and specifically live, than I'd have thought it possible for a House-that-Jack-built poem. Changing it to *wretched* at the end certainly is right" (419).

Bishop and Jarrell had just met in New York, their first meeting in almost six years, and Bishop may have pointed out the variant in conversation; but it is also very possible that Jarrell noticed it by himself, since around the same word, *wretched,* he had built one of the best poems of his middle period, "Seele im Raum" (1951). The change from *tragic* to *wretched* shifts the whole weight of the poem.[16] In *Nuova Corrente* the poem came full circle to where it began, at the heroic but almost inhuman purity of "tragedy," while now Pound's fall has less of a classical ring; it is less "literary" (remember that "This is a world of books gone flat"!), more human and painful. One cannot help thinking of F. R. Leavis's 1951 "Scrutiny" article-review of Pound's letters, reprinted in *Partisan Review* (where Bishop read it), which begins in this way: "One would say that the volume of *Letters,* in sum, made *tragic* reading, if only the disaster it records weren't accompanied by so much that is brutally without dignity, and where it is comic, often odious too. The disaster, in fact, was a long degeneration, and is *tragic* only in that there had been something so admirable and heroic about the hero."[17]

This, of course, is not offered as a source. But it may be a significant analogue, all the more so because Bishop herself puts us on its trail in her long and leisurely letter to Lowell of November 26, 1951, where she offhandedly remarks: "I thought the Leavis piece on Pound was excellent, but probably you won't" (*WIA* 129–30).

Lowell did not pick up on this slight provocation, which sets the tone for whenever the subject of Pound is touched upon in the Bishop-Lowell correspondence: Lowell always forthcoming, affectionate, sometimes exasperated but ultimately enthralled by the battered vitality and humorous resilience of the older poet; Bishop respectful, politely compassionate, occasionally amused, yet ready to undercut Lowell's generous enthusiasms. Sometimes she does so, even at the risk of sounding too rigid or irrelevant; as in a frankly far-fetched comparison with the life of Chekhov, to which "how petty Pound appears, how horribly 'flawed,' as you say—and almost completely lacking in natural human feelings": a verdict unusually without appeal, with which Lowell perhaps only chivalrously seems to go along (*WIA* 495, 500).

While Lowell kept corresponding with Pound (and Dorothy and Omar) and went to see him whenever he got the chance, whether in Washington, in Italy, or in New York, Bishop never saw him again after her 1950 visits to St. Elizabeths. She could have dropped in during September 1957, when she passed by Washington on her way to seeing Marjorie Stevens in Key West, but—as she wrote to Ilse Barker on January 6, 1958—"[I] couldn't bear to somehow. Well, I think I've expressed my mixed emotions about him in the poem."[18]

A few months later, when Pound was finally released from his confinement, Lowell's jolly reaction sounds like a spontaneous act of the sympathetic imagination: "Pound is out. Going to a Chinese restaurant and using a telephone for the first time in 13 years, he told his daughter-in-law 'the ancestral voice is once more on the air.' A joke, I think, not the beginning of a Jeremiad" (*WIA* 258). It is almost as if Lowell himself hadn't tasted Chinese food or heard disembodied voices in years. Bishop, on the other hand, seems capable only of what one may call, with an oxymoron, "detached sympathy." She is truly annoyed by Frost's self-serving public statements ("the Bad Grey Poet. I read some remarks of his about Pound—just what the public wants to hear, I'm afraid") (*WIA* 320), but she is also unsure whether her own relief at Pound's regained freedom may sound convincing, even to herself: all the more so because, right after his release, the rumor was spread that Pound might go to Brazil, where—as Bishop phrased it in a worried letter to Lowell of May 8, 1958—"There [were] too many crack-pots . . . already" (*WIA* 259).

It is very possible that Pound and Dorothy read Bishop's "Visits to St. Elizabeths," probably in *Nuova Corrente;* they may well have disliked it, but no reaction is extant. The poem was immediately a favorite of Lowell's. "I've read it aloud to people several times. Just as with the 'Prodigal' and 'Roosters,' you are very womanly and wise," he wrote on April 29, 1957, when he hadn't yet read "The Armadillo"—a poem that he later often paired with "Visits to St. Elizabeths"; one "of your peculiar triumphs," "overwhelming [when] decently read aloud" (*WIA* 249, 367, 543, 606). In his letter to Bishop of October 28, 1965, where he goes over his favorite poems in the freshly published *Questions of Travel*, he leaves "Visits to St. Elizabeths" for last, perhaps not only because it does come last in the book, but also because, in this way, its singular achievement is made one with the achievement of the whole collection. In Lowell's parenthetic reference to the old poet's birthday, it is almost as if Bishop's poem were a kind of prescient homage presented to a supposedly recovered Pound: "By the way, your rhythm and riming are extraordinary, and of course unobtrusive—and then Ezra is marvelous, you get bits of your old monument in it, nicely, and the whole is a success against every impossibility. By the way, I am talking on the educational TV with Marianne Moore about Pound for his 80th birthday. He seems to be completely sane now" (*WIA* 591).

Strangely enough, apart from his letters, Lowell did not write of his visiting Pound in St. Elizabeths until the late 1960s, recording his visits in two sonnets of *Notebook,* revised in *History:* "Cicero, the Sacrificial Killing" and "Ezra Pound" (and in a 1972 *New York Review of Books* memoir of John Berryman, whom he had taken to the Washington mental hospital, where Berryman, completely at ease, "saw nothing nutty about Pound, or perhaps it was the opposite") (Lowell, *Prose* 113). The fact is that, by the 1950s, Lowell had poems of "his own Bedlams" to write, no doubt influenced by the lesson of the *Cantos,* whether in the depiction and staging of characters, or through some elliptical allusions to Dante (as in the late poems "Home" and "Shadow"). Bishop's nursery-rhyme rhythms may do for the singular poem of a breezy, uncomfortable visitor, but not for the "life studies" of a poet who was all too often "visited" in turn, as an inmate of mental institutions. In fact, it may well be that the only rhymed couplet, at the end of the first stanza of "Waking in the Blue"—"as though a harpoon were sparring for the kill. / (This is the house for the 'mentally ill')" (*CP* 183)—is a conscious short-circuiting of Lowell's early grand mode (e.g., "The Quaker Graveyard in Nantucket") via Bishop's impersonal nursery rhyming, since neither style is serviceable as a sustained feature of Lowell's new and highly personal subject: the diminished day-by-day life in the asylum.

Dismissive at the beginning, Bishop, too, grew to like her Pound poem, which "expressed my feeling about him fairly well, I think" (*PPL* 345). She was clearly pleased when, in 1963, a young Ned Rorem set it to music, and the elderly soprano Jannie Tourel sang it at Carnegie Hall (a recital Bishop could not attend), but she was unconvinced by Cocteau's drawing for the cover of the music. "It must be one of his very last drawings," she wrote to Lowell on receiving the photostat: "The usual Cocteau thing, but a weird wreath of names around it: Ned Rorem, Ezra P, E. B., and Cocteau—(the only one I really like is E. B.)" (*WIA* 512). Occasionally she read the Pound poem in public and made at least one recording of it.

But one can be quite sure that "Visits to St. Elizabeths" would not have been the poem she would have chosen to read aloud, had she decided to attend the National Book Award ceremony at Philharmonic Hall in New York, March 5, 1970 (an award she received for her happily mistitled *Complete Poems,* 1969). Robert Lowell, who was on the stage to accept the award on her behalf, spoke of Bishop's "enormous powers of realistic observation and of something seldom found with observation, luminism (meaning radiance and compression etc.)" (*WIA* 669). Then he went on to regret that, amidst the complaints for some notable exclusions (he meant Nabokov's *Ada* and Roth's *Portnoy,* but gave no names), no one had noticed that "a much more important author, Ezra Pound . . . had published a little book in June [*Drafts & Fragments*], one of his good books and quite possibly his last," and rounded off his performance by reading "Visits to St. Elizabeths"—"the best reading Cal ever gave" (according to Giroux's report) (Millier 425). When Lowell went back to his seat followed by "decent applause," the voice of Kenneth Rexroth was heard (as reported in Lowell's letter to Bishop of March 11, 1970): "I announce that I sever myself from this antisemitic fascist performance" (*WIA* 670). He was instantly countered by the master of ceremonies, who announced in his turn: "I disassociate myself from anyone who could say what you've just heard was antisemitic or Fascist" (*WIA* 670). And while the audience seemed to side mostly with the master of ceremonies, the evening had an unpleasant aftermath. Lowell and his wife were awakened twice by the telephone ringing at five thirty in the morning and a voice on the other end of the line, "quite calm and clear," as Lowell describes it, who said, "this is the voice of the shofar (The Jewish ramshorn for war)." The second call warned him "to make peace with his God" and that "on this day he's going to die" (*WIA* 670–71). As he summed it up to Bishop: "It sounds buffoonish as I tell it, but that was not the effect, it seemed dignified and terrifying" (*WIA* 670–71).

Bishop wrote on April 8, sympathizing with Lowell, but also, no doubt, thanking Heaven she had not attended the ceremony: "I have received a rather strange note—my one repercussion, I suppose—asking me if I ever actually did meet Pound or if I made it all up" (*WIA* 718). (Of course, it is pure chance but not meaningless that her "one repercussion" touched on her one poetic dogma: accuracy of perception, imagination of the actual.) In the letter I have just quoted—one of his liveliest—Lowell sums up what he had said of "Visits to St. Elizabeths" on the stage: "a clear poem whose meaning was hard to determine, the tone was reverential mockery or mocking reverence" (*WIA* 670). Here, by way of conclusion, is the text of his actual speech, which brings together Pound, Lowell, and Bishop, and is probably the definitive commentary on her "St. Elizabeths" poem: "Ezra Pound was *not* a good politician, but he *was* a very great poet. I'm going to read one of Elizabeth's poems; it's about Ezra Pound. Nobody else could have written it. It refers to the times we used to go see him in the hospital in Washington. It's constructed in the form of 'The House that Jack Built,' and is one of those poems so perfectly clear that nobody knows what it means."[19]

NOTES

1. Quoted in Haffenden 212–14.

2. Mary Barnard to Ezra Pound, November 11, 1949, Brunnenburg, Tirolo di Merano, archives of Mary de Rachewiltz; quoted courtesy of Mary de Rachewiltz.

3. Marianne Moore to Ezra Pound, January 5, 1934 [1935], in Marianne Moore, *Selected Letters,* 339.

4. I was pleased that, when I showed it to her, the actress Monique Fowler made use of it in *The Other Life,* portraying Bishop as furtively tucking a bottle into her purse before going to see Pound; this marvellous piece based on the Bishop-Lowell correspondence is as good a dramatic re-creation of their friendship as any biographer or critic could hope for.

5. Mary McCarthy, "Books of the Year: Some Personal Choices," *Observer,* December 10, 1966.

6. Compare Lowell's letter to Mary McCarthy, December 16, 1967: "Interesting idea, that Elizabeth is a poet of terror. I have never been able to quite connect what I know of her life with the seemingly dispassionate coolness of the poems" (*Letters of Lowell,* 491).

7. Robert Lowell to Al Alvarez, February 15, 1961. On the Pound-Lowell connection see Beach, "Who Else Has Lived through Purgatory?"; and Ricks, *True Friendship*

8. Compare Lord Grey Gowrie's January 21, 2009, e-mail to Massimo Bacigalupo, acknowledging a publication on Pound by the latter: "I was riveted by the Ezra Pound booklet. I used to talk about Pound with Robert Lowell, who knew Pound well. I once asked Lowell who was his favorite poet writing in English. I expected him to choose T. S. Eliot, who published him and whom he revered, or W. B. Yeats. His reply surprised me: 'Oh, Hardy and Ezra of course. Because of the heartbreak.'" Quoted courtesy of Lord Gowrie and Massimo Bacigalupo.

9. "The prisoner of Pisa and Washington, great musician of poetry and maybe, in flashes, great poet, deserved the homage of a young man who is not enrolled in the 'chapel' of his political admirers" (E. Montale, *Sulla poesia* [Milan: Mondadori, 1976], 486, my translation).

10. "How different prose is; sometimes the two mediums refuse to say the same things. I found this lately doing an obituary on Hannah Arendt. Without verse, without philosophy, I found it hard, I was naked without my line-ends" (Lowell to Bishop, April 15, 1976, *WIA* 786); "trying to write prose—a hell of a job, it starts naked ends as fake velvet" (Lowell to Bishop, November 14 [1954], *WIA* 153).

11. In her *Elizabeth Bishop's World War II–Cold War View,* Camille Roman writes that the poem was completed "at least by early 1951 because Jarrell praised Bishop for it in a letter dated April 7, 1951" (119). But this letter (from which I quote later in this essay) is clearly postmarked April 7, 1957 (though the last cipher of the year can be mistaken for a 1) and makes reference to Bishop and Jarrell meeting in New York just a few days before, during her first visit to the United States in six years, in 1957.

12. VC 57.12.

13. The correspondence between Bishop and Rizzardi has been lost, though he quotes, in Italian translation, a few undated excerpts in the endnote to his "Visite all'ospedale di Santa Elisabetta."

14. *Nuova Corrente,* 5–6 (January–June 1956), 32. Apart from this major variant, the *Nuova Corrente* text varies from all subsequent prints in the title (where "St. Elizabeths" is written with an apostrophe and is not followed by "1950") and in stanzas 8 and 9, where lines 3 and 4 (respectively) begin with "over" instead of "across."

15. See note 11.

16. Bishop would employ again the word in connection with Pound at least once, in a January 1964 letter to Anne Stevenson: "I doubt that any American poet (except poor wretched Pound) ever bothered our government much" (*PPL* 863).

17. Emphasis added. *Scrutiny* 18 (1951), also published in *Partisan Review* (November–December 1951): 727, with the editors' note: "We are reprinting it because it seems to us to be of the utmost relevance to the discussion of Pound's position and influence."

18. Elisabeth Bishop to Ilse Barker, Barker Correspondence, Manuscripts Division, Department of Rare Books and Special Collections, Princeton University Library, Box 1, Folder 7.

19. Unpublished remarks given at Philharmonic Hall, New York City, Wednesday, March 4, 1970, which Robert Giroux related in his March 6, 1970 letter to Bishop (VC 44.4).

Elizabeth Bishop and Flannery O'Connor

Minding and Mending a Fallen World

GEORGE S. LENSING

The pairing of Elizabeth Bishop (1911–1979) and Flannery O'Connor (1925–1964) may seem a surprising and somewhat unexpected association: one a poet and the other a novelist and short-story writer; one a New England/Canadian/Brazilian sojourner and the other a rooted Georgia southerner; one a religious skeptic and the other a devout Roman Catholic; one homosexual and one heterosexual. Moreover, the two never met in person, though they did correspond intermittently, and Bishop once chatted with O'Connor on the telephone when passing through Savannah. Although they apparently had little influence on each other as writers, I want to make the claim that the connections between these two major figures are far from superficial, and the impact that each made upon the other was profound. In addition, their work shows surprising similarities, however different the ends to which they exercised it.

Each writer openly admired a quality in the work of the other that was paramount in her own, an unyielding commitment to seeing the world with a scrupulous accuracy and depicting it in highly sensuous language. For both, the precision of the eye (and all the other senses) in portraying the world comprises the foundation of their art. Characterization within their work is so various as to defy easy categories, but each shares a presentation that is gently tolerant of small human imperfections, especially as manifest among the working class, whom both knew well. O'Connor, more than Bishop, employs an unsparing satire on egotism, materialism, and human exploitation, but Bishop is also consistently attentive to the causes and victims of poverty and exploitation. As she says in a letter: "My outlook is pessimistic. I think we are still barbarians, barbarians who commit a hundred indecencies and cruelties every day of our lives, as just possibly future ages may be able to see. But I think we should be gay in spite of it" (*PPL* 863–64).

Bishop's agnosticism allows for little of O'Connor's more overt Christianity. Yet, each reflects the other in a method that draws liberally upon a symbology of

Christian objects, allusions, and parables. As I hope to show, such objects often set in motion certain sacramental and transcendent reverberations.

When O'Connor died in 1964, Bishop wrote to the poet Robert Lowell: "I feel awful about Flannery. Why didn't I go to visit her when she asked me to. And I hadn't even met her, or answered her last letter. . . . I feel awe in front of that girl's courage and discipline. I have some wonderfully funny letters from her—one about Lourdes" (*WIA* 552). Shortly afterward, Bishop wrote a brief memorial for the *New York Review of Books* in which she said: "I lived in Florida for several years next to a flourishing 'Church of God' (both white and black congregation), where every Wednesday night Sister Mary and her husband 'spoke in tongues.' After those Wednesday nights, nothing Flannery O'Connor ever wrote could seem at all exaggerated to me" (*PPL* 717). The idiot son of Rayber, whom Tarwater simultaneously baptizes and drowns in O'Connor's novel *The Violent Bear It Away*, is named Bishop—a character, she wrote Lowell, "named for me, I think" (*WIA* 309).

O'Connor's admiration of Bishop was no less fervent. "I have a great respect for your own work," she wrote, "though I am almost too ignorant ever to know why I like what I like" (*Collected Works* 1022). The two women did indeed share certain similarities: hardened by the catastrophes of life with a stoic toughness, living as writers outside the ordinary geography of their peers and often in isolation; keen observers of those around them—especially, for O'Connor, the blacks of Georgia, and for Bishop, the Brazilian working class, many of whom she knew during her many years living in that country. In one letter, O'Connor wrote, "I hadn't realized that life in Brazil might resemble life here in the South but I guess there are many similarities" (*Collected Works* 1021). Both lost their fathers at an early age. Both were skilled amateur painters. They shared a literary editor, Robert Giroux, who became a close friend to each. Both abhorred and satirized hypocrisy; O'Connor's fiction underscores Bishop's conclusion in an interview: "I don't like modern religiosity in general; it always seems to lead to a tone of moral superiority" (*Conversations* 23). Each had a great capacity for self-deprecation, as well as a humorous appreciation for life's absurdities. Though influenced by their respective religious upbringings, Bishop's memory of certain Protestant associations at times leaned toward the Catholic, while O'Connor's Catholic ones were shaped to southern Protestantism. Neither woman seemed capable of sentimentality in any form. Had they met, each would surely and quickly have warmed to the utter unpretentiousness of the other.

The figure who played a large role in both writers' lives and who often served as a conduit of information to each about the other was Robert Lowell. Bishop had met him in 1947, introduced by Randall Jarrell, when she was thirty-six and Lowell was thirty. Since the publication in 1989 of David Kalstone's *Becoming a Poet: Elizabeth Bishop with Marianne Moore and Robert Lowell,* we have been aware of the importance of this friendship. But with the publication in 2008 of their steady and massive correspondence in *Words in Air: The Complete Correspondence between Elizabeth Bishop and Robert Lowell*—covering a period of almost three decades—it is now clear just how profound and sustaining that friendship came to be. In addition, these letters make available for the first time extensive comments by each on O'Connor and her work.

While Lowell's connections to O'Connor were not as continuous or as pervasive, the friendship proved invaluable at a formative stage in O'Connor's career. The two met briefly in the same year that he met Bishop, 1947, when the acclaimed young poet spent four days at the University of Iowa; O'Connor, at the age of twenty-two, was a student in the postgraduate Writers' Workshop there. Their friendship blossomed, however, during the months in 1948 and 1949 when both were in residence at Yaddo, the writers' colony in Saratoga Springs, New York. Reading her work on her first novel, *Wise Blood,* Lowell immediately recognized her talent and set about trying to find a teaching position for her. At the same time, he was trying, at that point unsuccessfully, to persuade Bishop herself to join them at Yaddo: "There's a little Catholic girl named Flannery O'Connor here now, who will remain if she can—a real writer, I think one of the best to be when she is a little older. Very moral (in your sense) and witty—whom I'm sure you'd like. It would be a marvelous summer!!" (*WIA* 79). (Bishop finally went to Yaddo, but about four months after O'Connor had left.) Somewhat overwhelmed by Lowell's attention, O'Connor developed an emotional attachment to the young poet, even as she was encouraging him to reembrace his earlier Catholic conversion. Sally Fitzgerald, the close friend and later editor of O'Connor's work, reports: "Carolina Gordon stated the matter flatly: 'She [O'Connor] fell for him; she admitted it to me.' Much later, Edward Maisel [a musicologist, author, and Harvard graduate also at Yaddo] indicated as much: 'I lost her to Robert Lowell.' Lowell himself, of course, failed to notice" (415). Leaving Yaddo early in 1949, O'Connor followed Lowell and Elizabeth Hardwick, the woman he married in July, to New York, where O'Connor took an apartment. Lowell went on to introduce her to her future publisher, Robert Giroux, and to Robert and Sally Fitzgerald, who would become two of her closest friends and with whom she would later live and write for a few months before contracting lupus and returning to live the remainder of her shortened life in Milledgeville, Georgia.

At Lowell's encouragement, Bishop began to read stories by O'Connor in various magazines as early as 1949. Six years later, she reported to Lowell, "I've read most of these recent stories, and I think she's really pretty good, don't you?" (*WIA* 165).

Bishop initiated a correspondence with O'Connor somewhere around the beginning of 1957. Only six letters to Bishop are included in the collection of O'Connor's letters, and none of Bishop's to O'Connor has yet been published.[1] As a result, the published correspondence is one-sided. In the first letter, O'Connor responds to Bishop's indication that she was trying to get some of her stories translated into Portuguese and published in Brazil (*Collected Works* 1021).[2] In her letter, O'Connor introduced herself, only partially tongue-in-cheek: "She [her mother] and I live in the country a few miles outside of Milledgeville. The place is a dairy farm and I am glad to say that most of the violences carried to their logical conclusions in the stories manage to be warded off in fact here—though most of them exist in potentiality" (*Collected Works* 1021). Later that year O'Connor wrote to Betty Hester: "A very nice thing happened last night. Elizabeth Bishop called me up from Savannah. She was on a freighter going to Brazil where she lives and it docked unexpectedly in Savannah. I have never met her. . . . She seemed like a most cordial pleasant soul and it was one of those things that you just don't expect" (*Habit* 248).[3] A year later Bishop sent O'Connor a copy of her translation from the Portuguese of *The Diary of "Helena Morley."*

Later, an account of O'Connor's visit to the shrine of Our Lady of Lourdes in France followed ("The supernatural is a fact there but it displaces nothing natural; except maybe those germs" [*Collected Works* 1073]). She added that she had initiated some contacts with Emory University in Atlanta in the hope that they would invite Bishop to give a reading there followed by a visit to nearby Milledgeville. As it turned out, O'Connor's connection at "the Methodist college" was no longer on the staff there, and the invitation was never extended. In the summer of 1959, O'Connor succinctly described to Bishop her newly completed novel, *The Violent Bear It Away*: "My book is about a boy who has been raised up in the backwoods by his great uncle to be a prophet. The book is about his struggle not to be a prophet—which he loses" (*Habit* 344). In her final published letter to Bishop—though others followed—O'Connor thanked her for pictures Bishop had sent following her recent trip up the Amazon. Determined as ever to get Bishop to Milledgeville, O'Connor wrote: "Let us know if you are coming this way. We could likely come to Savannah and meet you and bring you up here" (*Habit* 344). In just a little over three years, the epistolary friendship had blossomed, though all the invitations and attempts to arrange a meeting remained futile. Bishop would later tell Lowell, "I think we have a lot in common" (*WIA* 437).

Unsurprisingly, Bishop responded eagerly in 1959 to Lowell's suggestion that she write a letter of nomination for O'Connor's admission in what is today called the American Academy of Arts and Letters. The attempt failed, but Bishop nominated her again in the following year. In between the nominations, Bishop read O'Connor's newly published *The Violent Bear It Away*. She wrote to Lowell: "That first section that was published somewhere before still seems superb to me—like a poem. In fact she's a great loss to the art, don't you think? And all through there are absolutely marvelous passages—conversations, bits of description—she's wonderful because it seems so effortless, and never a word wasted" (*WIA* 309). A week later, responding to Lowell's own assessment of the novel, she added: "Yes, the Flannery book is a bit disappointing, I'm afraid—one wishes she could get away from religious fanatics for a while. But just the writing is so damned good compared to almost anything else one reads: economical, clear, horrifying, *real*. I suspect that this repetition of the uncle-nephew, or father-son, situation, in all its awfulness, is telling something about her family life—seen sidewise, or in distorted shadows on the wall" (*WIA* 315). Bishop was sufficiently upset by the "nasty little notice of Flannery's book" in the *New Yorker* that she was going to write the magazine in protest: "It makes me really angry. They devote so much space to insignificant novels—and that notice wasn't even accurate, which they're so proud of being" (*WIA* 327–28). In spite of O'Connor's reiterated pleas for a visit, Bishop confessed to Lowell, "I'd like to go to call on her sometime, although I do find her a bit intimidating" (*WIA* 327).

It is clear from their correspondence that O'Connor's death from lupus in 1964 touched both poets deeply, both writing of their admiration of the work as well as the woman herself. Bishop immediately composed her short memorial essay for the *New York Review of Books*. In her remarks, she defines the meaning of the friendship:

> I feel great remorse now that I hadn't written to her for many months, that I had allowed this friendship to dwindle just when she must have been aware she was dying. Something about her intimidated me a bit: perhaps natural awe before her toughness and courage; perhaps, although death is certain for all, hers seemed a little more certain than usual. She made no show of *not* living in a metropolis, or of being a believer,—she lived with Christian stoicism and wonderful wit and humor that put most of us to shame. (*PPL* 717)

In an interview four years after O'Connor's death, Bishop declared: "The best of contemporary prose-writers is a woman—Flannery O'Connor—recently deceased" (*Conversations* 53). When O'Connor's letters were published in the last year of Bishop's life, Bishop received a copy from Giroux, who had edited them. She informed him:

> Thank you for the Flannery O'Connor Letters. I can't stop reading them—have until 2 a.m. for two nights now, to the detriment of my daily life. . . . The letters are wonderful, aren't they, and made me feel bad even more that I never got to Milledge-ville. (I think I was *afraid* of Flannery!) I get bogged down, naturally, in some of the Catholicism . . . but never mind, what an admirable and amazing young lady she was! I never dreamed of all that revising and rewriting and accepting of advice that went on. (*OA* 630–31)

Making sense of a world that often appeared overwhelming in its cruelty, poverty, loneliness, and materialism, both Bishop and O'Connor sought to give shape in their writing to an *ethos* for living in that world. ("But how to LIVE"? [*WIA* 661], Bishop asked Lowell in 1969.) One recalls, for example, the urban anomie of Bishop's New York in the poem "The Man-Moth" or O'Connor's similar presentation of Atlanta in the story "The Artificial Nigger." Though the weltanschauung that emerges for each is in some ways radically different, each sought in noticeably similar strokes to carve out a primary morality, what one might call a minimalist ethic for living honorably in the welter of the twentieth century.

In 1937, when Bishop was three years out of Vassar, she published a story in *Life and Letters Today* that in many ways could have been a model for later stories by O'Connor. In some ways it anticipates a particular O'Connor story that would appear sixteen years later called "The River." Bishop's story, "The Baptism," introduces three aging and unmarried sisters who live together as devout Presbyterians in a small town. The youngest, Lucy, however, has never formally joined the church. As the story unfolds, Lucy begins to have "visions" of Christ, visions that unsettle her older sisters: "Lucy was more conscious of his [Christ's] body than his face. His beautiful glowing bulk was rayed with a sunflower. It lit up Flora's and Emma's [the sisters] faces on either side of the stove. The stove could not burn him" (*PPL* 571). Lucy becomes increasingly absorbed with lengthy sessions of prayer and pious devotions. She upsets her sisters more when she decides that she will be baptized, but in the Baptist rather than their own Presbyterian church, two religions that Bishop herself had been associated with in her childhood. Though the narrative voice of the story never directly judges Lucy, it is clear that she is succumbing to a fanaticism, perhaps even insanity. The baptism by immersion occurs in March just as the frozen river begins to melt. Lucy catches a cold and high fever and dies a few days later after she has burned herself approaching the stove in their home as "God came again, into the kitchen" (*PPL* 573). In the story, Bishop presents and lets the actions of Lucy's fanaticism speak for themselves without further judgment. Though she had not been a churchgoer except during her childhood years, the story appears to be a kind of farewell to the religion of her devout grandparents in Nova Scotia.

O'Connor's story "The River" recounts the baptism of a young boy, Harry Ashfield, no more than four or five years old. He is neglected by his secular parents who seem only to tolerate his presence. On the day in which most of the action occurs, Harry is taken by his uneducated sitter, Mrs. Connin, first to her home, where the young boy is attacked by a pig, and then to a baptism in the river. The young preacher there, Bevel Summers, instructs the bystanders in the one true river, "the River of Life, made out of Jesus' Blood. That's the river you have to lay your pain in, in the River of Faith, in the River of Life, in the River of Love" (*Collected Works* 162). The young Harry is taken by Mrs. Connin into the river, where the young preacher baptizes him even as the impressionable boy seeks to be absorbed literally into the river of Christ. After the baptism, he is returned to his parents' home but, early the next morning, returns to the river alone, hoping once again to enter the river of Christ, only to lose his life by drowning. It is among O'Connor's most startling stories and connects to what many have called her menagerie of "grotesques." But O'Connor's Harry is not merely the fanatic of Bishop's Lucy. He seems somehow to have put himself in touch with radical but authentic Christianity. Of her goal as a Christian writer, O'Connor commented: "When you can assume that your audience holds the same beliefs you do, you can relax a little and use more normal ways of talking to it; when you have to assume that it does not, then you have to make your vision apparent by shock—to the hard of hearing you shout and for the almost blind you draw large and startling figures" (*Collected Works* 805–6). Although Bishop shrank from religious fanaticism, O'Connor often adapted it to her own religious ends.

Bishop in Brazil, where she resided for almost two decades, and O'Connor in Georgia lived in worlds defined by race and social class—often made manifest by servants in their own homes, and, in O'Connor's case, farmhands just outside the door. Each had a great respect and affection for these servant types, even as they astutely recognized how each class exploited the other for its own benefit. Here are a few lines from Bishop's poem called "Manuelzinho," spoken by her wealthy companion and lover Lota de Macedo Soares; under the title of the poem, Bishop inserts in parentheses: "*Brazil. A friend of the writer is speaking*":

> You steal my telephone wires,
> or someone does. You starve
> your horse and yourself
> and your dogs and family.
> Among endless variety,
> you eat boiled cabbage stalks.
> And once I yelled at you
> so loud to hurry up
> and fetch me those potatoes
> your holey hat flew off,
> you jumped out of your clogs,
> leaving three objects arranged
> in a triangle at my feet,
> as if you'd been a gardener
> in a fairy tale all this time
> and at the word 'potatoes'
> had vanished to take up your work
> of fairy prince somewhere. (PPL 77–78)

In O'Connor's "The Displaced Person," the admirable Polish farmhand, who does not speak English, observes one of the blacks stealing a turkey. He feels obliged to report it to Mrs. McIntyre, the owner of the farm, who seems as unperturbed as Lota in her response to Manuelzinho's petty thefts:

> The week before, he [the Polish farmhand] had come upon Sulk at the dinner hour, sneaking with a croker sack into the pen where the young turkeys were. He had watched him take a frying-size turkey from the lot and thrust it in the sack and put the sack under his coat. Then he had followed him around the barn, jumped on him, dragged him to Mrs. McIntyre's back door and had acted out the entire scene for her, while the Negro muttered and grumbled and said God might strike him dead if he had been stealing any turkey, he had only been taking it to put some black shoe polish on its head because it had the sorehead. God might strike him dead if that was not the truth before Jesus. Mrs. McIntyre told him to go put the turkey back and then she was a long time explaining to the Pole that all Negroes would steal. She finally had

to call Rudolph and tell him in English and have him tell his father in Polish, and Mr. Guizac had gone off with a startled disappointed face. (*Collected Works* 293)

Each account discloses a response to the servants' exploitations with both humor and good humor, even while they register exasperation and, finally, resignation. The narratives register a subtle truce between the social classes, a modus vivendi, allowing the system to function in the quotidian world each inhabited.

There is a brief scene in Bishop's classic memoir-story "In the Village," in which her personal counterpart in the story, a young girl five years old, is going through her daily routine while living with grandparents in a small village in Nova Scotia, the day in which the girl's mother (who is a stand-in for Bishop's own mother) is being committed to a mental institution. This woman's husband and Bishop's father had died a few months after Bishop's birth. The particular scene from which I am about to quote is almost incidental to the larger story, except that it seems to me that it could easily appear in an O'Connor story. The young girl is leading the horse called Nelly out to the pasture on the very day that the arrangements for the mother's committal are under way, arrangements unshared with the precocious young girl. The girl and the horse pass the home of Mr. and Mrs. Chisolm in a scene one could easily mistake for one by O'Connor: "Mrs. Chisolm's pale frantic face is watching me out the kitchen window as she washes the breakfast dishes. We wave, but I hurry by because she may come out and ask questions. But her questions are not as bad perhaps as those of her husband Mr. Chisolm, who wears a beard. One evening he had met me in the pasture and asked me how my soul was. Then he held me firmly by both hands while he said a prayer, with his head bowed, Nelly right beside us chewing her cud all the time. I had felt a soul, heavy in my chest, all the way home" (*PPL* 109–10). Bishop's Brazil and Nova Scotia show stark parallels with O'Connor's rural American South.

O'Connor's story "Revelation" (1964) and Bishop's poem "In the Waiting Room" (1971), as far as I know, have never been formally compared. Yet, their similarities are marked. Each is set in a doctor's waiting room where, in the story, a middle-aged farmer's wife, Mrs. Turpin, and, in the poem, a young girl named Elizabeth (the poet herself), undergo a traumatically imposed moment of self-revelation by which their lives are transformed. Mrs. Turpin's "revelation" is ultimately theological, while that of the young girl in the poem is very much of this world, and Mrs. Turpin and Elizabeth are very different characters. Even so, both, seated in a waiting room, undergo a wrenchingly painful moment of self-knowledge that redefines who they are—in their own eyes—and a new position in the world they inhabit.

Mrs. Turpin is a vain, self-righteous woman who repeatedly thanks Jesus that she is superior to the lower-class whites and the blacks (referred to in the thoughts of Mrs. Turpin as the "niggers") who live around her in the rural South. She quickly identifies and disparages the "trash" among the others in the waiting room. Here is a favorite O'Connor type, the vainglorious egoist who justifies herself through religiosity and smug superiority. Mrs. Turpin notes a college-age girl sitting near her reading a book and finds her ugly in appearance and rudely unresponsive, except for her withering stare, to all her questioning and eventually her provocative comments. The hostility eventually leads to the girl's hurling her book at Mrs. Turpin, striking her over the eye. A doctor and nurse quickly appear to treat her, but the young girl has one final weapon, her only comment to Mrs. Turpin: "Go back to hell where you came from you old wart hog" (*Collected Works* 646). The barb finds its intended target, and Mrs. Turpin cannot rid it from her thoughts as she and her husband return to the farm and their chores. Taking refuge in the pig parlor there, where she hoses down an old sow and her shoats, Mrs. Turpin questions God's intention: "'What do you send me a message like that for?' she said in a low fierce voice, barely above a whisper but with the force of a shout in its concentrated fury. 'How am I a hog and me both? How am I saved and from hell too?'" (*Collected Works* 652). As the sun sets and the story ends, Mrs. Turpin undergoes a dramatic moment of apocalyptic vision set against the sky, a "vast horde of souls" in procession "rumbling toward heaven": "There were whole companies of white-trash, clean for the first time in their lives, and bands of black niggers in white robes, and battalions of freaks and lunatics [her label for the girl in the waiting room] shouting and clapping and leaping like frogs" (*Collected Works* 654). At the end come her own counterparts, those who represent "good order and common sense and respectable behavior," and yet "their virtues were being burned away" in the vision. Those whom Mrs. Turpin has despised make up "the souls climbing upward into the starry field and shouting hallelujah" (*Collected Works* 654).

The young Elizabeth of "In the Waiting Room" is hardly puffed up with Mrs. Turpin's egoism. Almost seven years old, she is innocent of the lives of oppression and suffering around her. Hers is the waiting room of a dentist's office, and inside she hears the cry of her aunt, "an *oh!* of pain" (*PPL* 149). As she fingers through a copy of the *National Geographic* she is horrified by the pictures:

> A dead man slung on a pole
> —"Long Pig," the caption said.
> Babies with pointed heads

> wound round and round with string;
> black, naked women with necks
> wound round and round with wire
> like the necks of light bulbs.
> Their breasts were horrifying. (PPL 149)

Cumulatively, the cannibalism, the abuse of the babies and their mothers, the reality of the women's breasts, the aunt's cry of pain, even the awareness of the First World War then in progress overwhelm the young girl. In a sense, like Mrs. Turpin, a magazine, the *National Geographic,* has been flung at her also. And she is no less traumatized. "But I felt: you are an I, / you are an *Elizabeth,* / You are one of *them*" (PPL 150) — as if, again like Mrs. Turpin, she must now redefine her identity against a world that is alien, horrifying, and now completely reconfigured.

> The waiting room was bright
> and too hot. It was sliding
> beneath a big black wave,
> another and another. (PPL 151)

For both Mrs. Turpin and Elizabeth, their newly discovered worlds emerge first from their immediate presence in a waiting room, a setting of forced social presence and awareness. Here is where the poet and short-story writer seem especially similar. Mrs. Turpin, O'Connor tells us, "always noticed people's feet": "The well-dressed lady had on red and grey suede shoes to match her dress. Mrs. Turpin had on her good black patent leather pumps. The ugly girl had on Girl Scout shoes and heavy socks. The old woman had on tennis shoes and the white-trashy mother had on what appeared to be bedroom slippers" (*Collected Works* 635). The observations confirm in her mind her own superiority and lay the foundation for her later visionary humiliation at the end of the story. The young Elizabeth has the same angle of acute observation:

> I gave a sidelong glance
> —I couldn't look any higher—
> at shadowy gray knees,
> trousers and skirts and boots
> and different pairs of hands
> lying under the lamps.

> I knew that nothing stranger
> had ever happened, that nothing
> stranger could ever happen. (*PPL* 150)

Why, she will ask later in the poem, should she be one with these strange and distant figures? As in the O'Connor story, the encircling figures, their feet and knees and dress, cannot be evaded. For both artists, their characters' worlds undergo a necessary but radical inversion. As it turns out, both Elizabeth and Mrs. Turpin dramatically come to perceive a unity with human beings who previously seemed disturbing and alien—a discovery that goes to the heart of the larger work of both poet and fiction writer.

Aside from their thematic preoccupations, there is another, perhaps even more foundational similarity, and it has to do with how the artist's eye captures and interprets a highly sensory epistemology in response to the surrounding world. Grasping the world as it appears to the senses with the specificity of realism underlay everything Bishop wrote. As she once wrote to Lowell, contrasting her own style with his, her own dedication to accurate observation superseded every other consideration: "My passion for accuracy may strike you as old-maidish—but since we do float on an unknown sea I think we should examine the other floating things that come our way very carefully; who knows what might depend upon it? So I'm enclosing a clipping about raccoons. But perhaps you prefer mythology" (*WIA* 553). Reviewing Bishop's first book, Randall Jarrell said, "All her poems have written underneath, *I have seen it*" (235). In an interview, she offered, "I think I'm more visual than most poets" (*Conversations* 24). What Bishop admired in O'Connor's fiction was this same mode of observation, as she acknowledged in the memoir for the *New York Review of Books* just after O'Connor's death: "They [the stories] are narrow, possibly, but they are clear, hard, vivid, and full of bits of description, phrases, and odd insights that contain more real poetry than a dozen books of poems" (*PPL* 717). In her essay "The Catholic Novelist in the South," O'Connor noted: "The things we see, hear, smell and touch affect us long before we believe anything at all" (*Collected Works* 855).

There is a passage in *The Violent Bear It Away* that occurs early in the novel. Shortly after the death of his great-uncle, a self-proclaimed prophet, the young fourteen-year-old Tarwater leaves behind the cabin where the body of his unburied great-uncle and father-figure remains sitting crouched at the table where he has just died. The boy makes his way through the surrounding woods to the uncle's still:

> The birds had gone into the deep woods to escape the noon sun and one thrush, hidden some distance ahead of him, called the same four notes again and again, stopping each time after them to make a silence. Tarwater began to walk faster, then he began to lope, and in a second he was running like something hunted, sliding down slopes waxed with pine needles and grasping the limbs of trees to pull himself, panting, up the slippery inclines. He crashed through a wall of honeysuckle and lept across a sandy near-dry stream bed and fell down against the high clay bank that formed the back wall of a cove where the old man kept his extra liquor hidden. He hid it in a hollow of the bank, covered with a large stone. Tarwater began to fight at the stone to pull it away, while the stranger stood over his shoulder panting, he was crazy! He was crazy! That's the long and short of it, he was crazy! (*Collected Works* 357)

In this passage, the senses come prominently into play: the four notes of the thrush, the grasp of tree limbs, the smell of honeysuckle, and the visual cinematic representation of it all. The sentences are connected by a succession of conjunctive "ands," and the subordinate phrases and clauses are united by participles: "running like something hunted, sliding down slopes waxed with pine needles and grasping the limbs of trees to pull himself, panting, up slippery inclines." Highly sensuous, this passage possesses a crowded and cumulative force marked by O'Connor's control and precision. At the end, Tarwater arrives at the still, and the voice of the imagined stranger's climactic and pounding dismissal of the uncle: "He was crazy! He was crazy! That's the long and short of it, he was crazy!"

Bishop's "In the Village," from which I earlier quoted, depicts another child, five years old instead of fourteen, who also lives with a relative two generations older, her grandmother, in Great Village, Nova Scotia. The girl, of course, is Bishop herself. Her weekly task is to deliver a package of assorted personal items prepared by the grandmother to the post office from which they will make their way to the girl's mother, now committed to the mental institution. The incident itself is trivial, but behind it lurks the enduring tragedy of the young girl's loss, a loss subtly contained in the moment of the delivery of the package. The girl hands the package to Mr. Johnson, the postmaster:

> I have to go outside again to hand him the package through the ordinary window, into his part of the post office, because it is too big for the little official one. He is very old, and nice. He has two fingers missing on his right hand where they were caught in a threshing machine. He wears a navy-blue cap with a black leather visor, like a ship's officer, and a shirt with feathery brown stripes, and a big gold collar button.

"Let me see. Let me see. Let me see. Hm," he says to himself, weighing the package on the scales, jiggling the bar with the two remaining fingers and thumb.

"Yes. Yes. Your grandmother is very faithful." (PPL 117)

Like the passage from O'Connor's novel, detail is piled rapidly upon detail: The postmaster is very old. He has two fingers missing. He wears a navy-blue cap. This paratactic amassing of physical detail is Bishop's own way of viewing the world: "Everything only connected by 'and' and 'and'" (PPL 46), as she says in her poem "Over 2000 Illustrations and a Complete Concordance." Like Tarwater's inner voice (the stranger exclaiming, "He was crazy! He was crazy,") here, too, the details culminate in a dramatic exclamation from Mr. Johnson, "Let me see. Let me see. Hm,"—followed by participial phrases: "weighing the package on the scales, jiggling the bar with the two remaining fingers and thumb." Both of these passages present sensuous and precise detail with a similar kind of succinct rhythmic timing, supple grammatical and syntactical variation. Bishop's admiration for O'Connor's prose style was surely conditioned by her recognition of similar traits in her own occasional prose writing.

For all their similarities, in other ways their views of the world were profoundly different. O'Connor, for example, affirms a transcendent world of divine origin: "For I am no disbeliever in spiritual purpose and no vague believer. I see from the standpoint of Christian orthodoxy. This means that for me the meaning of life is centered in our Redemption by Christ and that what I see in the world I see in relation to that" (Collected Works 804–5). Whereas, as Bishop explained to Lowell: "I wish I had the 39 articles on hand. I also wish I could go back to being a Baptist!—not that I ever was one—but I believe now that complete agnosticism and straddling the fence on everything is my natural posture, although I wish it weren't" (WIA 161). That fundamental difference aside, I want to argue that both O'Connor and Bishop present a world that can be seen as manifesting a sacramental significance, or, for Bishop, something like a sacramental significance, as Sally Fitzgerald has observed.[4]

For these two writers, the objects of the physical world and the narratives that define and give meaning to that world often draw upon an overtly spiritual symbolism. Lionel Trilling, writing around the time of O'Connor's death, noted the frequent "secularization of spirituality" in contemporary American letters:

No literature has ever been so shockingly personal as that of our time—it asks every question that is forbidden in polite society. It asks us if we are content with our marriages, with our family lives, with our professional lives, with our friends. . . . It asks us if we are content with ourselves, if we are saved or damned—more than with anything else our literature is concerned with salvation. No literature has ever been so intensely spiritual as ours. I do not venture to call it actually religious, but certainly it has the special intensity of concern with the spiritual life which Hegel noted when he spoke of the great modern phenomena of the secularization of spirituality. (8–9)

These comments have valid application both to Bishop and O'Connor, except that Bishop embraces the "secularization of spirituality," while O'Connor seeks to make spiritual the secular.

Neither figure baldly presents a specifically religious homiletic, but both probe beneath and beyond the immediate realism of the physical world in quest of some manifestation of transcendent association. In the case of O'Connor, I am thinking of an object like her peacock in her great story "The Displaced Person," to which is directly attached a Christological significance. In "The Artificial Nigger," the story ends with the sudden and unpredictable appearance of a "plaster figure of a Negro sitting bent over on a low yellow brick fence that curved around a wide lawn." For Mr. Head, at the end of the day that has marked his troubled visit to the city with his young grandson Nelson, the figure becomes a powerful presence: "Mr. Head had never known before what mercy felt like because he had been too good to deserve any, but he felt he knew now" (*Collected Works* 229–30). A turnip-shaped cloud and a "guffawing peal of thunder from behind and fantastic raindrops, like tin-can tops" (*Collected Works* 183) become a supernatural censure of Mr. Shiftlet at the end of "The Life You Save May Be Your Own." O'Connor's narratives typically involve moments of epiphany in which natural phenomena and physical objects impose themselves dramatically as prophetic judgments, warnings, or recriminations.

Certain images in Bishop's poems also bear a revelatory quality, but with a calmer and less apocalyptic force than one typically finds in O'Connor. In "Crusoe in England," for example, Crusoe's fragile but life-sustaining knife, now consigned to a museum shelf at the end of the poem, "reeked of meaning, like a crucifix. / It lived" (*PPL* 156). In a different way, the miracle of the multiplication of the loaves hovers behind "A Miracle for Breakfast." She defines heaven and hell in the images of the Florida coast in "Seascape." The "celestial seascape" has "herons got up as angels"; it recalls a "cartoon by Raphael for a tapestry for a Pope: / it does look like heaven" (*PPL* 31). But the lighthouse "in black and white clerical dress" weathers the nighttime storm and, speaking in his own voice, redefines heaven as "something to do with blackness and a strong glare" (*PPL* 31–32). Christ's forgiveness of Peter's three denials on the night before the crucifixion not only informs "Roosters" but, at the same time, pulls the disjunctive poem into unity. The parable of the Prodigal Son in "The Prodigal," another poem of forgiveness and reconciliation, focuses on a character typical of many O'Connor characters: the lingering dissolution and near-despair of the prodigal: "But it took him a long time / finally to make his mind up and to go home" (*PPL* 54). In all of these cases, Bishop's images are not directing attention to the supernatural so much as drawing upon their symbolic resonances to indicate some kind of sustenance for this life or what she calls "the size of our abidance" in "Poem" (*PPL* 166).

Cheryl Walker notes: "To be of two minds was characteristic of Elizabeth Bishop. She could never quite relinquish the *desire* to believe, though a settled faith eluded her" (17). Walker goes on to quote from a previously unpublished letter from Bishop to the George Herbert scholar Joseph Summers, commending him for engaging with "all these insoluble and endless and nagging problems of man's relationship to God" (17–18). She adds that such problems are "*real.*—It was real and it has kept on being real and it always will be, and Herbert just happened to be a person who managed to put a great deal of it into magnificent poetry,—it is still real for all of us, after all" (18).

That symbolic but unsentimental intrusion hinting at spiritual immanence is nowhere better illustrated than in a gift Bishop sent O'Connor from Brazil. Here is O'Connor's description of it in a letter:

> I had a letter from Elizabeth Bishop a month or so ago saying that she was send-
> ing me a present by a friend of hers, or rather getting him to bring it back to the States
> with him and mail it from his home in Ohio. She hoped I wouldn't be too appalled
> at it, a crucifix, she said, in a bottle. She is much interested in the things made by the
> natives. So a few days ago it came. It's not a crucifix at all, she just don't know what a
> crucifix is. It is an altar with Bible, chalice and two fat candles on it, a cross above this
> with a ladder and the instruments of the crucifixtion [*sic*] hung on it, and on top of
> the cross a rooster. It's all wood except the altar cloth and the rooster and these are
> paper, painstakingly cut out and a trifle dirty from hands that did it. Anyway, it's very
> much to my taste. (*Habit* 518–19)

These kinds of primitive Brazilian artifacts were always favorites of Bishop, and she must have taken considerable pains to arrange its dispatch from Brazil to Georgia, confident that O'Connor would find it equally fascinating: "the kind of innocent religious grotesquery she might like" (*PPL* 716). To Bishop directly, O'Connor wrote of the artifact: "I am altogether taken with it. It's what I'm born to appreciate" (qtd. in *PPL* 716–17). The gift in many ways summarizes their mutual interest in a kind of "innocent religious grotesquery" that could be attached to a stark and unsentimental symbolism.

O'Connor's final letter to Bishop was delivered from her deathbed to Brazil by Ashley Brown, who was introduced to the poet through the letter. Brown was an English professor from the University of South Carolina who was beginning a year as a Fulbright lecturer at a university in Rio. He had known O'Connor for several years. As Bishop's biographer suggests, "perhaps because the two [Brown and O'Connor] were associated in her mind, and because she was so sad about O'Connor's death, Elizabeth made a special effort to meet and become friends with Brown" (Millier 359). Brown reports that, at their first meeting, Bishop queried him about O'Connor: "Elizabeth admired Flannery O'Connor tremendously and wanted to ask a few questions about her. [She wondered if] Flannery really was [the pious] Catholic she seemed to be. I said she was. Elizabeth was fascinated by someone who could be so totally committed to a religious idea as Flannery was" (Fountain and Brazeau 190–91). The Bishop who had told Lowell that "complete agnosticism and straddling the fence on everything" made up her "natural posture" (*WIA* 161) perhaps found in O'Connor another quality she found both enviable and daunting, her religious rootedness. In any case, relishing her gift of the bottled religious figures from Bishop, O'Connor wanted to return the favor, even though she had only weeks to live. Knowing that Brown would soon be en route to Brazil, where he would meet Bishop, she wrote, "I'm up here in the hospital else I would send you some peafowl feathers to take her for me" (Brown, "Bishop in Brazil" 688). The poet of sandpipers, roosters, and the bird of "Five Flights Up" who knows that "everything is answered" (*PPL* 171) would surely have prized such a gift with gratitude equal to O'Connor's: "what I'm born to appreciate" (qtd. in *PPL* 717).

NOTES

1. Robert Giroux reproduces five of the six letters that appear in *The Habit of Being* in his Library of America edition of *Collected Works*, but includes no additional ones.

2. O'Connor describes Bishop's attempt to introduce her in Brazil: "You were good to mention them [stories] to the editor of *Revista Contemporanea* and I would like to see some of them used" (*Collected Works* 1021). To Lowell, Bishop wrote at the same time: "I think I have it arranged that one of F's stories is to appear here in Portuguese—the best big literary supplement—they seem to be stalled on Salinger and Cummings now so I thought I'd give them a change" (*WIA* 300).

3. In a letter that followed the phone call from Bishop in Savannah, O'Connor wanted to correct some misinformation she had given her. I reproduce this correction here because it shows the same kind of deadpan, ironic humor that so often informs O'Connor's own fiction: "It was awfully

nice of you to call me up on your way to South America. Of course I misinformed you about the night Mae [*sic*] Sarton [the poet] was to be in Savannah. It was the next night so I hope you didn't seek out the performance. Two of the college teachers here [Georgia State College for Women in Milledgeville] attended. One reported it was over her head—she teaches sociology; the other said it was a great waste of time to take poetry that seriously when there are so many important *present-day* problems to be discussed—she was a Doctor of Education and was only slumming that night" (*Collected Works* 1062).

4. Sally Fitzgerald, who knew both Bishop and O'Connor well, notes: "Elizabeth was fascinated by sacramentals, possibly because they were quaint. She didn't seem to have a strong interest in Christianity, or any particular religion" (qtd. in Fountain and Brazeau, *Remembering Elizabeth Bishop* 382).

Words in Air

Bishop, Lowell, and the Aesthetics
of Autobiographical Poetry

RICHARD FLYNN

When Elizabeth Bishop left the United States in 1951 and embarked on her journey in the hope of satisfying her "immodest demands for a different world, / and a better life, and complete comprehension / of both at last, and immediately" (*PPL* 71), she had been unhappy and ill at ease in conducting the business aspect of poetry, exemplified by her disastrous year as the consultant in poetry at the Library of Congress. Writing to Lowell while on board the merchant ship *Bowplate*, Bishop remarks, "With me on the boat I brought your review of Randall [Jarrell's *The Seven League Crutches*] and Randall's review of you [*The Mills of the Kavanaughs*] & I've been brooding over them both" (*WIA* 130). Jarrell's review points out the many flaws in Lowell's long title poem, a poem about which Bishop also felt ambivalent, though she had offered extensive advice about it, much of which Lowell had followed (*WIA* 112–18). Lowell's generally laudatory review singled out Jarrell's "The Night Before the Night Before Christmas" as "the best, most mannered, the most unforgettable, and the most irritating poem in the book" (*Collected Prose* 89), the very poem Bishop had characterized nearly two years earlier as "*limp* & more suited for a short story": "When someone sends you something are you supposed to 'criticize' or merely appreciate?" she had asked Lowell (*WIA* 73).

Right after she confesses to "brooding" over her friends' reviews of each other, Bishop mentions writing "an I hope withering [review] of 'The Riddle of Emily Dickinson' for the *New Republic*." Bishop's review of this 1951 book by Rebecca Patterson is indeed withering; it condemns as reductive the book's thesis (that all of Dickinson's love poems were written for a woman, Kate Scott, with whom she had a yearlong relationship between 1859 and 1860). Bishop not only attacks Patterson's book, but asks why the whole genre of "literary detective-work . . . seem[s] finally just unpleasant." "Perhaps it is because," Bishop continues, "in order to reach a single reason for anything as singular and yet manifold as literary creation, it is necessary to limit the human personality's capacity for growth and redirection to the point of mutilation" ("Unseemly" 20).[1]

Bishop's discomfort with reviewing, however, by no means indicates that she was unconcerned with aesthetic matters; now that we have a fuller record of her previously unpublished notes and letters, it is clear that she generally conducted her most important critical investigations informally with trusted correspondents like Lowell, keeping those investigations well outside the public eye. Indeed, she may have found writing book reviews difficult precisely because the genre demands both adopting an authoritative tone and forgoing a certain amount of nuance in one's response to the work, given journalistic constraints. "The analysis of poetry is growing more and more pretentious and deadly," she wrote in her remarks for John Ciardi's *Mid-Century American Poetry* (1950). "After a session with a few of the highbrow magazines one doesn't want to look at a poem for weeks, much less start writing one" (*PPL* 687). Both Bishop and Lowell seem ambivalent at best about what Jarrell lampooned as "The Age of Criticism" (1952), but unlike their mutual friend, neither poet took to reviewing on a regular basis. Bishop at once admired and deplored Jarrell's role as prominent critic, writing to Lowell to say, "[Jarrell's] reviews infuriate me and yet that activity and that minute-to-minute devotion to criticism is really wonderful" (*WIA* 130).

For all of her hostility to what she deemed the deadly pretentiousness of the age of criticism, as well as her seeming insecurity about her own critical faculties, Bishop's undergraduate essays, such as "Time's Andromedas" (*PPL* 641–59), "Gerard Manley Hopkins: Notes on Timing in His Poetry" (*PPL* 660–67), and especially "Dimensions for a Novel" (*PPL* 671–80), had shown her early ability to grapple with difficult critical concepts and to engage in original analysis. Nevertheless, Bishop, to take her own adage in "Dimensions" to heart, wrote: "Bright ideas about *how* to do a thing are to be mistrusted, and the only bright idea which ever proves its worth is that of the thing itself" (671). Her tentative foray into reviewing during her year as poetry consultant proved unsatisfactory because she was disengaged from the poetry she reviewed. As Brett Millier points out, "Love from Emily," Bishop's brief review of another Dickinson book, *Emily Dickinson's Letters to Doctor and Mrs. Josiah Gilbert Holland* (*PPL* 689–91), "took her nearly a year to write" (225).

In October 1958, however, *Poetry* magazine published a review by Bishop that is uncharacteristically lively and enthusiastic: "I Was But Just Awake," a review of the revised edition of Walter de la Mare's anthology *Come Hither: A Collection of Rhymes and Poems for the Young of All Ages* (1957). Nearly forgotten until its inclusion in *Poems, Prose, and Letters*, the review appears at the height of Bishop's interest in childhood and autobiography as well as at a crucial moment in which she and Robert Lowell were negotiating important aesthetic issues involving the use of autobiography and the personal in poetry. In their different ways, each poet was insisting on rediscovering the importance of "real feeling" in the midst of what Randall Jarrell characterized in a 1957 letter to Bishop as "the era of the poet in the Grey Flannel Suit" (*Letters* 413).

Bishop, in particular, from her vantage point in Brazil, expressed impatience with U.S. literary culture, which she perceived as relatively bland and safe. Writing to Lowell in 1960, Bishop complained, "I get so depressed with every number of POETRY, *The New Yorker,* etc. . . . so much adequate poetry all sounding just alike and *so* boring—or am I growing frizzled small and stale or however you put it?" (*WIA* 344). Just as Bishop found *Poetry* magazine in the 1950s bland compared to its early days under Harriet Monroe, when it served as a principal venue for modernist experimentation, the tenets of the New Criticism were also beginning to seem ossified, enshrined as they were in the second edition of *Understanding Poetry.* Bishop seems to relish publishing in the staid pages of *Poetry* a rave review of something so unfashionable as *Come Hither,* de la Mare's idiosyncratic (and excellent) children's anthology.

In "I Was But Just Awake," Bishop takes particular delight in pointing out about *Come Hither* that "much of the poetry I admire is not to be found in it" (*PPL* 698). Finding that de la Mare's anthology tends to exclude the metaphysical poetry that often served as specimens for New Critical exegesis, Bishop welcomes his selection of fresh, childlike, and "frankly romantic poems":

> The book proper consists of songs and ballads, folk-poetry, and frankly romantic poems, all chosen for melodiousness as well as romance. There is nothing "intellectual," "metaphysical," or even "difficult.". . . Of Shakespeare, for example, there are only songs; of George Herbert, *Easter, Virtue,* and *Love* (the one that meant so much to Simone Weil). Donne and Hopkins are mentioned only in the notes; of Donne he says (and this explains many of the selections or omissions): "It is a poetry that awaits the mind as the body grows older, and when we ourselves have learned the experience of life with which it is concerned. Not that the simplest poetry will then lose any of its grace and truth and beauty—far rather it shines more clearly, since age needs it more." Blake, Shakespeare, and Shelley have the most poems; Coleridge, Keats and Christina Rossetti come next. (PPL 699–700)

She goes on to praise de la Mare's fondness for "'little articles,' home-made objects whose value increases with age, Robinson Crusoe's lists of his belongings, homely

employments, charms and herbs . . . what Randall Jarrell once called 'thing-y' poems, and never the pompous, abstract, or formal" (*PPL* 700). Aside from anticipating one of Bishop's greatest poems, "Crusoe in England," this describes Bishop's
own poetics of the homemade, an aesthetic she begins to explore seriously in her
1950s writing about childhood. While she delights in the frank romanticism of
de la Mare's selections, Bishop remains a fierce opponent of sentimentality in the
work of her contemporary poets and, most tellingly, in her own work. Reading the
work Bishop discarded, much of it collected in *Edgar Allan Poe & the Juke-Box,* one
is struck by the wisdom of Bishop's exclusions.

One is also struck by the ways in which the aesthetic judgments of the de la
Mare review illuminate Bishop's own writing about childhood. In the early to mid-
1950s, Bishop became immersed in recollections of her early childhood in Nova
Scotia—certainly subject matter with the potential for sentimentality—in work
such as the story "In the Village" (1953) and poems such as "Manners (Poem for
a Child of 1918)" (1955), and "Sestina" (1956). The work resists sentimentality primarily because of Bishop's insistence on presenting the child's-eye view without a
heavy layer of adult evaluation. She wrote to more than one friend, "It is funny to
come to Brazil to experience total recall about Nova Scotia—geography must be
more mysterious than we realize, even" (*One Art* 249; *EAP* 306). Despite expressing misgivings about even her best work, however, she not only understood that
"In the Village" is more of a realized work of art than "Gwendolyn" (1953) but also
had the wisdom to exclude drafts like "Where are the dolls that loved me so . . ."
(*EAP* 102), which, in my view, seems maudlin compared with both the stories and
with a finished poem like "Sestina."

Bishop's works of "total recall" were made possible both because of the relative
happiness and security of her early years in Brazil and the ordinary stock-taking
one generally engages in at midlife. Perhaps because her relationships with literary
friends in the United States had to be maintained primarily through writing, Bishop
also seems much more conscious of the direction she wishes to pursue in her work
during the 1950s and early 1960s (while at the same time, taking on assignments
like the *Diary of "Helena Morley"* and the Time-Life *Brazil* book in order to make a
living).[2] While she never expressed the ambition of a Randall Jarrell, who sought
to write "the sort of poetry that replaces modernism" (*Kipling* 51), she did, in collaboration with Lowell, seek to write a poetry that would escape the "'nice' careful,
dry and 'lovely'" work of midcentury poets like Richard Wilbur whose work displays a "kind of clever thinking out process that leaves me cold" (*WIA* 302). As her
guarded self-introduction in the Ciardi anthology betrays, she did not endorse his
vision of the midcentury poet as embodying "self-conscious sanity in an urbane

and cultivated poetry that is the antithesis of the Bohemian spirit" (xxix). *Life Studies,* she writes Lowell, satisfies her "craving" for "something new": "Your poetry is as different from the rest of our contemporaries as, say, ice from slush" (*WIA* 273).

Bishop's exasperation with her contemporaries, curiously enough, is that in the merely "adequate, sound-alike, boring poetry" there is an absence of real "feeling" (*WIA* 344). She reiterates to Lowell what a breakthrough volume *Life Studies* is, saying that it will "show ... that poetry does have some connection with emotions" (*WIA* 303). When Lowell reminds her, "But really I've just broken through to where you've always been and gotten rid of my medieval armor's undermining" (*WIA* 239), she demurs: "But 'broken through to where you've always been'— what on earth do you mean by that? I haven't gotten anywhere at all, I think. Just to those first benches to sit down and rest on, in a side arbor at the beginning of the maze" (*WIA* 247). Confessing that she is "green with envy of your kind of assurance" and lamenting that it is "hell to realize that one has wasted half one's talent through timidity," Bishop often claims the role of junior partner in the relationship. But as an advocate and an influence in the exploration of personal poetics, she does in fact lead the way. Her autobiographical story "In the Village" had such a profound effect on Lowell that he eventually versified it (unsuccessfully) as "The Scream" (1962). But more importantly, as Lowell himself acknowledges, it points the way toward "91 Revere Street" (1956): "I've got a big chunk of autobiography coming out in P[artisan] R[eview] this fall—fifty pages and hope you will approve, though it seems thin and arty after your glorious Nova Scotia mad mother and cow piece" (*WIA* 181). While Lowell often acknowledged the debt "Skunk Hour" owed to Bishop's "The Armadillo" ("I used your 'Armadillo' in class as a parallel to my 'Skunks' and ended up feeling a petty plagiarist [*WIA* 258]), I believe it is not claiming too much to say that without Bishop's "In the Village," there would not have been a *Life Studies.* There is an irony (perhaps intended) in Bishop's remark about Lowell's new autobiographical poems, "I've felt almost as wonderful a sense of relief since I first saw some of these poems in Boston as if I'd written them myself" (*WIA* 248).

This is not to say, of course, that Bishop's and Lowell's poetry is interchangeable. As Susan Rosenbaum argues in *Professing Sincerity,* Bishop's struggles with the ethical dimensions of self-presentation surface in her correspondence with Lowell surrounding the publication of *Life Studies,* and they come to a head with their disagreement about the ethics of using Elizabeth Hardwick's letters in *The Dolphin* (196–97). But as different as their poetry often is, and even though they found themselves disagreeing about the ethics of self-presentation, what seems striking in light of their complete correspondence is the extent to which they helped each other both to define and to pursue their particular excellences. Through a combination of admiration, fierce competition, envy, and genuine affection, they seem to have brought out the best in each other in terms of recognizing and encouraging their best work: Lowell's *Life Studies* and *For the Union Dead* and Bishop's *Questions of Travel* and *Geography III.*

Indeed, now that we have the complete correspondence between the poets, it is time for us to revisit our reading of their relationship, particularly the extent to which critics tend to play them against each other. Reading both sides of the story, it is clear to me that each poet recognized in each other's distinct virtues—that is, characteristics that distinguished a Bishop poem from a Lowell poem—ways of keeping their own characteristic faults in check. In the years since Lowell's death in 1977, as Bishop's reputation has increased and his has declined, critics have tended to portray Bishop's poetic virtues at Lowell's expense. Furthermore, they have tended to discount the virtues Lowell and his contemporaries recognized in Bishop's work—accuracy of observation, reticence, modesty of tone, what Jarrell described as its "restraint, calm, proportion," "personal and honest . . . wit, perception and sensitivity," and moral attractiveness (*Poetry and the Age* 234–35).

Understandably, her male contemporaries' association of these characteristics with the "feminine," accompanied as they often were with remarks such as "outside of Marianne Moore, the best poems written by a woman in this century" (Lowell, *Prose* 78) rankle contemporary critics as much as they rankled Bishop.

She had little patience with her fellow poets' sexism—and her unguarded remarks to Lowell about Jarrell's poem "Woman" makes her exasperation clear: "And Oh dear! Randall on the subject of women! Why didn't he think it over a little more! He can't really think all those clichés or Mackie would have left him years ago, I should think" (*WIA* 141).[3] Of course, she had earlier voiced similar objections to Lowell's cross-gendered performance as Anne Kavanaugh: "But it's at the end where she says, 'a girl can bear just about anything,' that I feel a real recoil. You may think this has all just to do with gender, but I don't honestly think so—it sounds to me as if the next line should almost go 'if she has a good big diamond ring'" (*WIA* 113).

Nevertheless, the characteristics of Bishop's poetry that Lowell and Jarrell may have associated with the feminine are characteristics that Lowell tried to cultivate in *Life Studies.* They also seem to be precisely the characteristics Bishop so admires in her famous jacket blurb for *Life Studies* because they temper Lowell's "now familiar trumpet notes" in order to produce a more emotionally complex verse that is still recognizably his own (*PPL* 707). In her 1962 essay "Some Notes on Robert Lowell," Bishop elaborates on her comments in the blurb:

> In *Life Studies,* published in 1959, the heavy-beat rhythms and trumpet sounds are modified, modulated. The lines still rhyme, but irregularly so, and their extension depends more on phrasing that is natural or breathlike than on strophic forms. These poems are almost always elegiac and autobiographical, on everything that is his, family, father and mother, wife (he is married to Elizabeth Hardwick, the renowned literary critic and novelist) and only child. Lowell's language is as grand, as moving, as brutal at times, as formerly—but the poems are full of "humor," of compassion, and of a simple affection for persons and places. (*PPL* 714)

In short, by incorporating some of the characteristics he most admired in Bishop, Lowell was able to remake himself as a poet. The publication of both poets' letters and of more complete editions of their poetry and prose in recent years complicates—or at least ought to complicate—our received narratives about their relationship with each other and their relative standing in literary history. For the last twenty years or more, advocates for Bishop have too often felt it necessary to construct a version of literary history in which the "confessionalism" of Lowell takes a backseat to the seemingly more nuanced personal poetry of Bishop. Paradoxically, the elevation of Bishop's reputation has relied to some extent on biographical readings that depict her poetry as more personal than it appears on the surface, unwittingly buying in to the "confessional" paradigm.

More than ten years ago, Thomas Travisano rejected the term "confessional" in his groundbreaking study *Midcentury Quartet,* proposing and articulating "a new perspective that would read Lowell, Jarrell, Bishop, and Berryman not as evincing a conflict between the reticent and the self-revelatory but as sharing a drive toward the self-exploratory" (66). In the years since Travisano's book appeared, and despite such eloquent defenses of *Life Studies* as Frank Bidart's afterword to Lowell's *Collected Poems,* "On 'Confessional' Poetry," the self-exploratory paradigm has not been embraced as much as it should have been and "confessional" has become a shorthand term used to dismiss a large number of poets. I myself have long regretted denigrating Lowell and Berryman in the last chapter of my *Randall Jarrell and the Lost World of Childhood,* and now charge those rhetorical excesses, as Robert Frost says, "to upstart inexperience" (341).

But in light of the growing published evidence, it will be harder, I hope, for readers to accept the truism that Bishop defined her "poetic practice against the example of her friend and poetic advisor, Robert Lowell," to cite Marilyn May Lombardi, who even goes so far as to describe Lowell's poems from the 1960s as acts of "literary predation" (140–41). Nevertheless, the old "confessional" paradigm that pits "the reticent and the self-revelatory" against each other in the fig-

ures of Bishop and Lowell has a long half-life. Among the many laudatory reviews
that attended the publication of *Words in Air* in 2008 are a number that reinscribe
the Bishop–Lowell correspondence itself as being conducted "Between Reticence
and Revelation," to borrow the title of James Longenbach's review in the *Nation*.
Michael Hoffman's review for *Poetry*, "The Linebacker and the Dervish"—at least
according to the headline on the Poetry Foundation's website—promises to "un-
cover a new way to read their mythologized friendship," yet it ends up reiterating
many of the old ways to read it:

> Lowell and Bishop are unmistakably and unignorably and quite intractably dissim-
> ilar—of that there can be no doubt. The letters might as well have been printed in
> different type or different colors, so little is there ever any question of who is writ-
> ing. . . . Bishop is acute, Lowell obtuse; Bishop sensitive, solicitous, moody, Lowell
> dull, sometimes careless, rather relentlessly productive; she is anxious, he when not
> shockingly and I think genuinely self-critical, insouciant; she is open to the world,
> whereas with him—and this is an understatement—"sometimes nothing is so solid
> to me as writing"; her poems in her account of them are fickle, small-scale, barely
> worth pursuing—and how many of them seem to get lost in the making—whereas
> his are industrial-scale drudgery and then quite suddenly completed. (359–60)

The supposedly intractable oppositions Hoffman insists on serve to diminish both
poets, playing them against each in ways that seem "tired / and a touch familiar"
(*PPL* 44). His comparisons become increasingly invidious over the second half
of the review, amounting to a litany of dismissive characterizations of Lowell—"a
unicorn who lives in an ivory tower," "the poet as house plant" (365), patronizing
and sentimentalizing in his response to Bishop's work, as well as self-consciously
"fraudulent" (366)—while at the same time delighting in Bishop's stance of
"brisk, tweedy, maiden-auntish, refusal" (364). Such caricature prompts Hoffman
to conclude, "In the end I don't believe that either helped the other's writing very
much" (367).

One would think that with Bishop's reputation secure these days critics could
finally abandon this tired stance in which "Bishop has been used as a club to beat
Lowell" (Longenbach, "Between Reticence"). Helen Vendler, who remains fond
of both poets' work, identifies the value of the complete correspondence as helping us understand "the often delicate negotiation back and forth between two difficult and distressed poets, determined to keep the current of their writing truthful, yet equally determined to encourage and praise" (Vendler, "The Friendship").
What Vendler identifies as a "delicate negotiation" between these poets is in many

ways at the heart of a reevaluation of Lowell's work which has not yet restored his reputation sufficiently.

David Kalstone's *Becoming a Poet* is still the indispensable account of the Bishop–Lowell relationship, and now that readers have access to the correspondence he relied upon, they can see how responsible he was in representing the then-unpublished record. But even such a sensitive critic as Kalstone describes Bishop complaining of Lowell's "prodigious assortment of adjectives" as stylistic habits of which she disapproved (207). However, the second appendix to *Words in Air* reveals a Bishop much more willing to admire such features of Lowell's style, in poems, prose, and letters: "He has a way in conversation, sometimes in prose writing or letters (I might quote from a letter to show what I mean here[)] of prefacing a name with adjective piled on adjective—I like this very much; sometimes I disagree with an adjective or two, but usually the others will be accurate, surprising, maybe, but suddenly new and absolutely right—you can take your choice—" (811). As Bishop implies here, if you can't admire Lowell's piled-on adjectives, you probably can't admire Lowell. Perhaps Bishop is simultaneously admiring and disapproving of this career-long stylistic feature of Lowell's work because its boldness is distinct from her own tendency to qualify, worry, or second-guess descriptions in the interest of accuracy. Her careful attention to his work, as in her extensive advice on Lowell's *Imitations* (1962), is not so much an attempt to contain such extravagance as it is an attempt to insist that Lowell's extravagance take place within the confines of translations that, however free, are free of "changes that *sound* like *mistakes*" (*WIA* 356, original emphasis). While Lowell is never the closely scrutinizing critic of Bishop's work that she is of his, his praise of her unique perspective and his admiration for her work—bordering on awe—provides her with much-needed affirmation and practical advice at crucial times in her career. Indeed, unlike Lowell, Bishop rarely seems to require corrective close readings; rather, because she is a severe enough censor of her own work, she requires encouragement.

In the oft-quoted final poem of Lowell's final collection, *Day by Day* (1977), Lowell struggles with the distinction between the "imagined" and the "recalled" in what had become for him a "threadbare art" (*Collected Poems* 838). In "Epilogue," he attempts to distinguish the

> snapshot
> lurid, garish, grouped
> heightened from life
> yet paralyzed by fact

from "the grace of accuracy / Vermeer gave to the sun's illumination" (848). This struggle goes back more than twenty years to his negotiation with Bishop to define the autobiographical aesthetic in prose and verse, both with and without "those blésséd structures, plot and rhyme" (838). Lowell plays the self-deprecating dismissal of his own work as a snapshot (complete with the piled-on adjectives "lurid, garish, grouped") against an accuracy he associates not only with Vermeer, but with Bishop. But as Bidart insists, "The power aimed at in *Life Studies* is the result not of accuracy but the illusion of accuracy, the result of arrangement and invention" (Lowell, *Collected Poems* 997). Furthermore, Bishop's renowned accuracy is equally the result of arrangement and invention. Ann K. Hoff discusses Bishop's "strict restraint of her reader, the care with which she recreates for the reader the experience of being just outside knowledge":

> By limiting the reader to the exterior of her memories, keeping them at the margins of knowledge, Bishop places the reader in the same untenable position she was in as a child. We know that something tragic, crucial, and life-changing has happened, but the adult voices speak in inscrutable whispers, and we cannot quite decipher them. We are helpless as a child, kept in the waiting room of Bishop's memories. Now adult and author, Bishop has gained entrance to these stories in full, filled in the gaps of her memories, but guards them and controls them jealously. In so reversing this power dynamic, Bishop regains ownership and authority over her memories, and by extension, over her traumatic childhood. (579)

Despite or perhaps even because of the differences in their poetry and prose, Bishop and Lowell are allies in their joint exploration of the aesthetics of autobiography. Their collaboration in this exploration intensifies in the 1950s and 1960s, as each concentrates on childhood recollections. Bishop's aesthetic—hinted at in the de la Mare review—is embodied initially in works of prose inspired by accurate observation, by "total recall," such as "In the Village." In January 1954, shortly after the December publication of "In the Village," Lowell praises the story:

> Your *New Yorker* story is wonderful. A great ruminating Dutch landscape feel of goneness. I could weep for the cow. I've been dragging up old conversations with you and wondering just how autobiographical this and that other two little girls story ["Gwendolyn"] are. I feel they are perhaps parts of a Nova Scotia growing-up novel—though of course they are rounded short stories. The second is much more considerable, but somehow it raises the first. So I think of some Education of E.B. or

E.B.'s Downward path to Wisdom. What KA Porter's childhood stories aim towards, or a super Miss Jewett. (*WIA* 151)

After a long break in the correspondence due to Lowell's manic episode following his mother's death, Lowell informs Bishop that he, too, is "trying to write prose— a hell of a job. It starts naked, ends as fake velvet" (*WIA* 153). By May 1955, he writes Bishop that he is "playing at starting my autobiography. . . . It's quite clumsy, inaccurate, and magical, but may work out passably. I like being off the high stilts of meter, and feel there's no limit to the prosiness and detail I can go into" (158). Bishop replies with encouragement: "Do please write an autobiography—or sketches for one. The two or three stories I've managed to do of that sort have been a great satisfaction, somehow—that desire to get things straight and tell the truth. It's almost impossible not to tell the truth in poetry, I think, but in prose it keeps eluding one in the funniest way" (*WIA* 161).

This exchange and a comparison between "In the Village" and "91 Revere Street" show that while Lowell draws his inspiration for attempting prose auto-biography from Bishop's example, his motives for doing so (getting off "the high stilts of meter" and allowing himself to be prosy, "clumsy, inaccurate, and magical") seem opposed to Bishop's avowed "desire to get things straight and tell the truth." The spare sensuality of Bishop's child's-eye view in "In the Village" (much closer to Jewett's "The White Heron" than Porter's "Downward Path to Wisdom") derives its power from the "'little articles,' home-made objects," and by inviting the reader to enter the child's world by flicking a fingernail "on top of the church steeple" at the end of the opening paragraph, she invites the reader to forgo adult evaluation in favor of the child's experience. Bishop insists on the freshness of the perspective, which escapes "the pompous, abstract, or formal," whereas Lowell's meditation on Mordecai Myers at the beginning of "91 Revere Street" plumbs the distance between the "Poor sheepdog in wolf's clothing" and the "true wolf" young Lowell had attempted to enlist "in the anarchy of my adolescent war on my parents" (*Collected Poems* 122). Myers's portrait, "mislaid past finding," exists only in memory, "in the setting of our Revere Street house, a setting now fixed in the mind, where it survives all the distortions of fantasy, all the blank befogging of forgetfulness. There, the vast number of remembered *things* remains rocklike. Each is in its place, each has its function, its history, its drama. There, all is preserved by that motherly care that one either ignored or resented in his youth. The things and their owners come back urgent with life and meaning—because finished, they are endurable and perfect" (*Collected Poems* 122). As this passage indicates, "things" are impor-tant to Lowell because of their emblematic function in historical and personal memory; they exist to heighten the family drama as the poet narrates the past. For instance, his father's "oak and 'rhinoceros hide' armchair" is "ostentatiously . . . masculine," and equally ostentatious in its overdetermined symbolism, its thick irony, that emphasizes the emasculation of the father and "only child" in the remainder of the memoir. It is not just the young Lowell, but "91 Revere Street" itself that is "drenched in my parents' passions" (Lowell, *Collected Poems* 127). David Kalstone observes that Lowell's memoir is "more brittle and visibly crafted than 'In the Village' and less exploratory and wild than his other pieces of autobiographical prose" (169). That is to say that "91 Revere Street" shows its seams; it is painfully self-conscious—aware that it plays to an audience just as young Lowell's expulsion from the Public Garden takes place "in the presence of my mother and some thirty nurses and children" (*Collected Poems* 137). But it is, after all, like a "Lowell poem, as big as life and as alive and rainbow-edged" (*PPL* 707). By contrast, "In the Village" collapses present and past tense and first- and third- person narration, but like "the echo of a scream" that "hangs over that Nova Scotian Village" it insists on our seeing (and hearing) the past moment without overt interpretation. Bishop's narrator all but effaces the adult "I" in favor of the child's eye—and ear. While for Lowell's more overtly retrospective narrator "things" are "urgent with life and meaning," Bishop's narrator wishes for the voices of her mother's "things," including the "frail, almost-lost scream," to be subsumed under the beautiful, elemental "*Clang*" of Nate with the blacksmith's hammer:

> It sounds like a bell buoy out at sea.
> It is the elements speaking: earth, air, fire, water.
> All those other things—clothes, crumbling postcards, broken china; things damaged and lost, sickened or destroyed; even the frail, almost-lost scream—are they too frail for us to hear their voices long, too mortal?
> Nate!
> Oh, beautiful sound, strike again! (*PPL* 118)

The poem Lowell later "derives" from this story, "The Scream," recasts the poem as a much less interesting monologue in which the speaker relates certain particulars of the story in the past tense, resulting in a somewhat maudlin self-pity exacerbated when Lowell has the Bishop speaker recall the precocious observation of his daughter Harriet, "But you can't love everyone, / your heart won't let you!" (*Collected Poems* 327). It is clearly a set performance piece and, in many ways it is a performance that misappropriates the story, despite Bishop's reassurance that "everything of importance is there" (*WIA* 402). Lowell himself understands that he has made "something small and literary out of something much larger, gayer, and more healthy. I let the scream throw out the joyful *clang*" (*WIA* 390).

Without the *clang*, Lowell's version of Bishop's story strikes a false note, resembling not so much an exploratory "life study" as it does an ordinary "confessional" poem of the sort that Bishop, in particular, came to deplore. Bishop's positive aesthetic influence fails to exercise its magic here when Lowell attempts to adopt Bishop herself as the speaker. Unlike Lowell's best work, it "magnifies," but fails to "illuminate" (*PPL* 707). In my opinion, "The Scream" suffers from what Travisano has characterized as Lowell's tendency to be "a poetic magpie, if ever there was one" (*WIA* xx). Lowell's defensiveness about the poem elicits Bishop's repeated, but somewhat hollow, reassurance: "No—*I was very pleased with 'The Scream.'* I find it very touching to think you were worried for fear I might be annoyed" (*WIA* 412). By contrast, in Bishop's visceral response to Lowell's "The Old Flame" (*Collected Poems* 323–24) (about his first wife, Jean Stafford)—"'The Old Flame' reduces me to tears" (*WIA* 402)—it is clear that she believes that Lowell has found the emotional center of that poem; its impact (particularly that of the ending) is so great that Bishop remarks, "Alas, it is too real for me to judge it as a poem" (*WIA* 403). Bishop goes on to say that these poems (which will appear in *For the Union Dead* two years later) pass her "test for 'real poetry,'" by making her "feel I *must* write a lot of poems immediately," an impulse that Bishop, unlike Lowell, knows she must resist: "Only they would come out, if at all, sounding like you" (*WIA* 403).

That each poet, in their best work, is able to learn from the other about "real poetry" without sounding alike is a testament to the importance of a collaboration that at its height seems nearly magical. The most famous example, in which Lowell's admiration for Bishop's "The Armadillo" allows him to discover the extraordinary leap of diction in "Skunk Hour" from the leisurely semi-humorous description of the first four stanzas to the stark and startling "My mind's not right" hardly needs to be rehearsed here. Almost as well known is the influence of Lowell's great poem "My Afternoon with Uncle Devereux Winslow" on Bishop's "First Death in Nova Scotia," but here, the reverse influence is instructive. Bishop's envious, self-deprecating letter to Lowell in which she says that he is "the luckiest poet I know" provides the background:

> And here I must confess (and I imagine most of our contemporaries would confess the same thing) that I am green with envy of your kind of assurance. I feel that I could write in as much detail about my Uncle Artie, say—but what would be the significance? Nothing at all. He became a drunkard, fought with his wife and spent

most of his time fishing . . . and was ignorant as sin. It is sad; slightly more interesting than having an uncle practicing law in Schenectady maybe, but that's all. Whereas all you have to do is put down the names. (*WIA* 247)

It is hard for one to believe that Bishop really thinks that the emotional resonance of a poem like "My Last Afternoon with Uncle Devereux Winslow" comes from just putting down the names. In the poem, Lowell plays the oppressiveness of the parents' "watery martini pipe dreams" and Edwardian bric-a-brac of *"Char-de-sa"* against a representation of the young boy's perspective that, while not entirely free of adult evaluation, comes much closer than "The Scream" to capturing the child-like point of view Bishop employs in "In the Village." While Bishop was to work on her memoir of her Uncle Artie, "Memories of Uncle Neddy," for years until its eventual appearance in the *Southern Review* in the fall of Lowell's death, her poem about the death of Uncle Artie's son, her cousin Arthur, "First Death in Nova Scotia," practically deconstructs the relationship between the child and the décor in "My Last Afternoon." Although the household objects in the Lowell poem seem to be heavily invested with a significance that the retrospective speaker understands (but the child in the poem does not), the ordinary objects in the Bishop poem (the chromographs of the royal family, the stuffed loon) are invested with a significance that only this particular, bewildered child immediately apprehends. Both poems play with warm and cold in their concluding stanzas, and the warmth in each poem proves illusory, but while "Uncle Devereux" concludes on a note of resigned acceptance—"Come winter, / Uncle Devereux would blend to the one color"—"First Death" concludes with what is from the child's point of view an unanswerable question:

> But how could Arthur go,
> clutching his tiny lily,
> with his eyes shut up so tight
> and the roads deep in snow? (*PPL* 122)

"First Death . . ." refuses the consoling wisdom of "My Last Afternoon with Uncle Devereux Winslow"—just as "Sestina" is also a bleak poem that refuses consoling wisdom—but it may be that it is that very element of uneasy consolation in *Life Studies* that Bishop envies.

The terms Bishop uses to praise the *Life Studies* poems—"sure feeling"; "that rare feeling of control and illumination"; "extended display of imagination" (*WIA* 246) "painfully acute and real" (263)—are also the terms that Bishop insists distinguish Lowell from his "better imitators," that distinguish Lowell's autobiographical verse from what would come to be called the "confessional." Anne Sexton's "kind of egocentricity is simply that," while Lowell's "has been made intensely *interesting* and painfully applicable to every reader" (327). Snodgrass seems to be

> really saying, "I do all these awful things—but don't you really think I'm awfully *nice*?" This is the masculine version of that "our old silver" feminine-thing[4] I wrote you about, too, I think, and it is the vast difference between you and one of your better imitators. You *tell* things—but never wind up with your own darling gestures, the way he does (he'd be giving Lepke home-made cookies or something). I went straight through *Life Studies* again and there is not a trace of it, and that is really "masculine" writing—courageous and honest. (*WIA* 359–60)

The Lowell of *Life Studies* becomes for Bishop such a touchstone, that it is unsurprising she would find some of the work after *Near the Ocean* (1967) somewhat disappointing by comparison. It is also significant that Lowell's sonnets, which he begins on the Fourth of July 1967, coincide with the end of Bishop's relative security in Brazil, culminating in Lota de Macedo Soares's suicide in September. One senses Bishop's growing impatience with the *Notebooks*—she doesn't "really know what to say at all" and is "overcome by the sheer volume" (*WIA* 654). And yet in the closing poem of *Notebook,* "Obit," Bishop encounters lines that seem to serve as a touchstone for her later work in *Geography III:* "After loving you so much, can I forget / you for eternity, and have no other choice?" In April 1969 she writes, "The ending is so good I wish I hadn't read it, since it is now predominant in a group of lines of yours that haunt my days and nights" (654). Later in a June 15, 1970, letter from Ouro Prêto, in the midst of the collapse of her relationship with "Suzanne," she is even more specific: "Those lines of yours, Cal darling—'After loving you so much'—etc.—I sometimes wish you hadn't written them or I hadn't read them. They say *everything,* and they say everything I wish I could somehow say about Lota, but probably never shall. I am trying to do a small book of poems for her, or about her—but it is still too painful" (677). It is in this letter that she sends Lowell "In the Waiting Room"—and wistfully, ironically, and perhaps unconsciously alludes to her productive period of "total recall" during the 1950s: "I just realized last night as the lights failed in the kitchen and I fried myself an egg by the light of the oil lamp, that probably what I am really up to is creating a sort of de luxe Nova Scotia all over again, in Brazil. And now I'm my own grandmother" (676).

Contrary to Lowell's improvisatory and magpie ways, Bishop internalized and gestated her stylistic influences over a period of years. The closing lines of "Obit" may have tarnished for Bishop after Lowell placed them at the end of *For Lizzie and Harriet* (1973), sequestering them from what Adrienne Rich called the "bullshit eloquence" of *The Dolphin* (1973). But they also seem to have acted as a genial epigraph that presides over her late poems about the art of losing, poems like "The Moose" completed at long last in 1972, "Poem" (1972), "One Art" (1976), and "Crusoe in England" (1971). A little over a year after Bishop's letter in which she voices her objections to *The Dolphin* (and appends several pages of specific notes for improving the poem), Lowell writes to Bishop about "Crusoe in England": "maybe your very best poem, an analogue to your life, or an Ode to Dejection. Nothing you have written has such a mix of humor and desperation; I find bits of the late Randall, his sour witty downgrading of his own jokes, somehow this echo, if it is, makes the poem more original and seals it with your voice" (*WIA* 755). In *Geography III*, in poems like "Crusoe," "Poem," and "The Moose," Bishop ultimately refuses to become her own grandmother. The "de luxe Nova Scotia," like the "proto-.../... crypto dream-house" in "The End of March" is "perfect! But—impossible" (168). The genesis of "Crusoe" goes all the way back to the Cuttyhunk notebooks of 1934: "A poem should be made about making things in a pinch—& and how it looks sad when the emergency is over" (qtd. in Millier 62). In "Crusoe," Bishop transforms the seemingly simple "little articles," "Crusoe's list of belongings," Jarrell's "thing-y poems," into the "poetry that awaits the mind as the body grows older ... when we ourselves have learned the experience of life with which it is concerned" (*PPL* 700). That Crusoe's once-loved objects no longer sustain him as he is "old" "bored," and "surrounded by uninteresting lumber" is heartbreaking—"How can anyone want such things?" (*PPL* 156)—but one can't help thinking that, had they lived longer, Bishop and Lowell undoubtedly would have given us more poems concerning the "experience of life," poems that would further articulate heartbreak and loss without giving in to self-pity.

One of the most heavily mythologized moments in the Bishop–Lowell relationship is the day in Stonington, Maine, 1948, when Lowell confesses in his August 15, 1957, letter that he had intended to propose marriage to Bishop—"asking you is the might have been for me" (*WIA* 226), a reminiscence Bishop at first ignores and then assiduously deflects as Lowell perennially alludes to it in letters and in the various drafts and rewrites of "Water." When he raises the issue once again in 1975, "as we near our finish" (776), Bishop admonishes him: "Please, *please* don't talk about old age so much, my dear old friend! You are giving me the creeps" (778) In addition to warning Lowell, "so *please* don't put me in a beautiful poem tall with long brown hair!" she notes: "In spite of aches & pains I really don't feel much different than I did at 35—and I certainly am a great deal happier, most of the time. . . . I just *won't* feel ancient—I wish Auden hadn't gone on about it so in his last years and I hope you won't" (*WIA* 778). What I am struck by most in revisiting their friendship and aesthetic collaboration is how they encouraged, admonished, cajoled, criticized, and conspired with each other to produce together one of the twentieth century's most significant conversations about "life and the memory of it." To reverse the terms of Bishop's "Poem," Bishop and Lowell were artists of equal stature whose visions coincided even though their "looks" were very different.

NOTES

1. While the annotations in *Words in Air* are excellent, in this instance, Bishop's Dickinson review has been misidentified as "Love from Emily" (reprinted in *PPL* 689–91 and in *CPr* 262–63). The correct citation for Bishop's review of the Patterson book is: "Unseemly Deductions," review of *The Riddle of Emily Dickinson*, by Rebecca Patterson, *New Republic* 127 (August 18, 1952): 20. It has now been reprinted (without the title) in Elizabeth Bishop, *Prose*, ed. Lloyd Schwartz, 264–65.

2. Unlike the Life World Library book, *Brazil*, Bishop's translation of the Brazilian childhood memoir was integral to her exploration of the childhood theme that surfaces in her work during the 1950s.

3. Bishop also expressed her distaste for Jarrell's "Woman" to Pearl Kazin: "Cal seems to be all wound up in teaching. Randall J. was married again, some time ago now—I haven't heard from him, but there's a dreadful poem called "Woman" in the last *B. Oscure* by him" (*OA* 241–42). One of the great pleasures of having the complete *Words in Air* is seeing just how frank the poets were to each other about even their best-loved contemporaries. Although the version of "Woman" Bishop read in *Botthege Oscure* was completely rewritten before its publication in *The Lost World*, its appearance there had a lot to do with Bishop's reservations about Jarrell's last book: "I dislike the ones on 'women'—more than you do, no doubt—and wonder where he *gets* these women—they seem to be like none I—or you—know" (*WIA* 573).

4. Bishop here refers to her remarks in a July 27, 1960, letter to Lowell: "That Anne Sexton I think still has a bit too much romanticism and what I think of as the 'our beautiful old silver' school of female writing which is really boasting about how nice *we* were. V. Woolf, K.A.P., Bowen, R. West, etc.—they are full of it. They have to make quite sure that the reader is not going to misplace them socially, first—and that nervousness interferes constantly with what they think they'd like to say" (*WIA* 333). This assessment of Sexton appears in *One Art*, but her similar criticism of Snodgrass does not—another example of the way the expanded record enriches our understanding of these judgments.

Part IV

The New Elizabeth Bishop and Her Art

Geography IV, or The Death of the Author Revisited

An Essay in Speculative Bibliography

THOMAS TRAVISANO

Imagine, if you will . . . Elizabeth Bishop, at the age of sixty-eight, visits a brilliant Boston cardiologist and receives timely medical treatment and advice, thereby avoiding what might have been her sudden death from a cerebral aneurysm in October 1979, at the height of her poetic powers. She is induced by this cardiologist to adopt a healthier regimen, including fewer cigarettes and much less alcohol, and so Bishop lives on into the 1980s, increasingly frail physically, but artistically still vigorous. At last, in 1986, when she reaches the age of seventy-five, her publishers, Farrar, Straus and Giroux, bring out what proves to be her final volume of poems. Let us call this notional book *Geography IV.* The reviewers send in notices that are almost universally admiring, and in a few cases, even reverent. But many of these reviewers, including several of the most admiring, admit to being startled by a new directness, sometimes even a certain rawness or indelicacy, emerging from the Vermeer-like surfaces of a poet they no longer refer to as Miss Bishop. These reviewers confess that in reading this new book, they have had to make adjustments to the expectations and preconceptions they had learned previously to bring to Bishop's work.

Thus began a paper I gave more than a decade ago at the 1998 MLA Convention with a title identical to this one. At the time I thought of developing the paper further, but it seemed more appropriate to await the publication of *Edgar Allan Poet & the Juke-Box: Uncollected Poems, Drafts, and Fragments.* The publication of this collection of nearly one hundred uncompleted, uncollected, or unpublished poems would make most of the poems under discussion in that earlier paper, which until then had only been available to scholars, accessible to the reading public. When that book, edited and annotated by Alice Quinn, appeared to significant fanfare and no little controversy in the spring of 2006, it seemed appropriate to return to the subject of *Geography IV,* our notional last Bishop volume.

Sadly, of course, Bishop never found that brilliant cardiologist who might have prolonged her life. Nor did she live to complete a new book of poems to follow up on her 1976 *Geography III,* whose nine original poems—including "One Art," "The Moose," "Poem," "The End of March," "Twelve O'Clock News," "Crusoe in England," and "In the Waiting Room"—confirmed her to be at the height of her powers.

However, Bishop's next published book of poetry was not our notional *Geography IV* of 1986, but the posthumous 1983 volume, *The Complete Poems: 1927–1979.* This was followed in 1984 by the *Collected Prose,* edited by Robert Giroux; in 1994 by *One Art: Letters,* edited by Giroux; in 1996 by *Exchanging Hats: Paintings,* edited by William Benton; and in 2006 by *Edgar Allan Poe & the Juke-Box,* edited by Quinn. Yet another major addition to the canon appeared in 2008 in the extensive Library of America volume: *Elizabeth Bishop: Poems, Prose, and Letters,* edited by Giroux and Lloyd Schwartz. Later in 2008 came a book edited by the present author with Saskia Hamilton: *Words in Air: The Complete Correspondence between Elizabeth Bishop and Robert Lowell.* Further collections of her letters, prose, and poetry are already in the works.

What I find intriguing about our notional fifth volume of Bishop's poetry are the questions it raises about Bishop's future as an artist, had she lived, and the vision such a volume offers—or is vision "too serious a word"?—of the arc of her development as a poet. Bishop was an artist whose development was always subtle, unpredictable, hard to characterize, and, for me, at least, fascinating. It was never marked by clear phases or styles, as was her close friend Lowell's, since each poem was sui generis. Yet that intricate evolution seemed to be leading her toward something new, toward poems that were gaining in sharpness and immediacy, sometimes at the risk of unmasking such characteristics as audacity, indelicacy, political anger, and a piercing pathos that had been lurking below the glittering surfaces of her earlier work. Where was her career going when she died so suddenly and with so many poems still actively in progress? That is the question I wish to contemplate in this essay. While there are no certainties, factors that might allow such an inquiry to proceed along plausible lines include her known work patterns, the poems she had already in the can, and the patterns of subject matter, tone, and theme that one can trace among the many completed, uncompleted, or fragmentary poems of her last period. The process of considering the future shape of Bishop's final book might be thought of, or so my title suggests, as "speculative bibliography."

The Oxford English Dictionary defines bibliography as: "The systematic description and history of books, their authorship, printing, publication, editions, etc." This might seem so precise and descriptive a science as to rule out the speculative altogether. But Bishop's work embodied a struggle of speech against silence, and this struggle toward difficult articulation aligns her with other writers — particularly women writing in the West or women and men laboring worldwide under political, cultural, or psychological prohibitions — whose cultural situation would have urged not just the use of coded language but a tendency to suppress, or to leave uncompleted or unpublished, some of their most provocative and compelling writings. For authors such as these, a creative approach to bibliography remains very much to the point.

Arguably, the first major work in the then-nascent field of Bishop studies was Candace MacMahon's excellent *Elizabeth Bishop: A Bibliography, 1927–1979,* published by the University Press of Virginia in 1980, the year after Bishop's death. And Bishop studies has maintained deep roots in the field of bibliography ever since. Many of Bishop's most important critics have acted as creative bibliographers, tracking down and publishing, or extensively quoting, important uncollected or long-fugitive texts by Bishop in prose and verse. *Edgar Allan Poe & the Juke-Box* is consistent with the adventurous spirit of Bishop scholarship present since its earliest days. Indeed, that adventurous scholarship helped to push the book toward publication, as Quinn acknowledges, and it is extensively and appreciatively cited in Quinn's notes. Many of Bishop's unfinished and uncollected poems, such as "It is marvellous to wake up together . . ." (*EAP* 44), "Dear, my compass . . ." (*EAP* 140), and "A Drunkard" (*EAP* 150) have long held a vital place in the everyday discourse of Bishop's scholarship. Moreover, so many of these poems are so interesting and even, in some cases, revelatory, that the appearance of such a volume may be read as a natural part of the recovery process for an author who left so much work of great value unpublished during her lifetime. Indeed, of the just more than nine hundred pages of Bishop's poems, prose, and letters that appear in the new Library of America volume edited by Giroux and Schwartz, only about two hundred pages were in print at the time of Bishop's death in 1979. The others remained in manuscript or were buried in the back issues of periodicals ranging from *Partisan Review* and the *New Yorker* to high school publications like Walnut Hill School's the *Blue Pencil* and North Shore Country Day's the *Owl.* I observed in my 1995 essay "The Elizabeth Bishop Phenomenon" that, since her death, "the Bishop canon is still expanding, at a rate that often seems to exceed her rate of production while she lived" (920). At this writing, the expansion of that canon shows no signs of abating, and my earlier remark appears, if anything, an understatement.

Based on her known work patterns, it seems reasonable to pencil in our notional date of publication for *Geography IV* as 1986, based on Bishop's well-established tendency to publish books of poems at roughly ten-year intervals (*North & South,*

1946; *Poems: A Cold Spring*, 1955; *Questions of Travel*, 1965; *Geography III*, 1976). At the moment of her death, Bishop had completed four new poems for the *New Yorker*, her regular venue. "Santarém," "North Haven," and "Pink Dog" appeared there in 1978, and "Sonnet" appeared there on October 29, 1979, just three weeks after her death. With four strong poems in the bank, Bishop already had a good start, and, according to our notional timeline, she would have had seven more years to complete *Geography IV.*

Some of the additional poems beyond the already-published quartet that might have appeared in *Geography IV* would of course have been entirely new, but based on her previous patterns, in which she worked and reworked poems, often over many years, it seems likely that she would have drawn on several poems already in draft. Those one hundred–plus poems in draft fall into four broad categories in terms of their degree of completion: first of all, active drafts—often in multiple versions—awaiting completion; second, back-burner poems and fragments awaiting a new burst of inspiration; third, completed poems she might have dismissed as occasional, trivial, or merely personal; and fourth, poems of risky subject matter, some of them completed or nearly so, but uncomfortable to Bishop herself in content and therefore possible objects of suppression. Several of the poems I am going to mention, including "Apartment in Leme" and "Salem Willows," exist in multiple drafts and, according to internal evidence, were being actively revised and apparently nearing completion. It would seem that only her sudden death prevented her from putting the finishing touches on these poems and sending them off to the *New Yorker*. Other poems on which she was working actively were full of promise, but still some distance from completion. Still other poems lay dormant, uncompleted but unabandoned, awaiting the kind of recurrence of inspiration that had led to the completion of two of the best poems in *Geography III*, "The Moose" and "Twelve O'Clock News," each after more than twenty years of artistic incubation. Still other poems bordered on disclosures—particularly disclosures about her family, her alcoholism, or her lesbian sexuality—that this poet, who favored "closets, closets, and more closets" (Fountain 330) was reluctant to make. It remains uncertain whether the new freedoms of the 1980s would have sufficiently encouraged Bishop to include such poems in her next volume. It is upon this range of materials, published and unpublished, nearly completed or fragmentary, that I draw for my outline of our notional *Geography IV.*

For that outline we can also draw upon certain broad categories of concern that Bishop explored in the quartet of poems published after *Geography III* and the others she was working on actively at the moment of her sudden death. These areas of interest might be termed: (1) "Brazil Reconsidered," (2) "Childhood Memories Extended," (3) "The Further Art of Losing," (4) "Abstract Self-Portraits," and (5) "Poems of Love and Sexuality." Thinking in terms of these groupings will help us envision the lines along which Bishop's career appears to have been developing.

I'll start with the category of "Brazil Reconsidered." Two of the four poems published after *Geography III* fit this category. While Brazil, where she lived for most of the 1950s and 1960s, had been the dominant focus of *Questions of Travel* (1965) and of the group of "New and Uncollected Poems" that appeared in *The Complete Poems* (1969), Brazil does not appear directly in even a single poem in *Geography III*, although it has, I think, an allusive presence in several of them, particularly "Crusoe in England" and "One Art." If we link the two late, published Brazilian poems, "Santarém" and "Pink Dog," which appear to return to Brazil with a new eye, with a poem being actively drafted, such as "Apartment in Leme," we may begin to recognize a newly explicit political dimension—specifically, a focus on poverty and otherness—emerging dramatically in this series of poetic reconsiderations of her long sojourn in Brazil. Each of these three poems was begun while Bishop still lived in Brazil, but each in its different way digs quite deep, and she appears to have been unable to finish them without the benefit of distance from Brazil in space and time.

Thus, as the day dawns in "Apartment in Leme," the poet observes:

> It's growing lighter. On the beach two men
> get up from shallow, newspaper-lined graves.
> A third sleeps on. His coverlet
>
> is corrugated paper, a flattened box.
> One running dog, two early bathers, stop
> dead in their tracks; detour. (*EAP* 135)

While in "Pink Dog," a "depilated" female dog suffers from scabies and emblematizes the otherness of the urban poor, here both human bathers and a "running dog" veer off to avoid the figure of a sleeping, homeless man. Yet "Apartment in Leme" also celebrates the power of the sea as a feminine presence that borders on and defines the geographical outline and emotional atmosphere of Copacabana: "Because we live in your open mouth, oh Sea, / with your cold breath blowing warm, your warm breath cold" (*EAP* 134). It was in Copacabana's Leme district that Bishop shared an apartment—overlooking the famous beach and Guanabara Bay—with her friend and lover Lota de Macedo Soares. Although the poem, which exists in more than thirty pages of drafts, was unfinished at her death, some lines are luminous, and it's hard to avoid the feeling that one is in the presence of a major poem in the making. Indeed, the fact that Bishop contemplated dedicating this poem to her close friend Robert Lowell, as she indicates in an August 2, 1965, letter, shows that Bishop herself thought highly of its possibilities. So is the fact that she regarded it as potentially "a bit better than 'The Armadillo'" (*EAP* 134), an earlier Brazil poem dedicated to Lowell that he held in particularly high esteem.

In published poems like "Santarém," "Pink Dog," and in extensive drafts like "Apartment in Leme," Brazil makes a dramatic return, not—as in *Questions of Travel*—as a locus of present experience, but rather as a nexus of memory: a lost continent, or a lost world, resembling now, in its imaginative presence and power, Bishop's long-lost Nova Scotia, a nexus to be explored through the defracting prisms and reflecting mirrors of memory.

The thematic zone I am calling "Childhood Memories Extended," though it involves no published poems in the final quartet, does involve a very large number of poems in manuscript. Some of these—such as the achingly poignant "Where are the dolls that loved me so . . ."—were waiting on the back burner, but several others were being actively drafted and redrafted. Of the poems Bishop was working on actively, "Salem Willows" was perhaps the most frequently reworked and the closest to completion. "Salem Willows" explores feelings of loneliness, isolation, and imaginative pleasure in the context of a partly nostalgic evocation of her Aunt Maud Bulmer, her mother's elder sister, an important female caregiver who tried to mitigate the early state of orphanhood and involuntary abandonment that Bishop suffered as a consequence of the death of her father when the poet was eight months old and the permanent emotional breakdown of her mother when the poet was five. Maud also appears prominently in the vivid draft memoir "Mrs. Sullivan Downstairs," which *EAP* includes in an appendix. There Bishop describes her impressions of Maud in some detail. "My aunt was small, worried, nervous. She was a clean housekeeper but not a very good one; things went undone often while she read a new magazine or a novel. The sewing machine was piled high with old *National Geographics* always, as far as I remembered it occasionally they were lifted off and deposited some other place while she made herself a dress. She did beautiful sewing. . . . My aunt and I loved each other and told each other everything and for many years I saw nothing in her to criticize" (*EAP* 203). Bishop lived for many years with Aunt Maud and her husband, George Shepherdson, in what Bishop describes in "Mrs. Sullivan Downstairs" as "a medium-poor section of a very poor town," i.e., Revere, Massachusetts. There Bishop continued to suffer from the asthma and eczema that had nearly killed her following her unwilling return, at the age of six, to the home of her paternal (Bishop) grandparents in Worcester, Massachusetts. Bishop would not become healthy enough to attend school full-time until the age of fourteen.

"Salem Willows" evokes a visit with Maud to a historic carrousel, famous for its beautifully hand-carved figures, in an amusement park in the nearby town of Salem. The poem's haunting rhythm and imagery evokes the seeming endless circuits of the merry-go-round's turning wheel in language that echoes and develops upon William Carlos Williams's famous "The Dance," a poem that begins:

> In Brueghel's great picture, The Kermess,
> the dancers go round, they go round and
> around. . . . (Williams 58)

Williams's (and Brueghel's) peasants "swing . . . their butts" energetically to the "squeal and the blare and the / tweedle of bagpipes," while Bishop's carrousel revolves more smoothly to "the coarse, mechanical music of the gold calliope," but also to the unheard, Keatsian music of the carrousel's "plaster people":

> From time to time, to the music,
> they'd raise a flute, but never
> quite to their lips; they'd almost
> beat their drums; they'd not quite
> pluck their upheld lyres. (EAP 164–65)

Bishop's poem evokes, with a child's eye, a turning world of ambiguous decorum in which it is the carrousel, and not human dancers, that spins on an axis, and the poem's observation comes not from outside but from inside its turning world. The draft version of "Salem Willows" closes thus:

> Around and around and around.
> Were we all touched by Midas?
> Were we a ring of Saturn,
> a dizzy, [turning] nimbus?
> Or were we one of the crowns
> the saints "cast down" (but why?)
> "upon the glassy sea"?

> The carrousel slows down.
> Really, beyond the willows,
> glittered a glassy sea
> and Aunt Maud sat and knitted
> and knitted, waiting for me. (EAP 165)

The poem's still point resides outside the "dizzy, [turning] nimbus" of the carrousel, resting upon the reassuring if perhaps uninspiring figure of the knitting Aunt Maud herself; Maud's quiet knitting is the only human—as opposed to mechanical—movement in the poem.

"Salem Willows," despite a number of magical touches, falls short—in its present form—of clinching the deal artistically by two or three turns of the screw. Still, like "Apartment in Leme," it exists in many late drafts, its texture and much of its language is characteristic of Bishop's work at its best, and it is hard to avoid the conclusion that, had Bishop lived a few more years, she would very likely have added "Salem Willows" to her long list of accomplished poems exploring the ambiguities of childhood experience as a locus, at once, of keen pleasure and excruciating loss. Perhaps, though this is more speculative, Bishop might have found the inspiration, as she was completing "Salem Willows," to return to and complete an elegy for Aunt Maud from the 1950s, begun in Brazil at a time when Bishop had launched her extensive reexploration of childhood experience in stories like "In the Village" and "Gwendolyn" and poems like "Sestina," "Manners," and "First Death in Nova Scotia." Her unfinished elegy for her aunt, "For M.B.S., buried in Nova Scotia," repositions Maud not as a Canadian transplant in an impoverished American city, but as one of many native residents of the communal graveyard in Maud's and Bishop's own beloved Great Village:

> Yes, you are dead now and live
> only there, in a little, slightly tip-tilted graveyard
> where all of your childhood's Christmas trees are foregathered
> with the presents they meant to give,
> and your childhood's river quietly curls at your side
> and breathes deep with each tide. (EAP 98)

Here, certainly, it is hard to avoid the inference that Bishop refers not just to Maud's "childhood's Christmas trees" and its deeply breathing river, but to Bishop's own remembered trees and river. And the poem hints at how intensely she yearns to recover and find placement in the world she had lost when she was so painfully removed from Great Village in 1917 by her unwittingly cruel paternal grandparents.

Other female caregivers appear in poems like "The Grandmothers," a poem that evokes the characteristic phrases of her "three grandmothers, (one 'great' one, understood)" (*EAP* 107), phrases that embody the aggressively assertive, resigned, or weary and dismissive views of life of these differing women: "My day will come," "Nobody knows," and "Ho-hum, Ho-hum, hum-a-day" (*EAP* 107–8). However, several of these poems in draft suggest an increasingly sharp-edged investigation of her relationship with her long-lost mother, Gertrude, who was permanently shut away in a mental institution when the poet was five. These include such poems as "Swan-Boat Ride," "A Mother Made of Dress Goods," and "A Drunkard." The last of these, in particular, seems to me potentially a great poem. Its composition history is hard to recover. In a February 15, 1960, letter to Lowell, she refers to a poem called "The Drunkard" as "a sort of sonnet" (*EAP* 344). Yet of the two drafts we now have, internal evidence indicates a composition date in the 1970s. Moreover, in its present form the poem is not a sonnet but a series of unrhymed verse paragraphs totaling nearly fifty lines. Unfortunately, any earlier versions do not survive. The poem vividly evokes a historical event, the Great Salem Fire of 1914 (which Bishop observed when she was just three years old) and which she describes as from inside her crib through a bedroom window:

> People were playing hoses on the roofs
> of the summer cottages on Marblehead neck;
> the red sky was filled with flying motes,
> cinders and coals, and bigger things, scorched black burnt.
> The water glowed like fire, too, but flat.
> I watched some boats arriving on the beach
> full of escaping people (I didn't know that). (EAP 150)

The poem, too, is characteristically Bishop-like in its unusual placement of the speaker—a three-year-old observer who experiences vividly yet who shares consciousness with an adult mind that has the powers of reflection and self-analysis. Along with its intense description of a historic conflagration in which more than fifteen thousand people were rendered homeless, the poem has a self-exploratory intensity that takes her to the brink of significant disclosures.

> I was terribly thirsty but mama didn't hear
> me calling her. Out on the lawn

> she and some neighbors were giving coffee
> or food or something to the people landing in the boats—
> once in a while I caught a glimpse of her
> and called and called—no one paid any attention— (EAP 150)

It is a further characteristic gesture of Bishop's to locate her own childlike pleas for attention in the context of a moment where others, the refugees of the fire, clearly need that attention even more. Possibly the key disclosures of bewilderment, guilt, or anger toward her mother for feelings of abandonment—and that abandonment's possible link, at the end of the poem, to an ongoing problem with alcohol—may have raised barriers to the completion of this powerful poem, but then, much of Bishop's most powerful work emerged when she pushed herself to or past the edge of self-censorship. It remains an open question whether the passage of years might have allowed Bishop to complete a poem she had begun in very different form in the 1960s and that she continued to struggle with through the 1970s and apparently up to the end of her life.

The poetic focus I've designated as "The Further Art of Losing" has a firm anchor in "North Haven," her beautifully incisive and poignant published elegy for Robert Lowell, who died in 1977. Here loss and the artist's problem of making are inextricably intertwined with the human problem of living. Another poignant poem in draft, and one that appears to be approaching completion, is "For Grandfather." This unfinished poem, begun in the mid-1970s, bids fair, in terms of its artistic potential, to surpass Bishop's earlier "Manners," which is also devoted to her beloved Nova Scotian maternal grandfather, William Bulmer. The poem begins by asking this long departed forbearer (he died in 1927), "How far north are you by now?" Then, in imagination, it finds him trudging in "splaying snowshoes / over the snow's hard, brilliant, curdled crust" (EAP 154) toward the North Pole—and, by implication, ever nearer to the realm of death. Bishop's mind follows her grandfather, and the poem crackles with characteristically observed detail—at once homely and surreal—and with characteristic questions:

> Aurora Borealis burns in silence.
> Streamers of red, of purple,
> fleck with color your bald head.
> Where is your sealskin cap with ear-lugs?
> That old fur coat with the black frogs?
> You'll catch your death again. (EAP 154)

The poem thus transitions toward direct address of her northward-plodding grand-father, a direct address that blends her personal mode of humor with an openly expressed affection that is rare in her published work:

> If I should overtake you, kiss your cheek,
> its silver stubble would feel like hoar-frost
> and your old-fashioned, walrus moustache
> be hung with icicles. (EAP 154)

In the poem's final stanza, the poet seems to be gaining on her grandfather, coming ever closer: close enough, amidst the endless frozen wastes, to hear, almost, his snowshoes as they move with difficulty forward:

> Creak, creak . . . frozen thongs and creaking snow.
> These drifts are endless, I think; as far as the Pole
> they hold no shadows but their own, and ours. (EAP 154)

This eerie mood is abruptly broken by the sort of sudden and alarmed excla-mation that ends so memorably her famous villanelle "One Art": "Grandfather, please stop! I haven't been so cold in years" (EAP 154). The association of cold with death and with a fantasy of travel through vast realms of drifted snow is remi-niscent of "First Death in Nova Scotia," one of her finest poems. Yet here the per-spective is not that of a child confused by the mystery of death but the perspec-tive of an adult wishing to annul a painful fact — the loss of her grandfather — yet ultimately forced by the logic of the poem, again as in "One Art," to acknowledge that death's immutable reality. "For Grandfather" to me feels nearly finished, and many poets would, I think, have been proud to be able to publish it even in its present form.

By contrast, still in an early state is her "Aubade and Elegy," a poem on the pain of losing the love of her life, Lota de Macedo Soares. Lota committed suicide by taking an overdose of tranquilizers and / or sleeping pills, and the fragmentary poem exists in its present form chiefly as an obsessive, forlorn refrain that laments the uselessness for Lota of Brazil's national drink and most famous export: "No coffee can wake you, no coffee can wake you, no coffee." Coffee is associated, too, with soil: "The smell of the earth, the smell of the dark roasted coffee" (EAP 149), and presumably, therefore, with Lota's burial in the soil of her native Brazil and, consequently, her eternal loss.

In many of these late poems, Bishop is cutting awfully close to her most intense and private feelings, and if our notional *Geography IV* had succeeded in presenting many of these poems in fully realized form, it would have been an extraordinary artistic achievement. As it is, these poems stand both as powerful and revealing biographical evocations and as works of art in the making whose potential for realization is so tangible, one can almost taste it.

Another category of potentially great significance to *Geography IV* is what I've termed "Abstract Self-Portraits." This had been, in a sense, a career-long Bishop specialty, beginning with early poems, such as "The Gentleman of Shallot" and "The Man-Moth," and continuing through such middle-period poems as "Sandpiper" and such later poems as "Crusoe in England." Among our final published quartet I would include "Sonnet" in this category. On the surface, this and the earlier poems may not look like self-portraits, and yet they explore issues central to Bishop's mental architecture while placing their heroes, allegorically, in emotional and epistemological predicaments that were native to Bishop as well. Specifically in "Sonnet," we find the emergence into explicit consideration of a long latent Bishop theme—the search for freedom in a world visibly marked by the risks of enclosure or entrapment. In this poem, Bishop's "Bubble in the spirit level" is, like her post-Tennysonian Gentleman, "a creature divided" as is:

> the compass needle
> wobbling and wavering,
> undecided. (CP 192)

I need hardly add that, after being "Freed—"

> the broken thermometer's mercury
> running away;
> and the rainbow-bird
> from the narrow bevel
> of the empty mirror (CP 192)

are versions of an alternative self: the self as unfettered traveler, a self that is "flying wherever / it feels like, gay!"

Among many Bishop drafts of abstract self-portraits that might have found their way into *Geography IV,* I'd like to focus on a back-burner poem that is one of my favorites: "Keaton," a dramatic monologue voiced by the screen persona of Buster Keaton, who, in his work as a silent-comedy star, was never enabled to speak. Keaton's stoic and unblinking screen persona was a figure with whom Bishop herself felt strong affinities.

> I will be good; I will be good.
> I have set my small jaw for the ages
> and nothing can distract me from
> solving the appointed emergencies
> even with my small brain
> —witness the diameter of my hat band
> and the depth of the crown of my hat.
>
> I will be correct; I know what it is to be a man.
> I will be correct or bust.
> I will love but not impose my feelings
> I will serve and serve
> with lute or I will not say anything. (EAP 119)

This dramatic monologue, along with many brilliant, spot-on lines, is riddled with those "gaps and empties" observed by Robert Lowell in unfinished poems fixed to Bishop's notice board, that are "waiting," as he so acutely put it, "for the unimaginable phrase" (Lowell, *Collected Poems* 595). It was such phrases, discovered by Bishop's deliberate but "unerring Muse," that enabled her, in Lowell's words, to "make[] the casual perfect" (Lowell, *Collected Poems* 595). The problem for our posited *Geography IV* is that in those poems that might have extended and completed the volume, these necessary phrases remain, for us, literally "unimaginable."

Bishop's Keaton soldiers stoically on:

> If the machinery goes, I will repair it
> If it goes again I will repair it again
> My backbone
>
> through these endless etceteras painful. (EAP 119)

Keaton—who was, like Bishop and Lowell, emotionally battered in childhood—resembles as well Lowell's Col. Shaw from "For the Union Dead." Keaton's screen persona is heroic, yet he "lost a lovely smile somewhere" (*EAP* 119), and, like Lowell's Union colonel, "he seems to wince at pleasure" and to "suffocate for privacy" (Lowell, *Collected Poems* 377). Moreover, like Col. Shaw, it seems as if he almost "cannot bend his back" (Lowell 377). Still unlike Bishop or Lowell, who faced an early expulsion from the paradise of childhood's innocence, Keaton's film persona seems somehow to cling to a foothold in that premodern paradise.

> I do not find all this absurdity people talk about
> Perhaps a paradise: a serious paradise where lovers hold hands
> and everything works.
>   I am not sentimental. (EAP 120)

Bishop never found that paradise where everything works, and for her the world was sad but never wholly serious. Still, like Keaton's screen persona, she was not sentimental.

It remains an open question how far Bishop might have gone in venturing to publish in our notional *Geography IV* poems representing the fifth and final thematic nexus to which I have referred, that is, "Poems of Love and Sexuality." This motif—and particularly the theme of love for other women—was without doubt extremely important to Bishop's unpublished oeuvre. Yet in her published work, only the most veiled and oblique examples—such as *A Cold Spring*'s "Insomnia," "Conversation," "Rain Toward Morning," "Argument," and "The Shampoo," or *Questions of Travel*'s "Electrical Storm" and "Song for the Rainy Season," or *Geography III*'s "One Art,"—appeared in Bishop's published pages.

Her more explicit and unpublished love poems, such as "It is marvelous to wake up together . . . ," "Dear, my compass . . . ," "Close, close, all night . . . ," and "Vague Poem (Vaguely Love Poem)" have been centerpieces of critical discourse on Bishop for many years now. Several of these poems remain in an artistically unsettled state, but such poems as "It is marvellous to wake up together . . ." and "Dear, my compass . . ." feel finished and complete. Another poem that appears to me complete, and that ranks, in my mind, as one of the best of her late poems, is "Breakfast Song," a poem that blends with complex simplicity a relaxed and pleasant eroticism with a stark confrontation with the immediacy of death:

> My love, my saving grace,
> your eyes are awfully blue.
> I kiss your funny face,
> your coffee-flavored mouth.
> Last night I slept with you.
> Today I love you so
> how can I bear to go

(as soon I must, I know)
to bed with ugly death
in that cold, filthy place,
to sleep there without you,
without the easy breath
and nightlong, limblong warmth
I've grown accustomed to?
—Nobody wants to die;
tell me it is a lie!
But no, I know it's true.
It's just the common case;
there's nothing one can do.
My love, my saving grace,
your eyes are awfully blue
early and instant blue. (EAP 158)

Yet the fact that this poem was discovered accidentally by her friend Lloyd Schwartz and cannot be found in the Vassar archive except for stray lines floating in the margins or reverse sides of the drafts of other poems suggests that Bishop intentionally suppressed it. Given Bishop's tendency toward self-censorship, especially in the areas of sexuality and the family, it seems reasonable to conclude that even our notional *Geography IV* might have left at least some "gaps or empties" in Bishop's published poetic oeuvre, though it is impossible to know for sure just how far that self-censorship might have extended in the more culturally accepting times of 1986. Still, no matter how extensive and inclusive, a completed *Geography IV* would almost certainly have left plenty of scope for a volume such as *Edgar Allan Poe & the Juke-Box.*

In his influential 1967 essay "The Death of the Author," Roland Barthes argued provocatively that "to give a text an Author is to impose a limit on that text, to furnish it with a final signified, to close the writing" (147). In Barthes's view, the author must be killed in order to accomplish the text's erasure from history, an erasure that will thereby free the reader: "The birth of the reader must be at the cost of the death of the author" (148). Barthes's essay, of course, speaks figuratively and no doubt hyperbolically, and in it he refers only to authors who had been long dead. By contrast, our discussion of *Geography IV* refers to an author whose recent and actual death left many poems of great artistic promise uncompleted. It is worth noting that in the years that followed Bishop's sudden departure from the scene, scholars have moved not to "close the writing" but to open it, both through a wide-ranging series of critical and biographical investigations and through a process of research and publication that has extended the Bishop canon exponentially and opened it, one might contend, to a range of readings that were impossible while she lived. Through these newly published texts, one can observe the function of the poet as maker, as we watch her poems take shape through a sequence of painfully, skillfully, and imaginatively reworked drafts. Here the author serves not as the passive conduit to an inevitably constructed text but rather as an active constructor and shaper of improvised and unpredictably evolving forms. And in fulfilling this function as author, a poet like Bishop serves in a way that is unique, and quite literally, irreplaceable.

What divides the posthumous and uncompleted poems of Bishop's *Geography IV* from her completed oeuvre is a handful or more of those unimaginable phrases. When the author dies, a peculiar and unique sensibility is lost that cannot be recovered by even the most strenuous, minute, or speculative efforts of the scholar, editor, critic, or bibliographer. Those final adjustments that Bishop made, which offer "just the right changes in perspective and coloring" (*CPr* 58) to bring the poem into its polished and inevitable-seeming published form, could only, one might suggest, be made by the living poet. In this sense, the death of the author is an all-too-real event, and death's finality leaves us, Bishop's readers, with a notional *Geography IV* that remains speculatively open as to its content, but that might have been opened further still had Bishop lived to complete, without in the process ever closing, her final volume.

"An Almost Illegible Scrawl"

Elizabeth Bishop and Textual (Re)Formations

JACQUELINE VAUGHT BROGAN

The wealth of the recent work on and by Bishop—from *Edgar Allan Poe & the Juke-Box,* to the previously unavailable material and reorderings in the Library of America edition of her work, to the remarkable letters between Bishop and Lowell in *Words in Air*—solidifies what has been, over the past twenty years, a growing understanding of the scope of Bishop's work and the complexity of her person. And part of this new understanding is that Bishop is, in fact, a deeply political poet, and moreover a subversive poet over any number of issues (including sexuality), in ways that her earliest critics seemed to miss or misrepresent almost entirely. This reformulated Bishop—the one generating this volume—allows us to take more seriously the subtle yet subversive ways in which she, all along, used traditional poetic conventions and forms precisely for political and feminist ends.

Although I began to broach Bishop's politically motivated manipulation of form as early as 1991, and Margaret Dickie rightly asserted, back in the 1994 essay "Text and Sub-Text," that while Bishop inherited a concern with traditional forms, she was interested in using "form as a means of layering varied meanings" (Dickie, "Elizabeth" 2), with the notable exception of "Sonnet," Bishop's deft employment of traditional verse forms and conventions has gone largely unexplored. Part of our reluctance to examine Bishop's purpose in turning to such traditional forms as sonnets, sestinas, and villanelles—to choose but three examples—may stem from her consistent disapproval of more radical verse. For example, in her review of *XAIPE* by E. E. Cummings (1950), now readily accessible in the Library of America edition, Bishop writes that "Often Mr. Cummings' approach to poetry reminds one of a smart-alec Greenwich Village child saying to his friends: 'Look! I've just made up a new game. Let's all write poems. There! I've won!'" (*PPL* 688). In a very early review of Edna St. Vincent Millay (1928), also available in the Library of America edition, Bishop had actually written, "While other modern poets continue to deplore the death of verse form and the unreality of rhyme and rhythm, and hail a 'new poetry' with coarse cheers, Miss Millay goes on writing poetry according to the ancient, honorable rules of the art" (*PPL* 640–41). In a relatively late letter to Anne Stevenson (1964), also reprinted in *PPL*, Bishop quite interestingly says: "I feel that both he [William Carlos Williams] & Pound, and their followers, would be vastly improved if one could lean on a sense of 'system' in their work somewhere . . . (After an hour of W. I really want to go off and read Housman, or a hymn by Cowper.—I'm full of hymns, by the way—after church-going in Nova Scotia, boarding-school, and singing in the college choir—and I often catch echoes from them in my own poems)" (*PPL* 862).

Such remarks as noted above might encourage a narrowly defined "aesthetic" and even conservative understanding of Bishop's recourse to traditional poetic forms and conventions, while missing her frequently innovative, if not subversive, uses of those various devices. Yet, at least in the letter to Stevenson, surely we can hear intentional irony. And, notably, the one poem with the word "hymn" in the title—the Hopkinsesque "Hymn to the Virgin"—is ruthless in its irony, approaching downright sarcasm:

> thus-wise
> Did previous paltry penny-clinkers come, but we bear ark-like
>   our great trust.
> What, take it not? Oh petulant and cranky princess, shall we
>   force it on Thee lust-wise?" (*PPL* 193)

Far from being traditional (or reticent and modest), Bishop's use of poetic conventions was always and continued to be one of her primary vehicles for making biting social commentaries. Quite frequently, Bishop seems to defer to traditional poetic forms in order to mask her encoded moments of personal and lyric compression—perhaps as her major poetic achievement, as we are only now beginning to fully understand. While this thesis could apply well to any number of poems clearly marked by fixed forms (such as her various sonnets, including the posthumously published one called "Sonnet," or the villanelle entitled "One Art"), my primary focus here is on Bishop's two remarkable sestinas—the relatively early "A Miracle for Breakfast" and the much later poem entitled "Sestina"—as constituting a concentrated *exempla* of Bishop's sustained social commentary made precisely through manipulating our expectations of traditional verse forms. What we may find now is that Bishop was thoroughly more modern, even more postmodern, than her contemporaries, though in ways somewhat differently defined than by Guy Rotella in *Reading and Writing Nature* or even by Thomas Travisano in *Midcentury Quartet.*[1]

Yet, in fairness to how we may have misunderstood or underestimated Bishop's poetic intent in times past, I think it accurate to say that the poet herself may have intentionally written in a particularly subversive and even *devient*[2] manner— deliberately creating an "*almost* illegible scrawl" (emphasis added)—that would encourage one kind of reading (or misreading) in her lifetime by almost everyone other than her most intimate friends (such as Margaret Miller or Robert Lowell, to name but two), but that would become open to very different readings by future readers over time. Such a strategy is indicated in the 1938 fable "In Prison," a work, published a year after "A Miracle for Breakfast," that actually defies genre categories and that I have elsewhere called her concealed poetic "manifesto."[3] Bishop's narrator claims that while in prison, her ultimate desire will be to "write on the wall" in this way:

> I shall adapt my own compositions, in order that they may not conflict with those written by the prisoner before me. The voice of a new inmate will be noticeable, but there will be no contradictions or criticisms of what has already been laid down, rather a "commentary." I have thought of attempting a short, but immortal, poem, but I am afraid that is beyond me; I may rise to the occasion, however, once I am confronted with that stained, smeared, scribbled-on wall and feel the stub of pencil or rusty nail between my fingers. Perhaps I shall arrange my "works" in a series of neat inscriptions in a clear, Roman print; perhaps I shall write them diagonally, across a corner, or at the base of a wall and half on the floor, *in an almost illegible scrawl.* They will be brief, suggestive, anguished, but full of the lights of revelation. *And no small part of the joy these writings will give me will be to think of the person coming after me.*
> (*PPL* 588, emphasis added)

I think it fair to say that a good portion of these remarks, while clearly describing the way in which Bishop will function as a poet, is "tongue-in-cheek"—meaning that her "commentaries" will include precisely "contradictions" and "criticisms," especially of social and political structures she finds confining.

In this regard, it is particularly revealing that she begins "In Prison" with this remarkable statement: "I can scarcely wait for the day of my imprisonment," adding, "The reader, or my friends, particularly those who happen to be familiar with my way of life, may protest that for me any actual imprisonment is unnecessary, since I already live, in relationship to society, very much as if I were in a prison"

(*PPL* 582). At this point in time, we might conclude that these remarks are barely veiled comments about her position in society as a lesbian woman in a time and place where that was largely unacceptable. And I would agree with that personal interpretation. But the total piece of "In Prison," especially with the first excerpt cited above, taken from a paragraph in the fable that Bishop actually titled "Writing on the Wall," seems to suggest that Bishop is also thinking deeply about her relationship as a poet, in her particular place and time, to poetic traditions which have preceded her, and without which she could not have produced the remarkable poetry that she did. Poetic conventions liberate and confine the writer, a fact Bishop clearly demonstrates. I therefore explore a few precise examples of how Bishop uses "fixed forms" and associated poetic conventions as ironic poetic "prisons" within which she is able to produce superficially reticent, but finally ruthless and reverberating social commentaries. Nowhere does the actual form of a poem prove more prison-like than in the poem self-consciously called "Sestina." However, to fully grasp Bishop's brilliant manipulation of form in this late poem, it is particularly useful to examine her earlier sestina "A Miracle for Breakfast."

As noted in the entry on poetic conventions in *The New Princeton Encyclopedia of Poetry and Poetics:* "Readers who are party to literary conventions may be very few indeed. . . . Readers who are ignorant of—or at least out of sympathy with—the convention must to some extent misinterpret a work that exemplifies it, and when the number of such readers becomes large, writers may abandon the convention—though of course works that exemplify it remain to be interpreted" (239). Bishop, I would argue, would feel that only a small circle of "readers"—or "friends," as she says above—would be familiar enough with certain poetic conventions she deploys to adequately interpret her poems. Furthermore, at least in a few instances, her use of particular conventions or fixed forms is intended to mask the real subject matter of the poems, making them deliberately unintelligible, even to certain friends. Such is the case of Bishop's insistence on "A Miracle for Breakfast" as a sestina, in her correspondence with Marianne Moore.

In a letter to Marianne Moore, dated January 5, 1937, Bishop writes, in reference to the poem: "It seems to me that there are two ways possible for a sestina—one is to use unusual words as terminations, in which case they would have to be used differently as often as possible—as you say, 'change of scale.' That would make a very highly seasoned kind of poem. And the other way is to use as colorless words as possible—like Sidney, so that it becomes less of a trick and more of a natural theme and variations. I guess I have tried to do both at once" (*PPL* 744). Most readers, perhaps, would not find the terminating words in this sestina to be particularly "unusual." They are "coffee," "crumb," "balcony," "miracle," "sun," and "river"—all of which, with the exception of "miracle," seem relatively colorless. The only word "used differently" is the word "crumb," which functions as the common noun in all but one appearance in the sestina, where it becomes a verb: "one roll, which he proceeded to crumb." The rest of Bishop's discussion of the sestina, written to Moore, is in fact a somewhat humorous defense of certain words, including "sun" and "crumb," as well as "gallons" and "galleries," which Moore had presumably criticized. Bishop's response is to keep her discussion fixed on the form (and not the content) of the sestina. The "trick" to this letter is that it deflects attention from the possible real objections on Moore's part to the actual subject matter. Specifically, responding to one of Moore's objections, Bishop writes, "The boisterousness of 'gallons of coffee' I wanted to overlook because I liked 'gallons' being near 'galleries'" (*PPL* 744), a comment that calls attention to the alliteration of the words and that masks the moment of sexual satiety that is buried in the stanza at hand and in the subversive strategy of the poem as a whole. This is a particularly deceptive strategy on Bishop's part, since, as we should remember, the earliest sestinas, as first devised by Arnaut Daniel, and then emulated by Dante and Petrarch, were explicitly love poems. But by the time Bishop was writing, and especially with the influence of Pound's well-known sestina "Altaforte" and Auden's own "Paysage Moralisé," the sestina had shifted in subject to one of social and political critique, a shift that Bishop superficially replicates in her own sestina. In this sense, Bishop's sestina does not seem to be particularly subversive as such, but rather a poem adhering to a new tradition established among leading modernist poets as to how the form could be used. In this case, "critical commentary"—whether of modern warfare or industrialization—had become the norm, a fact Bishop is exploiting.[4]

Formally, this sestina is not subversive at all, or at least not initially. It is a perfectly "natural" sestina, to use Bishop's word from the letter cited above, in which the relative financial ease of the speaker, as well as that of the man with the servant, is contrasted with others, apparently impoverished, standing in line for food and work. Published in 1937, in the midst of the Great Depression, "A Miracle for Breakfast" seems to provide a "legitimate" social commentary by clarifying the rigid roles assigned to economic classes or, rather, the relative freedom of the wealthy versus the passivity, dependence, and shocked scorn of the poor—all the while (and most importantly) masking the sestina's import as a love poem. While the wealthy man is crumbling his roll, with "his head, so to speak, in the clouds," the speaker of the poem intones:

> Was the man crazy? What under the sun
> was he trying to do, up there on his balcony!
> Each man received one rather hard crumb,
> which some flicked scornfully into the river,
> and, in a cup, one drop of the coffee.
> Some of us stood around, waiting for the miracle. (PPL 14)

I hear a particular echo here of Auden's 1933 "Paysage Moralisé," in which he writes:

> But dawn came back and they were still in cities;
> No marvelous creature rose up from the water;
> There was still gold and silver in the mountains
> But hunger was a more immediate sorrow,

suggesting that Bishop was intentionally trying to align her "Miracle" with that sestina in particular. While the speaker in Bishop's sestina also seems to identify with the poor, who receive only a single crumb and a single drop of coffee, elsewhere, we should note, she reclines in apparent luxury:

> Every day, in the sun,
> At breakfast time I sit on my balcony
> with my feet up, and drink gallons of coffee. (15)

Still, the poem seems to pair the poet and the poor, with its critique of the oblivious man, a fact that is reinforced by Bishop's implicit allusion to "the miracle" of Christ's feeding the poor with only a few fish and loaves of bread. In Bishop's sestina, however, that miracle does not occur. We could even say that the fixed form of the sestina corresponds to the reduced circumstances of people who find themselves with little hope of spiritual intervention or transformation. I should note, however, that this allusion was apparently unconscious on Bishop's part. For, in a letter to Anne Stevenson, dated January 8, 1964, Bishop writes: "You must be right about the Eucharist in 'A Miracle for Breakfast.' I had never noticed it myself until a Brazilian, Catholic, of course, translated that poem into Portuguese a few months ago and said the same thing to me" (PPL 863). Nevertheless, Bishop may have intentionally invoked and subverted another, related *poetic* convention—that of the "reverdie" and its expectation of celebrating the coming of spring. Reverdies, of course, like sestinas, were common forms for the Occitan troubadours, who had in fact "developed a set of generic concepts" in a total "system," by 1170 (Paden 851). In addition, we should note, a "reverdie" "celebrates the coming of spring. . . . By a natural association the reverdie began to welcome Easter as well as spring" (Holmes and Harrison 1045). In Bishop's poem, however, spring is not yet on the horizon—and certainly not Easter: while the speaker clearly desires a "miracle," the reality is that

> it was so cold we hoped that the coffee
> would be very hot, seeing that the sun
> was not going to warm us.

As noted, there is no Easter, no Son, no "miracle" of resurrection or transformation—other than the seemingly ironic reflection of light at the end of the poem, "on the wrong balcony."

Bishop's critique of the wealthy, oblivious man remains quite focused, for what is "not" a miracle in the poem is described this way:

> I can tell what I saw next; it was not a miracle.
> A beautiful villa stood in the sun
> and from its doors came the smell of hot coffee. (PPL 15)

Although apparently somewhat well-off herself, the speaker implicitly criticizes the wealthy man who is indifferent to the hardships of the poor below, hardships which the speaker of the poem at least sees and acknowledges. Moreover, like the speaker in Frost's "Stopping by Woods on a Snowy Evening," the speaker here has an aesthetic appreciation lacking in the wealthy man (and perhaps in the poor by dint of the weary repetition of poverty): she sees a "miracle" in the bird droppings, which she describes as "a baroque white plaster balcony / added by birds," so that her "crumb," her "mansion," is made "by a miracle, / through ages, by insects, birds, and the river / working the stone." Continued appreciation of such minute details then seem to provide the surfeit that allows the speaker to "drink gallons of coffee" each day.

Formally, the repetitions and elaborate patterning of a sestina seem to support the poem's themes. On the one hand, the daily drudgery or repetitive misery of the poor during and following the Great Depression is mimicked by the repeated, very common words—against that "miracle" that the aesthetic eye of the speaker perceives and that the poet achieves precisely in the elaborate patterning of the sestina. The only noticeable deviation from the expectations of the sestina form is that Bishop ignores the requirement, in English, of its being decasyllabic. Individual lines range in syllable count from the expected ten syllables to the fifteen syllables of the poem's last line. Perhaps, we might conclude, this minor deviation is Bishop's way of resisting the strictures of literary and cultural conventions, even while exposing them. Perhaps her use of the sestina form is slightly subversive, after all.

The preceding summary still misses what is arguably the poem's most essential subject matter—a subject which Bishop scrupulously avoids in her letter to Marianne Moore cited above. This sestina was one of the first poems that Moore helped Bishop to publish, and I would speculate that the real subject matter—lesbian love and sexuality—was intentionally suppressed by Bishop, not only for Moore's eyes, but for the majority (but not all) of the poem's readers. For example, Brett C. Millier, who chronicles the development of Moore's mentoring of Bishop, interprets the sestina in strictly economic terms: "This 'miracle for breakfast,' pressed by some longer, though indirect experience of Depression-era soup lines and hunger in New York and by the French surrealists as she read them intensely in Douarnenez and Paris in August and September 1935, became the sestina of that title" (Millier 80). Margaret Dickie, however, writing only one year after Millier, has a radically different understanding of the poem: in "Text and Sub-Text," Dickie interprets this poem, along with several others, as carefully encoded poems of lesbian sexuality. Or, as she would subsequently argue in *Stein, Bishop, and Rich*: "Writing at first under the eagle eye of Marianne Moore, Bishop seemed to restrain her expressions of desire, although . . . she encodes such expressions in the early packed 'A Miracle for Breakfast' or the strange 'Casabianca' or the surrealistic 'The Weed' and 'The Imaginary Iceberg'" (202). Here it is useful to take our eyes off the nominal form—that is, the fact that the poem is clearly a sestina, as described by Bishop in her letter to Moore—and off the nominal subject—that is, a kind of socialist critique that both Pound and Auden had recently employed—and to delve more deeply into other poetic conventions animating the poem. For "A Miracle for Breakfast" is not merely a sestina: it is also an "aubade" or "alba," a fact which the ironically invoked but frustrated expectations of the "reverdie" may help us to see.

In celebrating the coming of spring, the reverdie sings of "the new green of the woods and fields, the singing of the birds, the time of love" (Holmes and Harrison 1045). The irony of the first two categories is obvious: in "A Miracle for Breakfast," we are not in some pastoral idyll, but rather in the sordid reality of urban New York. There is no singing of the birds, only the "white plaster" (or bird droppings) "added by birds." But what of "the time of love," the third category we expect in a reverdie? Isn't the speaker alone, looking at the dread and poverty that many people experienced in the Depression era? Certainly, many critics have assumed so. For example, in her discussion of "A Miracle for Breakfast" as being Bishop's version of Wallace Stevens's "Sunday Morning" (with the addition of Depression-era concerns), Susan McCabe comes to the following conclusions: "I consider this poem her 'Sunday Morning' as it rejects orthodoxy and exults in the real of her own fictions and irrealities. . . . She claims this to be her 'Depression poem,' and in it she scorns the 'miracles' that do not really exist for the oppressed (*a community she makes herself a part of through her use of 'we'*) but merely taunt them" (McCabe 91, emphasis added). McCabe's observation is certainly true of the use of the pronoun "us" in the fourth stanza, where "Some of us stood around, waiting for the miracle." But the actual word "we" in the poem signals something else altogether.

The poem begins, "At six o'clock we were waiting for coffee / waiting for coffee and the charitable crumb," and concludes, "We licked up the crumb and swallowed the coffee" (*PPL* 14). Thereafter, in the rest of the poem, the word "we" virtually disappears (appearing only one more time, in the second line of the second stanza—"It was so cold we hoped that coffee / would be very hot"), so that the actual bedroom scene of the couple at dawn is barely recognized, if at all. Bishop's focus in the poem keeps our eyes trained outward on the wealthy man and the poor, just as the letter to Moore kept the focus on the sestina form itself. But, as Dickie recognized in "Text and Sub-Text," there is a buried love story of sexual desire here, one the speaker fears or cannot celebrate since she lives—"in relationship to society," as she notes "In Prison"—in prison, by experiencing "the time of love" as a lesbian.

This critical subtext to the poem is underscored by the time, "six o'clock" a.m., a fact which makes this sestina also an ironically evoked "aubade" or "alba," as noted above—I stress "ironically," for in an alba we expect a "dawn song, ordinarily expressing the regret of two lovers that day has come so soon to separate them" (Chambers and Brogan 26). If separated (a point to be discussed below), the lovers of this poem—the speaker and the companion who form the actual "we" of the poem—are parted not by the light of dawn, but by the glaring light of social and sexual norms that forbids this union. Whereas Pound can say, overtly, in the last line of his three-line poem called "Alba," "She lay beside me at the dawn," Bishop feels forced to mask her (*deviently*) traditional use of the sestina as a love poem under the surface appearance of an indictment of capitalism. Significantly, Bishop finds it easier to attack the prevailing economic system, an attack securely protected by the First Amendment, than to allude more than very obliquely to a same-sex relationship. It is also interesting to note that Pound himself thwarts the expectation that the lovers will be separated by dawn. For, however unorthodox

Pound's actual love life may have been, he is unabashed in his celebration of heterosexual love in the post-Victorian morés of the early twentieth century. In contrast, Bishop feels the need to suppress the real underlying nature and relationship
of her alba, a fact which encourages us to imagine that the lovers are forced apart
by social conventions. As such, "A Miracle for Breakfast" would seem to replicate
Juliet's famous complaint against the dawn in *Romeo and Juliet,* but with specific
gendered and social differences.

But are the lovers in this poem actually separated, after all? In fact, quite unlike
Romeo and Juliet, it would appear that the speaker of "A Miracle for Breakfast" and
her lover actually experience continued satisfaction:

> Every day, in the sun,
> at breakfast time I sit on my balcony
> with my feet up, and drink gallons of coffee.

This moment is not merely the result of aesthetic appreciation, as implied above:
it is a moment of emotional and sexual appreciation, even abundance, as well—a
celebration of the private life buried in the almost "illegible" alba, quite at odds
with the public stance that dominates the rest of this sestina. As Dickie also notes
in *Stein, Bishop, and Rich,* Bishop "came into her public audience not by coming
out as a lesbian in Rich's style, but by honing her craft so that she could express
without revealing her desire" (202). And the poem concludes, in what must have
been a very private communication at the time:

> We licked up the crumb and swallowed the coffee.
> A window across the river caught the sun
> as if the miracle were working, on the wrong balcony.

In actuality, "the miracle" of this couple's unconventional love may indeed be
"working" within the relationship and within the withheld "right" room obliquely
evoked in the poem. A superficial reading might regard the phrase "as if" as indicating that there is no miracle working in the poem or in reality, at all. An alternate,
and I would argue more correct, reading would be that the "as if" self-reflectively
suggests that "the" miracle is working, in the room from which the poet is writing,
and with the person with whom she is experiencing the full delight of tendered
and accepted love—even if economic relief is not in sight for the very masses
who might condemn this relationship. In this regard, I would say that the unusual
length of the last line (fifteen syllables) corresponds to the sexual and emotional

expansiveness the couple is experiencing, on a daily basis, despite the social conventions that would prohibit their union.

In concert with the traditional readings of "A Miracle for Breakfast," many critics read the later example of the form that Bishop titles "Sestina" in traditional biographical or formalist ways. For example, Susan McCabe deftly describes the many painful personal facts and events that animate "Sestina," asserting that ultimately the poem is positive, a valorization of human imagination and art. Citing the final lines from the poem, in which the "child draws a rigid house," placing a "man with buttons like tears" in the picture, before showing it "proudly to the grandmother," McCabe declares: "The 'rigid house' resembles the poem's proud form, yet testifies to the flexibility and adaptability of the imagination that can create new possibilities with limited materials. . . . Within limitation and facing the apparent finality of loss, the imagination empowers us with the potential for remaking. Tears of mourning irrigate a creative impulse—the child's recasting of a house—that tentatively helps shelter sorrow and painful memory" (McCabe 210–11). Brett Millier has a more cautious interpretation of the poem: reading the "Sestina" entirely in relationship to the more negative, biographical aspects of Bishop's childhood, Millier concludes that the child's drawing offers a "tenuous grasp on security," and that the "'rigid' form" of the house "reflects the insecurity of her makeshift home and her attempts to 'domesticate' it" (Millier 267–68).

While we cannot ignore the manifest biographical elements in the poem, "Sestina" is deeply involved with social critique. In this case, the "rigid house"—like the rigid form of the sestina itself—is emblematic of the rigid gender roles that the weeping grandmother, the "man with buttons like tears," and the child presumably endure due to social conventions that ultimately make of a home a virtual prison instead. As the grandmother and child sit at the kitchen table, underneath the "clever almanac" that "hovers," "Birdlike," above them both—uttering close-minded clichés, such as *I know what I know,*" the unchanging, unchallenged social scripts controlling their lives prove to be not fluid at all, but rather horribly confining. Bishop's social commentary is made then precisely through a poetic convention she ironically needs in order to demonstrate (and to rebel against) the social ones she wishes to critique. As noted above, "conventions both liberate and restrict the writer," a fact which Bishop thoroughly exploits to her poetic advantage. The poem, then, is a tour de force of expressing the gendered repressions that Bishop privately railed against most of her adult life.

Unlike the sestina "A Miracle for Breakfast," the strict form of "Sestina" is deeply involved in the poem's deepest theme. However, with its childlike tone, the remarkably banal terminating words ("house," "grandmother," "child," "stove," "almanac," and "tears"), and details like "Little Marvel Stove" and "jokes from the almanac," it is easy to miss the severe commentary Bishop is making about times past—and present—and especially in terms of gender roles. Here it is necessary to take the actual, rigid, underlying form of the sestina quite seriously (something which I believe Bishop intended, by changing the preliminary name of the poem from the personal "Early Loss" to the more formally self-reflexive one, "Sestina"). In addition, the envoi must use the other end-words, marked as 2, 4, and 6, in the middle of the last three lines, respectively. In other words, the sestina is remarkably "rigid" (like the house the child draws). In fact, as one critic has noted, Dante himself exploited the potential rigidity or "petrification" of the form in one of his more famous sestinas.[5] Once the end-words are determined, their future placement throughout the rest of the poem is entirely predictable, a point which Bishop is at pains to make thematically within the sestina in her depiction of social conventions, especially as determined by gender. "Scripts" or texts dominate the poem—the grandmother is reading from the almanac, the child is drawing pictures, and the objects within the poem purportedly spout such clichés as *"It was to be"* or *"I know what I know"* that encourage mindless adherence to cultural conventions (and that would discourage precisely the kind of "commentary" the poet is in fact making in the very act of using them). In this case, Bishop isn't subverting the form as such: instead, the form comes to embody the very situation as realized in actual life that she is critiquing—i.e., that of being "con-scripted."

This observation is borne out not only by the almost sickening repetition of domestic terms, but also by knowledge of just what kind of jokes "peopled," as it were, actual almanacs. A few examples will more than suffice to indicate the kind of gender bias, or blatant sexism, found in these most influential of books. In Benjamin Franklin's *Poor Richard's Almanac,* for example, we find that "After three days men grow weary of a wench, a guest and weather rainy" (1733), "A ship under sail and a big bellied woman are the handsomest things that can be seen common" (1735), and that "Three things are men most likely to be cheated in, a horse, a wig and a wife" (1735; qtd. in Stowell 223); even more disturbingly, the *Kentucky Almanac* of 1797 includes this remarkable "quip":

> Women are books and men their readers be—
> In whom oft times, they great errata see.
> Here sometimes we blot—there we espy
> A leaf misplac'd—at least a line awry:
> If they are books, I wish that my wife were
> An almanac, to change her ev'ry year. (Stowell 264)

Taken as a genuinely controlling script, for decades, even centuries, in actual rural lives, the jokes the grandmother is presumably reading from the almanac may be hardly funny—rather, they may be horrifying in the gendered codes and denigrations being passed down as tradition from one generation to another.

In addition to almanacs and cultural clichés, Bishop implicitly indicts the "largest" book—the Bible—as being part of this confining and enduring prison (notably, almanacs were commonly referred to as "weekday bibles"). In place of the "dove," the almanac "hovers," "Birdlike,"

> hovers half open above the child,
> hovers above the old grandmother
> and her teacup full of dark brown tears.

In contrast to that "cup of blood" that should have meant a cultural revolution, including liberation and salvation for everyone, the cup of tears that we have inherited is a legacy literally passed on at our mothers'—and fathers'—tables, an awful legacy that continues to ensure a sense of being damned in this life. This, of course, is an insight early explored by Bishop, not only in "Hymn to the Virgin," mentioned above, but in the remarkably complex poem "Over 2000 Illustrations and a Complete Concordance." There, the "gilt" of the biblical text is deeply entwined with our "guilt," which Bishop suggests should have passed away, if, at the "old Nativity," we could have "looked our infant sight away" (*PPL* 44–46).

Yet Bishop is not simply indicting "The Patriarchy" in "Sestina"—if that means merely showing the plight of women. As she does in other later poems, such as "In the Waiting Room," Bishop suggests in "Sestina" that people of all genders suffer from the same social imprisonments that constrict and conscript human lives. The man in the poem, with "buttons like tears," seems equally confined and limited by his presumed role as provider, as does the grandmother in the poem by her conventional role as nurturer. And, significantly, the "child" in "Sestina" is ungendered, implying that whether male or female, the grandchild is learning and repeating the close-minded scripts uttered by the almanac and stove and the grandmother herself—a fact that exposes how sexism is internalized and replicated, no matter what the gender of the child. This "commentary" is of an entirely different order than that made in the earlier "A Miracle for Breakfast," with its sequestered adulation of lesbian love and its surface indictment of the wealthy male. While the earlier sestina, presenting itself as social commentary, proves to be a deeply personal poem, the latter one, superficially a poem recounting a deeply personal experience, emerges as a very sophisticated social "commentary." How ironic, then, that the rigid form of the late "Sestina" would come to be, eventually, one through which Bishop would be quite silently advocating a kind of global liberation—in many ways well ahead of her time.

I would like to conclude with one final and rather obvious example here—the posthumously published "Sonnet"—the title of which, once again, self-referentially emphasizes its form. In this instance, we see yet another strategy on Bishop's part in her manipulation of poetic forms: in "Sonnet," her subversion (or, more precisely, inversion) of form mirrors the social commentary and change she wants to help create. Bonnie Costello has rightly argued that the compressed lines of this sonnet increase the intensity and energy of the poem (241). And, as Dickie has noted in *Stein, Bishop and Rich,* the whole poem "summarizes the imagery of her earlier work"—a fact that seems true as well (101). But what is finally most important is this sonnet's larger formal structure. While we expect, of a Petrarchan sonnet, an octave (often presenting a problem) to be followed by a sestet (perhaps resolving the issue in the poem), this structure is specifically *inverted* in "Sonnet"—with the six (half) lines coming first, and the eight remaining ones coming last (forming what is known as a "*reversed* sonnet" or "*sonettessa*"). In addition, the word "inversion," as many critics have noted, was used to identify and denigrate lesbians during the time that Bishop was coming of age and attending college, as well as a word in Portuguese that specifically means "homosexual" (as Bishop also would have known).

Actually, in "Sonnet," Bishop has fused the Shakespearean sonnet with the Petrarchan. While the structure may be a reversed Petrarchan sonnet, when it comes to rhyme, Bishop incorporates the Shakespearean sonnet, though in a highly irregular way. There are, notably, not five rhymes, as we would expect from this structure, but actually seven, as in a Shakespearean sonnet. However, they are so unconventionally dispersed that the latter octet is connected with the sestet (rather than being "divided," to borrow a word from the opening sestet)—with "broken" just echoing "wavering," and "bevel" clearly resonating with "bubble," "level," and "needle." Against the demands of structure—that decisive break we expect at the volta in a Petrarchan sonnet (even in an inverted sonnet)—Bishop insists upon a final description of self that is finally more integrated than surface appearances. Perhaps, at the end of her life, Bishop is using formal creativity to resist the strictures that might confine or "conscript" her through the label "lesbian," as well.

In "Sonnet," Bishop uses the palimpsest of the conventional Petrarchan form to highlight her somewhat *devient* escape from the prison within which she had clearly felt caught earlier in her life—in exactly the ways she said her prose "commentaries" would do, back in the 1938 fable "In Prison." There she says—or, more accurately, quite deliberately *writes*—of being "in prison": "I hope I am not being too reactionary when I say that my one desire is to be given one very dull book to read, the duller the better. A book, moreover, on a subject completely foreign to me. . . . Then I shall be able to experience with a free conscience the pleasure, perverse, I suppose, of interpreting it not at all according to its intent." Later she adds, "It is entirely a different thing from being a 'rebel' outside the prison"—in prison, being a rebel "is to be unconventional, rebellious perhaps, but in shades and shadows" (*PPL* 587, 589). I can't imagine a finer statement of Bishop's genuinely subversive poetics, ranging from subject matter to her unconventional manipulation of poetic conventions, the latter of which we are only now beginning to perceive as an integral part of her once private, yet now increasingly public, "system," emerging as they have from the archives into *Edgar Allan Poe & the Juke-Box, Words in Air,* and culminating in the Library of America's comprehensive *Elizabeth Bishop: Poems, Prose, and Letters,* which makes accessible, for the first time, an integrative reading of Bishop's work—both the previously published and the posthumous—in all genres. Frequently sequestered in the "shades and shadows" of poetic traditions, Bishop's particular rebellions emerge as an "*almost* illegible scrawl," the traces of which do prove finally legible, after all.

NOTES

1. In *Reading & Writing Nature,* Guy Rotella remarks that "Bishop is one of the least 'theoretical' of poets," a point with which I would strongly disagree, insisting that "the modernist revolution preceded hers and, although her own breakthroughs anticipate postmodern ones, the arguments for those came after. Bishop published no manifestoes and few explanations of her work" (198) a point which, as my subsequent argument shows, I challenge even more strongly. I find Thomas Travisano's account of Bishop's "postmodernity" much more convincing, focusing, as he does, on her prismatic, multiple points of view. Travisano does not, however, significantly address Bishop's use of poetic conventions that I am considering here (see *Midcentury Quartet*).

2. I am, somewhat humorously, copying Jacques Derrida's famous coining of the word "differance" years ago by introducing the word "devient" to mean both "devious" and "deviant," especially as the latter word *still* is used in the majority of major psychological studies to describe homosexuality. Indeed, Bishop did at times use poetic conventions in devious ways to simultaneously mask and reveal her supposedly "deviant" sexuality, as parts of the remainder of this essay will demonstrate.

3. See my "Elizabeth Bishop: Perversity as Voice," *American Poetry* 7, no. 2, 1990: 31–49; reprinted in Lomardi, *Geography of Gender.*

4. Although set in medieval times, following Dante, Pound's 1909 sestina "Altaforte" is a barely veiled complaint against the clearly patriarchal ideology promoting modern warfare. Particularly

relevant to Bishop's poem are the following lines (spoken by "Bertrans de Born," the promoter of strife): "I love to see the sun rise blood-crimson," and

> The man who fears war and squats opposing
> My words for stour, hath no blood of crimson
> But is fit only to rot in womanish peace
> Far from where worth's won and the swords clash
> For the death of such sluts I go rejoicing.

I note Auden's sestina, and its relevance to Bishop's poem, later in the essay.

5. See Teodolinda Barolini, *Dante and the Origins of Italian Literary Culture,* who contrasts Dante's attempt to make the sestina "Al poco giorno e al gran cerchio d'ombra" as "petrified verbally as the *petra* it describes" with Petrarch's "aims for greater fluidity, seeking ways to reduce the form's resistance" (202).

Words in Air and "Space" in Art

Bishop's Midcentury Critique of the United States

GILLIAN WHITE

In a 1957 letter of apology written to Elizabeth Bishop for the hypomanic episode he'd recently suffered while the two visited together in Maine, Robert Lowell dramatizes his sense of regret and defeat on the drive home to Boston:

> As I dully drove back over the Bango[r] toll bridge in my gray and blue Ford, the nut still rattling in the hub cap as though we were dragging a battered tin can at our heels, I looked up and a sign said, "When money talks it says, 'Chevrolet.'" (*WIA* 214)

Lowell doesn't elaborate on the anecdote, but given his choice to close the letter with it, we can assume he expected Bishop to feel its pathos: he illustrates with the Chevy ad's acquisitive bravado not just personal abjection but a being out of joint with a U.S. cultural moment defined by crass, cocky Madison Avenue copy.

Bishop seems to have registered the anecdote's import. In response, she avoids explicit reference to any of Lowell's overtly emotional confessions in his letter (including the confession of romantic feelings for her), opting instead to narrate her own automobile story. Like Lowell's, it is filled with pathos: Driving with Brazilian friends (this was Bishop's first trip back to the States since moving to Brazil in the early 1950s) from Manhattan to East Hampton later that same week, she reports:

> It poured and rained and the millions of automobiles on the endless highways *whished-whished* by, almost in silence. . . . There were super-highways and clover-leafs in 1951 [the year Bishop left the United States], but they have ex-foliated beyond my wildest dreams since then—they're really terrifying. . . . I still can't believe in any of it. . . . Every time I've made . . . a side-trip on this trip . . . I've come back depressed, I don't know why—I think it's mostly *automobiles*—and then I decide it's just some lack of vitality in myself that makes me feel so hopeless about my own country. . . .

But I really can't *bear* much of American life these days—surely no country has ever been so filthy rich and so hideously uncomfortable at the same time. (*WIA* 228–29)

This last assertion—"so filthy rich and so hideously uncomfortable"—is remarkably forceful rhetoric for Bishop, who tended to dislike hyperbole and cliché and, as Stephen Gould Axelrod notes, found it "difficult to broach political topics, even when writing to a rather political friend" ("Elizabeth" 844). And yet the statement is actually characteristic of critiques of "American life" Bishop made in letters to Lowell in the years surrounding her 1957 trip "home." Her admission that she "can't believe in any of it" suggests the power of a then ascendant way of life in the United States; Bishop can't believe in cars the way a person might fail to believe in God (*WIA* 229).

The recently published letters in *Words in Air: The Complete Correspondence between Elizabeth Bishop and Robert Lowell* make clearer than ever before Bishop's intense queasiness over U.S. culture at midcentury—the encroaching "slickness" of mass media into the literary arts, and the excesses and reach of high capitalism. This essay will explore Bishop's criticisms of the United States in her letters to Lowell with an eye to the important, subtle, and mostly inexplicit ways in which they inform her poetics of the era. Most importantly, the letters help show that Bishop's well-known concern for a poetics of "modesty" (articulated to Lowell in a 1958 letter—only a few months after her visit to the United States) can be regarded as a sharply *political* stance influenced by her midcentury cultural malaise (250). She diagnoses in a range of contemporary U.S. poetry (from "academic" poets to the Beats) a lack of "space" (250) and a glut of "self-consciousness" (335). Writing to Lowell in 1961 that a "real real protest" in contemporary poetry was needed, she exhibits concern that art should strive to create interpretive space by resisting and even protesting the rhetorical excesses of mass media shaping poetry's sound and its range of concerns (364). In striving to realize this space as "protest" in her own midcentury work, Bishop explores the processes by which discursive language shapes and even contests the idea of "voice"—another sign of excess, Bishop thought. Realizing the extent of Bishop's concern with what she regarded as social and cultural forms of immodesty in the United States will help to nuance the critical understanding of what about her work of the 1950s and 1960s can be understood as "political" or "socially conscious."

That Lowell and Bishop figure their concerns about the Maine visit around automobiles and ads for them places their exchange in a particular historical moment—one in which soaring postwar national confidence, often expressed as frank consumerism, made a modest social sensibility seem old-fashioned. We are helped to imagine Lowell and Bishop in the boom years of the mid-1950s, when both the advertising and the automobile industries, among others, swelled beyond previous imagining. The Federal-Aid Highway Act, which authorized the Interstate Highway System under Eisenhower's administration, was just a year old as Bishop and Lowell wrote; it marked the start of massive U.S. investment in the automobile-driven economy. As the cultural historian Juliann Sivulka writes: "Between 1945 and 1960 gross annual advertising expenditures quadrupled. Automobiles replaced packaged goods and cigarettes as the most heavily advertised product" (240). Chevrolet had the largest advertising budget in the ad industry in the period 1950–65 (Wicks); its generation of V-8 model cars is today iconic of those boom years.

Bishop's automobile story and her uncharacteristically bold generalization about "American life" obliquely acknowledge both Lowell's mix of mania and depression and also, perhaps, the limits of the fantasies about a happier life apart from wife and child he'd entertained while they were in Maine. By admitting her resistance to "her own country" (metonymized by the assumed "vitality" of modern automobility), she addresses the hints raised by Lowell's own vignette—that his spiritual malaise is symptomatic of, or even produced by, a larger cultural illness of excess ("filthy rich" so that we want our cars to talk money) whose consequences we may not have fully taken in (exfoliation beyond one's "wildest dreams").

And though in reply Lowell somewhat brusquely rejects the fervor of Bishop's condemnation of life in the United States, "wav[ing] a flag" (*WIA* 231) at her rhetoric, the personal, autobiographical poems he produced for *Life Studies* in the wake of the Maine visit and the emotional "energies" (Kalstone 189) it released actually confirm Bishop's diagnosis. In her blurb for his book, which Lowell thought indispensible to its success (*WIA* 290), she asserts that the poems "tell us as much about the state of society as a volume of Henry James" and offer "a chilling sensation of here-and-now, of exact contemporaneity." She finds them "aware of those 'ironies of American history'" acutely felt "in the middle of our worst century so far" (qtd. on 290). Later critics, including M. L. Rosenthal, A. Alvarez, and Stephen Gould Axelrod followed suit. Rosenthal, most famously, read "Skunk Hour" as definitive of a new "confessional" mode for its embodiment of the sociological through the personal: the speaker's "vulnerability and shame" become "an embodiment of his civilization" (82).[1]

. Bishop's being first to frame *Life Studies* as illustrative of the ways the personal is shaped by and expressive of larger social and political forces is notable, given the critical propensity, both over the course of her career and also for the first decade after her death, to regard her as a writer unconcerned with matters political, or, worse, as a writer who maintained a reactionary politics of privileged disinterest.[2] Since the late 1980s, a number of critics have helped us to dispel this misperception by magnifying Bishop's leftist interests. But these revisions have tended to identify the work's leftist politics with its receptivity to or interest in others—especially people of different classes or ethnic identities than Bishop's.[3] Yet while Bishop's social conscience is indeed important to any discussion of politics in her work, there are other, subtler and important ways in which her work can be read as political. For Bishop, to leave "space" (tonal and rhetorical) in a work functioned as a kind of politics, as resistance to a culture inclined to leave almost no such space.

Full registration of this poetic and its political force depends on our detailing Bishop's consistent preoccupation, in the years in which she produced the poems published in *Questions of Travel,* with the excessive wealth defining the quality and tone of American life. For Bishop, when money in the 1950s and 1960s United States talked, most of what it said was dismayingly powerful. Writing to Lowell about President Kennedy's inauguration (which Lowell attended), she bemoans its conspicuous wealth—a "Roman Empire grandeur": "I wish K weren't so damned RICH. It all turns my stomach, slightly" (352). After friends returned from the States in 1963, Bishop reports to Lowell that "they found the atmosphere there very Sodom & Gomorrah-ish . . . money money money and dreadful Negro troubles" (514–15).

Inextricable from Bishop's dismay over the disproportionate wealth of (white) American life is how she encountered it—as an infrequent traveler "home" and as a reader of popular American news and culture magazines, including the *Saturday Evening Post, Life,* and *Time;* Bishop was perhaps more alive to the cumulative effects of changes that, for a native, would have unfolded too gradually to seem shocking. She found it surprising to think of Lowell watching TV at his summer house (376) and complained about the ubiquity of television, and, implicitly, the U.S. consumer culture it so successfully exported abroad. Writing to Lowell of cultural changes in Nova Scotia and Brazil, Bishop complained: "TV aerials rise from the shingles. The dying out of local cultures seems to me one of the most tragic things in this century—and it's true everywhere, I suppose. . . . [In Brazil] . . . towns . . . [are] all dead as door nails, and broken-down trucks arrive bringing powdered milk . . . and TIME magazine" (401).

However, Bishop doesn't limit her criticism to "mass culture" or a "new money" aesthetic: for instance, she complains twice (in letters of 1952 and 1953) of the Library of Congress's new Poetry Room, funded by Gertrude Whittal, for its emphatic luxury: "I *saw* that Whittal 'poetry nook' . . . —and *ye gods.* I suppose everyone will soon have to resign. At least that seems like the only dignified thing to do. Yes, we do worship the dollar, that's all there is to say" (135, 144).

By 1960–61, Bishop was appalled by a glut of cultural production, including the "high" arts, and a consequent cultural torpor. Reading contemporary literary journals, she admits, "I get so depressed with every number of POETRY, *The New Yorker* etc. (this one I am swearing off of, except for prose, forever, I hope) so much adequate poetry all sounding just alike and so boring" (344). She continues: "There seems to be too much of everything—too much painting, too much poetry, too many novels, and much too much money, I suppose. (Although I certainly welcomed mine [from the Chapelbrook Foundation].) And no one really feeling anything much" (344).

It is not simply the wealth and reach of U.S. culture that Bishop flags in her letters to Lowell; it is also the "slickness" of an emergent cultural tone that felt inescapable, as her comment about the "adequate" and "boring" sameness of poetry suggests (448, 344). At various moments in the correspondence, she registers advertising's accentuation of that glib tone, and its potential effects on the tonal palette of art and even experience. She flags, for instance, a "fascination of extremes" (385) and trend toward "VULGARITY" that she supposes to be "defense[s] against the great American slickness, perhaps—" (448).

But it is in a parenthetical comment in making this point that Bishop reveals the extent to which she understood and critiqued a larger cultural logic operative in the 1960s United States. Indicating that she's not complaining about frank sexual subjects, she writes: "I read *Tropic of Cancer* in 1936 . . . and all the rest of them (Connolly's *Rock Pool* is a good one—and probably any day now it will be re-issued by Random House and all the critics will jump for joy, bring out their very frankest language, and it will be sold to Hollywood . . .)" (448). The aside addresses the then-new trend of reprising and remarketing work from previous decades, both in print and film, a practice that dominates the twenty-first-century culture industry. It also comments on the mainstream's co-optation of materials once thought "offensive," a trend indicative of a widespread commodification of culture. Bishop also complains about the pressure such a cultural economy put on self-presentation and the dominance of style, expressing the fear in 1960 (in the context of an event at Kenyon College) that the marketing of literary celebrity might supplant writing itself: "Why not just tape record everything, everything, and then cut it up into segments and advertise it madly, and not bother about art any more at all?" (316).

Bishop is not unique in expressing concerns about the powerful reach of advertising and the commodification of culture; these sentiments were ubiquitous in literary magazines and even mainstream publications at the time. As T. J. Jackson Lears has argued, the mid-1950s represented a peak of "alarm about manipulation in advertising," and expressions of indignation about the "unseemly economics of opulence" (as J. K. Galbraith put it in his essay by that title in 1952) were entirely common among the left-leaning literary set (Lears 251–54).

Yet Bishop's savvy about her own inevitable complicity in the economy about which she complains reveals a rather mature understanding of the moment, and may explain her urgent complaint to Lowell in 1960 that a "real real protest" was still necessary and yet ever more difficult to realize. For instance, after editors at Life World Library made unwanted changes to her prose book on Brazil (chiefly with marketing concerns in mind), Bishop identifies herself as powerless and complicit: indignant and yet just on the verge of sending in her contract, she complains with some humor: "It's like sending a snowflake to Devils Island, more or less. The article of 'The Madison Avenue Villain' in the last *PR* seems meant all for me" (386). Bishop references Robert Brustein's polemical essay "The Madison Avenue Villain" (1961), which rails against a marketing culture that, Brustein claims, turns "the objects of the intellect into commodities which can be sold across the counter like a bar of soap" (Brustein 199). Brustein identifies himself with a class of intellectuals who, he argues, should serve as guardians of the high-cultural flame — determined to save "truth and art" from their place "on the market block" (203).

Though Bishop shares some of Brustein's views, and even his tone, Brustein's argument "is meant all for [her]" because she cannot abide by its terms. While she clearly feels critiqued by his call for a "tremendous effort of the moral will" to ensure the "isolation of thought in places where thought is still free" (such as academic institutions, "little magazines," and "listener supported FM radio") (202–3), Bishop's wry comment to Lowell hints that this remedy is an unrealistic oversimplification of the economic-cultural situation at hand: no work by a poet supported by money from the Chapplebrook Foundation, or the Library of Congress, or (later) the Ford Foundation (even after railing against the unseemly wealth of the United States) can quite be taken as "isolated" or entirely "free."

Furthermore, the work of "teacher-poets" who did take "refuge" seemed to Bishop to risk intellectual and artistic sterility (*WIA* 365). She identifies academic poetry in the late 1950s with "formulated despair" and "careful stylishness" (267n), complaining to Lowell that both W. S. Merwin's and Richard Wilbur's poetry seem insincere, "proficient," and "glazed" (365), and, a year earlier, "'nice,' careful, dry, and 'lovely'" — marked by a "clever thinking-out process that leaves me cold" (302). Such epithets identify the "great American slickness" as being far more pervasive than Brustein imagined.

Indeed, an intense inclination against the totalizing effects of high capitalism seems to define Bishop at this point in her career. Taking issue with a point Lowell makes about modernism in his now famous *Paris Review* interview in 1961, she writes: "What you say about Marianne is fine: 'terrible, private, and strange revolutionary poetry. There isn't the motive to do that now'" (364). Bishop is fervent to push Lowell to a deeper awareness of his own point: "But I wonder—isn't there? Isn't there even more—only it's terribly hard to find the exact and right and surprising enough, or un-surprising enough, point at which to revolt now? The Beats have just fallen back on an old corpse-strewn or monument-strewn battle-field—the real real protest I suspect is something quite different. (If only I could find it. Klee's picture called FEAR seems close to it, I think . . .)" (364).

Given her view expressed in a letter from the year before, that the moment marked an economic and literary "late" and "decadent stage" (language evocative of Marxist theory), Bishop here articulates a cultural situation in which, contrary to what Lowell claims, the motive to stage a poetic revolt against dominant cultural modes is just as strong as (or even stronger than) it was for their modernist predecessors, even as (or perhaps *because*) a viable mode of protest had become so difficult to imagine (335). Bishop identifies a shift in the situation of language to effect, or even aspire to effect, cultural change. If for the early modernists, making language strange could "make it new" (and thus ideally effect new cultural situations), Bishop here hints that language, and "the private," no longer function as effective grounds for the "strange" to become visible: thus the difficulty of finding "a surprising enough, or un-surprising enough" form of revolt.

What Bishop protests in these examples is the absorption of aesthetic production into commodity production—one of the defining issues of Frederic Jameson's critique of the "postmodern condition" (Jameson 4). Indeed, we might very well call the conundrum Bishop describes "postmodernity"—a situation in which most forms of discourse, no matter how extreme, private, or "raw," feel (paradoxically) already absorbed by the tide of commodification—either quickly co-opted by the cultural mainstream or always already articulated in its terms. It is in this context that we can understand that Bishop rejects not indecorous roughness in the Beats' linguistic extremisms but rather a being stalled on exhausted cultural ground—being not "surprising enough." And it's important that Bishop's alternative mode is notably *not* to retreat into the "clever," "nice," or "careful" styles she associates with the academy, and which literary historiography might oppose to that of the Beats, a fact which strikes a blow to Ron Silliman's argument that Bishop is a key figure of a stilted midcentury "school of quietude" (Silliman). To the contrary, Bishop wishes to identify a new mode of art capable of addressing the cultural condition—one whose defining feature is the difficulty of opposing it—that she describes.

The question remains as to whether and how Bishop achieved her new mode, or how to describe it. In trying to answer this very question, Betsy Erkkila works against her own subtler claims about Bishop's midcentury interest in the limits of subjectivity, arguing that Bishop's search for an "exact point at which to revolt" results in the choice to interview the Black Panther Kathleen Cleaver in 1969 (Erkkila, "Elizabeth Bishop" 305). As interesting as the fact of that interview is, as an answer, it rather literalizes the meaning of "revolt," and misses the clearly aesthetic-political context in which Bishop critiques Lowell's interview comments.

Writing to Lowell a few years earlier, however, Bishop does make a rare explicit statement about her ideal poetic, and in terms that may help us understand the "revolt" she sought. She identifies "modesty" and *"space"* as *sine qua non* of effective contemporary writing and does so, notably, with reference to the work of Paul Klee. The link of the two comments through Klee gives us reason to believe that "modesty" and "space" factor into her sought-after mode of poetic revolt. She calls the "short instrumental pieces" of Anton Webern "exactly like what I'd always wanted, vaguely, to hear and never had, and really 'contemporary.' That strange kind of modesty that I think one feels in almost everything contemporary one really likes—Kafka, say, or Marianne, or even Eliot, and Klee and Kokoschka and Schwitters. . . . Modesty, care, *space,* a sort of helplessness but determination at the same time" (*WIA* 250).

Though critics such as Thomas Travisano ("EB and Indelicacy") and Jacqueline Vaught Brogan ("Perversity") have questioned "modesty" to describe Bishop's work (given the word's historically gendered connotations of prudishness or decorousness), *Words in Air* helps us reimagine the word's aptness to describe her particular response to midcentury cultural and aesthetic trends. The letters show that Bishop doubted the aesthetic priority being given to personality and voice, *im*modest for failing to leave interpretive space in the work of art. Indeed, as I'll now go on to show, the "modesty [. . . and] space" that Bishop calls for are consistent with her tendency (as Vaught Brogan has put it) to subvert the figure of "voice" then so central to an American poetic ("Perversity" 184–85).

Several months after writing to Lowell about modesty, Bishop congratulates him for the "strangely modest tone" of *Life Studies,* which, she admits, she finds surprising, "because [the poems] are all about yourself and yet do not sound conceited!" (*WIA* 273). She recasts this paradox three years later (in 1961), when she praises Lowell's work (especially in comparison to his better imitators, W. D. Snodgrass and Anne Sexton) for their "egocentricity," which in his work is "the reverse of *sub*limated" (327). "The reverse of sublimated" is key, especially in light of the "modest tone" and unconceited "sound" she earlier praised, for to sublimate is to refine material so that it sounds socially acceptable or likeable. This is to say that Lowell's work is "modest" and "modest" work an appropriately unsurprising revolt for its apparent willingness to leave space—to *not* control readers' intellectual or emotional responses to it. Sublimated work, on the other hand, employs "darling" gestures (as Bishop accused Sexton of doing) that enforce intimacy with the reader and assert personality. Such gestures share with the language of advertising that increasingly slick "self-consciousness" Bishop abhorred and in whose context modesty and "space" might seem, by contrast, revolutionary.

Allowing interpretive space, Bishop's midcentury work cultivates (revolutionary?) tonal ambiguity through which it can explore how discursive, public language shapes so-called "private" experience and "voice" in the first place.

Significant echoes from Bishop's epistolary critique of the United States resound as we turn to *Questions of Travel* (1965), in which many of Bishop's poems from the mid- to late 1950s appear. This is true on nearly every page of the collection's first section: the "demands" of the tourist in "Arrival at Santos" (the poem that opens that section) are "immodest"; she expects the landscape to correspond to her desires for

> a different world,
> and a better life,
> and complete comprehension
> of both at last, and immediately.

This is exaggerated rhetoric which, after an immersion in the letters to Lowell, seems very close to the tone and feel of advertising copy (*CP* 89). In the collection's second poem, "Brazil, January 1, 1502," we hear the letters ring in the "dream of wealth and luxury" the speaking-subject projects onto the psychology of the invading Christians (92). In the next poem, "Questions of Travel," the informing complaint is: "Oh, must we dream our dreams / and have them, too?" (93)—a question which, in the context of Bishop's concerns about "money money money" (*WIA* 515) and the trend to "madly" advertise "everything" (316), echoes her preoccupation with a glut of American products, and marketers' enticements to encourage consumer desire. In very clear thematic ways, that is, Bishop's poems, particularly in the *Brazil* section, seem informed by her explicitly stated political concerns about culture and the language.

Critics have not failed to remark the political nature of poems in *Questions of Travel,* though usually with a focus on poems in its "Brazil" section, a move coincident with the general critical tendency to identify politics in Bishop's work with a thematic concern with "others." And yet it seems important to entertain ways in which the "Elsewhere" section of *Questions of Travel* registers Bishop's concern with finding an "exact point at which to revolt" in the early 1960s. These poems witness her both inviting and refusing the expressionist and personal poetics of the newly popular "confessional" mode, in favor of what I'd call a meta-discursive mode—one, that is, in which "personal" language subtly reveals its discursive character. In other words, the mode is metadiscursive because it explores the nature of discourse as a shaping force on the personal.

In line with my claim is Mutlu Konuk Blasing's implication that what's notable about Bishop's poems, and "Brazil, January 1, 1502" in particular, is what I'd call their interpretive space. Blasing proposes that that poem *"leaves the reader room"* (*Politics and Form* 89, emphasis added) to question the poet's "rhetoric and representation" (in a poem that wonders broadly about the politics of representation), and concludes, "The poem tells its story by emphasizing the mediation of its own figuration" (89). I take Blasing to refer to the poem's overemphasis on its own discursive logic—the opening gambit of "Januaries, Nature greets our eyes / Exactly as she must have greeted theirs" (*CP* 91), and how the overemphasis on identity in "exactly" draws attention to the poem as just one more "representational surface" rather than as a straight rhetorical claim or as a container for some kind of knowledge.

The poem's exposure of the inherent limits of any rhetorical mode (even poetry) is powerful to the degree that we don't feel it has been imposed upon us, and it is this "leav[ing] the reader room" that I see constituting Bishop's answer to the difficulty of finding the "exact and right point . . . at which to revolt now" (*WIA* 364). Blasing doesn't historicize this tendency, but it does seem important to entertain the idea that for Bishop at midcentury particularly, the important ground of struggle for poets of her (and perhaps more so Lowell's) generation involved a tendency for cultural forms, under the influence of advertising and consumerism, to fail to allow any interpretive space. What's remarkable about "Brazil, January 1, 1502" is its refusal to function in the way that, in Bishop's view, most "personal poems" of the early 1960s did: either as covert self-promotion; as guilty justification for bad behavior; or as an author's claim to be victim (whether to family or history)—a move, Bishop feared, often mistakenly proffered as political awareness (386). Bishop's "Brazil, January 1, 1502," on the other hand, reveals the speaking subject as imbricated in a larger logic, one it both resists and by which it is implicated.

Let me turn now to several poems to explore some forms that "interpretive space" takes in *Questions of Travel.* "Arrival at Santos" (part of the collection's "Brazil" section, but one of the less explicitly "political" of those poems) constitutes a formal experiment that opens interpretive space for the reader, in part by disturbing our ability to identify in any comfortable way with the poem's speaking subject. Indeed, the poem invites and yet frustrates our reading it as a script for the "voice" of either the innocent tourist or the colonizing other; in spite of its colloquialisms and detail (notably, detail we can locate in Bishop's "real" life), odd shifts both in discursive modes and subject positions distance rather than create an impression of closeness between author and speaker, or speaker and reader.

This is all the more significant in that the poem acts as our introduction (our "port," if you will) to the collection: though in its final line, it promises a "driv[e]" to the interior, the poem (like the collection as a whole) in fact undermines the expectation that it will function as a revealing self-exploration in which speaking subject and poet are identified (*CP* 90). In other words, it invites and then fails to fulfill strong generic expectations that had been set, for most readers of contemporary poetry in 1965, by the success of Lowell's *Life Studies,* Sexton's *To Bedlam and Part Way Back,* and Sylvia Plath's *Ariel.*

It does so by emphasizing convention and artifice, beginning with a four-beat line evocative of nursery rhyme, privileging music over the prosy style that was then a strong gesture to "voice," especially for admirers of *Life Studies.* And though the poem tempts us to imagine it as a lyric monologue expressive of its speaking subject-poet's point of view, it just as often reminds us that the process of figuration is never *not* dictated (to some degree or another) by convention.

The odd interruption of "who knows?" in the middle of line three is one of several instances of address that both elicit and undermine our expectation of voice, establishing a colloquial tone whose very intimacy suddenly seems strange:

> Here is a coast; here is a harbor;
> here, after a meager diet of horizon, is some scenery:
> impractically shaped and—who knows?—self-pitying
> mountains (89)

We're thrown, because the purpose of the interjection is ambiguous: to what exactly does it refer? Is what's in doubt the mountains, or the self-pity; whose self pity?

Are we to hear the wisdom of the poem interrupting the figure of a speaker here, or is it the speaking subject herself? The apostrophe in line 7—"Oh, tourist"—is similarly eruptive, suggesting either a discourse switch (the emergence of a second "voice") or a moment of self-address. And the fact that it's only in the fourth quatrain that the first-person pronoun emerges asks us to think about who or what, if not "I," has been "speaking" all along (89).

Several times, the poem gestures overemphatically to being a "natural" real-time report of "arrival" (insisting that this or that is happening "now," for instance), thus clashing with its almost comic insistence on keeping its conventional rhyme scheme (*abxb* or *abab*); syntax spills over line lengths in a remarkably awkward effort to keep to the scheme, most notably in Bishop's famous choice to move the terminal "s" of "Glens Falls" to the beginning of a line to force an exact rhyme with "tall" (89–90). The "realness" of almost comically emphatic deictic gestures in such lines as, "Please, boy, do be more careful with that boat hook! / Watch out! Oh! It has caught Miss Breen's / skirt!" are undercut by steep enjambments meant to maintain rhyme: we can't forget that the poem is a construct (89).

The effect is a deconstruction of "voice" that makes it very difficult for me to decide, in performing the poem, how to "speak" it: form dictates one set of possibilities; shifting tone dictates another; shifts in discourse yet another. Or to put it in Bishop's terms, we lack either a strong rhetorical stance, or a "clever thinking out process" to interpret the scene's feeling tone for us; we are left with significant interpretive space with which to weigh the value of the "interior" that is (ironically) offered as a symbol at the end of the poem.

Thus while "Arrival at Santos" is muted and oblique in its political aims, placed in the context of Bishop's views on the most prevalent poetic tendencies of her day, the poem's leaving of such space for a reader reads as a political gesture, especially in contrast to the immodest cultural tendencies (the "egocentricity" and "self-regard") Bishop criticized in Sexton's and Snodgrass's work. What she objected to wasn't the revelation of intimate or shocking personal material (other forms of immodesty) (*WIA* 327). Rather, she disliked in both poets' works the relationship of their author-speakers to the ground of pathos in their poems; their work seemed to indicate primarily a concern with being "liked" (360).

To concern oneself so was to grant aesthetic primacy to expressive "voice" over and above more socially and culturally resonant forms. After suggesting to Lowell that both Snodgrass and Sexton are guilty of wanting poems to attest to their author's personalities, she subtly suggests that she takes this egocentricity (along with Lowell's mild dismissal of meter in the same letter) as signs of an "increasing self-consciousness" in the contemporary arts that served, rather than contested, the American cultural trend toward excess (333, 359). Qualifying his agreements with Bishop about Sexton's work, Lowell had added: "Meter is a puzzle to me now. . . . Something quite pleasant both to write and to read is added by meter, but it's something free verse doesn't want at all, and which seems to have little to do with experience or intuition" (331). In her reply, Bishop counters: "What you say about meter: . . . I have a theory now that the arts are growing more and more 'literary'"; that it is a late stage, perhaps a decadent stage, and that un-metrical verse is more 'literary' and necessarily self-conscious than metrical" (335).

Behind the exchange is a muted but significant disagreement about the source of art's power, and about the election of "experience" as art's source or payoff. Lowell's comment sets his idea of "experience" in an antithetical relationship to the conventional qualities of meter; an art of experience seems for him to be, by definition, expressive, and, he implies, "free." For Bishop, such a distinction (between "experience" and convention) oversimplifies matters: Notice that, in her reply, she calls the opposite of metered verse "un-metrical verse," not "free" verse, a move that highlights the conventionality of all writing. Further, she quietly marries Lowell's "intuition and experience" to decadence and the 'literary,' the latter being a word that both she and Lowell would associate with the stale narrowness of coterie (as opposed to concerns of broader social import) (*WIA* 390, 563–64, 726).

For it is notable that *Questions of Travel* not only does not jettison meter, but in fact emphasizes convention, poetically, metrically, and thematically. This happens at the broad structural level of the collection. Despite the opening poem's promise that we are "driving to [an] interior" (personal, emotional, geographic), with later poems held out as the longed-for antithesis to and relief from the "unimpressive" (because conventionally only necessary and "unassertive"), superficial impression ports make (*CP* 90), it doesn't take much to see the ways in which the collection's design in fact firmly deemphasizes personality and interiority, reminding us instead of the superficial, social qualities of all written material (and especially convention-bound forms).

If "Arrival at Santos" is the physical gateway or "port" to the rest of the "Brazil" section, then the physical "interior" toward which the section drives (its innermost part) is, at least in most editions, "The Burglar of Babylon," a ballad— perhaps the most conventional and least "personal" poetic form used in the collection (*CP* 112–18). Even given Bishop's placing of her autobiographical story "In the Village" at the center of her first edition, the story ends on a note that dispenses with the idiosyncratic historical detail of suffering that informed it—

"clothes, crumbling postcards, broken china; things damaged and lost"—in favor of a much broader point of view, becoming "the elements speaking: earth, air, fire, water" (*PPL* 118).

And just as "In the Village" prefers to transcend the personal, the collection as a whole subordinates it. For instance, what follows the story in "Elsewhere" is the poem "Manners," which explores conventional forms of sociality. And though the collection moves us, broadly speaking, from the foreign to the domestic through scenes of childhood, the final poem, "Visits to St. Elizabeths," is markedly impersonal and only vaguely "about" Bishop's visits to Ezra Pound during his incarceration at St. Elizabeths Hospital. Bishop subordinates her personal feelings about Pound to the conventions of the children's rhyme "This Is the House That Jack Built"—a form that presents us a diversity of perspectives (the sailor, the Jew, and so on) (*CP* 133–35). In most ways, Bishop's collection counters Lowell's implicit privileging of individual experience (and an "intuiti[ve]" stylistics of voice) over convention.

In fact, the poems in Bishop's second section of *Questions of Travel*, "Elsewhere," not usually those through which critics explore her politics, may nevertheless be read as political precisely for their focus on how discursive conventions, which inform how subjects reconstruct supposedly "authentic" personal experience, complicate the figure of voice. Several of these poems suggest the dialectical relationships of "interior" feelings and superficial "conventions," discursive practices and personal experiences, or, to put it another way, (personal) experience and the (social) language that describes it. In other words, I'm using the phrase "discursive conventions" (or discourse) in the by now familiar Foucauldian sense, to mean, as Stuart Hall describes it, language that "governs the way a topic can be meaningfully talked about and reasoned about" (Hall 72). Discourse, he explains, "'rules in' certain ways of talking about a topic, defining an acceptable and intelligible way to talk, write, or conduct oneself, [and also] by definition . . . 'rules out,' limits and restricts other ways of talking, of conducting ourselves in relation to the topic or constructing knowledge about it" (Hall 72).

Throughout "Elsewhere," Bishop emphasizes and makes strange the powerful, inescapable everyday discursive language that shapes our experience of experience. In these poems, "voice" is less idiosyncratic and particular; instead it is shown to be a weave of textual and conventional gestures, ritual phrases that Bishop makes foreign. In fact, many of the "Elsewhere" poems foreground their resistance to being "properly" voiced, again striking a blow to the midcentury interest in voice then so central to an expressive poetics of personality. This is a central concern of "Manners." The poem presents two characters, a grandfather hoping to share his conventional wisdom about the importance of manners, and a child (historicized as a "child of 1918") being educated to his worldview. The child dutifully repeats what the grandfather advises, a point the poem rather awkwardly emphasizes for us. Here are the first four stanzas:

> My grandfather said to me
> as we sat on the wagon seat,
> "Be sure to remember to always
> speak to everyone you meet."
>
> We met a stranger on foot.
> My grandfather's whip tapped his hat.
> "Good day, sir. Good day. A fine day."
> And I said it and bowed where I sat.
>
> Then we overtook a boy we knew
> with a big pet crow on his shoulder.
> "Always offer everyone a ride;
> don't forget that when you get older,"
>
> my grandfather said. So Willy
> climbed up with us, but the crow
> gave a "Caw!" and flew off. I was worried.
> How would he know where to go? (CP 121)

The poem only very subtly reveals the comic absurdity of the grandfather's logic of manners: notice that he does not offer a ride to the "stranger," only to a "boy we knew" (this fact emphasized by the line break's stress on "knew"), though he also insists that the children should "Always offer everyone a ride," something he's forgotten, perhaps (against his own command), since getting older (121). The poem ends up seeming less a "nostalgic eulogy for a passing life," as Margaret Dickie has claimed ("Race and Class" 53), than Bishop's complex and ironic exploration of the tension between the social worldview her generation (children of 1918) had inherited, and that view's mix of appeal, limitation, and increasing obsolescence for that now adult generation.

It is important that it is by adhering to convention, rather than by abandoning it, that Bishop's poem conveys its irony and ambivalence, which can't be said to be produced by "voice" at all. The poem's pounding, mostly three-beat line often creates a tension for the reader over what to stress, as with the line, "And I said it and bowed where I sat" (*CP* 121). Should we stress "I" or "said"?: If we want to stress the child's dutiful repetition, we would stress "I," but the previous lines have conditioned us, with their accentual beat, to stress "said." Stressing "said" rather emphasizes the force of convention to make us speak a certain way—key in a poem that repeats "said" or some synonym of "said" in seven of its eight stanzas. This ambiguity of stress is reasserted by the ambiguity of what exactly the child *has* repeated of the three slightly different things her grandfather says to say, in the second stanza, to the stranger. If the line is clumsy, it seems to attest to the mixture of feelings one might attach to having absorbed a grandfather's discursive education on manners. The poem underscores the only-ever-mixed value of such lessons by closing with a gesture to the historical conditions (chiefly the automobile age) that seem to render them comic, if not obsolete:

> When automobiles went by,
> the dust hid the people's faces,
> but we shouted "Good day! Good day!
> Fine day!" at the top of our voices. (*CP* 121)

Just as the grandfather seems (laughably) overinsistent on the importance of good manners when, in the fourth stanza, he anthropomorphizes Willy's crow's behavior, in this stanza, all three figures in the poem overinsist on a code of manners despite the fact that the mutual respect such behavior is supposed to convey is surely lost on the passing motorists. Given Bishop's attitude toward the automobile at this time, such moments seem her way of exploring—beyond expressions of indignation—the complexity of her dismay over the current pace and tone of contemporary culture.

And it is the fact that Bishop is not *only* nostalgic in the poem, *not* naively celebratory of "a social code that does not change," as Dickie claims (89), that makes it seem more deeply in tune with her concern to open interpretive space. In the space between the poem's adherence to convention (both thematically and prosodically) and its departure from it (in revealing the grandfather's hypocritical manners), we are offered a rather deep exploration of the process by which discourse asserts itself. The poem seems to know, for instance, that the children get out of the wagon in the last stanza because the grandfather has said to, not quite for the sake of "good manners" alone. Again the poem very quietly emphasizes the grandfather's power to command:

> When we came to Hustler Hill,
> he said that the mare was tired,
> so we all got down and walked,
> as our good manners required. (CP 122)

The fact of the children's willingness to repeat the lesson (without questioning its illogic) suggests the power of discourse to condition their worldview. This sheds an ironic light on both the poem's air of respect and its adherence to metrical forms.

What gets emphasized in the process *is not* a set of feelings that belong to a speaker, or, implicitly, to the poet. Rather, the poem focuses our attention on the scene of discursive education. While "manners" are no doubt something Bishop considered useful, she was also savvy to the way such phrases as "good manners" might be used to support any number of less homey agendas.

Such scenes of discursive education are emphasized in other poems in the collection, and perhaps most clearly in "First Death in Nova Scotia," where various technical choices emphasize discourse and also result (notably) in moments that resist clear tonal interpretation. We are tempted, by setting and choices of diction in the poem, to take many of its descriptive lines as very nearly spoken in the voice of a child who attempts, while looking at the body of her dead cousin, to embody or mobilize the culture's euphemisms for death:

> Arthur was very small.
> He was all white, like a doll
> that hadn't been painted yet.
> Jack Frost had started to paint him
> the way he always painted
> the Maple Leaf (Forever). (CP 125–26)

The addition of "Forever," and the parentheses around it, complicate our ability to "hear" particularities of a speaker's voice here. Who "speaks" the "forever" parenthetically added to what heretofore has seemed the child's imaginative description? Even if we try to take it as occurring within the real time or dramatized unfolding of the child-poet's thoughts, why has Bishop bothered to show us an automatic mental association (maple leaf recalling "Maple Leaf," and thus the old Canadian national anthem) occurring in this context?

That the word that comes to mind is "forever" of course fits a poem about witnessing a first "death," yet there is more at stake in these lines. Consider Bishop's awareness (inevitable given the mass-market magazines and television she was then encountering) of the efforts of marketing language to condition readers' responses. Such an awareness makes it possible to read the poem as exploring the child's susceptibility to discourse. The poem subtly suggests that the fantastic and symbolic images to which the child resorts are less imaginative deflections of the difficulty of her cousin's death, than indices of how children inherit culture, including sentimental discourses. For instance, the claim that the deceased cousin was "all white, like a doll / that hadn't been painted yet" reads, in light of the poem's falling into the old nationalist slogan, very like the details to which an anxious parent (and an anxious culture) resort to gloss hard facts of death and burial. For this is how one is disciplined to one's symbolic cultural norms: seeing each day the pictures one's parents have displayed (of important ancestors, celebrities, or of political figures), one is offered narratives that justify their presence. One takes these narratives as truth: from the child's perspective, the story that "the gracious royal couples" have invited one's dead cousin to be "the smallest page at court" is no less or more bizarre than the presence of the couples on the wall in the first place (CP 126).

That the poem wants us to register the gap between the child's psyche and the language that tries to manage it is suggested by the closing lines, the tone of which is almost impossible to gauge:

> But how could Arthur go,
> clutching his tiny lily,
> with his eyes shut up so tight
> and the roads deep in snow?" (126)

Who speaks these lines? They feel not genuine, given the poem's awareness of how insufficiently the explanation contains the death. However, they feel neither entirely rhetorical nor savvy, since the child, we understand, genuinely struggles to understand the strange logic he or she's been offered to explain the death (Arthur "the smallest page at court"). The lines, for this reason, are quite awkward to read aloud, for how to register their complexity, except by flattening our reading so as to mark only the pattern of three stresses per line — the purely conventional qualities of it? The line thwarts the identification of a locus of feeling or authentic experience in the poem, undermining its colloquial gestures (elsewhere) to "voice."

My sense of the importance of discourse in "Manners" and "First Death . . ." is reaffirmed by the surprising, seemingly unself-consciously uttered religious phrase that pops up at the end of "Filling Station": "Somebody loves us all" (128). This phrase is a key, oft-repeated slogan of evangelical Christianity, just the kind of phrase that Bishop might dwell on in notebooks or letters. Critics have struggled to read this line, some confident that it is spoken as dramatic monologue—sign of the speaker's disdain for the Christian idea that even the "greasy and saucy sons" are loved by Christ (or that we all have to be loved by someone). Is it enough to read it as a strange remainder in the poem—a gesture to the power of language to lead us down chains of thought almost against our will, in the way the language of an advertisement will linger in one's mind for years after hearing it? What constitutes genuine experience if the language with which one expresses or describes it is inherited and often already commodified for us?

Finally, it is in the destabilization of the ground of sympathy in these poems— ground that, if stable, would enable a reader's identification with their speakers— that leaves us interpretive space to identify the power of discourse at work. I read this as Bishop's "modesty"—refusal to arrange our understanding of the poem's implications, for if we don't fully identify with speakers, neither can we comprehend them fully as characters. Rather than striving to make familiar language a conduit of voice or expression of personality, Bishop's poems treat it as an object of analysis and wonder. This brings her poems into the same universe (somewhat surprisingly) with experiments from such quarters as the Language writers of the 1980s, who similarly believe that the most useful way to resist high-capitalist modes as they had infiltrated language was to disrupt habitual chains of syntax and rhetoric to allow readers more interpretive freedom. So quiet is Bishop's "unsurprising . . . revolt," however, that it has often slipped notice. Critics more inclined to champion her Romantic descriptive skills, or to recover personal confessions in her understated and often oblique poems, miss their more radical nature. The recently published correspondence with Lowell lets us see that "modesty [and] *space* in art" served as her (unsurprising enough) point of revolt. Bishop protested against a culture at risk of missing the rhetoric and tone shaping the sound of voices, a culture perhaps too inclined to be told what to feel.

NOTES

1. See also Alvarez 3–21; and Axelrod, *Robert Lowell*, 125.

2. Several critics have inventoried critical claims that assert or imply Bishop's being apolitical (see Erkkila, "Elizabeth Bishop," esp. 245–84; and Longenbach, "Elizabeth Bishop's Social Conscience" 467–86; see also Brogan's "Perversity as Voice," esp. 185–86).

3. See Dickie, "Race and Class," esp. 45, 58. See also Erkkila, "Elizabeth Bishop"; Camille Roman; and, in a view closest to my own, Axelrod's "Elizabeth Bishop and Containment Policy."

"A Lovely Finish I Have Seen"

Voice and Variorum in *Edgar Allan Poe & the Juke-Box*

CHRISTINA PUGH

Who can predict the half-life of a dead poet's unfinished works? And if they are disseminated for public consumption, who—or what aesthetic—may ultimately co-opt them? These questions have become more salient after the 2006 publication of Alice Quinn's *Edgar Allan Poe & the Juke-Box*. As is well known, Quinn's variorum edition has provoked its share of controversy in the literary world, largely regarding issues of authorial intent and a deceased poets' control over unpublished materials.[1] Perhaps the most famous objection was Helen Vendler's outrage that the "maimed and stunted siblings" of Bishop's published poems should be collected for the public to read ("The Art of Losing").

But I am interested in other, more globally aesthetic, questions that Quinn's volume raises. What is the nature, whether aesthetic or otherwise, of the literary world's investment in variorum or facsimile editions? In which particular ways do these editions redramatize, recharacterize, or reinscribe our hallucinated relation to a dead poet? Can lyric poems in manuscript format be co-opted by the thrall of the "unfinished" that is operative in a more experimental poetics? And is this experimental aesthetic actually imbued with a heftier conservatism than its proponents might allow, especially when it applies (or is applied) to the works of women poets in particular?

I will be addressing these questions by juxtaposing Bishop's manuscript work with the fascicles of Emily Dickinson and by suggesting that a recent movement in Dickinson scholarship may also affect the impact of *Edgar Allan Poe & the Juke-Box* on Bishop's reputation. Specifically, R. W. Franklin's manuscript edition of Dickinson's poems, published in 1981, has brought about a change in Dickinson studies—wherein critics' concerns have become arguably less "poetic" and more graphic or archival in their orientation.[2] And although the jury is still out regarding the lasting impact of *Edgar Allan Poe & the Juke-Box* on Bishop's critical reception, I will be arguing here that the publication of the variorum or facsimile edition as such, by canceling the terms and the sublimate sonorities (or fastenings) of poetic "voice," may paradoxically anchor the reader in a more conservative relation to the figure of the female poet in particular.

Before I begin to address these similarities, however, it is important to note the significant differences in the publishing history of Dickinson and Bishop, leading to corollary differences in the impact and significance of publishing their posthumous manuscript materials. As is well known, Dickinson published only a few poems in her lifetime; the first published collection of her work appeared in 1890, four years after her death in 1886. Bishop, in contrast, published four books of poems during her life. She also lived to see her poetry recognized by both the Pulitzer Prize in 1956 and the National Book Award in 1970. Any judgment about the impact of Bishop's newly published manuscript materials, then, must certainly be tempered by the notice given her work during her lifetime.

I want to argue, however, that despite Bishop's sizable "advantage" in lifetime published output, her work is still vulnerable to some of the same sorts of literary-critical co-options that we will see affecting the Dickinson materials, and that these co-options may necessitate a silencing of what we know as poetic "voice." In order to address the similarities between Bishop and Dickinson in this regard, we first need to ask whether the dissemination of manuscript materials can be compatible with the emphasis on poetic voice that the lyric tradition both assumes and promulgates. Is a concern with poetic voice really viable after poststructuralism? And if it is, can the publication of a manuscript edition serve to silence that voice?

Clearly, the dissemination of handwritten manuscript work would fall in line with the Derridean exhortation to treat writing as graphic trace rather than the logocentric transcription of (an ostensibly univocal) speech. But even in the wake of poststructuralism, the construct of poetic voice is alive and well in the criticism of the lyric, as seen in the work of W. R. Johnson, Mutlu Konuk Blasing, Susan Stewart, and Allen Grossman, to name only a few examples.[3] Voice has also remained the coin of the realm for many contemporary poets, especially those who see Bishop's work as seminal for the development of their own. As James Merrill wrote of Bishop, "Whether this voice says hard and disabused things or humorous and gentle ones, its emotional pitch remains so true, and its intelligence so unaffected, that we hear in it the 'touch of nature' which makes the whole world kin" (*Recitative* 129).

In Bishop's work, there is a significant relationship not only between voice and referentiality (Merrill's "touch of nature"), but between voice and "finish." It has become almost a commonplace to call Bishop a poet of assiduously polished surfaces, in which even ingenuous questioning shores up the poet's ravishing rhetorical authority. What is more, her poems often read as if in transparent service to extratextual visual acuity. As Lee Edelman has stated of the poet's critical reception, "They have cited her work . . . as exemplary of precise observation and accurate detail" (92); he goes on to quote David Kalstone's statement that Bishop was portrayed as a "miniaturist," with all the attendant enameling that the word implies (92). Though Edelman is ultimately critical of this miniaturist appellation—and we should also be wary of its gendered implications—few would disagree that Bishop was remarkably gifted in the precise rendering of percepts both empirical and imagined.

If we juxtapose the statements of Merrill, Kalstone, and Edelman, we can begin to understand the unusual ramifications of poetic voice in Bishop's work. By coupling the exigencies of precise detail with the creation of "kinship," we can see this poet's highly crafted "finish" as surprisingly tempered by the demands of communicative, nearly dialogic speech. The conjunction of filigreed, paratactic descriptive work (as seen in "At the Fishhouses" and "The Bight," for example) with "true" emotional pitch, in Merrill's terms, means that the patina of her finished poems is not only commensurate with, but also may in some sense constitute, the sonorities of an idiomatic conversational voice. Perhaps the best emblem of this unlikely balance was created by Bishop herself, who noted "the curious effect a poem produces as being as normal as *sight* and yet as synthetic, as artificial, as a *glass eye*" (xi, original emphasis, quoted by Quinn). In this passage, Bishop has combined the faculty of sight with its prosthetic simulacrum in order to define voice as both natural and artificial; such a paradox becomes the alchemy of what makes lyric poetry "work."

But the publication of poems Bishop chose not to publish—likely, in the poet's mind, "unfinished"—situates her in another arena, in which the visual thrall of the abandoned manuscript-in-progress chafes against the finish created by a mimetic, *extra*textual, referential impulse: the impulse, in other words, that guided her published poetic output. In *Edgar Allan Poe & the Juke-Box,* Bishop's referential visual register has often been exchanged for the "look" of the manuscript page itself. For this reason, it is almost wonderfully ironic that the first poem in the volume's "1929–1936" section is titled "A lovely finish I have seen . . . ," as if the past perfect were to act as an unwittingly elegiac commentary on the inviolability of the work in Bishop's *Collected Poems* and an equally pointed look ahead to the contents of the Quinn volume. As if proleptically aware of its own allegorical placement, the poem asks, "Can one accuse of artifice / such finishes and surfaces?" (11). Whether these "finishes and surfaces" refer to the contents of Quinn's volume or to *Complete Poems,* it is telling that the line rhetorically defends the "accused" value of artifice.

At the same time, however, the front matter of *Edgar Allan Poe & the Juke-Box* thwarts any vestigial expectation of "finish" that the reader might have had: the book's facing title page features a handwritten version of the poem "Edgar Allan Poe & the Juke-Box" slashed by a single stroke of ink. Before the book has even begun, then, it has visually allegorized its own title as a cancellation; the compilation has been named after a poem that Bishop "nixed." This canceled poem fairly refutes the gorgeous linguistic polish of the Bishop whose poems we knew, and yet Bishop herself is the author of it—the author, in a sense, of her own undoing. And the title page itself is hardly an anomaly. As Quinn notes in her introduction, the volume contains eleven other poem drafts that were "entirely crossed out by Bishop" in manuscript (xx).

From the outset, then, it is clear that *Edgar Allan Poe & the Juke-Box* necessarily "plays" Bishop differently—almost as a record on a juke box—from the music of her finished poetry. The erstwhile voice of the *Complete Poems,* a form of recto to the current volume's verso, is epitomized by the assertion of "Edgar Allan Poe" that "The burning box can keep the measure / strict, always, and the down-beat" (49). If legibility is allied with the productions of poetic voice, then the facsimile productions cannot keep such strict aural measure; on the contrary, they graphically capture one of our most obsessively legible poets in her transitional or self-canceling moments of illegibility. And if illegibility co-opts voice, as we will see in more detail later, then the public presentation of drafts with their variants renders Bishop vulnerable to co-option by a more experimental code of aesthetics than what she actually embraced as a publishing poet.

At this juncture, I want to clarify that my concerns are not so much with Quinn's manifest intentions around the drafts, insofar as her stated goal is to "provide an adventure for readers who love the established canon, enabling them to hear echoes and make connections based on their own intuitions and close reading of both the finished and the unfinished poems" (xv). Instead, I am more interested in the way that our current critical climate supports the aesthetic choices implicit in the very enterprise of facsimile dissemination, thereby opening the way to a set of receptions and co-options of the lyric—and of poetic voice—that we can see most saliently in the recent critical history of Emily Dickinson's work.

As I noted above, Franklin's facsimile publication of *The Manuscript Books of Emily Dickinson* in 1981 significantly redirected the study of Dickinson's poems. Since then, Dickinson criticism has turned away from questions of poetic voice and has instead embraced the problematics of the visual mark, cancellation, works perennially in progress, and the limits of legibility. Portrayed by critics as exemplary of writerly flux and resistance to finish, Dickinson's poems-as-manuscripts have become a newfound "open text," in the terms of the Language poet Lyn Hejinian: "The 'open text' often emphasizes or foregrounds process . . . and thus resists the cultural tendencies that seek to identify and fix material and turn it into a product; that is, it resists reduction and commodification" (43). In resisting "fix," the open text also necessarily resists what we have been discussing as poetic "finish."

Due both to this advent of textual scholarship and to experimental poets' recent interest in her work, it is fair to say that Dickinson's lyric output has been reborn as experimental: as visual marks that foreground process as such, in Hejinian's terms. Indeed, the criticism of Susan Howe, a poet often associated with the Language movement, has established Dickinson as a foremother of the experimental project; Howe ultimately allies the poet's work with "the space of silence" (170) rather than treating it as communicative speech or song. This is partially because, in her words, "these manuscripts should be understood as visual productions" (141).

And in her tellingly titled *Choosing Not Choosing,* Sharon Cameron has attributed a poetics of nonclosure to Dickinson, based largely on the way in which the poet's fascicle poems, in their presentation of variant words as foils and counterpoint to poetic lines, resist the choice of a "finished" line as such: "In Dickinson's fascicles . . . variants indicate both the desire for limit and the difficulty in enforcing it. The difficulty in enforcing a limit to the poems turns into a kind of limitlessness . . . for . . . it is impossible to say where the text ends because the variants extend the text's identity in ways that make it seem potentially limitless" (6). There is clearly a strong connection between Hejinian's openness and Cameron's "limitlessness." Yet to ascribe limitlessness to poems written in common and short meter is to ask that the reader's eye be trained away from the patently limiting circumscription of rhyme and metrical structures: those structures that, in a global sense, help to determine "voice" as it is often conceptualized in lyric poetry. Here, then, Cameron interprets the fascicles' variant words as destabilizing the very foundations of prosodic construction. This move is very much in line with the current direction of Dickinson studies, which has often myopically focused on microscopic aspects of the manuscript work, thus portraying it as a form of perennial Kristevan genotext (or text-in-progress) and eliding the components of prosody and sound that are indispensable aspects of poetic voice.

By taking Cameron's move as emblematic of a certain kind of reading, my purpose is to ask what happens when the values and modalities of "voice"—values often congruent with, but not fully identical to, prosodic structure—are exchanged for the more graphic values of "limitlessness" within the boundaries of the *same* poet's work. How could the notion of "limitlessness" speak to the poems in *Edgar Allan Poe & the Juke-Box,* for example? And how would such redressing serve to silence Bishop's recognizable voice?

For Cameron, as we've seen, Dickinson's retention of variants serves to create the limitlessness that then becomes representative of her oeuvre as a whole. Perhaps not surprisingly, the Quinn volume also includes many variants. In lines like "The chic dog and the not as chic leak / peak / street" (from "Rainy Day, Rio," *EAP* 133), Bishop is imbued with a veneer of experimental—even if rhyme-driven—undecidability that, when printed, transforms the finish of her published poems into a different poetics altogether.

This line also recalls Sally Bushell's discussion of Dickinson's structural "creative optionality" in her manuscript composition, wherein "the fixed frame establishes a factual structure of event and narrative, syntax and meter. The optional parts are limited to nuances within that frame and to subtle changes of tone and emotional register that affect the overall meaning at the level of feeling" (198). Even though Bishop seems primarily to be playing with assonance and near-rhyme here, the variants also proceed from nonsense to something approximating referential meaning: the singsong "not as chic leak" becomes, over the course of sequential wordplay, the almost referential "not as chic street"—which might describe a neighborhood that is not quite Fifth Avenue, for example. So if we decide to read these variants sequentially, they may indeed reveal something about the poet's aural process of composition. But the process itself would not have remained visible in the completed work; as we know, the "finished" Bishop was not a poet of wordplay, though she was also not averse to playing occasionally with prosody.[4] For Bishop, then, "creative optionality" would be a momentary artifact rather than a viable, process-driven poetics.

Thus the preponderance of variants in *Edgar Allan Poe & the Juke-Box* must read differently for Bishop than for Dickinson, who after a certain point chose to retain her variants as an integral part of her fascicle production. For this reason, the graphic attention extolled and practiced by Dickinson's most ardent textual readers has a different effect in the case of Bishop's poetry, since publishing the poems in *Edgar Allan Poe & the Juke-Box* does militate against Bishop's de facto intentions—and sometimes even overrides her textually manifested choices within the drafts themselves, as in Quinn's statement that "I feel there is nothing to be learned from omitting punctuation where it is clear she *would have* employed it" (xix, emphasis added). Though the volume spotlights the unfinished, there are evidently moments in which Quinn's editorial agency provides more "finish" than do Bishop's drafts.

More often than not, however, editorial selection and arrangement serves to intensify the appearance of undecidability in Bishop's unfinished work. Since the volume presents certain drafts in both print and facsimile forms, sometimes on facing pages, it provides a fascinating window into the aesthetics of editorial choice. In this case, the facing-page presentations serve to underscore the abyssal relation between each lettered surface and its textual, and technological, "other," thus opening a space for a more experimental poetics to reside.

As we saw in the line from "Rainy Day, Rio.," for example, recalibrating and "pasteurizing" handwritten drafts into print requires frequent use of the bracket and the virgule, diacritics that mark negative space in the manuscripts. Because these marks signify emptiness in the form of lacunae or aporia, they are closer in spirit to the indeterminate aesthetic of the "open text" than to anything resembling the Bishop of *Complete Poems*. In the print version of "Good-Bye—," for example, such a line as "Our eyes bleary & / /" is proleptically reminiscent of the blanks in Jorie Graham's *The End of Beauty* or indeed of Alice Fulton's doubled equal signs (*EAP* 13). Both of these prominent poets have worked with print diacritics as a way to resist particularization and semantic limitation. That neither of them would be claimed as "experimental" only reveals the degree to which aporia and undecidability have become accepted components of the mainstream repertoire that is available to the contemporary American poet.

These conditions contribute to the ease with which Bishop's unfinished drafts may be imbued with the experimental lure of the "mark." Perhaps we can see this best in drafts that inexplicably resist print recalibration altogether, as in a poem called "The Blue Chairs" (*EAP* 127). Here, we are given only a dubiously legible notebook page in facsimile reproduction, never a print "interpretation." Thus the visual mark was privileged over the poem's sense, with the page's verso ink perceptible in gusting layers of impenetrable hieroglyphs. Moreover, the choice to include the love poem "It is marvelous to wake up together . . ." as a photographed typescript also suggests that Bishop's creased paper and typewriter strokes might afford a more appropriate readerly "embrace" than a print version would allow.

When Bushell similarly aestheticizes a fragment from one of Wordsworth's ruined drafts of "The Prelude," we can better understand what is at stake in such choices: "When we respond to the page in isolation, it has a kind of beauty, I think, not only because of the evident fragility of the meaning it contains but also because of the unexpected and unintended enactment of its semantic meaning in its visual form" (90). This judgment presents as a familiar statement about form and content, but one that is enhanced by the element of uncorrected chance that occurs in the draft; for Bushell, it is the fragility of both letter *and* meaning that makes the draft beautiful. By aesthetically ratifying the values of the incomplete and the aleatory (or what exceeds the author's compositional intention, difficult as that may be to ascertain), Bushell is arguing that draft material can and should be interpreted literarily and not simply as steps in a writer's teleological formation of a work. It seems to me, however, that this argument could only be made in a climate that already supports the aesthetic of the unfinished-as-literary, whose values remain antithetical to the exigencies of poetic voice.

What is ironic in all this, of course, is that Bishop's status as a major reviser preceded the publication of *Edgar Allan Poe & the Juke-Box,* but in a very different capacity. For years, writing programs have fetishized her multiple drafts of "One Art" as a sort of mathematical proof that mainstream workshop pedagogy "works." Indeed, according to the traditional goals of the writing workshop, a student's multiple drafts will culminate in a finished poem that shows no traces of the drafting process. The rueful ease of Bishop's often-anthologized villanelle, having "vanished" its many previous draft versions, seems an emblem of those very values.

Similarly, in *The Writer's Home Companion,* Joan Bolker treats Bishop's multiple drafts as an object lesson about a necessary writerly teleology: "Judgments of our first drafts, of poetry or prose, are irrelevant, that what we need to do with our writing is to keep going, keep revising, keep moving the work towards what it is meant to be" (101). This is the second of two philosophies of revision that are driving these pertinent "looks" at Bishop's poetry: revision as synchronous value or limitlessness, as in the previous Cameron quote or in Bushell's discussion of Dickinson's "anti-telos" (196); or revision as means to an end, in Bolker's formulation. When Bolker categorically safeguards the draft from "judgment," she necessarily disqualifies it from the literary-critical judgments that Bushell promotes as appropriate for the reading of unfinished manuscript materials. Consequently, revision "plays" differently in *The Writer's Home Companion* than in *Edgar Allan Poe;* both texts reproduce Bishop's drafts of "One Art" for seemingly divergent purposes.

What we have, then, is a critical impasse regarding the proper status of revision in the literary work. I have been trying to show that due to the current critical climate, and in a manner analogous to Dickinson's rebirth as an experimental poet, Bishop is more likely to be conscripted by an "anti-telos" than to continue being associated with the teleological model epitomized by Bolker's comment. The moments of true illegibility in *Edgar Allan Poe* would go some distance in supporting this contention: illegibility, while only dubiously accessible by discrete criticism à la Bushell, is virtually disqualified from teleological process due to its apotropaic opacity.

There is an important sense, then, in which these moments of illegibility—in which the *non*transparency of the medium is offered for readerly delectation— become test cases in *Edgar Allan Poe.* Here, the impediment is the message. Consider, for example, the nearly occluded "(Florida Revisited)?" a poem whose title itself contains parentheses and a question mark. On the left-hand page, we have a copiously marked-up typescript that includes circlings, smudge marks, and crabbed ink handwriting. Facing this is a print version of the poem, whose lineation is supplemented by variant material placed close to the right margin. While, on one hand, the presentation reads as a testament to Quinn's arduous labors of deciphering ("Bishop's handwriting is challenging," she notes simply in the introduction [xviii]), it also shows the very unstable relationship between an effaced text and the necessarily indeterminate process of reading it. Here, transcription becomes the "wild surmise" of interpretation. Indeed, this very juxtaposition calls into question the distinction between process and product since the reader can see for herself how potentially inaccurate any such print choices might be; again, Hejinian's open text hovers over the presentation.

This problematic is palpably magnified in another poem, "Hannah A.," which the book also represents in facing pages of facsimile and print. The facsimile shows an inked notebook page that is marked and canceled beyond the point of illegibility. The print version of this poem, with only one bracketed stanza—less tentative in its presentation than many printed poems in the volume—opens a chasm of questions about intelligibility, legibility, and the degree to which these print poems become a product of Quinn's editorial labors. It is quite surprising to see the Rorschach-like facsimile—blotted, scribbled, and even fingerprinted to inscrutability—newly rendered in conventional print stanzas on the facing page, serenely (and cleanly) discussing "former birds who rested / on ice floes" (53). Given the visceral contrast created by these facing pages, the reader may well wonder whether the tidying act of "transcription" is more accurately an act of imagination.

Such questions exist in sharp contrast to Dickinson's editorial history, in which "faithfulness" to the fascicle (or even extrafascicle) markings is seen as accuracy— though, to be sure, an accuracy that is commensurate with perdurable undecidability. According to this line of thought, the earlier and more "finished" print publications of Dickinson's poems are revealed as products of her very editors. What *Edgar Allan Poe & the Juke-Box* shows us about Bishop, quite graphically, is that the closer we get to "original" mark, the greater the possibility for interpretive editorial largesse. Perhaps most powerfully, however, the volume also reveals the degree to which such largesse becomes the occupational hazard of any archivist interpreting illegible materials. Indeed, the draft of "Hannah A." suggests the degree to which archivist reading is a necessary fiction. One can only think that a premium has been placed on the inability to read.

But why? What is the market for illegibility? What, indeed, is the real interest in disseminating drafts of incomplete poems that can barely be deciphered? The stock answer is that the ephemera of a major poet should be made available both to a public readership and to the scholar. But illegibility is, as we've seen, a question of degree: the culling and presentation of manuscript material, particularly in facsimile form, necessitates formal and editorial choices. And as we've begun to understand, the illegible and the canceled were privileged in the facsimile productions included in this compendium. Quinn herself notes that in certain cases, the facsimile was the most "exciting" means of presenting the work (xv). I have been arguing here that the excitement of illegibility is, even if osmotically, the product of an experimentally driven critical climate that fetishizes what exceeds normative grammar and syntax, i.e., illegibility and "mark," as emblematized by the transformation of Dickinson from primarily a formal poet to an experimental one. But I also want to suggest that the re-dressing of both Bishop and Dickinson in experimental poetics may result in their critical—and in some cases, popular—redomestication as women poets. This is a reactionary move that would be worlds away from experimental values, and especially Language values, as such.

We can understand this better by looking more closely at the way that visual images and objects have functioned in the oeuvres of both poets. The deceptively marginal role of visual material in *Edgar Allan Poe & the Juke-Box* can, in fact, encapsulate some of the richest intersections between the Bishop and Dickinson manuscripts. There are two issues to be considered here: one is the inclusion of illustrative pictures next to facing poems; the other involves drafts of poems on which Bishop has drawn pictures. I am more interested in the latter problematic, in which the poem, "Dear, my compass," appears in *Edgar Allan Poe* only as a typescript containing childlike drawings of a barn, a goose, a swan, and a single bed. Here, as in similar cases just discussed, no print version of the poem has been included.

In the context of the volume as a whole, this presentation suggests that "Dear, my compass" cannot be separated from its accompanying drawings: that something essential would have been lost had the poem been presented in a nonillustrated print form.[5] Such a view dovetails dramatically with the materialist arguments of Virginia Jackson, perhaps the most celebrated of Dickinson's recent manuscript critics. In a trenchant critique of lyric voice, Jackson argues that we cannot interpret Dickinson's letter-poems without the objects (for example, the flowers or dead crickets) that the poet sent along with them in her correspondence. Jackson's complaint is that "the poems in bound volumes appear both redeemed and revoked from their scenes or referents, from the history that the book, as book, omits" (3). Clearly, she wants to critique the ostensible universality that the lyric—and its concomitant "voice"—has foisted upon Dickinson as its unwitting exemplar. But in doing this, she goes so far as to suggest that what Dickinson wrote may not have been lyric poetry at all, at least not insofar as our critical tradition has understood it: "But how do we know that lyrics are what Dickinson wrote?" (17).

I would suggest that there is much more at stake in Jackson's argument than a dismantling of lyric voice. By arguing that critics must take the metonyms and material contexts of Dickinson's poetic composition into account—the paper she used; the mementos she sent to Susan Gilbert Dickinson and others—Jackson is consciously relegating Dickinson's writing to the private, domesticated sphere of the poet's historical circumstances. What her argument doesn't address is the fact that such domesticated space has traditionally been the domain and arguably the ghetto of women writers. If Dickinson can *only* be viably interpreted in manuscript form, with the reader made aware of the original "props" around her writing, what does this really say about her viability as a major poet? Did Keats and Wordsworth need props?

Jackson's overemphasis on manuscript-as-materiality, in its refusal of a reductive universality, may thereby also refuse a (woman) writer the baseline universal of creating a text that can be widely disseminated; as Walter Benn Michaels explains, "the very idea of textuality depends upon the *discrepancy* between the text and its materiality, which is why two copies of a book (two different material objects) may be said to be the same text" (3, emphasis added).

Yet we can also contextualize Jackson's materialist approach by putting it into dialogue with other recent critical responses to Dickinson's manuscript materials. Take, for example, Marta Werner's seemingly opposing comment about editing Dickinson's fragments: "Never prepared for publication, perhaps never even meant to be read by anyone other than the scriptor herself, they are not so much 'works' as symptoms of the processes of composition, data—aleatory, contingent—of the work of writing" ("A Woe of Ecstasy" 27).

Werner's transformation of poet into scriptor—perhaps a body even *produced* by its writing—is notable both for its unapologetic universality and its radical commitment to a writing or "marking" that lacks a referential addressee such as Susan Gilbert Dickinson; these qualities are precisely what Jackson critiques as the reductive construction of the lyric throughout literary history. If anything, Werner's description creates an experimental sheen: far from referential, the *writing* is its own theater. But Werner's perspective also slips: if writing is "symptom" rather than communication, it retains the infectious, self-contained fascination of pathology. In fact, it is a remarkably short road from the "symptoms" of writing to the "weirdness," or worse, with which Dickinson has been imbued by critics and biographers.[6] In most cases, this characterization is a result not of Dickinson's writing but instead of her life choices.

The arguments of Werner and Jackson, I would argue, occupy two paradoxically complementary extremes on a spectrum of Dickinson textual criticism: while Werner's severely abstracted "scriptor" is by definition shorn of biography, Jackson's attention to the manuscripts' referential metonyms and material circumstances necessarily situates critical concern within the domestic or biographical realm. While the latter slippage is a fairly obvious risk, I am also concerned that Werner's superabstracted, textually created, and even transgressively experimental "scriptor," as generated within manuscript materials, could act as a screen for the retention of a very conservative relation between reader and (woman) poet: it could serve, in other words, to uphold the dubious category of "women's writing," a category that Bishop herself regarded with a measure of suspicion.

This is because even the materiality of writing-as-such, epitomized by Werner's point of view, often shades into an obsession with the gendered body—and life—that technologically produced that writing; the text is about the writerly conditions of its own production. Though metonymy is not as historicized for Werner as it is for Jackson, it remains foregrounded in her critical presentation; and metonymy is, as we know, the trope of bodily proximity par excellence. Even the neutered "scriptor," then, insofar as she or he is identified with marks rather than with voice, can play into the gendered assumptions that we have been critiquing here. As we have seen in both Jackson's and Werner's work, manuscript editions may elicit a reception that values muscular, social, or gendered personhood over an attention to lyric poetry as such.

In *The Shape of the Signifier*, Michaels has critiqued our contemporary tendency to read texts through the lens of identity politics and thereby interpret them as nothing more or less than bodily emanations of their authors' "difference." While his critique exceeds the narrow field of contemporary American poetry, I might also suggest that American women poets are particularly susceptible to these sorts of readings, even as the percentage of women writing poetry has steadily increased over the last twenty-five years or so.[7] It is arguable, in fact, that readers and poets are more likely to focalize the bodies and persons of woman poets; as a purely anecdotal example, Michael Hofmann's recent review of *Words in Air* quotes Bishop's fleeting commentary on eye shadow—out of a volume totaling over nine hundred pages of letters (363). And often body and text are commingled when a poet's idiosyncratic marks, as handwriting, are brought into the mix.

When body becomes confused with text, moreover, the variorum or facsimile edition can act as a sort of textual underwear, much as the ending of Billy Collins's "Taking Off Emily Dickinson's Clothes" suggests. In a blazon of incremental undressing that is reminiscent of Donne's "Elegy for His Mistress Going to Bed,"

Collins's speaker casts himself as a "polar explorer" who is blithely "sailing toward the iceberg of [Dickinson's] nakedness" (24). When he undoes the poet's corset at the end of the poem, however, the act becomes commensurate with a collective or public reading of Dickinson's works:

> and I could hear her sigh when finally it was unloosed,
> the way some readers sigh when they realize
> that Hope has feathers,
> that reason is a plank,
> that life is a loaded gun
> that looks right at you with a yellow eye. (25)

Here, Dickinson's presumably sexualized "sigh" is compared to the collective sighs of readers who internally "realize," or make real, some of her most famous lines. Thus for Collins, the fantasy of seducing the mythologized Dickinson is analogous to the reading act itself, if only via readerly symptom. Here, undressing the poet—the metonymic act par excellence—becomes a civic gesture on behalf of a discerning ("*some* readers") reading public. If Dickinson's body and poems are interchangeable to this degree, we must venture only a little further to render her undergarments commensurate with the Cavalier "delight in disorder" of unkempt draft formats. Collins's poem doesn't directly address recent Dickinson criticism, but it does suggest that we are all voyeurs of her irrevocably compounded text-body—whether we are heterosexual male (comic) poets or manuscript scholars of any gender or persuasion—and that this perennial undressing is not only pleasurable for us, but also what the dead-but-iconic Dickinson "wants." Have we also begun to undress Bishop?

To be sure, I am not suggesting that the variorum or facsimile edition constitutes a glass ceiling for women poets. It may be, however, that our readerly need for intimacy with what Dana Gioia calls "the author's hand" is more pronounced in the case of women poets, due to a larger acculturation that arguably still holds sway regardless of the empirical gender composition of the present literary world (46). This phenomenon is not far from what Simone de Beauvoir critiqued in *The Second Sex* as women's association with immanence and the limited life of the body.[8] More surprising, perhaps, is the way that the progressive experimental aesthetic—Hejinian's open text—serves this acculturated need by insisting on graphic mark, or what cannot be separated from the writing hand, rather than on the "finish" of duplicable text. This becomes a way of metonymically writing-in the (gendered) *person* of the writer, who is thereby prohibited from exiting the "footlights" of the text, in Barthes's terms (16).

But if we let graphic considerations replace or displace voice when we read lyric poetry, or the manuscripts of lyric poets, we do so at the peril of poetry itself—not because we thereby flout the poets' intentions, or because voice restores some chimerical sense of presence; but instead because the "finish" of a carefully crafted voice—whether formal or otherwise—allows for a necessary abstraction from the immanence of the body and its matter, an abstraction that is necessary for the creation of text itself. This abstraction is what W. R. Johnson has called "the transformation of the personal into the impersonal or, better, the tempering of the personal with the universal" (33). While such recourse to the universal has been widely critiqued as exclusionary, we might also consider reintroducing aspects of it as a corrective to the hallucination of too much personhood in the figures of these women poets. A silenced voice, in other words, inevitably leaves a remainder—of too much material matter.

NOTES

1. For a discussion of the nature of these disagreements, see Mokoto Rich, "New Elizabeth Bishop Book Sparks a Controversy."

2. For a discussion of this critical change in the focus of Dickinson studies, see Betsy Erkkila, "The Emily Dickinson Wars"; and Christina Pugh, "Ghosts of Meter: Dickinson, After Long Silence."

3. See Johnson's discussion of the "I-You" pronominal construction of Greek monody (3), as well as Blasing's assertion that "a convincing lyric subject" is one that "makes *audible* the shape, the 'beautiful necessities,' of the language" (35, emphasis added). Stewart and Grossman also emphasize the roles of sound and speaking in the lyric.

4. See, for example, her line break truncating the place-name Glens Falls as "Glens Fall / s" in order to create a perfect rhyme with "tall" in the cross-rhymed "Arrival at Santos" (*CP* 89). As this mock-dramatic enjambment shows, Bishop usually only "plays" with sound within (and sometimes as a metapoetic statement about) the formal confines of the poem in question.

5. I certainly do not wish to argue here that the poem actually *cannot* be taken out of its illustrative context. Such a claim would be immediately refuted by the reprinting of "Dear, my compass"—without its accompanying illustrations—in the Library of America's Bishop edition, which appeared in 2008 (251). Instead, I'm restricting my discussion to the construction and "philosophy" of *Edgar Allan Poe & the Juke-Box* itself, which was the first to publish the poem in a collection of Bishop's work.

6. For relevant discussions treating this portrayal of Dickinson, see Adrienne Rich, "Vesuvius at Home"; Sandra M. Gilbert and Susan Gubar, *The Madwoman in the Attic*; and Alice Fulton, "Her Moment of Brocade: The Reconstruction of Emily Dickinson" in *Feeling as a Foreign Language*.

7. See Jennifer Ashton, "Our Bodies, Our Poems" for a useful discussion of this changing demographic and its impact on the recent reception of women's poetry.

8. What Beauvoir means by "immanence" is, in short, this: "Woman? Very simple, say the fanciers of simple formulas: she is a womb, an ovary" (3). This association with, or reduction to, biological functions constitutes the "immanence" that for Beauvoir stands in stark contrast to the "transcendence" that is associated with male privilege. Though few would make such a stark statement today, many aspects of our cultural life (including "mommy wars" and significant opposition to abortion rights) suggest that women are still constrained by their cultural association with immanence, much as Beauvoir described.

Bibliography

Altman, Janet Gurkin. *Epistolarity: Approaches to a Form*. Columbus: Ohio University Press, 1982.

Alvarez, A. "Beyond All This Fiddle." In *Beyond All This Fiddle: Essays 1955–1967*, 14. New York: Random House, 1969.

Ashton, Jennifer. "Our Bodies, Our Poems." *American Literary History* 19, no. 1 (Spring 2007): 211–31.

Auden, W. H. *Collected Poems*. Edited by Edward Mendelson. New York: Vintage, 1976.

Axelrod, Stephen Gould. "Elizabeth Bishop and Containment Policy." *American Literature* 75, no. 4 (December 2003): 843–67.

———. *Robert Lowell: Life and Art*. Princeton: Princeton University Press, 1979.

Bandeira, Manuel. "Song for a Colored Singer de Elizabeth Bishop." *Tribuna da Imprensa*, August 1 2, 1953.

Bardi, Pietro Maria. "Calder and the Mobiles at the Coming Exhibition." *In Calder in Brazil: The Tale of a Friendship,* edited by Roberta Saraiva; translated by Juliet Attwater, 147–49. Sao Paolo: Cosac Naify, 2006.

Barnard, Mary. *Assault on Mount Helicon*. Berkeley and Los Angeles: University of California Press, 1984.

Barolini, Teodolinda. *Dante and the Origins of Italian Literary Culture*. New York: Fordham University Press, 2006.

Barr, Alfred H. *Cubism and Abstract Art*. New York: Museum of Modern Art, 1935.

Barthes, Roland. "The Death of the Author." In *Image—Music—Text*, by Barthes, translated by Stephen Heath. New York: Hill and Wang, 1977.

———. *The Pleasure of the Text*. Translated by Richard Miller. New York: Farrar, Straus, 1975.

Beach, Christopher. "'Who Else Has Lived through Purgatory?': Ezra Pound and Robert Lowell." *Papers on Language and Literature* 27, no. 1 (1991): 51–83.

Benítez-Rojo, Antonio. *The Repeating Island: The Caribbean and the Postmodern Perspective*. Translated by James E. Maraniss. 2nd ed. Durham, N.C.: Duke University Press, 1996.

Beauvoir, Simone de. *The Second Sex*. New York: Vintage, 1989.

Benton, William. *Exchanging Hats: Elizabeth Bishop Paintings*. New York: Farrar, Straus and Giroux, 1996.

Berger, Charles. "Review." *Elizabeth Bishop Bulletin* 13, no. 1 (Summer 2006): 1–4.

Bishop, Elizabeth. "The Art of Poetry, XXVII: Elizabeth Bishop." Interview by Elizabeth Spires. In *Conversations with Elizabeth Bishop*, edited by George Monteiro. Jackson: University Press of Mississippi, 1996.

——. *The Collected Prose*. Edited by Robert Giroux. New York: Farrar, Straus and Giroux, 1984.

——. *The Complete Poems*. New York: Farrar, Straus and Giroux, 1969.

——. *The Complete Poems: 1927–1979*. New York: Farrar, Straus and Giroux, 1983.

——. *The Diary of "Helena Morley."* Translated and introduced by Elizabeth Bishop. New York: Farrar, Straus and Cudahy, 1957.

——. *Edgar Allan Poe & the Juke-Box: Uncollected Poems, Drafts, and Fragments*. Edited by Alice Quinn. New York: Farrar, Straus and Giroux, 2006.

——. Elizabeth Bishop Collection. Vassar College Library. Poughkeepsie, New York.

——. *Elizabeth Bishop: Poems, Prose, and Letters*. Edited by Robert Giroux and Lloyd Schwartz. New York: Library of America, 2008.

——. "Letter to the Editor." *New Republic,* April 30, 1962, 22.

——. *One Art: Letters*. Edited by Robert Giroux. New York: Farrar, Straus and Giroux, 1994.

——. *Prose*. Edited by Lloyd Schwartz. New York: Farrar, Straus and Giroux, 2011.

——. "Unseemly Deductions." Review of *The Riddle of Emily Dickinson,* by Rebecca Patterson. *New Republic,* August 18, 1952, 20.

——. *Words in Air: The Complete Correspondence between Elizabeth Bishop and Robert Lowell*. Edited by Thomas Travisano with Saskia Hamilton. New York: Farrar, Straus and Giroux, 2008.

Bishop, Elizabeth, and Emanuel Brasil, eds. *An Anthology of Twentieth-Century Brazilian Poetry*. Hanover and London: Wesleyan University Press, 1972.

Bishop, Elizabeth, and the editors of *Life*. *Brazil*. New York: Time-Life Books, 1962.

Blake, William. *The Complete Poetry and Prose*. Edited by David V. Erdman. Commentary by Harold Bloom. Berkeley and Los Angeles: University of California Press, 1981.

Blasing, Mutlu Konuk. *Lyric Poetry: The Pain and the Pleasure of Words*. Princeton: Princeton University Press, 2007.

——. *Politics and Form in Postmodern Poetry: O'Hara, Bishop, Ashbery, and Merrill*. Cambridge: Cambridge University Press, 1995.

Bolker, Joan, ed. *The Writer's Home Companion*. New York: Holt, 1997.

Bower, Ann. *Epistolary Responses: The Letter in Twentieth-Century American Fiction and Criticism*. Tuscaloosa: University of Alabama Press, 1997.

Brogan, Jacqueline Vaught. "Naming the Thief in 'Babylon': Elizabeth Bishop and 'the Moral of the Story.'" *Contemporary Literature* 42, no. 3 (Fall 2001): 514–34.

——. "Perversity as Voice." In *Elizabeth Bishop: The Geography of Gender,* edited by Marilyn May Lombardi, 175–95. Charlottesville: University of Virginia Press, 1993.

Brown, Ashley. "Elizabeth Bishop in Brazil." *Southern Review* 13 (October 1977): 688–704.

——. "An Interview with Elizabeth Bishop." In *Conversations with Elizabeth Bishop,* edited by George Monteiro, 18–29. Jackson: University Press of Mississippi, 1996.

Brunner, Edward. *Cold War Poetry*. Urbana: University of Illinois Press, 2001.

Brustein, Robert. "The Madison Avenue Villain." *Partisan Review* 1961. Reprinted in *The Third Theatre,* 183–203. New York: Knopf, 1969.

Bushell, Sally. *Text as Process: Creative Composition in Wordsworth, Tennyson, and Dickinson*. Charlottesville: University of Virginia Press, 2009.

Calder, Alexander. *Modern Painting and Sculpture*. Published in conjunction with an exhibition at the Berkshire Museum, Pittsfield, Mass., August 12–25, 1933.

Cameron, Sharon. *Choosing Not Choosing: Dickinson's Fascicles*. Chicago: University of Chicago Press, 1992.

Chambers, Frank M., and T. V. F. Brogan. "Alba." In *The New Encyclopedia of Poetry and Poetics*, ed. Alex Preminger and T. V. F. Brogan, 26–27. Princeton: Princeton University Press, 1993.

Ciardi, John, ed. *Mid-Century American Poets*. New York: Twayne, 1950.

Cleghorn, Angus. "'Commerce or Contemplation': The Ethics of Elizabeth Bishop's Brazil." *College Quarterly* 7, no. 3 (Summer 2004). www.collegequarterly.ca/2004-vol07-num03-summer/cleghorn.html.

Collins, Billy. *Picnic, Lightning*. Pittsburgh: University of Pittsburgh Press, 1998.

Comins, Barbara. "'That Queer Sea': Elizabeth Bishop and the Sea." In *Divisions of the Heart: Elizabeth Bishop and the Art of Memory and Place*, edited by Sandra Barry, Gwendolyn Davies, and Peter Sanger, 187–97. Kentville, Nova Scotia: Gaspereau Press, 2001.

Costello, Bonnie. *Elizabeth Bishop: Questions of Mastery*. Cambridge and London: Harvard University Press, 1991.

De Lauretis, Teresa. *Technologies of Gender: Essays on Theory, Film and Fiction*. Bloomington: Indiana University Press, 1987.

Dickie, Margaret. "Elizabeth Bishop: Text and Subtext." *South Atlantic Review* 59, no. 4 (November 1994): 1–19.

———. "Race and Class in Elizabeth Bishop." In *The Yearbook of English Studies*, 44–58. Ethnicity and Representation in American Literature, vol. 24. 1994.

———. *Stein, Bishop and Rich: Lyrics of Love, War, and Place*. Chapel Hill: University of North Carolina Press, 1997.

Dickey, Frances. "Opening the Box." *Essays in Criticism* 57, no. 1 (January 2007): 73–81.

Dickinson, Emily. *The Manuscript Books of Emily Dickinson*. Edited by R. W. Franklin. Cambridge: Harvard University Press, 1981.

Diehl, Joanne Feit. *Elizabeth Bishop and Marianne Moore: The Psychodynamics of Creativity*. Princeton: Princeton University Press, 1993.

Dubrow, Heather. "The Marine in the Garden: Pastoral Elements in Lowell's 'Quaker Graveyard.'" In *Critical Response to Robert Lowell*, edited by Steven Gould Axelrod, 46–57. Westport: Greenwood Press, 1999.

Edelman, Lee. "The Geography of Gender: Elizabeth Bishop's 'In the Waiting Room.'" In *Elizabeth Bishop: The Geography of Gender*, edited by Marilyn May Lombardi, 91–110. Charlottesville: University Press of Virginia, 1993.

Ellis, Jonathan. *Art and Memory in the Work of Elizabeth Bishop*. Hampshire, U.K.; Burlington, Vt.: Ashgate, 2006.

———. "Elizabeth Bishop's Bone Key Poems." *PN Review* 34, no. 3 (January–February 2008): 37–40.

Eliot, T. S. *Complete Poems and Plays, 1909–1950*. New York: Harcourt Brace, 1980.

———. "Tradition and the Individual Talent." In *Selected Essays*. New York: Harcourt, Brace, 1950.

Erkkila, Betsy. "Elizabeth Bishop, Modernism, and the Left." *American Literary History* 8, no. 2 (1996): 284–310.

———. "The Emily Dickinson Wars." In *The Cambridge Companion to Emily Dickinson*, edited by Wendy Martin, 11–27. Cambridge: Cambridge University Press, 2002.

———. *The Wicked Sisters: Women Poets, Literary History and Discord*. Oxford: Oxford University Press, 1992.

Feirstein, Frederick. "Psychoanalysis and Poetry." In *After New Formalism: Poets on Form, Narrative, and Tradition*, edited by Annie Finch, 179–87. Ashland: Story Line Press, 1999.

Ferguson, Suzanne, ed. *Jarrell, Bishop, Lowell, and Co.: Middle-Generation Poets in Context.* Knoxville: University of Tennessee Press, 2003.

Fitzgerald, F. Scott. *The Great Gatsby.* New York: Scribner's Sons, 1953.

Fitzgerald, Sally. "Flannery O'Connor: Patterns of Friendship, Patterns of Love." *Georgia Review* 52 (Fall 1998): 407–25.

Flynn, Richard. *Randall Jarrell and the Lost World of Childhood.* Athens: University of Georgia Press, 1990.

Fortuny, Kim. *Elizabeth Bishop: The Art of Travel.* Boulder: University Press of Colorado, 2003.

Fountain, Gary. "'Maple Leaf (Forever)': Elizabeth Bishop's Poetics of National Identity." In *Divisions of the Heart: Elizabeth Bishop and the Art of Memory and Place,* edited by Sandra Barry, Gwendolyn Davies, and Peter Sanger, 293–308. Kentville, Nova Scotia: Gaspereau Press, 2001.

Fountain, Gary, and Peter Brazeau. *Remembering Elizabeth Bishop: An Oral Biography.* Amherst: University of Massachusetts Press, 1994.

Freud, Sigmund. "The Ego and the Id (1923)." In *The Standard Edition of the Complete Psychological Works,* edited by James Strachey and Anna Freud, 19:12–66. London: Hogarth Press, 1966.

———. "Introductory Lectures in Psycho-analysis, Parts I & II." In *The Standard Edition of the Complete Psychological Works,* edited by Strachey and Freud, 15:98–99; 170–73.

———. "Mourning and Melancholia (1917)." In *The Standard Edition of the Complete Psychological Works,* edited by Strachey and Freud, 14:243–58.

———. "Screen Memories." In *The Standard Edition of the Complete Psychological Works,* edited by Strachey and Freud, 3:322.

———. *The Uncanny.* Translated by David McLintock. New York and London: Penguin, 2003.

Frost, Robert. *Collected Poems, Prose, & Plays.* Edited by Richard Poirier and Mark Richardson. New York: Library of America, 1995.

Fulton, Alice. *Feeling as a Foreign Language.* St. Paul: Graywolf, 1999.

Galbraith, John Kenneth. "The Unseemly Economics of Opulence." *Harper's,* January 1952, 58–63

Gilbert, Sandra M., and Susan Gubar. *The Madwoman in the Attic: The Woman Writer and the Nineteenth-Century Literary Imagination.* New Haven: Yale University Press, 1979.

———. *The War of the Words.* Vol. 1 of *No Man's Land: The Place of the Woman Writer in the Twentieth Century.* New Haven: Yale University Press, 1988.

Giménez, Carmen, and S. C. Rower. *Calder, Gravity and Grace.* London; New York: Phaidon, 2004.

Gioia, Dana. *Disappearing Ink: Poetry at the End of Print Culture.* St. Paul: Graywolf Press, 2004.

Goldensohn, Lorrie. "Elizabeth Bishop: An Unpublished, Untitled Poem." *American Poetry Review* 17, no. 1 (1988): 35–36.

———. *Elizabeth Bishop: The Biography of a Poetry.* New York: Columbia University Press, 1992.

Greenhalgh, Anne Merrill. *A Concordance to Elizabeth Bishop's Poetry.* New York: Garland, 1985.

Gray, Jeffrey. *Mastery's End, Travel and Postwar Poetry.* Athens: University of Georgia Press, 2005.

Grossman, Allen. *The Sighted Singer: Two Works on Poetry for Readers and Writers.* With Mark Halliday. Baltimore: Johns Hopkins University Press, 1992.

Haffenden, John. *The Life of John Berryman.* Boston: Routledge and Kegan Paul, 1982.

Hall, Stuart. "Foucault: Power, Knowledge and Discourse." *Discourse Theory and Practice: A Reader,* edited by Margaret Wetherell, Stephanie Taylor, and Simeon Yates. London: Sage, 2001.

Hammer, Langdon. "Useless Concentration: Life and Work in Elizabeth Bishop's Letters and Poems." *American Literary History* 9, no. 1 (Spring 1997): 162–80.

Harrison, Victoria. *Elizabeth Bishop's Poetics of Intimacy.* Cambridge: Cambridge University Press, 1993.

Hass, Robert. *Twentieth-Century Pleasures: Prose on Poetry.* New York: Ecco, 1984.

Hayter, Stanley W. "Apostle of Empathy." *Magazine of Art* 39, no. 4 (April 1946): 127–30.

Heaney, Seamus. *The Government of the Tongue.* London: Faber and Faber, 1988.

Heidegger, Martin. "Building, Dwelling, Thinking." In *Basic Writings,* edited by David Farrell Krell, 319–39. New York: Harper: 1977.

Hejinian, Lyn. *The Language of Inquiry.* Berkeley and Los Angeles: University of California Press, 2000.

Hicok, Bethany. *Degrees of Freedom: American Women Poets and the Women's College, 1905–1955.* Lewisburg: Bucknell University Press, 2008.

Hochman, Jhan. "Critical Essay on 'Brazil, January 1, 1502.'" In *Poetry for Students,* vol. 6. Farmington Hills, Mich.: Gale, 1999. www.galenet.galegroup.com.

Hoff, Ann K. "Owning Memory: Elizabeth Bishop's Authorial Restraint." *Biography* 31, no. 4 (Fall 2008): 577–94.

Hofmann, Michael. "The Linebacker and the Dervish." Review of *Words in Air,* by Elizabeth Bishop. *Poetry* 193, no. 4 (January 2009): 357–67. www.poetryfoundation.org/journal/article .html?id=182649

Holmes, Urban T., Jr., and Robert L. Harrison. "Reverdie." In *The New Princeton Encyclopedia of Poetry and Poetics,* ed. Alex Preminger and T. V. F. Brogan, 1045. Princeton: Princeton University Press, 1993.

Howe, Susan. *The Birth-Mark: Unsettling the Wilderness in American Literary History.* Hanover, N.H.: Wesleyan University Press/University Press of New England, 1993.

———. *My Emily Dickinson.* Berkeley: North Atlantic Books, 1985.

Jackson, Virginia. *Dickinson's Misery.* Princeton: Princeton University Press, 2005.

Jameson, Fredric. *Postmodernism, or, the Cultural Logic of Late Capitalism.* Durham, N.C.: Duke University Press, 1991.

Janis, Harriet. "Mobiles." *Arts & Architecture* 65, no. 2 (February 1948): 26–28, 56–59.

Jarrell, Randall. *Kipling, Auden, & Co.* New York: Farrar, 1980.

———. "Poets." In *Poetry and the Age,* 220–36. Gainesville: University Press of Florida, 2001.

———. *Randall Jarrell's Letters: An Autobiographical and Literary Selection.* Edited by Mary Jarrell. New York: Houghton Mifflin, 1985.

Johnson, Alexandra. "Geography of the Imagination." In *Conversations with Elizabeth Bishop,* edited by George Monteiro, 98–104. Jackson: University Press of Mississippi 1996.

Johnson, W. R. *The Idea of Lyric: Lyric Modes in Ancient and Modern Poetry.* Berkeley and Los Angeles: University of California Press, 1982.

Jullien, Francois. *In Praise of Blandness: Proceeding from Chinese Thought and Aesthetics.* Translated by Paula M. Varsano. New York: Zone, 2004.

Kalstone, David. *Becoming a Poet: Elizabeth Bishop with Marianne Moore and Robert Lowell.* New York: Farrar, Straus and Giroux, 1989.

Keller, Lynn. *Re-Making it New, Contemporary American Poetry and the Modernist Tradition.* Cambridge: Cambridge University Press, 1987.

Kirsch, Adam. "Good Pickings." *Times Literary Supplement,* April 28, 2006, 3–4.

Klein, Melanie. *Love, Guilt and Reparation.* New York: Dell, 1977.

Lawrence, D. H. Introduction to *Bottom Dogs,* by Edward Dahlberg, vii–xvii. San Francisco: City Lights, 1961.

Lears, T. J. Jackson. *Fables of Abundance: A Cultural History of Advertising in America* New York: Basic Books, 1994.

Levine, Robert M. *Historical Dictionary of Brazil.* Latin American Historical Dictionaries. Vol. 19. Metuchen, N.J., and London: Scarecrow Press, 1979.

Lombardi, Marilyn May. *The Body and the Song: Elizabeth Bishop's Poetics.* Carbondale and Edwardsville: Southern Illinois University Press, 1995.

———, ed. *Elizabeth Bishop: The Geography of Gender.* Charlottesville: University Press of Virginia, 1993.

Longenbach, James. "Between Reticence and Revelation: Bishop's and Lowell's Letters." *Nation,* November 6, 2008, online edition. www.thenation.com/doc/20081124/longenbach.

———. "Elizabeth Bishop's Social Conscience." *ELH* 62, no. 2 (Summer 1995): 467–86.

———. *Modern Poetry after Modernism.* New York: Oxford University Press, 1997.

Lowell, Robert. *Collected Poems.* Edited by Frank Bidart and David Gewanter. New York: Farrar, Straus and Giroux, 2003.

———. *Collected Prose.* Edited and introduced by Robert Giroux. New York: Farrar, 1987.

———. "Epilogue." In *Day by Day,* by Lowell. New York: Farrar, 1977.

———. *History.* New York: Farrar, Straus and Giroux, 1973.

———. Interview by Fred Seidel. *Paris Review* 25 (Winter–Spring, 1961). www.parisreview.com/viewinterview.php/prmMID/4664.

———. *The Letters of Robert Lowell.* Edited by Saskia Hamilton. New York: Farrar, Straus and Giroux, 2005.

MacLean, Gerald. "Re-Siting the Subject." *Epistolary Histories, Letters, Fiction, Culture.* Edited by Amanda Gilroy and W. M. Verhoven. Charlottesville: University Press of Virginia, 2000.

MacMahon, Candace. *Elizabeth Bishop: A Bibliography, 1927–1979.* Charlottesville: University Press of Virginia, 1980.

Marter, Jean. *Alexander Calder.* Cambridge: Cambridge University Press, 1991.

McCabe, Susan. *Elizabeth Bishop: Her Poetics of Loss.* University Park: Pennsylvania State University Press, 1994.

McCarthy, Mary. "Books of the Year: Some Personal Choices." *Observer,* December 10, 1966.

McClatchy, J. D. *White Paper.* New York: Columbia University Press, 1989.

Menides, Laura Jehn, and Angela G. Dorenkamp, eds. *"In Worcester, Massachusetts": Essays on Elizabeth Bishop: From the 1997 Elizabeth Bishop Conference at WPI.* New York: Peter Lang, 1999.

Merrill, James. *Collected Prose.* Edited by Stephen Yenser. New York: Knopf, 2004.

———. *Recitative.* Edited by J .D. McClatchy. San Francisco: North Point Press, 1986.

Merrin, Jeredith. "Elizabeth Bishop: Gaiety, Gayness and Change." In *The Geography of Gender,* edited by Marilyn May Lombardi. Charlottesville and London: University Press of Virginia, 1993.

Michaels, Walter Benn. *The Shape of the Signifier.* Princeton: Princeton University Press, 2004.

Miller, J. Hillis. "Thomas Hardy, Jacques Derrida, and the 'Dislocation of Souls.'" In *Taking Chances: Derrida, Psychoanalysis and Literature,* edited by J. Smith and W. Kerrigan. Baltimore: John Hopkins University Press, 1985.

Millier, Brett C. *Elizabeth Bishop: Life and the Memory of It.* Berkeley and London: University of California Press, 1993.

Mindlin, Henrique. "Alexander Calder." In *Calder in Brazil: The Tale of a Friendship,* edited by Roberta Saraiva; translated by Juliet Attwater, 54–58. São Paolo: Cosac Naify, 2006.

———. "Calder, Smith and Sculptor." In *Calder in Brazil: The Tale of a Friendship,* edited by Roberta Saraiva; translated by Juliet Attwater, 120–23. São Paolo: Cosac Naify, 2006.

Monteiro, George, ed. *Conversations with Elizabeth Bishop.* Jackson: University Press of Mississippi, 1996.

Moore, Marianne. *The Complete Prose.* Edited by Patricia Willis. New York: Viking, 1986.

——. *Selected Letters.* Edited by Bonnie Costello, Celeste Goodridge, and Cristanne Miller. New York: Knopf, 1997.

Motherwell, Robert. *Partisan Review* 11, no. 1 (Winter 1944): 93–97.

Muldoon, Paul. *The End of the Poem.* London: Faber and Faber, 2006.

Mullins, Eustace. *This Difficult Individual: Ezra Pound.* New York: Fleet, 1961.

North, Michael. *The Final Sculpture: Public Monuments and Modern Poetry.* New York: Cornell University Press, 1985.

O'Connor, Flannery. *Collected Works.* Edited by Sally Fitzgerald. New York: Library of America, 1988.

——. *The Habit of Being: Letters.* Edited by Sally Fitzgerald. New York: Farrar, Straus and Giroux, 1979.

O'Donovan, Patrick. "Aldous Huxley's Island Paradise." *New Republic,* April 30, 1962, 17–18.

Paden, William D. "Occitan Poetry." *Princeton Encyclopedia of Poetry and Poetics,* edited by Alex Preminger and T. V. F. Brogan, 851–53. Princeton: Princeton University Press, 1993.

Page, Barbara. "Off-Beat Claves, Oblique Realities: The Key West Notebooks of Elizabeth Bishop." In *Elizabeth Bishop: The Geography of Gender,* edited by Marilyn May Lombardi, 196–211. Charlottesville and London: University Press of Virginia, 1993.

Palattella, John. "Extended Play." *Boston Review,* May–June 2006, 45–46.

Pedrosa, Mário. "Tension and Cohesion in Calder's Work." In *Calder in Brazil: The Tale of a Friendship,* edited by Roberta Saraiva; translated by Juliet Attwater, 124–36. São Paolo: Cosac Naify, 2006.

Plath, Sylvia. *Ariel.* London: Faber and Faber. 1965.

——. *Collected Poems.* Edited by Ted Hughes. London: Faber and Faber, 1981.

Pound, Ezra. *Selected Poems.* New York: New Directions, 1957.

Preminger, Alex, and T. V. F. Brogan, eds. *The New Princeton Encyclopedia of Poetry and Poetics.* Princeton: University of Princeton Press, 1993.

Pugh, Christina. "Ghosts of Meter: Dickinson, After Long Silence." *Emily Dickinson Journal* 16, no. 2 (2007): 1–24.

Quinn, Alice. "Interviewed by Meghan O'Rourke." *Believer,* March 2006, 77–84.

Rich, Adrienne. "The Eye of the Outsider: Elizabeth Bishop's Complete Poems, 1927–1979." In *Blood, Bread, and Poetry: Selected Prose 1979–1985:* 188–97. New York: Norton, 1986.

——. "Vesuvius at Home: The Power of Emily Dickinson." In *By Herself: Women Reclaim Poetry,* edited by Molly McQuade, 33–60. St. Paul: Graywolf, 2000.

Rich, Motoko. "New Elizabeth Bishop Book Sparks a Controversy." *New York Times,* April 1, 2006. www.newyorktimes.com.

Ricks, Christopher. *True Friendship: Geoffrey Hill, Anthony Hecht, and Robert Lowell under the Sign of Eliot and Pound.* The Anthony Hecht Lectures in the Humanities. New Haven: Yale University Press, 2010.

Rimbaud, Jean-Arthur. "Une saison en enfer." In *Rimbaud: Complete Works, Selected Letters,* translated by Wallace Fowlie, 198. Chicago: University of Chicago Press, 1966.

Rodman, Selden. *The Amazing Year: A Diary in Verse.* New York: Scribner's Sons, 1947.

Rogers, Dean, to Heather Treseler. "Re: 75.3." E-mail. October 6, 2008.

Roman, Camille. *Elizabeth Bishop's World War II–Cold War View.* New York: Palgrave, 2001.

Rosenbaum, Susan. "Collecting Elizabeth Bishop." *Twentieth-Century Literature* 53, no. 1 (Spring 2007): 79–87.

————. *Professing Sincerity: Modern Lyric Poetry, Commercial Culture and the Crisis in Reading.* Charlottesville: University of Virginia Press, 2007.

Rosenthal, M. L. *New Poets: American and British Poetry since World War II.* Oxford: Oxford University Press, 1970.

Rotella, Guy. *Reading & Writing Nature: The Poetry of Robert Frost, Wallace Stevens, Marianne Moore, and Elizabeth Bishop.* Boston: Northeastern University Press, 1990.

Rumens, Carol. "Caught in Mid-Creation." *Guardian,* review section, May 6, 2006, 18.

Samuels, Peggy. "Elizabeth Bishop and Paul Klee." *Modernism / Modernity* 14, no. 3 (2007): 543–68.

Saraiva, Roberta, ed. *Calder in Brazil: The Tale of a Friendship.* Translated by Juliet Attwater. São Paolo: Cosac Naify, 2006.

Sartre, Jean Paul. *Nausea.* Translated by Lloyd Alexander. New York: New Directions, 1969.

Schmidt, Michael. "Editorial." *PN Review* 32, no. 5 (May–June 2006): 1–2.

Schwartz, Lloyd. "Elizabeth Bishop and Brazil." *New Yorker* January 30, 1991, 85–97.

Schwartz, Lloyd, and Sybil Estess, eds. *Elizabeth Bishop and Her Art.* Ann Arbor: University of Michigan Press, 1983.

Sexton, Anne. *To Bedlam and Part Way Back.* Boston: Houghton Mifflin, 1960

Shapiro, Karl. *V-Letter and Other Poems.* New York: Reynal and Hitchcock, 1944.

Silliman, Ron. *Silliman's Blog.* November 14, 2005. http://ronsilliman.blogspot.com/2005/11/within-history-of-school-of-quietude.html.

Simic, Charles. "The Power of Reticence." *New York Review of Books,* April 2006, 17–19.

Sivulka, Juliann. *Soap, Sex, and Cigarettes: A Cultural History of American Advertising.* Belmont, Calif.: Wadsworth, 1997.

Skidmore, Thomas E. *Politics in Brazil, 1930–1964: An Experiment in Democracy.* New York: Oxford University Press, 1967.

"somebody loves you." www.somebodylovesyou.org/about/.

Stevens, Wallace. *Opus Posthumous: Poems, Plays, Prose.* Edited by Samuel French Morse. New York: Knopf, 1972.

————. *Wallace Stevens: Collected Poetry and Prose.* Edited by Frank Kermode and Joan Richardson. New York: Library of America, 1997.

Stewart, Susan. *Poetry and the Fate of the Senses.* Chicago: University of Chicago Press, 2002.

Stowell, Marion Barber. *Early American Almanacs: The Colonial Weekday Bible.* New York: Burt Franklin Press, 1977.

Sussekind, Flora. "A Geleia e o Engenho: Em torno de uma carta-poema de Elizabeth Bishop a Manuel Bandeira." *Papeis Colados* (Essay collection). Rio de Janeiro: Editora UFRJ, 1993.

Sweeney, James Johnson. *Alexander Calder.* New York: Museum of Modern Art, 1943.

Travisano, Thomas. "Elizabeth Bishop and Indelicacy." In *Elizabeth Bishop: Geography of Gender,* edited by Marilyn May Lombardi, 111–25. Charlottesville: University Press of Virginia, 1993.

————. *Elizabeth Bishop: Her Artistic Development.* Charlottesville: University Press of Virginia, 1988.

————. "The Elizabeth Bishop Phenomenon." In *Gendered Modernisms: American Women Poets and Their Readers,* edited by Margaret Dickie and Travisano, 217–44. Philadelphia: University of Pennsylvania Press, 1996.

————. "Emerging Genius: Elizabeth Bishop and *The Blue Pencil,* 1927–1930." *Gettysburg Review* 552 (Winter 1992): 32–47.

————. *Midcentury Quartet: Bishop, Lowell, Jarrell, Berryman, and the Making of a Postmodern Aesthetic.* Charlottesville and London: University Press of Virginia, 1999.

———. "'With an Eye of Flemish Accuracy': An Afterword." *Georgia Review* (Winter 1992): 612–16.

Trilling, Lionel. "On the Teaching of Modern Literature." In *Beyond Culture: Essays on Literature and Learning*, 3–30. New York: Viking Press, 1965.

Turner, Elizabeth Hutton. "'Our Adopted Ancestor:' America's Postwar Embrace of Klee." In *Klee and America*, edited by Josef Helfenstein and Turner, 224–37. The Menil Collection. Ostfildern-Ruit, Germany: Hatje Cantz Verlag, 2006.

Vendler, Helen. "The Art of Losing." *New Republic*, April 3, 2006, 33–37.

———. "Domestication, Domesticity, and the Otherworldly." 1977. In *Elizabeth Bishop and Her Art*, edited by Lloyd Schwartz and Sybil P. Estess, 32–48. Ann Arbor: University of Michigan Press, 1983.

———. "The Friendship of Cal and Elizabeth." *New York Review of Books,* November 20, 2008, online edition (subscription required). www.nybooks.com/articles/22078.

Walker, Cheryl. *God and Elizabeth Bishop: Meditations on Religion and Poetry.* New York: Palgrave, 2005.

Werner, Marta. "Flights of A821: Dearchiving the Proceedings of a Birdsong." *ebr* 6 (1997). www.altx.com/ebr/ebr6/6werner/Pages/6wern1.htm.

———. "'A Woe of Ecstasy': On the Electronic Editing of Emily Dickinson's Late Fragments." *Emily Dickinson Journal* 16, no. 2 (2007): 25–52.

White, Gillian. "Awful but Cheerful." *London Review of Books,* May 25, 2006, 8–10.

Wicks, Jan L. "On Top of the World: Chevrolet Television Advertising 1955 to 1965." www.eric.ed.gov:80/ERICWebPortal/searchdetailmini.jsp?nfpb=true&&ERICExtSearchSearchValue0=ED261366&ERICExtSearchSearchType0=no&accno=ED261366.

Williams, William Carlos. *The Autobiography of William Carlos Williams.* New York: New Directions, 1967.

———. "The Dance." In *Collected Poems*, vol. 2, *1939–1962,* edited by Christopher MacGowan. New York: New Directions, 1988.

Wiznitzer, Louis L. "Which Revolution for Brazil?" *New Republic,* March 19, 1962, 17–20.

Yenser, Stephen. "Poetry in Review: Elizabeth Bishop's Uncollected Work." *Yale Review* 94, no. 4 (October 2006): 173–87.

Zimmerman, Lee. "The Weirdest Scale on Earth: Elizabeth Bishop and Containment." *American Imago* 61, no. 4 (Winter 2004): 495–518.

Contributors

CHARLES BERGER is Professor of English at Southern Illinois University, Edwardsville. He is the author of *Forms of Farewell: The Late Poetry of Wallace Stevens* (1985), and has written numerous essays and reviews on modern and contemporary American poetry. He has been the recipient of a Guggenheim Fellowship.

JACQUELINE VAUGHT BROGAN is Professor of American Literature at the University of Notre Dame. She has authored essays on Wallace Stevens, Ernest Hemingway, Elizabeth Bishop, and Alice Walker, among others, and has written several critical books, including, most recently, *"The Violence Within/The Violence Without": Wallace Stevens and the Emergence of "A Revolutionary Poetics"* (2003). Brogan is also a poet herself, and her most recent work is a book-length experimental poem entitled *ta(1)king eyes* (2009).

ANGUS CLEGHORN is Professor of English and Liberal Studies at Seneca College in Toronto. Since 2004, he has served as the editor of the *Elizabeth Bishop Bulletin* for the Elizabeth Bishop Society. He has published articles on Bishop and Stevens, as well as the book *Wallace Stevens' Poetics: The Neglected Rhetoric* (2000), and guest-edited two issues of the *Wallace Stevens Journal* (1999, 2006).

JONATHAN ELLIS is Senior Lecturer in American literature at the University of Sheffield, England. He is the author of *Art and Memory in the Work of Elizabeth Bishop* (2006), as well as articles and essays on Paul Muldoon, Sylvia Plath, and Anne Stevenson. His next book is on twentieth-century letter writing.

RICHARD FLYNN is Professor of Literature at Georgia Southern University. He is the author of *Randall Jarrell and the Lost World of Childhood* (1990) and has published essays on Gwendolyn Brooks, June Jordan, Muriel Rukeyser, and others. He edited the *Children's Literature Association Quarterly* from 2004 to 2009. Recent essays include "The Fear of Poetry" in *The Cambridge Companion to Children's Literature* (2009) and "Randall Jarrell's *The Bat-Poet*: Poets, Children, and Readers in an Age of Prose" in *The Oxford Handbook of Children's Literature* (2011).

LORRIE GOLDENSOHN is the author of *Elizabeth Bishop: The Biography of a Poetry* (1990), *Dismantling Glory: Twentieth-Century Soldier Poetry* (2006), and the editor of *American War Poetry: An Anthology* (2006). She is currently doing research for a forthcoming project on how descriptions of dying have changed in American war poetry over the course of four centuries.

JEFFREY GRAY is Professor of English at Seton Hall University. He is the author of *Mastery's End: Travel and Postwar American Poetry* (2005) and editor of the five-volume *Greenwood Encyclopedia of American Poets and Poetry* (2005). He is coeditor (with Ann Keniston) of a forthcoming anthology of American poetry after the millennium. His articles on poetry and American culture have appeared in many journals, and his poetry in the *Atlantic Monthly, American Poetry Review, Mid-American Review,* and other journals. He has been an NEH Fellow, MacDowell Fellow, Geraldine R. Dodge Fellow, and two-time Fulbright Fellow.

BETHANY HICOK is Associate Professor of English at Westminster College. She is the author of *Degrees of Freedom: American Women Poets and the Women's College, 1905–1955* (2008), which focuses on the poetry of Marianne Moore, Elizabeth Bishop, and Sylvia Plath. Her essays and reviews on modern poetry also include articles on Wallace Stevens. She was a participant in a 2010 NEH summer seminar on Brazilian literature held in São Paulo, Brazil, and is currently working on a book on Elizabeth Bishop in Brazil.

GEORGE LENSING is Mann Family Distinguished Professor of English at the University of North Carolina at Chapel Hill. He is author of *Wallace Stevens: A Poet's Growth* (1986) and *Wallace Stevens and the Seasons* (2001).

CARMEN L. OLIVEIRA is a novelist and translator and the author of *Flores raras e banalissimas* (1995), translated by Neil K. Besner as *Rare and Commonplace Flowers: The Story of Elizabeth Bishop and Lota de Macedo Soares* (2003). She is author of the novel *Trilhos e Quintais* (1998), and a forthcoming collection of short stories,

Bátegas. She is working on a book with Barbara Page about Elizabeth Bishop in Brazil.

BARBARA PAGE is Professor of English (retired) at Vassar College, and an author of essays on Elizabeth Bishop and the Bishop Papers at Vassar, including "Shifting Islands: The Manuscripts of Elizabeth Bishop," "Off-Beat Claves, Oblique Realities: The Key West Notebooks of Elizabeth Bishop," "Elizabeth Bishop and Postmodernism," and "Elizabeth Bishop: Stops, Starts, and Dreamy Divigations."

CHRISTINA PUGH is Associate Professor and Director of Undergraduate Studies in the English Department at the University of Illinois at Chicago. She has published two books of poems: *Restoration* (2008) and *Rotary* (2004), winner of the Word Press First Book Prize. Her poems have appeared in the *Atlantic Monthly, Poetry,* the *Kenyon Review,* and other publications; her critical articles have appeared in the *Emily Dickinson Journal, Poetry,* and elsewhere.

FRANCESCO ROGNONI is Professor of English and American Literature at the Catholic University in Milan. The editor and translator of the Italian Pléiade edition of Percy Bysshe Shelley's *Works* (1995) and of the Italian edition of Robert Lowell's *Day by Day* (2001), he has written extensively on English and American authors, including Milton, Keats, Browning, Frank O'Hara, and Anatole Broyard, and on the Italian contemporary novelists Sergio Ferrero and Alessandro Spina. His collection of essays, *Di libro in libro,* was published in 2006.

PEGGY SAMUELS is Professor of English at Drew University. She is the author of *Deep Skin: Elizabeth Bishop and Visual Art* (2010). She has also published articles on John Milton and Andrew Marvell.

LLOYD SCHWARTZ is Frederick S. Troy Professor of English at the University of Massachusetts, Boston; coeditor of *Elizabeth Bishop and Her Art* (1983) and the Library of America *Elizabeth Bishop: Poems, Prose, and Letters* (2008); and editor of *Elizabeth Bishop: Prose* (2011). His most recent book of poems is *Cairo Traffic* (2000). In 1994 he was awarded the Pulitzer Prize for Criticism.

THOMAS TRAVISANO is Professor of English at Hartwick College. He is the author of *Elizabeth Bishop: Her Artistic Development* (1986) and *Midcentury Quartet: Bishop, Lowell, Jarrell, Berryman and the Making of a Postmodern Aesthetic* (1999), the principal editor of *Words in Air: The Complete Correspondence between Elizabeth Bishop and Robert Lowell* (2008), coeditor of *Gendered Modernisms: American Women Poets and Their Readers* (1996), and coeditor of the three-volume *New Anthology of American Poetry.* Travisano is the founding president of the Elizabeth Bishop Society and the senior advisor to the Robert Lowell Society.

HEATHER TRESELER is Assistant Professor of English at Worcester State University. Her essays and poems have appeared in *Harvard Review, Iowa Review, Southern Poetry Review, Boulevard,* and other journals, and in two collections of criticism, *Dunstan Thompson: On the Life and Work of a Lost American Master* and a *Salt Companion to John Matthias.* In 2010–11, Treseler was a Visiting Scholar at the American Academy of Arts and Sciences, where she began a project on post–World War II poetry and letter writing.

GILLIAN WHITE is Assistant Professor of English at the University of Michigan in Ann Arbor. She has published articles on Elizabeth Bishop's poetry in the *London Review of Books* and *Twentieth Century Literature,* and is at work on a book about "lyric shame" in contemporary American poetry and poetics.

Acknowledgments

Excerpts from unpublished notes by Elizabeth Bishop. Copyright © 2012 by the Alice H. Methfessel Trust. Printed by permission of Farrar, Straus and Giroux, LLC on behalf of the Elizabeth Bishop Estate.

Excerpts from unpublished letter to Al Avarez, February 15, 1961, and remarks given at Philharmonic Hall, New York, March 4, 1970, by Robert Lowell. Copyright © 2012 by Harriet Lowell and Sheridan Lowell. Printed by permission of Farrar, Straus and Giroux, LLC on behalf of the Robert Lowell Estate.

Quotations from the unpublished writings of Elizabeth Bishop are also used with the permission of Special Collections, Vassar College Libraries.

Quotation from an unpublished e-mail written by Lord Grey Gowrie to Massimo Bacigalupo used with the permission of Lord Grey Gowrie.

Quotation from Mary Barnard's letter to Ezra Pound used with the permission of Mary de Rachewiltz on behalf of the Pound Estate, and Elizabeth Bell, literary executor for Barnard's Estate.

Quotation from Elizabeth Bishop's January 6, 1958, letter to Ilse Barker used with the permission of Princeton University Library.

Excerpts from "Review of *The Riddle of Emily Dickinson*" and "Dimensions of a Novel" from *PROSE* by Elizabeth Bishop. Copyright © 2011 by the Alice H. Methfessel Trust. Farrar, Straus and Giroux, LLC.

"Manners" and excerpts from "Visits to St. Elizabeths" from *The Complete Poems: 1927–1979* by Elizabeth Bishop. Copyright © 1979, 1983 by Alice Helen Methfessel. Reprinted by permission of Farrar, Straus and Giroux, LLC.

"Composing Motions," from *Deep Skin: Elizabeth Bishop and Visual Art*, by Peggy Samuels, copyright © 2010 by Cornell University. Reprinted by permission.

"Geography IV," from *PN Review* 35, no. 5 (May–June 2009), by Thomas Travisano. Reprinted by permission.

"Postcards and Sunsets: Elizabeth Bishop's Revisions and the Problem of Excess," from *Resources for American Literary Study*, vol. 33 (2008), by Jeffrey Gray, copyright © 2010 AMS Press, Inc. Reprinted by permission.

Index